C000300471

Howard Spring was born in C[...] career as a newspaper errand bo[...] *Manchester Guardian* and develope[...] become the setting for several of [...] Spring took over the job of literary critic on the *Evening Standard* from J B Priestley and on moving to Cornwall at the outset of World War II he became literary critic of *Country Life*. His most well-known novel, *Fame is the Spur*, the story of a Labour politician's rise to power, was filmed by the Boulting Brothers and he continued to write until his death in 1965.

THERE IS NO ARMOUR

A novel by

HOWARD SPRING

HOUSE OF STRATUS

This edition published in 2000 by House of Stratus, an imprint of Stratus Holdings plc, 24c Old Burlington Street, London, W1X 1RL, UK.

www.houseofstratus.com

Typeset, printed and bound by House of Stratus.

A catalogue record for this book is available from the British Library.

ISBN 1-84232-359-8

CHAPTER ONE

ANATOLE LOP and Captain Marquick always came along together for the musical evenings, because the captain was blind and Anatole used to lead him, an arm crooked through his. There was a routine that never varied. On five days of the week – from Monday to Friday – my father took his lunch with him to the shop, which was on Oxford Road, just opposite All Saints Church. We were not badly off, but my father said we had to watch our P's and Q's – that is, he explained, our pence and quids. This doesn't sound much of a joke, and you could say of every joke my father made that it wasn't much of a joke; but what I remember of those days when I was ten years old and Blanche was eleven is this: that he was always making jokes, bad though they might be. We may have been as poor as church mice, but we were as happy as the day was long.

It was because we were hard up that my father took his lunch with him to the shop. I often watched my mother pack it, never without admiration for her neatness. There would be a few sandwiches, the meat cut from the joint which had to stretch over so many purposes – the roast, the sandwiches, the stew, the cold cut served with creamed potatoes, and what not. My mother would wrap the sandwiches in greaseproof paper, tucking the ends of the little parcel neatly in, and this she would tie round with thin string. (The paper and string came back day after day, to be used again and again.) Then there would be a lavish slab of cake, rich with fruit, that had been made either by her or Betsy Comfort. This was tied into a separate piece of greaseproof paper. There would be an apple, an orange, or a pear, according to the season of the year, with a wrapping of tissue paper upon it. Finally, there would be a bottle of beer. Father always bought his beer by the barrel, because it was cheaper that way. He had

1

made a strong wooden contraption that was kept in the scullery, and the barrel was rested upon this. It was an exciting moment for me and Blanche when a new barrel came and he removed the bung and put in the spigot. There seemed to us always the delicious chance of disaster, of a squirt of beer shooting across the scullery, of rushing and shouting and general disorder. However, this never happened. The small operation was performed with dexterity and despatch, and my father would look up with a grin and say: "Foiled once more, my dear children. The gratification of your passionate wish to see your old father make a fool of himself must be postponed to a later occasion." He would give Blanche's hair a playful tug, punch me in the ribs, and go out of the scullery whistling.

Well, it was from this barrel that my mother would fill the beer-bottle each morning. Sometimes she allowed me to do it. This was always a pleasure. There was a little lustre jug that held just a bottleful. I drew the beer into this from the spigot, filled the bottle, and put in the screw top, proud to have a hand in this important daily operation of seeing Father off to work. My mother would put the bottle into a small basket, tuck the sandwiches, the cake, the fruit, neatly round it, shut it up, and push home the skewer that held the lid down. Thus Father could eat his lunch in the shop and save a few coppers which made the difference between the price of this small meal and what he would have to pay in a restaurant.

When all was ready, my mother would shout: "Come along now, Father." It would be by now about eight o'clock. Somehow, it is the spring mornings I remember best. I see him come in from the passageway, where he has been putting on his black sombrero hat and taking up his blackthorn stick from the piece of drainpipe painted with irises that stood there. He was a man of medium height with a curling brown beard and dark laughing eyes. He would give my mother a kiss, shove the end of his blackthorn through the handle of his basket, and sling it over his shoulder. Then he would say: "Come, Tab." But Tab did not need to be called. She was always ready to run with him to the end of the street. Mother, Blanche and I would go out to the front gate to watch him set out. As he and the cat moved off, he would say gravely: "Thus Master Whittington set forth in quest of fame and fortune." It was one of the poor little jokes we always expected, and I remember how, when I was younger even than ten,

2

and one morning he had omitted the ritual, I screamed after him "Say it, Daddy! Say it!" He turned round gravely and said: "It." "No," I shouted. "Say about Master Whittington." He repeated the rigmarole, and I shouted excitedly to my mother: "Isn't he funny? Isn't Father funny?" as we watched him go, bundle on shoulder, down the street towards the Wilmslow Road that led to Manchester. The sky was a tender blue. In the small gardens pink cherry and yellow laburnum – that we children called golden chain – and lilac of mauve and white were riotous with blossom. It was a lovely little street, for there were houses on only one side. Facing us as we stood, there was a hedge and beyond it one splendid horse-chestnut tree, a dome of green lit by the flame of the flowers. And all was dewy. That, beyond everything, comes back to me: that all was dewy and sweet and sinless as we watched him turn, with a wave of the hand, into the Wilmslow Road and Tab come trotting back. It was the best part of a five-mile walk to his shop in Manchester. He did it on foot morning and night, in all weathers. "Poor Whittington! Poor Richard Whittington!" he would sometimes lament when there was a flurry of snow in the air, and in the morning darkness his bowed figure would be swallowed up before he reached the turning.

2

Thus, on five days of the week. Saturday was different. Father did not take his lunch to the shop, but came home and ate it with us. And in the evening Anatole Lop and Captain Marquick would come for the concert. I was taken occasionally to Father's shop, and remember it as a rather dusty down-at-heel little place where musical instruments were sold. Apart from what he sold, which, I imagine, was not much, he made a little money as a piano tuner. There was a youth with spectacles and many pimples, named Albert Critchlow, who looked after the shop when Father was out on his tuning work; and Father would gaily use him as a bogey when he wished to tease me. "Your name," he would say, "has a fine patrician sound – Edward Pentecost. When counting your mercies, which I admit, my dear child, are spiritual rather than material, remember that it might have been Albert Critchlow. Critch could so easily be crutch, and low is low whichever way you look at it. Whereas your name has the glorious ring of a celebrated occasion. Your eyes are clear, and do not look through a glass darkly like Albert's; and if you forbear to eat too many of Betsy Comfort's cakes and pasties, you may escape the pustular eruptions which suggest that minute moles are at work beneath the field of Albert's countenance."

He would flow on in this grandiloquent fashion when in the mood, and half of what he said passed over my head like summer wind over wheat, uncomprehended but warm and stirring.

Sometimes, when he came home, he would shout boisterously to my mother some such nonsense as this: "Dolly, the firm of Pentecost, which normally exists on the weekly sale of two yards of poor Tabby's gut and a lump of resin, has today veritably sold a musical instrument – to wit, one pair of castanets." Or it might be "One banjo to a nigger minstrel."

I know now that life for him, and for all of us, was precarious in those days, and thus the happiness of our lot appears the more miraculous. Saturdays were happy indeed. In the morning while he was away at the shop, my mother and Betsy Comfort had a great to-do in the kitchen. They made Cornish pasties and sausage rolls, and little cakes that could be eaten in one melting mouthful, being, as Betsy said, "light as vanity". They polished the best silver and washed the best crockery. They renewed all the flowers in the house, so that every Saturday seemed like an Easter morning.

Looking back upon it all, I often wonder how, our means being so straitened, things went along as they did; and the explanation is that everything was sacrificed to the home. Pennies were saved on lunches and by walking instead of riding, and our clothes were always shabby and pinchbeck. But we had a nice, though unpretentious, house, and inside it everything had to be just so. How my parents could afford to keep a treasure like Betsy Comfort was something I never asked myself, something only time was to reveal.

Well, there would be, on the Saturday morning, all this "fettling" as my mother called it, for she was a Lancashire woman, not Cornish like my father and Betsy Comfort; and, once lunch was over, my father would settle down to tune the piano. It was an upright with a fretwork front behind which was pleated red silk, and on either side was a candleholder into which a new candle was put each Saturday morning. The wood was walnut, and to this day I can see the smooth rhythm of the patterns made by the polished grain.

4

Blanche and I were never allowed to be in the room while Father tuned the piano. "Behind all mysteries, my dearly beloved offspring," Father would say, laying his little bag of tools on the carpet, "there are tricks of the trade. The tricks of the trade are for the old only. The young should accept the mystery with simple faith." And with hands laid gently on the backs of our necks he would push us out of the room. We would go up to our attic, and there we would be pursued by the often discordant noises of his work. These would give place at last to pleasing trills and arpeggios, and finally to the powerful strains of the Hallelujah Chorus. It was this that always announced that the work was done, that the tricks of the trade were over and the mystery re-established. "Now," he would announce, as we all gathered together at tea, "now let 'em all come." It sounded like a world challenge, but no one ever came save Anatole Lop and Captain Marquick.

I can still be enthusiastic about Didsbury. I have been back there of late and found the fairyland of my childhood laid waste, all its glories desolate. The buses rush by on the hard glassy surface of the road which then exhaled a tender dust as the horses shuffled along. Most of the fields are gone and platoons of little brick houses have made orderly and unexciting camps where Blanche and I used to pick the water buttercups and cuckoo flowers and see occasionally the flash of a kingfisher, like a piece of rainbow snipped off and flung through the morning. But even now something survives, some trees that must have been old when I was a boy, a few unplanned, uncovenanted nooks and corners where the whisper may still be heard and the mystery glimpsed. And there is still the Cock Inn, with the proud golden bird lording it as he did when he seemed the very monarch of my life's morning.

I have said that there was a routine which never varied, and my father's visit to the Cock on Saturday evenings was part of it. The piano had been tuned; and music for the night had been put ready; we had eaten our tea, and the supper on which my mother and Betsy Comfort had worked in the morning had been set out in the dining room. Then, at about five o'clock, my father would set out for the Cock. You had but to walk down our street to the Wilmslow Road, turn to the left, and there you saw it, a hundred yards in front of you.

This was the great South Road, the road, it seemed to me, of all romance, because it was the road to London. Where the Cock stood, the road's flowing continuity was broken. It widened out on one side to a small square. The flat façade of the Cock, with its golden bird and red window curtains that glowed so cosily on winter nights when there was snow on the ground, occupied most of one side, what with its main building and its stable yard. On the other side was another inn, and the space in front of the two contained a horse trough. In the angle between the two inns was a pathway that led to the church, a pleasing building of red sandstone, whose square tower looked across the low meadows through which the Mersey twisted and turned.

I never went into the Cock with my father. Sometimes I would be permitted to walk with him as far as this little square, and there we would linger until we saw Anatole Lop and Captain Marquick coming to the weekly appointment. They came from the direction of Manchester, walking slowly along under the high wall over which the trees dripped their branches. Their appearance never failed to fascinate me. On the wall in my father's shop were many pictures of composers and players of music. Among them was Paganini, and I never saw Anatole Lop without being reminded of the picture. Lop had a skeletal thinness, and this was emphasised by the close fit of his invariably black clothes. They were more a skin than a dress. The knobs of his knees and elbows stood out; and if one did not see his Adam's apple, this was because a black cravat was twisted round and round his throat, beneath the starched white wings that rose out of it to his very ears. He was as tall as he was thin, and this made Captain Marquick, who was not really a small man, seem as though he were a fat robin being conducted by a heron. This comparison came the more readily to my mind because the captain had a fancy for red waistcoats. If it were a summer evening and his coat was thrown open, you would see him gleaming from afar. Beneath his right arm would be the vast case of his cello; his left arm would be linked through Anatole's right; and from Anatole's left hand dangled the case of his fiddle. As soon as he saw them coming, my father would go into the Cock to order the drinks and I would return home to let my mother know that the visitors were thus far upon the journey. They would not delay in reaching us. Not one of them was a man who liked a long drinking session, but they were deep in friendship, and this weekly ritual was something that had arisen and was treasured as a part of the cement of it.

3

When you are following the road that runs from Manchester into Cheshire you cross a bridge over the Mersey. To the right of the quarter mile or so that you cover before reaching this bridge a few roads lead off. They were leafy and full of country quiet in my childhood. You could go into them and never guess that the life of Manchester was buzzing and humming five miles to the East, for you would see nothing but the few big houses – you could fairly call them mansions – that stood here and there back from the roads, hear nothing but the cheerful racket of lawnmowers and the singing of birds. These were the homes of wealthy Manchester merchants, and now and then you would see a carriage come out from one of the double gates, carrying some magnate's womenfolk to shop in the city.

Captain Marquick lived in one of these mansions. His father, the principal of the great cotton firm of Marquick and Marquand, lived there before him, and it was he who had the house built when he married. The huge place seemed superfluous a year later when Mrs Marquick died in giving birth to a son. But Marquick remained there, and there my Captain Marquick grew up. All his father's affection was concentrated upon him. This was not a smothering affection that sought to dominate and direct the boy's life. Young Marquick was allowed to choose his own way, and he chose to be a soldier. The year 1879 found him in Zululand, and it was during that war that a Zulu knobkerry deprived him of sight. All these things I learned much later, and I learned that he was thirty years old when that blow ended his soldiering forever. This tells me that in the year 1899, when I was ten years old and our Saturday night concerts were in full swing, he was fifty.

Marquick's father had married late in life. He was an old man when his son returned from Africa and he died not long afterwards. Marquick was a man of firm and resolute character. He set himself to overcome his disability, and especially he applied himself to music. At first he was a hearer only, an unfailing attender at the Hallé concerts and all other concerts that were going. This new art, of which hitherto he had known nothing, gradually took hold of him and became the dominant thing in his life. Now he must learn not only to listen but to perform, and thus it was that he made the acquaintance of Anatole Lop. Lop, an Alsatian whose life had been disrupted by the Franco-

Prussian war of 1870, had settled in Manchester as a music teacher, and he was also a violinist in Hallé's orchestra. He instructed Marquick in both the violin and the cello, but it was the cello that the captain preferred to play. These two had known one another for some years when the need to make a casual purchase took them to my father's shop. The three began to talk music, and when it was found that they all lived near together, my father said half in jest: "What with us and my wife, we could make a nice quartet. You must come and see us some Saturday night." It was out of this offhand invitation that the friendship between the three men arose. It was part of Marquick's determined character that he always walked to the appointment. He kept his carriage and pair and used them when he went to concerts in Manchester or anywhere far afield; but he had set himself to move under his own power so far as possible. Also, I think, knowing that we were poor, he disliked the ostentation of arriving in a carriage. I imagine it was for the same reason that he always allowed my father to pay for the drinks at the Cock. I often heard my father say, as though it were a commendation: "You'd think the captain hadn't a penny."

4

When I had returned to the house with the news that our visitors were on the way, there was what Betsy called a reglar confloption. You would think that nothing had been done all day and that I had reported the imminent descent of a totally unexpected party. The table in the dining room and everything upon it would be scrutinised. A chair would be shifted an inch nearer the table or withdrawn an inch from it. Knives and forks, laid out with what looked to me like perfect symmetry, would be edged this way and that; and nothing, I sometimes thought, remained to be done save taste the food itself so as to be sure that it was up to the customary standard. I went so far, more than once, as to make the gesture of seizing a pie or pasty with this intention, but Betsy Comfort was down on me like a shot. "You dare, Master Edward! You so much as dare! You get right out of this room now. I've seen you hovering about the door all the afternoon, looking surreptitous."

"But, Betsy," I would plead. "Just one of your fairy cakes. They're as light as vanity."

"That's as may be," she would return, unbribed by flattery, "but there'll be no fiddling nor fingering with my table till supper time."

Everything in the house was "mine" to Betsy. "I'll just give my brass a rub," she'd say, "and then I'd better make my beds."

My father would return with his guests in the midst of the confloption, and from that moment everything ran on the oiled wheels of custom. Our sitting room was at the back of the house. Windows, left open when these gatherings were in the summer, gave upon a short back garden, and beyond this garden the fields spread away towards Northenden and all the flat rural stretches of Cheshire. There was one tree in the garden – a sycamore of great age whose branches were perfectly shaped for holding a little hut. Between us, my father and I had knocked this together in the tree. It was hardly more than a box, but there was just room for me to get into it and to lie on some cushions I had begged from my mother. The side upon the west was open, and I was high enough up to see over the garden wall. While the musicians were taking their places, and Blanche was settling down on the old hassock in a corner, where she would sit all through the concert with her elbows on her knees, her chin cupped in her hands, and her great dark eyes broodingly watching now the fingers dancing upon the piano, now the bows surging over the taut strings, I would slip from the room and climb into my eyrie. Perhaps I shall never be nearer to heaven than I was then. Nailed to the wall on my right was a shelf with a few of the books I loved best. Hanging from the ceiling was an old iron lantern with a candle in it, and there was a curtain of sackcloth that I could draw to close in the westward side. But during those summer night concerts the lantern would be unlit, and the curtain undrawn, and I would lie there upon my cushions listening and watching. Listening to the piano notes rippling from under my mother's fingers, to Anatole Lop and my father wringing my heartstrings with their violins, to the solemn belly-notes of Captain Marquick's cello. Watching the daylight fade across the water meadows, and the western sky turn to a crimson smother behind the trees and church tower of Northenden, and the last swallows go and the first bats come, and the mist rise from the river, submerging the grazing cattle, filling the lower air with moving vapour that always made me murmur: "clothed in white samite, mystic, wonderful." Soon, even the church tower, for long now only a dark block upon the sky, would be quite withdrawn. There would be nothing but the night, and the first half of the concert moving to its end in a dying melody or a huge architecture of sound that seemed to be building palaces in the darkness.

There was always a pause, a hush, of no more than a few seconds, I suppose, but it seemed longer, before the world into which I had been carried away collapsed into a scraping of chairs, a cough, a few casual words. Everybody would be moving into the dining room where, by now, Betsy would have the tea and coffee on the table. I would enjoy the pleasure of watching Captain Marquick eat. He ate like anyone else, and the pleasure was in that. It was to be expected, or so it seemed to my childish mind, that a blind man would hardly know the way to his own mouth, but Captain Marquick knew it well enough, and never made a mistake in putting his hand on cup or knife, spoon or fork. It was difficult, looking at him, to believe that he was blind. He had been struck heavily across the eyes, and the marks of that blow had long since disappeared. But it had destroyed his optic nerves, so that the wide-open blue eyes which looked at you and at this and that with a fixed disturbing stare, as though searching you to the marrow, were not in fact looking at all. His other faculties, like those of many blind people, were developed to an unusual degree. He would congratulate my mother on her flowers, even when these had so faint a scent that to me it was imperceptible. But he would always name the flowers, and other things, too. I have seen him rub his hands on entering the dining room and exclaim: "Ha! You've made another of your lovely fruit cakes, Betsy!" and he was never wrong about that or anything else.

Blanche and I were packed off to bed before the second part of the concert began. Our elders returned to the sitting room, but we remained behind, picking at this and that choice morsel till Betsy chased us upstairs. "Come on now. Be off with you. I'm a working woman, I am, and I've got my dishes to wash. I never saw the likes of you, hovering about as if you could neither stand, go nor stay."

Reluctantly at last we would go, each taking one of the candles that stood on the small table in the passage. There were four of them: one for me, one for Blanche, one for Betsy, and one for my father and mother. Like everything else, they were renewed on Saturday mornings, and I was allowed to keep the ends for my lantern in the tree room. It was always to my tree room that I returned when I had got into bed. I would imagine that I was stretched out not on this mattress, but on my cushions there, with the sunset going down clear or stormy, and these imaginations had the power to put me quickly to sleep, sometimes before the fiddle-faddle of tuning had given place to music in the room below.

5

My mother, as I have said, was not a Cornish woman. Her maiden name was Sowler. That was one of the things, my father would say in his moods of heavy humour, that marriage had saved her from. "Sowler! What a name! It reeks of the Gadarene swine, my dear Dolly. You would long ago have rushed down a steep place into the sea if you hadn't been Pentecostally enlightened." She was a fair, blue-eyed woman, but Blanche and I took after our father. I do not know what my parents thought of Blanche, but for a long time to me she had been two girls. There was the girl I walked with to school and who, at home, went about gravely or sat hunched in a corner listening to the talk and the music, with her hair, which was a shining blue-black, tightly arranged in two plaits tied at the ends with crimson ribbon. They hung down her back when she stood, and when she sat they came over her shoulders and the ends lay in her lap. She was like the pool that she and I knew near Northenden: a pool in a wood, so shut in that the sunlight never touched it. The surface was always dark, unruffled and mysterious.

But there was another Blanche. I suppose I would be seven or eight when first I discovered her. It was a Saturday morning of high summer, and for once our father did not go to the shop. Our mother had not got up that morning, and Betsy Comfort was both worried and officious. In place of our mother packing the lunch basket for Father, there was Betsy packing it for me and Blanche and bidding us begone. "Off with you now! It's a lovely day, and we don't want to see you till teatime. You don't want to go so far you'll get lost, but keep out of the house." She pulled Blanche's plaits and said: "You look well after Master Edward, now, and keep away from the river."

We were glad to go. We were well used to being out on our own, though we had never before been sent off for a whole day in such circumstances of mystery. Neither had we before been entrusted with the precious lunch basket, and I remember how I tugged my father's big blackthorn stick out of the painted drainpipe, stuck it through the handle of the basket, and set off with what I took to be his resolute morning tread. He was not there to see us go. He had gone upstairs to my mother.

But we did not take the road my father took each morning. Leaving the house, we turned to the right, not, like him, to the left; and soon we were in the fields we loved so well. It would be about ten o'clock in the morning, mid-June, and there was a cloudless sky over our heads. In those days a few minutes' walk was enough to bring you from our house out among the hedges where the dog roses grew and into fields where pale blue harebells trembled and cuckoo flowers could be gathered in handfuls. As children will, we picked our bunches and tired of carrying them and left them to wilt where we threw them down. We wandered on and on, with no thought of route or direction, with the larks singing over our heads, and the sun strengthening, and the cattle lying in lumpy masses wherever a few trees gave them shade.

Blanche had little to say to me. Out in the fields she seemed to live a life of her own. One moment she was with me, and the next she was away with a darting, skimming run that seemed to take her over the field like a swallow. Wherever she went I plodded heavily after, carrying the basket, though by now I had given up the jaunty pretence of being a Whittington. The basket handle was clutched in one hand and the blackthorn trailed from the other, already a nuisance. In one of her swooping flights Blanche came near me and I called out to her to take her turn at carrying the stick and the basket. She paused long enough to say: "Put them down, silly. We can get them when we want them. D'you think I intend to cart those things about in my hands all day?" She was a little breathless and her eyes were shining. In a moment she was off again on her fantastic flight.

It was noon by now, and I was tired. I put the basket down in the shadow of a hedge and sat myself beside it. From the strip of shade I watched Blanche darting lightly about in the dazzling sunshine. She was like a dragonfly, loving the heat, stung by it into an ecstasy of beautiful movement. Her heavy plaits whipped about her like ropes. Then the languor of noon overcame me and I fell asleep. It can have been only for a little time, and when I awoke I could hardly believe that this was Blanche I saw dancing before me on a carpet of buttercups. She had untied her plaits and shaken out the dark cloud of her hair. She had tied together the two pieces of crimson ribbon, and these now encircled her waist, holding up above her knees the white cotton dress that had reached her ankles. She had thrown off shoes and stockings, and what met my opening eyes was the sight of her thin white legs and her dark hair whirring as she executed the final movement of some dance that had been going on for goodness knows how long. I hardly had time to take this in before a pirouette ended the performance, and laughing breathlessly she threw herself down at my side. She lay there panting for a time with beads of sweat upon her forehead, then sat up and said: "Don't you say a word about this to Mother. Or to Betsy. Oh! They don't know how mad I am." Then she drew on her stockings and her shoes, plaited her hair and tied the ends, and shook down her dress. We ate our lunch and wandered on, and for the rest of the day she was quiet, as though all that her body had to say had been said for the time being.

6

There were never any other children in our family save me and Blanche. The one who was born and died on the day when Blanche danced in the fields – I don't remember to this day whether it was a son or a daughter – had no successors. All of that day and of the few days that followed is blank to my memory save for Blanche's capers and Betsy's cross affection. There must have been a burial, but I have no recollection of it. My father was not the man to inflict a hurt on young minds. I can well imagine that he did all that was possible to make those few days pass over our heads as lightly as the circumstances allowed. One phrase out of that time sticks in my memory. I had climbed into my tree and sat there with a book on my knee and a box of crayons at my side. The book was full of drawings, and I proposed to give myself what then was to me a great joy. I intended to spend the afternoon colouring the pictures, making this drab black and white shine with the green of fields, the blue of sky and sea, and strong sepia of mountains. I sat there looking at my picture, deciding how to begin, when I heard my father and Betsy talking in the garden below. "It's a pity," Betsy said, "that we're so far from

Cornwall. You could have packed them off to Falmouth for a day or two."

My father answered rather crossly: "Well, we *are* far from Cornwall, and what's more, I'm not sorry." He turned and left her, and, peeping from my hiding place, I saw that his whole body was showing annoyance.

So now my picture, which was of a seashore, became for me a part of Cornwall, and I began to give it all the colour that that name evoked in my mind. I had never been to Cornwall. It was as a place far off in imagination, very bright: a place of sapphire seas and skies of burning blue, seabirds of a holy purity, and long rollers curling on golden beaches. It had for my imagination all the allure of the forbidden, the enhancement of that which never could be; because, though from time to time I heard Betsy and Mother speak of it with longing, they always fell silent when my father appeared. And if perchance he caught some fragment of their conversation, he became cross, as he had done just now with Betsy, and with a few brief words he would let it be understood that Cornwall was a place that would never see him again. And so that afternoon I put the heaviest indigo into the sea, rejoicing in the warm oily feel of the crayons, and the lightest bird's-egg blue into the sky, and romantic touches of orange into a castle crumbling on a crag. Beneath this I was daring enough to inscribe in capital letters the forbidden word CONWAL. I have the old book still, and often wish I had not disfigured its lovely drawings. More powerfully than anything else, it can recall to me the only shadow that lay over our singularly fortunate childhood. Still, these old tintings are not without their autobiographical value.

7

As I have said, I was seven or eight when I first watched Blanche dancing, and when I was ten the visits of Anatole Lop and Captain Marquick were already part of the household routine. These took place on Saturdays, and by the time I was twelve another institution had grown up amongst us. This was Sunday night reading. We did this only in the wintertime. They were unforgettable, those winter nights, with all five of us – for Betsy was included – sitting in a half circle before the fire and reading some well-loved book. The novels of Dickens were our favourites. My father would read the descriptive passages, and when it came to dialogue we would all chime in, taking a part each. I can recall now our huge delight when our mother, as Mrs McStinger, castigated the quailing Captain Cuttle of our father, and, too, the excellence of Betsy in such parts as Sairey Gamp's. Blanche quavering through the pathos of Little Nell, myself trying to snivel in a way which would not disgrace poor Smike: I shall never forget all this, or the hearty laugh with which my father would bang the pages of his book together at the end of the reading and cry: "Off to bed with these children, Dolly. The persecuted little martyrs — forced to submit to pianos and books and fiddles when they might be enjoying the advantages of modern science by seeing a magic-lantern show in a Sunday school." He would be already stuffing tobacco from his pouch into his pipe: the special pipe which he kept for smoking at home: a meerschaum with a curved amber stem and a bowl carved to represent a negro's head. I used to watch fascinated as the smoke rose up from where the negro's brains should have been.

I am trying to give you an idea of the sort of life Blanche and I lived. It was a life that owed everything to our home. School to this day remains dim and insignificant in my memory, but home is full of pictures exquisitely bright. Above the bedrooms there was an attic, and this was ours, inviolate. Neither my father nor mother would enter it save by invitation, and even Betsy was not allowed there to do the cleaning. What cleaning we thought necessary we did ourselves, and that was not a lot. It was a dirty, dusty, happy place, and we spent much time there on our own affairs, with a chalk line drawn to divide her territory from mine. I was beginning now not to colour other people's drawings but to draw for myself, and my territory was a litter of pencils, chalks, crayons and paper on the floor and drawings pinned to the walls. In Blanche's territory there was an old cupboard full of odds and ends of silk and satin that she would fabricate into garments. She would dress herself up in these and tread out impromptu dance measures. But it was not often that she would do this if I were about. For the most part, her dances were solitary. I sometimes surprised her at them, and then without a word she stopped and either ran downstairs or took up needle and thread and began to make another dress.

We had no friends of our own age. By standing on a box, opening the skylight, and pushing our heads through, we could see into the neighbouring gardens, and in the one next door we sometimes saw Luther Brimlow engaged on his silly games. He would hop on one leg up and down the garden path, which was the only place he had to play on, because the ground on either side of the path was stuffed with vegetables; or he would sit on a chair holding a hymnbook and singing:

> At the Cross, at the Cross,
> Where I first saw the light
> And the burden of my sin rolled away,

beating time with one hand and rolling his eyes horribly. Sometimes we threw horse chestnuts at him, but had to dodge down off the box before we could see whether they hit him or not. Once, to our horror, my mother asked Mrs Brimlow if she would like Luther to go with us on one of our walks, but she said No: she liked Luther to be where she could see what he was up to, and so did his father.

So our walks, which took us farther and farther afield, continued to be blessedly a concern for us alone, and one of them led us to Captain Marquick's garden gate.

Though the captain had for so long been coming to our house, none of us had ever been to his. My father thought this was as it should be. "He wouldn't want to emphasise the difference between his style of living and ours," he once said. Anyway, we children knew only that the captain lived somewhere on the other side of the Palatine Road, and it was along that thoroughfare that we were walking in the failing light of a February afternoon. There are several circumstances which help me to fix the date – an important date for me, as you will presently see. For one thing, the Boer War was being fought. In the lapel of the coat I was wearing – a double-breasted, brass-buttoned affair called a monkey-jacket – there were several portraits of British generals, insignia that no self-respecting British schoolboy was without at that time; and such was the innocence of those days that the presence of these portrait buttons in my lapel was literally the only impact of that struggle upon my imagination. But I can fix the date more closely than this because it was my birthday, and at breakfast that morning my father had said: "Well, Ted, this is your first birthday in the twentieth century, and your first birthday in the reign of Edward the Seventh. I hope you'll outlive the king, but I doubt if you'll outlive the century." This tells me precisely that the day was February 10, 1901, and that I had reached the age of twelve. An important age that was, in those days, for a boy like me, because twelve was the end of schooldays unless one were going on to some grander sort of school. For me, there was little hope of that, and that morning my father said: "Dolly, the next thing we shall have to consider is this young man's future. Shall we sack the dreadful Albert Critchlow and install our Ted in the shop?"

"We'll see," my mother said. "He can stay at school till the summer holidays, anyway."

"Ay, but let him stay at home today," my father commanded. "Let him go mitching to show the independence of his mature years."

This was said in the passage, as he tucked his stick through the handle of the lunch basket, and the next moment we were watching him go into the grey winter weather. It seemed to me, as my eye followed his light springy step down the street, that the sooner Albert Critchlow was sacked the better, and that few things could be more desirable than a lifetime of setting out each morning with my father, carrying a smaller stick and a smaller basket, with day after day of fellowship in the shop at the end of the walk.

But in the meantime here was this day of freedom to be got through. Blanche had done with school nearly a year before, and now helped my mother and Betsy with the housework, and so in the morning I had the attic to myself. I filled my pocket with horse chestnuts, climbed on to the box, and stuck my head through the skylight. But there was nothing worth a shot. One could not throw at Mrs Brimlow, who was pegging out clothes on the line, and there was no Luther to be seen. Of course, I reminded myself, he was at work. He had been at work for two years. He was fourteen, a big, gangling lad, but beginning to take exceptional pains with his appearance. Sometimes we saw him leaving his house as we watched our father go in the mornings, and Luther's stiff shirt fronts, upstanding white collars, and kid gloves made a deep impression on me and Blanche. In the winter he wore a bowler hat, and in the summer a straw boater with a black silk string fastened to the rim at one end and secured by a clip to his lapel at the other. If he saw us there, he would raise the bowler or the boater to my mother. His own mother would be watching his departure with pride and affection written all over her.

My feeling for Luther Brimlow, then, was one almost of awe, but at the same time of dislike. It seemed extraordinary that the boy whom we had watched hopping on one leg up and down the garden path, and singing the lugubrious hymns which he learned at the Plymouth Brethren chapel, should have developed into this superlative dandy. But though I was in awe of him I did not like him any more than I ever had done, and whenever I poked my head through the skylight the chestnuts itched in my pocket. We had a packing case full of them in the attic, gathered through several autumns from the gorgeous tree in the field that faced the front of our house. Sometimes Blanche made them into thick necklaces and anklets and bracelets that she used for her dances, and I loved them for their rich colour when new and their gnarled toughness in age. They would always be, to us, the appropriate ammunition to hurl at Luther Brimlow because, one tremulous October afternoon as we were gathering them with our feet rustling in the yellow and ochre leaves that littered the ground beneath the tree, there suddenly was Luther's pimply face poked through the hedge and Luther's voice taunting us: "Kids! Kids! Playing with conkers."

I remember the small incident so well. Blanche and I were so absorbed in our task that, as often happened when we were together, each had completely forgotten the other and was wrapped in childish self-communion. She was gathering the horse chestnuts into her apron, I into my pockets, and I am sure that to her, as certainly to me, this action was mechanical. Our minds were elsewhere, bemused by the tender autumnal sky, and the sun's gentle warmth, and the crackle and rustle of the beautiful leaves beneath our feet, and the haze of a bonfire that was burning nearby. But though thus apart, we had the power of flying together in one defensive organism, as swiftly as two drops of mercury become one when they touch. So now we glared back at Luther Brimlow's face sneering at us through the hedge.

"Who are kids?" Blanche demanded truculently.

"You are."

"Why?"

"Playing with conkers."

"Well, what do *you* do with yourself?"

18

"Sums."

I could see Blanche's fingers curling crisply round a chestnut, prepared for the throw, and my ammunition was ready, too. But, somehow, that answer stilled us both. We continued to glare at Luther Brimlow's face, but now it was not so much the face of the boy next door as of a monster outside the range of our comprehension.

Sums!

If, while we were eating cake, someone had announced a preference for coke we could not have been more astonished. And so, for that time, the enemy was able to withdraw, with not a shot fired from our side. When his face was beyond the hedge and he could be heard but not seen, he announced: "I've saved up one pound two and a penny."

It seemed magnificent, but still we had nothing to say about it.

"Bet you don't know what that would bring in at five per cent," the voice taunted us, and we certainly didn't.

"One and a penny farthing," Luther announced with triumph, and we heard him scuttle across the road to his father's house.

8

Luther Brimlow's father was a builder's merchant in a small way of business. On the Wilmslow Road, not far from the Cock Inn, there was a pair of double doors with "Jonas Brimlow" and the nature of the business painted on them. Within was a very small yard containing heaps of sand and gravel, lime, cement, and things of that sort. It always looked a disorderly place, and in a wooden shed, labelled "Office", was often to be seen Jonas Brimlow, a small disorderly man. I had once been inside the shed. On a Saturday, a couple of years before this birthday of which I am writing, I was walking along the Wilmslow Road when I passed some boys playing football in the street. It was possible, then, to do this without being suicidal. As I went by, the ball came in my direction. I made a run towards it, gave it a kick, and, to my own surprise no less than to everybody else's, lifted it beautifully over the wall into Mr Brimlow's yard. There was a moment of suspense as we waited to hear the hollow thud of bouncing leather, but we heard nothing of the sort: we heard the crash of breaking glass. I began to run away, but the boys, all bigger than I, seized me, propelled me towards the double doors, and pushed me inside. "You kicked it in, so you can go and get it out," one of them shouted. The push landed me in the arms of Mr Brimlow. I knew him, of course, and he knew me; but, till then, we had never been so close together. As I saw him that day, he was a hatless, round-shouldered little man with a ragged grey moustache and ragged grey hair untidily thatching his head. A dewdrop hung from his nose, and, holding me with one hand, he brushed it off with the hairy back of the other. He led me firmly but not roughly to the door of the shed labelled "Office" and pushed me inside. It was a cold blowy day, and the wind whistled bleakly through the hole the football had made in the window. Under the window was a table littered with papers, a few files, an inkstand, a blotting pad that had absorbed so much ink in its time that it was almost a solid black and could well have been the pad on which Mr Brimlow blotted the first invoice to go out from this office years ago. A wastepaper basket was overflowing on to the floor, and the walls were hung with calendars of many years past, as well as with the one for the year then in being. It looked as though nothing that got within those few square yards of room ever got out again – not a sheet of blotting paper, not a calendar, not anything. An oil stove made the place smell fetid.

Mr Jonas Brimlow shut the door and seated himself in an armchair whose cushion was a bundle of old newspapers tied together with string. He turned his small watery eyes upon me and wiped away another dewdrop from his nose. Then, without speaking, he pointed his pudgy forefinger towards a card hanging among the calendars on the wall. I looked and saw a liver-coloured card with lettering heavily embossed in silver. It read: *THOU GOD SEEST ME*, and above the words was a large silver eye, shooting lines of radiant vision all over the card.

Mr Brimlow spoke at last. "That's true," he said. "Absolutely and literally true. Thou God seest me. At this moment God is looking into this room. There are men, young Pentecost, who keep God for Sunday. There are men who keep God for home. But God is everywhere. In a man's business as well as in his chapel and his house. Might as well admit it. Might as well hang up the card. God is not only looking into this room. He is looking into my heart. And yours. Yes – yours."

His voice was slow and husky. His little fat hand kept rising and falling on the edge of his desk. "Now then," he said, "with God looking into your heart, tell me why you broke my window." He looked at me sadly – a soggy, moist-eyed, wet-nosed little man. But it was not as such that I saw him. No smiling implacable Buddha ever hypnotised a devotee as Mr Jonas Brimlow hypnotised me. I stared at him with fear amounting to terror. If he had, in the first place, seized me by the neck, given me a kick in the backside, and sent me sprawling out into the roadway, I should have got up and shouted derision. But now I could say nothing. My throat was dry; my lips were parched; I looked from the putty-soft hand beating the edge of the table to the silver eye streaming its sight down into the core of my heart, and I could say nothing.

Mr Brimlow sighed. "No answer, young Pentecost," he said. "I must answer for you. You broke my window because you are a sinner. No, do not shrink from the word," he exclaimed, holding up his wet-looking hand. "We might as well face the truth. No doubt you did not say to yourself 'I am a sinner, and therefore I will break Jonas Brimlow's window.' No, it's not so simple as that. You are a sinner. I am a sinner. All – all – are born in sin and iniquity. But some find Grace. I have found Grace. Mrs Brimlow has found Grace. With God's blessing, my son Luther is even now wrestling for Grace." He smiled with a kind intention. "You, too," he said, "may find Grace. Ask, and it shall be given unto you."

He got up, opened a drawer that was full of rubbish, and pulled out two dirty dusters. He twisted them into a ball and plugged the hole in the window. But it was not effective. He took my hand and held it near the dusters. I could feel the cold wind whistling through. "If God wishes to bestow His Grace," he said, "nothing can stop it. It will Come Through, just as the wind comes through those dusters. The wind bloweth where it listeth. Who knows, perhaps God led you to break this window so as to put it into my heart to give you this illustration. It could be that. It could be that God's Grace brought you here. But at the moment you are a sinner. Sin led you to play football, for such games are vanities. So, because you are a sinner, my window is broken. I do not complain. I have glass in stock. And putty. And I have been able to speak a word in season. Games are said to be good for the body. But the soul comes first. Boy, remember your soul. Now you may go."

I slung upon my head the cap that had been wriggling in my fist and began to make for the door. But Mr Brimlow's hand fell upon my shoulder. "One moment," he said. He rummaged among the litter of his table and at last turned up a folded sheet which he handed to me. It was headed "Sin, Grace and Pardon." He placed it tenderly in my hand. "And this," he said. Once more he began to rummage, this time in his waistcoat pockets, which seemed as full of litter as everything else about him. He placed on the desk a penknife, a piece of chalk, a twist of string, a stub of flat carpenter's pencil, and finally unearthed a sweet of that round streaked variety known as a bull's-eye. He handed it to me with a smile. It was hairy with fluff. "You must come and see me sometimes," he said.

When I got outside, the boys had recovered their ball and disappeared, and thereafter, whenever I passed Mr Brimlow's yard, I shut my eyes tight and ran like a hare.

9

As I stood on the box in the attic on my twelfth birthday, in the first year of this century, with my head through the skylight and my eyes upon Mrs Brimlow pegging out the washing, no animosity against the Brimlows was in my heart. I had by now buried that rather terrifying interview with the old man deep enough down for it not to worry me, and as for Luther, he and his starched shirts and bowler hats and stylish collars were more of a joke than anything else with us Pentecosts. If my father, setting out in his shabby clothes, with his greenish old sombrero, saw Luther going ahead of him, he would give a comical sigh as he hitched the basket over his shoulder and say: "It's a terrible thing for a man of my age to be shown up like that. I'll never be a smart city chap, Dolly. What a match you made! What a fool you were! Sorry?"

She would laugh uproariously. "Sorry, indeed! Thank God this family isn't likely to produce a little monkey-up-the-stick like that."

So altogether the Brimlows were something to be laughed at, and standing there that day, it seemed to me that, though I could hardly hurl a chestnut at Mrs Brimlow, I might well have a shot at Luther's shirts which she was hanging on the line. No sooner thought of than done. I had a pretty good quick-firing technique, and I had despatched four missiles before a cry from Mrs Brimlow made me realise that one of them had struck her. I leapt down at once from the box, confident that no one could guess where the chestnuts were hurled from. I fastened the skylight and was enjoying a tour of my art gallery when a purposeful knocking at the front door sounded through the house. I knew at once that Mrs Brimlow was at the door, and, stealing to the head of the stairs, I soon heard her voice in the passage. An extraordinary emotion shook me, an emotion such as none of the Brimlows had till then stirred in my heart. I ran back into the attic, threw myself to the floor and began to cry. It seems strange to recall at this distance of time, for I was not a crying sort. But my whole body was suddenly shaken with sobs at the thought that Mrs Brimlow was inside our house and that an action of mine had brought her there. No Brimlow had till then been over our doorstep, and I had a sense of having delivered the Pentecost fortress to the enemy. This produced in me an unaccountable sense of desolation and disaster.

Presently, Blanche came to the attic. "You've got to come down," she said. "Mother wants you." Then, seeing my condition, she was full of concern. "What's the matter?" she demanded, kneeling on the floor near me. "What are you crying for?"

"Who's crying?" I foolishly answered. "It'd take more than that old bitch to make me cry."

I suppose this language confirmed in Blanche's mind a sense of the seriousness of my condition, for I was not used to speaking words of that sort. She put her arm round me and lifted me up. Her arm was white to the elbow with flour, and I indignantly brushed the marks of it off my coat. "Don't mess me about," I said morosely.

Blanche laughed. "Betsy's teaching me to make fairy cakes," she said.

I gulped back my last sobs, and said: "She can teach you to make what she damn well likes."

Blanche looked hard at me rubbing my knuckles into my eyes, and said: "I know she's in, and the sooner you come down the sooner she'll be out again." Then I knew that Blanche had not failed me; she understood; and everything seemed better.

Mrs Brimlow was tall and raw-boned, with thin greying hair wrenched pitilessly back from her forehead into a meagre "bun".

Usually she wore *pince-nez* fastened behind her ear with a gold chain, but now these were in her hand, and I saw at once that the glass of one lens was cracked. I stood within the door, glowering at her with loathing. Everything about her infuriated me: that dry scraped-back hair, the thin nose, marked on either side with a red scar where the *pince-nez* rested, the scraggy neck which one sensed beneath the material held up round it by strips of whalebone: oh, the whole withered, desiccated, dry-as-dust appearance of the woman. I was so moved with emotion at seeing her standing by my cheerful and blooming little mother, so filled with a sense that her being inside our house was disastrous, that, when my mother took the *pince-nez* from Mrs Brimlow's hand, held them up, and asked gently: "Why did you do it, Ted?" I shouted vehemently: "Because I hate the sight of her."

There was a moment of consternation. Everybody was there: Mother, Blanche and Betsy. They stared at me with amazement, for I was not a badly behaved boy. Mrs Brimlow sank into a chair. "Well, I never!" she exclaimed, and no one else seemed able to say even as much as that. They all looked at me as though spellbound.

It was Betsy Comfort who broke the spell. She suddenly put an arm round me and pulled me towards her. "The poor dear!" she exclaimed. "He's overwrought about something."

I was. It had been at first a vague intuition of evil. Blanche's words had formalised it; but it was unlikely that anyone else present could have any idea of the turmoil that raged in my heart.

"Let him be, Betsy," my mother commanded. "Ted, I'm surprised at you. You must at least tell Mrs Brimlow that you're sorry."

"I'm not sorry. I wish it had been a conqueror," I said, glowering blackly. A conqueror was the most redoubtable of all conkers: a veteran years old, baked in the chimney to the hardness of mahogany, the smasher of all competitors in my childhood games. I thought of Luther idiotically hopping on one leg, and boasting about his sums, and wearing his stuck-up collars; I thought of Mr Brimlow and the terror he had once driven into my heart; I looked at Mrs Brimlow; and I wished it had been a conqueror.

Mrs Brimlow retrieved the cracked spectacles and put them on her nose. "Might have blinded me," she said. "At least I'll expect you to pay for the repairs."

"Yes, of course," said my mother. "And I'll talk to Ted. I'm sure he's as sorry as I am, Mrs Brimlow. But you know what children are. They don't like to say it."

"I know what *some* people's children are," Mrs Brimlow said darkly. "And I know what my Luther is. Jealousy's behind this, Mrs Pentecost. That's what it is – jealousy. I've seen your two sniggering behind Luther's back. But you wait – the pair of you. You'll see one of these days. You'll laugh the other side of your faces then."

She began rummaging in what I suppose would be called her corsage, and presently brought forth a letter. "This came this morning. This'll show you."

My mother held out her hand to take the letter, but Mrs Brimlow withheld it. "No, thank you," she said. "I'll keep this, if you please. If you should ever receive a letter like this, I don't suppose you'll be in a hurry to part with it. *If* you ever do."

She held the letter close to her spectacles and, as she read, ran it to and fro as if it were sandpaper and she was filing her nose. It was from the firm of stockbrokers who employed Luther.

Dear Mr and Mrs Brimlow,

it ran, so far as I can remember it.

> You will perhaps be surprised to receive this letter, but now that your son, Mr Luther Brimlow, has been for a year with the firm, we would like to take occasion to inform you not merely that he gives satisfaction, but that he shows a degree of talent unusual in one so young.
>
> Yours sincerely . . .

Mrs Brimlow folded the letter, and felt that on this high note she might go. She went. When my mother came back from shutting the door, she turned on me and said, without much anger: "You silly little fool. Wipe your nose. Betsy, give him a fairy cake."

10

It was a cold clear day without wind and the sky was winter-blue: just the day for a good walk: and after dinner Blanche and I set out. We went, as we almost always did, through Northenden, and visited the still, silent pool we knew just beyond it. We wanted to see if there were yet any signs of the water buttercups that we found there earlier than anywhere else, but of course it was much too early. They wouldn't be blooming till Eastertime. We always gathered a bunch on Good Friday and my mother arranged them in an earthenware pot that she called "the Truro bowl". I once asked her why, and she said: "Because your father and I bought it at Truro. We watched an old potter throwing these things on a wheel at the roadside and bought it on the spot." She added with a sigh: "But that was a long time ago."

I often wondered why everything to do with Cornwall – I knew that Truro was in Cornwall – was uttered with a sigh, a sense of reservation, of something far-off and forbidden: but such questions do not trouble the mind of a child for long, and certainly they were not with me on that frosty February afternoon. Blanche said: "We'll go back along the Palatine Road and see the horses."

We often did that. There was nothing but horses on the roads in those days, and we loved to see them. Certainly they were worth seeing: the huge creatures that pulled drays, and the smart ponies trotting so briskly along in front of tradesmen's light carts or farmers' traps and gigs; the polished handsome pairs that pulled the carriages of the wealthy, to say nothing of the hacks and other riding horses. And so we crossed the bridge over the Mersey and began to walk towards Manchester down that most attractive stretch of road with the winter-bare boughs sketched against the mauve sky on either hand.

A victoria with the hood up, drawn by one shining brown horse, was coming towards us, and at a crossing it was evident that the driver intended to turn. There was a moment of hesitation. We were asking ourselves whether we had time to dash across before the carriage turned, and evidently the driver was asking himself what these young fools were going to do – ought he to pull in the horse? – and all this brought the victoria almost to a standstill halfway round the corner. It was then that we saw who was sitting within, comfortably tucked up in a great bearskin rug; and Blanche said excitedly: "Why, it's Captain Marquick!"

Now I have said before that Captain Marquick's senses were acute. He instantly recognised the voice and shouted: "Hallo, Blanche! Is that Ted with you?"

The carriage was moving slowly all the time into the side road, and Blanche and I walked along with it. "Yes," said Blanche gravely, "it's the pair of us."

It was always "the pair of us" at home. "Now, then, what are you pair up to?" "Be off – the pair of you."

Captain Marquick laughed. "Well," he said, "the pair of you had better come in and have some tea. It's four o'clock."

There was no hesitation in our minds. We did not wonder what Mother would think of our absence; we put none of the questions that proper little children should have put. We were simply overjoyed and snatched at our joy with both hands. "Oh, thank you, Captain Marquick!" we cried together.

The carriage wheeled into the first gate on the left beyond the turning and we gladly followed. There was a short twisting gravelled drive with rhododendrons tall on either side, and then, in front of the house, a circular lawn with the drive going right round it. Away beyond the house were white stuccoed stables. The house itself was faced with white stucco, too. A flight of shallow steps led up to the polished mahogany front door under a porch from which a wrought-iron lantern hung down.

The coachman had descended from the box and lowered the step of the victoria. Captain Marquick threw off his bearskin and got down without help. He remembered what we had so cheerfully forgotten. He mentioned our address to the coachman and said: "Drive round there before you put the horse away. Present my compliments, and say that these young people will return sound in wind and limb in due season." And, turning to us: "Now, come in, the pair of you."

I don't suppose I shall ever forget a detail of my first visit to a house that was to become so familiar: the study opening off the hall into which the captain led us, walking so confidently, the glowing coal fire, the big brown leather chairs, the books and books and books that the captain could not read, and the pictures that he could not see. Lighted lamps were hanging from the ceiling, and a maid came in and drew the heavy crimson velvet curtains, shutting out the deepening February dusk and causing the warmth and happiness of the moment

27

to seem to wrap us round as cosily as the bearskin had wrapped Captain Marquick.

With her legs curled up under her in one of the chairs, Blanche said politely: "It's very kind of you to have asked us in, Captain Marquick. It's the best present Ted has had this birthday."

An exciting-looking wagon came trundling in. The maid who pushed it poured out the captain's tea and put it, with some toast and a piece of cake, on a table near his hand. She asked Blanche if she would pour out for herself and me, and Blanche importantly said yes, thank you, she would.

"So it's your birthday, is it, Ted?" the captain asked when we were alone. "And how old are you now?"

"'Twelve, sir," I said. "And I'll be leaving school at the end of the summer."

"And what are you going to do then?" he asked.

"I'm going to be an artist," I said.

Now why I said this I don't know. It sprang into my mind, a fully-formed notion, as unexpectedly as the notion that Mrs Brimlow, whom I had for so long looked on with indifference, represented something that I detested. I had for years now played with chalk and pencil, and, looking back, I see that even in those early days this was an occupation that gave me peace and tranquillity; but I had not, then, thought about the matter at all; yet out of the blue this answer came: "I'm going to be an artist."

Captain Marquick did not show any surprise, though I learned afterwards that at this moment he felt a good deal. He bit into his toast and said simply: "Well, yes, that would be an agreeable job if you felt up to it."

He had this charming way of talking to children as if he and they were of an age; but at that moment he did not pursue this matter of my problematic career. He urged us to eat of the great spread of toast and cakes and muffins and flattered Blanche by inviting her to refill his teacup. We talked to him about our life at home, and the Sunday night readings, and Blanche even related the horrible affair of Mrs Brimlow and her broken spectacles. Thus an hour passed most pleasantly by, and then Blanche said that she thought we should be going. Captain Marquick thanked us for coming, as though we had done him a great favour, and added that we must have some more meetings. The excitement which we had suppressed all this time broke out as soon as we were clear of the house. We ran all the way home, shouting and singing. The next day a parcel was delivered at our house, addressed to me. There was a note from the captain, apologising for sending a birthday present a day late, and hoping I would like his gift. It was a superb box of watercolours and brushes. I sometimes use the box still.

11

The consequence of this gift from Captain Marquick was that my activities in the attic came to light. Till now my father and mother had known nothing of what I was up to, but when Father, looking at my present, asked: "I wonder what made him send *that?*" I answered him as boldly as I had answered Captain Marquick: "Because I'm going to be an artist."

This was in the evening of the next day. I had gone to school, and, what is more, I was caned, I remember, for absenting myself without excuse the day before. When I came home at teatime there the box was. The captain must have gone into town early and ordered it to be sent out. My father saw it when he came home that night. He looked at me quizzically. "Oh! So you're going to be an artist?" he said; and Blanche, now that part of the secret of our attic had been bared, declared finally: "He's not *going to be* an artist. He *is* an artist."

"Hey! Steady on!" my father said. "These furtive and secret children of ours seem to have been up to some tricks unbeknownst to us, Dolly. But being an artist isn't as simple as that. What are *you* going to be then, Blanche? Queen of England?"

"I'm going to be a dancer," Blanche answered; and not to be outdone by her in generosity, I shouted: "She dances like a fairy."

My father and mother exchanged glances, but nothing more was said about these matters at the time. However, the next day, when my father came back from the shop, he handed me a packet of Whatman's paper and said: "One of these days you might like to show me what you're doing, Ted." I was greatly comforted by this gesture. It seemed to me to mean that "being an artist" was all right so far as my father was concerned. What I did not know was that, deeply against his will, he had made a concession to all that was meant by the word Cornwall

— a word which, I was beginning to understand, had dark and mysterious implications.

Once these things had been set moving, it seemed as though fate took a hand in the matter. That very weekend I collided with the mystery again. On the Saturday morning my mother gave me twopence and told me to go and get my hair cut. In the barber's shop there were a few people waiting their turn, and as I sat there with my feet dangling I passed the time by looking at the old newspapers and magazines with which the place was littered. Among them were several large "annuals" that had survived since Christmas, and sumptuous things the Christmas annuals were in those days, illustrated with fine plates in colour. It was these particularly that held my attention. Paintings and drawings of all sorts by now had a deep fascination for me, though few enough of them had come my way. It was strange, in a house so deeply dedicated to music as ours was, that neither Blanche nor I had shown any wish to play upon an instrument. We both loved the Saturday evening concerts, but on each of us the effect of the music was to release our dreams and desires in other directions. Blanche, as she listened, curled on her hassock, translated it all into dancing, and I, vaguely but irresistibly, into colour and flowing lines. Pictures were music to me, and in my attic art gallery were already, mixed up incongruously with my own daubs and scratchings, some coloured reproductions that I had torn from such publications as I now held in my hands. Printed beneath them were the artists' names, and some of these artists were called R.A. I had long pondered upon the meaning of these letters, and had at last decided that they meant Real Artist. All the current of my young hidden life was set towards reaching the excellence which would permit my pictures, too, to be called those of a "Real Artist".

And now, as I looked at this excitingly coloured annual in the barber's shop, I saw something that gave me almost a physical blow of painful excitement. One of the pictures was signed, in bold red paint at the bottom right-hand corner, with my own name — Pentecost. I sucked in my breath hard and the magazine trembled in my hand. It could not be — but it was. Kitto Pentecost. The line printed underneath left the thing beyond doubt. "The Fishing Fleet at Mevagissey. By Kitto Pentecost, R.A."

I felt as shaken and exalted as if I had beheld a miracle. Everything about the moment was magical. My own surname, and with "Real Artist" attached thereto! And that strange Christian name the like of which I had never heard before – Kitto. But hadn't I heard it? And there came flooding back to my mind the memory of one of the very few occasions on which I had heard my father use high words to my mother. I had come in on the tail-end of a dispute and heard him say "Damn the Kittos," and that queer foreign-sounding name had remained in my mind.

So what with my sense of exaltation and the feeling of having touched the fringe of a mystery, it was small wonder that I was wrapt away from that sordid little twopenny barber's shop on the Wilmslow Road, with the gas burning because the February morning was dim, and the fly-blown cigarette packets, and the bottles of sticky poisonous-looking hair oil ranged in front of the spotted mirrors. It was not till the barber shouted: "Hey! Come on! What is it? D'you want your beard off or just trimmed?" that I looked round and saw the place was empty save for him and me and a dirty little boy sweeping up snippets of hair from the oil cloth.

When he had done with me and I had paid my twopence, I stood there dithering. I wanted that picture, but for a long time dared not ask for it. At last I picked up the magazine and blurted out: "Please would you sell this secondhand? It's very soiled."

He took it from my hand and flipped over the pages. "Take it," he said. "It's time some of this old muck was cleared out." He rolled it into a tight cylinder, gave me a hearty slap on the backside with it, and then placed it in my hands. I thanked him breathlessly, and ran home with my treasure. I did not show it to anyone. I felt there was something about this picture that I had better keep to myself. I fastened it with drawing pins to the wall of the attic and placed a larger picture over it. This was nothing but a screen which, during the days that followed, I was continuously lifting to gaze at the brown sails and the blue sea of Cornwall – the forbidden, haunted land.

CHAPTER TWO

WE WERE on the way to Cornwall, and the cause of our going was, of all things, Luther Brimlow. It was much later, and only from a word here and a hint there, that I learned from Blanche what had happened between her and Luther Brimlow. Nothing would have happened at all if it hadn't been for our call on Captain Marquick and the present he sent me the next day; so I had better begin with that.

Both Blanche and I had declared ourselves. We had, as it were, thrown wide open the secret of the attic that we had guarded for years. Now we had to decide what to do about it, and it was Blanche's idea that we should ask our parents and Mr Lop and the captain to an entertainment. She would dance and I would display my pictures. We were puzzled about the captain because he would be able to see neither the dancing nor the pictures, but we felt that he would not like to be out of it, and in that we were right.

The idea that one of his precious Saturday night concerts should be sacrificed to childish folly at first horrified my father, but when Blanche was set on a thing she did not easily let go, and at last a compromise was reached. The show in the attic should be held in place of the first part of the concert; then supper would follow as usual, and there would be music after that.

Now that permission had been given, Blanche was like a being possessed. Save for the fag end of music, which I suppose she did not consider to be of much account, she and I must do everything. Our *début* must be a resounding success. The dim old attic, so badly neglected for so long, was now given the clean of its life. I was sent down on to my knees with a scrubbing brush, soap and water and made to work till the deal floorboards shone as white as the kitchen table. The skylight was polished, and two paraffin lamps were scrounged from Betsy and suspended from hooks. The tiny fireplace, in which never to our knowledge had a fire burned, was black-leaded till it gleamed like onyx, and a trial fire was lit to see if the chimney would "draw". It did, and then Betsy was cajoled into providing a scuttle of coal, to be ready for the night. In front of the wall facing the fireplace a hessian curtain was hung. This gave Blanche a space of a yard or so for a "dressing room" in which she could change between her dances. Upon the curtain I daubed scrolls and squiggles with a broad brush of white paint, and it looked, I thought, charmingly effective. We commandeered four easy chairs from rooms all over the house, and altogether throughout the few days before the Saturday we lived in a frenzy of excitement, taking care each night to lock the door and hide the key, for no eye save ours was to see what was happening before the hour struck.

But, scrounge, beg and pilfer as we would, there was one thing we were unable to find, and that was a fender. In front of the fireplace we had put the small rug from my bedroom, but, as fires were never lighted in bedrooms, there was no fender in any bedroom of our house, and Blanche said that if the attic was to be really as she wanted it, a fender there must be. She became a public plague and bugbear on the subject of the fender, asking casual acquaintances: "You couldn't lend me a fender, I suppose, just for one night? A very small one would do." It looked as though it would all be in vain, and then, on the Saturday afternoon, while I was on guard in the attic, I heard a clanking noise on the stairs, as though a knight in armour were ascending, and, opening the door, was amazed to see Blanche hauling along a fender. I ran out to help her, shouting; "Where did you get it from?" and she said calmly; "From Luther Brimlow". She sat down on one of our purloined easy chairs and began giggling.

I learned that she had been sent out to do an errand on the Wilmslow Road, and there she met Luther Brimlow who was coming home from the office, for this was the half-closing day. He was dressed up to the nines as usual, looking very important with kid gloves and a new cane. He raised his bowler hat and was about to pass by when Blanche blurted out her idiotic question: "I suppose you couldn't lend me a fender?"

I can imagine that Luther Brimlow was taken aback both by the strange request and by the fact that one of the Pentecost children had voluntarily addressed him. He came to a stand, and Blanche by now, she said, had regretted her folly and was anxious to fly. But she stood her ground, and Luther looked through his spectacles at her with those cold eyes that had whitish lashes, and he said: "A fender? What a strange thing to ask for."

"Oh, never mind," Blanche answered. "It was just for a game Ted and I are playing."

She began to move off, but to her annoyance Luther took her by the arm. "Don't go," he said. "There's no reason to be afraid of me."

"As if I ever would be," Blanche protested stoutly.

He smiled, and shuffled, and licked his pale lips. "I think I might be able to find one," he said. "You never know what old junk is knocking about in my father's yard. Let's go and have a look."

So they went towards the yard, which was not far away. The double doors were locked, for Mr Brimlow had packed up for the Saturday afternoon. Luther pulled out of his pocket a bunch of keys that were attached to a stylish chain, looking, Blanche said, like gold. He fitted a key into the lock of a wicket let into the big doors, and stood aside for Blanche to enter. He followed, and slammed the door. Blanche heard the lock snap to, and felt uncomfortable. To make conversation, she asked: "Does your father know you've got a key to the yard?"

"Oh, yes," Luther said lightly. "And to his office, too. I often come here at nights to study when I don't want to be disturbed at home. And sometimes I go through Father's books for him. His affairs were in a shocking state until I began to look into them."

He was pacing to and fro among the heaps of builder's material and rubbish of all sorts, fastidiously avoiding contact with anything. "Dear me, what a place it is," he said. "You might as well call it a marine store dealer's, and be done with it. Even at that, I could make it pay better than he does. If I were to buy the place up tomorrow and put a manager in, I could make something of it. Well, well. What is this? You see! You'll find anything here if you look long enough – anything that's no use to anybody. A fender!"

He pointed triumphantly with the end of his cane to a rusty fender protruding from a heap of old iron. Blanche at once pounced upon it and began to pull. He made at first to help her, then changed his mind, looking with solicitude at his gloves. "It will suit?" he asked.

"Oh, thank you," Blanche cried, "It's just the thing. A bit of blacklead and elbow grease and you won't know it."

She moved towards the gate, half-dragging and half-carrying the cumbrous thing with her. Luther walked at her side, unlocked the wicket, and stood there so that she could not get through. He took her by the elbow again, and began: "You wouldn't – I suppose you wouldn't –" But whatever it was he was going to say Blanche did not know. She saw a chance to slip through the gate and took it. "Thank you, thank you so much," she shouted, and ran for home, leaving him standing there.

When she had finished with the fender it certainly gave the room the added touch that we wanted. But all the same, I didn't like it there. I felt as I had done when Mrs Brimlow was in the house, that the sooner it was gone the better. Once, I had let the Brimlows in, and now Blanche had done it, too.

2

I am trying to tell you as quickly as possible what happened in two years, for I was fourteen when we first went to Cornwall, and Blanche was fifteen. I must not linger over details, and so I shall not describe fully the happenings of that Saturday evening. It was a success. A few pictures out of the occasion will ever remain in my mind. I shall see Captain Marquick sitting so patiently in one of the armchairs, with the firelight painting brightness upon his red waistcoat and his kind face smiling as he sensed the excitement though he was unable to share the cause. I shall see my father's sceptical grin – "What are the kids up to now?" it said as he entered the room – change to surprise and then to something which I was vain enough to call awe as he went the rounds of the "gallery". "You did all these, Ted? All on your own?" My heart was too full for me to answer. I nodded dumbly. I shall see us all sitting in our chairs at the fireside end of the room watching the curtain behind which Blanche had retired, and Blanche coming out, pausing for a moment in a long white muslin dress, with her dark hair trimmed into a coronet on top of her head and one crimson flower pinned upon it and another at her breast. I shall remember that as long as I live: the stillness of her in that moment of pause, her arms hanging down at her sides, her eyes closed, a look upon her face which moved me deeply, though I was too young to call it dedicated. I shall see her dance, and feel the quietness of everybody in the room, and remember the moment at which Anatole Lop, who had brought his fiddle up to the attic with him, caught the rhythm of the thing, got up without a sound, and began to improvise. That gaunt old skeleton scraping away at the catgut, looking, as Betsy used to say, like death warmed up, and the virginal girl in samite swaying and swirling upon the floor, till one wondered which was compelling the other: this, too, remains forever. Most astonishing of all, when I myself felt both excited and exalted, was to see my mother furtively wiping away the tears that were in her eyes.

This is enough – this is blessedly so much – to remember of that night. Blanche and I went leaping tumultuously down the stairs when it was over, and were already with healthy childish appetites tucking into supper while my father was carefully helping down the captain, who was not accustomed to moving about in that part of the house. Then, as usual, we were packed off to bed before the second part of the music, which tonight was the first part, had begun. And I was soon asleep. It took a lot in those days to keep me awake. I was aware of the tuning up and of the beginning of the music, but only vaguely, for my thoughts were elsewhere. They were on the picture by Kitto Pentecost, R.A., which I had removed from the attic and hidden in my bedroom lest anyone should lift its screen and see it. It was imprinted on my mind as a poem might be on someone else's memory. I recalled every brush-stroke, and slept happily in the vision of the Cornish sea and sun and the ships sailing in so bravely to the little port.

3

The course of our lives now changed rapidly and dramatically for me and Blanche. In some ways, I suppose, we were older than our years, but in others we were much younger (which largely accounts for our feelings towards Luther Brimlow, who was sophisticated in so much of which we were ignorant), and it would never have occurred to us that our entertainment in the attic would have consequences among our elders. But, of course, it did, for the four elders concerned were all of a sort to be moved by the spectacle of young lives unfolding as ours were. (But, for us, we had no standard by which to know that this unfolding was in any way unusual.)

It was from my mother that I learned of the debate which followed. Money was the trouble. My father's shop and his piano tuning just kept things together, and, not unreasonably, he had looked forward to the time when I would begin to earn some money. He did not share the notion, which has since become so popular, that a boy was a victim of social villainies, deeply to be pitied, if he had to leave school at twelve. "To leave school gives him a chance to begin his education – if he's the sort that education can matter to, anyway," he used to declare; and, without any sense of failing in his duty to me, he would have packed me off to work that year, either in his own shop or elsewhere.

There was, I learned, much discussion about my future and Blanche's, and all four of those who joined in the discussion took as their first point that Blanche must have professional training as a dancer and I as an artist. The whole thing was a question of ways and means. Education had so far cost my father nothing, and he would doubtless have said in his dry way that his children had been educated accordingly. "All they've ever learned they've learned here in this house." And that was true enough. He now declared that he could find the money for one of us to go to a teacher, but not for two. It was at this point that Captain Marquick took the matter in hand. Although he had no active part in the affairs of Marquick and Marquand, the firm that his father had founded, he was, by inheritance, the most substantial shareholder in it, and for him to get me a job in the office meant no more than uttering a word. This word was uttered, and I found myself, in that summer when I was twelve years old, an office boy in the firm's huge soot-blackened premises in Portland Street. Shall I ever forget the morning when I first walked up those steps, dodging the buckets of one charwoman as another polished the vast brass plate bearing one of the most famous names in the trade of Lancashire! It was like creeping through a rabbit hole into the rock of Gibraltar. Nothing, it would seem, literally nothing, would ever avail to breach that mighty fortress of ashlar blocks past which the lorries rolled with their bales spreading upon the air the never-to-be-forgotten smell of cotton! But I have lived to see it desolate, and the pigeons flying through its blind eye sockets to alight upon the dust and ashes which are all that remain within.

However, that is a thought of today, and the thought concerning us now is that of a boy of twelve in the first summer of this century. He was a boy receiving five shillings a week, and it is enough comment on our financial circumstances to say that this was an easing of the situation. He was a boy wildly excited by the knowledge that, when evening classes started at the Art School in the autumn, he was to attend them, and that Captain Marquick would pay the fees. And finally he was a boy whose sister was already attending Madame Gribble's Dancing Academy.

If Captain Marquick, more than the others, was my sponsor in all this, Anatole Lop was Blanche's. Poor Mr Lop was not able to do for her what the captain was doing for me. He had not the money to pay her fees. Somewhere there was a Mrs Lop, a mysterious person with whom he never appeared, but of whom occasionally he lugubriously spoke. I once heard my father say: "She leads poor old Anatole a pretty dance." In my childish imagination, Mrs Lop was a bold and beautiful creature, leading a gay expensive life at Anatole's cost, and, as it happens, I was later to discover that this was near enough to the truth, except that she looked brazen rather than beautiful, and made, in ways of her own, more money than Anatole would ever see. And all this did not prevent his being utterly devoted to her, as one might be to a poisonous drug that has become indispensable.

If Anatole was unable to do anything financially for Blanche he did all that otherwise could be done. It was he who introduced her to Miss Gribble (as Madame Gribble really was) and who entertained her with endless talk about dancing and the ballet. The ballet to Mr Lop was the greatest art in the world, and Blanche could not at that time have found in all Manchester anyone better able than Anatole was to give her constant injections of pride and humility, self-esteem and ambition – in a word to canalise the fragmentary and vagrant streams of her native genius.

At last I saw the fulfilment of my childish wish to walk daily with my father to Manchester. My mother now put up two luncheon baskets instead of one, and off we would go through the mornings of that fine summer, watched by my mother and by Blanche, who did not leave till later and then made the journey to Manchester by train. I am glad we had those times together. All that happened afterwards cannot destroy the glorious memory of them or alter in my heart the conviction that this companion of so many happy miles, and not the other man I was later to discover, was truly my father. But who shall sort out the mysterious and unpredictable ingredients of one human heart and say that this, not that, is the man?

With so gay a companion, the five-mile walk seemed nothing. First, there was our own leafy suburb which could smell in the dewy morning as if it were the country itself. Halfway along the Wilmslow Road, on the corner of Fog Lane, there was a house called the Priory, with iron gates and iron railings surmounting a low coping of stone. Here we always paused in the early part of the year to admire the snowdrops and crocuses, white, mauve and yellow, that grew in staggering abundance on the lawns. Then we came to the White Lion, where the roads flowing in from west and south became one that marched straight for the grimy heart of Manchester. But it did not become grimy all at once. There were trees enough, and pleasant gardens, for another mile or so till we came to Dickenson Road, where you could almost feel that a line had been ruled and that, once you had stepped over it, you were in Manchester good and proper. Little shops, little houses, little grey, mean streets opening to right and left were all that we could hope for now, but these had no power to depress me, for I was young. I was with my father, who was full of love and understanding, and ahead of me was the autumn when I would begin seriously to work to be a Real Artist. Soon we were at All Saints Church, with the cab horses standing on the rank just outside the thick dirty iron railings that enclosed the churchyard with its blackened and forbidding memorial stones. The dead were well battened down and strongly shut in, and past them at that early morning hour the living went in unheeding multitudes towards the day's work in the city which here finally and implacably closed upon us. I suppose it can never have been other than a barbarous and dismal spectacle, with the few wretched soot-poisoned trees of the graveyard reaching their stunted witch-like limbs into the air. But it did not then seem so to me; and whenever I think of it now I think not of its sad failure to achieve any sort of civilisation but of my own hopeful childish heart, and of my father standing there at the door of his little shop, which looked upon the graveyard, and of his pointing finger as he said: "Well, Ted, there it is. Soon now – eh?"

I did not need to look to know that he was pointing to the School of Art, the villainously ugly black block that stood on the western side of the graveyard. But was it villainously ugly to me then? Not at all. It shone with the radiance of young hope's gateway, and, bidding my father goodbye, I would go on with all the world singing about me, to the commercial citadel of Messrs. Marquick and Marquand.

4

So far as I remember, it was in the June of that year that I said to my father during one of those morning walks: "Father, what is an R.A.?" Anyhow, I know it was at the time when all the shrubs and trees that made spring so beautiful in our suburb had ceased their flowering. In the autumn, all would be lovely again with the turn of the leaf, but now there was the dull-green summer to get through.

He laughed. "Well," he said, "I suppose the answer to that depends on the answerer. There are some who would say it means a Rotten Artist."

But I knew he was chaffing me. "Really, though," I persisted, "what does it mean?"

"It means a Royal Academician," he said. "First of all, you have to be an A.R.A. That means an Associate of the Royal Academy. Then, if one of the academicians dies, and those who are left think you're good enough, they say: 'Let's make this associate one of us.' And there you are. Every year they have an exhibition at Burlington House in London. Anyone can send a picture along."

"Could I?"

"Yes. Then all the academicians gather together, and men in short sleeves hold the pictures up one by one, and the academicians say: 'Ha!' or 'H'm' or 'Pretty good' or 'Pretty bad.' Sometimes they say: 'Right! We'll show that one,' and sometimes they cover their eyes with their hands and groan: 'Take it away!' But to make up for all this sad labour they have one advantage. They can show their own pictures, good or bad, and no one can say a word about it."

I listened to all this with breathless interest. It was the first I had ever heard about it. "I thought," I said, "that R.A. meant Real Artist."

He grinned mischievously. "That's all a matter of opinion," he said. Then he added to my amazement: "I ought to know something about it. My brother Ted – the one you are named after – is an R.A. You'll probably run into his stuff some day. Kitto Pentecost he signs himself, though he's Ted to me. Edward Kitto he was christened."

"Kitto! What a funny name that is!" I said. "I've never heard the like of it."

"Then you've been lucky," he answered with a grin, "because you might have been condemned to read the novels of the Reverend Silas Kitto Hocking. Oh, there are Kittos enough in Cornwall. The name's as common as mud there. The county's full of names ending in O – Spargo and Pasco and all the rest of 'em."

I was highly excited. I was on the verge, I felt, of having a veil lifted, but I was sensitive enough to all that Cornwall meant in our house to know that this was ground on which I must walk tenderly. In as offhand a voice as I could command I said: "Why, Father! I never even knew I had an uncle."

"There are lots of things you don't know yet, young feller," he answered. "A chap who wants to be an artist and doesn't even know what an R.A. is evidently has a lot to learn."

I had the sense to know that this chaff closed the door for the time being.

5

Blanche, as I said, left the house later than I and Father. She walked to the Didsbury railway station and came into town by train. Madame Gribble's establishment was in a mean street in the heart of the city, not far from Marquick and Marquand's in Portland Street. Blanche used to wait outside the office for me to come out at one o'clock, and then we would wander the streets together for an hour, eating our lunch as we walked and content to wash the dry fare down with our own spit. We didn't ask much of life in those days. We became haunters of the Art Gallery in Mosley Street, where for the first time I saw a decent collection of pictures, and rubbed our noses against the windows of shops like Agnew's. It was there one day that we saw one of Edgar Degas' pictures of ballet girls. It filled us both with a deep satisfaction. It united in a few square feet of canvas the ambitions that were burning in both our hearts. Every day, until the picture was removed, we came to gaze at it. We strolled through the narrow alleys under the shadow of the cathedral where Manchester's past still spoke in a dying whisper, and in Tib Street we delighted our eyes with the marmosets and cockatoos, the pups and kittens, snakes and fish, that screeched and yapped and swam and slithered in the pet shops.

This daily hour with Blanche was as precious to me as the morning walk with my father, and it was with some annoyance one day, when I bounded down Marquick and Marquand's steps, that I found Luther Brimlow standing at the bottom, talking to her. I was annoyed, and yet impressed. There was no doubt about it: Luther was blooming with incredible speed from the moron, as we had thought him, who hopped on one leg down the garden path, to a fine figure of a young commercial man about town. How could I know, child as I was, that Luther had already found what Blanche and I vaguely hoped to find some day: the apt environment and expression of his particular abilities? He was, perhaps, a little too florid, too exuberant, but this was no more than a youthful rush to open his petals to his appropriate sun.

Anyway, there he stood, fully at ease, leaning on his cane, with kid gloves held in his hand. He greeted me easily. "Good morning, Ted. How is the world treating you?"

"All right," I said with a scowl; and my discomfiture was not diminished when I saw that Blanche was secretly laughing at both of us. My dark ferocity and Luther's overdone *savoir faire* seemed alike to tickle her humour.

But I could not understand this fellow, and I could not like him. On the Sunday before this, walking near our house in the cool of the evening, I had seen the members of the Plymouth Brethren chapel come out of their dingy tabernacle, form a ragged procession, and move off to the street corner. There they had held an open-air meeting, standing in a meagre circle while one member after another stepped into the middle and testified. Luther was there, quite at ease, between his moist little father and his whipcord mother. He was wearing none of the fine raiment that clad him now. He was lugubriously dressed and he looked lugubrious, shouting his "Hallelujahs!" and "Amens!" with the best of them. He even stepped for a moment into the ring and spoke a few words, telling how he had found "Grace", and thanking God generally that he was not as other men. And certainly to Mrs Brimlow he was not. She gazed at him as though a seraph had come down to utter truth in this world of liars. It was all confusing to my young mind. What was troubling me was beyond my definition, but I was bothered by a gulf which I apprehended between that young man and this one who so casually greeted me on the pavement of Portland Street. I was gripped with a fear lest Blanche and I should have our hour of companionship ruined by his company, but Blanche settled this by taking my arm at once and dragging me away. She waved a hand lightly to Luther Brimlow and wished him goodbye.

"Where did he spring from?" I asked morosely, when we were out of earshot.

"Oh, he was just passing by," she said. "His office is round the corner." Then she began to giggle. "He travels first class," she said.

"How on earth do you know how he travels?"

She giggled again. "I believe he's chasing me," she said.

I was horrified. The words themselves conveyed almost nothing to me, but I sensed a dark shadow wrapping them. And then Blanche told me that, as she was nearing the Didsbury railway station that morning, Luther Brimlow was going ahead of her. She had dawdled, so as to allow him to find a seat before she chose hers, and to her surprise saw him enter a first-class compartment. With relief, she took her place in her customary third, but just as the train was moving off Luther wrenched open the door and leapt in. They were alone in the compartment.

Blanche was not choice of speech unless there was some reason that made her wish to be, and she now cried to Luther: "You silly fool! Why did you do that? You might have been run over."

Luther had barked his shins against the step as he made his foolhardy leap, and he knocked the dust off his trousers with a newspaper that he carried. Blanche saw that it was *The Financial Times*. He sat for a moment looking rather white and shaken, both by her ferocious glance and by the sense of having indeed narrowly escaped an accident. Then he said, with an attempt at a grin: "I'd chance more than that for the pleasure of travelling with you."

Blanche did not answer this, but asked point-blank: "Why do you waste your money on travelling first class?"

"There's no waste about it," Luther answered. "I happen to be a little late today, and so I should have had a first-class compartment to myself. But normally I have plenty of companions. It pays to be seen travelling first. Mr Armroyd is often in my compartment."

Mr Armroyd was a member of the firm of stockbrokers who employed Luther Brimlow, and it must have been edifying for him to see his young clerk travelling first class and reading *The Financial Times.* Blanche, who had never thought of the social and commercial advantages of running into town with the bosses, had nothing to say about this. An uneasy silence fell between them, broken by Luther's saying: "I hear you're attending dancing classes."

Blanche nodded briefly: it was not a matter she could discuss with Luther Brimlow. "I'm sorry to hear that," he said. "I don't take the extreme view of my father and mother, who would be shocked if they knew I was talking to you now; but I think it's a sinful occupation, a pandering to the lusts of the flesh. It horrifies me to think of you showing your legs in public."

The distance between Didsbury and Withington stations is short. Already the train was slackening speed. As soon as it stopped Blanche got up without a word, leapt out and ran to a compartment farther down the platform. The rebuff did not prevent Luther from shouting after her: "Shall I see you at lunchtime?" She shouted back: "No. I always meet my brother." And this, I suppose, gave Luther the clue to be outside Marquick and Marquand's before I appeared. His presence there, and the story which Blanche told me when we had got rid of him, made me grim and resentful throughout the whole of our precious hour together, but Blanche was as gay as ever, full of disrespectful gibes about Luther and his family, acting almost as though the small adventure of the morning had given her, in its way, some pleasure.

6

As that summer wore on there was a good deal of strain between us and the Brimlows. The politicians of these later days, with their genius for wrapping up the truth in jargon, would say that our relationships had deteriorated. The fact is, we were ready for war. We never talked to them about our affairs, but things get out, and they knew not only that Blanche hoped to be a dancer in public but that I had a mind to be a Real Artist. Both these occupations were, in their view of life, at best levities, at worst sins. The Bible was full of women who danced men to perdition, and I suppose they saw not a pin between Blanche and Salome. They would hardly have been surprised to see her, wearing next to nothing, dancing down the street with a Plymouth Brother's head on an old tin tray. When we passed them, Mrs

44

Brimlow's mouth was a more rigid rat-trap than ever, and Mr
Brimlow's watery dog-like eyes almost overflowed with
compassionate condemnation. I can imagine, now in my later years,
how we were discussed. The musical evenings had been bad enough,
but now the older generation, not content with its own sins, was
consciously dedicating the younger to the worship of Baal. In their
imagination, our little house must have blazed with fires on impious
altars. I can well understand, too, knowing more now than I could be
expected to know then of the tendency of Luther's secret life, how all
the talk he heard inflamed an imagination already incendiary enough.
Just how contaminating an influence we were held to be I understood
one evening as the autumn was drawing on. Walking home alone from
my dreary and unsatisfying work in the office, I was passing the
Didsbury station when a train was discharging its passengers, and
among them was Luther. Though we had little enough to say to one
another, on such chance-met occasions as this we would walk home
together, and we were doing so that evening when we passed a
grocer's shop. We did not know that Mrs Brimlow was within, but she
saw us, ran out, and overtook us a dozen yards farther on. Without a
word, but with a look at me that was intended to shrivel me to dust,
she seized Luther's arm and drew him back with her into the safe
harbourage of the shop. That was all: a trivial matter: but he and I fully
understood the unspoken implications of it.

However, that of all nights was not one on which Mrs Brimlow's
tantrums could much affect me, for I was due, the next day, at Captain
Marquick's. That next day was a Saturday, which meant a free half-day
for me, and the captain had asked me to come alone and take tea with
him. The evening classes at the School of Art had now begun. I had
made my first few attendances, received many raps over the knuckles,
and in general had been shown that I was not quite the god-sent
genius that at times I had imagined myself to be. All the same, this had
not depressed me. Not a bit: it had fired me. It had awakened in me
something grim and resolute, and I felt now, more than ever, the
immensity of my task and the joy of measuring myself against it.
Luther Brimlow, who had an uncanny faculty of knowing, without
being told, what the Pentecosts were up to, was aware that I was
attending the school, and this very day – the day following that on
which his mother had snatched him from my contaminating embrace

he overtook me just as I had left the office. Happily, I reflected, it was not far to St Peter's Square where our paths would separate, he to ride stylishly home first class, I to peg along on Shanks' pony, picking up my father at the shop on the way.

"How are you getting on at the School of Art?" Luther demanded, when we had walked a little way.

I grunted some non-committal answer, and he said: "I can't understand why you want to be playing about with that sort of thing, Ted. What is there in it? Who buys pictures? Don't you ever think of making something of your life?"

No: I hadn't ever thought of that. The idea now came to me as something utterly new, and I asked childishly: "How d'you mean – make something?"

"Why," Luther cried expansively, "*be* someone – make money – get out of Kingsley Avenue. You don't want to spend your life there, do you?"

I could only ask him: "Why not?" It seemed to me a pleasant place, with the big chestnut tree in front, the open fields behind, and not far off the pool where the kingcups grew. But I didn't say all this. I only said: "Why not?"

Luther gave me a sly sideways glance. "I suppose it's the life classes that appeal to you. I'll bet you enjoy that – drawing naked women."

Now I was not likely for some time to attend "life classes". The words were there on the school syllabus, and I knew that this was something I should come to in time, but my imagination had not played around the matter as Luther's, evidently, was doing now. I looked at him and saw that his cheeks were red, and I mischievously told him that certainly the life classes were the thing. We had reached St Peter's Square, but he did not seem in a hurry to leave me. He was thirsting for information, and, urged by my imp, I gave it to him lavishly. At last I pointed out that if he didn't hurry he would lose his train. "Your mother will wonder what's become of you," I couldn't resist saying.

He gave me a confiding grin. "I don't worry about that," he said. "What I do is all right in that quarter." And as he moved off he added, half in admiration, half with reproof: "I must say you Pentecosts are a pretty hot lot."

My visit to Captain Marquick put this ridiculous incident out of my head. It was a delicious afternoon. September had been lovely, and now, though November was not far off, the season prolonged its golden dying. Trees, trees, trees. That, for me, was the glory of Didsbury. There were trees everywhere: beech and chestnut, oak and sycamore, Lombardy poplars like huge quill pens stuck nib-downwards into the earth: and now the flames of this late season were lighting them all, and the sky of periwinkle blue was serene and tender. The lawn in front of Captain Marquick's house had not been swept. It was like a patchwork quilt composed of every autumn shade: red and yellow and brown and umber; and under the walls of the house the chrysanthemums and Michaelmas daisies were in their glory. I stood there for some time listening to the silence. It was incredible that this enchanted garden could be so near to Manchester. Everything was so still that when a large crinkled leaf fell to the lawn at my feet I heard the faint sound of its touch upon those already fallen.

Someone within the house must have seen me standing there and told the captain that I had arrived, for my reverie was broken by his voice hailing me from the porch. "Hallo, Ted! Wait there. I'm coming out to you."

He came, swinging a key in his hand, and, taking my arm, he began to lead me round the big circular lawn. The leaves rustled beneath our feet. "I like that sound," he said. "It opens my eyes, Ted. That sound, and the feel of this mild sunshine, tells me the sort of day it is." He paused and lifted his face up to the light. "I can see it, you know," he said, "after twenty years. That's why I've never left this place, and that's why nothing here is ever changed. I know exactly how it all looks, in any sort of weather. We always have the same flowers in the same places. The Michaelmas daisies under the house now must be looking superb." We paused, and he passed his hands lightly among their mauve heads. "As good as ever," he said with satisfaction.

Just there, on the gravel path, was a curved white seat. We sat down with the last of the sunlight falling upon us; and Captain Marquick asked: "What do you think of these motorcars, Ted? It looks to me as though they're really going to be something."

He was like that. He knew about everything that was happening in the world, blind though he was. The daily papers were read to him

47

every morning, and he was quick to follow up anything novel or amusing. He talked to me now about motorcars, and how they were made to move, and how certain it was that before long they would be much improved and brought within general use. "I shall have one myself," he said, "as soon as I can manage it. The stables there won't be wanted for horses much longer, and anyway I've got only two now. In my father's day there were six. He used to ride down to Portland Street every morning, you know, have the horse stabled in town, and ride back at night. When I was a boy I used to have fine games in the lofts over the stable. They were full of harness and hay and straw. We had an old groom who taught me to make pipes out of straw. They didn't last long, but you could blow thin tunes out of them. Well, the loft is empty now. All we need can be kept down below in the stalls that the horses don't use, and I suppose even those will be cleared out soon to make a garage." He got up and handed me the large iron key he had been carrying all this time. "Come along," he said. "I want you to have a look at the old loft, Ted."

An outside wooden stairway with a handrail led to the loft. "You go first," he said. "I want you to open the door. Don't bother about me. I know these stairs all right. I've leapt up and down them like a goat ever since I can remember."

So I ran on ahead, turned the key in the lock, and threw open the door. I had guessed there was some mystery behind the captain's manner, but I had no idea what to expect. Certainly not this: not this spacious room with a large brick fireplace in which a fire was burning with a comfortable wicker chair on either side; not these tall windows, this easel, this long drawing table with its neat piles of Whatman's paper, its vase containing brushes, its tubes of oil paint. I stood just within the door, wondering what it all meant, when the captain came up and rested his hand on my shoulder. "Well," he asked. "How does it all look? I've got a pretty good general idea, but how does it all look to *you*?"

"It looks marvellous!" I burst out. "But what is it, sir?"

He began to laugh quietly. "Why, what do you think it is, Ted?" he asked. "It's your studio, of course." He walked over to one of the chairs by the fire and sat down. "Now shut the door," he said, "and have a good look round."

I could hardly move for the awe I felt. That was the only word to describe the emotion that had me in its grip. Sometimes I had allowed my imagination to play with a thought of the time when I would be a "Real Artist," and to conjure up the setting in which I would move. There had been in the *Strand Magazine* a series of illustrated interviews with celebrities, and among these were some Royal Academicians – Alma Tadema and Marcus Stone I remember among the others. There were pictures of them in opulent-looking rooms, and never had I dared to think that such surroundings would ever be mine. Now, at one stroke it seemed to me I had leapt beyond anything that my most extravagant hopes could have called up, and suddenly to my dismay, I was crying. I stood with my back to the room, looking down upon the leaf-strewn lawn from which the light was rapidly fading, and my shoulders began to shake and my lips to tremble. The captain was at my side in a moment. "Hey! What's all this?" he cried. "Come over here and sit down." He pushed me into one chair and let himself down into the other. "Now, what's the matter?" he demanded.

"You're so g-good," I stuttered. "You must have spent hundreds on me."

At that he laughed heartily. "I'll tell you what I've spent on you," he said. "A few quid for having the windows and fireplace put in. Everything else is old junk gathered from here and there about the house. The room was going begging. Why not use it? And remember this: if this studio is to mean anything at all – and I hope it will, Ted – it's you who've got to give it meaning. Not this place, which is nothing much, but what's done in it: that's the thing. Now go and open the door. I can hear someone coming up the steps."

As usual, he had heard before I did. It was a maid with crockery and food, a teapot and a milk jug, in a shallow basket. "Just leave it as it is," Captain Marquick told her; and, when she was gone, he said to me: "Now lay the table, Ted. I thought that we'd christen the room by eating in it together. It's your room. You're the host. Get busy and look after your guest."

So I pulled up a little table between the wicker chairs, laid out the things and poured his tea. I was more composed and tranquil, but all the same I seemed still to be living in a dream. The captain was full of the quiet satisfaction of a conjuror who has brought off a marvellous trick. He munched contentedly. "You will keep the key, Ted," he said, "and then you can come here whenever you want to. I've told the people in the house, and so they won't be surprised to see you coming and going. As you see, I've hung nothing on the walls. That's a matter for you. Please your own taste."

The walls were lovely: old brick whitewashed, with the new red brick of the fireplace standing out in contrast. I told myself that I would have Kitto Pentecost's picture framed and hung over the mantelpiece.

"I hear you're a rotten office boy," the captain said with a grin. I was glad he could not see my blushes. "I do my best, sir," I answered, "but I don't like the job."

"I'm not surprised to hear it," he said. "Ah, well, you'll have to put up with it for a bit longer, and see that you do it as well as you can. What I really wanted to say, and have done with it, was this. I wouldn't have wasted this place on someone who was not likely to benefit from it. I think you are. I am told you are, never mind by whom. But I've made inquiries, and people who ought to know what they're talking about tell me that you already show talent both with drawing and colour. I'm telling you this, Ted, once for all, because I want you to have confidence, but not conceit. You understand? I shan't make a habit of buttering you up."

I licked my dry lips. "Yes, sir," I murmured.

"Very well, then. Now the job's yours, to make what you like of it. We'll say no more about it, not now nor at any other time. I'll trouble you for another cup of tea."

When we went out again to the top of the stairway I carried the tea things and locked the door with an extraordinary sense of pride and possession. It was now dark, and instinctively I put down the crockery basket to give the captain my arm. He gently shook it off without a word, and I realised that in his strange world it was as light as it ever was. I wondered whether it was this very sightlessness that was seeking compensation by holding hard to one whose being depended on seeing intensely: seeing, even in what at first appeared to be the dark, the plum-bloom of the dregs of light, the ashen glimmer of the Michaelmas daisies, the frosty star-twinkle of a street lamp outside the garden. But, being a child, I thought this with one crude thrust of imagination: "Poor old Captain! He can't see, and so he wants me to."

7

I have said that our going to Cornwall was caused by Luther Brimlow, and I had better say how this happened. It was in the late autumn of 1901 that I became the occupier of the studio at The Pines, as the captain's house was called. Throughout that winter I worked hard at the School of Art, and when the evening classes there finished, being an office boy at Marquick and Marquand's became more than ever irksome. For relief, I worked passionately at my painting and drawing throughout the long summer evenings and during the weekends in the daytime as well. I was always finding some new example of the captain's thoughtfulness. My supply of drawing paper and brushes, crayons and paints, kept up like the drink in the widow's cruse, and during the summer a small bookcase appeared in which from time to time I would find a new volume, the biography of a painter, a book of reproductions, and things of that sort. But nothing was said, and I saw nothing of the captain except when he came to our house on Saturday nights.

In May of that year, standing at the window of the studio on a Sunday morning, I was overcome by the beauty of a hawthorn bush growing by itself on the edge of the lawn, with the pines, which gave the house its name, dark as a cliff behind its breaking foam. It took me an hour to put it down in oil – a tiny canvas; and I knew in my bones that, for the first time in my life, I had done something good. Also for the first time in my life, I signed the picture. It is one of those moments which, even now, can come back with all their morning glory undimmed. I can recall how, as soon as the thing was done, I stuck it on the mantelpiece under the framed reproduction of Kitto Pentecost's picture and then lay down on a canvas folding bed. The birds were singing joyously in the garden, and from the stable beneath me I could hear the occasional stamp of a horse's hoof and the snort of chaff being blown about a manger. I was pretending to read Vasari's *Lives of the Painters*, but in fact I was simply giving myself up to joy, to the sense of achievement, and again and again my eye would wander to the two pictures, one beneath the other, and I would think: "Well, uncle –" That morning he didn't seem so incredibly remote from me as he usually did.

I said nothing to anyone about the picture, and later had it framed. Much later again, I sent it along in the fearful hope that it might be hung in the autumn exhibition of the Manchester Academy. Not even Blanche knew anything about all this. It was the first secret I had had from her, but there was something about Blanche that summer that dimmed our old intimacy. I could not count on her being outside the office at one o'clock. Sometimes she would be there, and sometimes not. At first I waited for her; then I gave it up. If she was not there when I came out, I went off at once on my own affairs. Nothing whatever was said about this: there was no questioning on my part and there were no explanations on hers. To accept one another and to leave one another alone was a deeply-driven habit in our family. As the autumn came on, it was altogether exceptional for us to spend that hour together. I thought myself lucky if she appeared once a week. I say lucky because, whatever Blanche may have felt about me, I missed her.

I never inquired, and don't know to this day, whether it was by oversight or whether that was the way things were done, but I was not told that my picture had been accepted. I only know that when the day came for the opening of the Manchester Academy exhibition I dared not visit it, nor the next day, nor the day after that. I went each day and hung about near the formidable iron railings of the Art Gallery, but go in I could not. When I did go, I chose of all days one of drenching rain. There had been no threat of it in the morning and I was unprotected. Standing in a doorway I unwrapped my sandwiches and ate them looking out at the pitiless downpour. The drops exploded on the pavement at my feet, the gutters were running like rivers, and the waterpipes streaming like cataracts. When I had finished eating, I rolled the papers into a ball, booted them out into the street, put down my head, and ran. Resolution had suddenly come to me, and this time I was going to see that it carried me right through the sacred portals. There was not far to go, but in that sensational cloudburst it was far enough to cause me to arrive at the gallery looking like a wet dishcloth. Water squelched in my boots, it dripped from my hair and blackened my clothes. I rushed up the steps and through the doors. There I stood panting and gazed about me. But I had scarcely time to draw breath before I found myself confronted by a commissionaire who looked accusingly at the puddle spreading round my feet. "Hey! What are you up to?" he demanded. "What d'you think this is? A public shelter? You can't come dashing in here like that."

To my surprise, I was not afraid. I said simply: "I'm an exhibitor," and I knew that I was.

The commissionaire laughed. "Huh! You look it!" he said. "You look an exhibition – that's what you look." This little joke pleased him so much that he seemed much less official and forbidding, and as by this time I had ceased to drip so violently, I began to make my way up the stairs. The commissionaire walked at my side, his suspicions not completely overcome. "An exhibitor, eh?" he said. "Some might believe you. *Some*, I said. And come to that, some might not. I'd like to see your picture, that's all I say: I'd like to see it."

We had entered side by side into one of the galleries, and, as if instinct had taken me there, I walked straight to it. I was speechless. I could only stand and gaze as though spellbound at that square foot of canvas hanging in its own right among so many that seemed to me so splendid. The commissionaire looked down at me and was aware of my feelings. "That it?" he asked kindly. I could not answer. I could only point dumbly. "You did that? Your own very self?" he asked. I nodded. He stood back a pace or two, stroking his moustache and considering the picture. "Very pretty," he said. "That's what I call it – very pretty. Like a piece of cake?"

This surprising question brought me with a shock out of my musing. I was a boy, and indeed I would like a piece of cake. "Yes, please, sir," I said.

We went down the stairs, and now his attitude was different. It was that of a proud custodian. He took me into the tearoom, placed a coin on the counter, and said to the woman behind it: "Give this young gentleman a cup of tea and a piece of cake. He's an exhibitor."

Then he left me, and I sat down to enjoy the reward of my art: a piece of cake. I fear I was a more than usually unsatisfactory office boy that afternoon.

The next morning I said to Blanche: "Could you meet me this lunchtime outside the Art Gallery?" She said that she would. I did not tell her what I had in view. It was to lead her proudly to the picture, point to the signature, and then, when she was swooning with surprise, take her downstairs to the tearoom. Then, out of a few coppers I had saved, I would stand us both a cup of tea and a piece of cake. Then, perhaps, fortified by this refreshment, we would be able to return to the picture and withstand its emotional impact. I pleased myself all through the morning thinking of this courtly little plan. It would be the first time I had ever entertained anyone to refreshments. When one o'clock came I fairly flew towards the Art Gallery. Even the weather was in tune with my exuberant and expansive mood. The sun was shining, and over the dark valleys of the streets the clouds were light and fleecy as lambs. Ahead of me as I ran I could see the gleaming whiteness of St Peter's Cross, and then I saw something else, too, which suddenly collapsed my mood and slowed my running feet to a plod. There was Blanche, waiting where we had arranged, and with her was Luther Brimlow. So miserable did I feel, held in the grip of so sharp a revulsion, that I was tempted to turn down a side street and run away; but they had seen me and already were moving side by side towards me.

"Hallo, Ted," Luther exclaimed; and Blanche said with a rush: "I asked Luther to come along. You don't mind, do you?"

This was the first time I had heard her call him Luther, and my heart sank. He had for some time been glibly calling me Ted, but I had never called him Luther, and I shuddered now to hear Blanche do so.

I stood there for a moment in a savage silence, not knowing what to do or say. At last I stammered, speaking only to Blanche: "It was something I wanted to show you – something private."

Luther Brimlow smiled in his superior way, slapping one hand with the kid glove he held in the other. "Why make a mystery of it, Ted?" he demanded. "I can guess what it is. It's your old picture. I've seen it. I was in there the other day. I've already told Blanche about it. Not a bad little picture either, if it comes to that. A bit on the small side, perhaps . . ."

I felt as though the pavement were swaying under my feet. They had left me nothing – not even my secret. And Blanche had known! For a time I was too mortified to speak. Then I said: "Well, if you've seen it . . ."

"But *I* haven't seen it," Blanche cried.

I didn't want to show it to her now, and I didn't want to buy her a piece of cake. I turned and began to walk away, utterly miserable. "Oh, never mind, Blanche," Luther Brimlow said, "if he's going to be crusty, I'll show it to you."

They went up the steps together, and I buried myself in the black side streets with my heart as black as the stones. That *my* picture should be shown to Blanche by Luther Brimlow! It was more than I could bear. I could hear his vile voice as he pointed it out to her: "Not a bad little picture. A bit on the small side, perhaps . . ."

8

I was not the only one of the Pentecosts to make a first public appearance that year. It often happened that some of the children being trained by Madame Gribble were used to fill in chinks at our local pantomine, and thus, in the December, Blanche found herself for the first time upon the stage. There was nothing remarkable about it, and she gathered no renown. Just as my picture was one of hundreds, and attracted no attention, so she was one of a group who did some pretty dances together but, individually, were indistinguishable.

That, at any rate, is how it must have appeared to the public; but you may be sure it was not like that to the Pentecosts. My own renown in the family increased enormously. My mother walked into town, which was something she rarely did, and she, my father, and Blanche joined me in the lunch hour on a family tour which pretended to be interested in the exhibition but was not galvanised till my picture was reached. We all four stood there dumbly gazing at the hawthorn tree on that square foot of canvas, and then suddenly my mother bent down, hugged me close, and kissed me. I was glad we were alone in the room. As for my father, he said nothing at all, and I think that was because he could not trust himself to speak. Neither Blanche nor I said anything of her having already seen the picture. We both acted as though this were the first time she had looked at it. I knew that something secret had come into Blanche's life, and it was not for me to say anything about it.

When we had made a pretence of looking at some more pictures, my father took us all down to the tearoom, and there we lunched upon poached eggs on toast, cake and tea. It was the first time the Pentecosts had eaten out, so that we all felt it was an occasion of great celebrity. Indeed, the high mood of the moment was so strong on my father that when we got out into the street he was for calling a hansom cab and having my mother driven home in state. But she told him frankly not to be a fool. "It's a grand day," she said. "I'll walk."

It was a grand day, in every sense of the word. I felt as though I were walking on air; and when my father and mother had set off, leaving me and Blanche alone, and she suddenly took my arm and said: "It is a lovely picture, Ted. I do like it so much": why, then I thought my happiness could mount no further and I ran back to the office as if my feet were sprouting fiery wings.

But soon the concentration of family attention upon my achievement was switched off, and Blanche took the centre of interest. I need hardly say that there was a family party to visit the Palace Theatre for the first night. More than a family party, indeed, for Anatole Lop attended it and even insisted on being our host at a meal in a restaurant before the show. He, all along, had been Blanche's main sponsor, and now, he said, he must claim the privileges that went with the duties. Blanche was not with us at the meal, but Betsy Comfort was, and I remember how dear old Anatole, looking more than ever like death warmed up, raised his glass and said a few solemn words in which he was kind enough to remember me as well as Blanche, congratulating my parents on having twice the customary allotment of ugly ducklings, who, he predicted, were now, almost simultaneously, striking out on waters where their swanlike qualities would become apparent. He got it all rather confused and complicated, but everybody knew that he meant well, and we drank a toast to Blanche and tumbled out gaily to walk the few yards between the restaurant and the theatre.

I shall not say much about that December night, because I want to get on to the end of January. When Madame Gribble's Girls, as the turn was called, came on for their first dance, I had some difficulty in recognising Blanche, so much alike did they all seem except for the colour of their dresses. They were dressed in flowing chiffon of what we now call "pastel shades," every one wearing a different colour, and, as there were twenty of them, they made a pretty rainbow in the lines. At last I was able to pick Blanche out, but not in this dance nor in any other did she impress me as she had done that midsummer day when, waking out of a doze, I saw her with her skirt belted above her knees, dancing among the buttercups. However, they were all so young and unspoiled, so gaily enjoying their own performance, that there was something about them which must have struck the audience as virginal, as though they were flowers of a morning blowing about the stage, and they never failed to be warmly cheered.

This time we did have cabs. My father and mother, Betsy and Blanche, whom we had picked up at the stage door, set off in a four-wheeler, and Mr Lop and I followed in a hansom. We did not follow for long, because the eager little animal in our lighter cab soon went ahead of the old slow-coach pulling the others. At a corner in Withington I dropped Mr Lop, who paid for the cab, and then the hansom tore on at a great pace. When it had put me down, I had a quarter of an hour to wait before the others turned up, and as I paced to and fro in front of our house in Kingsley Avenue I was thinking of what seemed to me the strangest thing that had happened that night. In the press of people coming out of the theatre I had caught a far-off glimpse of Luther Brimlow's face. I was sure he had not seen me, and none of our people had seen him. The recognition disturbed me, because it reminded me again, with great force, of the secret that lay between me and Blanche. Brimlow's presence there was the more upsetting because I knew the violence of his parents' views about the theatre. Dancing, theatre-going, card-playing, even a game of football, were, to them, stages in an almost literal descent to hell; and I was visited by an uneasy presentiment that it must be something powerful that drove the son to defy prohibitions which the parents had proclaimed throughout the whole of his life.

It was midnight, and still: Christmas Eve. In a moment or two, I reflected as I walked up and down, we would be in Christmas Day. The full moon was up, sparkling on the rime that lay upon the leafless branches of our chestnut tree. It was very cold. I had just reached the junction of our street with Wilmslow Road when Luther Brimlow turned the corner, walking fast. We almost collided with one another.

"Well, Ted!" he cried. "What on earth are you doing out at this time of night?"

"I've been to the theatre," I explained briefly. "I've landed home before the others, and I haven't got a key. So I'm waiting."

He gave a light laugh. "The theatre! While I've been working my brain like a steam-engine."

I looked at the liar in wonder. "I've been in the old man's office," he explained. "I often work there at nights, you know, and this has been a long session. Bringing the books up to date for the year. And what a mess!"

We were walking back now along the street. I had nothing to say. "I closed down just before midnight," he said. "The old man wouldn't like me working on Christmas Day. And quite right, too."

To my horror, his voice now took on the nasal nauseous tone that I had heard in the ring on the street corners. He stopped walking and put a hand on my arm. "*Quite* right," he said. "The day of Christ's birth. Do you ever think, Ted, what that means to man? Do you ever think what it means to *you*? Ah, I wish I could be granted the right word to speak to you – to you and to Blanche."

The moonlight glittered on his spectacles. I gazed at him, fascinated, and I was afraid. Afraid for Blanche. Stark, frozen fear took me by the heart, a greater fear than I had known when his father had talked to me in the office. And then suddenly he was the debonair stockbroker's clerk again. He unbuttoned his overcoat and pulled a watch out of his waistcoat pocket. "Yes," he said. "Gone midnight. It's Christmas morning. Well, a merry Christmas to you, Ted." He held out his hand and I feebly shook it. "Excuse my glove," he said, took a key from his pocket, and went into his house just as the old four-wheeler turned in from Wilmslow Road.

9

One of Madame Gribble's Girls lived in Withington and one in a side street off Fog Lane; so it was in the course of things that these two and Blanche should walk home together each night after the show. When she had shed her second companion Blanche had only about a twenty-minutes' walk ahead of her, and this to some extent reconciled my parents to the arrangement. Not that they were altogether happy about it, even so. Blanche, throughout this year, had gained assurance. She had grown up quicker than I had. There was more than our secret between us. At Madame Gribble's she had made friends, and at Marquick and Marquand's I had not done so. Thus she had developed into a rather striking-looking young woman of *savoir faire*, while I was a good deal of a solitary savage. Despite her thus growing up, my father and mother were unhappy, in the beginning, about that midnight walk home. But soon custom dulled what apprehension they had felt. She was in by soon after midnight with regularity, and Betsy always sat up to make her a cup of tea and have a gossip.

It was towards the end of January that I was awakened from sleep by the sound of footsteps passing my bedroom door. A moment later there was a rapping of knuckles on the door of my parents' bedroom, and I heard Betsy's voice hissing urgently: "Come down! Come down, both of you!"

I sat up in bed, and heard my father and mother hurriedly pulling on some clothes and going downstairs. Then there was a noise of excited voices below, and, I thought, the sound of Blanche's crying. I got out of bed, put my feet into slippers, and pulled an overcoat on over my nightshirt. These excited voices, Blanche's crying, which I now clearly heard, this midnight alarm surging through the house: it all filled me with fear. I knew that something dreadful had happened, but I had not been called and I hesitated to go down. But at length I did. I flung open the sitting room door just as my father was exclaiming: "If I lay hands on the young swine I'll wring his neck." And I knew that he was talking about Luther Brimlow. I had time to get only a general impression of the scene. The fire was still burning, and in a chair near it Blanche was sitting with tear-stained eyes staring out of a face horribly white. Betsy was kneeling on the floor at her feet, with both her arms about her, so that Blanche's face looked at me over Betsy's broad shoulders. My father with trembling fingers was trying to light the tobacco in his negro-head pipe, and my mother, who seemed the calmest person there, had just poured out a cup of tea which she was carrying to Blanche. That was all I saw, for, as soon as I had appeared in the room, my father threw the flaming match into the fire, advanced towards me and hustled me out again. "Get straight back to bed," he commanded, and shut the door behind me. I obeyed him, but I did not sleep. After a long time I heard everybody come up to bed, Blanche going in with Betsy. Then it was again a long time before silence fell. My parents' voices rumbled on, and I could hear Betsy's soothing growls mingled with Blanche's crying.

10

I walked to work with my father as usual the next morning. Blanche had not appeared at breakfast. Nothing was said between us about the alarm during the night, nor indeed about anything else. My father strode along with a grim and frightening taciturnity, hardly saying goodbye when I parted from him at the shop door. This being wintertime, I was back now at my Art School classes, and so was absent from home that evening. Thus I saw nothing (not that I should have done in any case) of the dramatic three-cornered interview between my father and mother, Mr and Mrs Brimlow, and Mr Armroyd and Luther. I can tell you how the thing went from piecing together snatches of conversation and hints that fell here and there in the years that followed.

All that day, Blanche had remained in bed in Betsy's room. A fire had been lit there, and that in itself was an indication of crisis, for a fire in a bedroom was then, with us, almost unheard of. When my father had got home and eaten his supper, Betsy was left to look after Blanche and Father and Mother went next door to the Brimlows. They had hoped to find Luther there, but he had not yet returned from work. However, he soon came. My parents were hardly seated in the Brimlows' kitchen, and my father was still wondering how to open the unpleasant business, when the sound of a key in the front door was heard. Luther was not alone. He came into the kitchen pale and trembling, and with him was a tall well-dressed man who looked in a thoroughly black humour. Luther licked his lips and explained that this was Mr Armroyd, the stockbroker who employed him. Mr Armroyd began without preliminary: "I'm saving the police a job by bringing your son along myself, Mr Brimlow."

Luther immediately began to babble: "I can explain everything, Mother. It's all a mistake. It wasn't theft. It was nothing but borrowing."

It was at once to his mother that he appealed. Poor old Brimlow from the first was hardly in the picture. He got up trembling and pushed one of the wooden kitchen chairs towards Mr Armroyd, who sat down, leaving the old man standing. Mrs Brimlow did not lose her self-possession. Her narrow cunning face sharpened, and she said: "I think you and your husband ought to leave us, Mrs Pentecost."

My father answered her sharply: "I'm not so sure about that, Mrs Brimlow." And, turning to Mr Armroyd, he added: "My wife and I – we live next door – have just come in here to settle some matters that concern this young man. They may be related to what you have to say, and if we have your permission we shall stay."

"So far as I'm concerned," Mr Armroyd said briefly, "the more people who know about this young swine's tricks the better," but Mrs Brimlow, sniffing danger like a vixen, cried: "I won't have it! This is my house, and who stays in it is my business – not Mr Armroyd's or anyone else's."

Mr Armroyd said in a sharp, reminding voice: "Mrs Brimlow, I told you that I had brought your son along rather than permit the police to do it. If you are unreasonable, I shall have to change my mind. Then it won't be a question of your next-door neighbour knowing what has happened, but of everybody knowing it."

Mrs Brimlow was one of those fools who will not see reason. "You can say what you like," she shouted. "I won't believe a word of it. Our Luther's a good boy, and a hard-working boy, and a clever boy. What about your own letters? Haven't you written to say how good he was, more than once?"

Mr Armroyd's eyebrows shot up, and Luther said suddenly: "Oh, leave it alone, Mother. You'll do no good." But already Mrs Brimlow was rummaging in a dresser drawer, and she brought out three letters headed with the name of Mr Armroyd's firm. Luther made a snatch for them, but Mr Armroyd intervened quickly and took the letters. He gave a sweeping glance through all three, folded them carefully, and put them into his pocket. "These interest me enormously," he said. "It seems to me, Mrs Brimlow, that your son will go far in one direction or another. Picking from the petty cash is common enough with boys of his sort and at his age, but such a neat bit of forgery is unusual."

He looked with renewed interest at Luther, who was white and quaking. "Are you such a poor stick," he asked, "that you must bolster yourself up like this even to your own parents?"

There could he no doubt now, even in Mrs Brimlow's mind. She put her arms round her son and shrieked at Mr Armroyd: "You leave him alone! You slave-driver! You stingy old devil! Is it any wonder the poor boy steals when you pay him a wage I'd be ashamed to give to a washerwoman?"

Mr Armroyd shrugged. "I wondered," he said, "whether you knew how much he *was* getting. Since it seems you do – and I assure you it's a little more than the normal rate of pay – I'm surprised that one or two things haven't struck you. Your son dresses expensively for his situation, he travels first class on the railway, I've seen him at lunchtime in rather expensive restaurants entertaining a young lady . . ."

At that, Mrs Brimlow turned with a vinegar face upon my mother. "I'll bet that's that Blanche of yours," she cried. "I've had my suspicions – all along I have. She's turned my poor boy's head. She's led him wrong." She seemed in a frenzy. She pressed her hands to her narrow temples and cried: "Oh, why did God curse us with neighbours like you? Music and dancing and all the snares of the devil!"

Mr Armroyd intervened sharply. "Mrs Brimlow, I'm not going to have you flying off on a track of that sort. Believe me, I didn't come here tonight to listen to you abusing your neighbours. I came here to tell you that for a long time your son has been stealing considerable sums of money. I have learned from you that he is also a forger. Now listen to me, if you can stop your tongue clacking for a moment. Perhaps I had better not talk to you at all. You don't strike me as a person to be relied on. Mr Brimlow, what I'm saying now I'm saying to you. This young man has got to be cleared out of Manchester. He's flying a bit too high. Another thing about him I haven't told you yet. I've seen him at the Palace Theatre sitting in the orchestra stalls. Orchestra stalls are a bit expensive for a junior clerk, Mr Brimlow, even though I recently increased his salary to a rate higher than is usually paid. But I imagine he hasn't told you that. However, I did it, and I'll tell you why." He slapped the pocket containing the forged letters. "If I *had* written these letters they would have said just about what your son said of himself. He has shown exceptional insight into my business. If you like, I'll gratify Mrs Brimlow's vanity and say frankly that he's a prodigy. He could have gone a long way with clean hands. But in my office he's not going any way at all with dirty hands. Nor in Manchester, so far as I can prevent it. So now I'm giving you an ultimatum, Mr Brimlow. You'll send your son out of this town – a long way out – or the matter will be dealt with in a different fashion. I understand that the pair of you, and your son, are members of some strict religious body. I'm giving you the chance to save your names and his from scandal. And I want your answer at once."

Old Brimlow stood there looking like a sheep that has been stunned by a mallet; he couldn't open his mouth: and Mrs Brimlow took a deep breath and began to open hers. Luther himself cut in. Mr Armroyd's testimonial had brought some colour back to his cheeks. "Shut up," he said to his mother. And then: "I'll go. None of you need answer for me. I can answer for myself. I'll go." He spoke as though it were a relief, as though he had thrown off shackles. My father said that at that moment he even felt some admiration for him: he had become all of a sudden a man. There was a brief silence, and then Luther turned to Mr Armroyd and said insolently: "Don't you think the less said about the police the better?" And having let that sink in, he added: "I shall be gone by this time tomorrow. I may need you yet. If I ever do, I shall write to you."

The room then seemed full of thunder-threat. My father got up and said: "Since Luther is leaving the district, I shall say nothing about what brought me here."

Luther was now in full possession of himself. He had the audacity to hold out his hand to my father. "I am grateful to you for that," he said. "I am sorry for what happened. It was my fault, but no harm was done." My father ignored the offered hand, and he and my mother left the house.

Luther Brimlow kept his word. It was a long time before any of us saw him again.

11

It was not right to say that no harm was done. A great deal of harm was done that night in old Brimlow's office-shed, and the worst harm, as I am now able to understand it, was in Blanche's sense of shame and apartness. She was pale and apathetic and withdrawn. She must have felt herself disgraced and soiled, poor girl. The good looks which had begun to distinguish her faded away. She became plain, pallid and touchy. She would at times withdraw from us and be found in her bedroom quietly crying. She did not rejoin Madame Gribble's Girls.

Although I never heard the matter discussed, there must have been much discussion between my parents about this unfortunate situation, and the upshot of it all was that whatever reluctance my father may have felt about allowing his children to go to Cornwall was overcome. I was told nothing till an accomplished fact was arrived at: the dramatic fact of coming home one day and finding that neither Blanche nor Betsy was there. They had left that day, I was told, for Cornwall. They would stay there throughout the summer, and, what is more, when my summer holiday came, my mother and I would join them.

CHAPTER THREE

BEFORE EVER I met Kitto Pentecost, I felt that I knew him well. I had by now discovered more about his work than I had learned from the print given me by the barber. One of the Art School masters had affectionately pulled my ear and said: "Pentecost is a good name for an artist. Any relation?" and when I told him shyly that Kitto Pentecost was my uncle I could see that he was impressed. I added that I had never met him and that I knew next to nothing about him or his work, and my master said: "You ought to look in at Agnew's. They've got a lot of his prints. They'd be glad to show them to you."

So I called at Agnew's during a dinner hour, and the people there were most kind. They already knew me slightly, because it was to them I had taken my picture of the hawthorn tree to be framed; they were aware of my small success. When now they learned also of my relationship to Kitto Pentecost, they were interested and obliging. They produced a dozen coloured prints, and I found that Kitto was exclusively a marine artist. All were of the sea and ships, and I bought one showing a lovely barque with all her canvas stowed on the yards and her spars outlined against a greenish sky pricked by one pale star. I was then (and am now, for that matter, despite some clever young contemporaries) a lover of Tennyson's verse; and often and often, as I looked at this print pinned to the wall of my studio at The Pines, I would recall the words:

> Sunset and evening star,
> And, after that, the dark.

It seemed to me that Kitto Pentecost, with this picture of the old ship asleep on the water, her long voyage done, and the dusk deepening, had said this as beautifully as Tennyson.

And so, in the picture my young mind built up of my uncle, he was, first of all, something of a Viking. A roll in his gait and a blue horizon gleam in his eye, a nautical flavour in his clothes – a reefer jacket, perhaps, and a sailor's cap: thus I saw him. As for his background, this, I fear, was conditioned by those illustrated interviews in the *Strand Magazine* of which I have already spoken. No one who had reached the dignity of being an R.A. ever, I gathered from these, lived in less than marble halls, with every accompaniment of luxury and splendour.

In this bemused and fuddled state of mind, picturing a glorified able-bodied seaman living in circumstances of ducal distinction, I was on my way to make the acquaintance of my uncle. The day was in tune with my exalted mood. I had known – never having known anything but Manchester and Cheshire – how starved of colour my eye and mind had been. Cornwall had already painted for me a hundred pictures that I should see forever: headlands covered with corn that was the colour of the umber sand below; sea-rippled sand that was the colour of the corn and seemed, quivering under the heat, to have even its motion; water in which green and indigo achieved every miraculous combination; cottages in hidden lanes standing behind ramparts of blazing fuchsias and swamped beneath tides of honeysuckle; and over everything the midsummer insect droning drowsiness beneath a sky marked by nothing but hovering hawks and swooping gulls.

I had been born again. I don't know what Mr Brimlow would have said if he had heard me repeating to myself that I had been born again. I had Found Grace. I should not fail, later, to understand what frenzy had seized Vincent van Gogh when he left the plains and coal pits of Brabant and awoke among the sunflowers and oleanders of Arles. And that morning, though I was in the town, the magic seemed as powerful as if I were lying lonely with the seals on a rock amid the lazily-breaking tide. Falmouth's old grey buildings were expiring the heat of summer; what seemed to me to be, paradoxically, an exhilarating languor lingered in the narrow ways that led off from the main street to the waterfront.

It was one of these narrow ways that I was seeking. "You can't miss it," my mother had said. "It's right opposite the steps that come down alongside the parish church. Go down the little lane, and you'll see it right in front of you. An old grey building that used to be a chapel."

I was above the church now, and here were the steps twisting downhill behind it, a narrow gulch with iron railings on either hand, and behind the railings a careless tumble of gravestones and tombs upon the rising ground. Rough grass and docks and thistles grew abundantly among them, but these did not obliterate a name that leapt to my eyes.

Here lies
CAPTAIN JOHN PENTECOST
of the Packet "Termagant"
the victor in ten encounters with
French privateers,
Invincible in war, beloved in peace,
Who died at Falmouth March 7, 1825.

I stopped, and held on with both hands to the railings, looking at the oblong box-like tomb standing there amid the tall weeds under the noon sun; and I did not doubt that this was another of "us", another of the mysterious Pentecosts of whom I had known so little and who seemed now to be there for me to stumble over whichever way I turned.

Well, I reminded myself, I was on my way to meet one of them now, one who was living flesh and blood, not dry white bones as this sleeper in the tomb must be with the sun blinding down on his stone and on the triumphant weeds that grew about his monument.

And then I was out in the main street, and right in front of me was the short narrow lane leading to the waterfront and to this encounter with Kitto Pentecost, R.A., that I had already lived a hundred times in imagination.

My heart stood still; my feet came to a stand. I had never met an R.A., hardly, indeed, anyone who could be called an artist at all. I felt as meek and frightened as a fledgling angel summoned to his first encounter with the Lord High Seraph, accustomed immemorially to golden thrones and fanfares of crying cherubim. I began to snail my way down the path. At the end was a grey stone wall pierced by a green gate with a lush but barren fig tree half-hiding it. I looked up at the leaves drawing their firm classic outlines upon the hard blue of the sky. I was ready indeed to look at anything rather than open the small green gate. But at last I did so, stepped inside, and let it fall to behind me. I caught my breath at the wide and lovely view. The whole extent of Falmouth harbour, glistening under the noon sun, lay before me. To the right Pendennis Castle crowned its headland, and before me, across the water, the castle of St Mawes seemed to dip its feet in the tide. I could see the Carrick Roads running up to St Just, and on that windless day the blue expanse was full of ships standing on the water as though they were models exhibited on glass. From a splendid barque anchored in the offing to the red and green and white yachts scattered like dainty toys, there was no movement anywhere, save for a dinghy here and there being lazily rowed over the water and the gulls clamouring above garbage heaved overside. I was so taken up with all this, standing with my back to the shut gate, that I gave a great start when a voice said, close at my elbow: "You'll be Mr Pentecost's nevvy?"

Had this stranger said he was Kitto Pentecost himself I should not have been surprised. This was near enough to my notion of the man. "Henry Opie," he said, introducing himself; and Henry Opie was a broad, solid, red-faced fellow, clean-shaven, wearing navy blue clothes and a peaked cap fitted with a white linen cover. His reefer jacket had brass buttons and he carried a telescope under his arm. I now saw that just inside the gate, and to my left, was a white-painted wooden seat. It was from this that Henry Opie had risen. He had, apparently, been looking at the harbour through his glass. I said that I was Ted Pentecost, and he put out a huge red paw that enveloped mine and squeezed it hard.

In front of me was the old chapel that my mother had told me to expect. Like most of the buildings on the Falmouth waterfront, it was of grey stone, gnawed and pitted by the weather, roofed with slate that had been smeared over with cement. From where we stood, the land sloped down, and granite steps, succeeded by a short path, led to the chapel's green-painted door. But Henry Opie, going before me, did not open the door. Outside it, there were more granite steps, with an iron handrail. We went down these, and now we could no longer see the water. For here a tall grey stone wall, tufted with toadflax and topped by a chevaux-de-frise of valerian, flowering white and darkly red, shut out the view. This wall not only ran along the waterfront but completely enclosed a spacious oblong of garden. I told myself that it was such a garden as one might expect an R.A. to create. The walls, crumbling away like old cheese, were bright with climbing roses. Beneath them were beds, carelessly profuse, in which every sort of herbaceous plant seemed to thrive, and within these borders the whole place was paved with stone, and set with trimmed shrubs and charming figures in stone and lead. The old chapel filled in one end of this entrancing garden, and I saw now that it was not, as it appeared from above, merely of one storey, but that here, on the garden level, a basement ran beneath it, with a door and windows looking out into the paved and cloistral quiet.

"Neat – eh?" said Henry Opie; and I was to learn that thus briefly he had uttered his warmest praise. Had Henry ever aspired to anything so imposing as a family motto, he would, I feel certain, have chosen "Neatness is all." He led me now to a door which pierced the waterfront wall, threw it open and revealed the harbour in all its colour and spacious beauty. Outside the door, granite steps led down to the water which was lying almost without motion upon their base, the tide being full. A dinghy rode there, and this seemed to me the last touch of enchantment. Here, enclosed in a little space, was this private and domestic beauty; there, at the foot of the steps, was the escape from it out to sea. Out to wherever one cared to go on all the waters of the world. Henry complacently stroked his ruddy face, pleased to see my pleasure. "Now have a look at my quarters," he invited.

He shut the door, and we walked through the quiet garden to the other door leading into the basement. Beside it were two bushes: a eupatorium, which the butterflies love, and which was a-flutter now with a score of peacocks and red admirals, and a verbena that Henry squeezed and then pushed his perfumed thumb under my nose. How often thereafter did I squeeze verbena, and never without recalling that burning day when first I entered Kitto's house. This basement contained three rooms. Henry stood modestly aside as I entered, then followed and removed his cap. No sun penetrated here. He took me by the arm and spun me round so that I was facing the window. Now the garden took on a new beauty. It was like looking out of a cave upon a sun-drenched picture. This was the spot from which it all fell into harmony and composition. One saw how cunning was the apparent haphazard, how the shrubs and statues, the wreathed stone urns and the lovely wellhead all had a charming relation one to another. It was a tiny flawless world, deliberately created. "See," said Henry Opie, standing behind me, "no disorder. Neat. The Old Man hates disorder."

And to judge from this room, which was Henry's, so did he. There was not much in it, and, of what there was, a surprising amount was brass, twinkling with polish. A ship's lamp shone from a hook in the ceiling, like a radiant star hung under the dusky heaven; the curtain rods gleamed; the fender and the fire irons, the ornaments upon the mantelpiece, the ash-trays, a toasting fork and an old bed warmer: all were brazen and bright. A few pictures on the wall, in shining rosewood frames, were maritime. They showed full-rigged sailing vessels, becalmed like museum pieces or tossing in an inferno of wind and water; and there were a few photographs, too, of sailorly-looking men, all as neat as Henry Opie. In a recess near the fireplace was a raised bunk with the bedclothes neatly folded upon it. A few geraniums in pots bloomed on the windowsill. "We always took geraniums," Henry Opie said as he saw me looking at them; and it did not need much imagination to see in this room Henry's attempt to recreate as much as possible of that which, once upon a time, "we" did.

"Well, that's about all here," he said. "This is the galley."

If Henry's room gleamed with brass, the galley gleamed with copper. It was a tiny room, as neat as a new pill. A fireplace such as one sees in a ship's galley, shelves of crockery, copper pots and pans, cupboards of food: that was all there was to it, and it left little space to move in. I asked Henry if he cooked for my uncle; and he answered shortly: "I do everything for him. The Old Man would be lost without me."

A door from the galley led to the third and last room on the basement level. This was a dining room with windows on two sides. Thus, you could look out either upon the harbour or the garden, or, within, you could look upon the pictures that seemed to light up the walls; pictures which a glance showed me were Kitto Pentecost's.

"The Old Man don't eat here unless there's company, and that's not often," Henry Opie said. "As a rule, I carry his stuff up on a tray."

And, indeed, I thought a moment later, who, having the choice, would not prefer to eat, live, work, sleep and have all his being in this upper room? From the dining room a stairway ascended. Henry Opie had preceded me and knocked at the door to which it led. A voice piped: "Come in" and the next second, with the door shut behind me and Henry gone, I was alone with my uncle.

It was the north wall that looked over the garden, and in this wall were three large windows through which flooded the shadowless light. My uncle was standing with his back to the middle window, working at a canvas on an easel. He did not look at me. He made a vague gesture with his mahlstick and said: "Look around."

I looked, but I dared not move. I knew how I hated anyone to be near me when I was at work myself, and I almost held my breath in the presence of Kitto Pentecost, R.A., actually painting. I sank quietly into a chair and looked about me. It was a breathtaking room: the old chapel, undivided by any curtain or partition, handsomely proportioned, the roof rising high above my head in an inverted V to the ridge tiles. The walls were of stone whose rough texture showed itself through whitewash, and the beams which tied the walls together were painted a rich crimson. In the end wall was an enormous stone fireplace describing a half circle, and on either side of this was a tall window looking on to the harbour, but from where I sat I could at the moment see nothing save the burning blue of the sky. These windows, and the three in the north wall, let into the room a great gaiety of light. The south wall was blank and had bookcases fitted breast-high along its entire length, with all sorts of charming things in porcelain, glass and bronze standing on the topmost shelf. The floor was as brown as a peat stream and as gleaming as glass, and here and there rugs laid patterns of rich colour upon it. Glancing up nervously, almost afraid that my neck would creak, I saw that from the crimson tie beams lamps of curious shapes hung down, all different – silver, bronze, brass, iron. There was no curtain at any window, and this heightened the sense of space and of a cleanliness of light.

So much I observed, sitting like a mouse in my chair, and you may be sure that I had not overlooked my uncle. The first glance at him had slain my romantic dreams. A Viking — or, if not that, at least a bluff British sailor — someone infused with the essence of all those ships, all those tranquil or tumbling seas, that had entered into his pictures: that was what, ever since I had thought of him at all, I had built up in my mind. What I saw was a neat little fellow wearing a grey frock coat, with satin lapels of a darker grey, and trousers of black and white check. His boots were buttoned upon his small feet, and their uppers were of dove-grey cloth. His collar was a "choker," set off with a grey tie, and altogether his appearance was silvery. He was well-made, but on the thin side, and rather below the average height. Save for a dandyish moustache and an imperial, both silvery like his short well-dressed hair, he was clean-shaven. A black-rimmed monocle swung on his chest and a rosebud, backed by maidenhair fern, decorated his lapel. He was as spruce as a cat, as fastidious as a nice old maid, as lithe and modish as a dancing master. After his first words, which had not been accompanied by so much as a glance at me, he seemed to forget me altogether, and fully twenty minutes passed before he stood his brushes in a jar, put down his palette, and stepped back a pace or two from his picture. He seemed far more interested in the picture than in me. I wondered if he would call upon me to look at it, even perhaps to express an opinion about it, but he did not. He stood there for a long time, his head on one side, his eyes screwed up, the back of his left hand rubbing under his chin as if he were stroking forward an imaginary beard. Then he said aloud "Ah, well . . ." and at last came towards me.

"So you're Ted?"

I dropped down with relief from my chair. "Yes, sir," I said and held out my hand. He did not take it, and this left me a little hurt and puzzled. I learned later that he never shook hands with anybody. Like the rest of him, his hands were small and fine, and he had a fear lest some enthusiast should damage them. But I did not then know this. My hand dropped to my side and I stood there awkwardly enough, feeling that my first R.A., and my uncle at that, had rebuffed me.

"This is a very beautiful studio, sir," I said, for want of some other opening; and at that he laughed. "It suits me," he said. "It has all the qualifications. I got the freehold dirt cheap, made my alterations for no more than a couple of hundred pounds, and the rates are next to nothing. What more can you ask?"

He had a small piping voice, not my imagined bellow that would roar a hurricane down. He put a hand on my shoulder and walked me towards the tall window to the right of the fireplace. We stood looking down upon the harbour. During the last half-hour a breeze had sprung up. The moored ships were dancing on the water; a few had hoisted sail and were underway, ploughing white furrows upon the blue, and everywhere was the sparkle and animation with which a little wind can take a harbour out of its drowsy lethargy. "And incidentally," said my uncle, as though he had not ceased speaking, "there is that." He waved his hand towards it all: the lively water, the russet corn upon the Flushing hills, the sails, the flashing gulls, the dreaming castles. "All that," he said, "thrown in for luck. I'd call it a pretty good bargain."

We loitered at the window for a few moments, and then he said: "It's one o'clock. We'd better be off."

I had no idea where we were to be off to, but I humbly followed him as he went down the stairs that led to the dining room. In the garden Henry Opie was waiting with a large basket covered by a cloth. He went before us through the door heading to the granite stairway, and there we embarked in the dinghy. She was a varnished boat looking as if she had just come out of the shop. The brass rowlocks twinkled in the sun, and before pushing off Henry coiled down the painter as carefully as if it would not be needed for weeks. He sat on the bow thwart, my uncle and I in the stern, side by side, and that balanced the boat nicely. The basket was stowed amidships. Neither of them told me where we were bound for, and I did not ask. I was in a daze of happiness and placidly accepted all that was happening to me. Remember, until this journey to Cornwall, I had never seen the sea. I had never been in a boat, I had never imagined – or at any rate had never done more than imagine – such glowing sunlight, such colour, such entrancing movement as the short chop of the water under the freshening breeze. Above all, Kitto Pentecost, albeit silent and everything that I had imagined him not to be, was sitting at my side. His dove-coloured buttoned boots lay there on the bottom-boards alongside my seedy-looking scuffled shoes. I was happier than I had thought it possible to be, and when suddenly the barque which I had earlier noticed lying out in the roads began to unfold her wings, sail after sail running up to take advantage of this fortunate breeze, and when, taut and trim beneath the towering blue, she began slowly to move upon the water: why, then I should have been content to sit forever with Henry Opie's broad chest and powerful arms before me, the buoyant feel of the water beneath me, and my uncle at my side.

However, this was to be a very short journey indeed. Tied up to a large iron buoy in the middle of the harbour was a barge which I might have guessed had something to do with Kitto Pentecost and Henry Opie, for it was painted a gleaming white and here and there brass cleats took a dazzle from the sun. Henry Opie brought the dinghy carefully alongside this craft, throwing out small fenders encased in white linen so that her precious paint should not be scratched. Seeing that this was our destination, I sprang up in excitement, but Henry growled sharply "Sit down!" I subsided alongside my uncle, who had not stirred or spoken. A wire rail carried through stanchions ran round the deck of the barge, broken only at the spot where we had come alongside, and at this spot Henry now leapt aboard, with surprising agility for a man of his size, taking the painter with him. He gave it a turn round a cleat, hung out larger fenders and let down a short mahogany ladder, secured to rings in the deck by brass hooks that had the everlasting Opie twinkle. Then, the bows being held fast by the painter, he drew in the stern with a boat hook till the dinghy lay snugly against the ladder. Only then did my uncle rise and go aboard, and only then, too, did Henry Opie say reprovingly: "Remember you're in a ship. I don't care if it's a dinghy or the *Cutty Sark*, a thing that floats is a ship. So act accordingly. Now hand me that basket."

I did so, and, Henry still holding in the stern with the boat hook, I climbed on to the barge. I had been given to understand something of the etiquette of the sea; and I never saw Uncle Kitto go aboard his barge except with all these little manoeuvres performed just so, as though an admiral were entering his flagship. It was easy enough, with no more than the quietest bobble on the water and the barge giving us a lee. I have had time do some pretty sprightly leaping from heaving dinghies on to plunging ships since then; but this didn't matter to my Uncle Kitto. He would never embark unless the day enabled him to be dignified. "The sea!" I heard him say later. "Why, I loathe it. A horrible element!"When he wanted to observe the sea in agitation, he was content to do it from his studio window.

The barge was completely decked in, and the deck was white with scrubbing as my mother's pastry board, save where gulls had defiled Henry's notions of purity. But a mop dipped overboard, skilfully twirled till it rotated like a catherine wheel throwing off crystal sparks, and then vigorously applied, soon put that right. After this, an arrangement of pulleys was brought into operation to stretch an awning, striped in red and white, completely over our heads.

"Now, you stand by and take things as I hand 'em up," Henry commanded. Afloat, Henry always commanded. He opened a hatch and disappeared down a short ladder that led below decks. He passed up a folding table, canvas-covered chairs, glasses and cutlery, plates and a tablecloth of the finest linen. It looked as though lunch aboard the barge was to be no scratch meal, and indeed this proved to be so. Henry laid two places with great care. From the basket appeared rolls, butter neatly formed into yellow spheres as big as marbles, a dish of salad, sardines, sandwiches on a linen-covered plate, a bowl of fruit, a bottle of wine for my uncle, and a bottle of lemonade for me.

"That's the packet," Henry said, standing back and surveying the table as critically as I had seen my uncle surveying his picture. "Now I reckon you can look after yourselves."

"Yes, thank you, Captain," my uncle said. "Be back at about three."

Henry got into the dinghy and rowed away. "I didn't know he was a captain," I exclaimed with awe.

My uncle was putting salad on to my plate with silver servers. He laughed. "You'll find," he said," that every sailor in Cornwall is a captain, even if he's only the chief of two men in a dinghy. It's a pleasant fiction, and there's no harm in keeping it up, my dear Ted."

He put the monocle into his eye and smiled at me, and I knew I was going to like him very much. When Henry Opie came back and rowed us ashore, my uncle said goodbye and went at once into the chapel. I lingered for a while, looking round the garden, and then ran home feeling extraordinarily happy. He had called me "My dear Ted," and his last words had been: "You must come again. We'll have a talk about painting."

2

I say I ran home, and what I mean is that I ran to the house where my mother was. The house belonged to my great-aunt Sapphira Kitto, but she was not there: she was at Tresco Vean. It was at Tresco Vean that I had been reunited with Blanche after the long separation of the summer. At our little house in Didsbury her name was hardly mentioned – at any rate not in my presence: and I had received from her in the course of those months no more than a few sparse letters which told me little. They had the weariness and apathy that had made Blanche so pathetic a person in the short time between Luther Brimlow's going away and her own setting out for Cornwall. She told me something of Great Aunt Sapphira: that her house was "very grand," that she was "a regular old tyrant"; but there was no sparkle, no communication, in the letters; and all that this meant, had I but known it, was that Blanche was no writer. I have never in my life received a letter from her that was not as dull as ditchwater.

It would have been as easy for Betsy Comfort to bring Blanche home as it had been to take her to Cornwall, but my mother persuaded my father that she should herself go and take me with her. For once, the long feud of the Pentecosts and the Kittos was discussed in my presence. "Go if you like," my father at last reluctantly agreed, "but I shall not go. She's the worst of 'em, and till she's under Cornish ground you won't see my feet on it. I told her I'd never set eyes on her again, and I mean that now as much as ever I did."

"It's a long time," my mother said. "If there's a chance to let bygones be bygones you should take it."

"Bygones wouldn't be bygones for long, believe me," he answered. "If you want to start it all over again, go. You'll soon find she wants a finger in your pie."

"If you feel like that yourself," Mother protested mildly, "you might at least think of the children."

This was the worst thing she could have said. I have never seen my father so angry as he was now. "If you think me incapable of looking after my own children, say so and have done with it," he shouted. He violently knocked the tobacco out of his pipe into the hearth and turned to go out of the room. "The children are the last thing she shall interfere with. If what you're thinking about is getting her money for them, let me tell you I won't permit them to touch a penny of it. Not a penny."

We heard him in the passage taking up his basket and stick, and a moment later the door banged. So harmonious and kindly had our lives been, that the sound seemed to strike upon my heart. My mother was very pale. She got up from the table and went into the kitchen, and I could hear her crying there. I could not bear to see her tears, and I could not bear the thought of walking to town with my father that morning. So I sat where I was for ten minutes to give him a good start, and then I stole out of the house without a word, and walked the five miles with misery in my breast.

However, I see now that there was too much between my father and my mother for a sharp flame like this to consume their lives. It shot up that morning, but their love was not a dry withered thing that a brief anger could spread in and destroy: it was green and growing; and by the time my father came home that night they were both ready to act as though the morning's alarm had not been.

And what was this ancient feud of Kittos and Pentecosts of which a hint here and a word there had been reaching me during so many years? I learned all about it soon enough, and I might as well put it down here and have done with it.

Falmouth, when first I knew it, was already like an old warrior dreaming in the autumn sun. Its heroic days were in the past, and they were the days of sail. The lovely barque that I saw spreading her wings the day when first I met Kitto Pentecost might have been the ghost of Falmouth's golden days saying farewell and departing from a scene that sail would haunt no more. No more, at any rate, save as a lovely visitant, a rare *revenant*, something materialising out of a past that was over and done with, as a billowing dowager of the Edwardian prime might recall, in a ballroom of svelte and snaky moderns, the opulence of a mode that could be admired but never recaptured. There was no need now in Falmouth for the great sail-lofts and ropewalks, save to furnish the pretty trimmings of the cutters, ketches and yawls, the mere confetti of the ancient marriage of ships and the sea.

But it was not the fourmasters, the albatrosses of sail, but those lively kittiwakes the sailing packets, that made Falmouth the bustling port she once was. For a hundred years these 200 tonners, lightly armed, carried the mail to all parts of the world. Once the mail was aboard, they obeyed their standing orders to put to sea "whatever the wind was", and whatever, too, was England's relationship at the moment to France or Spain or America. Their orders were clear: to run when they could, to fight when they must, and to sink the mail rather than let it be captured.

They produced a great breed of men, and the high moment in the life of Falmouth, then, was when the sudden horn sounded to announce that a packet had arrived, and the town emptied itself upon the quays to watch the little ship come to her moorings, and to speculate from the tattered sails and hanging shrouds how many might be living and how many dead. And what news might she bring of victory or defeat? Falmouth in those days was the doorway into England, and the common talk of the town could be news that the dignitaries of London would not know till lathered horses had covered the distance from the West.

You will find all this in the history books, and you will find there the name of Captain John Pentecost of the packet *Termagant*. Who painted the pictures of the *Termagant* and the *Truculent* and the *Turbulent*, which I still have, I do not know. But they are lively pieces, although only one of them attempts to recreate a moment when the packet was in action at sea. This shows the famous fight between the *Termagant* and the French schooner *Julie* off Jamaica in 1793. The schooner's grappling irons have got a grip on the little *Termagant*, whose men are pouring musket fire into the *Julie*, standing indomitably beneath the rags of canvas and amid the snarls of rope and their own dead. But the most thrilling thing about the picture is that it depicts a moment when Captain John Pentecost performed the most astounding feat of his long battling life at sea. A shot from the Julie had unseated one of the *Termagant's* cannon, and here you see this giant of a man, with fire and fury all about him, grasping the cannon in both his arms and, with unhurried care, heaving it back upon its carriage.

From all I have read of the famous history of the packets, I take this engagement of the *Julie* and the *Termagant* to be the outstanding moment, though moment is hardly the word to use of a battle that endured throughout a day and a night, that ended with a handful of Frenchmen in chains, thirty and more dead, and the rest gone overboard, choosing to drown rather than fall into the hands of John

Pentecost. He brought the *Julie* into Falmouth, and with her he brought the beginning of the famous feud.

3

Miss Sapphira Kitto's house, where we were staying, was called Primrose Hill, and when I got back there that afternoon my mother and Blanche were out. Here for generations Kittos had accumulated their treasures, brought back by their captains from all the ports of the world. Carpets and tapestries, porcelain, paintings, furniture, trophies of outlandish weapons, and God knows what fantastic bits and pieces gave the place the look and smell of a museum, especially now that it was not often used as a house for living in. But, considered as a house, it was beautiful. It was perched upon a hill, and the back windows commanded a wide view of the sea. One of these windows, belonging to the library, was a lovely apse with a seat running round it, and I liked to come here, where no one else ever seemed to come, take a book down from the shelves and read.

I went straight to this room on returning from my first meeting with Kitto Pentecost because on the way home I had again passed the tomb of John Pentecost on the slope behind the church, and suddenly the words "John Pentecost" and "Termagant" had fallen into place in my mind. Back now in the library I took down the fat quarto volume, bound in faded blue leather, with the inscription on the spine: "Pentecost of the Termagant. Diary." I carried the book to the window seat and began to read, and for days thereafter I came back to it with fascination. It must have been, I thought, from this very window that Henry Kitto, looking through his telescope, saw the *Termagant* come round Pendennis Castle, and then ran out, shouting his orders to put the horses into the coach, and, leaving them to follow, hurried down to the quay. John Pentecost himself must tell of what had happened till then. Although the book, which is now on my shelves, is called on the spine "Diary", it is not a diary in the sense of being a record made as events unfolded. It is a story recollected in later years, and the part that concerns us now runs thus:

It was in the year before this that Henry Kitto, my owner, had visited his sugar plantations in Jamaica. God forgive me if now, an old man, I still find in my heart a grain of bitterness, but this I must

78

say, that Henry Kitto would never have made that voyage if his pocket had not been touched. But touched it was, and that alone was the reason why he put up with the discomforts of that voyage, for he hated the sea and was well content to let others win his fortune upon it. The story that came to my ears was that his manager upon the plantations was a slippery rogue, as he would need to be to get the better of Henry Kitto, but get the better of him he did, though only for a time, and after that voyage great changes were brought about there.

Such is the matter as I have heard it, and what I know of a surety is that it was during his stay at Kingston that he first met Martha Morden. Her father was a planter who lived on the island, an industrious man who looked to his own affairs, not one who was content to accept the profit of them and leave the labour to others. However, he was not rich. His affairs were small enough, and Martha Morden had little beyond her beauty of face and soul to commend her. They say he fell in love with her at sight, at a ball in Kingston, but he was ever cautious and did not conclude the matter. He sailed for home on but a half understanding, yet, being back in England, he now began to regret that he had not completely carried the thing off, and by letter all that was at last arranged. So it came about that when I sailed next for Jamaica in the *Termagant* I was to embark this lady and bring her to Falmouth. She was but twenty years of age. At that time I was forty, and Henry Kitto a little older.

We reached Jamaica without mishap, and when I had disposed of His Majesty's mails and carried advices to certain merchants, on behalf of Henry Kitto and other English men of business, I despatched an invitation to Miss Morden's father, asking that he and his daughter should visit the ship, to satisfy themselves that all was as it should be for the lady's accommodation. I had set my cabin aside for Miss Morden and a young half-caste girl who was to be her servant.

They came the next day and did me the honour to dine aboard and express themselves pleased with what they saw. I found Mr Morden, who was a widower, in a sad humour, what with the thought of losing his only child and his apprehension of danger. The activities of French privateers were much talked of in the island,

and I comforted him with a recital of our orders from the Post Office. "We must run, sir", I said. "Our business is to carry the mails and that is what counts – not our battle-wounds, but our lack of them. You have only to look at this ship to see that she is built for speed as a runaway." Miss Morden laughed at that, and said she understood well that British supremacy upon the seas depended upon our being hares, not hounds. She was a small dark woman, and I was much struck by her beauty and modesty.

When at last we sailed, we were for a time plagued by contrary winds, and a week's work found us not a hundred miles south-west of Jamaica. The half-caste girl now began to appear a little on deck. She had been very sick and Miss Morden had been her servant, not she Miss Morden's. I had ventured from time to time to look into the cabin, and was touched by our passenger's devotion to this foolish young creature, who at every sound of halliards slapping the masts or of feet running on the deck convinced herself that we were going to the bottom. It was the sight of Miss Morden stroking the girl's hand, or smoothing her forehead, or holding a spoon to her lips, that first touched my heart with feelings other than those which I should have felt for my owner's promised bride. I had sailed in one craft or another from the time when I was catching pollock off the Lizard at the age of ten, and I had never before had a woman aboard. To see the dainty touches that Miss Morden had made in my cabin where all had been rough and ready so worked upon me that the sunsets looked different and the birds that flew over the ship had never seemed so beautiful.

And so, when Miss Morden at last managed to bring that poor creature up on deck, and walked slowly to and fro with her, speaking encouraging words, I did not go near them and indeed made up my mind that I would not any more enter the cabin now that the patient was recovered and could do her duty by her mistress.

I was standing near the wheel, watching them as they walked down in the waist of the ship and making these good resolutions, when Miss Morden came up the ladder to where I stood and said: "Is it not good, Captain Pentecost, to see how well Rachel has recovered? We shall make a sailor of her yet."

I said formally that I hoped so, and then affected to be busy instructing Bob Uren, who was at the wheel, and who certainly needed no instruction of mine, and grinned at my embarrassment. Miss Morden did not go away, as I had hoped she would. She walked to the rail and looked back into the sunset, exclaiming at its beauty and calling one remark after another over her shoulder till out of politeness I was obliged to go and stand at her side. Then she said: "It is much on my mind, Captain, to have turned you out of your cabin. You must at least think yourself welcome there when opportunity offers. Pray join me at my supper tonight." I protested that my duty to the ship would not permit this, but she knew that this was a tarradiddle and pressed her invitation till there was nothing I could do but consent. "Be assured, sir," she said demurely, "that I shall immediately release you to your duty should a hurricane arise or a privateer become inquisitive. You will at once wish to give your orders to encounter the one and run away from the other."

The girl Rachel, now that she was recovered, attended upon her mistress' table that night, and when our meal was finished Miss Morden sent her out to walk upon the deck, for she had many personal things to ask me. She had never been in England and wished to know of the ways of life there, and especially in Cornwall; and there was much that she wished to know, too, of Henry Kitto. On these first matters I found myself chattering like a silly child, for, with her there so young and beautiful, my worn heart became young again and I was the child who had run barefoot about Mullion. I began to sing the praises of Cornwall above all other English counties, to tell her that the sea was coloured like precious stones, and that while winter lay upon other parts of the land there she would find the primroses peeping and the daffodillies dancing. "This would appear, sir," she said with a smile, "to be a paradise one had best explore with a poet for guide," and at that I felt foolish and said no more. But on the matter of Henry Kitto I had nothing to tell her save that all the beauties I had talked of were to be found at Tresco Vean. Then she would have me talk of my voyages, being filled like most landlubbers with the notion that our confined and tiring life was all rosy with romance. She would hear of my battles, some noise of which, I understood, had reached

Kingston, and I answered her as shortly as politeness permitted. Then the girl Rachel came peeping in and I bade Miss Morden good night.

I did not turn in then, but went up on to the poop and saw George Trounson bending over the binnacle light, and the glow of it making his face stand out in the darkness like a face in a picture. And I knew why, for the last few days, I had been noticing things like that, things which formerly had been commonplace and now seemed to have that poetry about which Miss Morden had twitted me. I wanted to go and open my heart to George, for he was a Mullion boy like me, and we had grown up together and sailed together, and once, in a dinghy that had had the bottom torn out of her when we were fooling round over the Manacles, we had nearly died together. But I merely laid my hand on his shoulder, which is a thing I had not done before, and said in a low voice: "All well, George?" and he answered: "Ay, ay, Captain," in the same quiet tones.

It was a night of full moon, and there was not much wind, but what little there was was with us and we were moving easily on our course. The peacefulness of the night gave me time to think, as sailors will, of a cottage where I could be near the sea, but not on it, and much foolishness of that sort, and presently I turned in.

It was at dawn that the mate, Bill Soper, shook me and told me that a sail had been sighted, and by full light there was no doubt that, whoever she was, she wanted to make our acquaintance. Even the little wind there had been when I turned in had slackened. We were moving too slowly for my liking, and when I had seen that the necessary orders were given for making the best of things, I stood right aft with a telescope to my eye intent on this stranger who was coming up on our starboard quarter. A voice just behind me asked: "Pray, sir, is this where we begin to run?" and I answered: "Ay, ma'am. But I fear we shall not run fast enough this time."

She begged me to let her look through the telescope, and I did so, standing at her side with my right hand holding the weight of it, and presently she said: "She is carrying the French flag." The morning air was cold. She was all wrapped up in a thick cloak of frieze, with a close-fitting little hat beneath which her eyes were shining with excitement.

"Shall we get away from her?" she asked, and I said: "We shall do our best, ma'am. We have no choice in the matter. Our orders are to do our best. You must understand that, though this ship belongs to Mr Kitto, we are the servants of His Majesty's government so long as we are carrying the mail. Our orders are from them, not from him, and the orders are clear. We must not fight unless we have to, and if there is danger of our being taken, we must sink the mail."

It seemed strange to be standing there explaining such matters to her, and to feel in my heart that now, more than ever, there was reason for showing a clean pair of heels. A fortnight ago I had not seen this woman. I had been able to think of taking her aboard as dispassionately as if she had been an additional sack of letters. Now what I was thinking of was not the fury of Henry Kitto should she fall into the hands of the French but the blow at my own heart.

The wind freshened during the morning and we ran under all we had, but pile her with every stitch as we did, we could not give the slip to the French schooner. I had to order Miss Morden to her cabin to take her meals. She was so excited that she wished to be on deck all day, but it was ever my way, when it seemed as though a fight would be forced upon us, to see that the men not only had their meals but ate better than usual. There was not much fear that thus we should run short: there would likely be fewer mouths to feed in the days that followed. So I insisted that she, too, should eat and also the girl Rachel needed much of her attention that day, for fear had made her sick again.

In the late afternoon the *Julie* managed to put a shot across us, and I knew now that there was no avoiding what must come. The sky was clear, the moon, when it came, would be full, and we should likely be at it all night. I ordered the mails in their weighted bags to be brought up from the hold and laid ready for the jettison if the worst came, and in a voice which I fear was rough with anxiety I ordered Miss Morden and her attendant to quit the cabin and go below decks. Now that we were within range the cabin might take a shot at any moment. I ordered George Trounson to take palliasses down and see that the women were made as comfortable as possible. The girl Rachel, her face dabbled all over with weeping, scurried after him, but Miss Morden did not go at once. She stood beside me on the poop, looking white but resolute, and I exclaimed with some heat: "I should regret it, ma'am, had I to order you to be carried below."

At that moment the *Julie*, which had been coming up with her bows on our starboard quarter, herself turned to starboard and thus sailed with us broadside on. She let us have her port broadside, and that was a devilish beginning to the fight. Three of their cannon-balls hit us. One smashed down the side of the cabin in which but a moment before the women had been sitting. Another cut the halliards of our mainsail, and the canvas came rushing down the mast, jammed halfway and began to beat angrily. The third was for poor George Trounson, who was coming up after seeing Rachel below. All this in the second while she and I stood stormily face to face, and in that second the anger spilled out of both of us as the wind was spilling out of the sail. Tears spurted out of her eyes. I saw them come like a sudden storm. One instant her face was white and dry, and the next the tears were streaming down. I put my hand on her shoulder and said gently: "You see how it is, my dear. This time we don't run." She said: "I must see to that poor man." Trounson had clutched for a moment at the coaming of the hatch leading to the hold. Then he had fallen backwards. She ran now and disappeared down the ladder and I turned to give my thought to what had to be done. I looked towards the *Julie*, and the smoke of the cannonade was rising lazily from her ports, letting me see, as it broke up, the mounseers jumping and cheering. In that moment the thought of Miss Morden went out of my mind. I thought of George Trounson's face looking so kind in the light of the binnacle lamp and of the day we wrecked the dinghy on the Manacles and when I was sinking George held me up till a fisherman picked us out of the water; and if our mainsail had not been mangled, if we could have run then and left her standing, I should not have done so, no, not if all the mails on the high seas had been in my charge. Our starboard ports had been opened and the guns run out. I ran down into the waist, shouting: "Mister, what are you waiting for?" and we answered the *Julie's* first word.

It was a strange sensation to be sitting there in the window-apse of Primrose Hill reading the living words of the man whose tomb, like a stone box, stood among the docks and nettles on the slope behind the church. I shall not here give his account of the battle that raged throughout that moon-bright night and under the sunshine of the following day. It was a battle of cannon-shot across open seas, and of musket-shot and the humming of cutlasses and the flash of pistols when the *Julie* threw out her grappling-irons, clamping her port side to the *Termagant's* starboard. Again and again each ship was boarded, and the boarders were driven back to their own place, only to surge forward again in another desperate and bloody rally. The crew of the schooner outnumbered the *Termagant's* by two to one. The canvas of both ships flapped in rags, the sheets and halliards were snarls of rubbish, and from time to time flames lit up the relentless scene. It was towards the end of the afternoon, when the débâcle had pressed itself once more over the grappled bulwarks on to the *Termagant's* decks, that Captain Pentecost, William Soper and Arthur Foot dropped overboard, on the captain's orders, swam unseen to the *Julie's* starboard side, and boarded her through an open port. Every man aboard her who was still alive was engaged in the last desperate mêlée on the *Termagant*, and the three of them, picking up pistols and cutlasses as they went, made their way through the fire and chaos of the ship and the dead and dying lying there and came up to the *Julie's* port bulwarks just as the handful from the *Termagant*, using the last of their strength, were once more hurling the invaders back into their own ship. At Pentecost's word, he and his two men let out a wild round of *Huzzas*, which caused the Frenchmen to turn in affright, giving the *Termagant's* crew the advantage they needed. They drove the Frenchmen on to the cutlasses and pistols of the frightful-looking dripping three, who desperately shot them and cut them down. This was the end. The crew of the packet made their last sortie, and the matter was concluded on the Frenchman's decks. There had been sixty-five men in the *Julie's* crew. Thirty-two of them lay dead here or on the *Termagant*; sixteen threw down their weapons and seventeen, looking at the terrible figure of Captain Pentecost, dripping with sea-water, running with the blood of a cutlass-slash across his forehead, and holding a red, reeking weapon in his hand, leapt over the bulwarks, choosing to drown rather than face what they imagined would befall them.

I put the sixteen mounseers who had survived to the task of dowsing the fires in their own ship, with Foot in charge of them (the narrative goes on). Then, when I had seen the mails safely stowed again, which was my first duty, and observed that what was left of our men were dealing with our own fires and doing already what could be done to make the *Termagant* shipshape, I ordered the cook into the galley to prepare such food as he could, and then went below. It had already been reported to me that Trounson was dead. I had seen Pasco and Hutchins go overboard cut about with so many wounds that they must have been lifeless when they struck the water. To cross the coaming of the hatch I had to lift my foot over the body of Alfred Cox, a Penryn boy making his first voyage with us, and the last, too, I thought bitterly, looking at his hands clutching his torn belly. Altogether, when I got down there into the half-light that fell from a couple of lanterns swaying with the ship's movement, and saw the worst, and Miss Morden kneeling by the side of Tom Hearn and winding a bandage about his bleeding arm, and the girl Rachel lying on a mattress, I was so filled with fury that I advanced upon her, seized her by an arm, and hauled her to her feet, shouting: "Rouse up, you black bitch. Rouse up and help your mistress. Is this a time to sleep?"

Miss Morden had cut the sleeves from her dress. Her long white arms were bare, and her hair was hidden by a white 'kerchief that she had wound like a turban about her head. She looked up for a moment from her task and said patiently: "The poor girl is dead, sir."

I had known this even as I shouted at the black girl. She was lifeless in my grasp. Her eyes, wide open with the terror that had killed her, glared insanely into mine. I let go my grip, and she thumped to the deck.

Miss Morden got up from her knees and said: "You are hurt. Let me see." There was a little pile of bandages ready to her hand, and I saw that these were made from garments which she had torn up. With one of them she staunched the wound in my forehead, and as we stood there face to face in that reeking hole I trembled to see that her arms were red with blood to the elbow. When she had tied the knot that secured the bandage we did not at once move apart. In that wavering, smoky light with the stink of blood in our nostrils, with five dead men neatly arranged by her hands to one side and six grievously wounded lying to the other, we looked for a moment into one another's eyes. God knows what was in my heart to say then. Whatever it may have been I did not say it. I only said: "This is not my first fight, ma'am, but it is the only fight in which my dead and wounded have been cared for. I thank you. And I am sorry I spoke so to the black girl."

"The poor child," she said. "She was soon out of it."

Then I went back on deck, pausing for a moment to look at the body of Alfred Cox, and yet not really seeing it, even when it suddenly twitched into death.

Captain Pentecost's narrative goes on to describe the next day's burial of the bodies at sea and the homeward voyage, which was made without further misadventure. As if to make up for what we had suffered (he writes) the weather was prosperous and we flew home like a pair of birds, the *Julie* and the *Termagant*. I saw little of Miss Morden during those days, or at any rate I spoke little to her. She had formed her own notions of what should be done, and I left her to do it. My cabin had been roughly repaired, but she would not use it. It was her opinion that below decks was no place for wounded men, and so she had them carried up and laid under an awning in the air. There were but four now; two had died. At nights, she had the four moved into the cabin. All day she was with them in the waist of the ship, where they lay upon mattresses, dressing their wounds, washing their bandages, fussing over what they should and should not eat, though God knows there was not much choice. It was strange to all of us to see how, before she would touch the men, she would wash her hands and arms up to the elbow. The wounded men, and not they only, followed her with their eyes as she soused her arms in a bucket of steaming water brought from the galley. In the Captain's cabin of the *Julie* there was much red wine and a fair amount of fresh fruit. She warmed the wine and soaked our hard tack in it. On this and the fruit, so long as it lasted, she fed her wounded men. They all strengthened quickly; they all recovered; and I thought of other fights I had been in and of the poor devils left thereafter to the darkness and roaches in the cockpit. We did not expect to see them live, and only a few tough ones did.

There is no joy to an English sailor like the joy of seeing English land again, and as we slid down the coast and all the familiar landmarks hove up and came abreast and fell astern – the Lizard, Coverack and the Manacles – I felt again what I had so often felt before: the beauty and the joy of life with bitterness at its heart. There were widows who did not yet know it, and fatherless who would look with round eyes at me who had come home without the men they had hoped to greet. I should look at those lambs and feel like a sheepdog who had allowed the ewes to fall into the grip of a wolf. I had been through all this often enough, and the premonition of it now made me quiet as the evening deepened and ahead the dark mass of Pendennis Castle shaped itself upon the sky. But I knew that this time there was more cause for sorrow than ever before.

Miss Morden's boxes had been packed. She was dressed for going ashore. From the poop I could see her down in the waist with a group of men about her, offering her the simple presents such men give: a carved shell, a mat made from ropes' ends, and such trifles. It was a quiet evening, and all the ship was quiet, because we held in our hearts the heavy news we had to tell. We hadn't seen the *Julie* since dawn. She had been more severely damaged in the fight than we and was limping. I had taken the precaution of mixing the crews. Some of the mounseers were with us, and some of our men were in the *Julie*, with Foot in command.

So now, I thought, this is the end of it and I shall see her no more, except maybe that she will glide into a room and glide out again when I am discussing with her husband how my life and many good men's lives may increase his fortune. I could not bring myself to go down to speak to her, but I stood there, willing her to come up those steps and speak to me – to say some last few words that I should remember all my life. But she did not come, and I know now that this was because she, also, was fearful that a few words would be too many.

We were round Pendennis Head, and the anchor was ready to be let go, and in the failing light we could see the Falmouth waterfront and hear faintly carried out to us the sound of the horn that told of our coming. Even as the anchor went down and the halliards were uncleated the water sprang into liveliness with dinghies pushing off from the shore, and in one of them, I knew, would be Henry Kitto. In my time I had brought much to that man from overseas, and I thought

88

with bitterness of the price that had been paid to bring him a wife. Dusky though it was by now, I could see him scanning the ship as his dinghy drew near, taking in the significance of the holes torn through our bulwarks, the charred wood and scorched paint. I was at the rail to receive him, and before he was aboard he shouted: "You have been in action, Captain Pentecost." "The mails are safe, sir," I assured him, giving him a hand up the ladder. "By God," he answered, "it will be no thanks to you if your passenger is, also."

Miss Morden stepped forward. "I am well, sir," she said, "as you see, and most happy to be in England."

"Most happy!" he shouted. "Most lucky would be a better word. Your orders are to run, Captain Pentecost, not to fight. And a fine time you chose to disobey them."

He was a slight man whom you would have known from his clean-shaven parchment face to be at home in a counting-house. His close-fitting black clothes were greenish with age. He had a reputation as a mean man, and so I had found him. He was also a man easily moved to anger when his interests were touched, though I had never known him angry in a generous cause. I shall not pretend that I had at any time felt a liking for him. In many matters I had felt for him much dislike, and all these old feelings gathered now into a knot in my heart, moved as I was by the thought of our encounter with the *Julie*, and of our dead, and of the parting with Miss Morden. He was the only owner I had ever served as captain, but in that moment I did not care whether I ever again commanded a ship for him or anyone else. I watched him striding up and down the waist, and this was not the first time I had witnessed this striding as a way of working up anger and imposing it on the beholder. I knew Henry Kitto and his ways pretty well. My own anger was cold and resolute, not like that striding bantam's, who must crow and bustle to nerve himself for a fight. "I am ready, sir," I said, "to discuss with you ashore the interpretation I put upon my orders, which come from the Post Office and not from you. Here, on my decks, in the presence of the men I command, I will thank you to hold your tongue."

I suppose it was not so much these words as the chuckle with which the men greeted them that infuriated him. Aware of the conflict between us, they had stopped their work and were all ears. Henry Kitto rounded upon them suddenly. "Get to your work! Get to your work, damn you!" he shouted, and I again intervened. "Permit me, sir," I said, "to remind you that this is not your counting-house. I am the one to give orders in this ship," and, turning to the men, I gave them the rough side of my tongue and sent them running.

There was no surprise in Henry Kitto's attitude to me, but I marvelled at his attitude to Miss Morden. She was standing a little apart, and he took no more notice of her than he might have taken of a piece of merchandise that I had brought from overseas. Nor did he speak of our fight or inquire about our dead and wounded men.

"Russell's wagon is waiting," he said to me brusquely. "When you have seen the mails into it, you will be good enough, Captain Pentecost, to accompany me to Tresco Vean."

Well, I might as well go there as anywhere else. I had no chick nor child. I was not bursting for drink or a woman. Mrs Treveal, with whom I lodged in a house on the terraces overlooking the harbour, would no doubt already be on the quay, and the matter could be explained to her. Miss Morden's trunks were already being rowed ashore. She and Kitto followed in his dinghy, and I got into another boat that was carrying the mail. It was fully dark by now, and as we drew near to the quay I could see the lanterns already lit on Russell's covered wagon and the horses waiting patiently in the warm night. The formalities of handing over the mail were soon gone through, Mrs Treveal was sent home, and, carrying a small bag with my night things, I walked across the cobbles to Henry Kitto's coach. The coachman was already on the box and Kitto was striding up and down, stimulating his impatience and importance. "Get in, man, get in," he cried testily. "Is Miss Morden to sit here all night under the gaze of these yokels?"

The news had got about that this lady who had come ashore was to be Henry Kitto's bride, and sure enough there was a knot of interested people, but this could hardly have discommoded Miss Morden for the inside of the coach was as black as a coffin. And so, as I got in, I was not sure whether it was by accident or intention that her hand brushed mine. Whichever it was, I was suddenly moved to take that hand and press it, and my heart leapt to my mouth as I felt an answering pressure. I knew from that moment how the whole matter would end.

We had five miles to go from Falmouth to Tresco Vean, five miles behind the clopping hooves, through a night moonless as yet, with the lamps showing a twist of hedge, a white gate, the grey end of a cottage. Even such glimpses were rare. For the most part, it was as though we were moving through a tunnel, and all the time I was thinking how oppressively this must lie – this dark end of the journey – on the imagination of a girl who already had endured so much.

We swung through the gates, and the tunnel darkened as we drove down the long road to the house, with the treetops meeting over our heads. Then we pulled up with a grinding of gravel, a squeal of brakes, and Henry Kitto leapt out and began hammering impatiently on the door. A manservant came, carrying a lamp, and Kitto shouted to him: "Show Miss Morden and Captain Pentecost to their rooms." Then, to us he said: "We shall dine in an hour's time." He had hardly given her his hand from the coach. He turned and disappeared into the house. Miss Morden and I looked at one another, she more marvelling than I, for I knew his ways. She had an exhausted look. I could have taken her into my arms then, but a housekeeper was there to show her the way, and I stood stock-still watching her painfully climb the splendid staircase.

Hot water was brought to me in my bedroom. I washed, but had nothing to change into. I sat down in my travel-stained clothes, waiting for the hour to pass. A sense of mystery, almost of disaster, oppressed me. Here was this girl who had come halfway across the world to meet her bridegroom. He had hardly spoken to her. Knowing that she had come through death and battle, he had asked nothing of her welfare and sufferings. Even for Henry Kitto, this seemed to me strange.

When at last we assembled, it was a gloomy and almost silent meal, though the dining room blazed with candles. I had expected that we three would dine alone, but a lady was present whom Henry Kitto introduced as Miss Magnus. She was young and handsome and splendidly dressed, more beautiful than Miss Morden if you take beauty to pieces and look one by one at eyes and nose, ears, mouth and complexion. But she seemed to me to lack the general sense of loveliness that Miss Morden had. Looking at pictures has never been a thing to come my way, but I can understand how one artist might get all his pieces right and another get some of them wrong, and yet this second one paint a picture that would smite you, and the other merely please you. Well, that is how I felt as I sat and looked at Miss Magnus and Miss Morden. Miss Morden was pale and composed, and this other lady was flushed with the same excitement and impatience which I had felt in Henry Kitto all through that evening.

When the cloth had been drawn and port wine put upon the mahogany and the servants were gone, Henry Kitto signed to the ladies not to follow them. He got up and locked the door. He leaned over my shoulder with the decanter in his hand, filled my glass with port, and then returned to his place at the head of the table. Standing there, he said: "Captain Pentecost, you will pardon a small deception. This lady, who *was* Miss Magnus a month ago, is now my wife. I invite you to pledge our happiness."

I could have killed him. Perhaps I should have done so; but one thing suddenly quelled the riot of emotion that had burst out in my mind. I looked at Miss Morden and saw that she was smiling. It was a smile such as I had not seen on her face before: a smile of profound happiness and relief. "Thank God," she said. The sincerity of the words startled us all. "You take it lightly, madam," Henry Kitto said with a scowl; and she answered: "It is only fair, sir, that the light conduct should not all be on one side."

"My conduct has not been light. On the contrary, it has been carefully considered," he began; and, my anger boiling up in me, I shouted to him: "Be silent, you dog. By the grace of God, you have done no harm; but that leaves you none the less vile and treacherous."

He looked at me coolly. "Your opinions are doubtless valuable, Captain Pentecost, upon matters that concern you. All that concerns you now is to discuss with me the return of Miss Morden to the Indies. That is the sole reason why you have been asked here tonight."

This notion that I existed for no purpose but to serve his ends, however unprincipled, stirred up my wrath again, and I threw the wine from my glass into his face. I strode to the door and unlocked it, and a moment later I was out of the house.

Now, twenty-five years later, an old man, I can recall the emotions of that moment, and I smile to think that, beyond anything else, I was tortured by the thought that I was old.

The highroad along which we had travelled from Falmouth runs just inland from the sea coast. It follows the bend of the coast as this turns in to form the wide mouth of the Helford River. From the road the land slopes down to the water in a number of lovely combes, heavily wooded, and landowners thereabouts have seen the beauty of these little valleys as housing sites. Tresco Vean was the loveliest of these houses. It was built of grey crumbly Cornish stone, reinforced in windowsills, doorways and at all angles with granite. It stood upon a platform at the head of the valley, and from here the land ran steeply down to the water. On either side were beechwoods, within them green thickets of rhododendron and camellia, hydrangea and fuchsia; and within these again was the long grassy walk to the water. It all made a small domestic paradise where one could be utterly undisturbed, and often enough during storms at sea or when I was brooding after the heat of fighting my thoughts would turn back to that delectable place and I would wonder at the arrangement of men's affairs which permitted one to remain snugly there, propped in his security by the danger and desperate action of others such as I.

But when I had flung out of Tresco Vean that night, it was not of such things that I was thinking. It was hard upon midnight, for it had been late when we arrived at the house, and the air in that small confined valley was dead and damp with autumn. My feet scuffled through the leaves that were thick upon the grass, and already the beech trees were far enough gone in their shedding for the full moon which had now risen to show with twigs scrawled upon her face. There was a sense of decay and of ending in every breath I drew, and the greatness of my years seemed heavy in my bones.

I can laugh at it now, but I did not laugh then. I was forty, a man without fortune, depending for his living upon following a dangerous trade. And this man loved a beautiful girl, twenty years younger than himself. Henry Kitto, I knew, was older than I, but he could pay for his pleasures, thanks to me and men like me. But what had I to offer to Martha Morden? I felt as miserable as if my lusty frame were crumbling into dissolution.

I reached the water and sat down upon the granite edge of the small quay there. The tide was full and quiet, and the moon-shimmer was hardly broken by a ripple. Across the river, the land rose up, shaggy with small twisted oaks.

So there was already a Mrs Henry Kitto. I marvelled at the man's duplicity, but now, in the knowledge of later years, I must put it down that his marriage to Miss Magnus was among the few generous and impulsive actions of his cold life. She was a bold and fascinating wench, an actress whom he first saw playing at a London theatre. He had already set out for London before the *Termagant* sailed for the Indies. The theatre was not a place he much frequented, but the need to be civil to business acquaintances took him there, and the mischief was done. Mischief enough it was, for she was light and impetuous and a scandal to all our neighbourhood before the end, but he loved her and forgave her – he who was as niggard of forgiveness as of all else and with her he knew times of stormy happiness that would not otherwise have lit him up.

But all this I could not know as I sat on the quay's granite eddy and looked at a dinghy motionless against the steps beneath me and at a quay punt moored out in the yellow moon-track. The people in Falmouth, on our landing, had pressed round Henry Kitto's coach, anxious to see Miss Morden, whom they clearly took to be his bride. He must have brought his wife home even more foxily than he did most things, but, once she was there, her concealment for a few months would not be difficult.

Well, there I sat as the night ebbed and the dawn began to show over the river mouth on my left hand. I had made a fool of myself. Never again, I thought, would I be able to command one of Henry Kitto's ships. Miss Morden was not for me, and now I had destroyed the possibility even of being entrusted with returning her to her father like a piece of merchandise that had come on approval and been rejected.

When the first light was in the sky, I got up, intending to retrace my way up the valley, past the house, to the highroad. The walk into Falmouth would be nothing. I might even find a cart that would set me on my way. So I rose and was stretching myself in the aguish mist-dripping morning, when a mocking voice spoke behind me. "Oh, so that's where you are. You look as grey, sir, as the stone you have been sitting on. You must be perished. Pray drink this."

It was Mrs Henry Kitto. She was wearing a long frieze cloak with a hood that covered her head, and she was sparkling with the distilled moisture of the morning. Her eyes sparkled, too, as if the moment had much merriment for her. Her gloved hand held towards me a silver flask. I took it and drank, and the fiery brandy did me good.

"You are kind, madam," I said, and she answered: "Yes – I think that at least can be said of me."

We looked at one another for a moment, and then she spoke impetuously: "Sir, I ask you not to think ill of me. I did not know of Miss Morden's existence until yesterday morning. She is as great a surprise to me as, I fear, I am a sorrow to her."

I could not but believe her. "He has treated you both very ill, ma'am," I said.

She waved that aside airily enough. "You need waste no sorrow on me, Captain Pentecost," she said. "I have means both to avenge and cure my own ills. As for Miss Morden, you must be dull indeed if you think she comes badly out of the bargain. I have talked to her for the past hour. And now, I pray you, talk to her yourself."

She turned at that, and beckoned, and my darling came out from among the trees that had hidden her, and with not a word spoken we were in one another's arms. The scrub oaks across the water were just catching the first gold of the sun, and birds began to stir in the trees, shaking down the cold dew.

I expected Mrs Kitto to withdraw, but she did not. Her bold eyes looked at us with a kind of mocking tenderness as though such scenes were not strange to her and of little account. Presently she said: "Miss Morden has breakfasted, and your breakfast is here, Captain." She indicated a basket lying among the bushes.

"You arrange everything, madam," I said. "I trust Mr Kitto approves of your provision."

"Mr Kitto," she said, "is still sound asleep, I think. He has not been consulted, but he will be informed"; and in those few words she stated the situation that was ever thereafter to exist between her and Henry Kitto. She was of a good heart, and with a better man she could have been a better woman.

"Come," she said now. "At these steps you see a dinghy, and out on the water is a little ship. They are both mine, for my husband would make me a sea faring woman – within narrow limits. I hate them both and have never used them. But would it not be appropriate, Captain Pentecost, that you and Miss Morden should at once embark upon your own element? Falmouth is not far away."

I rowed Martha out to the quay punt, and as the mainsail rings rattled up the mast I saw Mrs Kitto still standing upon the quay, and I could imagine the ironic smile at our romance which seemed so odd upon so young and lovely a face. Then a breeze caught us as I cleated down the sheet and we moved out towards the river mouth where the sunlight was merry on the water. We saw her still, waving a tiny handkerchief, and then she turned and began to climb up towards Tresco Vean.

4

I did not read any more at that time. Child though I was, I sat back deeply affected. I was sharply aware, as I had never been before, of the irony of time's passing. I gazed out of the window-apse and thought of the lusty captain groaning at the weight of his years, and so soon changing to joy and sailing out into the sunlight merry on the water. And what would it have mattered had he been twenty years older or twenty years younger? The sunlight was merry on the water today, and Captain Pentecost was a stone box full of bones on the hill behind the church. But was he as dead as all that? I turned over again in my mind some of the phrases I had read, so sharp and clear, so unlike what one would have expected from a man of that sort at that time, and I wondered how much of him lived on in Kitto Pentecost and in me, too.

John Pentecost had enabled me not only to read the thing but almost literally to see it. This, of course, was helped because I knew Tresco Vean. It was there that I had been reunited with Blanche, and the place was little changed. We were tired, my mother and I, when we reached Falmouth after our long journey from Manchester. We were limp and exhausted with the heat of that day of late summer, and it was like a sunrise to find Betsy Comfort awaiting us in the dirty little dead-end station. An ancient four-wheeler cab took us to Primrose Hill. When my mother had drunk some tea and eaten a little, Betsy announced forthrightly: "Now you'd better get to bed – the pair of you."

My mother was only too willing to be ordered to do something so sensible, but I was already revived and full of a boy's curiosity. "How is Blanche?" I demanded. "When shall I see my uncle? Where is my great-aunt Sapphira?"

Betsy and I were sitting in the garden, looking over the roofs of the town to the twilight settling upon the harbour. There were lights upon some of the ships, and a great stillness and serenity that made me think of my uncle's picture – "Sunset and Evening Star", as I called it to myself.

"You learn to contain your soul in patience, master Ted," Betsy answered. "What do you expect? Do you think the whole family is going to line up on parade just because you've arrived? You'll meet 'em all soon enough."

I thought," I persisted, "that Primrose Hill was my great-aunt's house?"

"So it is."

"Then why isn't she here to meet us?"

"Because she's got another house, and that's where she lives mostly. She's not the sort of woman who puts herself out to meet anybody, believe me. *You'll* have to meet *her* – *and* watch your P's and Q's when you're doing it, too. She's one of them as have got more money than sense."

Betsy was never idle. Beside her on the seat was a work-basket full of odds and ends that needed repair, and she paused now to thrust wool through a darning needle. "Blanche is all right," she said. "You'll see her tomorrow. I shall be taking you to Tresco Vean."

She looked sideways at me, and I knew that she understood that this, more than anything else, was what I wanted: to meet Blanche again. "She's all right," she repeated. "I've been keeping an eye on her. I've been seeing she's not put upon."

"Who would want to put upon her?" I asked.

"Why, her, of course – Miss Sapphira. A reg'lar old tyrant she is. She tries to put upon everybody. That was the trouble."

She went on with her darning for a while, then said: "The Pentecosts are all right – give their nuts away they would, if they wasn't screwed on tight enough. But them Kittos! They're getters, they are, not givers. Been gettin' an' gettin' an' gettin' for generations, which they can do so far as I'm concerned if it amuses 'em. But admit that this gives 'em the right to boss other people's lives – that I never will do. As for her, she's the last of 'em, and believe me, Master Ted, that's a strange thought, too, in these parts: the last of the Kittos. Why, they've been Lord God Almighty time out of mind."

At the bottom of the garden at Primrose Hill there is a mighty pine, a tortured giant of a tree that stands blackly against the sky, and through its ancient lattices you see the harbour in broken bits, shining on sunny days like mosaic splinters of glass, but now I looked on fragments of pewter, and over the tree bats were weaving their errant and unpredictable patterns. Very faintly from off the water came a sound we were not much longer to hear – the singing of a sea song as men trudged round, pushing the capstan bars. The moment is inseparably bound up in my mind with a sense that all the whispers and hints of mystery concerning Cornwall were about to thin like mist in the morning.

"How your father hated that woman!" Betsy suddenly broke out, and when I gently prompted her: "How should you know that, Betsy?" she cried: "Why, how could I help knowing, seeing that I was a little maid in her house at the time?"

She bit off an end of wool and spat it to the ground. "They couldn't keep away from one another, the Kittos and the Pentecosts," she said. "I've heard my mother speak of 'em, and my grandmother before that. The Pentecosts went to sea and worked the land and never had much more than two ha'pennies to rub together, and the Kittos had Tresco Vean and Primrose Hill and a counting-house in Falmouth and half the town besides. You'd say there was nothing between such folks, but they were always on one another's nerves and doorsteps. There was always something – arguments and lawsuits in galores. If it was nothing else it was a Pentecost cow breaking down a Kitto hedge – always something."

She yawned, and began to put her bits and pieces back into the work-basket. "Now off to bed with you," she said. "You've got me cawing like an old rook over an ellum."

She got up and shook out her skirts, then paused, her face full of recollection. "It was on this very seat," she said, "that I told your father I'd go with 'em. I'd forgotten that – on this very seat."

"Tell me," I said. "Whom did you go with?"

"Why, them two, of course – your father and mother." She sat down again and took the stuff of her skirt between her fingers, pleating it and looking into the past. "There was no one left then," she said, "not one of all them Kittos except Miss Sapphira."

5

At first, I did not see Miss Sapphira. I heard her voice from behind a closed door saying: "I cannot see the boy now. Tell him to go and play." I ran out of the house through the french windows which opened upon the terrace, and before me I saw the green dropping ground over which Captain Pentecost had shuffled through the autumn leaves so long ago. Here, where I stood on the stone pavement of the terrace, fuchsias bowed their heads over the rims of urns ranged in a formal row. Beyond them was the green grass, with the tall beech trees on either hand, and at the farthest point of perspective water flashed back a glint of sun. That was a long way off, and it was impossible to see the face of the girl in white who was walking uphill with this sun-glistered water behind her. But I knew it was Blanche. I leapt over the low parapet of the terrace and ran down to meet her.

I was glad that the meeting with my great-aunt Sapphira was postponed. I was unsure of what I wanted my attitude to her to be. There was so much I must ask Blanche first. How had she been treated? What did she think of the old woman? Was she the tyrant who had emerged in my imagination from Betsy's narrative of the night before?

There had come a time when there were only two of them – Sophie and Sapphira. The Kittos had shrunk to that. There were no men any more. All that generations of them had piled up was now in the hands of those two girls. They were twins, lording it like coeval queens, and adjoining Tresco Vean was the farm of James Pentecost, my grandfather. He was true to Pentecost form. He just kept body and soul together, paying his tithes, paying his rent to the Kittos, arguing with them about his rights and his wrongs, as Pentecosts had always argued with Kittos, and having little at the year's end save enough to start another year's grinding toil.

Sophie and Sapphira Kitto were fearfully aware of James Pentecost. He was a dark whipcord man of thirty, and according to the legend that had come down to Betsy Comfort they were both in love with him. He married Sophie, in whom, I should imagine, something of the blood and passion of the far-off Miss Magnus lingered on. It seems to have been a mad runaway affair that ended disastrously. Five years later James Pentecost and his wife were drowned off the Manacles when a squall capsized their sailing boat. They were washed ashore at

Coverack, locked in one another's arms. His mouth, Betsy said with a dramatic touch, was full of her hair. Sapphira Kitto did not attend the funeral. She had never forgiven her sister either for marrying a Pentecost or for preventing her from doing so. But she took charge of the children – my father and my Uncle Kitto.

I was learning a lot about my father. As I ran that morning down the green fall of the land, thinking of Manchester and the little shop, the smoky air and the sooty curtains that my mother must wash every week, I found it hard to believe that all this that now I saw had once been his. I stopped on the thought, and looked back. It was most movingly beautiful. The grey stone house slumbered in the sunshine with the bright flowers spread at its feet and the wings of the trees folded about it. They were slightly touched with autumn's russet and the first gauze of autumn was in the air itself, softening the outlines of everything, lending to the scene a faint touch of insubstantiality and mirage. Smoke rose in a lazy curl from a chimney, and I thought a window curtain stirred in that first-floor room which I knew to, he Miss Sapphira's.

How – why had he given up all that?

"He was always a one, was Mr Frederick," Betsy said. "Not like Mr Kitto. And that was a thing for you, if you like. It was little things like that that started the rows. Miss Sapphira always called him Kitto and he didn't mind it. You could have called him green cheese for all he cared, so long as you didn't interfere with his old painting. At it he was from the time he could crawl. 'I've always called him Ted, and I always will,' Mr Fred used to say, and sometimes at that Miss Sapphira would go blind raging. She was Kitto mad. I suppose because she was the last of 'em. I've seen her strike your father with her stick often enough over nothing more than that, and he standing there and smiling."

I can see now, clearly enough, those two boys growing up, the one wearing from the first the fragile but impenetrable armour of his gift, sliding without hurt between all chinks, enduring, without being aware that there was anything to endure so long as that which was entrusted to him came to no harm. But the other, my father, with no gift, but with an unconscious guarding of his integrity, was open to all winds, subject to all blows, breaking his skin forever on the rough outcrop of the old woman's pride and tyranny. They went to no school. They had a tutor now and then, but mostly they taught themselves what they knew. Kitto never had a lesson in painting or drawing.

So they grew up at Tresco Vean, with visits now and then to Primrose Hill, and life to one was paradisal and to the other perplexity and distress. Thus it went on till my mother took her father to die in Cornwall.

I have since seen, in the little church of Mylor, a plaque commemorating this grandfather whom I never knew. It reads:

Sacred to the Memory of
RICHARD SOWLER
Of Rochdale in the County of Lancashire
Who in this mild climate sought
relief of a consumption – alas!
in vain. He died on June the Sixth,
1880.

It was a day of fate, this sixth of June. I have since heard the story from my mother. They were staying at Primrose Hill then – my great-aunt Sapphira with Kitto and Frederick. The young men were in their early twenties. Kitto had had his first Academy success that year. His picture had been much talked of. Frederick, who had been trained to do nothing and had no natural gift, was living morosely on his aunt's bounty. She did not grudge it, so long as it was recognised as the grace of a Kitto overflowing to a Pentecost. On that June afternoon the young men were in the churchyard at Mylor. They had rowed round the point in a dinghy from Falmouth. Kitto was painting the little grey church, with the darkness of the centuries gathered into the great yew at its eastern end, and the brief glory of a summer's day lying upon the sea that flowed away beyond the churchyard wall. My father was lying in the June grass among the graves. The cracked bell that lives in a tower away from the church began to drop slow, spaced notes into the hot air, and this told them that a funeral procession was approaching. They stayed there in the sunshine while the service was held in the church, and when the procession came out they followed it through the grass that was rippling with heat and loud with the buzzing of transient unseen creatures. It was a poor procession. Four farm labourers carried the coffin. A girl wearing a black dress so ill-fitting that it appeared to have been borrowed for the occasion was the only mourner.

It was thus that my father first met my mother. When the parson's surplice had fluttered through a door of the church, like a white pigeon homing from the torrid heat, and the hired bearers were gone away, she remained looking down into the hole which an insensitive gravedigger was already filling, as though, now that the seed of immortality had been planted, no time must be lost in giving it a chance to grow.

Kitto and Frederick stood there, observing this scene: the earth-stained man, burned brown as a loaf from an oven, unselfconsciously plying his long-handled Cornish shovel, the boards and ropes of his craft thrown to one side among the broad leaves of the coltsfoot, and the girl, whose face was hidden by a black crepe veil, upright and unweeping as, thud by thud, with immemorial rhythm, the day closed upon what it had done with.

Suddenly she fainted, and Kitto has told me of his fascination as, undisturbed even by this, the grave digger went on with the practice of his ancient trade, as though he were the earth itself; intent on gathering its own.

The two young men took her up and carried her to the spring, enclosed in a small brick house, that ever bubbles in the midst of that churchyard. They laid her upon the ground, and while Kitto was filling his cupped hands with water, my father lifted her veil and looked upon her face for the first time. Then, for some reason best known to the fates that arrange the affairs of men, kneeling at her side he kissed her cheek. I suppose it was an impulse of pure compassion. Before Kitto had turned with the water, she opened her eyes and looked into my father's and smiled. Seeing her thus restored, Kitto did not dash the water into her face, but let it drip through his fingers, and then applied his cool wet hands to her forehead. She sat up, seeking my father's eyes, not Kitto's.

They walked with her through the churchyard to the thatched farm cottage that stands opposite the old granite mounting-block outside its topmost gate. Here for some months she had been lodging with her father, and here, for day after day, following the first encounter, my father met her. And it was hereupon that the last flaming row of Kittos and Pentecosts broke out. My great-aunt Sapphira was horrified at the notion of the marriage: more, I imagine, because one of the two Pentecosts she had in her grip would thereby escape than for any other reason. But, to her way of thinking, there were other reasons enough. Miss Sowler was a penniless nobody. Her father had been some sort of overlooker in a cotton mill, and what little he had saved had been expended in the last fruitless effort to save himself. And this was why my father found himself in Manchester and Betsy Comfort with him, and this was why the names of Cornwall and Kitto made him grind his teeth. It was Miss Sapphira who composed Richard Sowler's epitaph and caused it to be set up in Mylor church. Anything which even remotely concerned a Kitto must not be without its memorial, even a thing which finally broke her hold on the stubborn Frederick, leaving only the supple and self-sufficient Kitto to be by her side at Primrose Hill and Tresco Vean.

6

I had parted from a stranger, and I met Blanche. It was as though we were back in the days before she was one of Madame Gribble's Girls, before Luther Brimlow had broken through the wall that we had built against him. We ran to meet one another – she uphill and I down, and we met panting. We did not kiss – we never had done so – we did not even touch one another, but we stood and looked with smiles each into the other's face, and we knew ourselves for the allies we had been before. Her dress was white and filmy, down to her ankles in the fashion of the moment, and a white flopping hat was on her head. Already in the little time I had spent in Cornwall, I had lost my Manchester pallor, but Blanche, having been here through a whole spring and summer, had more than my holiday-maker's superficial cooking. Her skin was saturated with light and sunshine. She looked golden. And, too, she looked poised and assured in a way I had not known in her before. Indoors and outdoors at Tresco Vean there was a large staff of servants. She had become used to their ministrations, and accepted them as if they were her right, as if she were herself a Kitto, while I, all through that holiday, never ceased to feel irked and hindered by the presence of these people about me.

I remember how one morning as soon as I was dressed I knocked at the door of her bedroom and when she called to me to come in I entered and found her sitting in a dressing-gown before a mirror, brushing her hair. It was the most beautiful bedroom in the house, altogether an astonishing room to me, because I had always thought of a bedroom as a place where one slept and kept one's clothes and where there wasn't much room for doing anything else. But this room was a charming sitting room which happened to have a bed in it. There were easy chairs and a settee that would engulf three people, and all these were upholstered in rich brocade of a powder-blue colour fringed with gold. There were pictures and books, pieces of porcelain on the marble mantelpiece, and the view from the window was down the long sloping lawn to the water. My mother and I slept at the back. Most wonderful of all to me, Blanche did not keep her clothes in this room but in another opening out of it that she called her dressing room. Nevertheless, her tumbled bed was strewn with clothes, with a book she had been reading, with sheets of paper which suggested that she had been up early to write a letter. The sun was shining. I wanted her outside.

"Hurry up, Blanche!" I cried. "It's a lovely day to be out, and you haven't tidied your room yet." It was unthinkable in our little Manchester house that she and I should appear at breakfast without having made our beds and set our rooms to rights. "My room's all in order," I announced righteously.

She looked at me with a slow steady smile, her hand, holding the brush, arrested in the motion of smoothing her hair, which fell right down to her waist. The dressing gown had slipped up her arm, which was curved into a lovely arc the colour of golden honey.

Suddenly I felt very small, very insignificant. She was amused by me. She did not explain that there were things one left to the maids, which I suppose was the thought in her mind. She was amused, but she was also affectionate. She said: "Come in, I want to kiss you."

I approached her reluctantly, not being in tune with this mood, and she kissed me on the forehead. "Dear Ted," she said. "You're rather sweet."

She had one arm round my waist and she smelt of jasmine. Her dressing gown fell open, and, releasing me, she pulled it about her without embarrassment. I had seen that she had full firm breasts, and I felt confused and ashamed and very young. The breakfast gong sounded from the hall below. "It's too late now," I said, taking refuge eagerly in this commonplace. "We can't go out. And you'll be late for breakfast."

She went on brushing her hair. "Tell them to send it up," she said.

7

When I went down only my mother was in the breakfast room. Miss Kitto almost always breakfasted in bed, and when I passed on to the maid, with every fear of a dreadful rebuff, the message Blanche had given me, it appeared that no bones would be made about my sister's doing so as well. "Certainly, Mr Edward. I'll tell them to prepare a tray," was all she said, and she removed to a sideboard the things that had been set on the table for Blanche. Then, seeing that we had everything we wanted, she went out of the room.

"Isn't Blanche well?" my mother asked, rather sharply. I said that she seemed to me to be very well, and my mother made no further comment on the matter. But she was preoccupied all through the meal and had little to say to me. When she had finished, she went straight up to Blanche's room, but I did not hear then what passed between them. However, late that day, when Blanche was rowing me in a dinghy off the jetty at the bottom of the grounds (for she, after a summer at Tresco Vean, was at home with a boat and I was not) she suddenly shipped the oars and allowed the dinghy to drift idly. She said: "I don't want to go back to Manchester. I suppose I shall *have* to, but I don't *want* to."

My own heart was torn in two. I, also, did not want to go back to Manchester. And I did want to go back to Manchester. I did not want to leave these lovely woods, this sparkling sea, the sands that Blanche and I had run upon with the water curling round the rocks offshore in bands of amethyst and lilac and the white wild birds soaring and dipping. I did not want to feel that never again – or at any rate not for a long time – would I see my dry old Uncle Kitto, with whom I had had my promised talk on painting and watched him touching up with his own brush my childish canvases. But I did want to see my father again and walk with him the five miles to town and pour out to him all that I had seen and learned and felt in this brief magic time. And I did want to see our chestnut tree and go to the art school and apply in my studio at Captain Marquick's all that I had learned from Uncle Kitto. Oh, I hardly knew what I wanted and didn't want, so full was I of the acceptance of everything as it came. That, I imagine, is how it was with me, though then I could not unravel my web of thinking and feeling. There were moments when to go back seemed like torture, and others in which to turn from Wilmslow Road into our street, to run to the front door, came over my mind as if all the holiday had been nothing but a building-up to that lovely climax.

I looked at Blanche in perplexity. With a hand on either side, she was gently rocking the boat. A frown of concentration darkened her forehead. "Mother says," she burst out, ' that I'm getting above myself – too big for my boots. But what was the sense of sending me here if I wasn't to like what I found?"

I couldn't answer the question, but I was warmed by the confidence, by the feeling that she and I were talking together, as we always had talked, of what concerned us, so that even our parents stood outside our circle as something to be considered and discussed impartially. I remembered the day which seemed so long ago – though it could not have been so long as all that – when Blanche danced among the buttercups and conjured me to say nothing of it at home. Thinking of this, I said: "When you get back, you'll have your dancing again," believing that this would be the magic word to bring her to her senses. Nothing, I knew, would make me jump into the Manchester train more blithely than the thought of going back to my painting. All the greater, then, was my surprise and dismay when Blanche cried almost with disgust: "Dancing! Don't talk to me about that! A lot of good that would have come to. Dirty little dressing rooms with girls telling dirty little stories, and touring perhaps with some tenth-rate show, and staying in theatrical lodgings. I've seen what that's like. Have you ever been in Ackers Street? I have. I went there once with a girl who was lodging there." She gave a shudder of loathing. "Look at me," she said. "Do I look as though Ackers Street lodgings would appeal to me?"

I looked at her, and my mind looked at the girl in the lovely bedroom commanding that her breakfast be sent up. And in my childish way I think I understood that Blanche had sold her birthright.

"Besides," she said, "I *like* Miss Kitto. There again, if they didn't want me to like her, why did they send me to her? She's an old tyrant, and at times a regular old devil, but I like her, and, what's more, she likes me. When I answer her back, she says I'm a real chip off the old Kitto block."

She took up the oars and began rowing again, smiling to herself as though recalling scenes in which she and Miss Kitto had been embroiled. I had witnessed none of them, but I knew well enough that Blanche was a favoured person in the house. As for me, I was there on sufferance. Ever since our first encounter, my great-aunt Sapphira had hardly done more than say "Good morning" or "Please pass the salt". And what a chilly encounter that had been! I had heard at first, standing outside the door of her room, nothing but her voice commanding that I should be told to go and play. I had dutifully gone, and was nowhere near the house when at last she was ready to see me. I had to be searched for, and when I had been found and brought to the house the old woman's patience, I suppose, was on edge. Her room adjoined Blanche's dressing room, and had a door opening into it, and from that room she could go into Blanche's bedroom. They lived in one another's laps. But it would be hard to imagine anything more different than this room and Blanche's room, than this old woman and Blanche. The room was as cold and dull as an anchorite's cell. Tresco Vean and Primrose Hill were stuffed to overflowing with beautiful things, but nothing beautiful and nothing that ministered to physical comfort was in Miss Kitto's room. The walls were whitewashed, and there was not a picture upon them. The floor was covered with brown oil-cloth. The curtains, too, were brown – not a golden brown or a lustrous wallflower brown, but a downright dull repulsive brown that was almost black. And they were pulled nearly right across the window, so that the room was gloomy. The fireplace was of black leaded iron. Pushed into a corner was an iron bedstead that might well have accompanied a soldier on a spartan campaign. A couple of blankets were neatly folded upon it, as if awaiting a barrack inspection. This, literally, was all the furniture in the room save for a deal table scrubbed white and a kitchen chair. Hanging from the middle of the ceiling was an enormous ornate cage, shaped like a pagoda with a beautiful spire. It contained a grey parrot with a red tail. I have often heard and read of parrots that had a gift of speech, and I have often been asked to admire the sentences that tripped from parrots' tongues. But these have never seemed to me to be more than incomprehensible gibberish, shrill or chucklingly sardonic; and Miss

Kitto's parrot was like all the rest. He swung on his perch, and cocked a hard soulless eye at us, and occasionally shrieked and occasionally chuckled. He made the only spot of colour and movement in the room, and she took not the slightest notice of him. She took little notice of me, either. She did not ask me to sit down, and, indeed, there was nowhere to sit unless I had sat upon the soldierly bed, for she was sitting on the kitchen chair. She sat as straight as a ramrod at one end of the table and I stood at the other as though the court were about to pass sentence. Both her hands lay on the table before her, and I saw now that these did bring some colour and beauty into the room. They were lovely hands, long, fine and bony. There were jewelled rings on every finger. I have never seen so many rings or so many jewels on one pair of hands before or since. There was not enough light for them to flash, but they smouldered with various fire: diamonds, rubies, emeralds and amethysts. It was an astonishing thing to see lying on the scrubbed top of the kitchen table. For the rest, Miss Sapphira was as plainly furnished as her room. She wore dull grey right up to the ears, right down to the wrists. I never saw her in anything else. Her face was sharp and thin, with watchful black eyes, and the hair twisted anyhow upon her head was the cleanest-looking hair I have ever seen. It was a shining white, and I would not have been surprised to hear that it was washed and burnished every morning.

Our interview was brief. I stood there for a moment, looking at her hands, so powerful and richly adorned, lying under a small cascade of seed and sawdust that the restless parrot showered from the pagoda. She took no notice of this. Presently she said: "So you're Blanche's brother." And that, of course, is where I stood. I was not my father's son, and especially I was not my mother's son: I was Blanche's brother. In that capacity I was entitled to such consideration as she chose to show me.

"You're not a bit like Blanche," she said with satisfaction, and then, as though this were the one point she had wished to establish in her mind, she added abruptly: "Well, this is a good place for a boy to enjoy himself. I hope you will do so. Only a fool would want to go away from here."

She raised her hands from the table and fastidiously dusted off the birdseed and sawdust. "It came from Yucatan," she said; and I understood she was speaking of the parrot. "Perhaps you wouldn't believe it, but that cage is pure gold. Well . . ."

That "Well . . ." I saw, dusted me off like the sawdust, and, without having once opened my mouth to her, I turned and went out of the room.

8

I thought of this strange interview when Blanche remarked: "She says I'm a chip off the old Kitto block." I myself appeared to have been found so unsatisfactory that I had to assume I was nothing of the kind. "Anyway," I said, "we shall have to go home soon. My holiday is nearly over. If it hadn't been for Captain Marquick I shouldn't have had a fortnight – only a week like the other boys."

She seized on that. "How convenient for you! Of course, the other boys will hate you for it, but I don't blame you. Take what your friends can give you. And do *you* blame *me*? Do you agree with Mother? Shouldn't I take all that great-aunt has to give me – and enjoy it? How could I live with her at all – tell me, how *could* I? – if I were grudging and reluctant? After all, I'm not staying in a hotel and paying for my keep. I owe her something."

I didn't know what to say. I suppose, fundamentally, my attitude was that which Uncle Kitto had taken up all through the years. So long as he was allowed to get on with life as he wanted to live it, he hadn't cared much about Sapphira one way or the other. But I could not understand how Blanche could give up her dancing. When she returned with us to Manchester, as she would have to do soon, what was she going to do then? And that is what I asked her. "I don't know," she said. "Manchester! I think I shall die there. You should see London!"

The words slipped out of her mouth, and she realised at once that she had said too much. "Well," she said defiantly, "we *did* go to London – and why not? Where on earth do you think Miss Kitto bought the clothes you've seen me wearing? In Falmouth?"

"But Mother always got your letter from here – every week," I said.

"Oh, that sort of thing is easily arranged," she ran on. "It was old Sapphira's notion. I wrote four letters before we went, and one of the maids posted them, one each week." And then she plunged into an excited narrative, her face lit with recollected joys, talking of shops and hotels, theatres and hansom cabs and the moon shining on the river. And we at home had been thinking of her as a pale pining girl, brooding in her exile on the ills that she had suffered.

"But Betsy Comfort was here," I cried. "She must have known."

Blanche stopped rowing, attracted by a jellyfish that was floating past us like a tiny opened umbrella splotched with mauve rings. She tried with the blade of the oar to lift it out of the water, but it slipped back again and again. "Oh, Betsy!" she said, and began to laugh. "It was Betsy who posted the letters."

"But you said it was one of the maids."

"Isn't Betsy one of the maids?"

This answer seemed to turn my world upside down.

"Don't forget," said Blanche, "that when Betsy came down here with me she was coming home. The place is full of her friends and relatives, and she hadn't seen them for years. Sapphira simply gave her leave to do so, and she gallivanted about for a month while we were in town. What's more, she got engaged in be married, and she won't be going back to Manchester. I don't blame her."

Now we were back at the granite jetty, and while Blanche was making the dinghy fast I ran ahead with my mind in a turmoil. I thought of the beautiful room and the beautiful clothes that great-aunt Sapphira had given to Blanche, and now was able to add to those gifts others that were insubstantial but even more dangerous. I felt as though half the cords that attached me to my old life had been snipped and as though treasons were everywhere about me. Betsy took on in my mind the proportions of a perfidious fiend. Poor Betsy! She was the first person to open my eyes to the need for taking people as they are. She had given us nearly all she had. I saw little of her after that, and her life was hard and brief. But then, as I ran up the path towards Tresco Vean, I was in no forgiving or understanding mood. I didn't want to see anybody – not even Blanche, who was coming swiftly after me and calling upon me to stop. When a bend in the path hid me, I withdrew into some hazel bushes and stayed there till she had run past me. My mind was confused, angry and selfish, as in such circumstances a child's mind tends to be. "And what about Sapphira? She's a lonely old woman. Isn't *she* entitled to anything?" So Blanche had once asked me furiously; but now it was only what *I* was entitled to that concerned my mind. I was entitled to a world in which nothing changed. I was entitled to have about me people who remained as they were, who had no adventures that altered their relationship to the smooth pattern of my own being.

Well, if that was what I wanted, I didn't get it. I was only at the beginning of what was to flow from Luther Brimlow's rude love-making in his father's shed on the Wilmslow Road.

CHAPTER FOUR

I DID not say goodbye to my great-aunt. I wondered whether I
should walk up the stairs, knock at her door, and go in, and I hung
about in the hall for a long time, trying to bring my mind to this
sticking-point. But I could not do it. She had not sent for me, and I
had no sort of social address which would have permitted me to go
up, whether sent for or not, and do the job with casual efficient
manners. So, my few things being packed in a tin trunk that was now
in the porch, I did nothing at all. My mother had been up, and I
thought that when she came down she would say that it was now my
turn. But she didn't. She came down looking rather red in the face,
and merely said: "Where's Blanche? Is she ready?" Blanche was ready,
as unready-looking a ready as you ever saw. She was walking restlessly
and unhappily on the wide gravel sweep outside the front door, and
even as I put my head out to confirm this I saw the victoria coming
from the coach house which lay beyond a small island of trees and
shrubs. It pulled up at the door. We climbed in and drove away. As
Blanche had promised, there was no Betsy Comfort with us. Thus,
lugubriously, ended our first holiday at Tresco Vean. At Maenporth,
and again at Swanpool, little bays bite into the land, bringing the sea
almost up to the highroad, and here I leaned out to watch the white
combers thudding on the beach and to look my last for who could say
how long on the blue and white and gold of Cornwall.

It was late afternoon. The year was running out. Shadows
lengthened early and dusk came soon. I was filled with a sense of
things ending, but I did not know – none of us yet knew – how much
was ended for us all.

Primrose Hill was always ready to receive guests – Miss Kitto kept
an old man and his wife living there; and it was there that we spent
our last night. The next day we walked through a fresh autumnal

morning to the Falmouth railway station. My mother was of that breed of people who do not trust trains to run at the advertised times. Who knew but that one might take the notion of starting five, ten or twenty minutes before it was supposed to? Thus, we were there with half an hour in hand, and already my Uncle Kitto had come to see us off. I found this small dandified figure, with the swinging monocle and the flower at his lapel, immensely cheering, but I seemed the only one to do so. After the briefest of greetings, my mother got into the train, which was already standing at the platform, and Blanche followed her. He and I were left alone, and I was glad of that. We walked up and down, now in the shade of the canopy, now out in the sunshine, and we had little enough to say to one another. But there was nothing that we needed to say. There are people like that, people who can communicate without words, and Uncle Kitto was one of them. The only thing he said to me about painting in all that half-hour was "If you feel you can't live without it, Ted, for God's sake don't try to. I mean that – for God's sake. Work – technique – all that – well, that's something else. Perhaps we'll have a chance to go into that again some day. At the moment, I'm talking about first principles, if you know what that means. And now you'd better hop in. Your Mamma's getting anxious."

There were still five minutes to go, but Mother was looking out as though she expected to see me waving farewell at any moment. So I said goodbye to my Uncle Kitto, remembering just in time that he disliked shaking hands, and got into the compartment. He did not wait. He raised his hat and waved his ivory-knobbed malacca, and then for a few minutes there was nothing to do but contemplate that foul little station, so improbable a doorway to the light and colour of Cornwall.

2

It was raining when we reached Manchester late that evening. It was as though some mighty hand had ruled a sharp line between what we had left and what we had returned to. The sweet autumn weather had been with us as we travelled through Herefordshire and Shropshire. The orchards were jewelled with apples and the mighty stacks in the fields were like piles of careless gold. Over it all the haze of the season drew the blue veil that half concealed and half transfigured, for now we were in September, and a patchwork of umber and ochre broke up the dark green of the woods.

We came to Crewe under a blackening sky. Thence things worsened, and the day was no longer a decaying memory of summer but a premonition of winter. From Stockport on to Manchester was a crescendo of rain and blurred lights, glistening iron bridges, jarring points, slums and the rattle of shunting wagons. Finally, we drew into London Road station, the engine panting with distress, as if the huge black arch of the roof were the firmament of a world of despair. At Crewe, men had run along the tops of the coaches, lighting the gas lamps, but these made only a fitful gleam and our compartment had no more than an eerie mitigation of midnight. However, this was enough to show me that, as she stood up to pull her bags from the luggage rack, Blanche was crying quietly.

There was one thought in my mind to set against the dismal aspect of this homecoming; and it was that now I should see my father. He would be there to take off all our shoulders the business of handling luggage, and finding a cab, and getting home. His hearty: "Well, Ted—" would put all this in perspective, show it to be nothing more than a wet night in Manchester. And the day happened to be Saturday. Remembering this, I said to myself that now the Saturday night concerts would begin again. There would be Captain Marquick and Anatole Lop, the lighted fire and the curtains drawn against the night. But there would be no Betsy to prepare the supper.

My father was nowhere to be seen. We put the luggage down on the platform, and I searched for him there and beyond the barrier. But he was nowhere, and so, when we had delayed for a long time, my mother tipped a porter to carry the luggage out of the station and find us a cab. We had waited for so long that other passengers had snapped them all up, and, till one should return, we stood in an unhappy huddle, looking out at the rain-glistening cobbles of the station approach and listening to the clamour of the traffic through the premature night. "I don't understand it," my mother said. "I don't understand it at all."

There was so much that we did not understand and which, before long, we were to understand all too well.

3

I do not often go back to Manchester, but I was there in this year of 1946, and sentiment took my footsteps to All Saints, so that I might gaze on the ruined church outside whose railings I had spent hours drawing the old cab-horses and the cobbles on the rank there; and at the art school which surely is the most dolorous doorway there ever was to an enchanted world; and at my father's shop which stands there still, though transfigured and though musical instruments are not now sold in it. Then I began to wander in the maze of mean streets behind the shop, looking for his chapel. How had *that* fared in the crucifixion years? I came to it at last, treading the pavements that I had trodden with loathing so long ago: came, at any rate, to what was left of it, and that was not much. Hardly two stones were standing one upon another in a bomb-shattered desert. But the stone I was looking for was there, still carved with the words he had himself composed for it. "Erected in 1906 by Frederick Pentecost. Saved to serve." It was a blistering summer day when I looked upon this ruin. Nettles and willow-herb had seeded themselves and sprouted there as though paying the tribute of their meagre beauty to a soul's aspiration.

I have corrected myself here. I had written "to a soul's misguided aspiration." I have taken the word out. What do I know?

I wept as I stood in the torrid street and thought of the night when we returned from Cornwall.

4

When we reached our house there was no one in. We knocked the knocker, and banged with our fists, and looked the house front up and down in wonder and perplexity. There was no light in the window, no smoke coming from the chimney, no sound of movement. The old saying, a house of the dead, could have been used truly enough, for from this shuttered stillness there seemed to ooze a sinister and foreboding premonition that chilled us all. This was not the house we had known. We had come back to a place that had changed for the worse. That, I think, is what we were all feeling. Certainly it is what I was feeling.

The cab had long since disappeared round the corner, and we stood there with nothing more that we could think of doing, my mother exclaiming, as she had done at the station: "I don't understand it," and

Blanche looking as miserable as a half-drowned cat. The rain had not ceased to fall. At this deplorable moment the door of the Brimlows' house opened, and there was my father looking at us. "Ah!" he exclaimed. "I thought I heard something. It's you!"

"Why on earth didn't you meet us at the station?" my mother demanded crossly. "I wrote days ago giving you the time of the train. And what's the matter with the house? It looks like a tomb."

There was a smile in my father's eyes. "It *was* a tomb," he said, "but Lazarus is risen. Glory to the Lamb!"

We all three looked at him thunderstruck. He looked back at us, still smiling happily. "Come in out of the rain," he said. "Brother Brimlow will be pleased to break bread with you. We are reading the Word together."

"Fred," said my mother, "if this is a joke, it's the worst you've ever played. Don't keep us standing here. Come and open the door."

It seemed idiotic, this situation in which we found ourselves. The front gardens of those houses are only a few feet long. Between ours and the Brimlows' was a clipped hedge of privet. And there we were, my mother, Blanche and I, glaring over this ridiculous hedge at my father composedly smiling on the other side. The gas lamp inside the Brimlows' fanlight threw its glow down upon his face, and in this pool of radiance there swam into our vision the faces also of Mr and Mrs Brimlow. They took up their places one on either side of him; and so we stood – the three of them and the three of us, with the rain-sodden hedge between.

My mother was becoming furious with impatience. I suppose the idea of Mrs Brimlow as a witness of her discomfiture didn't help. She cried angrily: "Fred, come and open this door at once. Can't you see the children are getting wet through? And haven't you got a word to say to Blanche after not seeing her for months? Come on now. Stop playing the damned fool."

Then Mrs Brimlow spoke, the light glittering on the *pince-nez* that trembled on her nose. "Damned, indeed, he was," she said. "But thank God he's saved now. He's passed out of the house of bondage into glorious liberty."

She went so far as to lay a hand affectionately on my father's shoulder. Perhaps it was this gesture, more than anything else, that turned mother's annoyance into fury. "You can keep your glorious liberties to yourself, Mrs Brimlow," she shouted, "and if this is the house of bondage the sooner he comes back to it the better."

Now the moist-eyed Brimlow broke in. "Sister Brimlow speaks only in parables."

"She can speak in Hottentot for all I care," my mother snapped. "Come along with that key. How dare you keep me and my children standing here in the rain outside our own house?"

She was by now trembling with wrath. I had never seen her so angry, nor ever did I again. Among the luggage were walking sticks and umbrellas rolled up in a travelling rug. She stooped and wrenched out a stick and with one swinging blow stove in a pane of our front window. Then she reached inside, threw back the hasp, and pushed up the window. In an undignified flurry of long-laced boots, skirts and petticoats, she clambered through the window, knocking off her hat as she did so. Blanche and I looked at one another in amazement, our hearts chilled. The door flew open in our faces, my mother reached out her two hands, seized us, and jerked us into the passage. The door banged and the luggage was left outside in the rain. For a moment we all stood there panting in the darkness. Then suddenly my mother began to sob violently. She ran to the foot of the stairs and sat on the lowest step with her body shaking. Blanche followed and sat beside her, putting her arms around her and murmuring "Don't, Mother. Please, Mother, don't."

But my mother could not control her crying. The sobs tore out of her, and, after standing helplessly before them for a moment, I could put up with it no longer. I slipped past them and ran up the stairs to my room, banged the door behind me and threw myself on the bed. The room smelt stale and stuffy, as though no one had been in it since I went away. It smelt like prison. But I was too racked in body and mind to do anything about it, or even to get up and take off my wet clothes. No one came near me that night. It seemed endless and I did not sleep.

5

The next day was Sunday. I rose from my bed as soon as the light began to strengthen. No one was stirring in the house. In my misery, I went straight to the sources of my comfort. I climbed the stairs to the attic. In my "picture gallery" I would be among loved familiar things. It was not what it had been. Its glory had diminished since Captain Marquick's loft had become my studio, but I still kept there a few reproductions and a few of my own pictures on the walls, and on the long table were crayons and pencils and paints that I used now and then. Blanche, too, had had not much use for the attic since going to Madame Gribble's; but a few of her old dancing costumes were still hanging on hooks, recalling the days when all our dreams were secret and our aspirations hidden.

To this little sky-lighted room, then, I climbed that Sunday morning, seeking ease of my misery, and as soon as I opened the door misery closed with double thickness upon my heart. I could not believe that my father had done this: my father with whom I had rejoicingly walked morning after morning to town, who had seemed the very core and kernel of safety in all the troubles and dilemmas of my young life. But who else could have done it? There had been no one in the house but he.

Not a picture remained on the walls. Not only were the reproductions gone, but my own paintings, too. In the fireplace was a heap of charred paper and canvas. I turned it over with my toe, and fragments of colour disinterred themselves from the ashes. All had been burned. A strip or two of silk and satin showed how Blanche's dreams and mine had joined in a common cremation. Even my paints were gone, and my pencils and brushes. There was nothing left – nothing whatever of all that that room had stood for; but, my first anguish abated, I saw that there was something of what the room was intended to stand for henceforth. There was a new picture over the fireplace: a horrible oleograph of a Christ-like shepherd carrying a lamb upon his shoulders, and on the table were a few pamphlets. I turned them over listlessly. "Suffer Little Children." "And He called a Little Child." There were others, too.

Like all the rest of the house, the attic was stuffy and oppressive. The prison smell was everywhere. I pulled the chair under the skylight, stood upon it, and thrust my head out into the morning. It was beautiful. The rain had left the world washed and clean-smelling. I leaned my chin on the frame of the opening and breathed the sharp autumn air. Away towards Northenden the sun was catching house roofs and the tower of the church, and the glow this caused was muted by the mists rising off the water meadows. Here and there great trees were disentangling themselves from these misty scarves, and their rich autumn colours were most beautiful to see. I remained there for a long time, as the light strengthened and the mist dispersed and cattle became visible in the fields, stumbling up from their knees and turning their faces to the dawn. And, as if he were walking down there among them, my Uncle Kitto spoke to me. "If you *must* do it, for God's sake do it."

It was yesterday – it was not yet twenty-four hours – since he had said that. How, in that little time, the world had gone upside down! But had it? Had anything changed for *me* – the me inside these clothes and this skin, to whom Uncle Kitto was speaking so quietly out of the calm morning? And I knew that it hadn't. I received my first inescapable conviction though then, I had never read the words – that "neither death, nor life, nor angels, nor principalities, nor things present, nor things to come, nor powers, nor height, nor depth, nor any other creature, shall be able to separate us from the love of God, which is in Christ Jesus our Lord."

This was the intimation that flooded me as I stood at the skylight that morning, but I was to learn that my father's view and mine were different concerning the love of God.

I climbed down and looked at the little room again, and now it did not hurt me. For a moment I thought of adding the oleograph and the tracts to the pyre upon the hearth, but it didn't seem worthwhile. They meant nothing to me now one way or the other. I felt strangely calm, and indeed I could afford to be, for like (or unlike?) my father, I had received an intimation of immortality.

I was actually whistling quietly to myself when my mother came in. Towsled and dirty as I was, I was yet able to turn upon her a smiling face. She herself appeared to be worn out and unhappy. "Isn't Blanche here?" she asked. She looked about her in a dazed way, as though Blanche might be under a table or behind a curtain, or as if she might suddenly materialise from nowhere. "I wanted to talk to you both before your father gets up and I can't find Blanche high or low."

I said I would look, and Mother answered wearily: "Where will you look? I've looked everywhere. She's gone, and I don't blame her. I blame myself. I should have had more self-control."

She sat down on the wooden chair that was the only one in the room, and I sat on the floor at her feet. "I shouldn't have broken the window," she said with a pathetic self-accusation. "I shouldn't have lost my temper. If I had waited a little he would have come in. I'm afraid I frightened him. He stayed next door till I went to fetch him, after you and Blanche had gone to bed."

She talked to me for half an hour, her hand stroking my hair. She had gone in to the Brimlows, and there had been much talk, excited and exalted. From all this it appeared that on the day after my mother and I had left for Cornwall my father, feeling lonely, had strolled out into the streets in the cool of the evening, the day being Sunday. Had anyone whatever been there to give him companionship, said my mother, it might not have happened. But we were away; Anatole Lop had taken a summer engagement with a seaside orchestra; and Captain Marquick was in London. So there was no one, and there my father was wandering in his boredom about the streets. That no doubt was how he saw it then, but afterwards he took a more dramatic view. This aimless wandering he called his road to Damascus, and it was then that he saw a great light. At a street corner the members of the Plymouth Brethren chapel were holding their customary Sunday evening service. There had been in Manchester that week some sort of annual convention of the Brethren, and this had gathered together some of the more powerful preachers of the sect. One of these men had preached that night at our little Owen Street chapel in Didsbury, and had gone, after the indoor service, into the streets with the Brethren. It was just as this man had stepped into the ring and begun his oration that my father paused to listen. It was then, he explained seriously to my mother, that the light of God blinded him. He knew himself for a sinner, damned unless he could find Grace.

Since that morning when I sat in the attic listening to my mother's tired voice running on, I have read much of the life of Wesley, of the frenzied crowds in Gwennap Pit howling in confession of sin and crying for salvation. With these excitable Cornish Celts the preacher had some of his greatest triumphs; and if ever I am perplexed by the thought of my father's conduct I remember that he, too, was one of these. His behaviour followed the Celtic pattern established under Wesley. There in the public street he stood with the fear of hell in his heart, with the tears streaming down his face, and with his legs hardly able to support him.

When the meeting ended he begged the Brimlows not to leave him. They took him to their house and all that night they "wrestled" with him. They knelt upon the floor and prayed; they sat at the table and read the Word; Mr Brimlow engaged in exposition; and at four in the morning Mrs Brimlow mercifully brewed a pot of tea. But the light did not come, and when my father went to work the next morning he was a neurotic wreck, hardly able to drag one leg after another. He took a Bible with him to read in the shop, and in the small room behind it he terrified Albert Critchlow by falling upon his knees and crying: "Pray with me, Albert. Pray with me, and pray *for* me!"

All these details he remembered and recounted to my mother. They were precious to him, hard pebbles on his road to Grace.

The struggle for his soul went on all through that week. He spent the week at the Brimlows', eating and sleeping there, and seeking the way of salvation. Mr Brimlow went into the affair heart and soul. It had long been a matter of secret unhappiness with him that, apart from his son Luther, he had never been granted the privilege of leading a soul to Christ. Mrs Brimlow was already saved when he met her, and Luther had proved a backslider. Not that this eventually would matter, for a soul saved was saved forever. In God's good time, and through the inscrutable working of His will, a backslider recovered the lost ground. (All this I put down not in derision but as a simple statement of the affair as it stood. These were the things that the Brimlows believed and on which they built the edifice of their lives. These were the things which my father was to come to believe, too.)

The light came to him at five minutes past eleven on the Saturday night. He was never – at the time or later – in any doubt about the precise chronology of the matter, and it was, when the time came for doing such things, inscribed on the fly-leaf of the Bible he bought to mark the occasion.

It seems that that night the struggle had reached a tremendous pitch. Mr Brimlow was a limp rag and my father a sodden mass of misery. Mr Brimlow had read and expounded all that he could think of concerning salvation by Grace, and then, while Mrs Brimlow was in the kitchen preparing tea and ham sandwiches, he said: "I'll sing to you now, brother; and as I sing think of what I've been saying."

He began to sing the dirge I had often heard on the street corner:

"Over the line, hear the sweet refrain!
  Angels are chanting the heavenly strain.
  Over the line – why should I remain
  With a step between me and Jesus?"

Suddenly my father shouted: "I'm over! Hallelujah! I'm over!" And he was prepared ever thereafter to maintain – I heard him do so many times when he testified in public – that a light at that moment irradiated him, dispelling a darkness that for a whole week could be felt.

On hearing that triumphant shout, Mr Brimlow rushed from the room into the passage and yelled through to the kitchen:

"It's over!" Mrs Brimlow thereupon came hurrying in, carrying the plate of sandwiches in one hand and the teapot in the other. She placed her burdens on the table and at once sat down at the harmonium. She knew what the occasion demanded, and in a moment all three were singing:

"At the Cross, at the Cross, where I first saw the light
  And the burden of my sins rolled away;
  It was there by faith I received my sight,
  And now I am happy all the day."

Then they sat down and ate the sandwiches, or, as my father would henceforth always say, broke bread; and that, briefly, is how my father passed from death unto life.

6

My mother got up from the chair and said: "I'm not worrying about Blanche. She never wanted to leave Miss Kitto, and she's gone back to her. That's as plain as a pikestaff."

She was right. Before breakfast time a note, dropped mysteriously into our letter box by which we knew not what hand, came from Blanche. It was addressed to my mother and told her not to worry. It added that she was going back to Cornwall and that my father might as well leave her there. "I know," poor Blanche wrote, "that I am not what they call 'of age,' but I am of age enough to be sure that I cannot and will not put up with the sort of thing that happened last night. So please tell Father that, though he has the right to bring me back, even if he did so twenty times, then twenty times I would go away again." It was the most eloquent letter I ever saw from Blanche.

What had happened, I learned afterwards, was this. When I had gone to bed, Blanche went up to the attic. Before me, she had seen what my father had done there and had realised all that this was likely to mean in our lives during the years ahead. Fresh from a pampered and petted life, a life of ease and wealth and beauty, she was seized with a sickening revulsion. She resolved upon her course there and then and carried it out with precision. In the first light of day, even before I was up, she packed a few things and made her way to the house in Fog Lane of that girl who, as I have already recorded, was with her in the pantomime chorus. This girl's parents had gone the day before to Blackpool for their summer holiday, leaving her to follow on the Monday, and this stroke of luck suited Blanche well, for no explanations had to be made except to a featherbrained chit who was pleased with her *role* as conspirator. It was she who gave Blanche's note to the milkman to be dropped into our letterbox. What worried Blanche was the fear that our father would send watchers to the railway station to keep an eye on trains leaving for Cornwall, and indeed he did this, but without result. Blanche's friend was an experienced young woman. She had told her parents that work was the reason why she could not leave for Blackpool till the Monday, but in fact it was because a young man whose father kept a livery stable was coming to take her for a drive on the Sunday afternoon. They all three drove off together in the varnished trap, and that afternoon, when the young dancer and her *beau* returned to Manchester, Blanche was left behind in a Cheshire village not far from Crewe. She spent the night at an inn there, and went on to Cornwall from Crewe the next morning. She had more than enough money for the fare. Though she had said nothing to me or my mother about it, Miss Kitto had not kept her short. She telegraphed to Tresco Vean, and was not surprised when Sapphira herself turned up to meet her at Falmouth.

Years afterwards, I asked Blanche about the other girl. "Oh," she said, "she was not the sort of girl I wanted to have much to do with. I didn't give her my address, you may be sure. I told her my aunt was an old farmeress in Cornwall, and I never wrote to her once I'd reached Tresco Vean. As it happens, she did very well. She became quite a name in the music halls. I went once out of curiosity to see her when I was in London. As I had expected, it was a very vulgar turn."

"Blanche," I said, "there are times when I think strangling would be too good for you."

She shrugged her still shapely shoulders. "*Chacun pour soi*," she murmured. "*Sauve qui peut*. Strangling was always too good for me, little brother. But I've avoided it thus far, and please God I shall continue to do so."

She said it as piously as my father could have done.

7

What is loyalty? I suppose the loyalist sticks to a "cause" as often as not because this is a defence of something known and comfortable. My mother and I were "loyal" to my father in this way. From the first we accepted the new things that had come into our lives while doing all we could to keep the old.

We were already at the breakfast table when he came down on the Sunday morning. He was blithe and smiling. "Before we break bread," he said, "let us ask a blessing." My mother closed her eyes, and so did I. He asked a blessing, and when his meal was ended he said: "grace after meat." Then he exclaimed abruptly: "Let us pray" and, scraping back his chair, got on to his knees. We did the same, and he uttered a long, impassioned, impromptu prayer; and this was followed by a reading from the Bible. He began that morning at the first chapter of Genesis. As the months went by, we worked our way through a chapter a day, never more or less. And we came to know that all that he read there – ancient folklore, moving poetry, fantastic prophecy, the profound religious utterances of Jesus, the comments of the letter writers, and the mystic phantasmagoria of the Revelation: all this was not a majestic compound of disparate parts: it was one thing: God's word, simply and absolutely. If the Word said that at the beginning the earth and the heavens and all therein were made in seven days, then they were made in seven days. If the Word said that at the end Christ would come again, then, in literal and actual fact, the man who had walked the Syrian fields would come again. The Word commanded the saved to wrestle with the souls of the unsaved, and my mother and I had to accept that, too. We were wrestled with.

But, that Sunday morning, there were certain earthly matters that had to be dealt with. My father asked why Betsy Comfort had not returned from Cornwall, and, when he was told, he said complacently that the keeping of housemaids was an indulgence that could well be done without. He asked why Blanche was not down to breakfast, and said that he would require her presence there henceforth, as, at breakfast time, the means of grace would be provided. My mother handed him Blanche's letter. He read it with a frown, put it into his pocket, and said nothing. He never again spoke of the matter. I know that he did his best to prevent the flight, but Blanche was one too many for him. Thereafter, so far as he was concerned, she might have been dead.

When breakfast was over, my father stepped of old habit to the mantelpiece, took up his negro-head pipe, and began to charge it with tobacco. He struck a match and actually held it poised over the bowl when a groan shook him and he dashed the little light into the fireplace. "God help me," he cried. "God help me to overcome the frailty of the flesh." With that, he took pipe and tobacco pouch, put them into a small tin box, and went into the garden. From the scullery, where I was helping my mother with the washing up, I could see him digging a hole and burying his temptation. When the hole was filled, he stamped the earth down upon it angrily, and came into the scullery looking both sheepish and miserable. I have told how we always kept standing there a barrel of beer, and now he turned his attention to this. "Wine is a mocker, strong drink is raging," he quoted; and then, being always of an ingenious turn in small matters, he proceeded to deal with the beer in his own way. He brought in the garden hose, attached one end to the spigot of the barrel, and turned the tap. The "rose" at the other end of the pipe was finely punctured with a hundred holes, and, holding it aloft, my father propelled a dew of beer into the autumn air. For the rest of the day it smelt as though we lived in a brewery, but once the smell was gone, it was gone forever. He found no difficulty in giving up strong drink; but with tobacco it was another matter. The next morning when I woke I heard unaccustomed sounds in the garden, and, looking through my bedroom window, saw my father with a spade unearthing the tin box he had buried the day before. He took out the pipe and looked at it longingly. Twice he put it back and resolutely shut the box. Finally, he charged the pipe and lit it. There was a small arbour at the end of the garden, overgrown with honeysuckle, which now was decorated with clusters of autumnal berries. He went into the arbour and sat down and smoked contentedly. There was something reassuring about the calm morning, and the sight of him sitting there, and the blue incense curling out from under the roof of the arbour. But this did not last long. Presently he leapt up, put the still-burning pipe upon a stone, took up the spade, and battered the poor negro's head to pulp. Anguish seized me. The negro with his neat curls and flat nose and coffee eyes had for so long been associated with all the tranquil moments of life that I felt as though the blows raining upon him were failing upon my own heart. Even the fragments of his skull were spurned by my father's foot, ground into the soil by his heel, and the tobacco pouch was sent flying over the garden wall.

But this was not the finish of his battle with tobacco. At the end of every meal he would take an instinctive step towards the mantelpiece, and a week after the massacre of the negro I saw to my surprise that the fellow's twin rested in the old place in the ash-tray and that an ounce of my father's favourite shag was there alongside it. My father gazed at them as though they were an apparition come to haunt and tempt him. "Where did these things come from?" he demanded.

"You seem so miserable without them," my mother said reasonably. "I put them there."

There was a moment of silence and suspense. Anger that temptation should be laid under his very nose and a yearning to capitulate were wrestling in my father's mind. "Spurgeon was a great smoker," my mother wheedled. "He said he could smoke his pipe to the glory of God."

"Spurgeon!" My father spoke with contempt. "Spurgeon was a paid preacher." Nothing was more contemptible to a Plymouth Brother than a paid preacher.

"So was Jesus," my mother said, greatly daring; and on that he looked at her as though the final blasphemy had passed her lips. "You appear to have taken leave of your senses," he said coldly.

She answered cheerfully: "Not a bit of it, Fred, I've read the Bible in my time as much as you have, and I find no record that Jesus ever did His job as a carpenter after He began His job as a preacher. What did He live on then? He was taken in and given food and lodgings wherever He went, and someone must have provided His clothes. Well, then, what's the difference between taking money and buying all these things for yourself and not taking money but having them all bought for you?"

My father looked confused. "I must say you've got some queer notions," he muttered.

"Well, you have a smoke and think 'em over," she answered brightly, and began clearing the table.

I had myself, in even this short space of time, become so accustomed to hearing religion discussed as though it were nothing but a matter of certain facts which had or had not been stated, that I ventured to break into the talk. "The Bible can't forbid tobacco," I said, "because it was discovered by Sir Walter Raleigh." This erroneous notion was all that history at school had taught concerning Sir Walter.

Oddly enough, it was this piece of idiocy that turned the tide. "You're right there, Ted," my father remarked with obvious relief. "I hadn't thought of that."

"And I suppose," my mother shouted from the scullery, "you hadn't thought that Jesus provided the strong drink at the wedding in Cana?"

My father refused to be drawn on this new line. He put the tobacco into his pocket, the pipe between his lips, and gave me an embarrassed smile. Then he disappeared towards the arbour. Thereafter, he smoked without a sense of sin.

I hope I shall be forgiven for recording these trivialities. But they illustrate the basis of triviality on which my father conducted what he called his religion.

8

However, these things were in the future, and I was yet to experience what Sunday was to mean to me now that the Brimlows, whose entry I had so feared as a child, had become as it were firmly entrenched in our house. They were there not only metaphorically but in actual fact, for a great coming and going began at this time, we taking tea with them and they with us, visits being exchanged for reading the Word and prayer, and altogether a condition of things existing that could not have been much worse if we had knocked down the wall between the two houses. My father could never forget that it was the Brimlows who had wrestled him over the line, as though he were a rugby ball and they, against all the hosts of sin, had touched him down and converted the try by sending him sky-high to salvation.

No bell called us to service on that first Sunday morning, or ever. Bells were suggestive of steeples, and steeples of churches, and the less said the better about the misguided ones who frequented churches where paid parsons in popish dress whined through a preordained service and read a sermon. Not thus did the Brethren worship their God.

It was at a quarter to eleven that Mr Brimlow came through our open front door and shouted: "Are you ready, Fred?"

He was ready, and so was I, and so was my mother. Mrs Brimlow joined us in the street. For the first time in my life I set out to attend a religious service. For the moment I forgot that I was giving up much that had been precious to me. Sunday had been a careless happy day when Blanche and I wandered wherever we chose to go and did whatever we chose to do. There had been our kingcup pond, and the joys of the attic, and, later, there had been for me the secret retreat at my studio in Captain Marquick's loft. Indeed, all through my journey of yesterday, it had been towards this that my heart panted: to slip away as soon as breakfast was over and potter about in the studio. So much had so suddenly changed. As we came out into the street, the hole in the front window was an ugly reminder that things were not as they had been. But, even so, I was not at that time depressed. If something was gone, something new had come to take its place. I was young enough to look forward to it with eagerness and curiosity. I was going to my first religious service.

The outside of the Owen Street chapel was known to me well enough. But I must be careful of the words I use. Even "chapel", normally associated with religious dissent, was suspect to the Brethren. Baptists, Presbyterians, Wesleyans, Bible Christians, and goodness knows what other brands of breakers-away from the Established Church, called their assembly places chapels; but in them were practised abominations. Parsons, if they did not wear robes and surplices, wore their collars back to front; organs pealed, "Amen" was ritually sung at the end of each hymn, holy communion was administered with little cut-up cubes of bread and glass thimbles of wine, and baptism in some cases was a matter of mere sprinkling, and not of that complete immersion which alone, the Brethren held, did the thing as God willed it to be done.

For all these and many other reasons, the less said about chapels the better; and so, on the board to the left of the door was written Owen Street Meeting Room.

The outside of the meeting room was of stucco painted grey. It was just a box of that colour, with a door in front and three long windows on one side. Within depression deepened. There was nothing but the blank undecorated walls, with the windows high up as in a prison cell so that nothing could be seen through them, rows of varnished pine benches, and, in front, a rostrum.

My father and Mrs Brimlow entered first, walking side by side up the passageway between the forms. Mr Brimlow was behind them, and my mother and I followed, she holding my hand as though she knew that this place was striking a chill into my heart. We were about halfway down the length of the room when Mr Brimlow swung round and held out his arms to prevent our going farther. We pulled up sharp, and he pointed to a printed card tacked on to the bench at which we had stopped. It read: "Unbelievers, sit behind this seat."

"Come ye out from among them and be ye separate," said the Word, and the Brethren were obeying to the letter.

Mr Brimlow's moist hand fell upon my shoulder and his moist eyes looked earnestly into mine. "Who knows, Ted," he whispered, "some day you may be Over the Line. You may sit with the Elect." Then he followed the other two and sat near the rostrum. My mother and I edged our way into a seat behind the card and waited for the service to begin. I looked about me, nervous and unhappy. If this was a fair cross-section of humanity, then all was well with the world, for the sanctified sheep at the front outnumbered by ten to one the goats shrinking timorously at the back.

This was the only Plymouth Brethren service I ever attended. It was so long ago that the memory of it is faint, and if I do not dwell on its detail that is because I do not want to falsify. I can speak only of my feeling of misery, of hymns sung at the tempo of a dirge with no accompaniment of music, of several men who got up and delivered themselves of harangues which communicated to me no rhyme or reason, and this perhaps was because no speech was welcome there which did not spring spontaneously from the prompting of an agency called inadequately "the spirit". There was a collection box which disdained to circulate among the unbelievers, and a communion service which consisted in the passage of a loaf and a tankard from hand to hand. Each believer tore a piece from the loaf and took a sip from the tankard before passing them on. It all seemed designed to teach the Elect how high were their seats, and to impress upon us others our status as dogs unworthy to do so much as lick the sores of Lazarus.

All through the service, my mother, I thought, was pretty grim. During the hymn singing she stood upright as a soldier, gazing fiercely in front of her, but she did not add her voice to the others. When the congregation – but again I must be careful of my words and say when the Brethren meeting together in the name of the Lord – rose to sing their last hymn, she gave my arm a twitch and led me out of the building. She said not a word as we went home through the mild autumn sunshine, and it was not till we were sitting down to our cold luncheon that my father asked her why she had not stayed to the end. She replied forthrightly: "Because it gave me the pip, and Ted seemed to be suffering."

My father pointed to a card which he had tacked up over the dining room mantelpiece. "There is a guest present," he said. "Do you say that in the presence of our guest?"

The card read:

> The Lord is the Head of this House,
> The unseen Guest at every Meal,
> The silent Listener to every Conversation.

"I say in the presence of anyone you like," my mother declared vehemently, "that Ted was unhappy, and I'm not going to have it."

My father answered with what must have been, to her, infuriating calmness: "My dear, you must keep a sense of proportion. What is suffering? What is unhappiness? Haven't they been put into the world for a reason? Wasn't I unhappy? Wasn't I suffering? These are steps to redemption. 'Weeping may tarry for the night, but joy cometh in the morning.' Now eat your food like a sensible woman."

But the whole situation was too much for my mother. She suddenly broke down and began to weep bitterly. Out of her lamentations we picked up a muffled word here and there . . . Betsy gone . . . everything for me to do . . . Blanche driven away . . . and now Ted . . . Would he stay in such a home?

At last the crying stopped and she stood up and faced him, pale but firm again. "I won't have it," she declared. "Understand that once for all. *I won't have it* so far as Ted is concerned. I've gone on with you now long enough, wherever you've wanted to go, and I'll go on with you still. I'll go to your chapel or anywhere else as often as you like. But I'll not have Ted's life made a misery. If he wants to go with you, let him. But if he doesn't, then neither you nor your guest nor anyone else is going to make him – not so long as I'm here to stop it."

She walked out with her eyes flashing, and we heard her climbing the stairs to her room.

My father looked at me with a rueful smile. "Well, Ted," he remarked, "it looks as though the Devil has put some queer ideas into your mother's mind. Suffer little children to come unto Me, and forbid them not. Forbid them not. That's the point. She is forbidding you to find salvation."

The memory of her crying was in my heart, and the sight of her ravaged face. In that moment I hated him, and I was hardy enough to repeat what my mother had implied. "You've driven Blanche away," I muttered. I did not speak it boldly. I was afraid of him.

He laid down his knife and fork and looked at me steadily. "No, Ted," he said. "You must get that right. I have not driven her away. From the beginning I have been against you and Blanche or any of us having anything to do with the Kittos. I said what would happen. They would get their claws into you. And it has happened as I said. Blanche has been corrupted by wealth and worldliness. I have no doubt that long before you and your mother appeared on the scene the mischief was done. As I knew it would be. Well, she has made her bed and she must lie on it. I shall not interfere."

And yet he did. He had the station watched for days, but she had slipped between his fingers like a trout.

I got up and made for the door. "There is Sunday School this afternoon," he said. "It meets at two-thirty. I have spoken to Mr Brimlow and told him to expect you as a member of his class."

I did not answer this, but slipped through the scullery into the garden. A moment later I was outside the back door and running as fast as my legs would carry me to my studio in the loft at The Pines.

9

I have said that the captain had a way of leaving gifts for me in the studio. That afternoon there was one that set me off on the career I have followed ever since. It was a charming antique mirror: round, with a flame of dull gold foliage. When I came into the room, it was on the wall facing me. I walked straight up to it and looked at myself. I had never before taken much interest in my own appearance, and I suppose it was the change in my face which now compelled my attention. What had happened since last night had written itself in my mouth and eyes, but I was not aware of this. Why I was doing it did not enter into my thought at that moment. All that mattered was that I was scrutinising a face for the first time, not merely looking at one. That it was my own face was incidental. I spent the rest of the day, so long as the light lasted, in painting a self-portrait from this mirrored reflection, not knowing then that it was as a portrait painter that I should find what they call fame and fortune. I finished it, much later, and I painted in the mirror itself with its beautiful swags of foliage and bunches of berries. I wanted to put all that in because I knew it would please Captain Marquick, whose fingers must have run sensitively over this decoration as he was deciding whether to buy it. The picture was exhibited at the spring exhibition of the Manchester Academy in the following year. I am keeping well within the meaning of words when I say that I was amazed to find it bought for the city's collection. Moreover, I received two portrait-painting commissions as a consequence. I was launched. Perhaps I shot up too early and descended too soon to what my critics call the slick assurance of my present work. However, all that matters to this story is that I was already successful when young. I shall not enter into controversy about my own work, which I have done in accordance with my own lights; so let it be understood that I am using the word successful only in its worldly sense. In this sense, an artist is successful when he doesn't have to seek buyers but finds buyers begging for his time. I was in that position by my early twenties, and stayed there.

All this seemed far away that Sunday afternoon. I was a boy, and full of a boy's fears. So long as I was at work these had no power to oppress me, but they rushed in upon me as soon as I laid down my brushes. I remembered that I had been bidden to attend Sunday School and that I had disobeyed the order. I was afraid of my father. For the first time in my life I was afraid of my father. That the one I feared was the one I so deeply loved made my condition inexpressibly miserable.

The light was gone when I shut up the studio and went heavily down the outside wooden stairs. I had seen nothing of Captain Marquick, and there had been no movement in the house. Everyone seemed to be away, but someone must come in to look after the horses. I had heard them stamping and blowing beneath me throughout the afternoon. I did not go home. I guessed then it must be well past five by now, and at six-thirty, I knew, there would be an evening service at Owen Street. I did not intend to be there. I turned into the road leading to Northenden, and when I reached the bridge that crosses the Mersey the darkness was complete. I leaned upon the bridge, listening to the water pouring over the weir not far off, and I thought how often Blanche and I had passed this way towards our kingcup pond. Now she was goodness knew where and all my life seemed upside down. That I should wander where I pleased and do whatever my fancy suggested had been the very condition of my being, and now I could not look a moment ahead without seeing a wall of prohibition, a pathway of direction. Tomorrow I should have to present myself at Marquick and Marquand's. I should have to walk five miles to town, and the thought of doing this with my father became suddenly so disheartening that I leaned my head on the dewy iron of the bridge and wept. I loitered there for some time and then followed paths that zigzagged through the fields towards the Cock Inn. My idea was to reach the house after my parents had left it. No doubt I could get in somehow. There was, at least, the broken window through which I had watched my mother so ignominiously clamber the night before. Presently, crowning a rise of land, I saw lighted windows, and knew that these belonged to our parish church that stood a stone's throw from the Cock. As I drew nearer the sound of organ music came out into the night, and, seeing a few people going up the pathway between the tombstones, I followed them, hardly knowing what I was doing, and found myself in the church. The lighted altar and the flowers upon it, the music accompanying the processional hymn which was beginning as I entered, a bishop's robes (for I had stumbled upon a special service), the choirboys' surplices, the cross of silver wavering down the aisle: all this made up a revelation of beauty which instantly stilled the agitation of my heart. In its small way, it was my first taste of ritual, which is the application of a controlled and ordered beauty to those things which can never express but try thus to do so.

The experience was altogether tranquillising. I was so much in tune with it that, during the recessional, when the choir once more walked past my pew, I was not surprised to see among them the gaunt face of Anatole Lop, his long shoulders draped with a surplice that fell about him like a condor's folded wings. He was imparting a rich bass rumble to the hymn the choir was singing, and he recognised me as he went by, and gave me a wink that amounted to a gargoyle's leer. I was in a mood that could do with company, and so I hung about in the dark churchyard till Anatole appeared and took my hand in his hard grip. "Why, Ted," he said with a grin, "have you turned Anglican?"

I was dying to pour out to him my tale of misery, but fought the impulse and expressed surprise at seeing him there. It was all very simple, he said. He must needs turn an honest penny when he could, and, as his bass was passable, he had long been a member of this choir. If we hadn't known of it – well, what of that? It was something that didn't seem to matter much to him one way or the other.

We turned into that open square in which the Cock stood, and I found myself holding his hand like a child glad to have a protector. "Well," he said, "it's nice to see you, Ted, and we can go on together. I want to see your father before I go home. Did you know? – I've been working with an orchestra at Southport, but that's over now, and it's time we began to think about our winter programme for Saturday nights. Bach – plenty of Bach -that's what we'll have. I've got a letter from the captain. He'll be back next Wednesday. Time to get something fixed up. How's the painting? How did you find Blanche? When is she coming back? She's overdue to get on with her dancing, you know. I've been having a word with Madame Gribble . . ."

Dear Anatole! He ran gaily on, now and then giving my hand an affectionate squeeze that made it feel like a nut in a nutcracker. He didn't know that he was talking about a world that had fallen to pieces and that could never be put together again. I could not allow him to meet my father in this mood. We had already turned into our street when I said: "Anatole" – for so he liked us children to call him – "don't tell my father you saw me at church."

"My dear Ted," he answered, a harsh chuckle rasping his throat, "as you please. As you please. The secrets of your spiritual life are safe in my keeping."

"You'll find my father changed," I said, "Oh, Anatole, please don't be disappointed. But Blanche won't be coming back, and there'll be no more concerts, and nothing any more will be as it was."

I began to tremble, and he pulled me up sharp under the gas lamp that stood halfway between the corner of the street and our house. He bent down, so that you could almost hear his knees folding, and looked hard into my face. "No more concerts?" he said. "No more drinks at the Cock? And supper, and the captain . . . But, Ted – it was the breath of life to your father!"

"Please don't come," I said. "It'll only make you unhappy."

"We'll see about that!" he said resolutely, and snapped himself upright. So we advanced upon the house with the broken window, Anatole muttering to himself: "No more concerts! Nonsense! I never heard such nonsense!"

10

My father and Mr Brimlow were together in our sitting room. From the kitchen I could hear the tinkle of crockery and the sound of my mother's voice talking to someone whom I guessed to he Mrs Brimlow. My father did not at first speak to Anatole. To me, he said sharply: "Where have you been? Mr Brimlow was expecting you at Sunday School this afternoon, and I was expecting you to come with me and your mother to meeting tonight. Apparently, what we expect doesn't matter. It doesn't matter to you that those who could lead you to the Kingdom are willing and anxious to be at your service. You go your own way. You turn from the light."

He had begun harshly. His voice ended on a note of disappointment and despair.

"I didn't mean to stay away, Father," I muttered. "I – I – just did."

"What have you been doing?" he demanded, his voice becoming hard again.

"Painting."

"On the Lord's Day." This was from Mr Brimlow.

"On the Lord's Day," my father echoed, and he and Mr Brimlow nodded sagely at one another.

"Painting on the Lord's Day," said my father after a moment's reflection, "will cease. Indeed, painting will cease altogether."

It might have been expected that these words would sound like a knell in my heart. They did not. They sounded like nonsense. I knew that it was not in him nor in anyone else to stop me from painting so long as I wanted to paint.

Anatole Lop took the words more seriously than I did. He had been standing there uncomfortably with his old silk hat in his hand, occasionally brushing the nap with the inside of his sleeve cuff. He seemed utterly bewildered by what he was listening to. Now he said: "What's wrong with painting? You were so proud of Ted. What's come over you, Fred?"

"God has come over me," my father answered simply, and he seemed for the first time to become aware of the probable reason for Anatole's visit. He also remembered his manners. He got up and took Anatole's hat and put it on a chair. He introduced Anatole to Mr Brimlow, and he pushed him into his own seat. "Now, Anatole," he said, looking down at him, "I can guess what brings you here, and I thank you for coming, but we might as well clear the matter up and have done with it. There will be no more traffic with profane music in this house."

Angry colour stained Anatole's parchment cheeks. "Profane!" he stuttered. "Profane music! I was going to suggest a season of Bach."

My father looked at him pityingly, and then laid a soothing hand on his shoulder. "Ah, my dear old friend," he said, "we have had some good times together according to our lights. But if the light that is in thee be darkness . . . ? And that is what it was, Anatole – sheer blind darkness. Now, so merciful is the Lord, He hath put a new song in my mouth, even praise unto one God."

Anatole suddenly shot upright. His lean hands gesticulated furiously in front of my father's face. "Praise unto our God! Praise unto our God!" he shouted at the top of his voice. "What d'you think Bach is then? What d'you think Beethoven is, you bloody old fool?"

Hearing the angry voice, my mother hastened in from the kitchen, and behind her came Mrs Brimlow with the supper tray. "Oh, Mr Lop – you're back!" my mother cried. "Oh, if only you'd never gone away!"

This allusion passed over Anatole's head. He drew his worn frock coat about him with a starveling dignity. "One must work to eat," he said coldly; and, taking up his hat, he walked out without another word. "He's gone!" my mother exclaimed, and there was a desolation in the cry, which showed that more than Anatole had gone from the house. I myself felt as though the world were crumbling. Betsy, Blanche, Anatole – all gone. And in their place Mrs Brimlow, who was having the impudence to pour out the tea, and Mr Brimlow, who had been incapable throughout this episode of doing more than sit looking anxiously from my father's face to Anatole's with brown eyes that bulged and dribbled like a pig's.

I was hungry. I had eaten nothing since our cold midday meal, but I could not stomach food eaten with the Brimlows at that moment. I slipped out of the room and out of the house. A harvest moon was in the sky, its light falling full upon the noble horse chestnut which had been so peculiarly and comfortingly Blanche's tree and mine. I crawled through the gap in the hedge, and rustled among the fallen leaves, and stood facing the trunk of the tree with my cheek laid upon the bark and my arms thrown round it. The moonlight sifted through to the ground, and now and then a burr broke open, so full the season was of ripeness, and a conker plonked at my feet. My mind was riven by the strange new notions that were being thrust into it. Music was sin. Painting was sin. Dancing, no doubt, was the very worship of the devil. But merciful God killed the thoughts even as they came up to be looked at. I *could* not accept them. I had steeped myself for too long in another worship. Child as I was, I had for years so soaked my heart and mind in knowledge of the great painters – their lives and their works – that they had become to me the supreme arbiters, the final expression of all that was lovely and of good report. Time was to change much in my apprehension of them, but that night they stood about me like angels with shining swords. As, in the morning of that day, my Uncle Kitto's words had fortified me, so now in the night this host came to my aid.

I heard my father come to the door and call my name. I did not answer, but stayed clinging to the tree and saying to myself that I would not go back into the house until the Brimlows had gone out of it. They were there for so long that at last I scrambled back through the hedge and walked towards the Wilmslow Road. I turned left towards the Cock, where the moonlight fell in a great white splash upon the open space. The horse trough in the middle of it stood out as clearly as a table in a lighted kitchen, and sitting upon the edge of the trough, like an old black crow on a wall, was Anatole Lop. I approached him and saw that the bashed ruin of his silk hat was firmly held by his arm against his side and that his coat tails were in the water. He seemed unaware of this. He was muttering to himself, and I knew that he had been into the Cock and out again after a stay more prolonged than he was used to.

I could think of nothing to say but: "Hallo, Anatole."

Slowly and painfully his eyes focused themselves upon my face. He swung himself carefully down from the edge of the trough. The water dribbled round his feet from his soaking coat tails. He discovered his squashed hat, looked at it for a moment without recognition, and then laid it carefully on the surface of the water as though on a table. He swayed uneasily and then clutched me by the lapel of my jacket. "It's Ted," he said thickly. "Ted, I've been thinkin'. In the Cock. Thinkin' 'bout our immortal soul. Your immortal soul's in peril, Ted. Your predic – predic'ment's drastic. Drastic predic'ment – drastic rem'dies."

His skeleton fingers clutched my shoulder blades with demoniac force and the moonlight glittered in his eyes. In a loud voice he shouted: "Edward Pentecost, I baptise you in the name of Leonardo da Vinci, and of Michael Angelo and of Rembrandt, world without end. Amen. Plonk!" With that, he put his arms about me, swung me off my feet, and dropped me lengthways into the horse-trough. It was long enough to contain me – every bit of me. I came up gasping and spluttering and spitting out water. I clambered over the side and stood facing him, too shattered to speak. "Safe," he said gravely. "Safe for time an' eternity."

He took his hat out of the water and drove his fist into it, thus bringing it back to a semblance of its old shape. He put it on his head and gazed at me for a moment with water drops trickling down his face. He looked so sad that they seemed to be immortal tears. Then he turned suddenly and was very sick into the trough. I watched him speechless as he retched and groaned. Out of his vomit he muttered: "Profane! Profane music! Bach! Oh, Johann Sebastian!"

At last he stood upright and turned towards me, and now, if ever, he was death warmed up. He looked like some indecent thing salvaged by ghouls from a churchyard, save that his eyes shone with fierce lustre. "Don't forget what I called him, Ted," he said. "A bloody fool. Don't often swear. S'a bad habit. When s'not a habit, you mean it. An' I mean it. Bloody fool."

With that, he groped for his hat, which his retching had thrown to the other side of the horse-trough, put it on, and then took it off again in a wordless salutation as he bowed towards me. He went away through the moonlight a little steadier now on his legs, and I hoped he would safely find his way home. But he did not. He disappeared through the door of the Cock. I did not wait to see whether he was thrown out, but ran home shivering with more than the water's cold.

11

When I reached our house the Brimlows had departed and my father was gone to bed. My mother was sitting in the kitchen in an old wicker chair that had been Betsy's. She looked so sad and tired that I was ashamed of myself for coming in in so disgraceful a condition. But she was patient with me. I explained that I had been leaning over the horse trough when some louts had come along and thrown me in. She accepted this, and told me to go upstairs and take off my wet things and get into bed. I did so, and was no sooner in than there she was at the bedside with a bowl of hot milk that had bread floating on the top sprinkled with sugar. "Now get this into you," she said, "and listen to me."

She told me that there had been much debate that night between my father and the Brimlows concerning my future and my immortal soul. It had been unanimously and gravely agreed that painting was in the nature of making images, and this was something which the Word expressly forbade. "Take heed, Fred, while there is yet time," Mr

139

Brimlow ventured to say. "Already one of your children has gone the way of sin, and I wouldn't like to be too sure that God doesn't hold you responsible for that. Even if you didn't actively encourage her, you were standing by and consenting, like Saul when Stephen was stoned."

It seems that at this my mother flared up and gave the Brimlows the length of her tongue, with some biographical reference to their own offspring. Mr Brimlow's surprising reply was that Luther had come Over the Line. One gathered that however far he fell into the abyss, he was, so to speak, firmly roped to God, who in His good time would haul him on to the path again and conduct him to the summit. Blanche, on the other hand, had never been saved. She had dropped plumb into the void, and so far as one knew her immortal soul was shattered beyond redemption. It was a fine point, however, on which Mr Brimlow would not too dogmatically interpret God's mind, for His ways were merciful.

At this time my father had not discovered that the Word permitted him to smoke. He sat there torturing himself by sucking at an empty bowl, biting on a cold stem, and listening to Mr Brimlow settling my future on God's behalf.

"I had enough of it," my mother said grimly. "I told them that mischief enough had already been done in this house, but that it wasn't going to touch you. I told him that you would go on with your painting just the same as if your father had never lost his senses. I told them that if there was any hanky-panky with you – expecting you to go to their meetings or anything else – then I'd walk out of this house and take you with me. And so I would. We'd manage somehow."

Miserable as I was, I could not forbear to smile at the thought of my mother "telling them." I took her hand and hugged it tight. She drew it away testily. "There's no need for that sort of nonsense," she said. "You back me up. That's all I ask you to do. You get on with your painting. I'll find the fees somehow."

She gathered up my sopping clothes into a bundle, blew out the candle, and went downstairs.

12

A week later I found in my loft studio a letter that Blanche had addressed to me there. I knew her writing at once: what surprised me was to see a French stamp on the envelope. The letter was written in Blanche's usual unrevealing way:

Dear Ted, You'll be surprised to get this from Paris. What happened was old Sapphira was overjoyed to see me. I expect you guessed I'd be back at Tresco Vean sooner or later, and do you wonder it was sooner? Anyway, nothing would satisfy Sapphira but we must celebrate with a holiday. She said she used to love visiting Paris when she was young and gay but hadn't been there for years. She knows the place like the back of her hand, and we've been to all sorts of restaurants and theatres and dress shops. I asked her what's the good of Paris clothes in Cornwall, and she says isn't there London? So goodness knows what she's got in mind. In the meantime, Paris is good enough for me. It's divine in this autumn weather, so you can let Mother know I'm all right. You will know well enough why I don't address this to the house.

Love,

Blanche.

It had been a strange week. To begin with, I had not once walked into Manchester with my father. On the Monday morning he was ready to go a quarter of an hour earlier than usual. Standing in the passage, with his old blackthorn in one hand and his lunch basket in the other, he said: "Your mother has decided, Ted, that our ways must part. I am a parent unfit to have control of my child's destiny. If we walked to town together there would be a grave risk of my trying to open your eyes to the danger you are in. Indeed, I promise that I *would* so try. Your mother does not wish me to do this, and so we must walk alone. I shall go now, and you can follow in a quarter of an hour."

With that, he went; and we kept to this routine throughout the week.

Another thing which happened that week was that my father laid the foundation of his fortune. I use the word fortune relatively. He was never a rich man as the world understands riches, but he was soon to be what is called "comfortably off." He was always ready to give God thanks for this turn in his affairs and to explain how it arose out of his obedience to an Inner Voice. This Inner Voice explained to him

141

that to cease playing music in his own house would be a pretty piece of humbug if he continued to sell instruments of music and to go about tuning pianos. He therefore decided during that week, after much wrestling, that he must give up the job which had brought us all a scanty living. Mr Brimlow strengthened his feeble knees, as he put it, and counselled him to cast his bread upon the waters. It was in vain that my mother pointed out that her bread and mine was also concerned. The decision was taken to sell the shop. Fortunately for my mother, my father owned the freehold and, more fortunately still, a firm of provision merchants, who already had many shops in Manchester, wanted one more and wanted it there. It was a small place, but they had already bought the freehold of the premises next door. The idea was to unite the two in one shop.

Before his conversion, my father had got a good deal of fun out of this situation. The fact that they had attained half of their objective made the provision merchants anxious to close the whole matter, and Father had engaged in lengthy correspondence, beating up their price, but with no intention of selling. He was, in those days, literally uninterested in money. He would gaily read to us at breakfast time the latest letter from Clutterbuck and Freebody's solicitors and ask our help in concocting absurd answers, "*couched,*" as he would say, "couched, my dear Ted," in the idiotic jargon that they used. Now he put the screw on again, and obtained one more "positively final" offer of ten thousand pounds.

But this was not the end of the Lord's doings with him. The day after this offer was received he went out to tune a piano at a large house in Withington. This was to be his last job of the sort, his final tinkering with the sin of music. The house he went to was owned by a rich cotton merchant, a prop of the Hallé Society and of all musical matters in Manchester. He was himself a pianist of distinction, and knowing my father's deep love of music he always treated him as more than the man who came in to tune the piano. That day, as usual, they talked of many things, and in a confidential moment the cotton merchant told my father of a way to make easy money. Two important cotton firms were about to engage in a "merger." "Pentecost, beg, borrow, or steal some money," he said, "and get in at the beginning. Those shares are going to soar."

Saying nothing to any of us, my father called the next day upon a solicitor accustomed to handling such matters, and thereafter, apart from signing his name once or twice, he had nothing to do but wait. The money obtained from the sale of the shop was put into the new company. It was taken out again when the ten thousand pounds had become fifteen, and the fifteen were split up and invested here and there in five per cents. Thus my father's bread, cast upon the waters, came back to him after not too many days in the shape of fifteen pounds a week for which he had nothing whatever to do. He was never reluctant to cite this as an example of what happened to those who obeyed the Inner Voice. What Albert Critchlow thought of it all I do not know. He, too, was cast upon the waters, a minute and inconsiderable victim of commercial expansion, but whether he sank or swam I never heard.

13

Captain Marquick came back to Manchester on the Wednesday. When I got home from the office that night, my father was already there before me. He was not taking work seriously. He was merely dissolving partnership with the devil, and this did not seem to take much time. So there he was, and there, too, was Mr Brimlow, and with them were two others whose names I have forgotten – brethren who had been called in to discuss the matter of my father's baptism. He was anxious that this should take place as soon as possible. His impetuosity wanted to drive over all obstacles and land up in the inner courts of the redeemed. But it was not so simple as all that, I gathered from my mother. Those brethren who were now in the house had to be satisfied that he was sound on doctrine, and even then time must pass during which he must show not only that he had repented but that he had brought forth fruits.

My mother and I ate our high tea together in the kitchen. The sound of the debating voices came to us from the sitting room and cast a gloom upon our spirits. She did her best to be cheerful with me, but she must at that time have been hagridden by anxiety. My father had told her of his intention to give up the job by which alone our bodies and souls were kept together, but he had said nothing of his further plans, and the outlook for her must have been black indeed. Nevertheless, she did not at that critical time allow a tremor of anxiety to spill over in my direction. "You get upstairs to your attic," she said now. "Goodness knows how long this jawing will go on. You don't want to worry your head with that sort of thing, so get out of their way."

However, I did not want to go to the attic. I fancied that the smell of my burned pictures and of Blanche's dresses lingered there still, and, without having formulated the thought, I was horrified by a point of view which expressed itself in the burning of other people's idols. And so I am today, when all that is involved in the idea is apparent. I am busy enough if I seek out and tumble down my own false gods.

But it was not in this way that I was thinking that night. I was afflicted only by an unformulated repugnance, a sense that these mumbling voices coming through the wall were hostile and I took my cap off its peg in the passage and went out. I wandered through the autumnal streets, thinking of poor Anatole Lop as I passed the Cock, and, in no hurry, I came to the studio. There was not much I could do there. The light was gone and there was neither gas nor electricity. I lit the hanging lamp and sat down. On the wall was a print in startling colour that Uncle Kitto had given me. It was a picture of a man in a cornfield, reaping with a sickle. The sun blazed down, so that the corn looked like a prairie fire and one wondered if the man would be consumed. Also, the corn surged and tumbled so that it looked like a tempestuous sea and one wondered if the man would be drowned. An extraordinary picture that stirred my bones, and yet I couldn't size it up. Neither could Uncle Kitto. "It's by a chap called Van Gogh," he had said. "I don't suppose you ever heard of him."

I hadn't.

"Not my stuff at all," said Kitto. "But I don't know about you youngsters. It may say something to you. Try all the spirits, as Paul says. Well, there it is. Take it. He seems to have been an extraordinary chap by all accounts. He had an iron crown made with spikes round it, and he stuck candles on them and wore it to paint at night."

Well, I hadn't any such apparatus, and so there I sat in the quiet gloom, comforted by the sense of familiar things, but at the same time disturbed as I wondered what was to happen to me. Should I run away as Blanche had done, throw myself on Uncle Kitto's mercy as she had thrown herself on Miss Sapphira's? At the thought, all the glory of the holiday came flooding back into my mind: the ships on the lilac sea, and the light filling the chapel-studio, and Opie pulling us out to the barge, with my worn shoes lying on the bottom-boards alongside my uncle's lavender uppers. Such small absurd recollections suddenly overwhelmed me, and I got up and walked about angrily because I knew I was near to crying.

It was at that moment that I heard the captain climbing the outside staircase. "Well, Ted!" he cried. "They told me there was a light showing here, so I came to see how you're getting on. My dear boy! My dear boy! I'm so glad you're back!"

He came into the room with both his arms extended, brimming over with the friendliness of his welcome. I was so affected by this, coming as it did in the midst of a moment close to despair, that I fairly ran into those open arms, and he closed them about me and hugged me. "Well, well," was all he could say. "Well, well, Ted. So you're back. Good, good. I've been lonely. Is Blanche back, too?"

He found his way to a chair and sat down. I sat on the floor at his feet and leaned against his legs. "No," I said. "She came back with us, but she's gone again. Back to Cornwall."

I said this in so stiff and unnatural a voice that he sensed at once the trouble in my mind. "Come on, Ted," he said. "Out with it. What is all this?"

And then it all came tumbling out. I shudder to think of the exhibition of dismay and despair to which I must have subjected him; but, once started, I could not stop, and all that was in my heart flowed forth. He had to listen even to my account of my mother clambering through the broken window and of Anatole Lop baptising me in the horse trough. When I had told it all I felt cleansed, as though a boil had burst and discharged its poison. "That's all," I said. "And I suppose Blanche couldn't stand it. She'd been away too long. She and Miss Kitto had got used to one another."

Captain Marquick was silent for a long time. Then he said: "Well, I suppose I could have the concerts here. Anatole would come, and we could get some other people . . . still . . . it won't seem the same, Ted. It was more than the music. It was – well, I expect it was what the music was all about. However . . ."

Then he got up and shook himself. "But, there," he said, "how like me to be thinking of no one but myself! What about you? That's the thing. I must think it over. I must see your father."

145

14

I was at this time little more than a child, and I must hasten over the years that divided my childhood from my youth. When that winter came on, I gave up my work at Marquick and Marquand's and became a full-time student at the Manchester School of Art. This was in consequence of Captain Marquick's interview with my father. It did not take the captain long to realise that he might as well argue with a stone wall as with my father in the mood that was on him, and that mood – or let us do him the justice to put it thus, that intense conviction of being chosen by God – deepened as the years went by. It would, quite literally, the captain was given to understand, be compromising with the devil, pandering to evil lusts, if I were backed in my wish to paint or if musical occasions were continued in the house. The captain, who knew more than I did of the world and its odd ways, accepted this situation and told me that I must do so, too.

"So far as you are concerned, Ted, the point is this," he explained. "Short of using brute force, your father cannot stop you from pleasing yourself, and he doesn't seem inclined to do that. To that extent, you can count yourself lucky, for I've known men who held opinions like his and were not content with that. They insisted on trying to bend their families. I've known a boy thrashed black and blue because he read the *Pickwick Papers* on a Sunday, and I've known others who became experienced liars and hypocrites in order that their parents shouldn't know that they were committing dreadful sins like playing football and attending dances. Well, at least you've escaped that. When your father destroyed what he found in the attic, that was his way of saying what he wanted to say. Now it's said and done with. He won't help you, but he won't hinder you. So you see, it's merely a financial question."

We were not in the studio. He had invited me that night into the house. The air outside was chilly. A fire was lighted, the lamps glowed, and we sat with a tray of coffee things between us.

"Merely finance," said the captain with a smile. "Did you ever hear," he asked, "of the lady who financed Tschaikovski?"

I said no; and he added: "Quite a story, that is. You must read it some day. Then, of course, there were the Wedgwood brothers who gave Coleridge £150 a year, and I believe Wordsworth had a bit out of Raisley Calvert. Plenty of precedents. However, you'd better not start thinking of yourself as belonging to that order of people. No swelled heads, please. Still, you may become a pretty good painter. I hope so. Your uncle thinks you will. Did I tell you I wrote to him? No? Well, I did. He thinks you're worth encouraging. Let's not put it higher than that."

I can tell you, I was dying for him to come to the point. I had no inhibitions against receiving money. To get on with my painting I would have accepted money from him or from anyone else, then or at any other time. But he seemed diffident about what he had to say. When at last it came, it was simply this: that he was willing to pay for any tuition I received, and to allow me a small weekly sum for buying my materials. On my side, I would repay him by giving him ten per cent of my earnings, as soon as there were any, till the debt was cleared. All in all, it never amounted to more than a few hundred pounds. I realise now how gladly Captain Marquick would have handed me the money and left it at that; but he had both a delicacy about seeming to place me under an obligation and a fear of helping me to be a waster. As it turned out, the simple transaction tided me over, and, before either of us imagined that this would happen, I had paid back every penny.

15

In the following spring my self-portrait was bought for the city gallery, and you may be sure that the six lines about myself that appeared in the *Manchester Guardian* were posted with speed and pride to Blanche and Uncle Kitto. Blanche replied with an untidy letter about the winter she had spent in London with Miss Sapphira; and there came from Kitto the first letter I ever received from him, written in a thin elegant hand, in which he hoped I wouldn't take portrait painting too seriously. "A heart-breaking business, my dear Ted. You'll find the world full of lovely women whom you will want to paint and who won't be bothered, and rich men's wives with strings of pearls sawing the fat creases of their necks who need the attentions of a drill-sergeant rather than of a painter. But it is on these you will batten."

However, it was a rich man's mistress, not a rich man's wife, who was to have a decisive effect on my career. But that was some time ahead, and before I met Iris Randle I met Prue Cleghorn.

By sight, I knew Jesse Cleghorn well. Who in Manchester did not? Riding a bicycle and wearing a flat cap, he went about the city protected from disaster by the love of God. With dark eyes set deep on either side of a noble curving nose, with his hair longer than was usual, and with a beard that Moses might have envied, he appeared to commune with the infinite as he rode at a steady trundling pace over the granite setts. He could not be said to thread his way among the omnibuses and drays and miscellaneous traffic of the road, for his way never deviated. Rather, it seemed as though the traffic parted before him as the Red Sea parted for the Israelites. And this, as you watched him, you thought was only as it should be, for he was manifestly an archangel, engaged in archangelic contemplation, and if the hand of God did not clear his path, for whom should it be stretched forth? He was professor of philosophy at the Manchester University: a fact which occasionally engaged his mind sufficiently to cause him to pedal his bicycle through the big double doors and into the stony quadrangle; though he was more likely to plod on and find himself in the swarming heart of the city's commerce, like some bemused lemming irresistibly drawn to the deeps.

This was the man whose portrait I was to paint. Cleghorn was about to retire. The University Court had commissioned an "official portrait" from a Royal Academician; but it chanced that Cleghorn's contemporary students, moved by the love all must feel for the man, wished to present a portrait not to the university walls but to him, and as students are not able to command the services of academicians, they turned to the prodigy whose self-portrait had caused some comment. And so it was that I came to know Prue Cleghorn.

16

Two young men wearing Norfolk jackets and knickerbockers and no hats cycled out to our house. They were the official deputation from the students who wished to present the portrait to Jesse Cleghorn. Apparently, an inspection of my self-portrait at the City Art Gallery and a reading of what the *Manchester Guardian* had said had satisfied them as to my competence. Their object now was to discover whether I could paint a portrait for ten pounds. Would I not!

But already I had the sense not to express my gratitude too openly, especially as, when they set eyes on me, it was clear that my youth —

or should I say childhood? – astonished them. It was a Saturday afternoon in June. My father was out distributing tracts, which had become one of his ways for using his too abundant leisure. My mother was shopping in Didsbury village, and thus I was alone in the house. The two bicycles were propped at the edge of the pavement. The two young men, seeming to be identical twins – as, indeed, I discovered later that they were – with close-curling fair hair, blue eyes and open ingenuous faces, looked at me in perplexity when I had admitted that I was Edward Pentecost.

"Well, of course, we needn't have asked," one of them said. "We've seen your self-portrait."

When I gathered that it was they had come about, and apprehended from their attitude that spending ten pounds of other people's money was something they did not take lightly, I exclaimed: "Well, if you don't mind, I think we could discuss the matter better at my studio." This at once, I felt, put me on a different footing, and the young men seemed to think so too. "Ah!" they exclaimed in one breath, and turned briskly to their bicycles. "Hop on to my step," one of them invited, and I did so. The bicycles of those days had a small step projecting from the hub of the rear wheel, and, with one foot on this, the other swinging precariously in the air, and hands resting on the rider's shoulders, a passenger could make an undignified journey. And it was in this undignified way that I set off to clinch the bargain over my first commission. I called the directions into my rider's ear, and side by side through the June day, raising the June dust, with their bells giving many unnecessary silver calls, we sped to the studio.

Here I was playing on my home ground and felt at ease. I waved my hand to the wicker chairs and the young men fell into them and threw out their long legs clothed in brown stockings and terminated by cycling-shoes. They looked about and were obviously impressed. I felt that I should offer them cigarettes, but there were none so I invited them to smoke if they felt like it, and with identical gestures they pulled large curved pipes from their pockets, charged them and lit them.

I wandered about the room, feeling less young. At the Van Gogh print I paused. "Rather striking," I said. "Don't you think?"

They did.

"Do you know this chap Van Gogh?"

They didn't.

"A bit puzzling, I believe, to artists who are – well, shall we say in a groove? I was discussing him with my Uncle Kitto Pentecost, the R.A. That's a print of one of his pictures over there. Rather – well, playing for safety, don't you think?"

They agreed.

"Anyhow, he couldn't get anything out of Van Gogh. Still,"and I smiled, I hoped cynically, "we'll see."

When I had them in what I trusted was the right frame of mind, I cried buoyantly: "Well, now, this portrait of Professor Cleghorn."And after pondering for a moment and biting my thumb: "Yes, I think I could fit it in."

It was soon arranged, and I felt no shame for my bounce and brag, no disgust for having betrayed dear Kitto: nothing but youthful joy, a singing happiness; and when one of the young men (whose names I have long since forgotten) said: "Well, what about a run out into Cheshire?" I was ready for that or for anything. Standing now on the step of one bicycle and now of another, I was whirled between dusty hedgerows filled with hawthorn and honeysuckle to Handforth and Styal and many other villages, and we had tea in a cottage garden – bread and butter, cake and jam, cold meat and pickles and God knows what – and the young men bought great bunches of flowers and tied them to their handlebars. They had ceased to be a responsible delegation entrusted with the spending of ten pounds, and I had ceased to be a wonder child striving to keep his end up in a world of men. We sang as the wheels whirred and the rims twinkled in the evening light and the flowers on the handlebars wilted and absorbed the dust. They dropped me at the end of our street, and we heartily arranged to have many similar outings which never took place, and one said to the other: "He's lucky. He'll meet Prue."

"Ah – Prue."

It was the first time I heard her name.

They leapt on to their bicycles and went away to the silvery ringing of their bells.

17

Ah – Prue!

The silvery ringing of bells was the right fanfare and annunciation.

I had conspired with Captain Marquick in composing a letter to Jesse Cleghorn. So far as I remember, it ran something like this:

Dear Sir, – Some of your students have done me the honour of inviting me to paint your portrait. I should like to do this with the least inconvenience to you, and I should be glad therefore if you would consent to our going about the work in this way. I could call at your house at any time suitable to you and obliterate myself as far as possible while you went on about your customary affairs. This would give me an opportunity to make a series of sketches that would be helpful when it came to doing the final work. If we could arrange for two or three of these preliminary sessions, I should be deeply obliged. When the time came for the painting, would it be possible for you to sit in my studio at The Pines, Didsbury?

The old man replied with a charming letter, agreeing to all this and saying that he would be glad to permit me to perform my first obliteration on the following Thursday at three o'clock. If it were possible for me to materialise again at about four, perhaps I would join him in drinking a cup of tea. Thereover, we might discuss the sensation of obliteration – a matter which had always interested him.

I shall say of my portrait of Professor Cleghorn only this: that, while the "official portrait" which now hangs on the university walls depicts a morose Mosaic face backed by what could conceivably be the God-concealing vapours of Sinai, mine presented an old gentleman, done full length in carpet slippers, with a pipe in his hand, a background of shabby higgledy-piggledy books, and a quirk of humour glinting in the eyes. It was this first letter that told me to look for it, and I found it. That is, I found it when at last I found Professor Cleghorn. But that was not on the appointed day.

I called at three o'clock, as I had been told to do, at the small house in Withington, and the door was opened by a girl who seemed to be – and was – a few years older than I. I asked if Professor Cleghorn were in, and she said that he wasn't. Had I an appointment? I explained how the matter stood, and showed her his letter. She smiled gravely and handed it back to me. "I'm afraid," she said, "he's not good at remembering appointments. I've asked him to let me keep a diary, so that I can remind him of things, and that works for a day or two until he forgets to tell me. However, will you come in? He may be back, but you mustn't count on it."

It was a dark little house. When we entered the passage and she had shut the front door, I half turned towards her, waiting for her to lead the way, and saw her face in profile against the glass panel of the door. The panel was a tawdry mosaic of coloured glass set in a mesh of lead, such as you see in thousands of houses, but the light was behind it, giving it a swift romantic likeness to a stained-glass window, and Prue Cleghorn's face, imposed upon this, suddenly seemed to me beautiful. Then she moved, and the moment was gone, as they say, though no moment can ever go, as I know well enough, for that one is always there and I can take it up when I wish and look again at Prue in that instant of recognition. I thought her beautiful then, and I always thought her beautiful, though it was never easy to say why. She was of middle height, rather plump, with her uncle's dark brown eyes, and she wore her brown hair parted in the middle and twisted into a large round whorl like a Chelsea bun over either ear. Her nose was in none of the classic shapes, but was just a nose. Her lips were full and sensual. Her general impact in those early days was of brownness: hair and eyes and skin were brown: and of rich blood pulsing beneath it and suffusing the lips. One had a sense of an extraordinarily alive being, veiled by tranquillity.

I need not say that I did not arrive at all these conclusions in that first moment. I was aware only, as Prue led the way upstairs, that she seemed a nice girl and that she put me at ease.

"You'd better wait in my uncle's study," she said, opening a door from the landing. It was a room that had been designed as a bedroom – not large and jumbled up like an old ragbag. There were books everywhere: the walls were lined with them, the floor was strewn with them, the big writing table that filled the middle of the room was littered with them, and they lay even on the seats of the chairs. Prue removed some from a leather armchair set before the blackleaded iron fireplace, and said: "Well, make yourself as comfortable as you can. I'll bring him up at once if he comes in," and with that she went away, closing the door behind her quietly.

I sat there fascinated. Not a sound disturbed the stillness. The summer sunshine droned over the suburb. This street was a backwater into which not so much as a tradesman's cart or a nurse's perambulator seemed to intrude. I stood at the window and looked out, but there was nothing to see save the hot paving stones and the houses opposite sleeping with blinded windows in the sun and a tree or two that, in narrow front gardens, had survived from the time when hereabouts were fields and under these trees the sheep had sheltered and the cows had rubbed their flanks upon the bark.

I sat down again, glad of this breathing space. This room, this street isolated from the roar of the city, these books that were devoured and thrown away, these pipes on bookcases, on the mantelpiece, on the table: all this — the quiet girl, too? — seemed to me to be the *aura* of Jesse Cleghorn, and it pleased me to rest quietly in it. And never, all through my life, have I lost this feeling that I could work well only when there had been time and opportunity to live for a while in the ambiance of a sitter. O the portraits I have painted of this world's rushing busybodies! "I can give you half an hour tomorrow, Mr Pentecost, if you can be at my office at 3.13. Of course I can't promise that we shan't be disturbed." Politicians, businessmen, bishops: well, one does what one can and it must be left at that.

I began, as I sat there, to have already an idea of the picture I would paint. I got out of the chair and moved to the other side of the room and started slashing some lines on to my sketching block. The old sagging leather chair, with a lanky lay-figure roughly suggested in it, half the window behind the head, the bookcase alongside the window. There was a pair of carpet slippers near the fender, and I drew them again and again, and the fender itself, and the fire irons, and the opal-shaded paraffin lamp hanging from the ceiling. Time rushed by, and my mind was so precipitated into my work that I literally did not hear the door open and Prue Cleghorn come into the room.

"Oh," she said, "I'm sorry if I've disturbed you. I didn't think you'd be doing anything."

She was carrying a tray with tea-things on it, and I hadn't the address to take it from her hands or even to find a place for her to put it down. She looked at the writing table and said: "Do you mind pushing something aside? It's all so confused that it really doesn't matter where anything is."

I swept up some *Manchester Guardians* and *Hibbert Journals* and Prue set down the tray. "He's not back," she said. "I'm afraid you'll have to give it up for the day. But you'd better have some tea before going."

I was pleased that she didn't say: "May I see what you've been doing?"

She poured out the tea and said: "You must think me very rude. I haven't even introduced myself. I'm Prue Cleghorn. Professor Cleghorn is my uncle. I've been living here now for four years ever since my father died. What we shall do now I don't know – I mean now that my uncle is retiring from the university. He won't be going back when the new term opens."

I was munching rock buns with a boy's appetite and was not inclined to talk.

"I should like to go back to the Lake District," she said. "That's where I came from. My father had a shop at Keswick: clocks and spectacles and things. He was much younger than my uncle. As for my mother, I don't remember her, and I was an only child. So my uncle took me in."

I went on eating steadily.

"Good gracious," Prue said, "you haven't a word to say for yourself. Here am I giving you my life story and you do nothing but eat rock buns. All young men seem to be the same, though I must admit you're younger than most. My uncle invites them here in twos and threes, and as often as not forgets that he's done so, and then I have to give them tea and try to entertain them. And they haven't a word to say for themselves."

Then I spoke up mischievously. "Oh, yes, they have, Miss Cleghorn," I said. "But they say it when you're not there. Then they look into one another's eyes and say: "Ah Prue!"

"What *are* you talking about?" she asked.

Basely I betrayed my two young men. She did not smile. She laughed. Heartily, showing her white teeth and red tongue, she laughed. I was to learn to love her laughter, with its pulsing in the throat and its accent upon her sensual mouth. On these happy terms we parted. I had even recollected myself enough to carry down the tray and put it on the table in the passage. She shook hands with a firm warm clasp. "Now when he writes to you again," she said, "let me know the time of the appointment, and I'll see he's here. I hope you haven't wasted your afternoon."

I assured her that I had not, and went away feeling happy. When I came to the main road I saw Professor Cleghorn pedalling past a signpost which read: "To Cheadle and the South." This was the London road. How far he had gone towards the capital before realising that he wanted only to go home I do not know.

18

The portrait of Professor Cleghorn made no splash. For one thing, it was seen only by the few people concerned. Half-tone photography had not reached the newspapers at that time, and so the picture had no circulation. The philosophy students gave the old man a dinner at a second-rate hotel, which might have been the Berkeley or Savoy for all he seemed to notice, and Prue was there and so was I. Mr Cleghorn, who was always surprising people by lecturing about things – Shakespeare's heroines, for example – which were not supposed to come within the view of a philosopher, showed himself to be awake about painting. He talked of the Impressionists and even, to my amazement, mentioned Van Gogh. Van Gogh, he said, had once committed an outrage upon himself by painting himself without an ear; but this young fellow Pentecost, who had too early forsaken his mother's milk for turpentine, had committed an even greater outrage upon Professor Cleghorn: he had painted him without any pride, he had shown him as he was. "And to show a man as he is, is not only to show him: it is to show him up. This terrible infant," he declared, laying a hand affectionately on my head, so that for a moment I felt as if I were literally dwelling within the shadow of Jehovah, "this apparently corporeal boy, is undoubtedly a changeling. He exists not only here but also in fairyland. It was there that Hans Anderson observed him, squinting from the fringes of the crowd, and shouting with accurate but indecent perception that the Emperor was not wearing any clothes. Well, one may conceive portrait painting as having two functions: to put robes on to people, or to take robes off. Mr Pentecost seems to prefer the latter occupation, and so do I. As a philosopher, I should like to paint a portrait of the Infinite stripped naked. My!" – and he cast his wise old eyes up to the ceiling – "that would be a picture!"

It seemed to me a most exciting occasion, the first of the kind that I had ever attended. I owed so much to Captain Marquick that I had begged an invitation for him, and he accepted it. When it was all over, Professor Cleghorn mounted his bicycle and set a rough course for home. The captain's brougham was waiting for him outside the hotel, and he invited me and Prue Cleghorn to travel with him. It was the first time I had been in the captain's carriage, and I wished I was walking home with Prue Cleghorn. But I could not say so. In any case, she was carrying the heavy picture. I had given a generous ten pounds' worth. There was a lot of wood and canvas. Captain Marquick ordered his coachman to make a detour so that we could drop Prue at her door. There we found the professor, miraculously deposited by God. "Ha, Prue! Watch that coach closely," he said, "for at midnight it will turn back into a pumpkin."

At any rate, by midnight I felt that I turned back into a bumpkin. I tossed restlessly on my bed, the great occasion, to which I had long looked forward, deflated and done with, nothing of it remaining in my mind save a regret that I had not walked home with Prue Cleghorn. It was a long time before I saw anything more of her, except for casual meetings in the streets. Professor Cleghorn did not leave Manchester. I imagine that where he lived meant little enough to him, and that he could pursue his dreams as easily in the small house in Withington as anywhere else. I understood from Prue that he was working on his *magnum opus*, a survey and illumination of the philosophic thought of all times. Occasionally I saw him taking his afternoon exercise on his bicycle. Sometimes he would not see me; sometimes he would see me and not know me; once or twice he raised his flat greasy cap in a salute which I imagined to spring from a profound irony. All in all, there was no reason to suppose that Professor Cleghorn, Prue and I would have much more to say to one another. Nor had we for some years.

19

I was seventeen when we left Didsbury and moved into Hulme. There was no financial reason why I should go, for by that time I was self-supporting. If I had lived alone, it would have been a thin living, but I could have done it. I went because of my mother. It was she who throughout the past few years had borne the burden of my father's salvation. It had pressed in upon her from every direction. In his easier financial circumstances, there was no reason why someone should not have come in to take the place of Betsy Comfort, but it was his opinion that to employ a maid servant was to indulge in worldly ostentation. She respected – or at any rate accepted – this opinion, and cooked and sewed, scrubbed and mended. She had chosen her part. She had loved him; I suppose she loved him always. After the first hot moments of astonishment and disapproval, she allowed him to go his way and went obediently by his side. One thing only could cause her to fly again into the passion of resentment which had made her break the window, and that was when, as sometimes happened, the Brimlows inquired directly of me concerning the state of my soul or suggested to my father that he was not doing all that he should to secure my immortal felicity. Then she would sharply bid them to hold their tongues, and, if exceptionally nettled, would mention the straying from the fold of their own lamb.

As the years went by, the Brimlows were content to regard me as a brand unlikely to be snatched from the burning. Even their hints as to the corporeal and actual nature of this combustion left us unmoved – my mother and me. We felt we were always together in this, conspirators, breathers in unison, and in this fact was the best happiness we had in those days. We said little about it, but I was never unaware that the life she accepted was a conscious posing of herself between me and what she considered would be my spiritual ruin. My father, too, I think, realised the situation as it existed: that the uneasy truce could be maintained only so long as my freely-chosen doings were respected.

They were dull and dismal years. I would have left home and fared the best I could had I not felt that I owed it to my mother to remain. The worst of it was that my father was now, with no work to do, always on her hands. At the beginning there had been an effervescence about him. Something of the old unregenerate man bubbled occasionally through the new converted one. His silly little jokes would crop up as, one evening when the Brimlows were taking supper with us and Mr Brimlow as usual was tucking in with great heartiness, my father looked at his new friend's bloated stomach and began to laugh heartily. "Jonas," he said, "it just comes to me that if our good Lord made his second coming tonight, you'd need uncommonly powerful wings to go up with him."

157

The Brimlows were horrified, especially as I burst into a roar of laughter, entranced by the thought of Mr Brimlow battling heavily upwards against the pull of his paunch. They exchanged glances. Mr Brimlow pointed wordlessly to the card on the wall which assured us that the Lord was the unseen listener to every conversation, and then the pair laid down their knives and forks and marched into their own house. This was at a time when my father's baptism had been arranged for the following Sunday. It was postponed. He had to appear before a conclave of the Brethren, who gave him to understand that spiritual matters were not to be the subject of jest, and it was not till six months later that he had wiped out his ignominy sufficiently to be thought meet for immersion.

And so, from having been a man of many if not excellent jests, he changed into a morose and introspective person, touchily concerned that everything he did should be, as he put it, as if his last. "Well, so long as the Lord doesn't mind finding me on my knees with a bar of yellow soap—" said my mother. "You'd better get up to your study, Fred, and let me get on."

She was pleased that he had taken over what he called a study. This was the old attic that Blanche and I had once used. I never went there now, and I never went to the hut in the sycamore that he had so gaily helped me to build. It was falling into tatters like an old rook's nest.

My father, I think, could not fail to be aware that downstairs, with us, he lived on sufferance. And I hope that in the attic he found a release for his spirits. I think he did. In order to kill the boredom that his idleness imposed on him, he had taken to spending his afternoons in the distribution of tracts at house doors, and in pointing out the way of salvation to those who would listen. It seems to have occurred to him that these tracts could be bettered, and indeed this was not an unreasonable decision to arrive at; and from this it was not a long step to writing his own. This was his occupation in the attic. It was good for him, because to some extent it engaged his faculties; but I fear it engendered spiritual pride. The tracts were produced at his own expense by a cheap firm of jobbing printers. His name always appeared at the top of the page. "The Rock and the Quicksands. By Frederick Pentecost." "The Wreck and the Lifeboat. By Frederick Pentecost." So they went, and I have seen him open the proofs of these things at the breakfast table and apply himself to their correction with the pride and ardour that a master writer might bring to a major work.

It was his poetic fancy to make each of the tracts illustrate a verse from one of the doggerel hymns that the Brethren sang. "The Wreck and the Lifeboat," for example, was founded on this:

> Pull for the shore, sailor, pull for the shore;
> Heed not the foaming wave but bend to the oar;
> Trust in the lifeboat, sailor, cling to self no more;
> Leave the poor old stranded wreck and pull for the shore.

Our situation had its pathos. I recall this particular tract because my father, not without pride, handed a copy of it to me at the breakfast table one morning. He was so deeply aware of my mother's stand against his trying to influence my life, that he paused, I remember, with the strip of cheap paper held halfway towards me, as if he had, in the very act of handing it over, recalled that she might dislike his doing so. A look passed between them such as could have passed only between people deeply at one beneath their differences, for without a word said he had asked a question and she had answered it. It was only when the tract was in my hand that she said: "So long as you don't try *making* him read that sort of stuff . . ." and I saw that in her eyes were tears welling from her inability to be at one with *both* the people she loved. But I am sure there had not been in my father's gesture any wish to turn me from the paths wherein she wanted me to walk. It was pure pride of authorship, such as Dickens might have felt on handing a first edition of *David Copperfield* to young Henry Fielding Dickens. "One of mine," my father said with a relieved smile.

20

So our years went dully by until the time came to move into Hulme. That was in 1906. The thought of leaving our leafy suburb and moving into a slum in the black heart of Manchester appalled me. In this, as in everything else that he wished to do, so long as it did not concern me, my mother allowed my father to make his own decisions. She would go with him to Hulme. "You can please yourself, Ted," she said. "If you want to find lodgings somewhere else, do it."

I went with them because of her.

My father had adopted a motto. His tracts were now headed: "By Frederick Pentecost. (Saved to Serve.)" His letters, even about the most mundane things, were signed: "Yours in Christ, Frederick Pentecost. (Saved to Serve.)"

He did not intend that this should be an empty boast. It was his will to serve his Master by some art of especial significance; and over the supper table one Sunday night I heard the first rumour of his scheme. He explained to Mr and Mrs Brimlow that he felt called to take the Word to the outcast, and he had decided that Hulme was more outcast than Didsbury. It had been his habit now for some time to distribute his tracts there rather than in his own suburb, and as time went by he claimed to have led many souls from darkness into light. These were sheep without a shepherd. He intended to give them a fold wherein they might gather. Since his sale of the shop, he had been very conscious of the possibilities of financial manipulation, and the only occasions in those years when I saw him what he would formerly have called "hopping mad" were when, from time to time, news from the Stock Exchange was unfavourable. Apparently, it was beyond his comprehension that an omnipotent God who, according to all the authorities, took a personal interest in the affairs of Frederick Pentecost, should fail to rig the market so that he might more and more comfortably live on the labour of other people. It was not as though he "desired increase," to use his fine biblical words, for his own sake. He had set his heart on enlarging his assets sufficiently to permit him to build a Plymouth Brethren place of worship in Hulme. God did not withhold His mercy forever; the time came when the cash in hand enabled my father to carry out his long-cherished plan. A derelict fag end of land, till then dedicated to a hoarding whose boards flapped in the wind, to cats and squalling squabbling children and the thrown-out rubbish of mean streets, was now dedicated to his spiritual intention. A meeting room as drear and dolorous as that in Owen Street began to go up. With no ceremony, the stone was laid declaring that it had been built in 1906 by Frederick Pentecost (Saved to Serve). So that my father might supervise the work, we moved at once to our new house standing opposite the meeting room. It was as black and soul-deadening as all the houses thereabouts, and as it was a corner house at a crossroads, you could look in four directions and see nothing but identical houses, without gardens, reaching endlessly into the muck and gloom. You were at the junction point of a cross, and, look where you would: at the smoking chimneys, the stony pavements, the soot-darkened sky: you saw nothing but the crucifixion of hope and beauty, and Mammon mightily triumphant.

Here my father was happier than he had been for a long time. He would sit in the cramped front room watching the bricklayers across the road as proudly as Solomon could ever have looked upon the majestic upspringing of his cedarn temple. He would walk the streets with his tracts as confident of mission as Livingstone could ever have been in the darkness of Africa. I lived there with him and my mother, but I went my own way. It was for me little more than a sleeping-place, but for her it was a purgatory of dirt and discomfort in which she forever toiled with no hope of coming out at last into paradisal cleanness. As the building drew towards its end there was another of those pathetic happenings that could wring my heart. It was a Saturday afternoon. We had just finished our midday meal. Across the road, the workmen had knocked off for the weekend. I carried the crockery out to the kitchen, and when I came back my father was standing at the window, with the curtains parted, looking at his tabernacle. "See, Ted," he said, "the roof is on."

I stood at his side and looked at the meanly-proportioned little building, as inspiring as a toolshed. "Would you like to step across with me and have a look over it?" There was something so wistful in his voice, so desirous that I should approve of what he had done and share his pride in it, that I was touched by a sudden sense of the loneliness he must feel in the strange country his soul inhabited. He was as supplicating as a child asking an adult to take an interest in its sandcastle. "Yes," I said. "I'd like to see it. Let's go."

We crossed the road. A few children were playing among the brickbats and planks. They had made a trestle, and with a plank laid across it were enjoying a see-saw. A little girl sat on either end; a boy stood straddled in the middle, propelling the plank up and down with pressure of alternate legs. My father smiled at them and they shouted "Allo, Mr Pentecost," and when he had unlocked the door, they abandoned their play and came in after us. There was, as yet, nothing but the floor, the walls and a roof. The walls were painted a drab battleship grey, and texts were scrolled upon them. "Thou God seest me." "Prepare to meet thy God." "In such an hour as ye know not, the

Son of Man cometh." "Thou fool! This night thy soul shall be required of thee." It was all stern and admonitory, and my father stood looking upon it with a fond smile. The little girls had snuggled up to him. He held one by each hand. The little boy was playing with shavings, pulling them out and letting them jerk back like springs.

At the far end of the building was a raw hole in the ground, like a wide shallow grave. We looked down into it, and the sour smell of the Hulme soil came up into our nostrils. There was not so much as a worm in it. It was too sterile and acid for that. "It'll be lined soon," my father explained. "The baptism tank."

The little boy began to show interest.

"Will there be water in it, Mr Pentecost?"

"Yes, Jimmy."

"Will we bave? Will it be a public barfs?"

"No, Jimmy," my father patiently explained. "People's sins will be washed in the blood of the Lamb, and then they will pass through the water here, just to show that that has happened."

"Can we see the lamb, Mr Pentecost?" one of the little girls demanded; and my father answered gravely: "With God's grace, Edith, we will show you the Lamb. It was the Lamb who took a little child and set him in the midst."

"I see a lamb once," Edith said. "It was a Sunday School treat at Cheadle. It was white wiv a black face, and it sucked the sheep's tits, and waggled its tail like mad."

"You didn't ought to say tits," Jimmy reproved her. "Only like when you say tell-tale tit."

"I got tits myself," said Edith. "I seen 'em. They're beginnin'."

"You oughter be ashamed of yerself," said the staid Jimmy. He ran out of the building, kicking up the piles of sweet-smelling shavings as he went.

"I'll say it as much as I like," shouted Edith defiantly. She and her companions ran after Jimmy, Edith filling the tabernacle with her shout: "Tits, tits, tits! I got tits."

My father looked a little uneasy, and I quoted: "We have a little sister, and she hath no breasts; what shall we do for our sister in the day when she shall be spoken for?"

My father stood there prodding the edge of the baptismal hole with the toe of his boot. The dusty earth trickled down. "Ay," he said. "The

Bible's a queer book. It is so." And then, with defiance: "But mind you, Ted, the Word of God. Every bit of it."

I had already come to the conclusion that a woman's breasts were part of the word of God, which is the word of beauty; but before I speak of Iris Randle I must tell of the return of Luther Brimlow.

21

The new meeting room was to be opened on a Sunday evening, and for old times' sake Mr and Mrs Brimlow promised to make the journey from Didsbury and to assist at the ceremony. They were due at our house to take tea with us at four o'clock. It was a December day, and, by four, dark. I went myself to open the door when the expected knock came, and the light of the paraffin lamp hanging in the passage showed me that they were not alone. A tall man was with them, and he seemed taller because he wore a silk hat. It was not possible in the dim light to make out more of his face than that it was decorated with a moustache. When this person said: "Well, Ted. How are you? I'm Luther Brimlow," you could, as they say, have knocked me down with a feather.

In the imagination of all of us, Luther Brimlow, for years past, had been the prodigal son. We associated him with husks and swine. The prodigal's return was not in accordance with the storybooks. When he had placed his kid gloves in his hat, stood this on the hall stand, and followed his father and mother into our well-lighted sitting room, I looked at him with a surprise which I hope I had the address to conceal. Luther was a man of the world, self-possessed, easy in his manners, not bad-looking. He no longer wore the thick-pebbled spectacles that once disfigured his face. He was dressed with – well, restrained elegance, I suppose, is the right *cliché*. The thin gold chain across his waistcoat, the cuff links, the lavender silk tie: all the notes were right; none was stressed. He must have been six foot high. At that time, he would be twenty or twenty-one.

"See what I've brought!" was written all over Mrs Brimlow as she bridled under the lamplight. "This my son was dead, and is alive." Yes, very much alive was Luther.

I imagine that Luther's coming was a disappointment to my father, and an embarrassment, too. At a stroke, he and his meeting room disappeared from stage centre and retired to the wings. Neither Mr nor Mrs Brimlow wanted to talk of anything but Luther. Mrs Brimlow unpinned and passed from hand to hand the gold brooch that he had brought her. It was certainly something new in her experience of brooches. She had been accustomed to wearing a heavy cameo: this new thing, which presently I found in my hands, was simply a long strip of gold looped and twisted into an exquisite pattern. I was impressed by Luther's taste, and when my father had the hardihood to say that jewels and personal adornments were abominable in the eyes of the Lord, there was, ominously, not even an attempt on the part of the Brimlows to justify themselves. They merely looked fondly on their son, and it was to be understood that what he did was good in their eyes, whatever the Lord might think about it.

Luther's presence was, as I say, an embarrassment, too. My father and mother, I suppose, could not but recall the last time they had seen him: that winter's night when his fumbling with Blanche had taken them angrily into the Brimlows' house, and only the arrival of Mr Armroyd with the peculating Luther had scotched their thunder. The situation was not eased when Luther casually said: "I'm sorry Blanche isn't here, Mr Pentecost. I should like to have seen her. Do you hear anything of her now?"

My father answered darkly: "She has chosen her path and is walking in it."

Mrs Brimlow said: "Don't despair, Mr Pentecost. God's way is not our way, and it sometimes happens that those who go forth with sorrow return rejoicing."

The brooch had come back into her hand. She pinned it at her throat with satisfaction.

The tea was already laid in this room where we sat. My mother said rather grimly: "Well, we'd better get on," and chairs were drawn up to the table. Luther was attentive to his mother, and saw her comfortably seated. My father said: "Brother Brimlow, as the senior recipient of God's grace, will you ask a blessing?"

Four pairs of hands were folded in laps, four heads were bowed, as Mr Brimlow mumbled a few words, but Luther and I looked at one another across the table and he winked at me. It put us at once into a conspiracy. It said: "You and I, Ted, have this mumbo jumbo weighed up," and I did not like it.

When my mother was busy with the teapot, Luther said: "Do you know that story of the old parson who loved being invited to dinner? It was always his job to ask a blessing, and first of all he'd have a look round the table. If there was a good spread, he'd begin 'O Lord, for this Thy abundant provision . . .' but if things were a bit miserly, he'd say 'Lord, for these the least of Thy mercies . . .'"

Mrs Brimlow laughed. I don't think I had ever heard her laugh before, but now she laughed, and even behind Brother Brimlow's moustache a smirk of amusement could be detected. My father looked thunderous: he who had once loved just such little jokes as that. I could have wept at his humiliation. "We are thanking God for His blessings," he said. "We are doing it on the Lord's Day, and on a day when He has consented to the sowing of His seed in a new plot. It had been my intention that we should all get upon our knees and ask for His especial blessing upon this work. But if a prayer to God – which is what the asking of a blessing amounts to – is to be made the occasion of ribaldry, then perhaps we had better await a more favourable season."

Mr Brimlow at once took on the morose and dog-like air that indicated a deepening of his spiritual feeling. After all, he had been appealed to as the senior recipient of God's grace, and that had to be lived up to. Even Mrs Brimlow quenched her laughter and tightened her lips. Only Luther was unperturbed. Another wink flashed at me across the table, and he said: "That reminds me, Mr Pentecost – this new building of yours. What has it let you in for?"

My father was reluctant to discuss the matter, but Luther pressed him as keenly as some smart Levantine costing clerk might have pressed Solomon concerning the price of the cedars of Lebanon, and the firs and algum trees, the gold and silver, brass, iron and stone. And over it all Luther Brimlow shook his head. "I wish I'd known about it, Mr Pentecost," he said. "I reckon we could have knocked off twenty-five per cent." He spoke with authority, and, looking at him sitting there, figuring as the others went steadily through the cold ham, scones and all the rest of it, I recalled the gangling lout who had, so long ago, boldly answered "Sums" when Blanche and I asked about his master-passion. But Luther was no gangling lout now. No, indeed. He closed a slim book bound in red leather in which he had been writing, slipped into the pocket on the spine a thin gold-cased pencil, put it back in a breast pocket of his waistcoat and said: "I'm afraid you've been done," and with that he began to crumble a biscuit. He appeared to despise the plebeian plenty of our high tea.

At six o'clock my father and mother and the two elder Brimlows got into their coats, though they had but to cross the road, and though the first service in the new meeting room would not begin for half an hour. As the equivalent of the officiating clergy, they wanted to be there in good time. Luther dutifully helped his mother into her coat and handed his father the umbrella. Its appearance appeared to offend his taste, for he rolled the ungainly thing and fastened the band round it. Even then, it remained offensive and Luther shook his head over it. "I must buy you something better than this," he said. "Goodbye now, Mother. Mind how you cross the road. As Ted's not going, I shall stay here and keep him company."

"Very well. Give your old mother a kiss," Mrs Brimlow said fondly. He kissed her gallantly, and I reflected that never once since I had grown up had I kissed my mother. Over Mrs Brimlow's shoulder I caught Luther's swiftly-telegraphed wink. A moment later the door shut and we had the house to ourselves. We went back into the sitting room, which was stiflingly hot. "Whoo!" Luther exclaimed. "My God! Well!"

He took a thin gold cigarette-case from a breast pocket, sprang it open deftly, and held it towards me. "Smoke?" I shook my head. He tapped a cigarette thoughtfully on his thumbnail, lit it, and again said: "Well!" He walked lithely up and down, so far as the small crowded room would permit, and he reminded me of a tiger that has finished its polite public performance. He threw the hardly-tasted cigarette into the fire, and said: "Let's get out. I must have a drink. This town'll be the death of me. Manchester!"

"What's wrong with Manchester?" I asked feebly, knowing well enough.

"Wait till you've seen New York, Paris and London. Then you can ask – if you feel like it. I'm starving. Let's get out of this."

As soon as we were outside the front door a four-wheeler appeared, growling its way towards the cab rank at All Saints. Luther held up his furled, gold-banded umbrella. We got in and he named the most stylish hotel in Manchester. We sat in an almost empty lounge, for Manchester hotels were not much used on Sundays, and Luther ordered chicken sandwiches, fruit and a bottle of claret. When the waiter was gone, he sank back into the plush, stretched out his long legs, and sighed with relief.

"This is better," he said. "So long as there's a good hotel in a town, wherever you are you can be at home."

I was not at home. I had never been in such a place before: and for that reason I was the more impressed by Luther's ease. I was still afflicted by a hangover from my old dislike; nevertheless, I was unable to withhold admiration from this man of the world. He filled my glass, and I asked: "You've really been in Paris, and New York, and London?"

"Been in 'em and lived in 'em," he said. "I know 'em as well as I know Manchester."

He occupied himself for a while with the cress-fringed sandwiches; then he said: "It won't hurt you, young Pentecost, to know how to get on in the world. If your scheme is cut and dried and you stick to it — well, you can bring it off."

As soon as he was thrown out of Armroyd's office, he began to prepare his cut-and-dried scheme. He had come to the conclusion that America could teach him more of what he wanted to know than England could. But he did not go straight to America. He went to Paris. "I wanted to learn French," he said. "And take my tip, young Pentecost. When you want anything, go to the best place. That applies to everything, not only languages. Look at these shoes. They were made in Jermyn Street."

He had just enough money to get him to Paris, and there, I gathered, he literally starved and begged. At last, with some knowledge of the language, he began to get mean jobs: messenger boy, dishwasher and whatnot, that kept body and soul together. In his spare time he taught himself shorthand, and he never ceased his study of the financial papers which had become an obsession in England. "You despise all that, don't you, Ted?" he asked, filling our glasses again. "You're an artist, and so to Hell with Mammon. Ah! Believe me, there's an artistic satisfaction in understanding money and manipulating it that you'll never get out of your paint and canvas." He held his glass to the light and looked through the flowing wine as at a vision withheld from all but the devout. "Yes," he said. "Yes. You wouldn't understand that."

The wine was finished. He called for coffee and cigars. "And what with your coffee, young Pentecost?" he asked. "Cognac? Benedictine? Crême de menthe?"

I declined them all. The waiter pierced Luther's cigar, handed it to him, and struck a match. "Wait! Wait!" Luther cried. "You don't put a match to a cigar while the sulphur is fuming. Don't you know that, man?" He exhaled the first delicate tissue of smoke. "On second thoughts," he said, "not cognac. Armagnac."

When his French was perfect – "and I perfected it in what is universally held to be the best way," he said with an impudent grin – "if you know what that means" – I didn't – when his French was perfect he had been in France for little more than a year and had already made a few successful flutters on the Bourse. "But all that," he said, "doesn't amount to anything. Any fool can put a shilling on a horse. There's no more to it than that. It wasn't making money that interested me. It was manipulating money – flotation – promotion . . ." His voice trailed off. He looked into eternity, like a poet or a mathematician who has reached the point where mathematics are hardly to be distinguished from religion and philosophy. "Of course, I hadn't come to that. I've hardly come to it yet. On the fringes, you might say."

His story passed into regions that were then, and for that matter still are, so alien to me that I can hardly hope to make clear what it all came to. His master idea was to get to New York and study there the methods of financial jugglers. He knew that many rich Americans came to Paris for purposes both of business and pleasure, and now that he was master of the language his first attempt was to attach himself to one of these people as a secretary and general handyman, courier, and whatever else might be required. By impudence and perseverance he succeeded in doing this. Bilingual, stuffed with commercial knowledge, equally ready to type letters or to suggest a Bourse transaction, to order a dinner or take on his shoulders all the tedious details of an excursion, he was everything that Mr Hosmer Andrews could desire. "He was in oil," Luther said; "and that again is only selling. But it got me to the States."

Luther, it seems, put Mr Andrews wise to so many good things on the Bourse, that the American had the pleasant experience of returning home the richer instead of the poorer for his holiday. Luther went with him, and was cracked up by Andrews as a wizard. Soon, he was not a secretary but the confidential right-hand man of his employer. "I learned oil inside out," he said. "There was more in it than I thought. Still, fundamentally I didn't want oil." He said it as a man might decline a bun at a tea party. It was Hosmer's brother, the celebrated Horace Andrews – a name that even I had heard – who set him on his feet. Horace Andrews was one of those legendary people who play with the world's money. Banking, insurance, loans to governments, the promotion of grandiose operations of all sorts: these were the ingredients of the Horace Andrews game. "I didn't see him for a long time," Luther explained. There had come through a third party an offer of a job in the Paris office that "watched the Andrews interests." It was a small-beer job. It meant a heavy fall in salary, but it was what Luther wanted. It was a chance to be in, however humbly, on the impalpable, the mystic, manipulation of money.

"We'd better have some more coffee," Luther said, "and I do implore you to try this Armagnac. It's unexpectedly excellent."

It was all incredible. This hotel lounge, when first I entered it, these quiet lights and footstep-dulling carpets, these flowers in December and waiters gliding, whispering decorously, had seemed the final majestic peak of human amenity. And into this I had been inducted by the gangling lout who had hopped up and down the garden path, singing gibberish hymns, and recoiling from the fusillade of conkers that Blanche and I had directed from the attic skylight. Now this lout had become Odysseus, telling tales which I had to believe, and the hotel itself became inconsiderable as my mind painted in the background against which he had moved: strange cities, Circes, and sirens' songs. I sipped the Armagnac, and my excited imaginations were not diminished. It seemed at that moment the most natural thing in the world that Iris Randle should come into the lounge, accompanied by Sir Harry Banfil.

It was after a year of menial work in the Paris office – but not so menial at the end as at the beginning – that Luther Brimlow was recalled to New York and permitted for the first time to meet Horace Andrews. "We clicked," Luther explained briefly.

He crushed the end of his cigar into an ashtray, swallowed the last of the Armagnac, yawned as though suddenly bored by his own loquacity. "Yes," he wound up. "We clicked. I stayed with him over there for a year, and I don't think I wasted my time. Now I've got the London office – complete charge. You must look me up sometime when you're in town. The Andrews Finance Corporation in Threadneedle Street."

He got up, and the waiter came hurrying silently with the bill. Hardly looking at it, Luther tipped two golden sovereigns upon the tray and was casual about the change. Then, turning, he for the first time became aware of Sir Harry Banfil and Iris Randle. "Strewth!" he said. "What a stunner! And isn't that Sir Harry Banfil?"

I said that it was, and added that, if he liked, I'd introduce him. "If you like!" he cried; and then looked at me as though my offer to introduce him had been a bad joke.

"You couldn't."

"I could."

I led him across the lounge and introduced him to Iris and Sir Harry.

22

Iris was looking as beautiful and impudent as ever, and Sir Harry Banfil was looking what he was: a more developed and predatory man of Luther's own kidney. They also, I thought with a smile, should click.

Sir Harry Banfil was here, there and everywhere. His headquarters, I believe, were in London, but nine or ten months before this, I had received a note from him, asking me if I would call, upon a professional matter, at an address in St Ann's Square. It was still flattering to have my work called a professional matter, although I was not doing badly. I had already a local reputation. I reached the address I had been given on a day of bright winter sunshine. St Ann's Square was gay, with the shop windows full of coloured fruits, bright books, all the gleaming merchandise that we took for granted in those backward and uneconomic days. I lingered for a moment at Agnew's window, admiring a few paintings; I stood still, watching the pigeons tumbling against the pale blue sky over the church; I breathed the sharp clean wind that was blowing with a fragrance of coffee on it as I passed Parker's restaurant, and then I turned in at the address Sir Harry had given. The address was printed in dark blue, embossed on light blue paper. It wasn't at all the sort of thing you would expect to come from a business office, yet I knew Sir Harry Banfil to be what I vaguely thought of as a businessman. The doorway was between two shops. On the address-board I found what I wanted. "Third floor: Sir Harry Banfil." I noted that there was no one else on the third floor, and also that, while the other floors were occupied by commercial firms that stated their business, here on the third floor was nothing but this: "Sir Harry Banfil."

A lift took me up, and when the liftman opened the gate at the top I found myself not, as I had expected to do, in a passage of scrubbed wood or oil cloth, but in a small room, electrically lit, which was not usual in those days. It was a discreet illumination, too, and I had a sense of something furtive about the whole place, for the floor was covered with a thick black felt, and when the lift had descended, the gate clanging behind me, I moved with a disconcerting silence. In this room there was a secretarial desk with a typewriter upon it and a hardwood chair behind it, and a deep ottoman, upholstered in black with red piping. Nothing else. A door faced me, and on it was a card: "Please ring."

I stood still for a moment, and was aware that not a sound of Manchester's uproar penetrated to this secret antechamber. Then I pressed the bell.

Sir Harry Banfil himself opened the door. "Oh! You're Mr Pentecost, I suppose," he said. "You look very young. Come in."

I stepped into a large room, whose ample windows opened upon St Ann's Square, though we were too high up for me to see, from where I stood, anything of what was happening in the street. "Sit down," Sir Harry commanded. "Some tea will be here in a moment from Parker's."

I sat down, and noted that this large, light room was as silent as the anteroom. The windows were double. I noted, too, that Sir Harry Banfil had a liking for the Mephistophelian colours: red and black. The floor was covered by such heavy black felt as lay upon the anteroom floor. The doors, the window frames, were painted with red lacquer. The furniture was upholstered in red and black. The fireplace was an arch of red brick, and the very fire, burning briskly upon it, carried on the scheme with coal and flame.

The tea came. The tray was placed upon an immense red leather *pouffe* that stood between our chairs. It was for one only. "Don't wait for me," Sir Harry said. "I never eat at this time of day." He poured himself a drink of what I now suppose to have been brandy and lit a cigarette. He sat down facing me with the glass in his hand, one leg thrown over the other. He was a middle-aged man with a dark clean-shaven face and blue-black half-moon pouches under his eyes. His dapper shoes were small. It looked as though he had beautiful feet, and his hands were surprisingly long and fine, perfectly kept, like his clothes.

"Have you been to *Sinbad*?" he asked, referring to the pantomime at one of our theatres. I said that I had not.

"You might go along sometime," he said. "I'd like you to have a look at Iris Randle. Then, if the job appeals to you, perhaps you'd care to paint her portrait for me."

I tried to make it clear that I was not picking and choosing commissions. I was prepared to paint Iris Randle's portrait whether she was as beautiful as an angel or as ugly as sin, though, prudently, I did not put it like that. But Sir Harry Banfil was firm: I must see my sitter first. "And let me give you a piece of advice, Mr Pentecost," he said. "Painting, like everything else, has its business side, and business doesn't come to people who say they can't afford to pick and choose. If you can't pick and choose, you can at least pretend to be in a position to do so. As it is, you've laid yourself open. I could hire you for twopence ha'penny."

I remembered the silly game of bluff I had played with the young students of philosophy, but I did not feel like bluffing Sir Harry Banfil. I was rather afraid of him. I think he was aware of this. He put his brandy-glass down on a small table alongside his chair, leaned forward, and refilled my teacup. He patted my knee. "However," he said with a smile that revealed a sharp dog tooth on the right-hand side of his upper jaw, "don't think I shall take advantage of your youth. If you paint the picture, I shall pay you ten guineas anyway, and as much more as I think it's worth. And I shall *know* what it's worth. Come here and look at this."

I got up and stood with him facing the mantelpiece. "See that?" he said. "That's Cezanne; seen one before?"

I said that I hadn't, and he took me by the shoulders and wheeled me round. "See that? That's a Renoir."

We looked at the picture for a moment, and then he said: "All right, then. I know what I'm talking about. I've seen a bit of your work, so, if you take this commission, you've got yourself to thank, not me. Well, go to the show tonight." He took a wallet from his pocket and extracted two tickets for seats in the stalls. "Take a nice girl with you," he said. "An artist will never get anywhere without a nice girl." A grin bared his dog tooth again. "Be here the same time tomorrow."

I found Sinbad, whom I visited unattended by a nice girl, to be an impudent, attractive and vital young creature, strutting in silk tights, singing naughty and nautical songs, blessed with a voice that would have been nothing if it had not had the power to make even "Pass the salt" sound like an invitation to come to bed. She was a prodigious beckoner and winker, and would toss an invitation with a characteristic sharp twitch of her curly poll. These curls of hers were as black and unshining as ebony; her face was pale, and her eyes, when later I had a chance to look at them closely, I found to be of an intoxicating dark blue. Also, they were enormous. They burned in her head. Her small heart-shaped face was lit up by them.

The next day I told Sir Harry Banfil that I would like to paint the portrait. I said that my studio was at Didsbury, but he would have none of that, "Bring your traps here," he said. Why should Miss Randle traipse out to Didsbury? Look – the light is excellent. I shall be out of your way. I'm going to town tomorrow, and shall not be back for a fortnight. Miss Randle has a key and you can arrange the sittings to suit her convenience."

It sounded to me as though I was in for an exciting and dubious time. Sir Harry shook hands and led me to the lift. As the gate shut he said: "Old Bagley, Iris' dresser, will come to look after her."

Iris had never been painted before, and was annoyed by the method I suggested. She wanted to sit at once on some sort of throne, with me, brushes and palette in hand, slamming into the paint. I insisted on spending a few hours every night for a week in her dressing room at the theatre. I told her to take no notice of me whatever, and she certainly obeyed. She was sulky when she remembered I was there, but fortunately she tended to forget me, and she rushed breathlessly in and out, changing, swigging eggnog, blackguarding old Mother Bagley, I filled a book with swift impressions of her face and with entrancing "captures": the bend of her neck, the thrust of her arms through a garment half-on, half-off, the arch of a foot held out for Mrs Bagley to adjust a shoe. Sometimes she would remember me, pause at the door in her winged flight, turn, and thrust out her tongue. One night I made a drawing of her doing this. I went before she came back from the final curtain and left it on her dressing table, jabbed to a pin cushion. Years afterwards, when I had long forgotten it, it came back into my hands. She had written on it: "Dear Ted drew this." There was heartbreak for me in the inscription. Dear Ted, dear Harry, dear George and Rupert and Henry. Dear Iris! She was a generous woman.

I gave way to Iris on one point. I inspected her wardrobe and found a dress which I asked her to wear for the final painting. She agreed. It was of a light blue silk with a close-fitting bodice, a tight waist, and a skirt that billowed and spread at her feet. As I saw her, she would be seated in a straight-backed antique chair which I knew was in Sir Harry Banfil's apartment. The silk, catching the firelight (though the fire itself would be only suggested, not seen), would spray around her, with one shoe showing as she sat cross-legged. Her arms, coming out of the short puff of the sleeves, would be bare. One hand would rest in her lap; the other would hold a fan of black ostrich feathers, dropping rather tiredly at her side. It was to be a composition in blue and black, with her vivid face to light it up, and a dull-gold screen, embossed with apes, foliage and flying cupids, for background. And that is how it was painted, except, as I say, that Iris insisted on a significant change.

In this Manchester *pied à terre* of Sir Harry Banfil there was, behind the main apartment, a small bedroom and a bathroom. Mrs Bagley and Iris withdrew into the bedroom while I was setting up my easel and preparing my palette. The chair was in place with the screen behind it; the fire was blazing, throwing a satisfactory tremble of light on the spot where I wanted it. My footsteps were muffled as I moved. I could hear the whicker of the little banners of flame tugging upward from the coal. Not a sound came in from the street. Presently, Iris walked in. Ma Bagley was close behind her, full of loquacious protest. "You can't, luv. What'll Sir Harry say?"

Iris seated herself in the chair. "Shut up, Ma," she said, "you make me sick. I know what Sir Harry is paying for if you don't. Not that you don't. You do, you damned old hypocrite. Now," she commanded me, "get on with it."

She had shrugged her shoulders out of the bodice and was nude to the navel. Her body was as white as her face, and her breasts stood out with proud defiance. I knelt at her feet and arranged the folds of the blue dress. She was right. Not only was this what Sir Harry was paying for, but unquestionably this was how Iris Randle should be painted. She was no grand lady. She knew what she meant to men, and she was honest enough to admit it. She was a girl waiting half-undressed in the firelight, and I saw at once how the apes and cupids of the screen could be emphasised to lend their ironic significance. Iris was teaching me my job. As Sir Harry Banfil had said, an artist will never get anywhere without a nice girl.

23

I suppose, if I were a professional writer, I should know more or less how this writing was going to turn out. I should know, for example, how much of Sir Harry Banfil was to be in the book. As it is, looking back over the years, I am putting things down as they recur to my memory, and I shall say something here about Sir Harry lest, later, he disappear, too cloudy a figure. He was a lover of beautiful things. But is that quite right? Perhaps I should say that he loved to possess beautiful things. Most of all, he loved the process of acquiring them. If I say that he was a great artist in acquisition I shall not be far from the mark. When, a long time later, I visited his home in Hertfordshire, I was oppressed by its perfection. Everything was so right, and was so rightly placed, that I felt as I have often done in the presence of women whose beauty was flawless and whose minds were unruffled by thought. I have wanted to say outrageous things to them so as to see whether some authentic emotion, if only of horror or disgust, would disturb for an instant their assured and absurd self-control. So in that house, where not a rose was out of place in a vase, where a petal was brushed up as soon as it fluttered to the floor, where the cushions sat at precise angles and the ornaments were adjusted in unvarying lines, I wanted to commit some such outrage as knocking out my pipe on to the Aubusson or stubbing a cigarette into the basket held by a shepherdess from Meissen.

Going round this museum with me, Sir Harry Banfil showed all the knowledge one could wish of the worth of his possessions, but to every item there was attached some story of how he ran it down "dirt cheap," or beat old So-and-So to it, or duped some innocent owner who had not known its value. This rapacious background of the beauty that surrounded him seemed to him its crown and consummation; and I was not surprised to learn that he had acquired his wife "just at the right moment". He told me the story as he might have told of selling some shares as the bottom began to fall out of the market. "Believe me," he said, "if I'd waited another day Teddy Chalmers would have been there first." This was as we sat over our cigars after dinner. Lady Banfil, a younger daughter of Lord Crowborough, the brewer, had withdrawn. She was the sort of woman to whom I should like to have read some carefully-chosen chapters of Rabelais. They had no children.

It was difficult to discover what Sir Harry Banfil's occupation was, except that he had "interests". One heard people speak of "Sir Harry Banfil's interests in the North" or "of the Banfil interests in Germany", and he moved about a lot, looking after these interests. What concerns me is that he had a real interest in the art of painting, and, true to his tendencies, nothing pleased him more than to find promising painters and to buy their pictures before they were sufficiently established to command high prices. Time after time, in a perambulation of his house, he would pause, look at a picture, and say: "What d'you think I gave for that? A fiver, my boy. You wouldn't believe it, would you? I could sell it tomorrow for three hundred." Or some such comforting remark. The thought of his buyer's flair would make him grin, revealing the dog-tooth.

Like many men whose master bias is towards acquiring wealth, he liked to think that there was in him a streak of Maecenas, and now and then he would arrange an exhibition in London of work by his young discoveries. This would be not for the purpose of selling pictures, but to "give the youngsters a show," and I must admit that it was valuable, because the critics and dealers knew that Sir Harry Banfil did not buy rubbish.

Well, let me come to the point. Sir Harry was pleased with my picture of Iris Randle. He paid me twenty guineas for it, and it appeared, a couple of years later, in one of these exhibitions. Prue

Cleghorn agreed to lend to the same show the portrait I had painted of her uncle; and it was these two pictures that put the success of my career beyond doubt. But all this had not happened by that Sunday night in December when I took Luther Brimlow across the lounge of the hotel and introduced him to Sir Harry Banfil.

"Sir Harry," I said, "may I present Mr Luther Brimlow to you?"

Sir Harry seemed to wonder why I bothered him. "Mr Brimlow has just been appointed to represent the Horace Andrews interests in London," I added.

"Ha," Sir Harry said briskly, getting up and shaking hands with Luther. "Sit down, Mr Brimlow. Sit down. What will you drink? Have you dined?"

I caught Iris' eye, and she gave me a wink that some men would have paid a lot for.

24

She was back in our local pantomime, but our intimacy of the winter before had not been taken up again. I use the word in the sense in which it is absurdly used in newspapers.

"It was alleged that intimacy took place at a Cromer hotel." Intimacy took place! Darling, shall we be intimate? Well . . . !

What happened was this. Ma Bagley – old Mother Baggage, Bags, Bugs, or what not, as Iris chose to call her – was an efficient dragon during the six mornings on which Iris sat for me. On the last morning I said that there was nothing more now for Iris to bother about, but that I needed still to do some work on the picture. I would take it to my studio. "And where is that?" Iris asked. "Never you mind where that is," Ma Bagley said sharply. She was determined to earn the fee which no doubt Sir Harry Banfil was paying her. "You've done all that you need to do, and now let's be going."

"All right, all right," Iris said so angrily that I was aware of a profound perturbation in her, and I assure you that I had got to know and understand her pretty well during that week. I have said that, on the stage, she had an incomparable talent for invitation, and as she followed Mrs Bagley into the bedroom she turned at the door and gave that twitch of the head that had an unmistakable meaning. Let me admit at once that she had fascinated me. And I know now that she had intended to do so. A woman like Iris, with her body on view, needed no instruction concerning a thousand subtle ways of making it an allurement. I had thought her purpose was to mock and humiliate me. Now I knew that it was not. She had left her muff lying in the room, and as she withdrew through the door she pointed at it. I have sometimes wondered how large a part that carelessly-dropped pillar box has played in Iris' career. Anyhow, when she came out of the bedroom, dressed for the street, and picked up the elegant grey fur, decorated with a posy of sweet-smelling violets, my note was inside, and the look she gave me assured me that her fingers had found it.

I have not kept any of Iris' notes. For a woman who made a great success of love affairs, she scattered them with remarkable indiscretion. I remember that the first one to reach me, which came to the studio on the following Saturday morning, announced in her enormous dashing hand: "Ma B. has 'flu. Doc. says will be confined to bed 3 days. Sun. evg. 7 at Sir H.B.'s. I hv. key. Iris."

Her notes – they were never letters – were full of these absurd contractions, as though life was far too short to permit her to spell out a word.

Well, I don't know whether you are acquainted with Sunday evening in Manchester. And this was a winter evening, too. A light fog trailed its miasma through the empty echoing backstreets by which I made my way from St Peter's Square to St Ann's Square. A few prowling cats and dubious couples lurking in doorways were all I found to enliven my mortuary perambulation. In St Ann's Square the fog had thickened, as if it had drained into a lake. Service was going on in the church. Organ music surged out, and the windows were disembodied smudges of pale light hanging upon the darkness. The thought of the people gathered in the church made but the drearier the silence and emptiness of the square. Outside the doorway of Sir Harry Banfil's building I found Iris already waiting, hidden in a great fur coat that was pearled with drops from the condensation of the fog. She did not wait for any gesture on my part, but took me in her arms and kissed me. Her intoxicating smell banished the acrid odour of the night.

I had come to this assignation an inexperienced and innocent boy. I was in a mood both fascinated and frightened, and more than once, walking through those foggy backstreets, fright had almost overcome fascination, so that for two pins I would have turned and fled. But the fascination in the long run was the greater. I had no doubt what Iris' relationship was to Sir Harry Banfil, and there was fascination in that: in the thought of the kind of woman she was; and, too, in the thought of possessing her under the very nose, so to speak, of a rich and powerful owner. There was fascination in the thought that it was she who wanted me, for I had ever shrunk from women rather than sought them, doubtful of their reaction, unwilling to believe that I had anything to offer. But the primary fascination was Iris herself: her sheer magnetic vitality, which I had seen flaunting itself spotlighted before a thousand hungry eyes, stimulating, provoking, and at the same time – denying. So I fumbled my way through the dark Sunday evening streets, my knees uncertain and my mind in a turmoil, a most pitiful and perplexed lover, harassed by indecision about what he should say, what he should do. He had no precedents, that boy I was.

I need not have worried. Iris kissed me hungrily. Her frantic vitality took charge of everything, and I hung in her arms, with the blood thudding in my ears, and the organ music sounding odd and remote as though it were somewhere up in the air over waves that had submerged me.

Presently she let me go and said with a light laugh: "What do I call you, Edward Pentecost? Will Ted do?"

"Yes," I said, "if you like."

It was a shocking answer, and she looked at me narrowly with her enormous eyes. But she did not say: "Why, you poor child – what's the matter with you?" as she well might have done. If she had not been Iris. There was nothing motherly or compassionate about Iris. She said: "We've made a mess of things, Ted. We didn't remember that this front door would be locked. The place is a tomb. The only key I have is to Harry's flat, and we can't get in."

Again I was visited by a surge of feeling in which relief and frustration were mingled. Chance had come to help me: I could go. Yes, I could go, and toss all night on a sleepless bed, living over and over the moment when Iris kissed me.

"We could get a cab," I said. "We could go to my studio."

And that is what we did. When we got to The Pines, we stole like conspirators round the far side of the circular lawn, so that the noise of our feet on the gravel should not be heard in the house. We climbed the stairway on tiptoe, and when we were inside with the door locked, I drew the heavy curtains and lit a single candle. I was trembling so that I could hardly find the wick with the match. But Iris was experienced in putting such matters right.

25

I should be treating Iris Randle unfairly and ungenerously if from what I have written I allowed it to be supposed that she had seduced me. Any hesitation on my part was the consequence not of reluctance but only of inexperience. Sir Harry Banfil's interests kept him away from Manchester far longer than he had expected, and in the few weeks that were ours we met from time to time, and established the state of affairs which now, as I presented Luther Brimlow to Sir Harry, permitted me to understand all the implications of the wink which she flashed at me. It was not an invitation: it was an acknowledgement of past comradeship, not a suggestion of present delights.

Luther assured Sir Harry Banfil that he had dined, but he did not refuse another drink. More Armagnac appeared, and Harry Banfil took it that I was joining the party. I found a glass in front of me, and raised it to my lips when Sir Harry said: "Well, chin-chin, Brimlow. I'm glad to meet you."

And now, indeed, more than a little of phantasmagoria began to cloud the evening. I was no drinker, and already I had drunk what, for me, was a lot. The day had been altogether too exciting. Luther Brimlow's return, in a guise almost as incredible as that of Saul who went out chasing asses and came back a king; our truancy together while my father was opening his pitiful Bethel; the narrative Luther had poured into my ears: all this had powerfully affected my imagination, building up a romantic background against which, with an increasing vagrancy and undulation, waiters passed and hands appeared, pouring drink into glasses, putting down plates, striking matches, tapping cigarettes on thumbs.

A novelist friend once told me that when he is a little tight he sees things and people as they truly are, both in their physical appearance and their mental attributes, and has himself a tendency to say the things that are deepest in his heart; but when the fumes have cleared he cannot believe that things were either as good or as bad as he saw them.

So, now, I myself began to see things I had not seen before. I saw that Sir Harry Banfil's eyes were as hard and steady as a serpent's, black as onyx. I saw how aware he was of Luther Brimlow's intense awareness of Iris Randle, and how Iris knew herself to be the focus about which both these men's thoughts were glancing. And as she smiled now at the one and now at the other, I felt no twinge of jealousy and was happy in the conviction that Iris Randle was something I could take or leave with no heartbreak on her part or mine. I saw, too, that Luther Brimlow was as formidable a man as his story was intended to make me believe. I had had nothing against which to measure his story, so that its truth might be assayed; but now, watching him and Sir Harry Banfil, listening to their conversation, some of which might have been in terms of Euclid for all it meant to me, seeing their wariness of one another and attempts to influence one another: I knew that Luther was Sir Harry's match and that those two dreary old fowls the Brimlows had bred a cockatrice.

No one, after the first moments, spoke to me. I enjoyed an extraordinary sense of freedom and insight, as if I were sitting outside a bubble that floated before me, with those three enclosed within it, all their master motives painted in the nude.

This all dissolved and I came back to actuality – or should I say returned to mere appearance? – when a waiter began mopping with a napkin the drink I had spilled from an overturned glass. I was saying that I was sorry. I was apologising to everyone, especially to some strangers who had just come in. Sir Harry Banfil was laughing, dog-toothed, and dropping money on to a waiter's tray. "Well, then," he said to Luther, "that's understood. We travel to town together. The early train tomorrow morning." He turned to Iris and pulled her ear lightly. "Be a good girl while I'm away."

"Yes," she said. "While you're away I like a change." He could take that how he pleased. She was gathering up muff, handkerchief, all the impedimenta that always seemed to scatter about her. Between that and getting into a cab with Luther I was aware of nothing except trying to ascend a revolving door as if it a were a treadmill. All the way to our house in Hulme Luther said nothing. He had taken from his pocket the thin book in which, during teatime, he had calculated my father's waste expenditure on the tabernacle. Now from time to time he tapped his teeth with his gold-cased pencil, from time to time made a note. Arrived at our door, he got first from the cab, in full control of himself. He helped me out and then gave the cabman the address of the Brimlows' house in Didsbury. "I won't come in," he said briefly. "My people must have gone hours ago. It's eleven o'clock." He got back into the cab and it was driven away.

26

At our house in Didsbury I had owned a key and had come and gone as I pleased. I often let myself in when my father and mother were in bed; and had I been able to do this now all would have been well. But there was only one key to the door of the new house, and that was my father's.

My father had had to wait up for me, and when he came to the door he was already in an unhappy mood. My appearance did nothing to cheer him up, and I cannot blame him for that. The blame for what followed was as much mine as his. Perhaps I was the more to blame.

I did not then know what wretchedness he had already endured that night: a wretchedness two fold, for not only had the opening of the meeting room been farcical, thus mortifying his human spirit; but also he was in the mood, cast down from exaltation, which saw the affair as a chastisement from his Maker. He had made his offering, and God, he was at that moment convinced, had rejected it. Only thus was he able, then, to interpret the happenings of that evening.

I was not so drunk that I did not know what I was doing. My mind was alert enough, but my body was not under control. I lurched through the opened door and, when inside, took hold of the hatstand to steady myself. Looking at me sagging there, Father was filled with a sudden fury, for it was a drunken man who had debased him in the meeting room, and here was a drunken man delivered into his hands.

I had often heard him speak of the souls he had turned to the truth in Hulme, the sheaves he had gathered, the jewels in his crown, the brands he had plucked from the burning. There was no end to the figures of speech with which he lit up his accounts of these happenings. But if all these adherents had been swept together, they would have made a sparse showing in his meeting room, and by no means all of them came. Translating this situation, as was his custom, into the words that were "given him to say," he spoke from the text:

"Where two or three are gathered together in my name, there am I in the midst." They were hardly more than two or three, my mother told me. Including the four who had crossed the road from our house, eleven people assisted at that opening service. One of these was a young woman named Ruth Martin, of whom I had often heard as the brightest jewel in my father's crown. It was she who was accustomed to ask him in, during his trudging with tracts through the streets, to refresh himself with a cup of tea. They seem to have spent many happy hours together, arguing doctrinal points, reading the Word and praying. He was, I suppose, justified in looking upon Ruth as a jewel, for she was undoubtedly a reformed character. She was but twenty years old, and had been married for a year to a young navvy from Northern Ireland who liked Saturday night to be Saturday night, and it was not Saturday night to him unless he and his handsome young wife finished their pub-crawl as drunk as lords. My father changed all that. Nothing that Jack Martin now did was good in the sight of Ruth, and so he drank morosely and alone, and Saturday nights ended, as a matter of routine, with him roaring, and she pleading, and the buckle-end of his belt walloping her. Jack Martin had never met my father, but doubtless in the young navvy's mind there had grown up an image of a monster who perverted the thoughts of a man's wife, ruined a man's nuptial bliss, and poisoned the very springs of hops and barley. This fabricated monster increasingly oppressed Jack Martin's imagination, till he knew that peace would not come back to him unless he destroyed it. The opening of the new meeting room gave him the occasion he was seeking.

Ruth came to the meeting alone. The whole affair must have been lugubrious and depressing with that handful scattered about a building that would have held two hundred, but it was gone through with, and the congregation was singing:

> At the Cross, at the Cross
> Where I first saw the light . . .

when Jack Martin arrived, uproariously drunk. He joined in the hymn as he came rolling down the aisle, fitting his own words to the tune:

> At the Cross, at the Cross,
> I was playing pitch and toss.

This caused a good deal of confusion. Some were horrified. Some laughed loudly. But my father kept his wits. When the hymn was finished and Jack Martin sat down, waiting for another opening, my father began a harangue founded on Jack's profane words. The interrupter, he said, was perhaps not aware that at the foot of the Cross evil men had indeed played pitch and toss. And he went on to tell the story of the Roman soldiers dicing for the clothes of the man hanging crucified above them. He must have told the story impressively, for there was silence as he spoke, and even Jack Martin was subdued enough to wait for the end. Then he shouted: "I wouldn't do nothing like that. Don't you go blackening me, Mister."

"My young friend," said my father, "you are a sinner, and to be a sinner is to crucify Christ daily."

"You shut yer trap. I'm no more a sinner than wot you are. You been fillin' my wife's 'ead with them ideas. Wot the 'ell's a man to do with a woman who thinks 'e's a sinner?"

"You can come to the Christ who saved her," my father answered, and Mr Brimlow supported him. "Yes, my young brother, you can come over the line."

"You shut up, you beer-eyed spaniel," Jack Martin shouted. "I'm not arguing with you. I'm arguing with him. Wot's 'e turned my wife against me for?"

The small audience was now thoroughly excited. Some tried to push Jack Martin down in his seat. Some shouted: "Throw him out!" and some were frankly enjoying the row.

"Sister Martin," my father cried, "has not turned to me. She has turned to Christ. 'And I, if I be lifted up, will draw all men unto me.' I do nothing but humbly lift up my Master, as the fiery serpent was lifted up in the wilderness."

The fact that hands had been laid upon him infuriated Jack Martin. He shook off those about him like a dog shaking off water drops. He was fourteen stone of bone and muscle, ruddy, curly-haired and handsome. He glowered like a young bull, and then he charged. Clearly, he had reached the point where he saw that to bandy words would be to be worsted. He had no brains, so he used what he had, a fighting physique. He rushed down the aisle towards the small flimsy rostrum behind which my father stood and crashed into it like a rock hurled from an ancient ballista. The rostrum splintered. It, my father, and Jack Martin were mixed in a mad thrashing tangle on the floor. Mrs Brimlow seized the umbrella that Luther had looked on so scornfully and banged Jack Martin on the head. She might as well have flailed granite with straw. The few men in the audience tried ineffectually to intervene. Some of the women screamed. Ruth Martin prayed. Edith of the budding breasts, more intelligent than the rest, ran out and called in a policeman. He attempted to take Jack Martin into custody, but that fighting cock, inflamed by drink and an ancient cherished rancour, fought like a madman. With his helmet crushed under foot, his face bleeding, and an eye swelling, the policeman ran out of the meeting room and set his whistle shrilling through the dank Hulme air. Reinforcements arrived, and presently, handcuffed, fighting still, and glaring about him with blue bewildered eyes, Jack was half-led and half-carried by three policemen to the local lock up.

Most of the small congregation followed the policemen, so that nothing of the occasion should be missed, and then no one was left in the strange recovered silence of the meeting room save my father and mother, Mr and Mrs Brimlow, and Ruth Martin. They stood, panting heavily, around the wreckage of the rostrum; and suddenly Ruth Martin turned upon my father with her eyes flaming. "Damn you! Damn you! You interfering old sod!" she shouted, and ran out of the room calling: "Jack! Jack! I'm coming! Ruth's coming!"

27

This, then, unknown to me, was the emotional background of my father's mind as I stood there at eleven that night, swaying before him and holding on to the hatstand. I saw only that he looked tired. He passed his hand wearily across his eyes and said quietly: "Come in here. I want to talk to you." The door of the sitting room was open. The lamp was lit and the fire burning. I went in before him and fell rather heavily into a chair. He stood upon the hearth and looked down upon me. "I suppose," he said, "a drunkard finds it comforting to be seated?"

"Father," I said, "I'm sorry I've come home like this. I've been stupid. I've certainly drunk too much. But to call me a drunkard is nonsense. I'm no more a drunkard than you are."

With his left hand holding his right elbow, he kept on drawing his right hand down his face, as if trying to pull off a mask of utter weariness. I was by now fully alive to his look of sorrow and dejection. "Why don't you go to bed?" I said. "Is Mother gone?"

"Yes. I am glad to say that she is. It would have hurt her to see the consequences of the licence she allows you."

"Licence?" I cried, nettled. "What licence does she allow me? The only licence I make use of is the licence to work. And I work hard. I work harder than you do."

"Do not be impertinent," he said, sharply. "And don't shout. I have foolishly permitted you for years to go your own way. I see now that I was wrong in doing so, and God has punished me, God has humiliated me, God has rejected me. I have toiled here and I have toiled there. I have laboured in every part of the vineyard except on my own vine. My children reject Christ, and I stand by like a coward, watching them drive the nails into his hands and press the thorns upon his brow."

I never knew what to say to him when he was in this mood. I began weakly: "Father – please –" but he stopped me with a voice raised almost hysterically. "It must end! God has cast me out tonight. He has turned His face from me, for how can our Father in Heaven show His countenance to an earthly father so weak and sinful as I? My son, I must pray with you. Get down on your knees."

I remained sitting where I was, and suddenly his face was disfigured by a most human anger. He seized me by the coat collar, pulled me out of the chair, and sent me sprawling to the floor at his feet. "Are you incapable of getting up, you drunken young sot?" he shouted. "Then I shall help you."

I was sickened with disgust: disgust of myself and of him. I got on to my knees, with my hands on the carpet, and in this dog-like attitude was aware that he was down beside me. He was kneeling, with his hands convulsively twisting, his face upraised. He began to pray.

I could stand it no more. "Shut up!" I shouted. But still the fervent stream of petition flowed out of him, and froth edged his lips. "Shut up!" I repeated. "Shut up, will you!"

He went on praying, and so I tried to rise to my feet to go out of the room. But I was unsteady; I fell against him, and toppled him over. For the second time that night he was sprawling on the floor, at grips with a drunken man. This time he intended to be the master. He leapt up with surprising lightness and ran into the passage. He snatched his blackthorn stick from the stand, and by the time I was on my feet he was returning with this weapon firmly gripped. The sight of it sobered me completely. To consider it merely as a weapon was sobering enough. It was tough and weathered, garnished with knots where twigs had been pared away. But there was more to it than that. In that horrified moment of clarity, the old stick seemed the very symbol of all that had once been free and happy between us. This was the Whittington wand on which he had been accustomed to place his basket, sling it over his shoulder, and walk out of the garden gate with a joke upon his lips. It called to my mind opal autumn mornings in Didsbury, and Blanche and Betsy Comfort, and the small boy shouting: "Say it again, Daddy!" as some infantile jest sweetened the moment of parting: a small boy who could think of nothing lovelier in God's world than to have a stick like that, a basket like that, and to walk forever at his father's side.

And now here was this stick, here was this father, and sundering us I could almost literally see the dark river of estrangement and misunderstanding; and I knew that once that stick was laid upon my back all was over between us, forever. I stood upright, unable to make so much as a gesture of resistance, even of evasion. It was as though some such thought assailed him, too; for he came to a sudden stand within the door, the hand that held the stick fell limply to his side, and the other hand was drawn with that weary gesture down his face. We looked at one another for a moment; then he said in a reasonable voice, as if I would surely understand what he was about to do: "Ted, it is God's will that I should chastise you. If Abraham could lay his beloved son Isaac upon the altar . . ."

"Very well," I said.

He moved behind me suddenly, and the blow fell, and it was all over. I did not resist or cry out. I actually bowed my shoulders, and, once he had broken the spell that was upon his own mind, he struck again and again. I counted the blows. There were fifteen. Once when I was a child he had struck me in a sharp anger with a bedroom slipper. I counted then, and when he had done I said: "You sloshed me seven times, Dad," and we both laughed. I always remembered those seven blows to the body, and I always laughed. I knew now that I should always remember these fifteen blows to my heart and that they would be no laughing matter.

When he had done, he said: "You'd better get to bed. I shall stay here. I shall pray for you. Don't disturb your mother."

I went up to my room and packed a portmanteau. I heard him come up about an hour later, and I heard my mother's drowsy voice saying a few words to him. I lay on my bed fully dressed, sick in body and soul. My back throbbed. My stomach heaved. I was lucky enough before long to fall asleep. It was six o'clock and pitch dark when I awoke. There was nothing to do then but pick up the bag and walk out of the house. I was soon at London Road station, where I took an early breakfast in the refreshment room and felt better. My shoulders still ached, bruised and inflamed, but my mind was clear and easy. I took the first train to Falmouth.

CHAPTER FIVE

I T WAS on a fine June day in 1909, when I was twenty years old, that I married Prue Cleghorn at the parish church in Falmouth. Blanche was bridesmaid, and Uncle Kitto gave away the bride, for dear Prue had no man of her own family to perform the office for her. Kitto's servant Opie was my best man, and great-aunt Sapphira came into the vestry afterwards and signed the register. When it was over, we all ate a meal together in Kitto's studio. The table was drawn up to one of the great windows that looked upon the harbour. It was a drowsy day of midsummer heat and mist, so that the ships seemed insubstantial and the outline of St Mawes Castle across the water was little more than a tender smudge. After the meal, Sapphira and Blanche went up to Primrose Hill to change out of their wedding finery. They were catching a train to London that afternoon, and from there they were going to Paris, Venice, God knows where. They were eternally gallivanting about the Continent. Sapphira's coach would take me and Prue to Tresco Vean, which had been lent us for the honeymoon. Blanche looked very lovely and very rich. I wondered when she herself would be marrying. But I could not ask her anything about that. I did not feel close to her. The mellow ivory satin of her dress, crackling like five-pound notes as she moved, was unexpected at the ceremony which I had hoped would be simple. Prue's white muslin looked as if it didn't matter at all; as if an arm might crush it and nothing be the worse for that. Anyhow, she made no bones about it but came eagerly into my arms as soon as the coach was beyond the streets of Falmouth.

"Dear Ted," she said. "It was a lovely wedding."

"Happy?"

"I'm afraid to wake up."

189

"But you're wide awake *now*, darling. All this is real. Understand that? – *real*. Those round things out there with the tails sticking out of them are the buttocks of Aunt Sapphira's horses. This box that smells like the inside of a dustbin is Aunt Sapphira's coach. This is the road to Mawnan Smith. That is a hedge, and that oblong animal with knobs at the corner is a cow. All real."

"I don't believe it," she said. "We're being whirled through space on Pegasus."

"Not on your life, you late Miss Cleghorn. We're being whirled to bed by two most earthly horses. They seem to me to be damnably slow."

<h2 style="text-align:center">2</h2>

I hadn't stayed continuously in Falmouth since that winter morning when I had climbed into the train with my shoulders smarting. My flight from Manchester was an instinctive gesture of revolt, and the gesture having been made, I went back. I suppose I always shall go back to some great town or another. It is not only that a portrait painter needs to be where people are, though there is that, too. But I am not happy away from the stir and bustle of men. The love of it was born in my bones, and that is all there is to it. Roots in the soil; the virtue of mother earth; man made the town but God made the country: I know all about that, and I'm not prepared to make it a matter of philosophy. It's just that I like towns. Even the shabby disgraceful London of today – and I am writing in 1946 – a London which its own inhabitants began to strip of felicity long before German bombs helped the process: even this gives me a serenity I could never find in the country. Even a barbarous city like Manchester would be my choice if it had to be, permanently, that or the Cotswolds.

I remained in Falmouth for a year, and in the course of that time I learned a lot from my Uncle Kitto. I rented one room in a house on the terraces overlooking the harbour and I lived close to the bone. That I lived at all was thanks to Kitto who persuaded Sapphira to allow me to paint her portrait. The old woman was kind enough to me, and I think that was because she knew I had broken with my father. She never mentioned him or questioned me about my departure from Manchester but she showed a wish to cherish me, and that was something new. I lived at Tresco Vean for a fortnight while I was painting the portrait, and when it was done – with full justice to her wonderfully-ringed hands and to the parrot in his golden pagoda – she paid me fifty guineas for it, which was the most I had ever, then, received for a picture. I think this generosity was part of her campaign to attach a Pentecost to the Kitto interest. However, I packed up my traps and went back to my room in Falmouth. I saw little more of her during that year, or of Blanche.

"You don't mind, Ted, if Blanche is present during the sittings?" Sapphira asked at the beginning. "I must be read to."

I did not mind, and all through that fortnight Blanche was in the background, reading from French novels. I had had at that time no opportunity to learn French myself; and have always made heavy weather of speaking the language; so that I could not say whether Blanche read well or ill; but I judged that she read well, for she read ripplingly in a voice that pleased me. From time to time Sapphira would interrupt her, speaking in French, and they would have a conversation that was unintelligible to me. To my annoyance, they sometimes did this even at other times, when there was no question of instinctively continuing to speak in the language which Blanche had been reading. This gave me the feeling of being an outsider, of being treated like a child from whom secrets are deliberately withheld, of a tract of life common to those two but within which I had no footing.

One morning when Sapphira said: "That will do now, thank you, Ted" – for it was always she who decided when a sitting should end – I said to Blanche: "Your chattering away like that in French reminds me. I recently met an old friend of ours – Luther Brimlow."

I could at once have fallen through the floor, for as soon as I had spoken there flashed through my mind the circumstances in which Blanche had last seen Luther – circumstances which, I was sure, she would not wish to have recalled. It was simply of the boy next door that I had been thinking, and now I was sorry that I had spoken. I wondered how much Miss Sapphira had ever heard or might have guessed of Luther, for when Blanche had first been sent to Tresco Vean it was on the pretext of a breakdown in health caused by the climate of Manchester. Now Sapphira said: "Luther Brimlow? And who might that be?" and Blanche answered, with full self-possession: "Oh, he was a boy who used to live next door to us in Didsbury. Rather a horror.

Why my speaking French should call him to Ted's mind passes my comprehension."

"It wouldn't if you saw him now," I answered. "He lived in Paris for a long time and speaks the lingo like a native."

Nothing more was said about it at the time, but that afternoon when Blanche was mounted and ready to ride she called me, and I strolled along at her horse's side as she walked him down the long avenue leading from the house to the road. She was riding side-saddle, as women did then, and was beautifully habited. She wore a bowler hat and held an ivory handled crop in her gloved hand. For a time she said nothing, then, looking straight ahead, she suddenly asked "What is he like now – Luther Brimlow?"

"Terrifying," I said, meaning it.

"He always terrified me," she answered. "I was like a rabbit with a stoat when he was about. He fascinated me."

"You didn't like him?" I asked, amazed.

"Like him? Good heavens! What's liking got to do with fascination?"

She laughed, as if reminiscently. We had come to the gate, and I opened it for her. She saluted me with her crop, kicked the horse's barrel, and cantered away. She made a gallant figure between the hedgerows that were purple with foxgloves.

3

I had written at once to my mother on reaching Falmouth. How much my father had told her of what happened the night before I fled I do not know, and I took care not to lay it on. I merely said that he and I had had a sharp dispute which made it clear that we were better apart, and that accordingly I had gone. She, too, did not refer to the beating when she wrote, though I learned afterwards that she knew all about it. She simply said that she was not surprised and wished me luck. Thereafter we wrote to one another regularly, and it was one of her letters that brought me back. She sent me a cutting from the *Manchester Guardian* which reported an accident to Captain Marquick. He had gone in for one of the new-fangled motorcars, and this had scared a horse drawing a lorry loaded with bolts of Manchester cotton. There had been a bad smash up and the captain was now at The Pines with grave injuries to the head. He recovered and lived for many a day. I mention the matter only because it was this that sent me running back to Manchester. It was not Captain Marquick who died but Professor Cleghorn.

For some reason or another which I cannot remember I made that journey home by night, so that my truancy ended, as it had begun, in the refreshment room on London Road station in the grisly hours of a winter morning. I bought a copy of the *Manchester Guardian* from the sleepy youth who was pulling down the shutters of the bookstall and opened it as I sat over my coffee and eggs and bacon. There it was: Sudden Death of Professor Jesse Cleghorn.

How was it that in that moment I knew, with the unmistakable stab of certainty, that I loved Prue Cleghorn? It was to her, not him, that my thoughts instantly turned. We had met, as I have said, only infrequently and by chance since the night when the students gave the old man the portrait I had painted. A few words in the street, a conversation in a bus, once, but only once, quite a long talk when by accident we ran into one another leaving the Prince's Theatre where Henry Irving had been playing in *The Bells*. We walked together all the way to Withington. We were both exalted by the genius of what we had seen. It was a frosty night suited to our mood, with stars crackling in the black sky. We talked as youngsters will about things that can never be understood: what genius was, how it worked, how it conveyed its impression. She could give me more than I gave her, for she had the advantage of having lived years with Jesse Cleghorn's mind, but really we didn't get anywhere except into a liking for one another that was deeper than anything we had touched before. When we reached Withington she shyly asked me into the house, saying that her uncle would have finished his work for the day and would like nothing better than to sit up half the night talking. But I didn't go in. For one thing, I was a little scared by Jesse Cleghorn. He was a man immeasurably beyond my mental range. I don't mean only then, but at any time. He could talk to the youngest child and the most awkward youth without giving any impression of being more than a kindly and likeable person; but, for myself, I had always the sense of what he truly was behind these agreeable externals, and I felt rather like a pebble conversing with the ocean. And, too, there was the long walk back to Hulme. So we parted there, and I feel that if we hadn't, if I had stepped over the threshold, we might have continued in this new and deeper understanding and I might never have seen Iris

Randle again. But there it was. I said goodbye and did not after that
see Prue before leaving Manchester a year later.

This was on a Monday night, and it chanced to be the very night
after I had taken Iris for the first time to the studio. That was another
reason why I did not improve this occasion with Prue. The affair with
Iris, so impetuous and unexpected, had knocked me off my feet into
a whirl of feeling which left no room for anything else. As I walked
back to Hulme I thought with a temperate pleasure of Prue's
companionship. I had had next to nothing to do with women. It was
agreeable to find that one of them could talk so sensibly – even with
a warm enthusiasm – about the things nearest my heart. But I thought
also of Iris Randle and how she had said the night before: "You darling!
Do you know how lovely it is to do this for someone who doesn't pay
you?"

4

I think that what finally fused my heart and Prue's was a phrase I read
in the *Manchester Guardian* as I sat there in that dead and desolate hour
of the morning with my breakfast congealing before me on the cold
marble table and the sickly gaslights buzzing. Professor Cleghorn had
died in his sleep, which I hope will be my happy fortune, too, when
the time comes. He had gone to bed at midnight. "At eight o'clock,"
the newspaper said, "his niece, Miss Prudence Cleghorn, who had
kept house for him for some years, took a cup of tea to his bedroom,
as was her custom, and found that he was dead."

Do you know, Prue, that it was just these simple words that opened
my eyes; opened them literally, so that I saw you lay down the cup of
tea, draw back the curtains upon the lugubrious Manchester morning,
and then, taking up the tea again, turn to the bed. And there he was,
the man who, I gathered now from these words I was reading, was
greater even than I had known or guessed. Here were the tributes,
from universities and learned societies, from men whose names were
known and reverenced throughout the world. They called him master.
And here was the record of the books he had written, of the range of
his thoughts into heights and depths, and there was he, lying on the
bed with his head perhaps fallen to one side, all surmise and
speculation done with; and it is not him that I see, it is not his
greatness in life or majesty in death that moves my heart. It is you,

standing in the flat winter morning light with a cup of tea in your hand.

5

I never spoke to my father again after that night when he thrashed me with the blackthorn stick. When I left the railway station it was not with the intention of going to the house in Hulme. I was not worrying over-much now about Captain Marquick whose accident had called me from Cornwall, for the *Manchester Guardian* assured me that he was "progressing favourably and was out of danger." My first concern, therefore, was to find cheap lodgings, and I remembered a jibing phrase Blanche had used the first time I was at Tresco Vean. "Can you imagine me in rooms in Ackers Street?" I couldn't.

It was not a prepossessing street. Just beyond the University, it ran off the main road. Most of the houses were rookeries of cheap rooms where theatrical birds of passage alighted for a night or two and then were gone. I had no difficulty in finding accommodation there. I knocked at the door of the first house I came to showing a fly-blown card "Rooms to let," and there I hired a bed-sitting room on the first floor. It was a small back room floored with cracked oil cloth, furnished with an iron double bed, a rickety chest of drawers and washstand, a small table under the window, a chair with a broken leg precariously splinted with a piece of packing case, and nothing else. Beyond the window the desolation of the winter morning dripped upon the sour soil of a row of backyards.

In the afternoon I went to see my mother, trusting that my father's habits would be unchanged and that he would be out distributing his tracts. He was. Mother received me without much emotion. She did not even kiss me. Her life in Hulme had not improved her looks. She was pale and worn, and that did not surprise me. What surprised me was that she had, as they say, let herself go. It was nothing much. Her hair was a little untidy. Her hands were neglected. The room we sat in lacked that final and inescapable air of cleanliness that had been the seal of her Lancashire housewife's pride. I thought of the polish of the furniture, the glitter of the brass and silver, in our old Didsbury house, and of the flowers that somehow managed to appear even during the dark winter months. We ate an early tea together, so that I could go before my father returned, and that gave me the greatest surprise of all, for we ate shop bread.

"Why, Mother," I cried, "are you *buying* bread now?" and I recalled the major operation of bread-making in the old days: the warm smell of the dough rising in the big red earthenware pan before the kitchen fire, the sweet taste as teeth broke through the new brown crust.

"I can't do everything," she answered shortly. "Don't forget, I'm the burnt offering to the Lord."

She said it without bitterness, even with a trace of humour, but I could see that she felt keenly the situation in which my father's frenzy had placed her. She was without any domestic help. She had lost both her children. She must endure, alone, the prayers and readings of the Word that daily went on, and the solemn discussions of visiting Brethren, and the services in the meeting room across the road.

"Did you ever hear of Aaron?" she asked. "There's a hymn they sometimes sing over the way:

> 'You can be like faithful Aaron,
> Holding up the prophet's hands.'

There was a fight going on, and for some reason which I don't understand the Israelites could keep it going only as long as Moses held up his hands. He got a bit tired of it, poor old lad, and so Aaron got hold of his hands and kept them up. Well, that's me. I have every sympathy with Aaron. I think he was pretty tired, too, before the day was out."

She got up and began to clear away the tea things. I went into the scullery and washed as she dried. "Mother," I said amid the rattle of the crockery, "would you like me to come back? I shouldn't mind. I'd put up with it."

"Don't talk daft," she answered sharply. "What sense would there be in throwing away all I've done for you? Don't forget, he's not the only Moses. Your hands have got to be held up, too. It all means a bit of overtime for Aaron, but I can put up with it."

She was smiling now as she played with this fancy of hers and developed it, and it came to me that of late she hadn't had much to smile about.

"How's Blanche?" she asked, wiping her red forearms on the roller-towel behind the door.

"A perfect lady," I said lightly, and suddenly the difference between Blanche's lot and my mother's came over me in a burst of illumination so sharp that I was appalled. I thought of Blanche as I had seen her tit-tupping daintily down the road, curled like a luxurious cat on a sofa with a yellow-backed French book in her hand, strolling in the garden at Tresco Vean, snipping the dead roses from the bushes.

"She doesn't write to me," my mother said. "I'm no great shakes at writing myself, come to that. When you see her, give her my love."

6

They were committing to the earth one of the great spirits of our time, a man whose thoughts had been of an immensity I can never hope to understand, but all the same this rude gash in the ground was as harsh and bleak and uncompromising as if it were a pit for any rubbish. In the church, a service was going on, but I did not attend it. I waited there by the grave, and looked at the names on the stones that surrounded it, names of no renown, among which his would bloom illustriously. The rain was falling in torrents, making channels in the piled-up clay, sending a score of pigmy waterfalls dancing over the edge, and occasionally carrying down a little rush of earth and pebbles. I remembered being told that when the tomb was put over William Morris' grave someone said: "It will be a roof for the old man," and I wished that all this were done with, that the old man had his roof, and that we could leave him quietly there in his dark house.

They were coming now from the church, and I stood aside, with my overcoat collar hunched up under my ears, to catch a glimpse of Prue. That was what I had come for, not for the dead but for the living. I was filled with an absurd presumption, as though I alone stood between her and the misery of the occasion, as though my presence could blind her eyes to the finality of that ripped earth, as though she had but to see me to fly to me forever.

She was not there. The parson came, sending the immemorial words of the committal service flying out through the veil of rain that an umbrella, held over his head by a boy, dropped round him like a curtain made of frail glass cylinders. Behind him trudged men in black, all with black, glistening, cascading umbrellas, save those who carried the coffin, and on the coffin's lid the rain, redoubling its fury at this moment, danced in innumerable fountains with a pelting sound that could be clearly heard. The men whose business it was to lower the coffin into the grave took a careful grip with their feet upon the clay, churned almost to pottery-slip. The wet ropes slid through their hands, and a sense of haste filled the moment. It was almost as though the elements were out to receive an elemental. It needed only fire to complete the picture. As it was, air, earth and water were in spate, and the clay was carried down with no need for a spade. Wet gobbets plunged into the hole after the coffin.

Prue was not there, and I was glad she was not there. I remained for a time when everyone else had gone squelching away save the men who were now tumbling the sodden earth into the hole. The death announcement in the *Manchester Guardian* had said: "No flowers." But, lying upon the ground under the full fury of the rain, waiting to be placed on the mound when it should be completed, was an untimely bunch of pale blue hyacinths, tied with white ribbon threaded through a card. I walked to it and bent down to read what had been written. "Au revoir, Prue."

Au revoir! Who but Prue would have written that! I walked away wondering with what hope she fortified her heart in this dreadful hour.

7

I did not take any steps towards meeting Prue. In the course of my life I have taken few conscious active steps towards doing anything except getting on with my work, and I did that only because it was the one thing I wanted to do. I have gone through life with the very real feeling that this was the kingdom I must seek, and that, if I gave to it all that I had, then whatever else was added to me, little or much, would be all that I needed. There was much that I wanted, but I have always had the sense to know that my wants were one thing and my needs another.

So now each morning I left my frowsty room in Ackers Street, took my breakfast at a cheap eating house near the university, and then walked to the studio at The Pines. Sometimes I worked there; sometimes I didn't; but I was always there so that I could work if work demanded to be done. I would first call at the house and have a few words with Captain Marquick, who was now well enough for this, but not for anything more. One morning, as I arrived, I found Anatole Lop leaving the house. He explained that he had been saying goodbye to the captain, for he was "severing his connection," as he put it, with Manchester. The fact was, as I learned afterwards, that Anatole's volatile wife had finally severed her connection with him. Till now, she had been content to make her lovers incidental, and, infatuated with her as he was, Anatole had accepted the situation. But at last what he had long feared had happened: some lover had been powerful enough to detach her completely and she was vanished without trace. And so Anatole was going. He had taken the job of music master at a boys' school in Yorkshire. I never saw him after that morning, but then we spent some hours together that I would not call happy, but that I am glad to have experienced. They were too reminiscent for happiness. In the studio I made coffee, and the old man smoked his pipe and talked: of his childhood in Alsace where his father had been overseer in a vineyard, of the disruption of his life as a music student in Paris by the war of 1870, of his flight to England and his life there. "I've been happy in England, Ted," he said. "I was very happily married – you didn't know I was married, did you?"

"No, Anatole," I lied.

"She's dead now," he said. "Well, I had that. I'm not complaining. I had that, and I had some lovely times with the captain and your father. Of course, it all went wrong, as you know, poor boy, to your sorrow. I wish it had gone a bit better for Blanche, How is she?"

I told him, and he shook his head. "It sounds well," he said, "but it's not good enough for Blanche. You know, Ted, while you've been away I've been round once or twice to see your father in Hulme. This mania for saving souls – I can understand it. I felt like it about Blanche. Of course, it's selfish in a way. But when you're getting old, d'you know the loveliest thing that can happen to you is this: to find someone young and beautiful and to have a hand in helping her to become everything she could be – as a writer, a dancer – anything you like – to feel her as a sort of late bloom on your own tree; and to know that she – well, you can't expect love, can you? – you're lucky if you feel that she likes you a bit."

Dear Anatole! I know that in your way you loved her. I hope that you will not be too unhappy; but I fear that you will, and that little

wanton boys will mock your reverend skeleton and give you anything
but love.

8

It was my custom at that time to buy a few sandwiches at the eating
house where I breakfasted and to have these for my lunch at the
studio. Then in the afternoon I would walk for a couple of hours. That
day when I had said goodbye to Anatole I walked through Northenden
and Baguley to Cheadle and back along the main Wilmslow Road to
the Cock at Didbury. It was not an inspiriting walk, for it was through
sodden fields and under the dripping winter trees. It was a walk full
of a sense of loss and loneliness, of a pause and halting place in my life,
and when I came to the double doors of the builder's yard with the
name Jonas Brimlow painted upon them I could not help thinking of
the days when the Brimlows had been nothing to us but comic
enemies, simultaneously disliked and derided. Something in the
appearance of the door made me halt. It was its brightness that caught
my eye. It had always been dull and down-at-heel. Now the name in
new white paint twinkled upon a field of fresh green. The wicket
opening through the big doors was ajar, and I thrust my head inside.
The disorder that I had known there was gone. Nothing was to be seen
that could be called junk. Everything was neat and well arranged.
Yellow planks were stretched under a lean-to. There were mounds of
bricks and tiles, gutters and window sashes, crates of glass, rolls of
sheet lead: everything that a builder's merchant could require, and all
in apple-pie order. The dilapidated shack that had served as an office
was gone, and in its place was an attractive brick building, with the
chimney smoking cosily and a telephone wire attesting such "modern
conveniences" as Mr Brimlow had never dreamed of.

As I took in all this, a young man stepped out of the office and saw
me there. He came to the wicket and asked politely if there was
anything he could do for me.

"No," I said, stepping into the yard. "Forgive me for sticking my
nose in. I used to know Luther Brimlow, and I wondered if he was
about."

200

"No," said the young man, "he's in London. We don't see him here once in a blue moon, but you never know when he'll appear, so we're always on the top line."

His eyes twinkled as if to suggest: "You know what a sharp 'un Mr Luther Brimlow is."

He led me into the office, invited me to sit in a comfortable leather chair near the fire, and gave me a cigarette. I looked about at this place so different from the shack in which I had had my terrifying interview with Mr Jonas Brimlow. Everything was tip-top, modern, efficient. Nothing was superfluous. No notice assured the visitor: "Thou God seest me."

"Look at these steel filing cabinets," said the young man proudly. "The latest. Sent from America."

He seemed glad of company and busied himself at a gas ring in a small tiled cubbyhole opening off the main room. He placed a cup of tea and biscuits on a table near my chair, as affable as if I were about to order material for a hundred houses.

"I thought this was Mr Jonas Brimlow's business," I said. "I see his name's still on the door."

Well," he answered, "it is and it isn't. Mr Luther put me in to reorganise it. The old man only looks in now and then to sign cheques and so forth. And even that's something new to him. Believe it or not, he did all his affairs in cash till we took over. Of course, all the profits are his. Mr Luther laughs at this place, even as it is now. It's not so much as chicken feed to him. He just does it for the sake of the old man, and I suppose because he can't bear to see any business run badly."

"I'm not surprised at that," I said. "He seemed wide awake when I last saw him."

"Wide awake! Believe me, he never sleeps. It's lucky for me he bothers with his father's affairs at all, because it's given me a chance, I can tell you. The profits this year are already doubled, and Mr Luther has challenged me to make this the biggest thing of its sort in Manchester within five years. That's what he's like. 'Get it done,' he says, 'or you can get out.' By this time next year I reckon there'll be a clerk and an office boy as well as myself. What I'm aiming at is to get this place on its feet and then be invited by Mr Luther to work for him in London."

Yes; he seemed a keen and go-ahead young man. I wished him luck and told him not to bother to let Mr Brimlow know that I had called. I continued my walk by strolling along our old street. The dusk was coming down, and as I passed the Brimlows' house I saw, the curtains not being drawn and the gas lit, Mr Brimlow sitting in an easy chair by the fire reading the newspaper and Mrs Brimlow pointing to a table at his side where a maid in cap and apron was putting down a tea tray. Then I was past the house, but the brief glimpse was burned into my mind. I thought of my mother's arms reddened by labour, and it seemed to me an agreeable thing when a prodigal son not only returned but brought his own fatted calves with him.

I walked back to the studio and found there a letter that had come by the afternoon delivery. It was from Sir Harry Banfil telling me that he was arranging an exhibition of paintings by his "young discoveries." He added: "I shall show your portrait of Miss Randle. If you have one other painting that you would like to exhibit, I shall be pleased to show that, too, if I think it of the standard required."

I made up my mind to call in the morning upon Prue and ask her to lend me the portrait of Jesse Cleghorn.

9

It was now about three weeks since the funeral of the professor, and so it seemed to me that I might, without appearing intrusive, call upon Prue. After breakfast the next morning I walked out to Withington. To reach the house where Cleghorn had lived, you turned to the left just before coming to the bottleneck of the old village street, and then you turned right into the quiet byway where the house stood. I was making this right turn when a four-wheeler cab, with luggage piled on the roof came out of the byway, and before it went past me I had time to see Prue Cleghorn sitting back in a corner with her eyes closed. In a moment she was gone. I watched the cab till it turned into the main road and headed for town, then, with no object now, I strolled slowly on towards the house where she had lived. It was as dead as the professor. The curtains were down from the windows and I could look straight through into the empty front room where straw and shavings and crumpled paper made a desolate disarray. In the window was a newly-hung notice: This House to Let.

So she was gone. The cab was headed towards the centre of the town and thus towards the railway stations, and the luggage piled on top spoke of a journey. Whither? I did not know. Prue had said that her relatives in the Lake District were dead, and whether she had any others I had not been told. I turned away from the house feeling as desolate as its own empty rooms and blind windows. Prue was gone. Anatole was gone. The captain was too ill to be a companion. My father might as well be dead, and to visit my mother was to risk an unwanted encounter with him. In all Manchester there seemed no one to turn to; and as I told myself this I remembered that there was Iris Randle. The thought of Iris went to my head like fire. For the first time I wanted her: her sparkling life and impudent gaiety, the almost frenzied vitality that she could pour into the dull void of this moment. If she wanted to. If she wanted to see me at all.

Well, I would find out. Only a few nights ago I had seen her strutting and winking and beckoning on the stage, her silken tights flashing, her great hungry eyes black in her pallid face, a devastating version of Jack the Giant Killer, and certainly apt to kill the Giant Despair who now oppressed me. I had sent a note to her dressing room and been bidden to see her, and had listened to her racy abuse of Sir Harry Banfil, who had found another mistress. I hadn't stayed long, but she had kissed me hungrily, and taken my face in her two long bony hands, and gazed into my eyes. There was something hypnotic in her stare, as though she had the power to suck you down willy-nilly into whirlpools. But she contented herself with pushing me from her, slapping me lightly on the cheek, and saying: "Go home now, little boy, before I eat you," and I had been glad to go.

I knew that, when in Manchester, she always stayed in that hotel where, a year ago, I had made Luther Brimlow and Sir Harry Banfil known to one another. I went there now in great haste, wrote a note, and sent it up, asking her to have lunch with me. Presently the telephone rang at the reception desk and the clerk there said to me: "Will you go up, sir, to room 705?"

The lift shot me up, and when it had descended I found myself gazing down such a long, hushed and somehow sinister corridor as one might walk endlessly and silently in a dream. Silently indeed I walked along it, my footsteps muffled by the mossy carpet, and the only light fell from a shaded electric lamp here and there. Now my brazen confidence was gone and I dawdled towards the door I was seeking and knocked timorously. She called to me to come in, and I entered, shutting the door behind me. The room was warm and full of her perfume. The curtains had not been drawn back from the windows, and an electric table-lamp by the bed made a gentle glow. I stood just within the room looking at Iris, who was sitting up in bed.

"Well," she said, "this is a nice time to disturb a girl. It's only half-past eleven."

"Iris —" I began huskily.

"So you want me to lunch with you," she broke in. "Lock the door. We'll talk about lunch later."

10

It was nearly one o'clock when I woke. I had slept soundly, but towards the end of my sleeping I dreamed. I was gazing down a long red-carpeted corridor, and at the end of it was a four-wheeler cab piled with luggage. I ran after it, but it turned the corner, and when I reached the corner I passed to another corridor like the first, and the cab was disappearing once more. I ran and ran, down corridor after corridor, gradually drawing nearer to it, and slowly the cab itself changed into a coach of glass. Inside it I could see Prue Cleghorn, dressed in all the splendour of Cinderella at the ball. She leaned out and waved to me to run quicker, but Iris Randle, wearing tights and a silver-buttoned coat, sat on the coachman's box, whipping up the horses. Finally, I turned a corner and ran full tilt into the pair of them, sitting on a pumpkin. Professor Cleghorn, wearing academic dress, was standing by with my portrait of him under his arm. He asked me which girl I really wanted, and I answered idiotically: "Priris." Then he pulled my picture from under his arm, raised it aloft like a butcher's cleaver, and cut the pumpkin into two. A coffin was inside. The professor lifted the lid, sat down in the coffin, raised his velvet doctor's hat courteously and said: "Au revoir." He then lay down at full length and pulled the lid shut. The pumpkin closed round it, and Iris said: "Well, I suppose that's that." "Yes," said Prue, "and no hard feelings." Between them, they rolled the pumpkin away down the corridor, and torrents of rain began to fall.

The splashing rain woke me. I sat up dazed in the perfumed dimly-lighted room. The sound of splashing was coming through an open door. It was the door of a bathroom, and Iris was in the bath, singing heartily. I got out of bed and strolled into the bathroom and looked down at her soaping herself vigorously. "Gosh!" she said. "I feel the better for that!" She gave me a *gamine's* impudent grin. She was always like that: silent and intense in passion, and then relaxed into gay and irresponsible chatter. "You'd better have a bath when I've done," she said, "and then be off."

"What about lunch?" I asked.

"Nothing doing," she answered. "I'm fixed up."

11

When I reached the studio the next morning a large flat parcel, addressed to me, was leaning against the leg of my drawing table. Opening it, I found inside the portrait of Jesse Cleghorn and a letter from Prue.

> Dear Mr Pentecost, – Will you do me a great kindness? You have, of course, seen from the newspapers that my uncle is dead. This leaves me without relatives and (though this has nothing to do with you) without money, or, at any rate, with no more than will see me through a few months. I haven't yet decided what I shall do, and indeed I'm not sure that there will be much deciding about it. Chance will have to take me in hand and find me work of some sort. I have given my uncle's books to the university library and have sold the furniture in the house, and now I am going to stay for a while with a friend in Keswick. Your beautiful picture of my uncle is one of the few things I want to keep, but I shall find it a rather embarrassing possession until I have some place to settle down in. And so the kindness I ask is that you should look after it for me for the time being. It would not be a nuisance hanging on your studio wall? Perhaps it would even occasionally remind you of him and me. I should like to think that it was so. But don't hesitate to say if you can't do this, and I'll put it in store.

The letter ended with her address in Keswick and told me that she was mine sincerely.

I sat down at the table with the letter propped up before me, examining minutely the small carefully-rounded letters of her writing, as clear as a printed page, but rather formal, unrevealing, almost "copybook" in character. It told me nothing that would amplify the phrases on which my imagination seized: "Perhaps it would even occasionally remind you of him and me. I should like to think that it was so."

I wrote at once to Keswick, making my letter as formal as hers, and a few days later received her permission to show the picture in London. I decided that I would go myself and take the picture with me. I had not yet been to London. Blanche and Miss Kitto were there. Harry Banfil was there, and Luther Brimlow was there. Perhaps it was time that I too was in this place that seemed to draw all men to it.

12

Luther Brimlow said: "Listen to me, young Pentecost. Years ago you painted a hawthorn tree. Remember? I believe it was the first thing you ever succeeded in showing. It was pretty good, but a bit on the small side. You hated me for saying that, didn't you?"

I nodded and inhaled the rich aroma of my visitor's cigar. He made the room seem shabbier than it was, and God knows it was shabby enough. It was little better than my room in Ackers Street, Manchester, but it was in London. The traffic roared by and the day was dun and forbidding, but it was in London. I had looked for a room as soon as I alighted at Euston, and I had found this on the Euston Road. I couldn't sleep at night for the noise, and I was living on slops and scraps, but I was in London, and I was happy. I had been to Bond Street and seen my two pictures in Sir Harry Banfil's show. I had spent hours wandering round the National Gallery and the Tate and the Wallace Collection. I had seen semitic-looking bearded Edward driving down the Mall with his queen at his side, her head tight with ringlets, her throat banded with pearls. I had leaned over the Embankment in the daytime and mingled with the West End crowds in the dusky lamplit night, and come back to this noisy dingy lair, feeling happier than any man had a right to be.

And then one afternoon I had seen the hansom stop, as I dawdled idly at the window, and there was Luther Brimlow climbing out of it wearing a frock coat and top hat and carrying his elegant cane.

"Harry Banfil asked me to see his little show," he explained, "and I got your address from him. So here you are, in London at last. Well, well."

He seemed amused by me, and I hated him for it, and he began talking about the picture of the hawthorn tree, which made me hate him the more, for it recalled that humiliating moment when he had walked away with Blanche.

"You've learned better," he went on. "You've learned where the money is, Ted. You stick to portraits, and stick to London. D'you know anything about Rembrandt?"

Coming from Luther Brimlow this seemed to me a facer. "Well, do you?" he persisted. "Have you ever seen his picture called the Board of the Clothmakers' Guild?"

I said that I had seen reproductions of it.

"Well, that's something. I've seen the original in the State Museum in Amsterdam."

Amsterdam! Where hadn't he been?

"The point is this, young Pentecost. There you have not one portrait but six, and a starchy-looking lot of Plymouth Brethren they are, too, come to that. But Rembrandt knew his stuff. He got in with the commercial people – that is, the people with the money. Well, I'm offering you your life's chance to do the same thing."

Suddenly it seemed as though the place he was sitting in struck for the first time upon his imagination. He got up, abruptly. "Look," he said. "This is important. Let's go somewhere to talk about it."

I followed him into the street and he stopped a passing hansom with a wave of his stick. We drove to the Palladian Club in Pall Mall. An attendant greeted him with the right mixture of familiarity and deference, took his hat and stick and my shabby bowler. Luther led me to a nook where leather chairs were hospitable in front of a fire, and an admiral, painted by Sir Joshua Reynolds, looked down upon us. Tea and muffins came silently. "Now," said Luther. "Let's get down to it. Harry Banfil and I are both agreed, and I think we can carry the others with us."

The others, I gathered, were fellow members with Sir Harry Banfil and Luther Brimlow on the board of Consolidated Textiles. This was a newly-formed company, with headquarters in London, and it had been in the first place Sir Harry's idea that in the large panel over the fireplace in what I gathered was a palatial boardroom there should be painted the members of the board. He and Luther Brimlow had discussed the matter while walking round Sir Harry's exhibition in Bond Street, and the presence of my pictures there had suggested my name.

"And don't think you're the only pebble on the beach, young Pentecost," Luther said, lighting a cigarette. "Sir Harry's in touch with a lot of young painters, and believe me I had to work to persuade him to think of you. But I owe you that much for introducing me to him. Not that it wouldn't have come sooner or later," he added complacently.

I was dumbfounded. It was such a commission as I could not have expected to get for years. I babbled my thanks.

"Hold hard – hold hard!" Luther laughed. "The job's not yours yet. There are four other people to be persuaded, and I dare say they've all got their own ideas. However, we've made a start. By the way, Ted, you'd never guess whom I saw the other night."

"No," I said. "Who was it?

"Blanche!"

He refilled the teacups, and added after a moment: "I could hardly believe it at first. She looked stunning. She was dining with a dry-looking old duck at a restaurant I sometimes go to."

"That would be her great-aunt," I said.

"I had no idea she was in London."

"Well, I don't suppose she'll be here long. They're everywhere, those two."

"I'd like to meet her again, Ted, now that she and I have both grown up. What kids we were!"

Yes, indeed! And what a kid I felt still, confronted either by Blanche or Luther! Looking at him now, I could by no manner of means think myself back into the old derisory relationship in which he had once stood to me. He was my patron! That fact alone overcame me with incongruity. Luther Brimlow my patron! To get the conversation on to ground where I might be more level with him, I told him of my recent visit to Didsbury and of my talk with the bright young man in his father's office.

"He's all right for what he's there to do," Luther said briefly.

"He's ambitious," I told Luther. "He wants to come and work for you in London some day."

"Well, he might at that," Luther answered. "I've got him pretty well weighed up and there might be a corner for him. But he'll never amount to much. A five-hundred-a-year man. That's the most he'll ever come to."

Luther laughed heartily at the notion of anyone who called himself ambitious ending up at five hundred a year.

13

I had come to London with no intention of staying there. Of course, I had for a long time told myself, I should set up in London one of these days. But this had always been said with that consoling absence of a time limit with which a sinner tells himself that he will turn to grace or a beggar that his ship will come home.

Now, all of a sudden, the thing became practical. It happened like this. There had been excellent notices in the newspapers of Sir Harry Banfil's show, and I was encouraged and Sir Harry impressed by the way in which my two pictures were chosen for special comment. There was luck in this. Professor Cleghorn had been dead only for a short time, so that he was, as they say, still news, and here was a portrait of him that had not been seen before. Naturally, the critics turned some attention upon the picture of so notable a man, and my work thus gained perhaps in interest over some of the rest. Moreover, I was myself unknown in London, and Sir Harry had been clever enough to feed the critics with stories of my youth. So, what with one thing and another, there it was: the famous sitter, the hitherto unknown painter, the "infant prodigy". From the professor, attention went on to Iris Randle, though in the catalogue she was not mentioned by name. "Woman in fireshine" was the designation; and I felt that Sir Harry would not have shown this intimate picture at all if he had not now done with Iris.

However, all this was not helping me to live, except with a buoyant life of the spirit, an exaltation which made those first days in London so crystal and coldly glittering and free of dross that, winter though the season was, I recall it as though it were tender-leafed and virginal. I was doing no work. I was merely and bountifully *being*, asking for the moment nothing better than to exult and taste and see. One morning

I took my coffee in a cheap eating house and then turned from Piccadilly into Bond Street. Then, I thought I could never tire of walking up and down that street's magic length, gazing into the windows of the picture dealers and the sellers of furniture and porcelain and jewels and lovely clothes. I had recently taken to smoking a pipe, and as it happened it was into a tobacconist's window that I was looking that morning, receiving a lesson in how a humble vice could be elevated to the status of a luxurious and costly art. Luminous briars, whose price would have kept me in tobacco for a year, pigskin pouches, cigars like torpedoes, tobacco jars of rich wood and porcelain, cigarette boxes of gold and silver, plain, chased, enamelled or engraved, even matchboxes with intricate monograms upon their precious metal: it all made up a vision of the recondite and superfluous that held me fascinated till a sharp blow upon the shoulder brought me back to the winter street and the thin sunlight that filled it. I swung round and confronted my great-aunt Sapphira, whose umbrella had conferred the accolade. She had just alighted from a cab. "I thought it was you," she said, "and happily it is, or I should be prosecuted for assault." She looked at the window that had held me. "Rubbish," she said. "Sherlock Holmes kept his tobacco in an old slipper, and you can do the same."

She expressed no surprise at seeing me there, though I had not let her or Blanche know that I was in London. I had heard from Blanche just before leaving Manchester and knew that they were staying at Brown's Hotel in Albemarle Street, which was always Sapphira's London headquarters.

"Wait here," Sapphira said. "You are not fit to come into a ladies' shop. I have called to collect Blanche. She is trying on some clothes."

She marched into a shop next door to the tobacconist's, and I waited for three-quarters of an hour. When she came out, she said: "Good gracious! Are you still here? Well now, you can show us these precious pictures of yours. We've been reading about them in the newspapers."

Blanche said: "Oh, Ted! I'm so glad! You're famous!" and Sapphira, eyeing me up and down, reproved her: "Don't talk nonsense, child. Famous! Look at him!" But there was a twinkle in her eye, as there was apt to be when she had a Pentecost to herself.

I was glad to cross the road with them to the gallery, for it would have taken a lot to tire me of looking at the pictures that Sir Harry Banfil had assembled there. Thinking back upon it now, I am still compelled to admire his *flair*, for of the young men whose work was shown with mine half a dozen are among our finest artists today.

The window was of that discreet luxury which Bond Street knows so well how to use. It was floored with daffodil-yellow carpet and backed with a half-circle curtain of pale ancient green velvet. In this select *enclave* was an easel, and on the easel was my picture of Iris Randle. There was nothing else in the window.

I had not known that this had happened. When last I had looked at the window, a Cotswold landscape by Adrian Woodrow stood upon the easel. I felt my throat contract and my hands go clammy. There I was, picked out and isolated in the eyes of all men in one of the half-dozen most famous streets in the world. I felt as though the gaze of every saunterer was upon me, and my knees went weak. Thus, I imagine, some modern dramatist might feel when for the first time, flaring across the façade of a famous theatre, he sees his name in lights.

We all three came to a stand in front of the window, and I could not speak. It was Blanche who broke the silence. She saw the signature and cried: "Oh, Ted! It's yours." She impulsively put her arms about my neck and kissed me, there in the street. Sapphira poked her with the ferrule of her umbrella, "That will do! That will do!" she said; and added after a moment: "H'm! An impudent baggage if ever I saw one."

I scarcely heard her, and I scarcely saw the impudent baggage on the easel. What I was seeing was a Manchester street, and me, when I was Marquick and Marquand's office boy, released for the dinnertime and munching a sandwich as I stood, with Blanche at my side, gazing into Agnew's window. How godlike, how unapproachable, had seemed the Real Artists whose works we looked on then! And now –!

Well, now it still seemed a dream rather than reality. I could only say to Blanche, as casually as my dry lips could frame the words: "Remember Agnew's?"

She gave me a look which showed that she remembered Agnew's and that she understood what I was feeling in that moment. This made me happy as we pushed open the door and entered the gallery.

14

Sir Harry Banfil came to the gallery while we were there, and I introduced him to Miss Sapphira Kitto and my sister Blanche.

"Sir Harry Banfil? Sir Harry Banfil?" said Sapphira, searching her memory. "Aren't you chairman of Consolidated Textiles?"

Sir Harry said that he was.

"I thought as much. I've got some money in it."

"I congratulate you, Miss Kitto," said Sir Harry.

"H'm! We'll talk about that later. Mind you behave yourself."

"Luther Brimlow also is on the board of Consolidated Textiles," I said to Blanche.

"Brimlow? Brimlow?" said Sapphira, who had a great capacity for storing names in her memory. "Where have I heard that name? Weren't you and Blanche speaking of him at Tresco Vean? Who is this Luther Brimlow?"

Sir Harry said with a smile: "We don't quite know yet, Miss Kitto. The years will tell. At the moment he's a young man who thinks that some day he will buy me out, lock, stock and barrel."

"Oh, a clever young man, is he? Mind he doesn't play the fool with my money, Sir Harry."

"I shall be on the spot," Sir Harry promised. "I'll look after you."

He was in a charming mood. "I've got some good news for your brother," he said, turning to smile upon Blanche. "Brimlow has already talked to him, I believe, about the possibility of a good commission coming his way. Well, it's all fixed. Yes," he added, laying his long thin hand on my shoulder, "the job's yours, Mr Pentecost. Where will you work?"

I hadn't thought of it. I had had, as I have said, no intention of staying in London. And now here it was.

"But – but I've got *nowhere* to work," I stammered.

"Then you had better let me help you," said Sir Harry. "Look. This man." He pointed to Adrian Woodrow's picture. "He's finished. He doesn't know it, poor devil, but he's finished. He's got a very nice studio in Chelsea, but, for himself, he's gone off to Capri. Consumptive. He thinks he'll recover there, but he won't. I know, because his doctor told me so. I've been looking after Adrian. He was a promising man. I did what I could for him – doctors and what not – but it's no good. He's asked me to let his studio for a year or two, till he comes back. But he won't come back. So you'd better have a look at the place. Here's the address."

Masterfully, in this offhand way, Sir Harry disposed of my future.

"I can't afford a London studio," I objected.

"Young man," he said, "you had better start learning what are the things you can't afford *not* to have."

15

Sapphira took me back with her to Brown's for lunch. Afterwards, she said to Blanche: "Amuse yourself for half an hour, child. I wish to speak to Edward alone."

This sounded serious. Putting together all the odd times I had spent in Sapphira's company, they didn't amount to much, but they had been enough to teach me that when she called me Edward she had something important to say. We went up to her bedroom, and she said: "Now light your pipe if you want to, though I'd rather you didn't, and listen to what I have to say. Sit there."

I left my pipe in my pocket and sat in the easy chair she had pointed out. She sat down on a straight-backed wooden chair facing me.

"I'm going to talk about money," she said, "which is the most important thing in the world after land. So don't interrupt me. You look disgraceful. I'm almost ashamed to bring you into this hotel. It's time you took yourself in hand. And you can. You were not born to be a pauper."

Her heavily-ringed hands were lying in her lap, and she considered them for a moment before going on.

"I don't know how much your father has permitted you to know about your own family, and when I say that, I remember that you're a Kitto as well as a Pentecost."

A Sowler, too, I thought, a proper mix-up; but I knew that my mother was less than nothing to Miss Sapphira.

"I expect," she said, "you know precious little about your grandmother, who was my sister. We were twins, but I had the luck to give the first howl. I was half an hour older than she was, and when our father died that turned out to be important, because his will, which he had made before we were born, and which he never altered, laid it down that almost everything he had was to go to his eldest son, and that, if he had no son, his estate was to be divided between his daughters. But not equally."

We were interrupted by the arrival of a waiter, bringing the coffee she had ordered to be served in the bedroom, and when he was gone, she said: "We're a queer lot, we Kittos, as I expect your father has told you often enough. For generations we've ruled the roost in our parts, and we've dutifully gone to church and sagely nodded our heads every time the parson read: 'Woe unto them that join house to house, that lay field to field.' We've thought how rightly that applied to everybody who wanted to buy or sneak half an acre from us. But we never sold land – not a solitary rod, pole or perch. And that was why my father left the greater part of everything to his eldest daughter. She would be a catch – something to tempt some worthy man to settle down with her and go on in the way of the Kittos. He was even to change his name. It was all laid down: whoever married me would have to become a Kitto.

"Do you find that funny?" she shot at me suddenly. I said hastily that I didn't. "I should think not," she said, wagging her old head. "Pour me some coffee. Black."

I did so, and she raised the tiny cup to her lips in that strange hand of hers, glittering with precious stones.

"I don't want to talk about myself," she said. "I want to talk about my sister, your father's mother. She was as mad about money as any Kitto of the lot. Her share was smaller than mine, but she was a well-to-do woman, and she made a will that concerns you, which is the only reason why I'm talking to you now. It's time you learned about these things.

"The one thing the people in my family can't bear is to think that a time will come when their descendants will be nobodies. That is to say poor. It's the same thing with us. And so we try to legislate for the future. We go in for entail and so forth, if you know what I mean. I suppose my sister thought that her children would be all right. They would grow up under her own care. Being a proper Kitto, it was succeeding generations that she thought of: which means, as it happens, you and Blanche."

As I knew, my grandmother, after all, did not see her sons grow up. She met that tragic end at sea with her Pentecost lover, and when her will was read, I now learned, it was found that my father and my

Uncle Kitto were to have five thousand pounds each when they came of age, and that all the rest of her money was to be tied up in a trust fund to accumulate for the benefit of her sons' children, who would all, on reaching the age of twenty-one, become equal sharers.

"What your father did with his five thousand I don't know, and I don't care," said Sapphira; and I was glad to be able to break into the monologue and enlighten her. A lot of it, I said, had gone on buying a little Manchester shop which he had lately sold at a great profit and invested the money.

"Well," said Sapphira, "that's the first sensible thing I ever heard of his doing, but it's rather late in the day for him to start. Your Uncle Kitto spent a lot of his on that ridiculous chapel place that he lives in. However, let them be, and think of yourselves for a moment. What it comes to is that there'll be twenty thousand pounds, more or less, to be divided between you and Blanche in a few years' time. That's not a lot, but if you have it in decent investments it should bring you in ten pounds a week each."

She paused for a moment, then said abruptly: "Just get up now, Edward, and look at yourself in that mirror."

I did so, rather sheepishly, and she said: "Honestly, do you think you're fit to look at?"

Well, I thought, people seem to think my pictures are, anyway, and that's the main thing; but I did not say this to her. I said jokingly: "I've seen more prepossessing specimens."

"Take yourself in hand," she said. "I don't know what you, or Kitto for that matter, get out of this painting business. It's not what I would have chosen for you, but I was never asked. However, your uncle at least sets you the example of not looking like a dustman's son dressed in the day's finds in dustbins. If you are to associate with people like Sir Harry Banfil and his Mr Luther Brimlow, or for that matter with me and Blanche, you owe yourself a little attention."

I knew that the old girl was doing her best to be kind. She was speaking to me for my good, and I was not offended.

"You must take this studio we have heard of," she said. "Of course you'll need money. Now this is the point of everything I've been saying. You must be seventeen years old. In about four years' time you will have ten pounds a week, and mind you do that. Don't fool about and fritter away the capital. To be independent is to be cock of your own dunghill, however small it is. And never forget it was a Kitto who made you so. I expect your father has already forgotten it was a Kitto who gave him his shop, and consequently everything he has now. Well, I'm rambling from the point again. I could do this for you: I could see the lawyers who are concerned with this money and arrange that for the next four years you should have five pounds a week. If then, when you are twenty-one, you continue for another four years to draw only five pounds instead of ten, you will be straight. Do you grasp that?"

She spoke as earnestly as if I were a dull child having its first lesson in the mystery of money, which I saw obsessed her. I assured her that I grasped the point, and that I would be grateful if she would make the arrangements she had suggested.

"All right, then," she said. "I think that's all. With what you make as a painter, you should manage to get along. But live within your means and find a rich wife." She said this quite gravely. She opened her reticule and took out two five-pound notes. "Buy yourself some clothes," she said. "And don't forget: a man like Sir Harry Banfil can be more than your patron as a painter. You might get some good financial tips out of him. Well, God bless you, boy. I'm glad you're doing well. Kiss me."

I kissed her cheek, and said: "Thank you. And thank you for all you've done for Blanche."

She waved her ringed hand that seemed almost too heavy to lift. "Don't talk nonsense," she said. "Have you ever thought what Blanche has done for me? Well, now, I shall get into my bed. I don't mind lying, and I don't mind sitting, but I hate lolling. Ask Blanche to excuse me this afternoon. Get a cab and take her to see this studio."

16

Manchester, after this, was no longer my home. I went back from time to time, but less and less often; and when my father and mother were dead years would pass between one visit and another. But I did not know the cut was to be so clean and complete when I took my place in the Manchester train the day after Blanche and I had visited the studio.

It was Blanche's idea that the cab should set us down by the riverside at Chelsea and that we should walk about and savour the district before approaching a place that might mean so much, one way or the other. It was three o'clock when we got out of the cab, and, the day being grey and overcast, there was already a premonition of night as we walked the damp pavements and looked upon the darkling water. It was a long time since we had been alone together, away from the influence of Miss Kitto. I said this to Blanche. At Tresco Vean or in Falmouth there had always been the sense of the old woman's presence, of her wealth, of everything proceeding out of her bounty or caprice.

"I'm surprised she has permitted us to be out of her sight," I said.

Blanche laughed. "I think," she said, "she knows that I'm safe. She's snatched my soul from the burning, as Father would say. She's converted me from being a Pentecost and made me wholly Kitto. Praise Sapphira from whom all blessings flow; praise her, all creatures here below. Isn't that it? Well, I *don't* mind."

"Don't you ever want to see Father and Mother again?" I asked.

She did not answer for a moment, and then she said: "I think that's an unfair question. What has wanting to do with it? Will wanting give me back the father I knew? If you mean the father I have now, I don't want him. You've told me enough of what he's like. Well, I don't want that. And even if I could go back to what we used to know – the concerts and the dancing, and – oh, all the *fun* and *joy* of it – well, what's the good of asking me that now? You can't go back, and that's the long and the short of it."

We walked on in silence for a moment, and then she said with feeling: "For goodness' sake don't be sanctimonious about it. You've left him yourself. What difference does it make that your lodgings are only five minutes' walk from his house? You've left him as decidedly as I have. What does the *distance* of it mean? Nothing. You know that as well as I do."

Yes, I knew that, and there was no answer I could make. "But Mother –?" I insisted gently.

"Oh, God!" cried Blanche, "do you have to rub it in? D'you think I don't see her a thousand times climbing through that window and crying at the foot of the stairs? But what can I do about it? I'm a kept woman – don't you understand that? – and kept women do as they're told."

I was sorry I had started it; but, for the comfort of my own soul, I had to go on. I had to wrest one more answer from her.

"That's a horrible thing to say," I protested. "And it would be true only if you remained with Sapphira because of what you can get out of her. I don't believe you do. It may have seemed like that once. But I don't think it's true now."

"No. It's not true now, Ted," she said more gently. "I'm glad you believe that. I've always feared that you despised me."

"You fool. Why should I?"

"There's been reason enough."

"Let me tell you something. This afternoon I thanked Sapphira for what she had done for you, and she answered: 'Do you ever think what Blanche has done for me?' "

Blanche stopped in her tracks and looked at me with a smile lighting her face. "She said that?"

"Those very words."

"I'm so glad. So glad, Ted." She put her arm through mine, and snuggled warmly to me. "Now, before it gets dark, let's find this studio."

17

We were looking for a place with the delicious name of King's Mistress Yard, and it did not take us long to reach it. You turned into a street off the Chelsea Embankment and found, not far along it, an opening into a small space roughly rectangular. This is King's Mistress Yard. There are three small houses on the right, and on the left there are two small houses and the pub called the King's Mistress, carrying a portrait of Nell Gwynn for its sign. She was a rather dingy Nell that night when Blanche and I first looked into the yard. Years later I gave the old house a new one, using Iris Randle in her prime as my model. There was a legend that the pub stood on the site of a private house at which Nell used to meet a lover. Certainly, it was a discreet little yard, and as we stood there a lamplighter was touching his flame-tipped rod to its only gaslamp. The light fell charmingly upon the bare branches of a noble plane tree which stood amid the cobblestones and drew their patterns upon the white wall of the house that filled in the third side of the square.

The upper rooms of this house were to be my home for many years. It was a two-storeyed place whose flat white façade was enlivened by light green paint at doors and windows. Sir Harry Banfil had given me a key, and it was with a considerable flutter of the heart that I opened the door on the extreme right of the house. This led to a stairway giving private access to the upper rooms. There was a good-sized studio whose window looked into the branches of the plane tree, through which now the cosy lights of the King's Mistress began to glow. This studio occupied the whole front of the floor. Behind it was a small bedroom, a small kitchen, and a box of a place that contained a bath.

Blanche and I lit the gas in every room and wandered, enchanted, through the small domain. I could not believe that, even with five pounds a week added to what I might earn, I could afford the place. But it turned out that I needed to have no anxiety on that score. It was a close scrape for a time, but time passes.

When we came out into the yard it was too late to think of looking up the agent. "Leave it to me," Blanche said. "I'll see the agent tomorrow. You get back to Manchester and clear up your affairs. And give my love to Mother," she added.

18

Clearing up my affairs sounded a grand process, but it involved little more than telling my landlady in Ackers Street that I should be gone in a few days and saying goodbye to my mother and Captain Marquick. I arrived in Manchester on a Wednesday evening. The next day I frittered away in sentimental journeys to Didsbury and Northenden, in visiting the art gallery in Mosley Street, in seeing at night the show in which Iris Randle was appearing. I did not call on her. I had no desire whatever for her company that night. But when I got back to Ackers Street I wrote a letter giving her my address in London. I had no doubt at all that the studio in King's Mistress Yard would be mine. And it was. A letter came from Blanche the next morning: her customary letter which seemed like the condensation of a précis:

> Dear Ted, – All fixed now with the agent in Chelsea. You can go in there any time. Sapphira is pleased to think you are going to settle down and make a lot of money like a good Kitto. Except Kittos don't make money. They just lay two sovereigns together and let them breed. You should have heard her and Luther

Brimlow discussing the stock market! What an extraordinary person he has become! Well, we move off any moment – our plans indefinite. Florence to begin with, so don't know when we'll be seeing you again – or Luther Brimlow for that matter. But Sapphira has promised to let him know where we are.

All love,

Blanche:

So they had met Luther Brimlow. But what a damnable unrevealing letter it was! How? Where? When? It left me frustrated and fuming. I didn't want them to meet Luther Brimlow, but what had it to do with me? And yet – the little runt, hopping on one leg up and down the garden path, chanting his hymns and glowering from behind his pebble glasses! But it was no good trying to bluff myself like that. This was not the person Blanche had now met, and I knew it. She had met someone whom I felt to be both powerful and dangerous; and between her and him there had once been something of whose depth and extent I had no knowledge, something which might, for all I knew, have left a smoulder that could again be fanned. I was tempted to intervene. What did she know of Luther Brimlow? What ought she to know? She had left us, to make that first journey to Tresco Vean, before we heard the story of those forged letters and that petty theft. Had anyone ever told her of that? I was pretty sure not, for the family policy, in the few letters exchanged, had been to say nothing of the Brimlows. Well, ought she to be told now? Was it fair to let her think Luther Brimlow something that he wasn't? But, also, was it fair to Luther to dig out an ancient fault for which, charity would suggest, his industry and energy had long since atoned? Damn it all, man, I said to myself, how would you take it if someone decided to warn Prue Cleghorn that you were the sort of person who slept with the first willing woman he found?

The argument barged to and fro in my head. I did nothing, but it left me feeling bothered and irritated when I went to call on my mother. What a pass I had come to, I thought, in all my relationships! There I was, dawdling on the corner of that miserable Hulme street, ready to withdraw from sight the moment I should see my father leave the house, but resolved, with a stubborn inflexible righteousness that at once possessed and appalled me, not to go to the house *till* he had left it. He was a punctual man, and I saw him come, his beard, which he no longer trimmed, flowing patriarchally down the front of his black overcoat. The pockets were stuffed with tracts. He took a turn which would bring him straight to where I was hovering, and so I moved hastily into the little fly-blown corner shop whose paltry display had given me an excuse for my loitering. I asked for some tobacco, and as it was being reached down from the shelf I watched him go by the window.

"There 'e goes," said the woman behind the counter. "Reg'lar as clockwork – rain, 'ail or snow."

"Who?" I asked truculently.

Mr Pentecost – 'im as just passed the winder. Takin' 'is tracts to the ungodly."

She grinned maliciously, and I said: "Well, a man could be worse employed." I banged the shop door behind me, furious both with her contempt of him and with my feeble word of justification. I looked along the street in the direction he had taken, but some by-lane or alley had already swallowed him, as this black and godless sprawl of Hulme, I thought, would swallow without trace his feeble voice crying in its wilderness.

I went on then to the house, found the door ajar, and walked in. My mother was not in the sitting room or kitchen, so I climbed the stairs, and from the landing I could see into the back bedroom which my father used as his study, for the door was wide open. My mother was there with her back to me, and she had not heard me come. I watched her for a moment, busy at the small writing table placed beneath the window that faced me. She poured ink from a bottle into the inkwell. She took up scattered heaps of tracts and shook them down into neat piles. She dusted the pen tray and put a new steel nib into the pen. She fluffed up the cushion on the wooden armchair. I was deeply moved to see her performing these devotions, and guessed that my father would not be aware that they had been done. It was almost as though I had unwittingly intruded upon a worshipper in a silent church, and for another moment I stood there fascinated, looking at the leaden light falling through the window, and the grey fish scales of the roofs beyond, washed over by the brumous and almost palpable atmosphere, and at the woman serving her altar. Then I stole back down the stairs, and I knew far more about my father and mother than

I had ever known before. There had been in my mind a half-formed idea of asking her to come with me and share my life in London. In my youthful folly, it had seemed to me that anything would be better for her than to live here in Hulme the sort of life my father had ordained. Now, suddenly, I was appalled by the magnitude of my misunderstanding and presumption. I slammed the front door behind me noisily, as though I had just come in, and shouted up the stairs: "Anyone at home?"

She came, almost running down, gladly, her face lit with welcome; but I should never again be so foolish as to suppose that I was indispensable to her peace.

19

I have read over what I have written thus far, and it seems to me that I have a bad habit, which a trained and able writer would avoid, of getting myself lost in a labyrinth of detail and not marching resolutely forward with my story. Here I am, still not twenty years of age, and I shall be writing till doomsday if I deal with all my life in this fashion of small particulars. Now, at any rate, I shall let some years flow over my head, and take up my story on an April evening in 1908. On that evening I met Prue Cleghorn again. It is strange to say – but it is true – that she had passed completely out of my mind. When I left Manchester I was perplexed about the portrait of her uncle which she had entrusted to me. I wrote to her, at the address in Keswick which she had given, and said that I was leaving Manchester for good. The portrait would be as safe in a London studio as in a Manchester one, and so I would take it with me. Would she let me know when she wanted it back? I heard from her six months later. She wrote to say that a Professor Blackstock, who had held a chair of philosophy in a Scottish university and had been a friend of her uncle, had retired and gone to live near Keswick. He had just begun to write a book on Jesse Cleghorn's life and work and she had been engaged as his amanuensis. "While the work goes on," she wrote, "I shall be living with Mr and Mrs Blackstock. I have a lovely little room, with a view of Derwentwater, and so now, for the first time since leaving Manchester, I shall have my own den to creep into and I am gathering some of my things into it. It has been most kind of you to look after the portrait for so long. Will you now be so good as to send it to me? It is the chiefest of my few poor treasures."

And so the portrait went. A note of thanks reached me from Prue, and then I heard from her no more. So long as the portrait had been hanging on my studio wall in King's Mistress Yard, I had often thought of her and of the exciting days when a ten-pound commission could flutter my heart. But now I thought of her less and less, and the preoccupations of my new life, themselves so exciting to begin with, settled down into a steady routine of success. It was not yet the success which permitted me to pick and choose my sitters, but it was already enough to leave me few idle moments, and to give me the satisfaction of knowing that the prudent arrangements that great-aunt Sapphira had made for me were unnecessary after all. I could live, if not yet in luxury, then already in more than comfort, on what I earned.

Sometimes, it was to me a horrible thought that I owed this more to Luther Brimlow than to anyone else. It was he who had persuaded Sir Harry Banfil to give me my first important London work; and other things followed from that. I did the work well; the portrait of Charles Conlow especially satisfied me. He was the most impressive-looking member of the board: his face was more like a musician's than a financier's. Conlow himself was so pleased with the portrait that he commissioned me to paint his wife, dazzling in diamonds, and his pretty, ingenuous daughter. These women spoke to their friends about me, and I had the wry satisfaction of knowing that my repute was passed along from one to another as women pass along news of a dressmaker they have discovered.

This must not be a catalogue of commissions. I want only to show that, after I had been for a little time in London, the ball was rolling, and financially I had nothing to worry about.

I did not wish to see more of Luther Brimlow than I could help, but it was impossible to avoid him altogether, especially as great-aunt Sapphira had formed what appeared to be a firm friendship with him. He had followed her and Blanche to the Continent just at the time when I was settling in London, and in the following summer he had been invited to Tresco Vean. He called upon me in my studio on his return, brown and fit-looking, and talked of riding and sailing with Blanche. It was clear that I should not be able to write him off easily.

We were soon Ted and Luther to one another. I had to suffer his rather ostentatious charity. Comfortable though I was, he seemed to find pleasure in regarding me as a poor acquaintance who had to be helped, and this, I am sure, was his way of asserting himself in revenge for those years when Blanche and I treated him as a laughable ninny of no consequence. He would bring a valuable piece of porcelain and casually leave it on my mantelpiece, and on my birthday, which he must have learned from Blanche, a gorgeous set of ancient damask curtains arrived at my studio from a Bond Street shop. The devil of it was that the man had developed a taste in such matters. I had not even the satisfaction of privily damning him for a philistine. Nothing came from him that did not please me as a possession, though I was displeased to receive gifts from such a quarter. But there was nothing I could do about it without a rudeness of which I was not capable.

20

I drew my curtains across the window at four o'clock, pausing, before giving the final tug, to look into King's Mistress Yard. As I had done so often, I congratulated myself on the pleasant places in which my lines had fallen. In a few moments it would be dark. Now the yard was dusky, with the colour of the doors on either hand just discernible: yellow, blue, red, but all beginning to dissolve into grey. Snow had fallen during the afternoon; the one gaslamp and the lights from the King's Mistress shone upon a pattern of footprints that gave the quiet place the air of a forest clearing where animals had been at play but had now withdrawn into their lairs. I sighed with pleasure at the thought. There is a part of me that belongs to caves and solitude. I cannot see a night watchman, isolated in his box, with the brazier burning, the lamp lit, and the long night before him, without a feeling of envy. Give me a candle and the works of Shakespeare, I am disposed to say, and that will be enough. I am aware, though, as now when I close the last chink of the curtains, that there is pose in this. The lair to which I retreat is that of a too luxurious troglodyte. Still: here is solitude, which I love, wherever and of whatever sort the cave may be.

The studio walls were golden, and the carpet, like these curtains that Luther Brimlow had sent me, was of green faded to sage. Over the red brick fireplace was a picture of the sea breaking upon the Manacles, those cruel rocks not far from Tresco Vean where, I recalled now, stretching myself in a long Minty chair, Captain Pentecost had once had the bottom torn out of his dinghy and narrowly escaped drowning, and where my Kitto grandmother and her Pentecost lover had lost their lives. My Uncle Kitto had given me the picture as a settling-in present. Below it on the mantelpiece were two porcelain pieces that Luther had left there one night: a Leda and Swan and a wise-looking Chinese mandarin. My books were in recesses on either side of the fireplace, and I took out *The Adventures of Sherlock Holmes*. I might talk to myself about Shakespeare, but for a comfortable lazy evening at home I usually chose Conan Doyle.

It was pleasant to sit there, listening to the silence broken by nothing but the flames whispering in the grate, and to enjoy this anticipation of hours of my own company, which I was young and healthy enough to think the best in the world. Even to get up presently and make my tea on a gas ring in the kitchen seemed an unnecessary intrusion of energy, but I did it, and, when I had eaten, I washed up, lit my pipe, and settled to my book, as cosy as a cat in a household that rightly revolves round its comfort.

At about seven o'clock I heard the sound of wheels turning into the yard and of a horse's hooves striking softly upon the snow-muted cobbles. I hoped to goodness this was not someone calling upon me, and the next moment hope died. The bell jangled at the head of the stairs, just outside the door of the studio. I looked sharply towards the curtains. They were firmly drawn, and they were so thick that not a ray could penetrate them. "Damn it," I thought. "Let 'em ring. Let 'em think I'm out." The bell jangled again, and, throwing the book impatiently to the floor, I went downstairs. As soon as I had opened the door, Iris Randle shouted to the driver of the hansom cab: "All right. You can go." She embraced me and said: "Well, so this is your lair!" and walked upstairs.

It was a long time since I had seen Iris, and there had been no reason to suppose that I should see her again. But I had not been unaware of her career. There was a paper popular at that time called *The Pink 'Un*, scurrilously addicted to gossip and innuendo concerning the theatre, the racecourse and finance. It was not on my subscription list, but Luther Brimlow was addicted to it as firmly as to *The Financial News*. So far as I knew, he had not met Iris after that one encounter, when I introduced him to her and Sir Harry Banfil in Manchester; but he remembered her, and more than once he had called my attention to paragraphs concerning her in *The Pink 'Un*. If they were to be believed, her cap had now been thrown over higher windmills than Harry Banfil could command. It was only in such moments as this that a hint broke through of the Luther I had known long ago. His salacious sniggering over *The Pink 'Un* at once recalled to me the ugly youngster who had reproved Blanche for showing her legs in public and had sounded me about the delights of painting from the nude.

Before I was up the stairs, Iris had taken off her hat and coat and stretched herself in my chair by the fire, as possessively, as much at home, as though this were her own boudoir. I looked at her with curiosity, almost expecting to see upon her the marks of what my still naïve imagination could interpret as moral degeneration. She was lovelier than ever. She had fattened a little, which was not, in those days, a thing to fill a woman's heart with dismay. Her face, when first I knew it, was bony, with the dark eyes sometimes brooding and sometimes flashing in the sockets of the skull, and her complexion was pallid. It still was, and her eyes were still amazing. I have studied many women's eyes in my time, but I have never known other eyes like hers: so black and burning and hungry. But, at this time, she had lost the angularity of her face. There was a little flesh between the skin and the bone, and this emphasised the magnolia pallor and smoothness of the skin, which had been too tight. Oddly enough – and I could hardly repress a smile at the thought – she looked more of a lady, less of a guttersnipe. I could not imagine her now quarrelling vulgarly with Ma Bagley. She would imperially command. Her experience of ducal parties at which the most august persons were present – if without their wives – had not been ineffective.

Iris was not unaware of my prolonged scrutiny, or, I imagined, of the reason for it. She was quick-witted.

"I hope you approve," she said.

"You are very lovely, Iris."

"I need to be," she said simply. "There's a lot of competition. Now sit down here."

She indicated the floor alongside her chair, and when I had sat down, leaning against the chair with my carpet-slippered feet to the fire, she stroked my thick rough hair and said: "You are very soothing, Ted. You are the only man I know who doesn't think I am something to be paid for; and even you, I fear, are becoming prosperous. I shall be driven to find a stevedore or a night watchman for my last resort. My father was a stevedore. They are nice people – simple and brutal."

She had told me from time to time that her father was a sergeant-major, a Dean of the established church, and a window cleaner. He was in fact, as I later discovered, but not from her, a member of a seaside concert troupe; and she was the result of his liaison with a boarding-housekeeper's daughter.

It was not difficult to divine from her languid hints that she was, as she sometimes called it in the theatrical world, resting: that is to say, she had ended one affair and not yet begun another. So far as her stage work went, she was as far as she could ever get on the line she then followed. She had just been engaged to play the lead in a West End musical show: it was the celebrated *Girl in the Gondola*.

I am not yet an old man: I have some way to go before I shall be sixty; but at times I find it impossible to believe that the world once existed as I have known it. Such changes! There was no telephone in my studio. Nor was there electric light. In the streets you rarely saw a motorcar, and mews had not yet become flats because they were still mews, with coachmen living in the upper rooms and horses on the ground floors. By day and night the streets were full of hansoms and broughams; cockaded footmen stood behind, stately coachmen held the reins and laid the whips delicately upon the lovely horses; and the West End, when dusk had fallen, was full of opera hats and white shirt fronts and the rustle of women's skirts. They sounded as though they were forever walking through autumnal leaves. It was a time of lovely women, and, in so far as the theatre was concerned, it was a time when women were "girls". There were Gaiety Girls, and Gibson Girls, and the Girls at Daly's. The renown of these girls was deeper and wider than the renown of the film players of today, because they were not shadows. They were seen, amply, in the flesh, the embodiment of a cult of light-hearted gaiety that flamed to its zenith in the years before it ended forever, merging into the regimented exhibition of "revue". Connie Ediss and Ada Reeve, Marie Studholme and Connie Gilchrist, Gertie Millar and Iris Randle: they were the West End queens in the few hectic years before the johnnies and the mashers departed to come back, if at all, transmogrified by filth and by wounds of body and spirit into other men facing another world: the

227

world we know, in which those tawdry but fascinating lamps are out, and no others have yet been lit.

Except as a spectator, I was not much concerned with that world, and as I sat there that night on the floor at Iris' feet and she excitedly told me of rehearsals and dresses and of the splendour of this great opportunity that had come to her, I was more amused by her enthusiasm than stirred by any sense of the occasion itself.

"You are a damned old sobersides," she reproved me. "Doesn't anything about me excite you except the thought of going to bed with me?"

"Not even that tonight, Iris," I said.

"I believe you," she answered. "You know, Ted, you're that distressing thing known as the marrying sort. Some day you'll settle down with a wife and rear a family." She got up, and I helped her on with her cloak. "Ah, well," she said. "When that time comes will be my opportunity. I shall have to see what I can do with you then."

She went to the window and pulled back the curtains. "This is a nice little retreat you've found," she said. "And that's a nice-looking little pub on the corner. Shall we have a drink?"

I pulled on some snow boots and an overcoat and we crossed the yard. Standing here as it did on an open space, with the light falling through red curtains, the pub made me think of the Cock Inn at Didsbury and of all that was mixed up in my mind and experience with that place. Iris and I sat companionably in an alcove, with a fire burning, and I supposed there would soon be a thousand mashers in the West End who would give their ears to change places with me. But I was unexcited, aware of Iris only as a friend whom I liked and valued. My thought was rather with fiddles and 'cellos sounding through our old house and with dear Anatole, tight as a newt, exasperated as a saint at the sight of sin, picking me up and dropping me into the horse trough.

I sent a boy to scout for a hansom cab, and when it came I put Iris in and wished her good night. "Cheer up. You'll soon be dead," she said facetiously. She leaned out over the apron and kissed me soundly on the lips. Back in the studio, I felt lonely.

21

I suppose if anyone now chose to revive a musical comedy of the prime as a "period piece," then The *Girl in the Gondola* would be as likely a choice as any. But what "revival" can revive a day that is dead? I could not bear to attend such an occasion, if it ever presented itself, because I should find nothing but the bones. The spirit can never come back: the spirit of that "first night" when I was young and the world did not yet know that it was old.

It was Luther Brimlow who took me, and we sat in the stalls. That, in itself, was a testimonial to the rise of Luther's star. To get a stalls ticket for a first night at Henley's Theatre was as good as to get into the Royal Enclosure at Ascot, but I did not know that then. *The Girl in the Gondola* was to open on a Saturday, and on the Monday night before that Luther turned up at my studio, bringing, as he so often did, a parcel which his dignity did not permit him to carry up the stairs. He paid his cabby a shilling to do it for him.

"A little present, Ted," he said when we were alone. "Open it."

"Luther," I protested, "you are bringing me far too many little presents. Those curtains came on my birthday, which was in February. It is now but early April. Let me be frank. You are putting me in your debt in a way I can't return and that I don't like."

He laughed, and shrugged off the protest. "We were boys together," he said.

We weren't; we were boys as far apart as I could make it; but I could hardly say so, and I hacked with annoyance at the string of the parcel. It contained a decanter and half a dozen tumblers.

"Waterford," Luther said complacently.

"I wish you wouldn't do it. But I thank you."

He clapped me on the shoulder. "That's better," he said. "Now have the decanter filled on Saturday night. I shall call about six. I intend to show you the town. You know, Ted, you're still hanging back too much in your shell. You must get out and be known, and a first night at Henley's is one of the occasions for doing that. You'll find the bench and the bar, Harley Street and the Church, to say nothing of Debrett, the turf and one or two financiers. I've got two tickets and we'll make a night of it, beginning here with a drink at six. I suggest White Horse."

"I haven't got the clothes for such an occasion."

"Then it's time you had. You've left things rather late, but if I have a word with my tailor he'll do a rush job."

"Thank you, I shall manage somehow, if I come at all."

His face went grave. "Listen, Ted. Even I did not find it easy to get those tickets. I had to pull one or two strings. Between you and me, I managed to give a few tips in the right quarter. Well, now, the tickets are in the bag, and believe me, there are plenty of people I could take with me. But I'm asking you. This isn't just going to a show in the off-hand way in which you looked into the old Palace in Manchester. This is a great social occasion. This is something that will help to put you on the map – where Blanche's brother ought to be."

"What on earth has it got to do with Blanche?" I demanded, unable to keep resentment out of my voice.

He looked at me with a queer glint in his eye. "I'm not going on my bended knees to you," he said sharply. "Do you want to come or don't you?"

"Very well," I said. "It will be fun to see how Iris Randle makes out."

"I don't care what your reasons are. I'm asking whether you want to come."

"Yes. I will."

"All right, then." He paused for a moment, and added: "Look, Ted. For God's sake try and be a bit more cordial with me. I want to be your friend."

I am always too weak-willed to argue. I often consent by my silence to the most outrageous opinions, while damning them in my heart. "Very well, Luther," I said. "You must forgive me. I'm not a sociable animal, and I don't suppose I ever shall be."

His self-confidence was restored and he patted me on the back. "We shall do our best with you. At six, then, on Saturday."

22

It was an incredible Luther Brimlow who presented himself in King's Mistress Yard on the following Saturday night. I was not displeased with my own appearance, but I was not prepared for his. He had the advantage of me in figure, to begin with. I was then, and have remained, stocky and thickset. Luther was slim and six feet high. His evening clothes fitted him like a scabbard, and he looked as keen as a sword. His tall hat carried his height impressively upwards, and he wore a cloak, lined with red silk, fastened at the neck by a silver chain passing from one to other of a pair of small silver lion-heads. He carried an ebony cane, mounted with a silver knob. A gold-rimmed monocle swung from a ribbon of broad watered silk. He had passed deliberately and consciously out of the status of a merely well-dressed man, and become a dandy, a masher. And yet, looking at him as he stood in my room, I hesitated to apply to him either of these words, which seemed to me to suggest something trivial and without significant purpose. Beneath even these trappings, Luther looked formidable. The vulture was not obscured by the feathers of a bird of paradise.

It annoyed me that he was having an effect upon my mind and conduct. For example, it had seemed to me that a man who understood the art of entertaining would not put this lovely Waterford decanter crudely on the table. He would have a silver salver, and I had found a beautiful one in an antique dealer's shop. There it was, and I was distressingly conscious of it, and of its significance: I was trying to live up to Luther Brimlow. I hoped he would not notice it, but he did. His eye missed nothing. He threw his cloak on to a chair, laid his hat and gloves on it, and walked straight to the table. He removed the decanter and tumblers and took up the salver. He examined the chasing and peered at the maker's marks. "Excellent, Ted, excellent," he conceded, like a master pleased with a pupil's progress. I was glad that he said nothing about my clothes. Doubtless, he thought them merely adequate, beyond or beneath comment one way or the other.

I gave him a drink and he settled down in a chair. "There's no hurry," he said. "I've told the cabby to wait. Well, here's to you, Ted. May your palette never be dry."

I lounged against the table with my glass in my hand, looking down at his pomaded head, perplexed as usual by the feeling that I had nothing to say to him. More than any man I have known, more even than Sir Harry Banfil, he gave me this feeling of belonging to a race which did not live in my world.

Driven to desperation, I asked presently: "How are your father and mother, Luther?"

"On velvet," he said. "Or what is velvet according to their lights. I don't see much of them, but that youngster Ormsby, who's in charge for me down there, looks after them well enough."

I remembered the youngster Ormsby, and my conversation with him in Mr Brimlow's office.

"Ormsby? That's the ambitious boy who wants to come and work for you in London, isn't it?"

"That's the man. But I've got other notions for him. He's a bit too bright for what he's doing, and I shall hand his job over to someone else soon. I think he can help me politically."

This was something new, and I suppose my face showed my astonishment.

"I can never make out why it should be so," Luther went on, carefully considering the dregs in his glass, "but people think an M.P. is a safe and trustworthy fellow. They really do. It's odd. However, it's something to think about. When you're associated with finance, anything that increases public confidence in you is worth thinking about. Still, those are affairs for the future. It just occurred to me that this man Ormsby might make a good political agent. Well, now, let's be off. I've ordered dinner at Kettner's."

It had been a capricious season. Earlier in the week there had been flurries of snow, but now it was April embracing May. Even in that sundown hour, there was a little warmth in the air, and a gaiety, a promise, that stirred the heart. As we rattled through the streets Luther said: "I hope you will join us after the show in a glass of champagne at Rule's. I've asked Iris Randle."

I had not known that he was well enough acquainted with her to do that, and surprise kept me mute.

"You don't seem enthusiastic," he said. "Believe me, Ted, it wasn't easy. There was a lot of competition. Sir Harry Banfil, for one, is after her again. He sold out there a bit too soon. He didn't realise that the market would be rising. Well, I shan't be sorry to let Sir Harry Banfil know that he's not God Almighty."

It was a preposterous evening. Everything was excessive and outsize. We could, to begin with, have walked from Kettner's and gone straight into the theatre; but this was not Luther's idea of how such an occasion should unroll itself. We took a hansom cab and joined a line of carriages that stretched in a crawling queue right out of

Leicester Square. We moved forward inch by inch through the bright streets, past pavements thronged with the idle and the curious and the envious, scarecrow hungry faces, and vacant faces, and patient faces that looked as if they were ready to wait for a long time; and Luther sat back, wrapped in his splendid cloak, smoking a cigar, his hat tipped slightly to one side. It all became to me more than a little phantasmal, and when at last we were in the theatre and pushing our way through a burst of heat and noise and light towards our seats, the impression of the outsize and barbaric became overwhelming. You don't see such sights today, and you never will again: the tiers rising like cliffs glittering with precious stones, the splendid fabrics that were worn, the white bosoms, the icy sparkle of diamonds, the coloured fire of rubies and emeralds, the bracelets, the collars of pearls, the tiaras, the fans fluttering, the silks whispering.

Luther leaned towards me, his eyes shining with excitement. He pointed out duchesses and bookmakers, statesmen and financiers. "Everybody who's anybody," he said. "I wouldn't like to guess, Ted, what the jewels in this house would fetch in Amsterdam." A few people recognised him and spoke to him. He waved to Sir Harry Banfil, who was in a box with the Conlow family. He was in a fever of satisfaction at being in the right place, among the right people, at the right time.

The lights went down, the curtain swung up, and the stage made upon my mind the same stunning impression that everything seemed to make that night. It was at once trivial and opulent, worthless and captivating, crowded with skill and beauty put to ignoble, frivolous uses. We listened for the first time to songs that errand boys whistle to this day, sundered by so much from that; we applauded everything, for everything was perfect within its intention; and we applauded nothing more than Iris Randle singing *Stars in a Velvet Sky* and *Dennis, you're a menace in a gondola in Venice*, songs so innocuous in themselves, so charged with invitation as Iris sang them. I never hear them now without thinking of that hot excited night, of how, when it was all over, I saw Luther and Iris drive away in a cab, with another following them, loaded with bouquets, and of how, after all, I did not keep them company, for other company than theirs suddenly presented itself.

23

Luther was not a man who left things to chance or grasped at ragged ends. Everything he did was what he called "organised". If he were taking no more than a journey to the suburbs, the train times there and back would be noted in his little red-leather book and he would be on the train half a minute or so before it left the station. So, this night, all was in order. There was a four-wheeler cab with a well-tipped cabby waiting at the stage door. "Get in, Ted, and wait," Luther commanded. "I'll go up. I've got the old boy organised."

I got into the cab and watched him make his way through the crowd of gapers round the stage door. The "old boy" evidently expected him, touched his forelock, and let him in. I settled down to wait, leaning back into the cab, for I disliked the inquisitive stare of all those eyes. But, unseen, I could see, and suddenly I saw a face that brought my heart to my mouth. At first I could not believe it. I had thought her far away, in Cumberland; and then, when I saw beyond a doubt that it was Prue, I could not believe my own heart. It began to thump uncontrollably, and my mind was filled suddenly with a sense of happiness and release. It was, more than anything else, a sense of contact. All through that hot excited evening I had had contact with nothing: not with the occasion, so brightly fluffy, so febrile and spurious; not with the people about me; not, assuredly, with Luther Brimlow. In theory I was having a night in a million, everything, as they say, slap-up and of the best. In fact, deep down and till now unrecognised even by myself was a lonely ache that repudiated the whole occasion and drew nothing out of it. Seeing Prue, I felt a wave of sheer happiness flow suddenly over me. I wanted to leap out of the cab, take her in my arms and embrace her. But all I did of this was to leap out of the cab. I went up to her, raised my hat, and said: "Good evening, Miss Cleghorn."

For a moment she looked at me, obviously not knowing who I was. Then she laughed. I have said before that when Prue laughed she laughed wholeheartedly, and she did so now. Her laughter rang out there in the street, and her throat pulsed. "Well!" she said at last. "Well!"

"Yes, I know," I said. "If you like, I'll never wear them again."

"They don't suit you," she said. "You look like nothing on earth."

"Neither do you, for that matter," I answered. "You look like something dropped from heaven."

So she did, to me then. I'm no good at describing women's clothes. I can only say that she was wearing something that seemed to wrap her up in brown fur, like a little animal in the winter woods, and that her brown eyes shone from under some tight-fitting brown fur casque. She looked utterly out of place in that sophisticated London street, under the dazzling urban lights.

"I'm waiting for a friend," I said. "He may be some little time. If you care to get into the cab, we could talk till he comes. To begin with, you could tell me how you came to materialise outside Henley's Theatre."

"Oh, that's simple," she answered. "I was passing by. I saw the crowd. I stopped. As simple as that."

We were in the cab now. "Not simple at all," I said. "Utterly miraculous. You were passing by. Do you often pass by Leicester Square when you set out for an evening walk in Cumberland?"

"Oh, we left Keswick a month ago. We're living in London now – my professor and his wife and I. We have rooms in Lincoln's Inn."

She went on to tell me of the life she was leading, and as she talked I took her hand in mine and rubbed my thumb up and down the smooth exciting skin. Now and then I pressed her finger warmly. She gave me no answering pressure, but she did not take her hand away. She said that the book "her professor," as she called him, had been writing about Jesse Cleghorn was now finished, and that other work was on the stocks. Her professor had decided that he could not remain in the country. There was much that he wanted to write in his retirement, and he had to be near books. She was remaining with him as his secretary, and much of her time was spent in the British Museum, tracking down references and copying from original sources. "It's rather dull," she said. "But I like my professor, and one must live."

She took her hand gently from mine and pulled on her large beaver gloves. "I must be off," she said. "My professor's wife will wonder what on earth has become of me. She's never lived in London before – and neither have I, if it comes to that. But I'm not quite so frightened as she is by the modern Babylon."

235

We got out of the cab, and I said: "She's right, of course. You should have a protector. Allow me to walk with you as far as Lincoln's Inn."

Prue looked at me, and again her merry laugh broke out. "Well," she said. "So long as she doesn't see us . . . If she saw me walking with you, she'd think I'd been overtaken by a fate worse than death."

"I could throw away the hat," I volunteered. "I think that's the worst. It hides my essentially honest face."

"You certainly look like something out of a George R. Sims melodrama," she said, looking at me quizzically; and I answered righteously: "I can't say. I've never seen one."

"Then you've missed a lot," she answered. "My uncle and I went to all of them – *The Lights of London, Man to Man* – oh, every one. We always took a bag of nuts, and had a great time. He had wonderful teeth. He always cracked the nuts for me with his teeth and gave me the kernels. We finished the play with our feet crunching ankle-deep in shells."

This absurd little memory suddenly made her grave and withdrawn from me. I could understand that Jesse Cleghorn, whose delicious lectures on the heroines of Shakespeare I had heard, would find a rich ironical satisfaction in eating nuts as he watched the plays of Mr George R. Sims.

A sudden surge forward of the crowd round the stage door announced the arrival of Iris Randle. She came with a great armful of flowers, with a triumphant tempest of silks and a waft of perfume. She knew what was expected of her. She waved her hand. She cried: "Thank you, my dears – thank you all, very very much," and with a kiss of the fingers and a flurry of skirts she was inside the cab. Luther followed, he, too, carrying flowers, and quite a conservatory of them came shining after in the hands of menials. "Get another cab," Luther commanded. A whistle brought one, and the flowers were loaded into it. I plucked Luther by the sleeve, and he turned testily. When he saw who it was, his face cleared and he said: "Oh, it's you, Ted. I'd forgotten you."

Clearly he had. He was on top of the world, and there were only two people in it. "Look, Luther," I said. "I think I'd better go straight home."

"Oh, but – are you sure?"

He sounded relieved.

"Yes," I said. "Off you go now. Iris is not a woman to be kept waiting. Thank you for a lovely night."

He needed no urging. He got into the cab, and off they went. The crowd began to clear, and I said to Prue: "Now, let's be off."

"Who was the swell?" she asked.

"Oh, a man I used to know in Manchester. And the woman was Iris Randle, the actress. He's taking her off to supper."

"Well, well," she said. "The night becomes more and more George R. Simsian. I feel we should buy some nuts."

We did. Shops kept open at all hours in those days, and we bought nuts, and I cracked them with my teeth and gave her the kernels as we wandered eastward along the Strand. It was a lovely night, and we had little to say to one another till we parted near Temple Bar. Then I said: "Look, Prue. I often wanted to go after you into Cumberland, but I never took the trouble to do anything about you because I knew we should meet sooner or later. Well, we've met, and I'm glad. Are you?"

"Yes, Ted. Very glad."

"Give me your address," I said.

I wrote it in a notebook, and then I said: "I'd like to kiss you, Prue, if you'd like to kiss me."

She didn't answer, except by coming into my arms. It was a lover's kiss, and when she stood away from me she sighed with happiness.

"Good night, my darling," I said. "I'm sorry for your professor. He's going to lose a treasure."

I watched her disappear into the darkness of Chancery Lane, and then began to walk aimlessly about the streets.

24

I had noticed an eating house in the Strand, near Villiers Street, with the satisfying notice in the window: "We keep open all night," and I brought up there after a desultory round that had taken me through Fetter Lane and Holborn and then away to the left down the road we now call Kingsway: the dull dead road that was to show how completely we had forgotten the art and craft of building. We have forgotten so much, in this world in which I am now writing. We are thrown back, each one of us of an older generation, upon remembering individually, recalling the brief bright sparks that made our own fires. Let me remember now my first love letter to Prue. I

ate steak and kidney pudding in the Strand, and drank coffee, and then
I began to walk again. My head was full of a daze of lovely thoughts
that made no coherent sense but were the only thoughts I wanted
then. They flowed through me not like charted constellations but like
the nebular beauty of the milky way. It was one o'clock when I went
out into the Strand. The roar of the town was muted but not
suspended. "All that mighty heart is lying still," Wordsworth wrote on
Westminster Bridge. But it never does lie wholly still, and as I walked
down Piccadilly, with the light of a gaslamp falling here and there on
the first tender green of foliage, I could hear the beating of it, as
sometimes on a June night you hear a nested bird sing a few drowsy
notes in its sleep.

I wandered on through Knightsbridge to Kensington, and there I
came up sharp against an apparition of beauty that made me stand. In
a garden an almond tree was in full flower, and the standard of a street
lamp lifted so near to it that the light was in the very heart of the rosy
blossom, giving to beauty's self such pure translucence that I
wondered why, since so many people will deck themselves in
diamonds to watch a ballerina dance, there was no crowd here to see
this miraculous pose in mid-air; the wide-flung skirts of beauty
hanging over the dark stage of the street.

It was while I was leaning against a gate, looking at the tree from
the opposite side of the street, that one of those odd creatures who
inhabit the night of London came upon me. He was all made of
wildness, a thing of tatters torn to shreds, a being hardly arrested on
the fortunate side of madness. White hair flowed down his shoulders
and a white beard down his chest. A shepherd's smock, patched and
filthy, clothed him, and in his hand was a shepherd's crook. But this
bucolic suggestion was denied by his tall silk hat, a battered dustbin-
relic of a hat, round which was tied a broad band bearing the word:
"Repent!"

He hailed me while he was yet some way off: "Hey! You, for whom
Christ died," and when he had come up with me he thrust into my
hand some bills that he took from a satchel round his neck. They bore
the simple inscription: "The Covent Garden Mission. Shepherd
Hamlin calls to the Lost Sheep: "Repent! Repent you! Repent you
all!"

He looked at me with an eye that glittered frostily. "Well, here you are," he said, "all dolled up in purple and fine linen, too drunk to stand up straight, unable to find your way home from your whoring and wine-bibbing. And what do you care about the agony of the Christ? Not a thing. Not a damned farting thing."

I couldn't help it. I began to laugh. He was too much for me: this Ancient Mariner, this Wandering Jew, this scarecrow made up of the rags of a dozen outworn scarecrows. "Laugh!" he cried. "Laugh your ruddy eyes out! You'll laugh the other side of your face when you feel Old Nick's red-hot toasting-fork stirring up your bleeding bowels. Then you'll howl for your sparkling Moselle, and not a blasted drop of water will you get not as much as a fly could pee. Then you'll cry for the soft bosoms of your molls and doxies, but what will your bed be then? Ha! Sizzling clinkers, my boy, sizzling red-hot clinkers!"

I contemplated in silence this unexhilarating destiny. There was nothing I could say to him.

"Why don't you answer back?" he demanded. "You stand there like a ruddy stuck pig. How can the Lord give me words to speak unless you answer back? Ha! It's different in Covent Garden! They answer back there quick enough. Every morning at four o'clock, there you'll find me, the Shepherd of my sheep. Poor bloody wandering sheep they are, too, bleating their little bits of cheek and impudence. But God makes me a match for 'em. But you! You haven't got the guts of a farting louse. Not a word to say for yourself. Not a word to say for your own boss, His Farting Satanic Majesty."

He paused, as if waiting to see whether his taunts would strike any fire out of me, but they did not. "Well," he said, "I must be off on my Father's business. Got a fag?"

I gave him a cigarette and held a match for him, but he was so hairy, so like a haystack, I feared I might set him alight. He inhaled deeply and blew the smoke out through his nostrils. Then he handed me a card inscribed "Henry Hamlin, M.A. (Oxon). Shepherd of All Souls." He said: "So long, hell-fodder. See you at the dividing of the sheep from the goats," and went shambling away round a corner.

I was left alone with my tree, and with a sense, greatly deepened by this strange encounter, of my need of Prue, of her beautiful sanity in this insane world. There were two of Shepherd Hamlin's bills in my hand, each with one side blank, and, taking out a pencil, I began to write to Prue. I sketched the lovely tree. Its branches and blossom filled the top half of the paper; its trunk ran down the middle, and I wrote my letter on either side of the trunk. "Underneath this lovely tree in Kensington, 3 a.m. This is to tell Miss Prudence Cleghorn that everything beautiful will always make me think of her, always make me want to stop and write to her, as I stop and write now beneath this tree. There is nothing that I want to write *about*. I want only to write, to say: 'Here I am beneath an almond tree in flower, thinking of Prue Cleghorn.' The first time I ever heard her name was when a student in Manchester said: 'Ah, Prue!' And that is all I want to say now: 'Ah, Prue!' Edward Pentecost."

I folded the sheet, then folded the second one so that its blank side was out. I enclosed the first one in this, tucked in the ends, addressed it, stamped it, and dropped it in a letterbox. I thought of Prue sitting in the British Museum, "copying from original sources," as she had said, and the thought sickened me. Original sources! Look at this tree! Isn't that an original source, a regular dynamo of power? What was it Wordsworth had said: "To me the meanest flower that blows can give . . ." Yes, Prue, there are plenty of original sources that you and I shall visit together.

The dawn was breaking when I got back to Chelsea. Streaks of silver light were coming here and there on the river, as though its sluggish lead had been newly scratched. I thought lazily for a moment of Luther Brimlow and wondered what sort of a night he had spent. But I was by now too exhausted in body and mind to think long of anything. I could hardly crawl up my stairway, and once I had got into bed I did not leave it again that day. Nor did I leave again the rest I had found in Prue. She insisted on remaining with her professor until the time of our marriage, and he gave us one of his two-volume works for a wedding present. It was called *Post-Kantian Influences in European Philosophic Thought*, but we never had an aspidistra to stand on it, and so it served no purpose at all.

CHAPTER SIX

MR AND MRS BRIMLOW were not present when Luther married my sister Blanche in the autumn of 1911. I cannot recall everybody who was in the church in Hanover Square, but I was there with Prue, and Sapphira was there, and I remember Sir Harry Banfil and the Conlows, and a lot of people who, Prue said, were probably Old Throgmortonians. It was everything that our own wedding had not been. All the trimmings were sewn on regardless of expense. There were press photographers, a reception at the Ritz, and, the next day, plenty of fluffy writing by the newspaper society gossipers. It was from them that I learned we had been honoured by the presence of three peers and two peeresses. Only Sapphira, Prue and I were at Victoria to see Mr and Mrs Luther Brimlow leave for the Continent. Luther had sent on his Rolls Royce car. He was proud of himself as a driver. He would pick up the car in France, and the honeymoon was to be spent touring. Motorcars, even in 1911, were still uncommon enough for this fact to excite all the gossip writers.

As she had been all day, Blanche was cool – Prue said icy – at the station. Luther was more excited than I had ever known him. There had been a lot of champagne at the Ritz. I wondered if he was thinking of that day so long ago, of which Blanche had told me, when he leapt into her compartment of a moving train at Didsbury, only to find Blanche in flight as soon as they reached the next station. Had he then gritted his teeth, made up his mind that he would have her some day? I now knew Luther and his invincible perseverance well enough to think this not improbable. There was about him no tenderness, no sense of humility in the face of good fortune; only a sense of triumph, of an overcoming.

Blanche had said goodbye to us all rather formally and settled in the corner of the compartment. Luther lingered on the platform, though the porters were already running along the train, banging the doors. Sapphira gripped his sleeve tight in her jewelled hand. "You look after her," she said. "Understand? I'll have no nonsense."

"Now, really," Luther laughed, "do I look a nonsensical type?"

"I don't know about that," Sapphira said. "I don't altogether trust you financiers. Those shares Sir Harry Banfil recommended have dropped two points."

"Are you still listening to poor old Harry? Really, my dear, we shall have to transfer *all* your money affairs to the family."

"Well, never mind that now. You look after Blanche, or I'll never forgive you. Get in. The train's moving."

It was, and what remained in my mind out of the moment was the curious fact that Blanche was still sitting in her corner. I should have expected her to be at the window, crying: "Come along, Luther. Do hurry. You'll be left behind." But she did nothing of the sort. She was just sitting there, looking in front of her. At the last second Luther leapt on to the moving train and hid her from me, so that I could not see whether she looked up and smiled at him.

Old Sapphira snivelled and touched her eyes with a bit of cambric. "Well," she said. "I hope they'll be happy. I'm sure I've done my best for her."

2

Sapphira urged me and Prue to return with her to Cornwall the next day, but I could not do this as I had work in hand. However, it was interesting to find the self-sufficient old woman almost pleading with us. She must, I thought, be looking forward with no pleasure to a time of loneliness. I had come to like her. There was nothing of ogress in her now, so far as I was concerned. No doubt my father had had cause enough for his dislike, but we are not all of a piece. Fortunately for most of us, we have a little that some can love if much that others must hate. And we do not remain constant, immutable. I had loved my father, and I could still love the memory of the boyish man swinging out of the house in the morning with his basket on his shoulder. But it would have been nonsense to pretend that I loved the man my father was now.

I did what I could to ease Sapphira's departure into loneliness the next day. I attended on her at Brown's Hotel after breakfast, and travelled with her to Paddington. It had been a summer of drought and great heat, that summer of 1911, and though it was now October, and early in the morning, the air was dry and brittle as though the earth's waters had all been driven down to their deepest springs and the scorched crust was gasping for breath. I feared Sapphira was going to have an uncomfortable journey. I got a luncheon ticket for her and bought her some newspapers and magazines, and then stood at the open door of her compartment, talking to her as she fanned herself with her handkerchief. The train was due to leave at half-past ten, and there was a quarter of an hour yet to go. She patted the seat alongside hers and said: "Come and sit down, Ted. Tell me what you think of Luther. Extraordinary name! Makes me think of bulls and diets of worms. You've known him a long time, I understand."

"Not really," I said. "I knew him a long time ago, but that's another matter. We were born in the same street in Manchester and grew up in next-door houses, but, frankly, we didn't get on together very well. We hadn't much in common."

"You haven't now, if it comes to that."

"No, I suppose not. Well, Luther left home when he was quite young, and I didn't see him for years. He travelled a lot, and when he came back he – well, he rather staggered me. You know how it is. When you've known someone as a child who didn't strike you as remarkable, it's rather disconcerting to find him turning up as a notability. Luther is certainly that – in his way."

"Where did he get his money from?"

"Good gracious! What do I know about money? Where *do* financiers get their money from? I don't even know whether he's got money or whether he's all façade."

"Oh, he's got money all right," she said. "And he's only at the beginning. Do you think I did right?"

"How do you mean, Aunt?"

"In letting Blanche marry him. In pushing her into his arms if you like to put it that way."

"Did she need pushing?"

"She did and she didn't. When he wasn't about she never talked of him, and she never wrote to him. Not that she writes to anybody. She

243

can't write. But when he was there he seemed to fascinate her. *He*
wanted *her* all right. No doubt about that."

"I think he's wanted her for a long time."

"Well," she answered piously, "we must leave it to God. At least,
Blanche will never know poverty. Now, you've still got a few minutes.
Just get me a smelling-bottle, will you?"

There was a chemist's shop on the platform. When I had brought
the bottle she immediately began to sniff at it. "Ah! That's refreshing,"
she said.

"Do you feel all right?"

"Well, yes and no. It's been a dreadfully hot summer, and I must say
I've found London trying. And a fashionable wedding isn't a rest-cure
at my age. But there's nothing to worry about. Just a spasm now and
then. One expects it at seventy-five."

"You don't look it, Aunt," I assured her.

"Well, I must say Blanche gave me a new lease of life. I hated it
when it was first proposed that she should come to Tresco Vean. But
it was the best thing that ever happened to me. We had some lovely
times together. But that's all over now. I don't suppose I shall leave
Tresco Vean again. Mind you and your wife come and see me as soon
as you can. She's a nice little thing. And bring some children with
you."

I said I would do my best.

The whistle blew. I got out and spoke to her through the dropped
window. She had the bottle to her nose. "You're sure you're all right?"

"As right as I can expect to be," she said. "Don't fuss. I shall go to
sleep after luncheon."

She got up to wave as the train pulled out. Her hand was still
fluttering as the train curved out of sight. That was the last I saw of
her. She was found dead in her seat by the attendant who came along
shouting: "First lunch!"

3

It was a rather dreadful situation, because I couldn't let Blanche and
Luther know. They had left no itinerary with us. Their scheme was to
motor wherever fancy took them. "We may spend the whole month
in Paris, or we may settle for a week in a village no one's ever heard
of, or we may not pass two days in the same place," Luther had said.

"We don't intend to write to anybody, and there's no reason why anybody should write to us."

I myself learned of Sapphira's death from a paragraph in the *Westminster Gazette* that evening. "A woman passenger was found dead this morning in a first-class compartment of the Cornish Riviera Express which left Paddington at 10.30. She was alone in the compartment, and was discovered to be dead by a dining-car attendant. There is no reason to suspect that death was due to anything but natural causes. From papers found in her handbag she is believed to be Miss Sapphira Kitto of Tresco Vean, near Falmouth."

So I had to leave my work after all. Prue and I travelled down by the night train. We breakfasted in a Falmouth hotel, and then went along to Kitto's old chapel. He was serenely at work, as though nothing had happened, but he put down his brushes and we went out into his paved garden and sat in the mild autumn sunshine among his statues and tub-bushes. He was wearing a tussore silk suit, with a pale blue silk tie, a panama hat, and white buckskin shoes. Henry Opie brought out coffee, and Prue and I began to cast off the jaded sense of our night's journey. Uncle Kitto said that there would be an inquest at noon, and that he would give formal evidence of identification. He had already seen Sapphira's body, he said, and it had been removed to Tresco Vean. I suggested that I ought to give evidence, as I had been the last person to see her alive. I could testify that she had been feeling unwell.

"My dear Ted, why bother?" he asked. "No one knows that you saw her off, and nothing you say will make any difference one way or the other. You and Prudence stay here and rest yourselves. I'll join you at lunch."

"Well," I said, "it was a nice way to die. After all, seventy-five's a good old age. She'd had her time."

"Who told you she was seventy-five?" he asked.

"She told me herself."

Kitto smiled and lit a cigarette. "I wonder why it is?" he mused. "It's one of the world's deepest mysteries – why women lie about their ages, or at best say nothing about them at all. There's more than vanity in it. If it's a horror of the passing of the years, why don't men lie in the same way? And why do women begin this sort of thing in their

245

twenties? One is not much afraid of the years in one's twenties. One feels immortal. You know, Sapphira was eighty-one."

Eighty-one. Certainly a good old age. All the more reason, I thought, for the shock the old woman had suffered at the clean cut with the beautiful youth that had refreshed her withered years.

When Kitto was gone, I asked Opie's permission to use the dinghy, and I rowed Prue upon the harbour, which was as smooth as silk. It was good for both of us. The calm loveliness of the day flowed like a sedative along our nerves. Too much had happened too quickly: the wedding, Sapphira's death, the sense of frustration at not being able to reach Blanche with the news, the precipitate sleepless journey to Cornwall. We came back refreshed, plunged our hands into the verbena bush at Kitto's door, and inhaled the fragrance.

After lunch, Kitto said: "Tell me about this man Brimlow your sister has married. Who is he?"

I told him what I could, which was little enough, for what did I know of Luther Brimlow after all? I had never met Luther Brimlow. I had met the person who signed his name with those two sets of letters, but what had that to do with Luther Brimlow? This was no more than to meet a bloodhound benevolently on view at Cruft's. I had never seen him on the trail. What did I know of anybody? I had talked to Jesse Cleghorn, but what had that brief glimpse through a dark window shown me of his immensities?

So, as Prue and Kitto and I sat there, relaxed in easy chairs, looking at the tranquil day shining on the water, I felt as if Kitto had said: "Tell me about Falmouth harbour." What shall I tell you about – this bright passing moment, or the day when a St Mawes fishing-smack sighted on the horizon the white cloud of the Armada; or of how Benjamin Franklin landed here from America; how Captain Pentecost brought in the *Termagant*; how the *Queen* transport pounded out her life after the Peninsular War; or how Lieut. Lapenotière came ashore from the *Pickle* and hurried east behind his sweating horses to wake a sleeping Ministry with news that Nelson was dead and that England lived?

"Luther Brimlow?" I said. "He's what they call a financier, I suppose. I never know exactly what that means."

"I thought you'd known him for years," Kitto said, "but you're not very enlightening. I must say I didn't take to the fellow. I met him once or twice when he was staying at Tresco Vean. He and Sapphira became as thick as thieves. She's babbled to me a lot about him since then, and I can tell you one thing: under his advice, she's been reinvesting nearly every penny she had. I hope the feller's sound."

"Well," I comforted him, "if being sound means having the ability to turn sixpence quickly into a shilling, I should say he's all right."

The verdict had been "Death from natural causes". Kitto and I attended the funeral, and afterwards a Falmouth solicitor read the will to us in the dining room at Tresco Vean which I liked to fancy was the very room in which Captain Pentecost had thrown his wine into Henry Kitto's face so long ago. The will confirmed what I had expected, and what Kitto had expected, too, I imagine. Sapphira had left everything, without qualification, to Blanche.

4

In this year 1911 I was twenty-two years old, Blanche was twenty-three, Prue twenty-four, and Luther, I imagine, twenty-five. We were a nicely-graded set of young people, gathered round the dining table in Luther's house in Bedford Square. Work on the house had been going on for some time before the marriage and had continued while Blanche and Luther were away. When Prue and I arrived, that evening late in November, Luther took us round before dinner with a pride that had some warrant. The place was electrically lit and centrally heated. The appointments were all of the best: at once elegant and beautiful. I had never known Luther so human as when he showed us that house. He was so pleased, like a child displaying the contents of a Christmas stocking. I feared I might even begin to like him a little.

A week before the dinner we had received a letter from Luther inviting us to "christen", as he called it, his home and Blanche's. He wrote from Dijon, of all places, saying that he was moving on at once to Paris, where a few days were to be spent before the crossing to England. He gave the name of the hotel where he and Blanche would be staying, and thus, at last, I was able to write to Blanche and give her the news of Sapphira's death. I had not seen her since her return. She was not visible when Luther received us and showed us over the house.

We had finished the tour and were standing round the fire in the drawing room, drinking a glass of sherry, when Luther's manservant came in and said to me: "Madam would be pleased if you could spare a moment, sir." I followed him up the stairs; he tapped at a door and left me.

Blanche called: "Come in." It was a charming room, like all the others. In King's Mistress Yard we had to edge our way between the bed and the wall. Here, everything was spacious; you could walk freely. A fire was burning, and Blanche was sitting on the stool before her dressing table, buffing her fingernails. She was dressed in white satin. It shone under the quiet light dropping from a crystal chandelier above the dressing table.

She put down the buffer and rustled to her feet, looking somehow even taller than she was. She was much taller than I. She put a hand on each of my shoulders and gave me a formal kiss on the cheek. "I wanted to have a word with you, Ted, apart from the others," she said. "Tell me about Sapphira."

She sat down again and I stood on the bearskin before the fire and told her what there was to tell. It wasn't much. In my letter I had said nothing about the will. Now I told her of that, too. To my surprise, she began to cry quietly. "Why *me*?" she asked. "Why everything to *me*? Oh, I used her shamefully. Her life had been so dull, and I helped to make it happy. It's as though I sold her my years, and she felt she had to pay."

"Nonsense," I said. "Look at it reasonably. She was an old woman who'd led a life utterly selfish and autocratic. I'm sick of the feud Father waged with her, but there's something in his point of view. She wasn't happy unless she was twiddling other people's lives round her little finger. She wanted to wear people like all those rings she had. And when you went there, that's what she wanted with you. But it didn't work out that way. You gave her a bit of humanity. Why," I smiled, "you made her something that even I could begin to like. It would have pleased her to give you everything she had, so as to make you in her own image, but you, who seemed to have nothing, had something that she would never have had by herself. She had it at the last because you gave it to her. It was something she could not have bought with all her money." I managed another smile. "If anyone left *me* a fortune," I said, "I'd try hard to look on the bright side of it."

She had got up and dried her eyes. She walked over to where I was standing, looking most poised and regal for one so young. She said a surprising thing. "Ted, you are a nice person, you know. I'm afraid anyone could bluff you. Still, it would be comforting to look forward to a life lived with someone like you."

Before I could answer this the gong sounded, and she said: "Let's go down now. Luther likes punctuality."

5

During dinner Luther said: "We were terribly upset, Ted, terribly upset, to get your letter about Miss Kitto's death. If she'd lived a few more years, she'd have been a really rich woman."

"That she missed that certainly makes the thought of her death more bitter," said Prue.

Luther looked at her coldly. "Don't misunderstand me, Prudence," he said. "I am not associating the two ideas. Perhaps it was unfortunate that I expressed them together. All I wanted to say was that she had taken me into her confidence, and I had been able to show her that her money was not so well invested as it could be. She had permitted me to begin putting that right."

"Well, now you can go on," Blanche said. She had recovered her self-possession. "Ted has been telling me about the will. Great-aunt left me everything."

I think this is what Luther had been waiting to know. "Most generous of her," he said. "Ted, a little more of this saddle of mutton. Prudence, the redcurrant jelly is at your elbow. Most generous, but not unreasonable. After all, my dear, you gave her some of the best years of your life."

"I gave her no more than she gave me," Blanche answered. "And now she's given me everything."

"Well," said Luther, busy with the carving-knife, as if the pleasing thought were in his mind that Miss Kitto had cut up well, "there was, after all, no one else."

"Nonsense," Blanche said sharply. "There was Ted, and there was our father, and there was Uncle Kitto, to say nothing of hospitals and orphanages and homes for strayed animals."

Luther smiled upon her forgivingly. "It pleases you to make light of a serious matter, my dear," he said. "I repeat that, in effect, there was no one – no one, that is, who had counted in Miss Kitto's life as you had. One thing I regret is that Tresco Vean is so far from London."

Blanche looked up in surprise. "What is regrettable about that?" she asked.

"Well," said Luther, "a place in the country is a great asset. It's most valuable for entertaining and so forth at weekends. But it should be handy. Buckinghamshire or Hertfordshire at the farthest. Cornwall's at the end of the earth. People would never bother to get down there just for a weekend. I imagine that if you wanted to dispose of it, Tresco Vean would fetch a decent figure, and you could acquire a handier property with the money."

"Dispose of it!" Blanche cried. "Dispose of Tresco Vean!"

She seemed too astonished to say more, and Luther said soothingly: "It was just a passing thought, my dear. If it doesn't immediately appeal to you, perhaps you'd turn it over quietly in your mind and we'll talk about it later. After all, a place three hundred miles away isn't of much practical use to people whose affairs keep them in London. And the cost of maintenance would be high. If we had a place nearer at hand – why, with the car, we could be out of town every weekend."

Blanche said: "If I am to be in Tresco Vean but one day a year, I shall keep it."

"At least," I backed her up, "it will be a useful lodging to lend to your indigent relatives. I've no doubt Prue and I will be glad to keep it warm for you now and then. After all, we have an affection for the place. We spent our honeymoon there. Now, tell me about *your* honeymoon. Where did you get to?"

We didn't learn much about the honeymoon. We learned nothing more than the names of the places they had been to, and the number of times the car had broken down, and what hotels had been stayed at. All palatial, I gathered. I thought of our own honeymoon, and of how, at times, even the quiet kindly walls of Tresco Vean had seemed intrusive. I had awakened one night and found the full moon shining in at our window, and I had wakened Prue, and we had dressed and gone out. For hours we had wandered in the woods, inhabited, it seemed, by pallid tigers as the moonlight threw stripes of shadow across the white clearings. We watched a badger grunting down a path, and smelled the rank odour of foxes, and heard the wary birds stirring in their nests. Death was abroad as well as life, but it had no sound save life's own last cry that rang out once or twice. And when that happened, Prue would clutch my arm and tremble, for there is no mistaking that sound, no misunderstanding that the death of a rabbit is Death, the voiceless, unseen and only immortal.

There seemed to have been no nights like that during Blanche's honeymoon, and when, late that evening, Prue and I were crossing Bedford Square, and I said to her: "Well, my darling, how did you think Blanche was looking?" she answered: "Like someone walking in her sleep."

6

It was about two years after this that Prue and I left King's Mistress Yard – that is, as a place to live in. As soon as we knew that Stephen was on the way, we began to look round for a more spacious house. There was never any doubt in our minds that it would be a boy, and it was.

Luther settled all the details about the house in Hampstead. It was kind of him to bother with us at all, because I had flown in the face of his principles and of all that Sapphira had tried to hammer into my mind. In a word, I was not living on the interest of money. I got hold of the capital that Sapphira had told me about so solemnly that day in Brown's Hotel, soon after I had first come to London, and proposed to buy my house with a large slice of that. Luther was shocked that I had not left the only capital I had to brood like an old bird in a hen-run, producing regular eggs, but had slaughtered it improvidently for the table. I had not even consulted him about it. I had put the thing through and then told Blanche, who then told him. Prue was out when he called on me at the studio and let me know what he thought of me.

"It's a small matter, Ted," he said. "Forgive me if I know all about it, but I'm like that, you see. I can't help ferreting into the ins and outs of money. I know it's a matter of a mere ten thousand, because that's Blanche's share, and I know you were equal sharers. Well, that's ten pounds a week, as the money was invested. I could have made it more for you – with perfect safety, too – if you had done me the honour of giving me your confidence." He looked rather hurt and haughty as he said this. "I never bothered you about it because the sum is a bagatelle. You must please yourself. However, when it comes to buying the house, I should like to be of service to you. Even in so small a transaction there are plenty of roguish tricks, and I think I know them all."

I told him that once I had found what I was looking for, I would be glad to leave the rest to him. This pleased him, and I believe that he did, in fact, save me a small sum of money on the transaction. He was as happy about this as if he had propounded a masterly scheme for saving the Bank of England from dissolution. The amount at stake never seemed to matter to him. The companies with which he was involved at this time must have had a capital value beyond what I can imagine, yet he was prepared to saddle himself with my small affair. Luther was not a mean man. In many ways he was more reckless with money than I could dare to be. He bought almost anything he fancied, but immediately something arose in the nature of a "transaction", in which wits were pitted against wits, he was as sharp-nosed as a fox to smell out a pennyworth of advantage. It was a matter of principle with him not to be outwitted when dealing with his own kind.

I remember that it was a most unpleasant November day – the day in 1913 when Luther called on me. Prue had gone to visit her professor's wife in Lincoln's Inn. I think she wanted proudly to let her know that now, beyond doubt, Stephen Pentecost's annunciation had been made. It was this impending fact that clouded Luther's mind, too, and made him think me, I imagine, financially unfit for fatherhood. I pottered round in our little kitchen, made tea and toast, and brought them into the studio, where we sat before the fire. The room was darkened by falling rain. I assured him that my income from painting had risen steadily ever since I had been in London. During the last two years it had been a thousand a year, and I saw no reason why it shouldn't soon be more. That was one thing that had made us decide to take a new house. It was becoming difficult to combine work and domesticity under this small roof. When Stephen was born it would be impossible. This would be a studio only. I should come to and from Hampstead on the Underground.

Luther was rather inattentive to all this. He thought me, I knew, a man whose decisions were to be deplored, but who would make his own decisions nevertheless. There was no point in wasting time on such a man, and clearly his thoughts were elsewhere. Suddenly he asked: "Do you ever think of the state of Europe, Ted?"

"In what way?" I asked, rather puzzled.

He looked at me, frankly irritated, and for the first time in all my knowledge of him, stated what he thought to be my opinion of him, and challenged it. He got up and began to walk about the room, coming to rest at last at the window. He looked out into the desolate little winter yard and the pouring rain and spoke with his back to me. "Sometimes you make me sick," he said. "You spend your life here, day after day, smearing pigments on to a bit of wood and transferring them from that on to bits of canvas. And it gives you a hell of a feeling of superiority. You're an artist. You're above the marketplace. A man like me is a carnal animal, concerned with nothing but rootling in the mud."

"Oh, come –" I protested.

He swung round and went on vehemently: "Don't interrupt me. I'm telling you the truth for once. I'm telling you that you're as blind as a bat. You can't see what's under your nose. If there's one thing that holds this complicated world together it's trade and finance. All you artists, and all the hot-headed fools who never had two pennies to rub together and yet know exactly how the enormously difficult affairs of the world should be conducted: you all spit the word financier as though he were some kind of a snake poisoning the veins of life. Let me tell you what a fool you are. Finance is the life-blood of the world. If you want a true internationalist, go to a financier. If you want to know what is *really* happening in the world, and what is about to happen, ask men like me. I can tell you one thing: we're boiling up for a pretty mess. Believe me, I, and men like me, are thinking pretty hard in these days, and we don't like what we're thinking about."

He sat down and became calmer, and I poured him some more tea. He drank it and said: "I have decided now about the moment for going into politics. I shall wait till the storm blows over. The men who've been in government, or even in Parliament, during a war, are not likely to be much liked when the war is ended. Then is the best chance for new men. I shall still be young."

When he was gone, I sat there for a long time wondering whether he had taken leave of his senses. To me, nothing whatever was apparent to give substance to the things he had said. Life was smooth and calm. And yet I could not exorcise the word he had left suspended in the air. War . . .

The word was exorcised before long. It ceased to trouble me and it seemed not at all to have troubled most people. We passed into 1914, and on a May morning of that year Stephen was born. When I was told that I might see him and Prue, I went upstairs, and the bedroom was as quiet as a harbour after storm. The nurse opened the door for me and then withdrew. I seemed to see the bedroom with new eyes. The window was wide open, and the muslin curtains were soundlessly shivering in a warm tremble of air. A bowl of red tulips stood out against the white of the wall, and from above the mantelpiece the portrait of Jesse Cleghorn looked down with an interest at once benevolent and satiric. My feet were soundless on the thick carpet. I saw all this, I say, with new eyes, because in my mind I was wondering: "How is it going to look to *him?*" He was lying in the crook of Prue's arm and I could see nothing of him except the round top of his skull, covered with fine ruddy down. I kissed Prue, and she smiled and said: "He's ginger." Then her eyes closed, and I knew she wanted me then no more. I walked to the window and looked out through the curtains' transparency to the Heath, which was separated from our house only by a road, and on the edge of the Heath there was a great chestnut tree in the glory of its bloom. There had been, I remembered, such a tree opposite our house in Didsbury, and I hoped that this tree in Hampstead would be as happy a thing for Stephen as that one had been for me and Blanche.

Had been . . . It was all over and done with save for a few memories in my heart. I was twenty-five, and I was filled suddenly with a hatred of the thought of the days when Stephen would be twenty-five. Would all this, then, be but memory for him? Would Prue and I be as far from him, in place and mind, as my father and mother were from me?

I turned to the bed again and saw that Prue had opened her eyes. She was watching me intently; and when I stepped to the bedside, kneeled down, and placed my head on her knees, she said: "You were staring out so fiercely at nothing, Ted. What were you thinking about?"

"I was defying the years to take Stephen away from us. I was thinking of the time when he'll be as old as I am — twenty-five."

"What a terrible great age," she teased me, ruffling my hair. "Twenty-five. I wonder what sort of a world it will be for him then? It will be nineteen thirty-nine."

Stephen roused himself and for the first time displayed to me his creased and crumpled face. I stared at it in fascination – my son's face. He closed his eyes, clenched his fists, and began to howl.

7

It was about a month after this that Blanche motored out to Hampstead to see me. During the honeymoon Luther had taught her to drive, and she now had her own car. "I've brought you a few things, Ted," she said. "Come and get them."

In the car was that picture I have spoken of, by an unknown artist, showing Captain Pentecost in the heat of battle lifting a gun back on its carriage in the *Termagant*. There was also Captain Pentecost's diary, which had been in the library at Primrose Hill. I carried them into the house, and Blanche said: "They're yours, if you want them."

Prue had begun to take gentle walks. She was out now on the Heath, with a nurse pushing young Stephen's pram. This was a sumptuous affair, the gift of Luther Brimlow. He was an odd fellow. He had arranged with the people from whom he bought the pram that they should tell him the exact moment of arrival. And there he was, his car pulling up at the tail of the delivery lorry, to hand the thing over with a flowery little speech to Prudence, as he would always call her. I took him aside afterwards, and once more made my protest against receiving gifts. "Look here, young Pentecost," he said, reverting with a twinkle to his old form of address that he knew annoyed me, "Uncle Luther has certain rights in the matter of his nephew. There's an art in receiving a gift graciously."

But I was not in a gracious mood. "Damn it all," I said, "I'm not a pauper. I can keep my own wife and child. I've got more work on my hands than I know what to do with, even though I've raised my price."

"Yes," he said, knowing everything as usual, "but the people you paint are nearly all obscure rich people. No one's ever heard of 'em."

"What the devil has that got to do with it?" I asked irritably. "A picture doesn't depend for its success on the sitter, but on the artist. Who ever heard of the old Jewish women Rembrandt painted?"

"Come off the high horse, my boy," he advised me. "Look at the pictures of Shaw and Thomas Hardy that John has painted. That's what you want to go after. A picture of someone whose name is known all over the world is discussed and reproduced. It does you a lot of good,

a picture like that. What about Lloyd George? All the people without
money love him and all the people with money loathe him. And he's
got a fine head to paint. I'll have a word with him, if you like."

I did not say: "Don't talk rubbish. How can you possibly know
Lloyd George?" I looked at Luther and understood something of what
Blanche had meant when she said that he fascinated her. The first
world war, which destroyed so much, destroyed among other things a
certain formality in clothes. As late as that summer of 1914 men of
business were still togging themselves up like tailors' dummies; and
Luther was wearing, as he spoke to me now, the frock coat, striped
grey trousers and careful tie of his kind. His silk hat lay on the hall
table. It was essentially the same outfit that he had worn on that night
when he appeared so unexpectedly with his parents at my father's
house in Hulme; but now he wore it with a difference: like a seasoned
soldier, not a rookie. And there was just the same difference in his
face, too. He was confident, assured, a man who had tried himself and
knew himself. His eyes had hardened. His small moustache was neatly
clipped over his iron mouth. I knew that whatever else he might need
to lie about, there was no need for him to lie about the influential
people he came across and worked with. So I merely asked: "Since
when have you been meeting Lloyd George?"

"Oh, for some weeks," he said. "Even you, Ted, in your queer
world, must have heard that Lloyd George is Chancellor of the
Exchequer, and it may have occurred to your mind that there are
problems on which a Chancellor finds it useful to consult financiers.
As a matter of fact, I was breakfasting in Downing Street this morning.
Riddell was there with a few new stories. Even in Downing Street, it
seems, one gets a long way with a few new stories."

He was in Downing Street this morning, and now here he is in
Hampstead, delivering a pram. Yes, he fascinated me. I said lamely: "I
can't make you out, Luther."

He laughed outright – something he rarely did – and slapped me
condescendingly on the back. "You never could, young Pentecost." he
said. "Well, I'll speak to L.G. about the portrait."

8

Blanche stood in our little hall, slapping one hand lightly with the gloves she had drawn off. She looked tired and discontented. "You couldn't give me a sausage on a tin plate, could you, Ted?" she asked.

"If you need it," I said, "I think I could. I know there were some sausages left over from breakfast, and our cat Jezebel would part with her plate for a quarter of an hour. But is the matter urgent?"

She walked into the sitting room and sat looking out through the open window. "Oh, I'm just tired of being the perfect hostess, that's all," she said. "Splendid dinners in June are a bit too much. However, that's nothing to do with you. How's Stephen?"

"Powerfully lunged and vociferous. But why have your affairs nothing to do with me?"

"Well," she said, "they haven't had, have they, for years and years. I shall go down in history as the woman who made her own bed. Well, I've been to Tresco Vean."

It was now nearly three years since she had inherited the estate, and this was the first time she had visited it. I had caught from time to time rumours of the dispute that had never ceased between her and Luther on the subject of selling the property. But she had had her way.

"Did Luther go with you?" I asked.

"Oh, no. He hates the place. It's his Naboth's vineyard in reverse. However, I've put Primrose Hill in the market. I don't want a house in Falmouth. I just brought away a few things, and the rest can be sold. I knew you liked that picture, and you once bored me to tears with Captain Pentecost. So you'd better have his diary."

"Thank you," I said. "It's a fascinating book. You should read it some day."

"Oh, to hell with the Kittos and Pentecosts," she said. "They can stew in their own juice so far as I'm concerned. I'm Mrs Luther Brimlow."

She had not yet been married for three years. I had been married longer, and I was watching the Heath anxiously for the return of Prue and Stephen. I could not bear to have them out of my sight.

9

But they had to be out of my sight for a long time every day. I went forth to earn our bread as punctually as my father had done from the

257

small house in Didsbury. My sitters came to the studio in King's Mistress Yard in the mornings. At one o'clock I had a snack in the pub, and in the afternoon I did the work that had to be done when the sitters were absent. It was a routine life, almost a hermit's. I saw little of the hordes of artists who surrounded me in Chelsea. I was never one either for fruitless chance acquaintances or for the froth of "bohemianism". Over my glass of beer and sandwich in the King's Mistress I passed the time of day with a few of my fellow painters, but I managed, I hope without offence, to decline all invitations to parties in studios and such organised buffoonery as the Chelsea Arts Ball. Even my father could hardly have found fault with my exemplary bourgeois existence.

I did not paint the portrait of Mr Lloyd George. He soon had other matters to think of, and so had we all. It was in the King's Mistress that I read of the shot at Sarajevo: the loosened pebble that started the landslide whose rocks, with more and more vehemence, are hurtling about us as I write in 1946.

Joe Jefferson, the cadaverous landlord, whose blue-scraped lantern jaws made me think of Anatole Lop rather than of the conventional picture of "mine host", said, as he handed me my tankard: "Another bloody Archduke gone west, Mr Pentecost," and I answered lightly, turning the paper over in search of more interesting matter: "Ay, so it seems, Joe."

"Ah-well," said Joe, who was something of an anti-monarchist, "it all helps to sweeten the air a bit."

Well, we were to smell the sweetening of the air soon enough. I took the tankard and my plate of sandwiches to my customary table, and Francis Chellew was sitting there. He was the only one of the pub's clientele that I had exchanged more than a few words with. He was tall and fair, with startling blue eyes. The bones of his face were all visible beneath the skin. A small trimmed moustache was the ripe-corn colour of the curls that snuggled in a close casque to his fine head. I thought him overbred, like a prize greyhound. It was his Cornish name that first led me to take some notice of him. He was older than I: about thirty, I should say. In a few conversations I had learned that, despite his name, his family had not lived in Cornwall for generations. His father was a retired admiral turned farmer somewhere in Essex. "I shouldn't mind the farming," Chellew said to me one day, "but to hell with the sea. I loathe it."

But Admiral Chellew was of the third generation to serve in the navy, and he wanted Francis to carry on the tradition. The boy was sent, willy-nilly, to Dartmouth, and ran away at the end of six months. There was a great deal of fuss, but the affair was smoothed over and the authorities agreed to take Francis back. Francis put up with it for another month. Then he ran away again. "My father took the skin off my backside and sent me to Marlborough," he said. "I didn't like it, but I put up with it. The same with Oxford. I had a good enough time, but what the hell —"

I asked him what he *did* want to do, and he said he didn't know. His mother was dead, and when he was twenty-one he inherited from her a small sum which gave him about three pounds a week. On this, he lived somehow in a bed-sitting room. "The devil of it is, I can't touch the capital. It's tied up. If I could lay hands on that, I'd have a bust. Travel. That's what I'd really like to do – have a gorgeous bust. Then perhaps I could settle down and do something."

I discovered that afternoon what Francis Chellew really wanted. Oddly enough, this was to be a statesman, but I don't think he ever knew it. Another thing I discovered about him was this: that what he called a wish for a grand bust was a frantic desire for the bright eyes of danger.

"Well, Pentecost," he greeted me that day as I sat beside him. "You see it's on the way at last."

I looked at him, not understanding; and he said: "This affair at Sarajevo. What's the betting that it's the first squib of the European Brock's benefit?"

It was on my tongue to say: "Good God, man, what rubbish you talk," when suddenly I recalled what Luther Brimlow had said not long ago: "I can tell you one thing, we're boiling up for a pretty mess." I did not speak. I looked at Chellew sitting opposite me, and for the first time I was aware of his face, in the full sense of awareness to me as an artist. It had real beauty, and fineness, and the intelligence that does not often live with beauty. He had always seemed to me a haphazard person; and now for the first time I wondered whether he was ineffective merely because he was like some new machine that is doing nothing only for lack of being applied to what it could magnificently do. In any case, I was aware with certainty that Chellew was not the man to whom one might casually say: "Oh, don't talk balls."

I answered him lightly: "You don't share Joe's opinion, then, that an archduke more or less is a small matter?"

"Oh, as for that," he said, "I'm with Joe. The trouble is that this particular archduke was the safety catch on the rifle. Well, the safety catch is off now, and the rifle's loaded."

"Figures of speech!" I said impatiently. "I could never abide them! What are you getting at?"

"Well, in a word, it's the chance Germany's been waiting for. Don't you agree?"

Don't you agree! What did I know about it? I was suddenly overwhelmed with a sense of my own ignorance. To men like Luther Brimlow, and to men, so different from him, like Francis Chellew, things were clear that were dark to me. Events were unrolling themselves, and were there to be observed; and not I, not one in a thousand of men, bothered to be acquainted with the dynamite and the matches that could blow us sky-high.

"I can't agree or disagree," I said. "I know nothing about it."

Chellew looked at me as if he were dispassionately considering an entomological specimen. "H'm," he said. "It's a pity."

We ate and drank in silence for a while, and when I rose and said: "Well, I must be off," he answered timidly: "If you're not desperately busy, if you could spare an hour, perhaps you'd care to come to my room? I could put you wise to a thing or two."

It was a small cramped room that had forgotten human comfort. There was not even a curtain to the window, and that did not matter, for a blank wall faced it a dozen paces away. A canvas bed was folded and leaning against a wall, with a sleeping-bag near it. "I live on active service," Chellew said with a smile. The floor was bare boards. Apart from the folded bed, a deal kitchen table, two wooden chairs and a chest of drawers made up the furniture. This spartan scraping down to the bones of things did not apply to books. They were numerous but there was no bookcase. They filled the mantelpiece; they stood on the chest of drawers; and those that were left over were along the skirting boards on the floor, with the tides upward. Pinned to the wall were maps. One was an immense map of Europe. Here and there were detailed maps of particular areas.

"How do you like headquarters?" Chellew asked with a diffident smile.

"Well, for myself, I prefer life to be rather more padded."

"So do I," he answered, pulling out with his foot a chair for me to sit on. "For example, I like warm baths, but I haven't had one for a year. I use a canvas bucket of cold water and sponge myself all over. However, there's no point in mortifying the flesh except to prove to yourself that you can do it. The thing is that the flesh doesn't matter much one way or the other. So why not indulge it if you want to? At the moment, I find it necessary to live like this, and so I'm doing it. I know now that it can be done."

"Why do you find it necessary?" I asked him.

"Well, I'm a territorial lieutenant. We'll be among the first to go. I imagine that conditions in the field will be worse than anything I can devise for myself here, but I'm preparing myself as well as I can."

"You seem pretty sure that it's coming."

"I'm absolutely sure not that it's coming but that it's here. Fill your pipe if you'd like to. I don't smoke."

I filled my pipe, and Chellew began to walk up and down the room, talking. Now he would pass to the map. "Here, you see. That's where I reckon they'll try to break through, and don't talk to me about the inviolability of Belgium. Belgium will be violated." Or he would bend down to the floor and take up a book. "You know Clausewitz, of course?" "You've read Bernhardi?"

I shall never forget that hour. I listened to the voice of doom talking coldly and dispassionately through the beautiful mask of Francis Chellew. I have never had a deeper sense of being in the presence of a dedicated man. History, geography, strategy, tactics: he had considered them all in the light of something that was to him as inevitable as the coming of tomorrow's daylight; and when he had done talking of that, his voice warmed and he talked of society as it was and as he hoped it would be when the war was over. I discovered in him a passionate addiction to justice and liberty, a love of people, a burning desire to free them from the snares of their own fears and consequent hatreds.

"Forgive me," he said at last, a charming smile lighting the wintry beauty of his face. "I tend to forget myself. I don't see many people. I'm a bit of a hermit and things stew in my mind. I've made you the victim of the boil-over. If I could go home now and then I suppose it would be different. But my father and I don't hit it off."

I looked at him in wonder. He was trained down to bone and muscle. He was clearly as hard as nails; but I had also the sense of a man mortally exposed. "I dare not be soft," he had said at one point; and I know that he dared not because it would be so easy for him to have his heart on his sleeve. I was afraid to touch him emotionally, just as I was afraid to touch Stephen's egg-shell skull beneath which I could almost see the convulsions of the brain. Another thing Chellew had said was: "I used to read a lot of poetry, but I've given that up. For the time being, I belong to Sparta, not Attica."

"You've given up too much," I thought. "For you, it's fortunate the moment has come, or something would break. Even as it is . . ."

And there I was, conceding that the moment had come.

"If for once," I smiled, "you can bear the silken dalliance of a comfortable chair, let's go round to my studio and have some tea."

He was glad to come, and when we had had tea I made a few sketches of his head. It was a fascinating head to draw. Quixote, I thought, was like this when young.

"I'd like to paint you," I said. "Would you have time to give me some sittings?"

"I can't afford it," he answered.

"I'm not after a commission," I assured him. "The first woman I ever went to bed with had been kept by a rich man. She said how pleasing it was to go to bed with someone who could pay her nothing. I was too young then to know that it's a wretched life if we can't occasionally give away the thing we do best."

"I see what you mean," he said, "but I've never been to bed with a woman. I hate promiscuity. However, if you'd like to paint me, I'm not busy at the moment."

He had risen to go when there was the sound of a motorcar stopping under the window, and a moment later Blanche came in. "Hallo, Ted," she said. "Oh, I beg your pardon. I thought you had sitters only in the morning."

"Let me present Mr Francis Chellew," I said. "This is Mrs Luther Brimlow, who also has the privilege of being my sister Blanche."

They shook hands. There was something nervous, high-strung and unreleased about the pair of them, I thought. Chellew went at once. He didn't have even to pick up a hat, for he did not wear one. He just went, with an air of flight, escape.

Blanche laughed as we listened to his step running down the stairs. "Sorry," she said, addressing the closed door. "I didn't mean to startle you." She turned to me. "Did you ever see such a bolt? He went like a stag that had sniffed danger in the breeze. Who is he?"

"A remarkable man," I said, "who will die famous in old age or unknown in youth."

"Well," she answered, "plenty are going to die unknown in youth if what Luther says is right. He's been giving me the creeps today. Have you read this news in the papers about the assassination of an archduke?"

I made some more tea and we talked for half an hour. As she was pulling on her gloves, Blanche looked down at the drawings of Chellew's head scattered on the table. "He is a remarkable-looking person," she said. "I must say he gave me quite a turn. Did you notice his eyes?"

"That's part of my job. I'm going to paint him."

"Well, it's not part of mine," said Blanche, "but I noticed them all the same. When do the sittings begin?"

"At once, if I can get him along. If he and Luther are right, there won't be much time."

"You can take it from me," Blanche said, "that Luther is always right – in matters like that."

10

We were soon to become used to the sight of uniforms in the streets, but I was surprised when Chellew turned up in uniform for his first sitting. He looked a different man. A racehorse browsing in a pasture looks different from a saddled and bitted racehorse dancing impatiently at the starting tapes. There was that difference in the two Chellews. But he was as shy as ever. He was as biddable as a child when I began to pose him.

"Do I have to keep absolutely quiet?" he asked.

"Oh, no, you can talk. But try not to shift about."

"Thank you, Pentecost. Or would you mind if I called you Edward? I haven't many friends."

"Anything but Edward," I begged him. "Ted will do."

"Well, Ted, I thought when I got home the other night that I'd been rather rude to your sister. Did it seem so to you?"

"Not particularly. You were a bit abrupt, perhaps. But I shouldn't worry about that."

"You might tell her I'm sorry," he said, like a small boy apologising for rudeness at a party. "I never got on well with people, and lately I've been a deliberate recluse."

"All right. I'll give her your apology. That is, when I see her. We don't see a great deal of one another, Blanche and I. She's very much a married woman, you know. She entertains a lot for her husband. He's a financial bloke, if you know what that means, I'm never sure. His language is foreign to me. Holding companies. Operating companies. All that sort of thing. I can never make out what it all adds up to."

"I expect he's a very rich man."

"Yes. And Blanche is a rich woman in her own right – if anyone has a right to be rich without having done a thing about it. She inherited an estate in Cornwall and a lot of money from an ancient relative who took a fancy to her."

"That's hardly surprising, Ted."

"No. I suppose not. Try not to fidget."

"I thought she was a very beautiful woman," he said with difficulty, and he blushed like a girl.

Looking back upon it all now, I can say this: nothing that followed surprised me. Since the evening when Blanche and Francis had first met, the European situation had worsened. Therefore, I could not pretend to be taken unaware when, the work for that morning being over, Blanche's car turned into King's Mistress Yard just as Francis Chellew and I were leaving my studio to go to the pub for a snack, and Blanche said to me: "Oh, Ted, I had to come and see you. I must talk to someone. I hardly see Luther at all nowadays, and when I do he's nothing but a voice of doom. I've come to drag you off to lunch somewhere."

The words tumbled out of her mouth – the first excusing words that came to her – and her eyes were devouring Francis Chellew as he stood there tongue-tied, stroking his moustache with the end of a little leather-covered stick that he carried. In his uniform he looked very handsome.

"Where do you want to go to?" I asked.

"I've booked a table at the Café Royal," she said. "I could get you there by one. It's only half-past twelve now."

"All right," I consented; and Chellew said: "Well, don't let me keep you. I'll pop in here and get my sandwich."

I was not surprised, I say, by anything: not even when I noticed that Blanche's fingers, resting on the handle of the car door, shook a little and that she moistened her lips before saying: "Would you like to come too, Mr Chellew?"

"Oh, you must excuse me," he said. "Really, I couldn't go up to town dressed like this. It would be – a bit ostentatious."

He saluted, and began to move towards the pub. I took a pace after him and grasped his arm; and I have often wondered whether that was not the definitive gesture, whether, if I had let him go, that would have been the end of the matter. But I had seen Blanche's crestfallen face, and I said: "Look, Francis. You can be in your room, changed, and back here in hardly more than five minutes. We'll wait for you."

"Yes," said Blanche. "There's no hurry."

"You'd really *like* me to come?" he asked, leaving me out of it and speaking to her.

"Yes," she said.

"Very well," Chellew answered and hurried away; and that was that.

I don't know whether he noticed, as I did, that the table which Blanche had booked in the Café Royal was laid for three. I went back to Hampstead after the meal, and left them there drinking coffee and brandy.

11

Through those appalling days when the world rocked in uneasy balance before toppling over, I worked on Chellew's portrait, and, having to observe him as closely as I did, I was aware of the tension in him, betraying itself by long silences and occasional hectic outbursts of speech, by a ticking of the clenched jaws, and by the sudden starts with which he would come to, out of some far reverie, if I spoke unexpectedly.

On the last day of the sittings he said impetuously: "Surely to God, Ted, it's *natural* to be joyful! The devil of it is, I've been afraid of joy all my life. I can't give myself to it. I fly my own nature, as if I were a leper."

The job was done, for good or ill, and I laid my brushes down in a dish of turpentine. I propped the wet palette against the wall. I pulled off my smock, and I stood looking at the picture. I did all these things slowly and deliberately, postponing the words which I knew he was expecting from me. He was older than I was, but he was like a child waiting for instruction.

It was a day of heavy heat. Even in the spacious studio, with its windows wide open, the atmosphere was oppressive. Chellew remained sitting where he had been posed. I turned my back on him and stood at the window, looking into the hard dark-green leaves of the plane tree. Not a breath moved them. Only my eyes, not my mind, saw them. My mind was in a far-off day when Blanche had stripped off her stockings, rolled up her dress, and danced madly in a field alongside the Mersey. "Don't you say a word about this to Mother. Or to Betsy. Oh! They don't know how mad I am!"

What did I, either, know about her madness? How mad was she now? All I knew was what I could divine from Chellew, and he seemed to be in hell.

What was I to say to this man, my elder? Cheer up, my boy? Follow the dictates of your heart? It'll all come right in the end?

I turned towards him. "Francis," I said, "is there anything I can do to help you in any way?"

"Yes," he said. "I've got my call-up. I join the battalion tomorrow. Will you stow my books here while I'm away? There's nothing else worth bothering about. I've told my landlady she can keep the rest. But please look after my books."

"Yes," I said, "I'll do that, Francis. Are you sure that's all?"

"Well," he hurried on, "perhaps you'll think it an awful cheek – you may think it altogether irregular – but if I were to write to Blanche, could I address the letters here?"

"Yes."

"You don't think it would be wrong of me to write to Blanche?"

"I'm not your judge."

"Well, so long, Ted," he said.

"I could come and see you off tomorrow."

"Please don't. I have a horror of goodbyes."

We shook hands and he ran out of the room. From the window I watched him cross the yard. He didn't look back, and he hadn't bothered to give a glance at the finished portrait. He was on my mind for the rest of that day, and I had not shaken him off when I awoke in the morning. I decided, despite his wishes, to go to the station and say goodbye. But Blanche was there before me, and, seeing her without being seen, I did not say goodbye to Chellew after all. I turned in my tracks and took a taxi to Chelsea.

12

I suppose it was some scheme that had been concocted between Blanche and Francis, but the letters were not addressed to Mrs Luther Brimlow. They were addressed to Miss Blanche Pentecost, c/o Edward Pentecost, Esq. Francis must have written his first letter in the train, for it reached me on the morning after his departure. Thereafter, the letters came daily, and on some days there were two. I began by enclosing them in envelopes and sending them on to Blanche, but one afternoon she appeared in the studio and asked me not to do this. "Luther is likely to wonder," she said, "why there is this sudden burst of brotherly communication. After all, you are on the telephone and so are we."

She seemed to me to be drawn and reckless-looking. She tried to carry the situation off with bravado, but when I handed her the letter that had come that morning, she took it with a shaking hand, hurried to the window, and tore it open with an unashamed eagerness. I watched her covertly, and saw her face become composed and a smile light her eyes. It was a situation so delicate, so touch and go, that I felt doubtful about venturing so much as a word. However, when she had read her letter several times, and seemed disposed to read it once again, I said: "You never gave very good value as a letter writer, Blanche. One of the last things old Sapphira ever said to me was that you couldn't write if you wanted to."

She said gravely: "Well, the old dear was right about that. With a pen in my hand, I'm like a swan on dry ground. But all I need to say to Francis I can say in three words, and I say them every day."

I had finished work for the day, and I sat by the fire smoking while she pottered about in the kitchen making tea. She wheeled it in on my little trolley and sat opposite me. We had now been at war for a month. "Francis is a captain already," she said.

"He could hardly avoid it," I answered. "They must be creating officers wholesale, with all these thousands of recruits coming up."

"There must be more in it than that," she said touchily; and I understood that I must say nothing that even obliquely diminished Francis. "Yes, there must be," I quickly agreed. "I never met a man in any job so resolved as Francis to do the job as well as it could be done."

"He is incomparable," she said simply; and I decided that I had better leave it at that.

We arranged that henceforth I should keep Francis' letters, and that Blanche should call at Chelsea as often as she could and pick them up. "I don't know," I said, "what we shall do if I go away myself."

"What do you mean – go away?" Blanche asked sharply.

"I mean join the army."

"But, Ted, you couldn't!"

"Why not? I'm twenty-five. I'm as robust as a young ox."

"But you're married, and you've got a child. What on earth would Prue say?"

That, indeed, was the question. For more than a week now this worm had been gnawing my guts. The posters in the streets – your King and Country need you – the ragged platoons of civilians in caps and bowler hats and straw boaters, in tweeds and broadcloth and rags, marching with what they could muster of military swagger behind bands; the daily news in the papers; the orators at recruiting meetings on every street corner; all these things, and, too, a surprising and unsuspected wish to march with my fellows, had tormented me, made my work a burden, and told me that, sooner or later, there would be no resisting the small sucking eddies that would soon become a vortex. There was another thing, too, of which I said nothing to Blanche. That morning, for the first time, I received a letter from Francis Chellew. It was like him to go straight to the point:

My dear Ted, – I imagine that you will find it difficult to stand
out against the spirit that we feel everywhere in the country
today. I know that you are married. So are many of our officers
here and many of our men. This letter does not seek in any way
to influence you. You must make up your mind for yourself. All
I want to say is this: that *if* you decide to join some officers'
training corps, it would be a great pleasure to me, when your
training is done, to try and get you into this battalion. I think it
could be managed. We need officers badly. Think it over.

Sincerely,

Francis Chellew.

The half sheet of writing was almost brutally abrupt. It contrasted
significantly with the thick wad that was contained in every letter
addressed to Blanche. But it heartened me. I knew in my bones that I
should join the army. To be with Chellew suddenly seemed very
desirable.

13

Prue was crying. She was not, thank God, one of those women who
smile bravely, put a good face on it, as they say, and repress all the
emotions of their hearts. I had told her, and she was crying.

Stephen was a good child. As a rule, when he had been put to bed,
he slept and we heard no more of him till the morning. But that night,
just as we had got into bed at eleven o'clock, he gave a great cry – so
unaccustomed that we both got out of bed and went over to his cot,
which was in a corner of our bedroom. His cries continued for a
moment. Prue took him up in her arms, crooned a few words to him,
and he fell asleep. She laid him back in the cot and we heard no more
of him. It was a strange interlude, as though an adult had struggled
with a cry out of a nightmare, found familiar things about him, and
fallen back upon sleep. But what, I wondered, could furnish either
dream or nightmare for so young a child? There was no experience of
the past, no threat from the future. Or did the young mind return into
a past that we had forgotten, range already into a future physically
unexplored?

Prue and I got back into bed, leaving the dim bedside light burning.
We lay with my arm under her shoulders. I looked up at the gentle

light suffusing the ceiling and I thought of her and Stephen. Such experiences as this which we had just gone through wound them about my heart. It was nothing great, as greatness is usually apprehended, nothing startling or sensational, that made the warm and beautiful texture of our lives. It was the recurrence of such little moments as these, gentle flowers of shared experience opening about us day after day. It would be hard to leave them.

"Prue," I said. "I have decided to join the army."

I felt her body go rigid in my arms, and then she began to cry. I did not feel that words could comfort her, nor, it seemed, did she feel that words could express her grief. So we lay there clinging to one another till her crying ceased. The last sounds of her sobbing reached me after her eyes were closed and she was asleep. It was inexpressibly moving, this sound of Prue crying in her sleep, and before putting out the light I lay there for a long time thinking of this world of madmen cheered on by waking women who cried in their sleep.

But Prue did not cheer me on. The first thing she said to me in the morning about my resolve to join the army incredibly was this: "Ted darling, you should go and say goodbye to your father."

We had breakfasted, and Stephen had been fed, and I was pushing his pram along a path on the Heath. Prue was walking at my side. It was a morning of autumn's best. We shall not forget it, those of us who lived through it, the ripe ironic beauty of that autumn of 1914. On the Heath awkward squads of recruits were marching and doubling in the golden sunshine. Now that my mind was made up, I could not bring myself to face the routine of work in Chelsea. The day was like an opal, and I asked nothing better than to be here on the Heath with Prue and Stephen.

Prue's words shattered my lazy aimless enjoyment of the moment. "Do you think so?" I asked.

"Yes. Don't you?"

"Yes."

Prue had not met either my father or my mother, but I knew that for some time now she and my mother had been exchanging letters every week. Not long before this, sitting at her writing desk, Prue had looked up and said: "I'm sending your love to your mother, Ted."

"Good," I said.

"And to your father," she added. She looked at me with a question in her eyes. "Very well," I answered reluctantly.

"You see, Ted," she explained, "there's Stephen now. I don't want him to grow up in an atmosphere of hate."

"That's a strong word."

"Well, let's not quibble about the word. I'll send him your love."

Because of this, I was not surprised when Prue suggested that I should go to Manchester. I went the next morning. I arrived at noon, lunched in the town, and in the afternoon walked out to the house in Hulme. Even now, though I had come to say goodbye to my father, I was reminding myself that this was afternoon, and that, if his habits were unchanged, he would be out distributing tracts.

Travelling up, as I had done, through the ripe loveliness of England, through fields of stooked corn and orchards red under the reddening woods, the hideousness of Hulme struck me like a blow. The very tenderness of the day, the sun shining benignly and without much heat, seemed ironic, almost spiteful. The rows and rows of identical houses, regimented into endless vistas of squalor, unrelieved by so much as a stunted laurel or privet, the doors opening straight off the pavements, the listless litter shrivelled by the abounding sun of that year: all this, seen anew after long absence, afflicted me with a poignant sense of waste and futility; and with more than this. For, as never before, I saw my father's life dissociated from its effect upon mine. I saw it as, I thought, it must appear to him: as a stupendous but gladly accepted sacrifice, a conscious putting aside of so much that had been so joyful: his music, his delight in trivial amusing things, his love of the trees and fields that had been about us in our house in Didsbury. All these he had loved and left to give himself to a thankless job in this desert that had once known trees and water and was now made hateful and sterile by greed.

Thinking these things, I was glad that Prue had put it in my heart to come, and I hastened to the little house, telling myself that, even should he be out with his tracts, I must stay till he returned, however late that might be.

I did not see him. I saw my mother and the Brimlows. It was three o'clock when I reached the house; a four-wheeler cab was at the kerb. My mother and Mr and Mrs Brimlow were standing in the passage, dressed for going out.

271

"Well, Ted!" my mother said in her undemonstrative way, but I would not have this coolness. What I had been thinking had made me emotional. I took her in my arms and kissed her. "Where's Father?" I asked.

"About the Lord's business," said Mrs Brimlow sharply; and Mr Brimlow said: "Ay. Wist ye not that I must be about my father's business?"

"Where is Father?" I repeated, addressing my mother, and she said: "I'm afraid you're unlucky, Ted. He's attending a religious conference in Newcastle. He won't be back for a week."

"He's a power in Israel," said Mr Brimlow. "To think it! I little knew what was in store when I was privileged to lead him to the mercy seat. Eh, Mother?"

"Ay," Mrs Brimlow rejoined. "It was a happy day when you all went off to Cornwall and left him in the hands of God's mercy. It was a terrible tussle, but he came over. How is our dear boy?"

Listening to these two had been like returning to an outgrown nightmare. Mrs Brimlow's question brought me back, reminded me, almost with a shock, that marriage had related me to these people. Their dear boy was married to my sister Blanche, who was burning with love for Francis Chellew.

"He seemed well when I last saw him," I answered. "But I don't see much of him. The war keeps him busy."

Mr Brimlow laid a hand on my shoulder. "If you can spare the time, Ted," he said, "you'd better come with us. We're taking your mother off to tea."

My mother gave me a look of invitation, and I said: "Thank you. I'd like to come, if I may."

Mr Brimlow chuckled. "If I may . . . Hear that, Mother? Anybody'd think he was a stranger. You're one of us now, Ted my boy. Almost my son. God help me some day to lead you into the light, like your father before you."

We got into the cab. The Brimlows sat facing me and my mother, and I was able to take stock of them. They seemed fat with content. Mr Brimlow's eyes were still rheumy and he still tended to drool and dribble. Mrs Brimlow's steel *pince-nez* looked like the very pair I had splintered with a conker long ago. But despite these touches of familiar appearance, they were embellished and adorned in a way that was new to me. They were evidently spending money on themselves. And then there was this cab. The idea of taking a cab from Hulme to Didsbury would have been startling in the old days, and, to break a heavy silence, I said as much.

"Yes," said Mrs Brimlow. "And that reminds me, Jo. You'd better enter it before you forget."

Mr Brimlow took a small book from his pocket and made a note. "We're not kept short," he explained, "but Luther expects an account rendered."

This seemed to him the most natural thing in the world, but I was overcome with a sense of shame at the thought of the old man accounting to Luther for every penny he spent. No, indeed, Luther would not keep them short, but he would demand a strict reckoning. "To cab, conveying Mrs Pentecost to tea, Hulme to Didsbury, 10s."

"You are fortunate to have such a son," I said.

Old Brimlow tucked away his book and looked up with glistening eyes. "He's the light of our lives," he said simply; and Mrs Brimlow added: "After the Lamb."

"Ay," said Mr Brimlow, "after the Lamb."

The autumn dusk was already settling upon the city as we went clopping along the road that offered me at every moment matter for nostalgic thought. It was under these trees of Fallowfield and Withington that I had walked day after day with my father in his boyish buoyant mood of a Whittington. Here I had watched Jesse Cleghorn cycling towards the city that stands four-square, not seeing the profane confusion through which his charmed life moved; and along this road, I recalled with a catch of the breath, I had driven in a cab like this, hot with anticipation, cold with apprehension, to that first encounter with Iris Randle at my studio. I wondered idly how long Iris would remain attached to Viscount Moreton Hampstead, the blue-eyed boy, younger than herself, to whom she had been married for a year.

All along this road it was as though I were saying goodbye to my youth; and when the cab drew up at the Brimlows' house, and I saw next door, in the house where we had lived, a strange face watching us through the window, I felt as though treason were afoot. While my mother and those two went indoors, I asked to be excused for a moment, and I clambered through the gap that was still in the hedge and stood under the majestic tree that had been almost a presence in my childhood and Blanche's. Always, in that part of Manchester, the dusk is bloomier than elsewhere, for the light strains through the perpetual exhalation of river mists, and images have the tender texture of photographs taken through gauze. This is especially so in autumn, and it was so that night, with the great tree sheltering me beneath its russet canopy and offering to my feet the always good sense of the humus nourishing its enduring life with its recurrent deaths. Looking up into the branches, I saw the heavy crop of fruit, the toys of our childhood, but now, in my valedictory mood, the pledges of an immortality that would endure when I had left this scene forever.

In the Brimlows' front room a light sprang up, and I laid my hand upon the bark of the tree and let it rest there for a moment as though I hoped that something of myself would enter into it and abide with it, and then I crossed the road and went into the house. Mrs Brimlow, who didn't miss much, had been watching me through the window. "That's the tree you used to get the conkers from," she said, and I knew she was reminding me of the day when, in my sin and iniquity, I had batted her in the eye with one and refused to apologise. "Ah, well," she said, "I don't suppose it'll be there forever. If that field comes into the market we'll buy it. I expect Luther'd advance us the money. Then we'd soon have it down. It darkens the house."

A fire had been lit, and my mother was sitting on one side of it and Mr Brimlow on the other. A couple of little tables were on the hearthrug between them, and this, too, I thought, was a measure of the Brimlows' advance into gentility. No longer the hearty spread of a Lancashire high tea, eaten sitting in to the dining room table. A capped and aproned maid came in with a tray; Mrs Brimlow whisked the curtains across the window; and we sat down to eat a few fancy cakes and fingers of buttered toast. But not before Mr Brimlow had said as unctuous a grace as if this were the Lord Mayor's banquet. It might all have been funeral baked-meats so far as I was concerned, for a more lugubrious repast I have never shared. The Brimlows had no conversation, and I was never any good at using light chatter to relieve a moment that didn't engage me. It was not till the maid had been summoned by a bell and the tea things had been removed that Mrs Brimlow said briskly: "Now, Ted, tell us all about Luther."

"It's rum," said Mr Brimlow, "to hear you call him Ted, Mother. It's rum to think that all of us, sitting here by God's grace round the fire, are related. It didn't look likely, not so long ago."

It seemed rum to me, too, and I didn't like being reminded of it; but Mrs Brimlow took it all in her stride. "There's one thing we can be assured of," she said, "and that is that what God wills to be done will be done. I don't say that, if I'd been consulted about a wife for Luther, I'd have picked Blanche; but I wasn't consulted, so that's that. The Lord's will be done."

"I can well imagine," I said, "that finding the right wife for Luther gave the Lord an anxious time. If we feel that He did His best, we shouldn't complain."

Mrs Brimlow shot a suspicious look over her glasses, as though she smelt blasphemy in this; but she only said: "I'm not complaining. I have faith in Luther."

"And in the Lord."

"And in the Lord," she accepted firmly; leaving me with the feeling that Luther and the Lord made a combination that could never fall into error.

I had not, since the war began, seen Luther, and Blanche, whom I saw almost every day for reasons that would astonish the Brimlows, told me nothing about him. It was as if, so long as Francis Chellew lived, Luther was dead to her. So I said: "I should like to be able to give you news, Mrs Brimlow, but really I see nothing of Luther in these days. You probably gather more from his letters than you can get from me."

"We don't get letters from *him*," she said with an odd mixture of pride and pathos. "The letters come from his secretary."

"Yes," Mr Brimlow broke in, "we've got nothing to worry about or complain of. We are kept regularly informed as to Luther's health. I am a simple man, and I've been used all my life to handling simple business affairs. But I can well imagine the sort of affairs Luther is called on to handle – vast – international" – his pudgy hands waved in the air, indicating vague continents – "and I suppose that leaves him little time for letter writing."

Again I caught the note of pride and regret, and I wondered whether these two had any notion of the sort of cockatrice they had hatched.

We entered then upon a good session of Luther-worship. Mrs Brimlow produced a book into which was pasted all she had been able to gather of cuttings about Luther's wedding and references to him that were becoming more and more frequent in the press. Another big city deal, another merger. It must have been double-Dutch to her, but this, I guessed, whether she herself guessed it or not, was, more authentically than the Word of the Lord, the word that spoke to her heart. This was her bread of life. It was a pity, I thought, that the record did not begin with those forged letters of long ago. That might help her to avoid disappointment in the long run. But I dismissed these thoughts as ungenerous and suggested to my mother that it was time we should go. It was past six o'clock.

Old Brimlow got up heavily. "Well, Ted, it's been nice having you. We don't see too much of the younger end these days. Give our love to Luther, and, mind, if there's any bit of news about him that you can spare a minute to tell us, we'll be glad to hear it."

I told them nothing of my intention to join the army. I merely said, as we parted at the gate: "Goodbye for the moment. I'll be seeing you again."

"D.V.," said Mrs Brimlow, looking as if she would not be much upset if D. did not V.; and with my arm through my mother's I walked along to the Wilmslow Road. She was silent for a time; then she said: "I suppose you've come to say you're joining the army."

I tried to carry off the moment lightly. "Since when have you had second sight, Mother?"

"Second sight!" she snorted. "Half one's usual sense is all that's necessary. You were asking for your father as soon as you got to Hulme. I don't suppose you'd have been doing that if you hadn't wanted to say goodbye. You pig-headed Pentecosts! You've left it too late, as usual."

She said this not in anger but as a statement of fact; and she was right enough, it seemed to me, to kick the Pentecosts if she wanted to. Much good they had done her.

A few moments' walking took us to the Didsbury railway station. "We'll take a train to town," I said. "Let's not spend the evening in that wretched little house."

"It wouldn't hurt you," she objected, "to pass a few hours in the way I pass my life."

The remark brought me up short, pricked the bubble of my fine intention. We were to travel to town first-class, have a good dinner at the Midland Hotel, and go to a show. I would let her see that Luther Brimlow wasn't the only son who looked after his parents. Her few words stripped me naked, showed me the egotistical fool I was.

"Would you rather go home?"

"No."

"Are you unhappy?"

We faced one another under the lamp burning outside the station. She looked more dour and suffering than I had known her before. "It depends on what you mean by happiness," she said. "If you mean does living in Hulme give me the willies, well, it doesn't. It's nothing new to me. It's the sort of place I lived in before I met your father. I'm used to it. If you mean am I disappointed with your father and the life he's given me, I can only say he's got the right to lead any sort of life he chooses. And you can take it from me there's something in a man who chooses, even if he chooses what doesn't suit you. A man like that is better than all these gormless tykes who have everything chosen for 'em by the bosses and the brewers."

"Well—" I began; but she broke in again: "Let me tell you this, Ted. Few of us are all of a piece. Your father's the man I married. If the piece of him I've now got to live with isn't the piece I knew first of all, well, it's a piece of the same man anyway. It was the whole man I married, and you can take it from me it was a pretty good man at that. As for happiness — well, find it if you can. I get along. You've heard me grumble more than enough, but I've got plenty to be thankful for. Now let's stop nattering and have this bust you're set on."

And so we did. We ate the last dinner that she and I were to eat in Manchester together, and then we went to the second house at the Palace. The customary music-hall gaiety was heightened to a hectic flush. There were many uniforms in the audience, and all the women performers showed the lust for driving males to the slaughter that was more marked in that war than in the one just ended. They smirked and strutted and cajoled, promising kisses and hinting at more satisfying favours for those who were in the King's uniform by Saturday night. It was all faintly disgusting. If it had to be done, I thought, how much better Iris Randle would do it than these grimacing chits. Iris would know what she was talking about.

When we got back to the little house in Hulme the fire was out. I lit it, my mother made a pot of tea, and we sat there talking till far into the morning.

"I wish you and Prue could see something of one another," I said.

"Well, we can't," she said flatly. "This is no place for her to come to, especially with a child. Your father'd drive her mad preaching at her morning, noon and night. And I can't leave him to go to her. So that's that. Live your own life, Ted, and leave me to live mine."

CHAPTER SEVEN

ALL OF us, except Luther, were down at Tresco Vean in the summer of 1919: Blanche and her daughter Frances, my mother, Prue, Stephen and myself. Luther was visiting his father and mother in Manchester, but the letter which Blanche had received from him that morning was not dated from the house in Didsbury. It came from the Midland Hotel. The old people, I imagine, waited upon him there in such time as he could spare them. To say that he was visiting them was, in any case, hardly a true statement of the case. His affairs had taken him to Manchester; seeing his father and mother was something fitted in.

What Luther's affairs were it was becoming, for a financial ignoramus like me, increasingly difficult to say. During the war he had been abroad a good deal – to the United States and to South American countries especially – buying this, that and the other thing on behalf of the British Government; and his patriotic endeavours had not impoverished him. At any rate, while the war was still being fought, he had succeeded in buying Greenlands, an estate not far from St Albans, with all its contents. It had belonged to Lord Doverdale, an eccentric bachelor, the last of his line, who intelligently abandoned its splendours for the snugger comfort of a service flat in London. Occasionally, Lloyd George escaped from the pressure of Downing Street to Greenlands for a weekend, after Luther had bought the place. Blanche told me she had never met the Prime Minister, and I was not surprised at that. The greater part of Luther's life was conducted behind a veil of reticence that amounted to mystery. I often wondered how much, by now, he and Blanche had in common.

Did Luther imagine that they had Frances in common? It was something I could not ask. Prue and Stephen were running towards the blue glimpse of water which Blanche and I, sitting in deck chairs on the grey stone terrace, could see at the bottom of the narrow valley that made the garden. It was down there, on the old granite landing place, that Captain Pentecost had waited through the night years ago, and found his love in the morning. My wounded leg was aching abominably, and it pleased me to sit with Blanche, doing nothing, thinking of those long-off days, of Kittos and Pentecosts, and soaking in the sun. The low wall edging the terrace supported here and there stone urns that spilled cascades of pink geraniums into the sunlight. Overhead, gulls on motionless wings floated against the blue. It was just three years ago, I reflected, on as lovely a summer day as this, that I had given Francis Chellew a boost up into the lorry that took him to the railhead where he would catch the leave train. That was in early June of 1916. Frances was born in March of 1917. All I knew of a certainty was that Luther was himself in London during those June days, and that Blanche had once said to me: "Luther never met Francis. He didn't know of his existence."

I turned my head lazily at a sound behind me. Miss Nethersole, the brown-uniformed Princess Christian nurse, was pushing the pram out through the french window on to the terrace. Blanche at once leapt eagerly to her feet. Miss Nethersole put a finger to her lips. "She's asleep, madam." She placed the pram so that the raised hood shaded the child's face, and, sitting upon a rigid chair, began rather severely to knit. Blanche stood looking down at her daughter, who had the curling golden hair of Francis Chellew.

2

Chellew was like a child going home from school, filled with the foretaste of delightful doings. We were in a rest area, in a village that remained comparatively civilised and unbroken. It had been possible to clean ourselves up. We had been enjoying the luxury of baths, and I remember a cressy stream that, just before a bend, deepened into a pool under trees. The sun shone through the trees. They splintered its light into shafts that pierced the water and lay in quivering spangles upon the golden gravel that made up the bed. The water was just deep enough for a dive, just wide enough to permit three strokes before the other bank was reached. Francis and I went there every day and plunged naked into the cleanness. It asperged us of our bodies' filth and our souls' horror. He had plunged before me, and reached the other side, and clambered out, clutching the grasses and the down-drooping branches of trees. He stood on the bank facing me, but not looking at me, looking up into the sunbeams netted in the canopy of leaves. His look became fixed and faraway, and I knew that he was thinking of his leave, as a soul in purgatory might think of purging's end and paradise beginning. He was thinking of that, and of Blanche. He had said to me, a few days before: "Ted, this leave it's to be everything," and I had known what he meant. It had not been everything in any leave before that. I told him that I had done what I had promised to do. I had written to my friend Joe, the landlord of the King's Mistress pub. Joe had the key of my studio. His wife went in occasionally and gave the place a wipe over. For this leave, I told Joe, the key was to be handed to Major Chellew, who would be living in the studio for a week. Francis and I both understood the significance of this.

And now I stood there watching his naked body that was to be Blanche's: the casque of golden hair that was shedding water into his blue eyes, the ropey muscles of his arms, the virile stance of his legs. The livid scar of a flesh-wound tore a red line down his right thigh. Suddenly, his mind seemed to drop like a plummet back into the moment, and he shouted: "Come on!" His words shattered my reverie, and, feeling a shame of my staring, I plunged.

Two days after this I stood with him outside the quartermaster's store, waiting for the lorry. We had served together for eighteen months. I knew Francis now as I had known no other man, and there were times when it was in my heart to wish that some sudden stroke of fate would remove Luther Brimlow to a better world or a worse: I hardly cared which. A thousand things done and endured had made Francis my brother. I thought, as I stood there with him in that road which was a cutting through chalk, and as I looked at the chicory flowers trembling on its topmost edge against the pale blue of the Picardy sky, that whatever joy Blanche might feel at his coming could not be greater than my sorrow at his going. Then the lorry came, and I boosted him up into the back of it, and in a haze of chalky dust he set off for the railhead.

There is not much more to be said of Francis Chellew, except insofar as the life of Frances will go on saying it. We had already moved up nearer the line when he rejoined us. The bombardment that preceded the battle of the Somme had begun. For a week the world shuddered around us and the night horizon was molten fire. We moved into our final positions, worming our way through the brown bowels that had been cut into the tortured earth, and there we waited. On the night before we went over I was making my rounds, a second lieutenant, and I ran into Major Chellew and saluted him and he returned my salute. Francis was apt to be formal and strictly according to the book on such occasions. He asked: "All well?" and I said: "Yes, sir." He squeezed past me in the narrow trench and I was going on my way when he called quietly: "Ted!" I turned back and he held out his hand. "I shan't see you again till the balloon goes up," he said. "So long, and all the best."

I took his hand. "The same to you, Francis," I said.

It was still rather formal; and then he said: "Look, Ted, you know as well as I do that tomorrow's going to be bloody hell – the hottest bloody hell we've had so far. And so I'd like to say – just in case – Thank you. Thank you for everything."

He went on, rather bowed, for the parapet was low, and disappeared round a bend of the trench. I never saw him again. All his brightness was dissolved into nothing when a shell hit the trench the next day. There was not a finger of him left to be buried. The news of his death reached me in hospital, where a bullet was prised out of my splintered shinbone. It was from the hospital that I wrote to Blanche. I knew that already the casualty lists would have given her the bitter news, and so my letter to her was nothing but these two lines by Julian Grenfell:

> But Day shall clasp him with strong hands,
> And Night shall fold him in soft wings.

This was Blanche's answer:

> Dear Ted, – I'm sorry to learn about your wound, the news having reached me through a friend of mine who is engaged to your Lieutenant Fletcher. Let's hope it will mean the end of the war for you. Write often. I can do with letters.
> Love.
>   Blanche.

Not a word about Francis, nor did she ever say a word about him, except on one occasion when she told me that Luther had not known of his existence. Later, I asked her if she would like to have the portrait of Chellew that I had painted, and she said with a bright smile: "No, thank you, Ted," and nothing more.

3

Getting my leg right was a long and beastly business. In fact, it never got right: it is not right to this day. But by the spring of 1917 I was moving about on crutches, and by the summer I was walking with a stick. The hospital I was sent to was a pleasant enough place – a large house with a good garden in Hampstead. This was most convenient for seeing Prue, and I saw my mother also. For the past year she might as well have been a widow. My father had left home in fulfilment of a mission to which he felt called. He was wandering the country, staying here for a week and there for a week, wherever large camps of soldiers were to be found, preaching at street corners and distributing tracts. And so my mother at last felt free to leave Hulme. She came and spent a long holiday with Prue in the summer of 1917, and it was while she was there that we heard of my father's death.

It was a strange and terrible death that gave a nobility to his end. He had made his way to the north-east coast and divided his ministrations between the soldiers and the miners of the village in which he lived. He lodged in the cottage of a miner who was one of his converts, and there, like Vincent van Gogh in the Borinage, he entered into the lives of those he had come to save. After the disaster, my mother received a long letter from the man he had lodged with, and from this I was able to see the manner of his life in those last days. Preaching on the street corners and outside the pubs, he was treated with good humour and tolerance but was not taken with any deep seriousness. He had to put up with rough banter, but underlying it there was a liking that amounted almost to affection, and his teasing was only such as might have been addressed to a friendly dog that, at bottom, one is fond of.

It was to be expected, though, that there were a few who resented him and all that he stood for, and it was one of these who tried to quarrel with him one night in a public house.

I could have wept when I read of the public house. My imagination flew back to the Cock at Didsbury, and I wondered whether, in the last few days that were permitted to him, he thought of Captain Marquick and Anatole Lop arriving through the autumn dusk, and the fiddles tuning, and the passionate rush into a joy not yet esteemed diabolic. And, if he did, did memory bring comfort to him, there amid strangers in that strange land? Probably not. If he thought at all of us and of those days, he thought, I imagine, of a bright enchantment from which he had been delivered by grace; or perhaps, even more contemptibly, Beethoven was – a piece of smelly cheese no longer able to lure him into the devil's trap.

It was his habit now to go into the public houses in the hectic half-hour before closing time, when the bars were dense with smoke and the air was full of the hubbub of fuddled conversation. He would order his glass of ginger ale, talk to the miners and soldiers, and press his tracts upon them; and one of these which he had written, called *The Friend of Publicans and Sinners*, started the row.

It simply came to this: that a miner who hated him for what he called a "creeping Jesus" told him he'd be a bloody sinner himself if he had to work in the bloody pit all the hours God sent. With this, he used the tract to mop up the beer that had slopped upon the table, wrung it out, and threw the sodden gobbet into my father's face.

The stupid incident at once caused a great commotion, as such things will in such a place and at such a time. Some began to shout against the man who had thrown the missile and some were for him. Let the creeping Jesus keep outside, where he belonged, some said; and the sturdy British cry: "A man got a right to express his bloody opinions, in 'ere or anywhere else," was not slow to come up in answer. It was closing time, and the landlord was glad to sweep the argument out into the gutter. There it bandied to and fro, and the cause of the trouble kept up a monotonous cry: "Let 'im come down the bloody pit 'imself. Let 'im come down the bloody pit 'imself. Then 'e'll see. 'E won't be so ready to call a poor bugger a sinner because 'e wants a drink."

"Brother," my father answered, "I'll come down with you any day."

I know nothing about pit-head procedure. How it was wangled I cannot say; but my father went down the pit the next day. Only two men of the shift came back, and one of them was the man who wrote to my mother. None of the bodies was recovered. The area in which the explosion took place was sealed off after a few days had been spent in rescue efforts. There was no funeral either for Frances' father or for her grandfather. The one was dissolved into the bright air. The other was shut deep in the gloomy earth. And none of these three ever saw the others.

4

Many incredible things happened during the war, but, even with all that I had experienced of these oddities, I was staggered when a nurse told me that Major Brimlow had called to see me. And there, indeed, Major Brimlow was, his Sam Browne glistening like the hide of those conkers I had hurled at him through the attic window long ago, his slacks creased to knife edges, the crown upon his shoulder twinkling, and, what is more, the red tabs of a Staff appointment brightening the morning. I saluted him not without irony and said "Good morning, sir." The irony was wasted. He returned my salute punctiliously, then said: "Sit down. Don't let us stand on ceremony."

I sat upon a canvas chair in the garden. Luther walked up and down on the lawn before me. He was carrying new kid gloves and the same kind of little leather-covered cane that Francis had taken with him wherever he went. I remembered how we had come out of my studio, and Blanche was there with her car, and as she spoke to me Francis looked at her, stroking his fair moustache with the end of the cane. Major Chellew, the weathered rock of a man whom I had depended on to shelter me in my difficulties and dreadful fears. Major Brimlow. It didn't make sense.

"Well, Ted, I've only got ten minutes or so," he said. "I must be in France by the morning. They've found me a new job. Traffic this time. The P.M.'s fed up with the tangle things are getting into. He's asked me to have a shot at straightening it out. I insisted on rank. Must have authority in dealing with things like that. I think I've got the trouble pretty well weighed up already. Shouldn't take me long once I get on the spot."

I wished him luck.

"How are you feeling now?" he asked.

"Bored to tears," I said. "Thank God I shall be out of this next week. The doctors have promised me that."

"How would you like to be out of the army altogether?"

"It'd suit me down to the ground. But the mills of God dash round like turbines compared with the mills of the army. Some of the men here are waiting for their discharge from the Zulu war."

"What do you think of these war artist chaps?" he asked. "Nevinson – Muirhead Bone – that lot."

"I haven't seen what they're doing, but I've no doubt they're doing it well enough."

"You're going to have a chance to join 'em," he said. "I hope you won't think I'm pushing my nose in where I'm not wanted, but I dropped a word in the right quarter. If you want it, you can be out of the army and doing that sort of thing before the year's much older. We ought to have portraits of the army commanders, corps commanders, all the big shots. You could do that as well as the next man."

"I could do it a damned sight better than the next man," I said. "But all the same . . ."

"No buts about it," he broke in, silencing me with a wave of his cane. "I must be off. Don't get up."

And, indeed, he had to be off. A military chauffeur appeared at that moment, saluted, and reminded him of an appointment. "Well, thank you, Luther," I said. "It's kind of you."

He raised his cane in salute. "One does what one can," he said. He walked away looking well content; and he had good reason to be, for he had shown himself once more how Luther Brimlow was important enough to do for Ted Pentecost what Ted couldn't do for himself.

5

It was not till the late autumn of 1917 that I found myself in France again. That had been a dreadful year, with the bloody battles raging to and fro in the mud of Passchendaele. Forward or backward there was no hope. We were bogged down in the middle of despair. To keep sane, some sort of physical movement was necessary, some pretence of doing something that had at least the appearance of pushing this awful Sisyphus rock to a summit. Luther Brimlow found it in a new mission. I heard from Blanche that Lieutenant-Colonel Brimlow had left for the Italian front "to do God knows what," she said. For me, there was no such release. This was the war's most bitter time. So long as I had been a soldier, I had had my daily round, my necessary task of keeping myself alive, my swift alternations of fury and boredom, but the grey texture of the boredom could at least be embroidered with the pattern of routine, the trivial duties that fill the hours.

Now there was nothing but desolating thought. I painted a few portraits of harassed and worried men who had little time to spare; I sketched the abomination of desolation, peopled with moving files of huddled soldiers, with turning wheels and drooping horses; and here and there the indomitable spirit of man broke through in a picture of a cheerful Cockney with a quiff and a mouth-organ, slogging through a weeping landscape, carrying someone else's rifle as well as his own. In such brief glimpses I found more hope than in my pictures of commanders wearing rainbows on their chests.

A savage and desolate mood possessed me as autumn changed to winter, and physical pain was added to my spiritual misery. My leg, at unpredictable moments, would flame with agony, and as I had no intention of delivering myself to the doctors again, I said nothing of this, but it made me morose and I gained a bad reputation. So we passed on into that drear November when I met Iris Randle again.

She was still Iris Randle. I imagine that to be the Viscountess Moreton Hampstead gave her no more satisfaction than to be Irene Roberts, which in fact was her name. She, and no one else, had created the woman whom the world knew as Iris Randle, and that was the woman she prized. She had remained on the stage after her marriage, and she had remained as Iris Randle, and it was Iris Randle who organised the most popular party of entertainers moving behind the front.

I attended the show ostensibly to make some sketches that would perpetuate those heartbreaking occasions when youth threw itself fanatically upon joy in odd inches of time snatched from leagues of timeless tribulation. But, in fact, I went because I wanted to see Iris Randle again.

It was a filthy night, hissing with rain that drummed on the tin roof. The Nissen hut had a cold frostiness, and the wet, steaming soldiers, whistling, stamping, smoking, singing, filling every seat, standing in a packed cohort round the door, sent up an exhalation that dimmed the lights and gave to the moment a quality of phantasmagoria. In the intervals when the rain relented for a moment I could hear the distant thud of guns, calling up a picture of the wild wasteland of mortal peril, of cosmic disorder, out of which these few hundreds had for a while been gathered in.

I leaned against the wall halfway down one side of the hut, with a sketch block in my hand but with idle fingers. In the front rows there were a few red-tabs and other officers, looking as if they had walked out of Savile Row. Behind them were the anonymous files who saved the sum of things: wrapped in smelly fleeces, in reeking overcoats, in glistening oilskins, topped with the cocky hats of Australians, or the flat tin helmets of those days, or peaked caps; and under all these lids were eyes bright with excitement as they seized this moment like thirsty men seizing cups of wine. Up in front was a rude platform, veiled now by a curtain of flimsy black cloth. And the rain beat down as though the roof were being flailed by metal rods, and now, even through that insistent din, we could hear the thud of guns, the crump of exploding shells.

Someone began to sing, and soon everybody was singing. They sang that roses were blooming in Picardy but that there's never a rose like you, and they sang:

> "I want to go over the sea
> Where the Germans can't throw bombs at me.
> Oh, my! I don't want to die;
> I want to go home."

And as they were singing this, the curtain rustled softly apart, and Iris was standing under a light. She was wearing a dress of loose flowing black, a filmy thing that seemed almost liquid, and she rose beautifully out of it, having, because of her slenderness, an appearance of tallness, though she was not tall. Her face was white and her dark eyes were cavernous. She had a great black hat upon her head. She was all black, even to her enormous eyes, except for the white glimmer of her face. And she was crying, crying unashamedly.

I shall never forget it: the great enthusiastic shout that went up, ending the men's singing, as they saw her there, the shrill whistles that pierced the blue waving fug, the stamping feet, the clapping hands; and then that moment of embarrassment and indecision when they saw that she was crying, that slow, painful wavering away of all sound into silence, a silence that grew and deepened, till they might all have

288

been dead men, and there was nothing but the tears falling from Iris' eyes, and the rain on the roof, and the far-off menacing mutter of the guns.

6

"You see, Ted," she said, "I was standing there, waiting for the curtain to go up, and I heard them singing 'I don't want to die.' Oh, God! The things men sing."

She was leaning against me in the car, shuddering. My arm was round her.

"Kiss me," she said.

I kissed her.

The night was as black as pitch; the rain was still falling. Occasionally the car went through a pothole and a wave parted, surging up alongside either door, hissing by, as though we were in a cutter at sea.

I shouldn't read poetry," she said. "Not that I do – much. Not poetry nor anything else. Did you ever hear of a chap called Coleridge, Ted?"

I said that I had heard of him.

"One of our girls carries a book by him wherever she goes. I found it lying round and had a read at it the other day. Did you ever hear of a poem called *The Ancient Mariner?*"

I said I had heard of that, too. And then, dropping her conversational voice, and speaking with the husky thrilling tones into which she could put infinite meaning, Iris said:

> "The many men, so beautiful!
> And they all dead did lie:
> And a thousand thousand slimy things
> Lived on; and so did I.

You shouldn't read things like that, Ted. Not now. They hurt too much. I was all set tonight. Honest, I was as right as rain. And then I was standing there, waiting for the curtain to go up and they were singing 'I don't want to die!' and those damned words came back and smashed me like a mallet – *the many men, so beautiful: and they all dead did lie*. And I couldn't help it, Ted; the two things hitched up, and I started crying

289

my eyes out. Bloody poets! They ought to be stopped. They know too much. I'll bet that Coleridge was a one."

"He had the brow of a god and the mouth of a satyr."

She said surprisingly: "Well, so have we all, more or less."

The Viscountess Moreton Hampstead put a tiny scented handkerchief to her eyes, and said "God! I bet I'm a sight!"

She relaxed comfortably upon my shoulder and I squeezed her waist. "Thank God I can still get along without corsets. Can you feel that?"

"'M." She was as slender as a reed.

Her professional pride came back. "How was I, Ted, once I got going?"

"Splendid. The whole company gave 'em a grand evening."

"I'm not talking about the whole company. How was I?"

"Never better."

"You're an old blessing, Ted. You were always my best comforter. I think you understand me; the me crying over that old poem, and this damned silly stuck-up me worrying about whether I was better than the others. You're not exciting. You're just comforting. You were born to be a comfort to women in their moments of distress."

It was dark in the car, but I could tell from her voice that she was now even laughing a little. "Thank you, Iris," I said. "You appear to be one of these poets who know too much."

I knew that her eyes were straining to see my face. "You're not cross? You're not annoyed that I said that?"

"No. I'm not an easily annoyed person. Besides, it was rather complimentary."

She got hold of my hand and held it tight. I could feel that her long, brittle fingers were burning. "Stay with me tonight," she whispered.

I put both my arms round her, and she began to kiss me hungrily.

The car splashed on through the dark wet night, into the dark wet streets of Amiens. Late though it was, the dining room in Iris' hotel was packed with a noisy crowd of officers and women. Corks were popping, wine was flowing, loud and uninhibited voices were raised in speech and laughter. Iris gave one look at the room and said: "No, I think not." She led me straight to her bedroom, which was stone cold and had the icy propriety of middle-class bedrooms the world over. "Smoke a cigarette and wait a moment," she said.

She went away, and ten minutes later she returned, followed by a waiter bearing a tray that contained a cold chicken, salad and bread. Iris herself carried a bottle of champagne. When the waiter was gone she locked the door.

We ate and drank and talked for a little, and then Iris got into bed. I went to the dressing table, a solid bourgeois piece of furniture, squatting under a naked electric bulb with its heavy mahogany prinked with geegaws of lace. It was like a mammoth wearing silk pants. I was fumbling with my collar when my eye fell upon a piece of paper lying there and, willy nilly, I could not but read it: "Regret to inform you . . . Second Lieutenant Viscount Moreton Hampstead . . . killed in action."

I took it in my hand and turned to the bed. Iris was sitting up, with the sheet drawn to her chin, as though, incongruously for her, she wished to hide her nakedness. But she was only protecting herself from the cold. She saw what was in my hand, and her eyes burned like coals in her tragic face, staring at me over the parapet of white sheet.

"When . . . ?"

"Just before I left for the concert."

I had never seen him, but I understood he was little more than a boy.

The many men, so beautiful!

I stood there in the cold room, supporting myself with one hand on the mammoth's flank, with the words buzzing in my ears as though they would never cease. They seemed both the epitome and the epitaph of the tragedy we were living through. I could feel my cheeks tic-ing, and the paper was trembling in my hands. In Iris' eyes I read the desolation of a woman who would give everything, while tortured by knowing that her gift was but the last breakfast of the doomed man.

She dropped the sheet and held out her thin arms. "Come, Ted. I'm so cold and tired and empty."

7

We parted the next day. Iris, with her half-dozen men and women, moved on I never learned where, and I spent a day of misery in Amiens. I was twenty-eight, and that day I felt a hundred. Physical and mental ills combined to pull me down. The pelting rain ceased during the night, but the morning was damp and miasmic: the sort of weather which to this day makes me aware of the trouble in my leg. I had an ash stick with a thick pad of rubber for a ferrule, and I pottered about Amiens with this, feeling like Lazarus on his first day out of the tomb. Iris' insight had taken me down among the dead men, and the mould still clung to me. At some time during the day I wandered into the cathedral. Far away, at what seemed the point of infinity, a service was being conducted at the high altar. Colour and warm mellow light, the tinkling of bells, the murmur of voices. It seemed as remote as paradise, as intangible as a dream, confused by the shuffling of the throng about me, soldiers in blue-grey and khaki, civilian men and women, chattering, gawping, amid a tawdriness of painted wax and paper flowers.

I fled from a place whose meaning, if it had any, I was in no condition to apprehend. Outside the great west door I slipped on the damp pavement and crashed to the ground. A flame of agony shot through me and caused me to cry out. I tried to get up but found it difficult. Several people came forward to help, and finally I was lifted up by a young priest. I stood shakily, testing my leg. No great damage seemed to be done. I could rest on it, though with pain. The priest stood by with a hand under my elbow. "Thank you," I said. "I think I'm all right."

It was but a small affair, and everyone else had drifted away. This man looked no older than I was. His face was lighted by an attractive smile that puckered the skin about his grey eyes. It was hale, ruddy skin. He might have been a young farmer. He spoke to me in good English. "You look as though you are in pain."

"Please don't bother. I am all right. Pain! If this leg were all of it!"

He looked at me curiously. "There is something else then?"

"Isn't there something else for everybody?" I broke out impatiently.

"Yes, yes. Would you like to tell me about it?"

He had taken his hand from under my elbow. I flexed my knee once or twice and decided that I was all right. Tell him? What was there to tell him?

"No, thank you. It's nothing talk can cure."

"As you wish," he said. He held out his hand. "God bless you."

He was moving on towards the west door when I called after him: "One moment!" He turned and came back, still smiling, as though

292

ready either to go or come at my will. There seemed such a true
humility in him that my heart winced at the thought that I had been
rude to him. "Forgive me," I said, "if I seemed brusque. Don't blame
me. Blame my leg."

"Ah, your leg!" he said. "What a hard life that poor leg is going to
have! It will have to bear the weight of all your sins. It is most
convenient to have such a leg."

He looked at me with his shrewd grey eyes smiling, and I felt a
fool. I felt that I had been seen through. And then I was smiling
myself, smiling at the thought of a tyrannical Ted Pentecost carrying
this leg through life, cherishing it as an inestimable possession, a
shock-absorber that would keep all unpleasantness from him. Stephen
would be noisy and Prue would say: "Hush, darling! Think of your
poor father's leg." Or Luther Brimlow would call and be told: "You
can't see Mr Pentecost today sir. 'Is leg's troublin' 'im something
excruciatin'."

I caught the young priest's smiling eye, and suddenly we both burst
out laughing. "Come," he said, "let us drink some coffee in my
lodgings."

The lodgings were not far from the cathedral. Except that there
was no bed in it, the room we entered was like the room in which I
had spent the night in Iris' arms. It was small, cluttered with heavy
mahogany, prettified with mats, runners and every other fal-lal of
lace. My companion threw his big hat into a corner, sat on a horse-
hair sofa and pulled out his pipe. Some coffee was brought. "There is
good cognac in it," he said with a smile. "I thought perhaps you needed
it."

Certainly it was heartening, and we sat there puffing our pipes and
smoking companionably for a time without speaking. Then he said:
"Well, I am glad to be out of uniform and back in these clothes."

I looked at him in surprise. "You have been a soldier? – you, a
priest?"

"Oh, yes," he said. "Didn't you know that! Many of our French
priests are soldiers. I was a *poilu*. I was wounded, and now I am out of
it."

"You look very fit."

"Yes. But I, too, have a leg, so to speak, if I care to make use of him.
Forgive me, I tease you too much about that."

"Where did you learn your English?" I asked, for I had never heard of a foreigner speak our tongue so well.

"In England. I was at school at Stoneyhurst. My parents had a little farm. They were poor, but with great ambition – for me. They wanted me to be a priest for one thing, a linguist for another. They denied themselves everything, and they sent me to school in England."

"They must be proud of you."

"They are dead. I learned that yesterday. I have seen their farm – or what was their farm. God rest their souls." His hand flickered a cross upon his breast.

There was no fire in that little room, and the dun November light leaned heavily on the windowpane. The afternoon was closing in. The young priest's face was in shadow.

"How terrible," I said. "How terrible," feeling the words absurd, inadequate. "After all they had done for you."

"But they had done it," he said quietly. "Isn't that what matters? They loved me, and they did what their love demanded."

"That's one way of looking at it."

"Is there any other?"

I got up in sudden anger, my mind aflame with a searing vision of the many men, so beautiful, the men I had known and hadn't known: Rupert Brooke and Julian Grenfell, Francis Chellew and young Moreton Hampstead, yes, and this man's bucolic parents, squashed flat, I supposed, among their pigs and geese and apple trees. "Oh, God damn it all," I cried, "you take it too easily. We're being swatted like flies on a wall. What sense is there in any of it?"

"In any of what?"

"In anything that's happening now."

"Ah, that!" he said calmly. "Sit down."

I sat down, and he refilled my coffee cup and his own, recharged his pipe and lit it. In the darkening room his sensible peasant's face was illuminated for a moment by the flaring match. I was still rebellious. A line surged up out of memory: *There is no armour against Fate*, and I spoke it aloud.

"There is no armour against Fate."

"Yes," he said, "that is true. Can you recall the whole verse?"

I couldn't; and he said: "I read – I still read – much English poetry. That line is by James Shirley. The verse goes like this:

> The glories of our blood and state
> Are shadows, not substantial things;
> There is no armour against Fate;
> Death lays his icy hand on kings:
> Sceptre and crown
> Must tumble down,
> And in the dust be equal made
> With the poor crooked scythe and spade."

Neither of us spoke for a moment; then he said: "Your poets are very fond of this idea that everybody dies: kings and peasants, golden boys and chimney sweeps. 'Dust has closed Helen's eye.' They say it beautifully, but it's obvious, isn't it?"

"It's obvious," I said, still savage, "that he's right when he says there is no armour against Fate."

"What do you mean by Fate?"

"Well, what do *you* mean by it?"

"God. There is no armour against God."

"God! And what do you mean by God?"

"Love."

It was quite dark now, and he lit a candle in a cheap enamel candlestick on the table. He pulled the curtain across the window. "This is what men have come to," he said. "We have to hide the light of a ha'penny candle from our brothers, because we do not know that Fate is God, and that God is Love."

The light got hold of the wick, grew, and flung his shadow hugely on the wall. "My son," he said, this man no older than myself, whose calm made him look younger, "my son, there is no armour against Love.

"You said," he went on after a moment, "that there is no sense in anything that's happening now. But there is, you know. There is complete logic in it, cause and consequence. We are witnessing nothing but man's own sins coming home to roost. You can't put this on to God's shoulders, my son. This is your doing, and mine."

"You speak confidently about God." I could not keep the hint of a sneer out of my voice.

"Yes," he said quietly. "I can do that. I know very little about God. Even Moses on Sinai was permitted to glimpse only His hinder parts.

But to know the least thing about God, to have the faintest glimmer of knowledge of Him – this candle's light against the sun," he said, cupping the yellow crocus of flame with his hand so that its glow showed me a deep scar I had not noticed before – "even to have that is to have a great confidence."

The quiet smile came back into his eyes. "You practical English," he said, "were greatly excited about the Angels of Mons. It is a pity that so excellent a people should allow itself to be hoodwinked by nonsense of that sort. There were no angels at Mons. There is no God walking these battlefields. There is nothing but man's hatred flying in God's face. But yet – even here – yes, I saw God's face once."

He began to tell me of how a section of trench in which he found himself was pestered from a German sniping position. This was nothing but a few shattered walls among the rags of what had once been trees. It concealed a marksman of extraordinary skill, so that no Frenchman dared show an eyebrow on pain of death.

"I was sent out at night to deal with this. I need not tell you of that crawl through the midnight, of how I sank into the mud like an eel when starshells lit up the desolation. I was as black as the night itself when I got behind those walls and went forward upon him from the rear. I have an owl's eyes," he smiled. "It is a gift. That is why I was sent. I could see there was but one man."

But the sniper was wary. He had rigged trip-wires to the rear of his position. "And so, when I stumbled to my feet we were face to face. He lunged with his bayonet."

The priest held up his hand and showed me the wound.

"I gave a grunt of pain and he of horror. 'I have hurt you,' he said in German. We stood there facing one another and panting with the shock of the encounter. We were shapes to each other, not faces. 'Is it bad?' he asked, and I said: 'It hurts a bit.' I took out my field-dressing and he dropped his rifle and bound up the wound. I said: 'I was sent to kill you, but I had better go now.' 'I had forgotten,' he said, 'that you are my enemy.' We looked at one another though we could not see one another's faces, and he said: 'What is your name?' I told him, and he said: 'Mine is Gottfried Muller. I am twenty. My father is a stonemason. You had better say that you killed me. I shall not fire for the next few hours. They will think someone else has been moved into the post.' 'You still have to explain to yourself why you do not kill me,' I said. 'This hand makes me helpless.'

"He pondered this for a moment, then said: 'Perhaps it is because I have spoken to you. When I stabbed you I spoke to you involuntarily. I suppose that was the mistake.'"

This seemed to be the end of the story. "And that was when you saw God's face?" I asked.

"Yes."

"I am a practical Englishman," I said. "I haven't yet worked out what you mean."

"My son," he said patiently, "I have told you that God is love. Nothing else. Love. Gottfried and I delivered ourselves naked to love. And so we did not kill one another."

"We shall see much armour in the days to come," he said after a pause. "These things we see about us now – tanks, aeroplanes – when the war is over they will be developed to something we can hardly now imagine."

"Oh, surely," I cried, "we shall have learned better sense than that. If we don't know now that there's no way out down that road we shall never know it."

"So you *do* know that?" he said. "That is all I have been trying to say to you. Hold on to that knowledge."

"Everyone knows it. When this war is over you will see men turning everywhere from violence."

His face was inexpressibly sad. "I do not think so," he said. "I see nothing to lead me to think so. Men will pile up mightier and mightier armour, and so their last case will be worse than their first. *There is no armour against Fate.* You think that means that what must come must come, and that we might as well grin and bear it. I think it means that the love of God is seeking us out, and that, do what we will, it will find us in the end. It will find us when we throw ourselves unarmed and naked upon its mercy. And that will be when our first thought is to bind up one another's wounds and tell one another our names."

"What is *your* name?"

The smile came back to his grey eyes. "You are too literal," he said. "Please permit a little of the hocus pocus that you English are so ready to charge to my religion."

8

I had not seen much of Stephen. The child who uttered a cry in that night when I told Prue that I should join the army had not known me or my name. If I was anything to him at all, I was a shape, familiar and, I hoped, reassuring, but not so familiar as his mother's shape or the shape of Amy Lingard, our little maidservant. I comforted myself with the thought that I was perhaps third on Stephen's list of well-known unfrightening shapes. I used to leave Hampstead for Chelsea before he was out of his cot in the mornings, and, often enough, he was back in his cot and sleeping before I returned at night.

The first time he saw me in uniform, he howled; the familiar shape had altered. It was not until the end of my leave that he began to accept me. It was comforting to know that later, when Amy Lingard joined the WAACs, he howled at her, too. Prue was left alone to cope with him and the household until late in the war, when my mother came to Hampstead, thinking it was but for a visit, and remained, after my father's death, as a member of our household.

I did not see the boy grow up, as Prue did. I saw him at widely-separated times, so that he was always a new person. During one leave he was able to speak a few words; during the next he was able to speak a few sentences; and by the time I came home finally, no longer either soldier or war-artist, he was able to babble freely. By now, the idea of fatherhood had entered his mind. I was no longer a shape: I was his father, though for some time he was on his guard with me, as he was not with his mother and grandmother. With them, it was a matter of sheer tyranny. With me, there was a defensive interval during which he weighed up the chances of imposing his tyranny.

There was the episode of the bear. Prue, my mother and I were all out on the Heath. It was a beautiful day in the late summer of 1918. The war was going well: there was hope in the air: we felt things were rolling to a good conclusion. Into the pram we had packed Stephen and Broobroo the bear, as well as sandwiches and Thermos flasks of coffee. We were going to have a good long session in the sunshine. Broobroo was mangy, one-eared, and blessed with startling eyes, made of buttons, one blue and one white. Despite these disadvantages, he was deeply loved, and, like many deeply loved persons, he was shockingly treated.

There were rugs, too, in the pram, and we spread these out on the grass in a place where a clump of gorse bushes was at our backs and the land before us rolled away in a fine exhilarating prospect.

When we had eaten our lunch, Prue and my mother lay on the rugs and dozed. Stephen, with a lead of string attached to Broobroo, began to pull the creature hither and thither upon the turf. I sat upright and looked at my son.

He was fair, fat and sturdy. The hair lay upon his head in tight red curls. I should have been perplexed by that carrot nob if my mother had not told me that just such hair as this had been her father's: that ancestor, already legendary to me, who lay in Mylor churchyard, where, so long ago, my mother, standing at his graveside, first met Kitto Pentecost and my father.

Stephen's face was like a plum pudding, so mottled with freckles the colour of sultanas, from out of which his eyes shone with a candid blue. He was wearing nothing but sandals and a tight blue bathing-slip that his grandmother had knitted. It was so tight, and the wool of so fine a texture, that the child's genitals were defined, like the genitals of a male ballet-dancer wearing tights. (One reason why I can never take ballet seriously is that these fellows make me think of bulls pretending to be fairies.) But I was pleased to see Stephen's genitals. I was proud to have a man-child.

He had known nothing but war. The sun drowsed me, and I sat there half awake thinking of this. He had been awakened into life by the blast of a trumpet. The earliest things his eyes had rested on had been men marching, and his father in uniform – his Army, too. He had heard bugles blowing in forlorn sunsets. To me, when a child, war had come as a rumour. Captain Marquick had been blinded in the Zulu War. That was one of the first things I learned, and a fine romantic thing it seemed to me. I could imagine the Union Jack flickering over some remote mêlée in which lusty black men laid about them but were no match for the conquering whites, so that a Marquick could go down blinded into the dust with at least the sense of being on a side that was at once just and victorious.

A remote mêlée . . . That was the thing: it was remote. And the Boer War, so clearly remembered: that was remote, too. I had lived through it, but I had never seen a soldier who fought in it. But to

Stephen war was not remote. His ears had literally heard the tramp of men, the call of bugles.

There were a few lullabies that Prue had always to sing to him before he would go to sleep; and now, when he and she are gone to sleep forever, I can hear as I write her clear small voice in a verse of one of them:

> O fear not the bugle, though loudly it blows,
> It calls but the wardens who guard thy repose;
> Then hush thee, my baby, and sleep while you may,
> For strife comes with manhood and waking with day.

I hear the verse now, and I heard it then as I sat half-awake on the Heath, and it brought me wide awake and caused me to look at my son as though I should already see him in manhood, waking with day.

Stephen was sitting on the turf, holding Brooboo under his left arm, and with his right hand he was feeding grass towards the bear's mouth. He brought to the operation a concentrated earnestness that made him oblivious of me and apparently of everything else under the sun. I let myself down to full length on the rug and watched him from under my lashes. The bear would not eat and Stephen began to jab his nose with the grass, muttering "Eat! Eat!" The bear was obstinate. Stephen threw him angrily to the ground, kicked him towards the bushes where we lay, picked him up, and hurled him into the gorse.

He stood there, looking down at us, all apparently asleep, and, with a mother's instinct for the nearness of her child, Prue opened her eyes and sat up. The movement woke my mother. She sat up, and I decided that I had better sit up, too.

"Broobroo in the bush," Stephen said, pointing.

"How did he get there?" I asked. "Did he jump?"

"He flew. Daddy get him."

"He couldn't fly. He's got no wings."

"He had wings *for once.*"

Prue got up. "I'll get him."

Stephen stamped his foot. "No! *Daddy* get him."

I didn't stir. I was determined to resist the tyrant. My mother got up next, and was reaching a hand towards the bear when Stephen shouted: "No! Not Granny. *Daddy.*"

The string-lead attached to Brooboo was lying near my hand. "You can get him yourself," I said, quite persuaded now that Stephen has thrown the bear into the bush for no other reason than to command me to get him out. I handed him the string. "You've only got to pull."

He threw down the string and said with quick decision: "*You get Broobroo.*"

I began to pack the cups and Thermos flasks into the basket. I rolled up the rugs. "Time we were going home," I said. "Broobroo will fly after us."

I bent down to lift Stephen into the pram, and then he stooped, caught hold of the string, and pulled the bear in after him. All the way home he considered me under lowered lashes, and as we were turning into the house he said: "Broobroo didn't fly. I *froo* him."

"Yes," I said. "I know that."

There was the beginning of an understanding between us.

9

And now Stephen was five and Frances was two: Stephen, disappearing down there with his mother towards the water, Frances lying in her pram under the shadow of the old grey house that Luther had wanted to sell. My mother came out from her after-luncheon nap, and, as was her way, went straight to the pram and looked at Frances. Then she came and sat between me and Blanche. "I can't see bit of Brimlow in her," she said. "Not a bit. Not a bit of Pentecost, either, come to that." She had said it before.

"Perhaps the Sowler strain predominates," Blanche said lightly.

"Nor Sowler, neither," my mother said in her matter-of-fact way. "I knew my father's people pretty well, and there were never one owt like her."

Blanche smiled across at me. We were tickled when we caught our mother out lapsing into a spice of Lancashire speech.

"Ay," Blanche mimicked, "t'little lass is a reight mystery. Let's leave it at that." She had covered the moment, but she at once got up and went into the house.

Miss Nethersole came across and asked my mother if she would hold a skein of wool while she wound it; they fell into a chatter about children; so I took up my stick and left them. I wanted to see how Stephen and Ernie Lingard were getting on.

Amy Lingard was now demobilised from the WAACs and had returned to the house in Hampstead as easily as if she had been away for no more than a weekend holiday. Her service had taken her to France and Italy, but she came back as complacent and roly-poly as when she went away. "Them foreigners!" she would say darkly. "I had nothing to do with *them*. I kept myself to myself." And I was certain, without her telling me, that wherever Amy went was forever Pudsey.

But Amy returned to us with an anxiety named "our Ernie." Our Ernie had joined the navy. Like many a man from the midmost parts of England, he had sailed the seas as competently and unconcernedly as though descended from generations of Vikings. What worried Amy and the whole Lingard family was that he wanted to go on sailing the seas. He had returned to Pudsey, given it one look, and gone off to find a ship. There were still, then, a few sailing ships in the world, and Ernie had embarked as a seaman in one of them, a coal ship plying from Lancashire to Cornish ports, and he had learned to love sail as he had loved everything else that moved on water. It was his announcement that from his small coaler he meant to go on to one of the great four-masted Finnish barques that threw the Lingard family into consternation. We had just reached Tresco Vean when a letter came to Prue from Amy begging her to ask me to rescue our Ernie from this fate worse than death. His ship was at Falmouth. Would I try to make him see reason?

The *Dick and Harry* was not at Falmouth. She had crossed the harbour and gone up the Percuil River, that delicious bit of water that, at low tide, ends in mudflats lying in silence among green round-bosomed hills. Even at high water you navigate carefully there unless you wish to spend six hours on the mud, hearing the curlews calling, watching the stolid herons and the busy redshanks and oyster-catchers, and the duck and swans flying over. You might do worse.

But as far as the hamlet of Percuil there is always water, and there, disembarking from the ferry that had brought me from Falmouth, I found the *Dick and Harry* discharging her coal. There is a tea garden there, with a lawn edging the tide, and there I sat, drinking my tea and watching the primitive operation: the osier baskets swinging up out of the hold and tipping the coal into carts alongside. The horses stood patiently on the beach with the sun raining down upon them, flashing upon the river, and lighting the trees on the opposite bank out of whose green coolness now and then came the long-drawn cry: "Fe-e-r-r-y!" Then the ferryman would come from his thatched cottage and row his dinghy across to bring the passenger. A few small yachts, blue, green, red, were bobbing in midstream. A leathery-looking old gentleman, mahogany-skinned, silver-haired, seventy if he was a day, wearing nothing but a pair of khaki shorts, had anchored his dinghy just off the beach and sat smoking a pipe and holding a rod.

It was extraordinarily peaceful. Even the coughing of the donkey-engine on the *Dick and Harry*, the rattle of the winch, seemed charming sounds, embraced within the wide serenity of the afternoon. On her deck a man was squatting with oakum and a caulking hammer. The tap-tap of his work was as pleasing as the sound of a woodpecker tapping a tree.

I thought of all I had been through, of all that Ernie Lingard no doubt had been through, of all that poor tormented Europe had been through, and I thought of this that men might have in peace, and I marvelled at the huge insanity of my species.

But it was not an afternoon for thought, or a place for thought, and before long I was asleep in my deck-chair on the lawn.

I was awakened by a hearty voice demanding "a coop o' tea to wash out t'coal-doost," and, opening my eyes, I had no doubt that this was our Ernie. He was wearing dungaree trousers and a coal-stained sleeveless vest stuck to his back by sweat. And he was the image of Amy: short, broad and good-tempered looking. The very man, I thought, for the job in mind.

Now that the war was over, and now that Luther seemed inclined to spend as little time at home as he had done when his "missions" were taking him hither and thither, Blanche was becoming more and more attached to Tresco Vean. She intended to spend all her summers there with Frances. She announced that she would never send Frances to school. She would be educated by governesses. "At least they can pretend to educate her," Blanche said. "So long as she stays with me, I don't care what they do." It was clear enough to me that, after eight years of marriage, there was not much between her and Luther. Francis Chellew had perhaps destroyed what there was, though I prefer to think that he had destroyed nothing, but had created something in what had been a void. However that might be, there seemed little doubt that Blanche intended to build her life around

Frances, and to build it largely here at Tresco Vean. "And every summer you and Prue must come and bring Mother and Stephen. Frances and Stephen must grow up together." Already she was living in the future; better, at least, I thought, than living in those few snatched moments of love which, I suspected, comprised all that she thought worth while in the past. She had bought a quay punt, one of those handy cutters that carry a mainsail, a foresail and a jib, and the little ship was riding now on the water at the foot of the garden with the name *Frances and Stephen* painted on her counter. There were a few dinghies tied up at the steps. Well, someone would have to look after these things, and teach the children to sail, and in the winter lay up the boats and keep an eye on them, and turn them out spruce in the spring.

Just across from the gravel sweep at the front door of Tresco Vean were the stables and coach house from which I had often seen old Sapphira's coach come and where Blanche had kept her riding horse. No horses or coaches were there now. They were charming buildings, built at a time when an outhouse was not allowed to lack dignity. In one end Blanche had had a garage made. The other end she proposed to turn into living quarters for her boatman; and as soon as Amy's letter came I had marked our Ernie down for the job. His family feared the thought of the great barques – plunging through mid-ocean. Well, it would be easier to get drowned from a quay punt off Rosemullion or the Nare, but they wouldn't know that.

I sat in the garden at Percuil and looked at Ernie. His forearm was tattooed with a red rose nestling in green leaves, surmounted by a scroll bearing the name Rosie. His neck rose out of his shoulders like a squat red tower, supporting a round head whose nondescript hair was shaved almost to the skull. Strength and serenity seemed to radiate from him. He brought his tea to a table near my deck chair, and, never an inch from his heel, followed a deplorable dog. It was black and fat, short-haired like a terrier, but with a pug's lugubrious prominent eyes. They were brown and watery, like Mr Brimlow's. The dog was altogether like Mr Brimlow. If Mr Brimlow had had a tail, it would have been like this dog's: two inches of misery, perpetually curving inwards. The dog planted itself on its stern and looked up into Ernie's face. "God! What a man!" it was saying. It was perpetual adoration.

"That's a nice dog," I said.

Ernie looked down and patted the dog's head. "Ay, it is an' all," he said. "That's t'finest gun dog in England."

"Do you do much shooting?"

"Nay. Ah've never shot owt in ma life. It's a fooil's game, shootin' things. But all t'same, Ah'm not so daft Ah don't know a good gun dog when Ah see 'im."

He tore off a piece of bun and handed it to the dog. The dog ate it, and said: "Oh, all-beneficent provider! Oh, man!"

"Ah reckon," said Ernie, "that if Ah *was* so daft as to go shootin', that dog'd show 'em a thing or two. Eh, Nobs?"

Nobs said: "Oh, Master! For you I would tear eagles out of the sky."

"Ay," said Ernie, dismissing the matter, "that's a dog, that is." He munched his bun stolidly.

The *Dick and Harry* lay on the beach just under the garden where we sat. You could have thrown a stone aboard. The donkey-engine had stopped coughing; the winch was no longer rattling. A man wearing a fringe of whisker under his chin climbed through a hatch on to the deck and looked up into the garden.

"Eh! You – Lingard!" he shouted. "Come on. Time we started cleaning up this muck. An' leave that bloody dog on shore. I'm tellin' you, an' I'm tellin' you for the last time. If I find it aboard when we get goin', I'll chuck it overboard in mid-ocean."

A tear squeezed itself out of the gun-dog's eye and a tremor ran through its frame. The voice from the deck was evidently known and feared. "Oh, All-powerful! Save me!"

Ernie consulted a wristwatch. "Ah'll be there in fifteen minutes," he said, "an' not a second before. What d'you think this is – action stations? Ah've got a right to eat." He added, as a ringing afterthought: "An' Ah'm bringing t'dog."

The whiskers disappeared down the hatch, and Ernie said "You'd not think it to look at him, but that's finest skipper in sail."

"He doesn't seem to like your dog."

"Nay. T'dog's a bone of contention, as you might say. Skipper's got a dog in Bootle as is not a touch on Nobs. There's jealousy in it. Ay, jealousy."

He pulled the gun dog's ear, and the beast shivered in ecstasy.

"So your name's Lingard. That's odd. My wife's got a maid named Amy Lingard. In Hampstead."

Ernie got up. "Well, Ah'm damned!" he said. "It's a small world. That'll be our Amy."

Whiskers came up again through the hatch. He was carrying a shotgun. "See this, Lingard? I'm going to shoot a few seagulls when we get to sea. Your gun-dog'll have a chance to show what he can do."

"Nay," Ernie shouted. "Don't be daft. A well-bred dog'll know better than to go after carrion."

"You come aboard."

Ernie again consulted his watch. "In five minutes. This chap knows our Amy."

Whiskers grinned. "Ay. Finest girl in Pudsey, I suppose."

"If she was t'worst, Ah'd back 'er against t'finest girl in Bootle." He added seriously: "She *is* t'finest, come to that."

<h2 style="text-align:center">10</h2>

There had been some question about Ernie Lingard's duties. Looking after a small cutter and a few dinghies didn't seem much to occupy a man's time, especially in the winter, when they would be beached. He said that he would find plenty to do keeping things tiddly. Tiddly was Ernie's master-word. Now that his quarters in the coach house had been fixed up, we began to understand the almost infinite implications of tiddlifying. Everything that could be painted had been painted. Everything that could be shone was shining. New mats made of cunningly twisted rope appeared on the floors, and outside the walls flowerbeds were contrived within neat edgings of stone. Trees which I remembered lying torn out of the ground even in Sapphira's day had their limbs sawn off, their trunks split, and finally came to rest, in piles as neat as the bricks in a builder's yard, within one of the outbuildings. When he had nothing else to do, Ernie could be found contemplating the house itself and promising to make the paintwork tiddly as soon as we were all gone away. His huge fingers were skilful with the smallest tool, even a needle. He had embroidered the words *Frances and Stephen* on his blue jersey so effectively that Stephen, who had begun to read, was stunned with admiration, and therefore on Stephen's own blue jersey Ernie had inscribed a similar legend. It was a cause of some dispute with Prue, for, so far as Stephen was concerned, she was a nudist. She liked to see him walking about in nothing at all, drenching his body in sunshine; but the jersey was more than he could resist, and he was often to be seen, running between the house and the water, wearing nothing but this garment which attested him a member of the crew of the *Frances and Stephen*.

When Blanche had gone into the house, I left my mother, holding Miss Nethersole's skein of wool, and Frances sleeping in her pram, and wandered down the shallow valley of the garden towards the water. It was very hot. There had been no rain for a long time, and the moisture-loving hydrangeas were hanging wearily. But here and there among them the flame trees stood up worshipping the sun and flaunting their clouds of scarlet. It was a great year for butterflies. Red admirals, painted ladies and peacocks veered and tacked in impalpable currents and eddies of the air, and humming-bird hawk moths flashed with their dazzling rushes from flower to flower, plunging their long threads of tongue deep into heart after heart.

The path to the water climbs a little on to the hill on the left, making a stony way through the undergrowth of scrub out of which the graceful beeches grow. Their bare elephant-grey trunks in the springtime are like the pillars of a temple, and the temple floor trembles with the azure of bluebells. But now the stems of the bluebells were sagging everywhere into the leaf mould, and there was nothing but a green coolness and a quiet. I sat down to rest for a moment on a rustic seat, because my leg was troubling me a little, and my leg made me think of the war and of the priest at Amiens. He was a recurring voice speaking out of the backward abyss. For weeks on end I would not think of him, and then, perhaps on waking in the dead of night, perhaps in some such suspended moment as this, he would be there again, warning me to watch foolish man, rattling about the world in the armour of his pride.

I soon dismissed him. It was easy to dismiss him that day. It was easy amid all that appearance of beauty to cry "God's in His heaven; all's well with the world." I don't know that I gave much thought, if any, to God in His heaven or anywhere else. The world itself seemed fair. The war's nightmare was ended. It was a long, long time since Joe had told me in the King's Mistress that another archduke had been bumped off. And there, now, we were: Prue and Stephen and I, Blanche and Frances, and somewhere there was Luther, who at least seemed inclined to leave us all alone and go a-whoring after his own gods, whatever they might be. No, it was easy to shake off so slender a shadow of oppression. I walked on, out of the coolness, on to the grass-grown granite jetty. The sun slammed down upon me, withering the grass, burning the stone, chipping flakes of dazzling silver off the surface of the water. And from the little ship, lying offshore at her moorings amid the drench of light, I could hear Stephen's clear penetrating voice saying: "Pintle . . . gudgeon . . . counter . . . sheet . . . halliard . . . block . . . truck . . . thimble."

Ernie was running over the parts of a ship and her gear. He and Stephen had not yet been to sea, nor, said Ernie, would they go till Stephen had learned all these lessons and had learned, moreover, to swim. I sat kicking my heels against the jetty wall, and thought with satisfaction that Ernie was good for the boy. When Ernie was put in charge, he was in charge, and that was that. There would be no tyrannising over Ernie. The cutter looked lovely. She had been tiddlified up to the nines.

Presently they came ashore in the dinghy: Prue, Stephen and Ernie. Ernie had retired to the forepeak and put on a bathing suit. Now, in the shallow water inshore, Stephen removed the jersey which was all that he was wearing and Ernie took the swimming lesson in hand. Stephen had come on during the holiday. From twenty yards out he managed to make a scrambling breaststroke plunge to the shore. He stood on the beach with the water streaming out of his hair and down his naked body, and I had a sudden poignant vision of Francis Chellew standing thus naked on a stream's edge beneath trees in Picardy.

"I'm good," Stephen crowed boastfully. "I did it."

Ernie stood in the water with a hand on either hip and looked at him scornfully. "Ay," he said, "You did it as far as it went, but that's not far. You'll have to do better than this. With t'finest little cutter in Cornwall you'll have to be t'finest little swimmer, too. An' you're not that yet – not by a long chalk."

The black dog had crawled morosely out from the shade of a clump of briars and stood shivering violently in the sunshine. Shivering in all weathers was its supreme accomplishment.

"I can swim better than Nobs," said Stephen. "Make Nobs swim."

"Nay," said Ernie. "Ah'll not force t'dog to do what he doesn't want to do. If Nobs wanted to, 'e'd swim like a porpoise. Ah doubt if you'd find any dog swim better than Nobs if he set his mind to it. But Ah'll not force 'im."

"You'll not force me," Stephen said fiercely.

"Nay, that's a fact. Ah won't," Ernie promised placidly. "And Ah'll not take thee sailin' till tha can swim from here to t'ship."

Stephen plunged back into the water and began to swim out to where Ernie was waiting. He now swam with sufficient self-possession to see what was happening ashore. "Nobs is afraid!" he shouted. "Look! He's shivering. Shivering in this weather."

"Ay, he is an' all," said Ernie. "Ah'd like to see another dog as could shiver in an 'eat-wave."

CHAPTER EIGHT

T HIS IS not a book of justification. What happened between me and Iris Randle is not something I want to justify. I merely put it on record. It would perhaps be agreeable to depict myself as an always and wholly faithful husband, but I was not. I remember that Francis Chellew once said to me: "I don't like promiscuity." Neither do I, and I don't think I could be called promiscuous. But I begin to justify myself . . .

In 1924 Prue bore our second and last child, a girl. The birth was accompanied by dangerous complications, and I was taken aside by our doctor, who spoke of symptoms of eclampsia. Prue was very ill indeed, and the child died two days after birth. This was in May. In the middle of July Prue was fit to travel, though she was still anything but well and had some traces of exophthalmic goitre. (But these at last completely disappeared.) Blanche and Frances, who was then seven, were about to leave for Tresco Vean, and my mother and Prue travelled with them. They went in Blanche's Daimler. Blanche had become as ardent a car driver as Luther. They seemed to me to be leading a queer life, that pair: he with his Rolls Royce and she with her Daimler; he with Greenlands and she with Tresco Vean. For the winter months they lived together at the house in Bedford Square. But Luther was never found at Tresco Vean or Blanche at Greenlands.

I saw the party off that July morning. I did not expect to be able to join them till August, for I had a number of commissions to look after. In a week or so I should meet Stephen, who would be back from school, and put him on to the Riviera Express at Paddington. At Falmouth, he would be met by Ernie Lingard, who would take him on to Tresco Vean. Then there would be nothing at all between me and my work.

The day that I saw the Cornish party off I had an appointment with a sitter at eleven o'clock. She was a woman who was much in the newspapers at that time. She was the young and very beautiful daughter of a famous peer. She had been a mannequin; she had appeared in the chorus of a musical show; she had an antique furniture shop; and she was to be found with a new lover every month or so at whatever happened to be the favoured nightclub of the moment. She organised spectacular shows for charity at the great hotels and was known to make a handsome profit out of them. She had been arrested drunk and incapable in the streets of Mayfair, following a night when she and a crowd like her had brawled around that region, the men wearing schoolboy clothes and the women gym skirts and sailor hats. Her face was as serene and innocent as a Madonna's, and she was a complete bitch. You couldn't pick up a "society" magazine without finding her photograph in it, or read a column of the nauseous muck called society gossip without learning where she had come from and "gone on" to the night before. This was Claire Fayling. She is dead and forgotten, like the inebriated decade she lived in. I don't know where the portrait is that I painted of her. It was handsomely paid for by the son of a brewer, whom she left almost as soon as the cheque was in my bank, and who was killed soon after when trying to break a motor speed record in France.

It was an exhausting morning. The girl was a chatterer. "I expect you've heard the most dreadful things about me, Mr Pentecost." She loved her unsavoury reputation and hinted at enormities that had not been publicised. She had known Lord Hugh Brymer, the young poet who was killed on the Somme on that awful day of butchery that saw the end of Francis Chellew. She babbled about her love for him and would have me believe that her life was a reckless descent into hell by a woman who could never forget. "But they didn't die in vain, Mr Pentecost, Hugh and all the other wonderful men like him. They bought us our freedom." It seemed to me an enchanting thought that Francis Chellew and Hugh Brymer, to say nothing of one or two Toms, Dicks and Harrys, had died to give Claire Fayling the freedom to dance and drink and fornicate and peddle cocaine. I say she exhausted me. All the same I was glad to paint her; she was the loveliest rose-leaf creature; but I wasn't sorry when her brewer came in an enormous Bentley at half-past twelve and took her away.

I lunched at the King's Mistress and talked to Joe about the new signboard I had promised him. We were friends of many years' standing now, and "Mr Pentecost's chair" was an institution in the corner where snacks were served. I was also, I should imagine, apart from Joe himself, the oldest inhabitant of the yard. The war and the few restless succeeding years had brought many changes. It seemed a long time ago since Sir Harry Banfil had directed a shabby youth, who had not intended to stay in London, to have a look at the studio of an artist who had gone away to die in the sun. Joe was the only man with whom I could trust myself to exchange a few words now and then about Francis. When we were speaking of Francis one day, Joe made an oblique remark which showed that he was not unaware of what had happened during that leave in 1916. "Well, I reckon a man's entitled to a bit of happiness if he can find it in this bloody world, Mr Pentecost."

But we didn't discuss Francis that day. It was now eight years since he had died, and skin was growing over the old wounds. Literally, it was. I no longer had to carry a stick. It was rarely that my leg reminded me that it wasn't all that a leg should be. Down at Tresco Vean I could scramble in and out of a boat with the best of them, and I had learned, if something went wrong, to keep the pangs to myself.

That day it was the frowsty old signboard that we discussed, the reputed portrait of Nell Gwynn. It was so old and weather-beaten that the features were hardly decipherable. "It'd be a bloody funny king," said Joe, "who'd want a mistress like that. Something is indicated more like the bit of stuff I just see coming out of your studio. The Fayling woman, wasn't it?"

I said that it was. That publicised face could hardly be mistaken. "A peer's daughter," Joe pondered, sucking his moustache into his hollow cheeks in a way he had; and added philosophically: "Ah, well, a tart's a tart the whole world over. I think what we want on the old board is a good tartish face. I leave it to you, Mr Pentecost."

I began work on the board that afternoon. I didn't need a sitter, but the face that began to evolve was Iris Randle's. It was so unmistakably Iris Randle's that no one seeing it and knowing her could have any doubt about it. The least I could do, I thought, was to get her permission. I had better ring her up. I put down my brushes as this idea came into my mind, and I found that my heart was beating a little quicker than was usual. I was possessed by a not unpleasant feeling of excitement. I was alone in London.

Alone in London.

I have a mind that finds itself most strangely jolted into reminiscence by odd combinations of words; and now it occurred to me that *Alone in London* was the title of one of the old melodramas that used to go touring up and down the country. I had never seen it; but thinking of it made me think of the night when I had first found that Prue was in London. I had walked with her down the Strand, and she had told me how she and Jesse Cleghorn had loved to spend a night laughing at a melodrama.

My hand was actually on the receiver of the telephone as I stood there with these thoughts passing through my mind: thoughts of Prue at the moment when my heart was bumping pleasantly at the thought of Iris. I thought of Prue's long illness and of the little wizened body of her child that had died, and I felt overwhelmed with misery and loneliness. I lifted the receiver.

2

I don't know whether Iris ever met young Moreton Hampstead's people. Hers was a runaway match. She never used her title, and by now it was beginning to be forgotten that she had one. She was older than I, and at this time I was thirty-five. I don't suppose Iris was much, if anything, under forty. We had met occasionally since the war ended, but never by intention. All the same, when we did meet, we were intensely aware of one another. Our feeling for one another had never burned itself up in a passion, never in that way been consumed and done with. If it was volcanic, the volcano had never erupted.

The years had not diminished Iris' haggard beauty. If anything, they had added to it. Hers had become a haunted and haunting face that I could never look on without emotion. I did not feel that Iris would ever believe that men had died to give her freedom. If she, and life too, had done with them, she had not done with their ghosts. *The many men, so beautiful.*

Her work had changed, too. She no longer appeared in pantomime and musical comedy. A year ago Alexander Durnford had written the first of his plays. Durnford had gone straight from school at Marlborough into the army. He was a youth of flaming enthusiasm and patriotism, who saw all life as black against white and the war as a crusade against anti-Christ: He lost both his legs, and his life now was lived in a wheeled chair. But he lost more than his legs: he lost his faith and idealism, and he turned upon mankind with the savage intensity of a betrayed lover. You will find some of his poems, written when he was a subaltern, in those collections of the works of soldier-poets that were so popular while the war lasted. It is instructive to compare that morning music with the snarl of his first play: *Not Mentionable in Despatches.* You will find in the comparison all the gulf there is between 1914 and human history ever thereafter. It was in this play that Iris first showed herself to be a straight actress of deep emotional sincerity. She, like Durnford, was no duck off whom the waters of tribulation smoothly flowed. They absorbed. They were well matched, those two. She was now appearing in Durnford's second play, whose ironical title was *England Helped Me.*

3

We kissed when we met, but we were now in the time when a kiss was not necessarily either a sign of affection or a Judas betrayal. It was an automatic action, like shaking hands. I didn't relish that fashion: I like a kiss to be a kiss and to mean something. I think Iris had this feeling, too. The last time I had met her, before this, had been about a year ago. There had been a few of us at the Savoy Hotel, and I had brought Iris out to see her into a taxi. She had given me that brushing of the cheek and smack of lips into the air that goes for a kiss nowadays and had stepped towards the cab. Then she had turned, come back quickly, and kissed me full on the lips. "Good night, old darling," she said. I treasured the moment. I often relived it. I don't like meaningless gestures. There was no meaning in Iris' kiss this day a year later when we met in her flat in St James' Square.

I had heard that Moreton Hampstead had left her a lot of money, and she must have been earning a good salary as an actress. The flat was opulent in the modern way. Evidently, Iris had handed the job over to an interior decorator, and the all-white craze of the moment had gone to this person's head. Crossing the carpet, one almost expected to leave footprints in the snow, and the bearskin rug seemed so much at home that it would not have been surprising to see it look up and howl for fish. A picture by Cezanne over the fireplace, a few

Bow and Chelsea figures on the mantelpiece beneath it, the coloured leather spines in a bookcase: these were all that cheered the arctic waste. I suggested to Iris that she should have a flag flying to indicate the exact position of the Pole.

Iris was not amused. She seemed to have something on her mind. Her maid brought in tea, and we sat at the window looking down on the great plane trees in the square. The flat was on the top floor. When the maid was gone, Iris poured out the tea, and asked: "Why did you ring me up?"

What could I say? "My dear Iris, because I realised that there was no one to supervise my doings, and I was bored, and Prue's illness has made me a celibate for two months, and I thought of you and found my heart pleasurably thumping." No, I couldn't say that.

"My darling, do I have to have some cut-and-dried reason for wanting to see you? Do I have to come about the gas or electricity, or to tune the piano?"

She shrugged her lean shoulders impatiently. "If a sheer loving impulse brings you," she said, "I must say it operates with extreme infrequency. It's a year since we last met. Now you walk casually in. Do you find me the sort of woman you can put down and take up just how and when you please?"

There was a tremor in her voice, a slight shaking in her body. I took her thin fingers into mine, but she withdrew her hand abruptly. "What is the matter?" I asked her; and to my surprise she fell on her knees by my chair and buried her face in my lap. I lightly stroked the white skin where the topmost vertebrae moulded themselves beneath it, and at that she shuddered violently. Then she began to cry.

I got up and lifted her up with me. I led her to the great white settee before the empty fireplace. I sat down and pulled her on to my knees and put my arms round her. Her head went down into my shoulder. "Now," I said. "Tell me."

"It's Alec," she sobbed. "He wants me, and, O, Ted! He *needs* me, too. But I can't."

I was horrified, and clasped her rigidly. Alexander Durnford! I had met him. He was an indomitable man. In his wheeled chair he would go everywhere. I had seen him propelling himself round art exhibitions. I had seen him in public restaurants, adjusting the wooden tray in front of his chair on which he had meals served. The face of the young enthusiast who had flamed into battle with a song was wry and sceptical, but it was still a face of extraordinary beauty, with a plume of dark hair sweeping across the wide brow above the pain-shocked eyes. I could imagine Iris' feeling for him. I could imagine that he was the first man who had wanted her, and whom she had wanted, to whom she had said no.

She got off my knees, dabbed her eyes with a handkerchief, and said: "Give me a cigarette."

I lit it for her, and she walked to the window and stood with her back to me, looking down into the square. I was moved by a profound compassion for her. I wondered if she had by now forgotten how many men had wakened on how many mornings with their arms beneath her shoulders. What had she sought from them all? What had she tried to give to them all? Joe had said the signboard needed a good tartish face, and I had begun to paint the face of Iris Randle. Looking at her now, I wondered whether I had ever known a woman who so completely failed to be what I understood by that word. She had given and given; and now she had reached the limit of what she could give.

She turned round and said: "It would help him so much if I could. But I can't – I can't! I've gone over it all in imagination, and I can't."

I, too, went over it all in imagination, and shuddered. Durnford's legs had been severed at the hip joints.

"I'm beginning to feel," Iris said, "that I can't go on much longer if he stays about. He turns up wherever I am, and he says he intends to go on doing so. He even comes to the play. Night after night."

"That must be very difficult for you, my dear."

"Difficult! If it goes on much longer there'll be a complete dry-up one of these nights. Do you know the play?"

"No."

"There's a moment when a blinded soldier meets his girl again for the first time. He's wearing a great bandage across his face, with two holes cut in it. Not because this is going to do him any good, but because his face is too hideous to be looked at. He talks as though everything between them is to go on as it was, and the girl, who knows that it won't, can't bear to say so. And so she talks, too, as though nothing is different. I'm the girl. You see, the thing is the contrast between what she's saying and what she's looking. He can

316

hear the false joy in her voice, but he can't see the real horror in her eyes. You see?"

Yes, I could see; and I could see how this situation would devour Iris' very heart, for she would be seeing more than that girl and that man. She would be seeing the many men, so beautiful, the world over, shorn of legs and arms and eyes. No one would know more than she how much greater than ever now was their need for what women could give them, or feel more profoundly the urge to give it, or recoil with a sharper despair before the impossibility of the giving.

"So you see, Ted," she said simply, "I'm in despair."

She walked about, lean, hungry and unhappy. "Sit down," I said. "Sit down here by me."

She did so obediently. "I think I shall go to America," she said, "as soon as this play comes off."

"Why America?"

"Because I've been asked to go and make films there."

We weren't, then, at the moment when anybody who had had any kind of success was asked to go to America to make films. The films were still silent, and half of Iris' appeal was in her voice. This had become more and more so as the years went by. Her intense sexuality had once expressed itself in a swaggering physical invitation; but now she permitted a good deal to pass unexpressed, to be assumed. And one assumed it mainly from the way her husky voice said things. I told her that she would lose half her personality in Hollywood. She didn't bother to answer. She laid her head back on my shoulder, and to my surprise was soon asleep. Presently the maid came in and took away the tea things, but Iris did not wake. I had caught her at a moment of physical and emotional exhaustion. My own head began to nod, and soon I was asleep, too.

I awoke to find Iris standing on the bearskin, looking down at me, and laughing. She was altogether different now. The tiredness was gone from her face; she no longer had the appearance of seeing ghosts. She reached down a hand, which I took, and she pulled me upright. We faced one another for a moment, then she put her arms round me and we kissed – this time with meaning, with more meaning than there had ever been before in a kiss between me and Iris.

"Why were you laughing?" I asked.

"I was thinking."

"I'll bet you were."

"I was thinking of Ma Bagshaw in Manchester. Remember her?"

"Yes."

"She looked a regular old procuress, and probably was one. But who guarded my virtue like a dragon."

"Then dragons are less efficient than one is led to believe."

"Well, naturally, you can't allow them to dominate you. But I was thinking—"

"Yes; you've said that."

"This girl here. She looks like a little Quakeress, and she allows me to spend the afternoon sleeping in a strange man's arms."

"She's probably pure-minded. And moreover, she realises that the strange man is middle-aged – all passion spent. He proved to be nothing but a sleeping draught."

She took my face between her thin hands and looked at me with great tenderness. "It was what I wanted, Ted. It did me a lot of good. You're an understanding old dear. You don't rush things. And I like that. I suppose I *am* getting middle-aged—"

"Here! I didn't say so. I said I was."

She shook her head. Her black hair, which hadn't a grey thread in it, had been cut to a bob, so that her whole head was shaped like an opulent flower. She put her finger on my lips. "Not another word about it. Now you want to make a dishonest woman of me. Isn't that what you came for?"

"Yes."

She took me by the arm and led me to the door. "*A ce soir*. Come to my dressing room at the theatre at ten o'clock. Wear a dinner jacket. We'll eat somewhere and dance."

4

We ate somewhere and we danced. I was not much of a dancer, but it was not necessary to be. The nightclub we were in was the supreme candle for the moths of the moment. A royal duke might come in any night. None came that night, but the place was as crowded as one would expect a place to be where such a miracle might happen. It was not a big place: nothing but a fairly long narrow room. The band occupied almost the whole of one end. Small lamp-lit tables were down each side, and on the strip of floor in between what was called dancing took place. It did not matter that I could not dance. I found that to hold Iris close to me and gyrate was to do as much as the conditions permitted to be done. Holding Iris was like holding a pliant reed. I could feel that now, as when I held her in a car sloshing through a filthy night towards Amiens, her body was self-supporting. She was wearing soft black crepe silk, with a crimson flower and crimson shoes. Her mouth was crimson in her white face. She looked very tired. Her head was resting on my shoulder. "He was there again tonight," she whispered. I knew she meant Alexander Durnford.

The saxophones stopped their moaning and there was a scatter of applauding hands. "Let us sit down," she said.

Some newcomers, evidently of consequence in that place, were being conducted through the crowd standing up and waiting for the next dance. One, in icy satin, was my sitter of that morning, Claire Fayling. Her face looked more than ever like an opening rosebud preserved in ice. The young man who had called for her with the Bentley was in front, ploughing a way for her with a rugby footballer's shoulders. Behind him came a girl in green with green eyes and a vicious face, and following her was Luther Brimlow.

Why should I feel that sudden sharp pang of hatred? Why should my heart say: "Here! What about Blanche?"

Well, what about Blanche? What about Prue?

The four went by our table to one on the other side of the room, up near the band.

"Do you know the girl in green with your brother-in-law?" Iris asked.

I could not help asking: "What do you know about my brother-in-law, Iris?" I knew that she knew him. I remembered the night when I had watched him disappear with her in a cab, and I had walked away with Prue. But it was not her way, so far as I had discovered it, to speak to one man of another. Or to speak of a man's woman. She had never spoken of Prue or Blanche. A relationship with Iris was unique and self-contained. But she was living in conditions which must have concealed from her little that was happening in this disintegrating layer of society.

"Oh, I know plenty about him," she said impatiently. "If you mean, has he ever been one of my men, the answer is No. I cut him off pretty quick. You see, Ted, with me, there has to be *something* about a man. I may love him, or just like him, or respect him, but there's got to be *something*."

"And with Luther Brimlow there was nothing?"

"Nothing but loathing – and well, if you like you can call it fear. But I'm talking about that girl in green."

"I don't know her."

"That's Christina Lake."

"Good God!"

"Yes," said Iris. "As you say, good God!"

Looking back now, more than twenty years later, it is difficult to believe in the reality of some of the people who were to be found then in the swim of fashionable life. No one could have failed to hear of Christina Lake. A few months ago her career had been dragged through the courts and publicised in the newspapers. She was the daughter of a clergyman in the West country, and from her mother, a younger daughter of a wealthy businessman, she had inherited enough money to start her chosen career. It was a career of folly and dissipation all too common at the time, and Christina Lake's only distinction was that where others were foolish she was frenzied, and where others were dissipated she was dissolute. She lived, as was the way with so many girls like her, in a mews, and it was leaning from the window there at two o'clock one morning that she shot with a revolver at a lover foolish enough to be importunate when done with. He was but slightly wounded, and no doubt this would have been no more than another of "the beautiful Christina Lake's" talked-of exploits if a passing policeman had not heard the shot.

As it was, there was a mighty washing in public of Christina's filthy linen, a Roman holiday with a twenty-two-years-old Messalina from a Devon rectory as the centre piece. She was shown to have been fuddled with drink for three days before the shooting, and presumably incapable of knowing what she was doing. This happy fact, together with her youth, enabled her lawyer to build up a picture of an innocent fly caught in the web of this wicked world; and if Christina Lake did not walk from the court without a stain on her character, at least she walked from it. Iris, who would know about such things, said that she had been in a nursing home for some months, and that this was her first reappearance in society. "It was one of those nursing homes that eat up thirty or forty pounds a week," Iris said, "and the little bitch had run through every penny of her own money. Can you make a guess who paid for her?"

I looked at the table up there near the band platform. A waiter was pouring champagne, and I saw Luther put a hand over Christina Lake's glass. They were too far away for me to hear what was said, but the other two could be seen to laugh, Christina to protest, and Luther to shake his head vigorously. He took up a carafe and filled her glass with water.

"Yes," I said, "I could guess who paid."

"You'd be right, and he hasn't done paying yet. It was because she thought she had a hope of him that she shot Bertie Wontner. Poor little devil. He hadn't a penny."

I hoped that Luther had not seen me, but now the floor was clear, for Miriam Morris, one of the attractions of that place, was about to sing. Luther sat back and looked around him, fingering the stem of his champagne glass. He saw me, and raised the glass in greeting. I returned the salute with my hand. When Miriam Morris had finished singing, I said: "Let's go now. A little of this goes a long way with me." I felt I had had more than a little.

It was nearly two o'clock when we got to the flat in St James' Square. Iris' Quakeress, in her pretty grey demure apron, was still up. "Is there anything else I can do for you, my lady?" she asked.

It was something of a shock to be thus reminded that Iris was a viscountess.

"No, my dear," she said. "Go to bed. Everything that has to be done now I am quite capable of doing for myself."

5

"Let me congratulate you, my dear Ted, on having a charming and self-reliant son," Luther said mockingly.

I looked at him aghast, and at Stephen standing by his side: the plump ruddy schoolboy in grey flannel trousers and a purple blazer bearing his school crest. Stephen looked at me — with smiling, confiding eyes.

"The boy can look after himself," said Luther. "He should make his way in the world."

"It was nothing," said Stephen; "nothing at all."

"Sit down and tell me about it," I invited them, and they sat down on Iris' great white divan.

"It seems," said Luther, watching me carefully, "that Stephen expected his father to meet him at Waterloo, but doubtless the pressure of business prevented you, my dear Ted, from keeping the appointment. You have a terribly busy father, Stephen. These artists are here, there and everywhere."

I turned to the boy. "I'm sorry, Stephen. I did forget. Absolutely. Still, it's never happened before, has it?"

"No doubt," said Luther, "there's never been so compelling an engagement elsewhere."

I think Stephen uneasily sensed something underlying this back chat. "Oh, it was nothing, sir," he assured me. "Uncle Luther's exaggerating the whole affair. When you weren't at the station, I just hopped into a taxi and got driven to your studio."

"Hear that!" said Luther with delight. "Just hopped into a taxi. Now tell me this. How many boys of ten do you think would have the sense to hop into a taxi? They'd just stand on the platform and cry their eyes out. Why, Stephen, I shudder to think what I was at ten. A puny, silly chap who was rightly regarded with contempt by all who knew him. Isn't that so, Ted?"

"What happened then?" I asked the boy.

"Well, I couldn't get any answer when I rang the studio bell, so I went into that public house there and asked if I might use the telephone."

"A man of initiative," Luther inserted. "Never defeated."

"It was simple enough. There was no answer from Hampstead, so I rang up Uncle Luther, and was lucky enough to find him in."

"And Uncle Luther, having a pretty good notion where Father was likely to be detained by business, brought you along. That's the whole story."

"Well, Stephen," I said, "you acted with great common sense. And thank you, Luther, for bringing Stephen here, rather than calling me there. It showed great consideration."

He looked at me levelly. "Thank you, Ted. I'm glad you appreciate that."

"I do, believe me. I shall remember it always."

6

It was on a Monday night that Iris and I returned from the nightclub to St James' Square, and it was on a Friday, at about noon, that Luther confronted me there with Stephen. The days between, and the nights, too, I spent with Iris. This was the first time that we lived for days continuously together. Fate, or fortune, or what you will, helped us to those days. I took some pride in being businesslike where the business side of my profession was concerned, and on the Tuesday morning I was at my studio as punctually as though the night before had been like any other night. I was no sooner arrived than the telephone rang, and there was Claire Fayling, telling me that she could not keep her appointment. She was to have been with me each morning that week, and now she had to say that she was going out of town at once. She had no apologies to make; one didn't apologise for much, or to anyone, in those days. She had been invited to join a friend's yacht. They might go to Cowes, or they might go to the Mediterranean; and, wherever they went to, when they came back they were all going on to Scotland. So she would have to let me know later when we could get on with the portrait. And that was that. Her bored voice trailed off, and she hung up.

That was how I was given the liberty of those days with Iris. They were simple and enjoyable days. Each morning we got up rather late. We stayed in the flat until about eleven o'clock; then she drove us in her two-seater car out into the country. We lunched wherever we found an attractive inn, and we loafed through the afternoon. Once I took her in a punt on the river. Once we swam in a roadhouse pool. We would be back in time for her to change for the theatre. I took her there on the Tuesday, Wednesday and Thursday nights and sat through the show. Then we had supper at her flat and went to bed. Throughout the three days the weather was superb. Iris lost her strained and tired look. I had known her now for twenty years, and throughout that time I had met her so infrequently, at such wide-spaced intervals, years sometimes passing in which I would not see her at all, that she seemed always at a new point of development, and thus she had the advantage of being at once an old friend and an enchanting stranger. What pleased me with her now was a capacity for calm that I had not supposed her to possess. My presence with her permitted her to forget, or at least not to be overwrought by, the shadow of Alexander

Durnford, which obstinately refused to be withdrawn. She was able to take the moments of those three days as they came, and they came happily and beautifully, full of air and sunshine and sensual enjoyment. She was utterly restful.

Thus it came about that I forgot my appointment to meet Stephen at Waterloo station. We intended that day to take luncheon at an inn near Hungerford, but we were later in starting than we had been on other days. Returning to town on the Thursday, Iris had complained that the car was not behaving well, and we arranged at the garage to have it overhauled. It would not be ready till noon, and Iris had gone to bring it round just at the moment when Luther turned up with Stephen. I was glad when Luther went, leaving me alone with the boy. I hated myself as I lied to Stephen.

"Look, Stevo," I said. "I'm terribly sorry to have forgotten you. I had an appointment to meet a lady here about painting her portrait, and the one thing put the other quite out of my head. All over and forgotten?"

It was our catchword when we had been at cross-purposes and had come together again.

"Absolutely," said Stephen. "There's no need to treat me like a child, anyway. What's easier than to hop into a taxi and give an address?"

He walked about the room with his hands in the pockets of his long flannel trousers, nonchalant, a grown-up, he hoped, capable of handling crises. "You were not the only one," he said, with a laugh. "Bugsby was forgotten, too. There's always someone."

"Bugsby? What an unpleasant name!"

"Well, that's what we call him – Bugsby or Bugs. His name's really Begbie. An awful wet. There was no one there, and he started to howl. Of course, he's only nine."

"What happened to him?"

"Well, I had to organise something for him. So I got him a few bars of chocolate out of the slot machine, then I wrote his name and address on a label and tied it into his buttonhole and handed him over to a station policeman."

"Good. Bugsby will be all right, then. And when you'd looked after him you began to think about yourself?"

"Oh, well, I wasn't in a panic."

"Captain Pentecost couldn't have done better."

"Shall we have some more of him tonight?"

"Yes, and then tomorrow I'll see you off at Paddington."

"As you wish," he said. "Don't bother about me if I'm a nuisance. I'm capable of buying a ticket and getting into a train."

"No bother. It'll be a pleasure."

"Good then. What do we do now?"

"Well, I'm afraid I'll have to wait till this lady turns up. She's late. I hope she's not in the habit of forgetting appointments, too. Then we'll go and have some lunch somewhere."

"Good. I'll have a Neapolitan ice for my sweet."

"Anything you like."

Iris came in, looking as trim and taut as a girl of twenty. She was wearing a sage-green suit. Her hat, gloves and shoes were all of French-mustard yellow. I was glad that she was an actress, quick on a cue. "Good morning, your ladyship," I said. "I'm afraid I was rather early for our appointment."

She looked at the watch as big as a postage stamp on her wrist. She shook hands with me. "I'm afraid it's I who am a little late, Mr Pentecost," she said.

"Forgive me for having my son here. I've committed a grievous sin against him. I should have met him at the railway station this morning, but this appointment put it out of my mind. However, as you see, he found his way here."

Iris smiled at the boy and said: "Well, I mustn't keep you long, Mr Pentecost. If your son can be happy here for a few minutes, we can go into my room and discuss our affair."

So we left Stephen sitting on the couch and went into her bedroom, and there I explained what had happened. She put her arm round me and smiled sadly. "So after all the day is in pieces, Ted."

"Yes."

"Well, thank you. You've been lovely to me, my dear."

"Do we meet again?"

"Not by appointment. We've never made appointments, you and I. Let's not begin."

I kissed her. "Have you made up your mind about America?"

"Yes. I'm going when this play comes off. That's in a month's time. It'll go on tour then, but without me."

"Don't stay too long, my dear."

"It won't matter to you. You've got that lovely boy, and you've got your wife. D'you still love her?" She had never before mentioned Prue.

"Yes. Very much."

"How strange that is. Because I believe you love me."

"I do. You must believe that, my darling."

"How strange."

"Yes. But there it is."

She took herself out of my arms, and echoed: "Yes. There it is."

Then we went out into the sitting room, Iris talking with bright animation. "So if you could finish the portrait before I go to America, Mr Pentecost . . ."

She sailed early in September, and before her ship reached New York Alexander Durnford had rolled himself out of his prison-chair, rolled himself along the floor of his flat, and rolled his head into a gas oven. It was a method of suicide popular in those days. A year later, the remembrance of his end brought great crowds to his third, posthumous, play, that despairing cry called *England, My England*.

7

That night Stephen and I had the house at Hampstead to ourselves. Amy Lingard had followed the motorcar party by train into Cornwall. We didn't go home at once. After lunch we went out to Richmond and hired a dinghy. Stephen despised it. There were red plush cushions on the seats, fancy oars, a scrolled back to lean against in the stern, and strings to the rudder. The idea of having any sort of rudder in a dinghy was all wrong to Stephen, and the long rakish shape of this boat was all wrong to him, too. A dinghy, to him, was a tough and tubby little vessel, furnished preferably with wooden thole-pins instead of rowlocks, and with sturdy oars that could, if need be, dig a boat along through a bit of sea. And, decidedly, it should *not* have a rudder and it should *not* have red plush cushions. Red plush didn't go with a certain amount of bilge water slopping round naked toes, or with an old rusty tin-can bailer, or another old can containing bait or fish hooks or rolls of gut.

Stephen stood on the landing stage at Richmond and looked at the boat I had hired, and expressed all he thought about it in one phrase:

"I should think you'd keep this thing tiddly with a vacuum cleaner, not with an old mop."

Ernie Lingard had taught him the importance of being tiddly. He had taught him more than this; he had taught him the importance of worship. I doubt whether, at this time, there was any matter on which Stephen would have accepted my view in preference to Ernie's. It was Ernie who had taught him to swim, who had taught him to sail the *Frances and Stephen*, who knew where to dig lugworms and where the fish lurked who were suicidally partial to these singular delicacies. Ernie had taught him to gut fish and bring them home clean for the kitchen, how to make knots and splices, how to hit a conger-eel over the head with a mallet, and how to distinguish the cries of gulls who were hovering over a shoal of mackerel from the cries of gulls who were out merely to make a fool of you. Ernie had taught him, one day of sudden squally gusts when they alone were in the boat and the jib carried away and its tatters snapped like whips in the wind, and Stephen was inclined to be a little frightened, that one didn't panic but quietly and swiftly did what the occasion demanded. Ernie had taken down the handy-billy auxiliary engine, bit by bit, nut by nut, and bolt by bolt, washed it all in paraffin, anointed it in oil, and before Stephen's fascinated gaze had put it together again so that it went like a song. And perhaps the most astonishing thing of all was that, last summer when Stephen arrived at Tresco Vean panting for the holiday's delights to begin, Ernie had taken him down to the quay to show him a new dinghy, trim and tiddly as a kittiwake, floating on the water.

Stephen knew at once. "You made it!" he exclaimed, awe-struck, and Adam on the seventh day of creation could not have stood in more humility before his Maker.

"Ernie looked with a happy yet deprecating grin at the little clinker craft, the white enamel of her outsides, the pale green within, the varnished oars, the coiled painter. "Ay," he said. "Ah reckon you'll go a long way before you see a more reliable little boat than that. Ah wouldn't mind venturin' to France in a boat like that."

Ernie, when are we going? When *are* we going?"

It was an old question. Ernie had promised that *one of these fine days* he and Stephen would really do some sailing. "We've messed around between 'ere and t'Lizard long enough, Stevo," he declared. "Us'll have a real do. Us'll sail to France."

327

It was understood that this concerned only them. Neither Blanche nor Prue was much interested in sailing, though they could be induced to go out on a fine day. "They like sailin' on a day when there's no wind to sail with," said Ernie contemptuously; and Stephen, picking up the mood, answered: "Ay, that's like women." So they were counted out of the French trip, and Frances was too young, and somehow I didn't matter much. I was content to leave it to Ernie Lingard. He had taken his time before allowing Stephen to sail at all; and I could trust him not to make this voyage till the boy was fit to make it.

It was not only in the summer holiday now that Stephen came to Tresco Vean. He was not content to arrive when the year was at the top of its joyous shout and to find everything prepared for his lordly use and occupation. He had been thinking for a long time, I could see, of Ernie with the boats pulled up in the boat-shed, working away with scraping-tool, blowlamp, sandpaper and paintpot, and these were joys he was determined to share. And I had learned that when Stephen was determined, he must have reason, not excuse, before he let go. We could give him no reason that satisfied him why he should not go down to Tresco Vean for his Easter holiday, and he had gone down, both last year and this year. When he came back, I gained an impression of his holiday from the enrichment of his vocabulary. I learned of dowels and chamfers, and could picture the scene in the boat-house, the wood behind it floored with the azure of bluebells, the air within resinous with the hyacinth curls of wood falling from the bench, heavy with the stink of the gluepot, and stifling with the exhaust of the blowlamp. There they would be, Stephen in his blue dungarees; Ernie, whistling through his teeth, his sleeves rolled up to show the name Rosie tattooed on his arm; the black dog, divorced forever from his life's work with a gun, squatting on his haunches and taking the scent of the pine-curls for adequate incense in this temple where there was nothing to do but worship.

During the Easter holidays I often thought of those three, and of the bond strengthening between them, and I was inclined to be envious of the dog. I would have liked to share his silent corner and take my fill of those precious moments, slipping away and away, hours falling one by one like the wood shavings, not ever to be put back, my son's days stripping off his life like leaves from a tree, and I not there to count them over. Or is it only now, in retrospect, that I attribute to

328

myself emotions I did not feel? – now when the brooks in Vallombrosa are strewn with leaves not autumnal, and we have waked to see the green woods of spring naked and to hear no song in the brakes?

It would be a poor world, anyway, if we were rancorous about joy we cannot share; and I was not rancorous but pleased, if with a pang at the heart of pleasure, when I thought of the blowlamp falling to silence, and the shavings swept up for the day – "Leave the place tiddly, Stevo" – and those two, with the dog at their heels, walking up the path through the edge of the wood in the dusky bat-light, with the blue of the coppice hyacinths shrouded in the deepening blue of evening, and the daffodils shining, and the great drooping wings of the beeches new-feathered with green. The drooping boughs would brush their faces with cool fingers, and on the rough path, I think, Stephen's small hand would take Ernie's work-worn paw, and they would think nothing of the awful fact that another day was closing behind them its dark irrevocable doors. Thrushes and blackbirds would be in the trees, singing their praise-God vespers, and Ernie's hut would be before them, with hours yet for talk of what they had done today and what tomorrow should be done; and I think they would be content.

8

Well, all this was the background of Stephen's remark as we stood on the landing stage at Richmond. "I should think you'd keep this thing tiddly with a vacuum cleaner, not with an old mop."

What summer days the thought of an old mop called back to memory! An old mop swabbing the seats of the dinghy as we put the kettle aboard, and the bottles with the day's water supply, and the oilskins and Cornish pasties, the bathing suits and paper screws of tea and sugar, the cups and the towels, all the paraphernalia of a day that might take us anywhere, to land on any beach, lazing upon its gold through the blue and silver hours. An old mop, its handle resting on the gunwale of the *Frances and Stephen*, its head whirling like a crazy chrysanthemum, throwing out sparkles of water and nacrous fish scales as we cleared up on the homeward journey. An old mop that would serve at a pinch to fend her off a quay, or to swab sea boots, or be, in general, the useful dilapidated charlady of all things tiddly.

It was no wonder that Stephen got into the boat at Richmond with a frown on his face, exclaimed, "You row!" as though he could not be bothered to propel such a craft through such water, and settled on the cushions in the stern with the obvious intention of spending a thoroughly disparaging afternoon.

But it wasn't too bad. Water is water and a boat is a boat, and boats and water were too deeply bitten into him by now for him to be altogether unhappy. If the afternoon was not exhilarating, at least it was agreeable. It was what I should call a thoroughly Birket Foster afternoon, with everything pleasant, pretty and smoothly flowing. It was Nature that had never known a mad king's beard on a blasted heath. It was Nature in gingham, smiling under thatched eaves at the pretty ways of the ducklings.

We found a waterside tea garden and had tea and boiled eggs, bread and butter, cake and jam. We threw crumbs to the finches instead of chucking fish guts overboard to the screaming gulls. Then we rowed back to Richmond, and I did a bit of fancy feathering with the oars, arousing Stephen's contempt.

It was being a day most different from the one I had looked forward to when I woke that morning in Iris' bed. But it was a good day all the same. I felt that I shouldn't see much of Stephen that holiday. There had been hints that the voyage to France might take place. And so I was glad to have him there, sitting bolt upright because this sissy boat was made for lolling, his blazer and shirt thrown down beside him, his young but already sturdy body brown as a well-baked apple pie. We didn't say much, but it was good to be together in the sunshine with the river smell in our nostrils: the used smell that seems to belong to the busy affairs of time, so unlike the salt and bitter indifferent smell of the sea's eternity.

I was in no hurry to return to Hampstead. We went to town and had dinner in a quiet restaurant, and even then, so entrancing was the evening after the heat of the day, and the emotional shifts and changes that it had brought me, we walked for an hour on the Heath before allowing walls and a roof to close upon us.

"And now for Captain Pentecost," I said.

The old diary that I had read so long ago at Primrose Hill and that Blanche had given me after Sapphira Kitto's death, was one of the strongest bonds between me and Stephen. A year ago I had begun to read it to him when he was in bed, both because the sort of books I liked to read to him were few and far between and had long been exhausted, and because I wanted him to know something of his forebears. It had at once fascinated him, because so much of it was about the sea and because some of it was about Falmouth and Tresco Vean. Last summer we had made a pious pilgrimage. He had wanted to stand, as near as could be, on the spot where Captain Pentecost came ashore with Henry Kitto and handed the mailbags over to Russell's van. He wanted to see the captain's tombstone in the tumbled graveyard climbing behind the parish church. He would look for long moments at that old picture I had showing Pentecost heaving the gun back on to its trunnions.

So now it was with a pleasant expectation of renewing a deep intimacy that I proposed a session with Captain Pentecost. Stephen had got into bed. The bedside light fell upon his face, and now he did not look the reliable dealer with problems who had brought comfort to Bugsby in the morning. In his pink-and-white striped pyjamas, with his hands resting on the counterpane, he looked adorably young and defenceless. There was dirt in his fingernails and he had not bothered to brush his hair: it made a ragged red halo in the light. It was gratifying to feel that he would long need my strength and support. I sat in the chair by the bed and allowed the ancient pages to fall open.

"Do you think, Daddy," he asked in a serious voice, "that I could be allowed to read the book myself tonight?"

I was taken aback. "Why, yes, Stevo, by all means if you'd like to. I thought it would be fun to read it together. And, of course, reading handwriting is not so easy as reading print."

He held out his hand for the book and turned the pages here and there. "I can read it easily. He wrote very well." He granted me a smile. "Really, the letters you write to me at school are far more difficult to read than this."

"Very well, then . . ."

"I think it's rather childish to be read to at my age."

"All right, Methuselah." I tumbled his hair. "But don't read too long. Put your light out soon and go to sleep. You've had rather a tiring day and there's a long journey in front of you tomorrow."

His face lit up. "Yes! By this time tomorrow I shall know all that Ernie's been up to. Here." He handed me the book. "I don't think I'll read. I'll have a good sleep. I expect I shall dream of Tresco Vean."

"All right. Good night, old son."

I did not kiss him. He disliked it. I stood at the door till the light snapped off and I could hear the sound of his burrowing like a healthy little animal down into the bed.

I went downstairs, feeling desolate in the empty house. I told myself that this was the effect of the summer twilight, when I had always hated being between walls. Perhaps it was; and perhaps there was more in it than that. Anyway, I could not abide being in the house and I felt no desire for sleep. I shut the front door quietly and crossed the road to the Heath. It was hot and moonless, but with the day's light pulsing tremulously in the west and every path and bush clear enough to make walking possible. And so I walked, and I went into Jack Straw's for a drink, not because I wanted one but because I was feeling lonely. I was just as lonely when I came out, and I went home at a good lick, because my heart was saying that I was a thoughtless fool to have left alone a child who needed me. I ran up the stairs and opened Stephen's bedroom door, ready to rush in and comfort him. I could hear him breathing easily in his sleep, and then I went next door to my own room and got into bed, glad that the day was over.

I prepared breakfast the next morning for the two of us, and as he was eating it, suppressing a manifest excitement, Stephen said: "Please don't bother to come to the station if you're busy, or if you don't want to. Just put me into a taxi and I shall be all right."

I had not slept well. I was feeling morose, and his determination to be a grown-up man of the world jarred on my spirit. "Doesn't it occur to you, Stevo, that I might *like* to come to the station with you, and that even if I were busy I might still think it worthwhile?"

He looked at me for a moment in surprise, then jumped from his chair and ran round the table. "I'm sorry," he said. "Please! Please come."

He was irresistible. I put an arm round him and squeezed him to my side, then pushed him away. "Go and finish your breakfast. You can't make that long journey without something in your stomach."

And so, at Paddington, we parted on a happier note than I had expected. I asked him if he wanted anything to read, and he said, No – he would spend the time practising knots. He produced from his pocket a small handbook on the subject and a coil of rope's ends that he laid out on the seat.

The hands of the great station clock moved on to 10.30. "I shall see the sea," he cried, "soon after Exeter! I wish school was near the sea."

"It's a good thing it isn't, or you'd learn nothing."

He looked down at his bits of rope, itching to be fiddling with them. Then the green flag waved, the whistle blew, and the great train gathered its strength together with a few deep-throated coughs and began to glide out of the station on its way west. On its way to the *Frances and Stephen*, and Ernie Lingard and the black dog, and all that Stephen's young heart knew by summer.

There was nothing to do. Nothing at all. It was a Saturday morning. Today and tomorrow were mine. Next day I had a sitter who, I expected, would keep me busy till the Friday. Then, on the Saturday, I should make the visit to Tresco Vean. But today and tomorrow . . . I remembered Iris Randle and went into a telephone box, feeling in my pocket for coppers. But I didn't telephone her. I came out again, feeling dry, empty and exasperated, and for no reason that I could give myself I took the next train to Newbury and spent the weekend walking in the country. I ate at pubs. I slept on Saturday night under a haystack, and late on Sunday night I crept into bed at Hampstead.

9

The next Saturday I travelled alone to Tresco Vean. It had been a dullish week. My sitter was a provincial lord mayor whose fellow citizens did not think quite enough of him to go to the expense of commissioning an R.A. to paint him. They decided to make do with an A.R.A., which I then was. I dealt with the job as faithfully as I could seeing that the sitter did not interest me, and I finished Joe's signboard, and I thought of Iris Randle. But I felt no desire to visit her, and she can have felt no desire to visit me, or she would certainly have done so. There was a paragraph in the theatre gossip column of an evening paper: "Alexander Durnford's *England Helped Me* ends its successful run at the Cosmopolitan on the 29th. The play will then go on tour with the complete London company with the exception of Iris Randle, who, I understand, has signed a contract to make several films in Hollywood and will be leaving for America as soon as the play is withdrawn."

My lord mayor had given me a death-dealing cigar and gone off to enjoy what was left of another day in London. I sat by the cold fireplace of the studio listlessly looking down this gossip column when another item caught my eye: "The latest Financier to interest himself in the London theatre is Mr Luther Brimlow, whose money, I understand, is now behind at least three leading houses in the West End. Mr Brimlow's remarkable career is outlined in 'City Personalities' on another page."

I turned to "City Personalities," which on former days had dealt with Mr James White and other men of that sort. There was Luther's portrait, set in the midst of a column article. It was a recent photograph and a good one. It showed Luther at Ascot, wearing a grey top hat and morning clothes, a flower at his buttonhole, binoculars across his shoulders. My eye slipped down to a paragraph near the end of the article. "Whether Mr Brimlow will be as sensationally successful on the turf as he has been in the City remains to be seen, but with Eclat, Morning Tide and John Silver he begins his turf career with a trio that many an owner might envy."

How little I knew of this brother-in-law of mine! This was the first news that had come to me of Luther's "turf career". Blanche had never told me of it. It was possible, I thought, so queer had that household become, that she knew nothing of it. I put the paper into my pocket, took up the finished signboard for the King's Mistress, and strolled across to the pub. I had asked Iris if she minded my doing this, and she answered that in a world of false prophecies another wouldn't matter.

It was no day to sit indoors, and so, when I had eaten my snack, I went down to the Chelsea Embankment and strolled up and down for a moment on that spot where, on a dun winter evening, Blanche and I had gone long ago to take a breather before looking at the studio Harry Banfil had recommended. So long ago that I felt infinitely old: before I had married Prue, before Blanche had married Luther, before Francis, before everything that was now revealing itself as formative and crucial. Before all of that – except Iris.

I took the crumpled paper from my pocket, seeking knowledge of Luther. It seemed likely to me that, if he had not written it, he had at least carefully supplied the sifted facts. His early financial genius was noted. "James Watt, gazing at the kettle on his mother's hob, does not suggest a more prophetic moment than that in which we see young Luther Brimlow, with few, if any, advantages of parentage or education, watching the ebullitions of the world's markets."

Yes: a pretty enough rendering of Luther going up first class from Didsbury to Manchester, with his eyes glued to *The Financial Times*, sparing a glimpse and a thought now and then for Blanche's legs.

All Luther's youth was here fairly enough, if shorn of the nefarious things that I knew, and my mother knew, and the old Brimlows knew, but which, I suppose, were known then to no one else in the world save to Luther himself.

The article showed the young Brimlow, not kicked out, but adventuring into the world, driven by a hunger to be among what was charmingly called "formative financiers, the formidable few whose nod and beckoning vibrate between Throgmorton Street and the Bourse and flutter the tapes of Wall Street."

Excellent; but so far I had learned nothing new about Luther Brimlow, about the boy I had known so closely, wilting in the arid summer evenings on the street corners of Didsbury, shouting in unison with the rest "Glory – glory!" while those other Hosannas were bubbling unseen in his deepest wells.

Reading on, I did not get much light, for financial information never enlightens me. But I did get a muddled impression of realms beyond my comprehension in which Luther was moving; I did seize the fact that now, at somewhere near forty, he was, by those whom such things interested, esteemed to be a dynamic power, so intercoiled with a complication of "interests" that he must be watched with fascination, as one watches, in a whirl of machinery, the crucial wheel which, thrown out of gear, will bring all the delicate adjustments down in chaos. Flotations and promotions, finance corporations, holding companies, promoting companies, operating companies, insurance, cotton mills, theatres, mines: a miasma of information, half-understood or not understood at all, coiled through my mind as forebodingly as, on that day when Blanche and I had first stood here, the winter evening mists had coiled upon the river.

Finally: "Mr Brimlow has political ambitions. He is married to the only sister of Mr Edward Pentecost, A.R.A. They have one daughter."

Oh! they have, have they?

10

I went straight back to the studio and rang up Luther's house in Bedford Square. I was bored, completely at a loose end, in the mood when one wanders into the Park, and falls asleep on a bench, and wakes up to find that the respectable-looking girl who has seated herself aloofly on the other end is in a mood to open an unrespectable conversation. So I thought of Luther. It would be interesting to meet him again. He was, as I had expected, not at home, but I was given a telephone number in the City, and there I was given the number of a West End club whose porter told me that Mr Brimlow had just left and gave me another number. I ran him down at last, and he was in a breezy mood. "As it happens, my dear boy, I *am* free tonight. Come and have dinner with me. You'll meet some old friends of yours . . . No, wait till you meet them . . . You'll be surprised. Seven-thirty. Don't bother to dress."

So I was not, I supposed, to meet anyone whom Luther considered to be important. In fact, I met his father and mother. I had not seen the old people since the day when I had gone up to Manchester to say goodbye to my mother before joining the army. In the meantime my father had died, and, so separated was I from the Brimlows in everything save the accident of my childish association with them, that the old man gladly seized on this event, now no longer poignant, as a lifeline. He was alone when I arrived in Bedford Square. Luther was not back from whatever concerns occupied him, and Mrs Brimlow was somewhere upstairs. The evening was hot; the windows were open on to the baking pavements of the square. Old Brimlow got up heavily when I went in and took my hand in his sweaty palm. He seemed immortal. I could detect no change from the moist-eyed, drip-nosed old horror who had terrified my childhood.

"Ah, Ted, my son," he wheezed, "so your dear father has passed away." He gazed at me as though expecting to see sorrow's devastation in my face.

"Yes," I said, "he's dead."

"In the body," Mr Brimlow amended. "Absent from the body; present with the Lord."

"Well," I said, as cheerfully as I could, "it's a long time ago now, Mr Brimlow."

"A thousand ages in Thy sight are but an evening gone," he assured me. "He might have died only yesterday."

"Yes, that's true enough."

"Or he might be still alive today."

"Oh, yes."

"In such an hour as ye know not the Son of Man cometh. That's the point, Ted. In such an hour as ye know not. It behoves us to be prepared. We must be wise virgins."

I thought of that wise virgin Christina Lake, and I wondered what this doddering old fool really knew about his son.

"Luther's late," I said.

The tired dog-like face lit up. "Luther!" he murmured and it was as though he were invoking the Holy Ghost.

"I suppose you don't see much of him nowadays, Mr Brimlow?"

"Very little, my son, very little. He has been called into strange ways. He has been called to be a friend of publicans and sinners. His light shines in dark places, and for the moment the darkness comprehendeth him not. But it will. Yes; it will."

Well, that was one way of looking at it. Was old Brimlow fooling himself, or was he trying to fool me? I suppose I shall never know. The repetition of words had worn such grooves in his mind that he could roll anything he liked along them.

Through the window I saw Luther's car draw up. He leapt out, left it standing at the kerb, and ran into the house. We heard him go straight upstairs, and soon afterwards he came down and into the room with his arm round his mother's shoulders. She was astonishing. I wish I could describe clothes as well as I can paint them. What can I say about her except that she was *deluxe*? She made me think of the cheap poems, the utterly bogus claptrap, of Ella Wheeler Wilcox bound in limp purple leather with gilt edges and a title in gold. She did her best to *sail* into the room. Her mean eyes glittered at me from behind her spectacles as suspiciously as ever, and her mean nose was pinched and white. Her grey silken clothes rustled. There were rings upon her fingers, and some sort of jewelled ornament adorned her brow. As she moved, new black satin shoes with glittering buckles peeped out from beneath her skirt. I thought of the phrase Betsy Comfort had once used of Anatole Lop. Mrs Brimlow looked like "death warmed up".

Her entry was clearly aimed at me. It was a phrase flung defiantly in the face of the boy who used to pelt Luther with conkers: "Well, what about him now?" It was he, it was his power and glory, that she was bringing into the room. She was content not to exist save as an affirmation of her son; and I knew that, whatever might be the mystery of Mr Brimlow's mind, there was no mystery about this woman's. Luther did not fool her, and never would. She understood him in every tortuous twist of his being, and she would not for a moment have him other than he was. If he had been the biggest crook unhung and she had known it – as she would have known it – still, she would have been with him to the end.

"Well, Ted!" Luther cried. "What do you think of my little mother?"

"I think she's just the sort of woman you should have married."

Mrs Brimlow shook hands with me. "Nonsense," she said. "Luther should have married a duchess. He could have done if he'd waited a bit."

Well, that told us Pentecosts where we stood in the good woman's eyes, and I would have left the matter alone; but Mrs Brimlow went on: "I don't understand your sister at all. Sticking to a house hundreds of miles away from her husband. I think she should be here looking after Luther's establishment."

I thought so, too, but it was not for me to enlighten Mrs Brimlow on the difficulties in the way of this.

"I've never once so much as set eyes on my granddaughter," she went on. "I should have thought a grandmother was entitled to some say in the child's upbringing."

I could have said: "Ah, my dear Mrs Brimlow, that's something you'll *never* have – not if I know Blanche," but I merely said smoothly that I was sure she and Frances would meet some day.

"Frances!" she snorted. "I was not even consulted about the name. Why on earth was the child called Frances?"

"Just a whim of Blanche's."

"Blanche's whims are too much pampered," Mrs Brimlow started off again; but Luther broke in pacifically: "Well, so are yours, little old Mother. You must blame your son for that, not Blanche. He can't resist pampering the whims of beautiful ladies."

It was difficult to say which was the more horrible: her self-satisfied smirk or the wink Luther flashed me over her shoulder. "Well," he said, "I think we can now go in and eat."

I had once or twice been at some stylish dinners in that Bedford Square dining room where Luther had the two lovely Boudins that I would have stolen from him, given half a chance. He liked to have an occasion to spread himself, and I imagine it was the gratification of this instinct, rather than any real regard for me, that had caused him to arrange a dinner here that celebrated my becoming an A.R.A. God knows, becoming an A.R.A. doesn't amount to much, but any hook was good enough for Luther to hang an occasion on, to assemble a company which illustrated the range of his associates. There were a couple of R.A.s, including old Kitto, who chanced to be making one of his rare visits to town, a celebrated actor, a novelist, a playwright, an architect famous not only for his art but for his excellent after-dinner stories, and the women these people brought with them. "You see," Luther was obviously saying to me, "you despise me as a mere financier. Well, I can get as many as I want of your own sort any time I want them." It was a lavish dinner, with a wine matching every course and cigars a foot long.

That was the sort of thing Luther could do when he wanted to, I was thinking, walking over to peer at the Boudins, as I did whenever I entered that room; but now he struck the note of almost holy austerity. I had got into the habit of seeing all he did as a series of gestures; and his gesture now seemed to be saying: "You know, my dear parents, that the chances of life have drifted me into company and into ways far removed from yours. But here is what I love: to get back to the sort of simplicity that belongs to our old life together."

We sat at table, and Luther said: "Will you ask a blessing, Father?" and old Jonas Brimlow mumbled the words I had often heard him mumble before.

There were no servants present. At the sideboard Luther carved a cold shoulder of mutton, and we helped ourselves to potatoes and salad. No wine was served. There was a pot of tea for Mr and Mrs Brimlow. Luther and I drank water. A cold apple pie with cream followed the mutton, and Mrs Brimlow approved of the crust, whereupon Luther dutifully gave her a second helping. The conversation was trivial and domestic. Luther inquired about the small house in Didsbury where the old people still lived. In my time there they had rented it. Now, I gathered, he had bought it for them. They reported on the progress of decorations, a new bathroom, electric fittings. This visit to London was to permit them to be out of the way of the workmen.

"What d'you think of this pair, Ted?" Luther demanded playfully. "I told them they could go where they liked while the work was on. They could have lorded it at Gleneagles, or gone on to the Continent, regardless of expense; but nothing would do for my little old Mother but to come here."

He tweaked her ear; and I wondered whether she had not asked of him the hardest thing of all. He took from the breast pocket of his waistcoat the little gold-bound leather-covered book that always lived there, and made notes about things they wanted done. Then he said: "Let's go up to Frances' room."

Frances did not spend much time in this place, but there was a room on the second floor at the back of the house which was set aside for her use. I had amused myself daubing the white walls with pictures to please her. I had worked under her command, and nearly all the pictures were of her life at Tresco Vean. There was the cutter in full sail. There was the magnolia that climbed as high as the house, with flowers blooming upon it like chalices one day and alabaster saucers the next. There was Ernie, and the absurd dog, and there was Stephen. "Make Stephen *big*," Frances commanded; and there he was, life-size.

Frances was not much of a child for toys, and there were none in this room; but there were many gay books, a few comfortable wicker chairs, and there was a small white upright piano.

"Make yourselves comfortable," Luther said, and the Brimlows sat down and looked at what must have seemed to them a strange room indeed. I, too, sat down. The dusk was deepening. It was very shadowy up here. I was bored to tears and wondered how we were to get through the rest of the evening, when Luther seated himself at the piano, struck a few notes, and then turned on the stool towards his parents. "I thought we'd have a few of the old favourites," he said, and began to sing, accompanying himself:

> "Abide with me, fast falls the eventide;
> The darkness deepens, Lord with me abide."

Presently the Brimlows raised their voices with his. I, too, joined in.

It was an extraordinary moment. The corners of the room were webbed and clotted with the gathering dark. What light there was fell upon the white piano and upon Luther's face which I could see over the top of it. His face, too, looked white in the thickening gloom. His head was thrown back; his eyes were closed, and he strummed like an automaton. Old Brimlow sat coiled up like a spider in a dark corner. His elbow was on the arm of the chair, his face in his hand, and his voice mumbled through his fingers. Mrs Brimlow was upright, her face enigmatic in the dusk. The buckle on her shoe, the ornament in her hair, the spectacles upon her nose, caught an occasional glitter as the day beyond the window stirred on its deathbed.

I was caught out on the words after the first verse, and could do no more than contribute a bass humming, but the Brimlows, all three, were word-perfect. Almost without a pause, Luther passed from Lyte to Newman. "Lead, kindly light, amid the encircling gloom," they sang; and this time I knew the words better and was able to sing right through to the end:

> "And with the morn those angel faces smile
> Which I have loved long since: and lost awhile."

There was not now even a glimmer to stir a twinkle on Mrs Brimlow's foot. The walls were black. The magnolia tree and the dog, Stephen and the ship and Ernie Lingard were all there somewhere in that blackness watching this strange scene; this prodigal whose father had not awaited him but had arisen and journeyed to visit him in full career in the far country. Useless to speculate on the secrets of those three hearts: how much of emotional memory, how much tug of a natal cord, how much camouflage and cover. Beyond the dark window, upon the façades of unseen houses, a light or two began to appear. I sprang to my feet and shook myself as if to be rid of clinging webs of black crepe. "Let's have some light," I said, but old Brimlow answered: "No, no. I like singing in the dark. Let's go on singing in the dark."

So I thanked Luther for his entertainment, made my excuses to the old people, and left them singing in the dark. I was glad that I should soon be joining the summer gathering at Tresco Vean. I had bought a book on knots and splices, and had been practising. I was anxious to show Stephen that I was not a fool.

CHAPTER NINE

A LWAYS IT seemed to turn out that I journeyed down to Cornwall alone, and there was always something to occupy my mind, something that had to be done to keep up with Stephen. And, as time went on, with Frances, too. There was usually a lot of impedimenta with me, and so the change at Truro into the Falmouth train was a nuisance. But once Falmouth was reached, there would be the three trusties, all now wearing jerseys emblazoned with the name *Frances and Stephen*. They would fall upon my store with joyful shouts, and in their hands it seemed nothing. I would look vaguely round for some bag or parcel, to make some pretence of being self-supporting, but everything had been cleaned up and there was nothing to carry but my ticket to the barrier. Then, outside the station, there would be Stephen's car, with that absurd dog Nobs sitting in it, shivering and addressing to everybody who cared to look at him an apology for committing the crime of being alive. Stephen's car was a dreadful bone-shaking contraption that he had bought with a fiver I gave him for a birthday. Its engine had died years before, but he and Ernie Lingard had breathed into it a dubious breath of life that was liable to become stertorous, asthmatic, and to fail altogether in moments of crisis. But to me, who cannot tell a carburettor from a sparking plug, it was wonderful that this corpse, which had mouldered in the grave for so long, should even go through the motions of being alive, and so I had christened it Lazarus, and this name was painted in red on the bonnet. With Lazarus and Nobs trembling each with an independent tremor, yet in unison, we would swerve away to the seafront, Stephen masterfully at the wheel and Ernie, watchful but seemingly negligent, beside him, shouting: "It fair beats me how that dog took to t'car. You'd go a long way before finding a dog like that – naturally mechanically-minded." He would stroke Nobs' head, and Nobs, shivering upon his incurved inch of tail, would look up with tears of gratitude rolling down his face.

Well, there we were upon the Falmouth front, with the hotels on our right and the sea pounding upon the level sand on our left. "Captain Pentecost wouldn't know this place," Stephen would cry, carelessly lifting a hand from the wheel to wave it towards the trim, seaward-looking buildings; and, indeed, save for Pendennis Castle on the frowning hill behind us and the headlands stepped out one after another into the westward sea, with the cruel teeth of the Manacles ripping the smooth blue summer silk, there was little indeed that Captain Pentecost would have known.

But we soon left all that behind: the coloured confetti of bathers rushing across the yellow sand, the white bathing huts, the wave uncurling itself like a perpetual undulent lazy feather; and we slid past Swanpool shimmering in the sunblaze, margined with an army of green reeds, and put Lazarus to the test of the climb beyond the bay where the little freshwater stream forever frisks with the vast skirts of the ocean, like a puny human life toying with the problems of immense unknown eternity. Up Lazarus would go with a grinding of teeth, and we holding our breath till he had made it, living still, but perilously near a return to the tomb; and then it was a switchback past Meanporth, past the absurd endearing blood-red lion on the pub at Mawnan Smith; past the gateway with the zoological improbability of a putty-coloured fox upon either gatepost, and so to Tresco Vean at last. Behind us the magnolia would be offering up the glory of its great cream flowers, and before us, down the long vista of the little valley, we would glimpse the sea – so small a fragment it looked, blue and tranquil, but the sufficient entry upon any adventure. Prue would be there, and Blanche and my mother, and the children and Ernie, who always ate with us now as of right, and some odd Miss Smith or Jones or Robinson, a changing creature, an unabiding phenomenon, someone charged with teaching functions towards Frances that were never seriously esteemed or permitted to interfere with the fun of the fair.

So many of these occasions I seem to recall, with the heat beginning to drain away from the afternoon, and the birds silent, the torrid blue of the noontide sky deepening to indigo, the whole day seeming to close in upon us slowly like folding wings, only the children eager and impetuous for restless life, shouting: "Tomorrow! Tomorrow! Ernie, what shall we do tomorrow?"

2

It was thus, in most summers, that my holiday began, but in 1927 there was a change. I had enjoyed the journey as usual, once Slough was left behind; only a fiend who not only lived in hell but liked it could enjoy the region between Paddington and Slough. Except, of course, for the sense of escape, of being away for a time from the Sloughs and all they stood for. The punts looking so cool under the grey lovely bridge of Maidenhead; the streams and canals thick with cresses and yellow nenuphars that the bobbing coots and moorhens breasted aside as they swam; the great tiled barns; the white horses carved on the lean flanks of the downs; Glastonbury Tor and holy Athelney standing over the sedgy flats of Somerset; the crumbling red coasts of Devonshire, and finally Cornwall: little fields, little woods, little valleys, little streams: the place of minute beauties and intimate personal loveliness.

Then there we were in the late afternoon going over the viaduct into Truro, with the town smoking below us, and the dumpy cathedral doing its literally level best to aspire, and far away, a silver arm reaching through the mauve mist of the evening, the river: so called, but in fact the sea, a bit of all the salt water there is, anywhere, in all the earth.

I had assembled my gear in the corridor, ready to transfer it to the Falmouth train, and I stood at the window, watching the long platform and the people on it slide past me, and thinking that now it would not be long before I met Nobs and Lazarus and the trusties. Then, to my surprise, there was Frances, running past the bookstall, running with the train, and Ernie Lingard running with her.

Perhaps it was because I had not expected to see her there, but at that moment I saw Frances very clearly, and I thought: "My word, young woman, you're going to be a beauty some day. You're going to break a few hearts."

She was wearing sandals and brief shorts of pale-blue linen, and a boyish-looking short-sleeved shirt, wide open at the neck, and, I suppose, nothing else. Her long legs and arms were golden, and her hair, arranged in two plaits, thumped upon her back as she ran. The summer had bleached it almost lint-white. As the train slowed, she slowed, too, and began to look at the faces in the windows, and it chanced that we came to a standstill with her and me confronting one another, looking into one another's eyes, and hers were of the mauve of scabious, incredibly candid and unafraid. She was ten. Stephen, then, was fourteen.

I got out and kissed her and shook hands with Ernie. "Why this change in the programme?" I asked. "Where's Stevo?"

They smiled at one another in the manner of conspirators, and Ernie began to pick up my bags. He set off with them towards the gate marked: "Way Out."

"Here! What's all this? Aren't we getting into the Falmouth train?"

I was following Ernie, a bag in each hand, further hindered by Frances' arm tucked through mine. Ernie did not condescend to heed, much less to answer, my question. He put down his bullet head and bored his way through the crowd towards the gate. "You'll see," Frances said. "It's a surprise." Through her arm I could feel her body jumping with excitement. "It's top of the tide," she said, "and high springs." She had begun to know all about such matters and their connection with what you could or could not do in a boat.

In the square outside the station Ernie was piling the bags into a taxi, and a moment later we were off. But we did not take the road towards Falmouth. We dropped down the hill into the town, and in no time at all had pulled up at the quay built around the farthest reach of the water I had looked at from the train. It is a spot I have always liked, especially at high tide when the water lies against the grey stone wall of the dusty flour mill, thick-grown in all its ancient crannies with valerian and other weeds, and the gulls swoop over the water or swim upon it with the swans that love to gather there. The hot summer air has always a slight vibration from the coughing of some old engine which, concealed within the mill, shoots its asthmatic breath out through a pipe to hang in little clouds. A few trees grow among turf on the quay, which pushes a blunt rounded granite nose into the water, and that day, sitting upon a bollard on this quay, was Stephen. He did not see us come, for he was looking westward into the distance from which the water flowed in, flooding the channel that at low tide is grey mud inscribed with the squiggles of a few tricky twisting channels, and in which, even at high tide, it was well to observe the buoys if you carried more than a foot or two beneath you. All I saw was his white-shod feet, his khaki shirt and shorts, and his copper nob flaming in the sunlight. There was one small unaccustomed note in the picture he made: tucked into his belt was a fistful of cotton-waste.

"Ahoy! Coming aboard!" Ernie shouted; and on that Stephen leapt up and came towards us. He shook hands with me gravely, took the bags from me, and said: "This way, sir."

He followed Ernie down the steps. And there she was, what I had more or less guessed I should find when Frances spoke of high springs: a motor-launch, shining like something to which for a week past the whole British navy had applied its conception of the tiddly. Her outsides were gleaming white enamel with gold lines finishing at the bows in a bit of scroll and flourish. Her wheel, her cleats, her portholes, shone like gold. Up forward her anchor lay upon the cabin roof attached to a rope that had been coiled down with mathematical precision. She was about thirty foot long and fairly beamy, and she was held off the quay wall by snowy canvas-covered fenders fore and aft. From the engine box in the middle of the cockpit came a gentle purring.

"Cast her off," Ernie shouted, and up on the quay Frances untied the rope, threw it aboard, and ran down the steps. Stephen took the wheel. Ernie threw the engine into gear. Frances and I fended her off from the wall with our hands as she began to move slowly forward. "We're going home by water today," she said, and I answered: "Yes, my child, that had seemed to me probable."

Beyond an expression of admiration which was obviously called for, I said nothing more. Clearly, all three were bursting with information which I was sure they would want to impart in their own time, so I left the time to them. At the moment, nothing was more important to them than to make a stylish and efficient getaway which would leave no grins at the antics of landlubbers on the faces of the curious lining the quay.

It seemed to me that they did creditably. "In with those fenders," Ernie commanded; and Frances leapt to it, detaching the ropes from the cleats and stowing all neatly away beneath the seat which made a half circle round the cockpit.

"She's only crawling," Ernie confided, coming and standing at my side. "Got to go slow in water like this. Wait till we get out. That's an engine, that is. Not many like 'er. And economical. Now, Stevo. What's the drill?"

"Coming out of a river, round buoys on the starboard, conical buoys on the port," Stephen chanted.

"That's the lad," Ernie approved. "Keep it in your noddle. You never know when you'll need a bit of knowledge like that."

The launch zigzagged to and fro in the buoyed channel between low banks held from dissolution by thousands upon thousands of fasces of hazel rods stuck upright into the edge of the land. For a long time here the sea had fought to win the land and men had fought to defeat the sea. Soon we had passed this tricky patch and come to deep water. The land rose steeply on either side, densely grown with little oaks, and the water in between was deep enough to float a battleship. High in the air above this lovely gulch a pair of buzzards hovered, swooped, climbed again; and along the water's edge a heron flapped slowly from one rock to another. Ernie gave the engine a turn of speed, and the standard at our stern woke up and began to stream.

"Well, I must say this is a nice way to come home," I cried.

"Ay; better than goin' through t'tunnel into Bradford," Ernie conceded, with a grin. "That's a stinker, that is."

"Now I suppose I'd better explore the ship." I stepped forward to open the cabin door, but Frances leapt in front of me, shouting: "No! Wait till you're called. You'll be called when everything's ready." She went in and shut the door behind her.

"This is all very mysterious, Ernie."

"Ay, it is an' all, but Ah'm sayin' nowt."

"Would you like to take her for a bit, Dook? She's easy on the wheel."

So I took her, and looking back over my shoulder was amused to see Stephen bending earnestly over the engine, wiping this and that with his handful of waste, his freckled face knotted up in concentration. "Beautiful! Beautiful!" he murmured, wiped his hands, and joined Frances in the cabin.

"What are they up to in there, Ernie?"

"You might as well ask t'Chancellor for his secrets on t'day before Boodget," said Ernie firmly. "Ah'm saying nowt."

Later, Frances stuck her head through the cabin door. "You can come in now." I handed the wheel to Ernie and ducked into the cabin.

Dunlopillo mattresses softened the tops of the lockers that made seats on either hand. Between these there was just enough room for a long table, and on the table a meal was set out. "Going home this way," Frances explained, "you'll be rather later than if Lazarus had met you at Falmouth. So we thought we'd better provide dinner."

I wondered how much I was going to enjoy this dinner. It had been prepared on two primus stoves, and the air was poisonous with fumes of paraffin and methylated spirit. On one of the stoves water had been boiled to make tea, and on the other, liver had been cooked in a frying-pan. The children had done their best to achieve *chic*. A green linen cloth was on the table. There was a vase of wild flowers. I edged into my seat and Frances sat at my side. Suddenly she hugged my arm and cried excitedly: "Look! Look! Hadn't you noticed?"

She pointed to the crockery on the table, and I saw that every piece, every cup, saucer and plate, was inscribed "The Dook." I don't remember how it started, but this absurd name was mine, as far as the children went.

"We named her after you!" Frances cried. "Didn't you notice her name when you came aboard?"

I was ashamed to say that I hadn't.

"Daddy said," Frances explained, "that we could call her what we liked, and he'd have the name put on to the crockery."

"So Daddy gave you the launch?"

"Yes," Stephen broke in. "Uncle Luther had her sent round for Fran's birthday."

One of Luther's typical lavish gestures. Cost him a pretty penny, I reflected.

"It's a bit hard to take a present from him and name it after me," I objected.

"Oh, I don't know," Stephen answered with insight. "Giving it was what he wanted. He wouldn't care after that. And he doesn't know who the Dook is. Probably thinks we worship Wellington. Coming up."

He carried the pan of liver to the table and dished it out on to the plates. A pile of bread had been cut, and Frances poured out the tea. The fumes began to dissipate as air blew down through the skylight and out at the open door. I enjoyed the meal more than I had expected to. I was hungry. Halfway through, Stephen went out to the wheel and

Ernie came in to eat. The bread and liver were followed by bread and strawberry jam, and then there was the fun of washing up. I washed and Frances wiped. Then she opened a door in the forward end of the cabin and proudly displayed the W.C. tucked into the peak of the bows. She gravely pumped away at the handle, to show me how it was done, and said: "You'd better practise a bit. If you don't leave it right, you could have the whole place flooded."

After that, I had to see every locker and cubbyhole, examine every bit of gear, praise the lighting system that Ernie had installed. I had to be told the difference between navigation lights and riding lights, and I had to admire a scheme for installing a small searchlight, so that moorings could he picked up when *The Dook* came in after dark.

By the time all this had been gone into, we had crossed the Carrick Roads, we had left Falmouth on our right and come round Pendennis Head. Before us stretched the open sea. *The Dook* began to lift and rock a little and the air freshened. "You'd better put some clo'es on, Fran," Ernie said.

"I'm warm enough," Frances objected.

Ernie went into the cabin and came back with a thick turtle-necked sweater. "Come on," he said.

She looked rebellious, and without a word Stephen began to pull on a sweater. Frances puts hers on, too.

It was a lovely evening. The light was level as we made the starboard bend into the wide mouth of Helford River. The tide was running out strongly when we came to moorings: new moorings that had been laid down alongside those of the *Frances and Stephen*. Up on the foredeck, Stephen deftly hooked the buoy aboard, and there followed the always pleasant sound of the chain coming in through the fairlead: voyage done, harbour won. "Finished with engines!" Stephen sang, making the chain fast round the cleat, and Ernie stilled the engine with a touch. Stephen leapt down from the foredeck. "Fran, take *The Dook* ashore, and then come back with a dinghy. Ernie and I want to have a look at one or two things in the engine."

So Frances rowed me ashore, and when she was gone back to the launch I walked slowly up the hill through the wood towards the house. Rough seats stood here and there along the path, and from them Blanche rose and greeted me.

"Well," she asked, "how did you like the great adventure?"

"Very much; but I hope you haven't assumed that I shall now want no dinner."

"We've heard of nothing but bringing you home by water for the last week. Ernie and those children have been scrubbing and polishing since dawn, and as much thought went into your bread and liver as the head chef at the Savoy would give to an international banquet."

"Ther're a sweet pair of kids. I thought Frances was looking lovely."

"I made her take a bath before starting. She was oil from head to foot. Stephen's gone mad on engines, and that means that she's mad on them, too."

"Doesn't the poor old *Frances and Stephen* get a look in now? She seemed reproachful as we came to the moorings."

"Oh, yes. She's not neglected. Frances made her first trip to France in her with Stephen and Ernie a fortnight ago. They just looked into Dieppe and back again. They ride and swim, sail and take out the launch. That more or less makes up their life down here."

We had not moved from the seat. We had stood dawdling on the path, and now Blanche sat down again. "I wonder how long it can last?" she said.

"Well – how long *does* youth last?"

"No," she cried. "No, Ted, I don't want a sentimental answer. It's not a question of youth. It's a question of finance."

"Ah! Now Luther's wife is talking." I sat down beside her. "What is it, Blanche? Anything wrong?"

"Well, look at this place. It takes a lot of money to run it. Yes, let me talk like Luther's wife for once. I've never done it before. I just took everything as it came along. There was Sapphira to do the worrying to begin with. Not that there was much to worry about in her day. This isn't like a farm or any other self-supporting place, though from what I hear farms aren't having all that easy a time now. This place is unproductive. It's got to be kept going by money that comes in from outside itself. And, as you know, it's kept going well. I should hate to see it shoddy and shabby. It's better than it was when Sapphira had it."

That was true. In Sapphira's day the gardens were a wilderness. Now they were a show place: not that they were ever shown except to us favoured few. The house had been a place that could be lived in comfortably. Blanche had gone through it and weeded out everything that offended her. She had installed an electric lighting plant. She had had every corner redecorated, and the rooms had an expensive austerity of period furniture. I had often thought the place was costing her a pretty penny; but this had not worried me. Since that day when I had wandered on the Embankment at Chelsea reading in an evening newspaper the story of Luther's financial career, his splendour had sharply increased. It was a time when the wolves of society were in full cry and Luther was a leader of the pack. One heard, for example, of disasters in the cotton trade, and out of these and such affairs he seemed to skip nimbly, richer than ever. His cronies were beginning to feel a draught. I had read in the newspapers that "Mr Luther Brimlow, Conservative M.P. for the Irwell Division of Manchester, has bought Sir Harry Banfil's famous collection of modern paintings," and not long after that there had been an account of Sir Harry's bankruptcy proceedings "assets nil". But Luther went dazzlingly on, manipulating millions, and there seemed no reason to doubt that he was one of the richest men in the country.

How all this affected Blanche I did not know. Her relationship with Luther appeared to be purely formal. She spent the winter months in Bedford Square, and she and Luther were seen together occasionally at some dinner or at the opera or theatre. But I didn't imagine there was much, if anything, more than façade in all this. To put it bluntly, I thought they had not been to bed together for years. Nevertheless, with a millionaire in the background of her existence, and one with whom there had been no overt scandalous breach, I had supposed that Blanche need never worry about money. And there was the fortune Sapphira had left her.

"I'd sell the whole place up," Blanche was saying, "if I couldn't keep it in the way I want it to be kept. You know that ever since I married him Luther has wanted me to get rid of it. He's never had the slightest use for the place, and so I've not allowed him to spend a penny on it. I've always insisted that Tresco Vean was my affair and that I'd pay for it."

"Well, you're not finding that difficult, are you?"

"No. Not at the moment. But more difficult than it used to be. I know your views about money, Ted. You've got some queer moral scruples about living on investments, haven't you?"

"Well, living on investments means living on other people's labour. I don't like doing it. So I spend what I earn, and when I want some more I earn some more. That's all it comes to. It horrifies Luther. He's offered once or twice to put me on to what he calls a good thing or a dead cert, and he thinks I'm mad when I'm not interested. However, we've had all this out before."

"Yes. But you see I *can't* earn. There's nothing I can do. And so everything I have here depends on what my investments make. And though I'm not worrying at the moment, they're not making what they used to. I saw my man last time I was in town, and he didn't seem happy – not about anything. That's all I meant when I wondered how long this could go on. Perhaps I'm shying at a shadow."

"I expect you are."

"Still, there is another thing. Do you read *Country Life?*"

"I see it at my club occasionally."

"Last week, in the notes about property, it said that Greenlands was coming into the market."

"Good lord! That *is* something. I thought Luther was devoted to the place. He's spent thousands on it."

"It made me shudder. When these men start selling things . . ."

These men! A nice way to speak of your husband, Blanche. Still, she was right. Sir Harry Banfil had sold his collection of pictures, and he hadn't lasted long after that.

"It made me wonder," Blanche said, "why he sent that expensive launch down here for Frances' birthday. He's never given her a lavish thing like that before."

"My dear, I don't follow . . ."

"Well, earning goodwill . . . Getting a footing . . ."

"I thought a footing in Tresco Vean was the last thing he wanted."

"So did I. But he's here now. He arrived unannounced by car an hour ago."

I stood up, astonished and shaken. There was even a trembling in my limbs which recalled to me a day of long ago when my childish folly had first permitted Mrs Brimlow to cross the threshold of our little house in Didsbury. I had thought of her as the enemy within the gates, and something of the same feeling visited me now. Luther at Tresco Vean! I gave Blanche my hand and raised her from the seat.

With the same feeling of defensive conspiracy that had been ours then, we now walked up to the house together.

3

Luther Brimlow's career was so remote from anything which I could even begin to understand that, had it not been for a hint from him, I should have missed the significance of a point that came to my mind as Blanche and I walked to the house. Many years ago he had talked to me about his wish to enter Parliament. He had said that this could be useful to a financier, because the investing public felt that Members of Parliament were to be trusted. He hadn't put it so bluntly, but the impression that remained in my mind after that conversation was that sheep's clothing was useful wear for wolves. Now I did not know which companies, corporations, combines and what not Luther controlled, but I did know *some* of them, and it had interested me to ponder on the names of the directors. One thing leapt to view. Luther had for a long time finished with the Banfils, the Conlows, and men of that sort. The directors of his companies now were all men whom one would hardly expect to know a thing about finance on Luther's colossal scale. Their names were all fairly well known. They had evidently been handpicked as decoy ducks. An ex-colonial governor, major-generals, admirals, a fine collection, it seemed to me, of worthy simpletons. They would accept what Luther had to say, because they wouldn't know what he was saying. They were the polished red apples on the front of the stall. What went on behind the healthy picture they presented to the public was Luther's affair.

These ideas had been in the back of my mind for some time. Blanche's obvious alarm at her husband's unexpected appearance sharpened them and brought them to the front. But it was a false alarm. Luther went away in the highest of spirits the next day.

However, that was an evening of exceptional interest. From the terrace, Prue saw us when we came out from the bit of woodland, and she hurried to meet us. We embraced, but she, like Blanche, seemed to have Luther rather than me on her mind. "I'm afraid you've come to a bit of a madhouse, darling," she said.

What had happened was this. Blanche had left the house to meet me soon after Luther had arrived. It might have been expected that Prue would come to meet me and that Blanche would stay with her

353

husband; but to expect this would be to miss the inwardness of the situation. Ever since the birth of Frances, Blanche had instinctively fled when Luther approached and it is not too much to say that between her and me there now once more existed that defensive anti-Brimlow alliance that we had known as children. On the surface, it was less crude and savage; it was conducted even with charm and civilised consideration; but it was there. And so I for one was not surprised that it was Blanche, not Prue, who escaped as soon as possible.

Luther had not been at Tresco Vean since his marriage, but he knew the place in Sapphira's day. He would remember the old dovecote, a charming octagonal building of grey stone isolated from the other outbuildings, and he would remember, too, that at Tresco Vean the only telephone stood on a table in the hall. There could be no whispered confidences over the telephone in that house. Everything one said was bawled into the public ear.

"As soon as you'd gone," said Prue, "an electrician arrived from Falmouth. Luther seems to have arranged something with him as he came through. The man's there now, taking a telephone extension to the dovecote."

We looked at one another in amazement. We stood still, reluctant to go forward and learn what we all seemed to feel might be the disagreeable truth. At that moment Luther himself appeared on the terrace and began to walk down towards us. We went forward to meet him. He shook hands with me.

"Well, Ted."

"Well, Luther."

That was all we said. With that, he seemed to wipe me out of account and took Blanche's arm.

"You ran away, my dear, before I had a chance to say a word to you. I'm afraid I've been taking some liberties with your property. You must forgive me. You gave me no chance to consult you."

"Prue has just told me that you've had a telephone line taken to the dovecote."

"Yes. Damn the telephone. But there it is. I can't take even a day's holiday away from it."

"But it was there – in the hall."

He stroked the fingers of the hand lying on his arm. "Yes. But, my dear – my affairs are hardly public property. The servants . . ."

"I see."

"I have sometimes to spend as much as half an hour at a stretch on the telephone. It would be a nuisance to you all to have me shouting away in the house."

"Yes. I suppose so."

"Forgive me, won't you, but I've had a chair and a small table taken out to the dovecote. I may have to spend some time there . . . Ah! There's that fellow . . ."

The electrician, in blue dungarees, had appeared on the terrace. Luther ran forward eagerly, and the rest of us more slowly followed.

"It's OK, sir. Like to give a trial ring?"

Blanche shrugged her shoulders. She and Prue went indoors. I followed Luther and the electrician to the dovecote. The line was tested and approved. Luther passed a tip into the man's hand, and he drove off in a rattletrap two-seater. I went into the dovecote and looked around. A long trestle table had been carried out there. Upon it was the telephone, a sumptuous attaché case inscribed L.B., and a three-branched candlestick, furnished with new candles. A few spare candles lay alongside. A wooden kitchen chair stood by the table. I pointed to the candles. "Expecting an all-night session?"

He turned the question off. "D'you remember, when I was a kid, how I used to spend all-night sessions putting the books in order in my father's shack? I used candles then. Happy days! Can't remember using them since."

He was wearing city clothes. He grinned at me uneasily, and I thought he was anxious for me to be off.

Blanche appeared at the door. "Dinner will be ready in ten minutes. You've just got time to wash. Ernie and the children are in view."

"You needn't tell them I'm here."

"But aren't you coming in to dinner?"

"No."

"They'll see you in the morning."

"Maybe. In that case I hope it will be a pleasant surprise for them."

"Shall I send you out some sandwiches and a bottle of beer?"

"Please don't fuss," he said, and for the first time there was a note of petulance, annoyance, in his voice.

"Very well," said Blanche, and added, with a shrug: "Good hunting."
Then we left him and saw the door shut and heard the bolt pushed
home. It would not be a comfortable place for him. The only light was
through the holes, high up, that the pigeons used. There had been
none for a long time, but recently Frances had introduced three pairs
of white fantails who palatially inhabited this house that would hold
hundreds of birds. These were fluttering uneasily about, alighting now
and then, taking off again, disturbed by this intrusion into their
domain. We left them to their pink-toed strutting upon the tiles, to an
indignant puffing-out of chests, and a constant melancholy crooling.

"What do you make of it all?" Blanche asked uneasily.

"I think we shall know more in the morning. Better do as he says,
and tell the children nothing."

So we passed the word to Prue and my mother, and dinner went
off uneasily. Happily, there was no lack of matter for conversation
with the children. The performance of *The Dook's* engine, which had
seemed to me smooth enough, was apparently engrossing their minds
as deeply as something – who knew what? – was engrossing the mind
of the man – lonely, unhappy, I imagined – shut away behind the
bolted door of the dovecote. What had he to talk of, and to whom,
that he must discuss at so great a distance and in such suggestive
privacy?

"It's nowt that a new gasket won't put right, so don't worry, Stevo.
An' we'd better have t'plugs out an' clean 'em."

We might as well not have existed, we four grown-ups, for all we
mattered in the exciting little world that these three occupied. They
chattered of water-cooling and the petrol feed. "An' I don't altogether
like the way she takes up when she goes over to oil. A bit slow."

My late arrival had put the meal back, and it was dusky in the
dining room. Stephen, I suspected, had done little more than give
himself a casual rub with his hank of cotton waste, and Frances looked
as if she had not even done this. She had come to the table in her
shorts and shirt, and there was a greasy smudge down one side of her
face. She was sitting between Ernie and Stephen, and her face turned
constantly from one to the other, loving and admiring them both. I
felt suddenly a great gladness that no drop of her blood flowed from
the being of the man shut up with whatever his secrets might be in the
dovecote. But what power he might have to harm her! My heart was

unhappy. I thought of the gentle birds hovering out there in the gathering dusk, frightened by this alien presence in their accustomed place.

My mother and the children went to bed at ten. For another hour, Prue, Blanche and I remained in a state of extreme tension, talking merely in order to talk about *something*. None of us mentioned Luther. Each of us was thinking of nothing else. Suddenly the telephone bell rang in the hall, and so sharply had telephones entered our consciousness that we all leapt as though a bomb had exploded among us. As it happened, it was nothing but a caller who had been given a wrong number; but the incident brought our emotion to a head. Blanche got up, said: "God, I feel a wreck!" and without another word went upstairs.

Prue said: "I think I'll go, too. You won't be long, Ted?"

"No, darling. But I think I'll sit up for a bit."

I watched her disappear round the bend of the stairs. The clock in the hall struck eleven. I opened the front door and went out.

The night was warm and still. There was just enough light for me to see what I was doing. The window of Ernie's room at the end of the old coach house was lit, and as I stood there the door opened and Ernie was silhouetted against the bright interior. He came in my direction, and I walked to meet him.

"Ah!" he greeted me quietly. "That you, Mr Pentecost? Ah were just comin' to see if anyone were still up."

"Why? Anything wrong, Ernie?"

"Look at t'dovecote."

The squat tower was dark against the sky, and the perforation of holes running round it stood out as small ports of dusky light. I could see the white ghosts of the pigeons still tumbling about uneasily in the darkness.

"Looks as though there's someone in there," said Ernie. Ah've tried t'door. It's locked on t'inside."

I took him by the arm and began to walk away from that telltale gleam.

"There's another thing. Ah looked into t'garage, an' there's a Rolls Royce there. A fair beauty."

We were walking away from the house, along the tree-bordered drive that led to the highroad. Ernie had seen so much that I thought I had better take him into my confidence.

"You've never met Mrs Brimlow's husband, have you, Ernie?"

"Nay, he seems a reight mystery man."

"Well, he arrived unexpectedly for a short stay while you were on the way to Truro to meet me this afternoon. Unfortunately, a holiday for him doesn't mean what it does for me. He can't leave his affairs behind him. He's got to be in touch with all sorts of people by telephone. So he's set up a small office in the dovecote and had a telephone extension taken out there."

"Ba goom! Quick work," said Ernie.

It was, and I wondered uneasily why it had to be so quick.

"Ah should have thought 'e'd be more comfortable inside. Plenty of spare rooms in that great 'ouse."

"He doesn't want to disturb people," I explained lamely. The moon was rising. It was pleasant and cool out here under the trees. Ernie stopped to light his pipe, and the match showed me his face, puzzled but trusting.

"Well," he said, with a laugh, "'e certainly 'as a taste in motor launches. Gosh! The engines in that boat!"

"I'm afraid engines are not in my line, Ernie. Is there anything exceptional about them?"

"They're terrific," he said briefly.

We had turned and wandered back to his room. I went in and admired its neatness and home-made comfort, and when we had chatted for a few more moments he said: "Well, Ah'll turn in. So long as everything's all right . . ."

I said good night and walked on to the terrace, wondering whether everything *was* all right, what strange drama was being enacted in the straitened seclusion of the dovecote, what spirits were being summoned up, and for what purpose, by the telephone wire so hastily laid. The quiet moonlight lay upon the tubs of blue and white agapanthus, the stone urns spilling out sprays of pale pink geraniums. There was the moving sound of curlews calling down on the water where *The Dook* lay with her terrific engines. I thought a lot about those terrific engines.

"Ah! You're up still!"

I swung round and faced Luther. I had not heard his crepe soles on the pavement. He spoke softly.

"I was restless. I couldn't sleep."

"Ah, sleep!" he said. "By gosh, Ted, I shall sleep soundly now. But first of all I must eat. I'm starving. D'you know your way about the house? Could you find the larder?"

There was a relief, a gaiety, about him that had been absent earlier. I said I'd see what I could do, and we went into the house together. I led him to the larder and we made some sandwiches. "I'll join you. Shall I make coffee?"

"No! We'll celebrate. Wine!"

"What do we celebrate?"

He looked at me for a moment without speaking; then he said in a low voice: "Deliverance."

He was pale and seemed to me overwrought, like a man who has emerged from a difficult place after a hard struggle; but he caught himself up again into gaiety. He slapped me on the back, and said: "Where's the wine-cellar? I expect you know that, you old devil."

There was nothing that you could call a wine-cellar. We didn't drink much at Tresco Vean; but I led him to a cupboard where Blanche kept a few dozen bottles, and he ran his eye quickly over them. There was one bottle of champagne, and he pulled it out.

"Champagne!" he said. "That's what the moment calls for."

"It's Blanche's last bottle," I said.

"What of that? When I get back to town I'll repay her with a dozen of the best."

He was increasingly cock-a-hoop. We went into the lounge and he promptly drained a glass. He ate hungrily, and I left most of the bottle to him. It increased the gaiety of his spirit, and presently he said "I should imagine that's the first transatlantic telephone call ever to go out of these parts."

"Gosh! Have you been through to America?"

He looked at me sharply as though he had already said too much. He poured the last of the champagne into his glass and drained it down. He got up. "I must get some sleep. Where are they putting me?"

I took him to the room that had been prepared for him, and went to my own bedroom. It was half-past one, and Prue was still awake.

She sat up in the moonlit bed. "Darling, whatever's the time? I seem to have been waiting for you for hours."

I kicked off my shoes and sat on the bed with my arm round her. I felt exhausted, as though I had just come out of some hard physical struggle. Prue sensed this, and leaned over to take a cigarette from the box on the bedside table. She lit it and put it to my lips. "You poor darling," she murmured.

"He's gone to bed," I said presently. "It was nearly one o'clock before he finished whatever it was he was up to."

"And what can that have been?"

"I can only guess. And my guess is that he rushed away from London knowing that the odds were about fifty-fifty that he'd never go back."

Out in the night a heron gave his sudden cry, like harsh fabric violently ripped, and I saw the white pigeons tumbling through the air in the moonlight. Poor creatures! They couldn't get over that intrusion into their home.

"Unless he'd been *taken* back," said Prue.

And, of course, that is what had been in my mind all the time. Now that it was stated, I could look at it more calmly. I could look at it without feeling a pang for Luther Brimlow. But Blanche? Frances?

"Well, anyway, I gather that he's pushed the boat off the rocks. He's afloat again. He's cooked something up."

"For the time being," said Prue.

"The time being is all I propose to concern myself with at this time of day," I answered. "I'm dead beat."

I stubbed out the cigarette, undressed myself, and got into bed.

4

My father had spent more than twenty years of his life in this house. I had never heard him speak of that time, but my Uncle Kitto had often done so, with a quiet chuckling appreciation of Aunt Sapphira's civilised tyranny. I gathered that one lived to a schedule, and years later, during my own brief visits to the place while she was alive, she was still relentless. One went to bed, got up, and ate meals according to a plan as immutable as Bradshaw's timetable. If you missed a meal, you missed it, and that was that. It was gone, like a train departing on time, and there was nothing to do but wait for the next. Blanche alone had contrived a kind of "most favoured nation" understanding with the old woman. She could do as she pleased with small risk of giving offence; but, especially towards the end, when she realised what she owed to Sapphira, and found some real affection for her, she was careful to observe all the old girl's quirks and crochets.

However, now that she was the mistress of Tresco Vean, the house was a lawless place. Stephen and Frances, for example, as often as not, were missing at breakfast time. The day could not be too long for them. They would scratch up a meal as soon as they were out of bed, and this might be at six in the morning if the day were fine. If they were not back when the rest of us sat to table, no one bothered.

I didn't sleep well during the night following Luther's session in the dovecote, and I was up at six o'clock. I went to the kitchen to see if I could find a cup of tea, and did so. I carried it out on to the terrace. The morning was dripping with dew and sparkling with sunshine. The cobwebs hanging from the geraniums were jewelled and shining like purses of most delicate mesh. It was going to be a lovely day.

When I had finished the tea and lit a pipe, I strolled over to Ernie's room. The door was open, and he was there, with a bare torso, scraping away at his face in front of a piece of looking glass standing on the mantelpiece. He sponged his face, pulled on a sleeveless singlet and a thick white sweater.

"Good morning, Ernie, what's the drill?"

"Good morning, Dook. Well, it's an early start. We're going to get those engines shipshape before breakfast."

"Have breakfast before you start, and do your trials out at sea," I suggested. "And you could run in to Falmouth and give the crew lunch there. They always like that. You needn't be back till this evening."

He lit a cigarette and looked at me shrewdly. Ernie was no fool. "An' keep my mouth shut, eh?"

"I think that would be a good idea, Ernie."

"OK, Dook. Ah'll come along an' see if t'crew's awake."

We strolled across the gravel to the house. The children were already in the kitchen, boiling eggs. Nobs was squatting on his tail, regarding them mournfully. He sat up, hanging his forepaws, when Ernie entered. "Look at that!" Ernie cried. "Fair *asking* for breakfast.

'E can all but talk, that dog can. Ah could train 'im as a show dog if Ah gave my mind to it."

He pulled Nobs' ears, and commanded the children: "Eat up now. Us'll not be back vor breakfast. There's a long day in front of us."

They set off at seven-thirty, and I walked with them as far as the quay. There was already a breath of autumn in the air. The tide was full and lazy. Scarves of mist waved like long white farewell arms across the face of the scrub oaks on the farther bank, where a couple of herons stood at the edge of the water, looking dejected, with their heads sunk into their shoulders. It was a morning when one felt a touch of dissolution. Behind me I could hear drops of water falling from the trees: an insistent saddening sound. There was no other sound and no movement, till the engines of the launch began to throb and the buoy splashed into the water. At that, the shy herons rose and winged away in their slow stately fashion, low down to the water, moving towards the open sea. Presently the throbbing rose to a roar. "Terrific engines," I thought: and *The Dook* began to move out of the river. She was soon beyond sight and hearing, and I walked back towards the house, glad that the children were away from – well, what? It was difficult to put a name to my feelings, but I thought of Stephen and Frances, looking in their heavy white sweaters, which were glistening with moisture, like lambs that had come through a dewy night. I thought of Stephen, resolute and stocky, giving her a hand into the dinghy, and of her legs, so long and slender, with their brittle-looking insteps, exquisitely feminine like a doe's, lifting over the gunwale. I felt that these two had nothing to do with Luther Brimlow, and that it was a good deed to put them, if only for a day, as far away from him as I could.

So pondering, I walked back to the house, my shoes soaked with dew. Here and there on the bramble fronds was a stain of yellow, umber, purple. The house seemed to be asleep and the sunshine falling upon it was strained through a silver screen. I stopped beneath the magnolia and pulled down a bough. The dew from the great flowers rained into my face. They were so full you could have drunk from them. The petals were as cold as chastity.

I walked on to the dovecote. It could be bolted only from the inside, and so I was able to enter. The expensive polished attaché case, which last night had seemed so incongruous lying in this place of gloom and cobwebs and bird droppings, was gone. Curiosity took me to the garage. There was Luther's Rolls Royce, companionably alongside Blanche's Daimler and Stephen's Lazarus. I peeped through the window at the ivory and silver fittings, the red leather upholstery. I tried the door. It was locked.

"Well, what do you think of her?" Luther asked.

He had come upon me silently as he had done last night on the terrace. He was dressed, shaved, spruce-looking. In my flannel bags and blue sweater, I seemed a creature of another world. Luther took out a gold cigarette-case, and lighted his cigarette from a gold lighter. He took a key from his pocket, opened the car door, and with the same key opened a locker beneath a seat. "There it is," he said, with a grin. Then he locked the door again upon the attaché case.

I asked him if he had slept well, and he said he had never slept better.

"Well, shall we go in and find some breakfast?"

"Thank you. I've had breakfast. Will you give my apologies to Blanche and Prue? I'm afraid this has been a rather unceremonious visit."

He climbed into the car, and I decided on a shot in the dark. "I was sorry to see from the papers that you're giving up Greenlands. You must be attached to the place."

He considered the burning point of his cigarette for a moment, then said: "I'm not giving it up. I shall cancel the instructions as soon as I'm back in town." He added after a while, "One should never panic, Ted. I've had a few bad moments, and they've taught me a lesson. Never panic. There's usually a way out."

"Out of what?

"Out of anything."

He started up the engine and held out his hand. "Au revoir, Ted. Don't forget my apologies to the women. But I really must be off. When I get back to town I shall be up to the neck."

I watched the car out of sight and then went into the house.

5

There are times when a thunderstorm seems inevitable. The air thickens and grows hot; the sky becomes a congested purple; and in the trees the birds twitter with apprehension. And then, perhaps, the threat drifts away. A coolness and sanity come back; one feels liberated. Something unpleasant, possibly disastrous, has after all decided to go elsewhere.

Some such feeling was upon us that morning. It was nearly nine o'clock when Blanche and Prue came down to breakfast.

"Where's Luther?" were Blanche's first words.

"Round about St Austell by now, I should imagine," I answered. "I saw him off. He presents his apologies. Urgent affairs call him to London."

Blanche was turning over the letters beside her plate.

"Well, as long as he's gone . . ." she said, absent-minded.

"He's not selling Greenlands after all."

She went on fingering the letters; then, realising that I had spoken, looked up apologetically. "'M? Oh – isn't he? Good. So long as he's gone . . ."

"Where are the children?" Prue asked, and I told her that they and Ernie would not be back till the evening.

"I must say," she said, "that parentage has few responsibilities in these parts. I sometimes wonder what we are here for."

"To enjoy yourself, my dear." Prue, without responsibilities, was apt to be restless. "Your only responsibility now is to realise that you have no responsibilities, and that there's a lot to be said for sweet do nothing."

Blanche had finished with her letters. She looked up brightly. "Don't fuss yourself, Prue," she said. "Now, what shall we do today?"

The question was answered for us, because at that moment Frances and Stephen came clamouring into the room, demanding breakfast. Ernie followed more slowly.

"How many breakfasts do you children want in any given day?" I asked. "And what's brought you back?"

"As many as we can get," Stephen said, with a grin; and Ernie answered: "She weren't behavin' well. Nothing much. Us can put it right in a tick, but Ah didn't want to be stuck out there with engine failure. So we coaxed 'er 'ome to get some tools."

The children had taken their places at the table and were disposing of the odds and ends of toast, marmalade and coffee. Stephen stopped munching to say: "I'm not sure that boat's not too posh, Ernie."

"There's summat in that," Ernie agreed; and Frances said: "I think so, too."

"It's rather like Uncle Luther," Stephen added impudently, and Prue, with a quick look at Blanche, reproved him. "That's no way to speak, Stephen. It was kind of your uncle to give you the boat."

"He isn't my uncle, really," Stephen insisted. "An uncle is the brother of a father or a mother. Well, he isn't your brother or the Dook's. He's only the husband of a father's sister. That makes him no blood relation at all."

"Well – !" said Prue.

"Oh, don't worry about me," Blanche laughed. "I agree, Stevo. He's only my husband."

And now Stephen did look a bit ashamed of himself. "I'm sorry, Auntie," he said. "I was rude. But," he firmly added, "the boat is posh."

To be tiddly was one thing: it was to be *comme il faut*, to be all that a boat should be. To be posh was another thing: it was to be superfluous, redundant, cursed with the vulgarity of excess like diamond rings worn over kid gloves. Often enough I had heard Stephen and Frances dismiss craft out of hand with that one damning word: posh.

Ernie was sitting in the window seat with a cup of coffee in his hand. I was amused by the discomfiture in his honest face.

"Well, Ernie," I chaffed him, "this is a nice thing! Are you letting down the standard of the fleet?"

"It's nowt to do wi' me," he defended himself. "Fact is she's nowt but a marvellous engine in a fancy 'ull. Ah don't like 'er, an' that's flat; and now that Stevo says she's posh – well, Ah say so, too. But Ah didn't want to speak seem' she's a present from Fran's father."

Then, out of this mildly ruffled sky, came the lightning stroke of the morning. Frances said with great deliberation: "He's not my father."

Prue and Ernie laughed. Such a seemingly senseless remark could be to them a laughing matter. I stole a look at Blanche. She was staring at Frances as if seeing a ghost. As for me, I could see Chellew standing behind the child's chair.

No one spoke, and Frances repeated solemnly: "He's not Stephen's uncle and he's not my father."

I was afraid Blanche might be betrayed by her emotion into saying something irrevocable, or even that she might collapse; so I pushed back my chair, and said: "Come on now, everybody. Breakfast has been knocking about, off and on, for the last three hours. There'll be a strike if we don't give the staff a chance to clear away."

Ernie and the children went out on to the terrace. Prue's sense of responsibility took her upstairs. "I must make the beds," she said. My mother, as usual, was breakfasting in her room; and so Blanche and I were left alone together. She sat down heavily in the window seat from which Ernie had risen.

"What do you think she's got in the back of her mind?" I asked.

Blanche shook her head. She looked white and ill. Earlier that morning I had been reflecting how a threatened storm had blown over, leaving us in happy calm. Now it was back, and burst with a vengeance.

"Should we try and find out what she was talking about, or treat it as a silly remark, like Prue and Ernie?"

"I'd like to know," she said. "That is, if you can find out without making things worse."

"Are you all right? Is there anything I can do?"

"Well, I had a rotten night. I slept with my door locked. It made me feel like a prisoner. And now this . . ."

"Take a couple of aspirins and lie down for a bit."

"No. That would make everybody wonder. I shall go for a walk."

When she was gone I went on to the terrace, for I saw from the window that Stephen was alone.

"Hallo, Stevo!" Where are Frances and Ernie?"

"They're gone to feed the hens."

"Well, what's the scheme for the day?"

"It's a bit vague. I expect we'll go sailing. We seem to have gone a bit flat on motor-boats."

"Let's go and have a look at the poor thing," I invited. "What with the meal aboard and one thing and another, I hardly saw her yesterday."

So I got him to myself aboard *The Dook*. I filled my pipe and sat on the seat in the cockpit. The day's heat had come and the boat hardly stirred on the water, which was a dazzle of silver. I watched him, wearing nothing but shorts, poking about with this and that.

"Well," I said at last, "uncle or no uncle, it's a handsome gift in its way."

"Yes," he agreed, "in its way, I suppose it is."

"You were a bit hard on poor Uncle Luther."

"I don't much like him, you know," he said as though discussing a pup offered for his inspection. I had pulled off my sweater and singlet. He looked at me approvingly, "I'll bet his body's as white as a shark's belly," he said, as if this were the final condemnation. "Well, here's for a plunge," he added; and, swiftly unbuttoning and dropping his shorts, he climbed on to the gunwale and entered the water like an arrow. He trudgeoned over to the *Frances and Stephen*, held on to the bobstay for a moment, and then came back with a breaststroke. I helped him up over the ladder, and as he stood beside me towelling himself he said: "That's a queer idea Fran's got that he isn't her father."

So here it was, without my having to probe for it.

"Queer!" I said. "It's crazy! Where does she get it from?"

He was towelling his red nob, and his face looked out at me mischievously. "From you," he said. "You put it into her head yourself."

He enjoyed my astonished look. "D'you remember – how you gave us tea in your studio during last winter holiday?"

I did, very clearly. It had been a most enjoyable hour, for I had been painting Frances' portrait, and this was the occasion for showing them the finished work. It was on an easel with a cloth over it, and after tea by the fire we made a little ceremony of inviting Frances to unveil the work. I was pleased when both the children exclaimed with delight; and then, as I always do in such a moment of exultation, I felt in my pocket for my pipe. I found that my pouch was empty, and I asked the children to stay there while I crossed the yard to get some tobacco from Joe at the King's Mistress. He was talkative as usual, and I was away for a quarter of an hour or twenty minutes. Stephen now artlessly revealed to me what had happened during this time.

When they had satisfied themselves that I had done Frances justice, they began to poke about the studio. Hanging on the wall in a rather dark place was the portrait of Francis Chellew that I had painted in 1914. In 1916, when Francis was dead, I had offered this to Blanche, but she would not have it. I knew that she had burned all his letters. She would have nothing that physically represented Francis, though a score of little incidents, from the day of his death till now, had made me aware that he was vital in her heart. Neither at Tresco Vean nor in Bedford Square had I seen a photograph of him. That morning, listening to Stephen, who had now thrown himself down from the cockpit boards and was soaking in the sun, I suddenly knew why. From the moment she felt the child within her, Blanche must have been aware that it could no more fail to have the image and superscription of the man she loved than the hot wax can fail, when cool, to have the mark of the die that has been pressed into it. There would be, then, sufficient reason why every trace of Francis Chellew should be out of the way.

Stephen, busy with a book of sketches which he was ruffling over on the rug before the fire, called Frances to examine something that amused him in it, and when she did not answer, he turned round and found her gazing entranced at the portrait of Francis. He walked to her side, looked at the picture, and said:

"Gosh! He *is* like you, isn't he?

He was. I realised now that, all through the time when I was painting Frances, I had been aware of Francis. He and I had seen so much and done so much together, and we had *been* so much, each to the other. These days, now drifted far down the stream of time, came back. The line of memory tautened, and they were there on the hook. I could feel them tingling through me; I lived them again in exultation and bitterness as that young lovely face floated demurely before me till I scarcely knew whether she or Francis was sitting on the chair. The likeness had always been obvious; but it was not till now, not till I carefully and professionally scrutinised the face, that I saw how close it was, how fundamental, in the very bones. And I think that, hardly knowing what I was doing, it was the image of Francis in Frances, rather than Frances herself, that I sought to paint. She was the sweet contemporary glass behind which the ghost of my dead friend moved. I understood now why it was that Blanche, who saw the picture a week later, stood aghast before it for a moment, turned away, and would not look at it again. And yet it was the portrait of a fresh and lovely child. I was satisfied on that score.

It seems that Frances now switched on the lights to examine the picture more closely; and she then took the canvas of herself from the easel and stood it on a tallboy which was beneath the portrait of Francis. Seen together like that, they must have said something to the heart of the child who was, after all, deeply and emotionally implicated in the situation. Chellew's eyes looked down into hers, and I should be a worse artist than I am if they had nothing to say. She responded to them; and they may have called subconsciously to her awareness those other eyes to which, I knew, she had never responded: Luther's shrewd and worldly eyes, his iron jaw, his general cast of countenance which was as human and consoling as a cash register. Whatever may have been the strange turmoil in the child's mind at that moment, she said to Stephen: "My father."

When I returned from the King's Mistress, the portrait of Frances was back on the easel and the children were turning over books on the hearth-rug. Frances said no word to me, nor, I gathered now from Stephen, had she again, till the hint of this morning, referred to the matter. From the studio we went into town, met Blanche and Prue for dinner, and then attended a pantomime. "Not *Peter Pan*, please," Stephen had begged. "I hate the silly little squirt. I *want* to grow up." He was a normal boy; and all through that evening Frances was a normal happy little girl. No one would have guessed what questions had been stirred beneath the surface of her mind.

Well, this was the story I should have to take to Blanche. There was one good thing about it: Stephen, not any more than Ernie or Prue, seemed to take seriously what Frances had said. His only curiosity was as to Francis' identity. "It certainly was a remarkable likeness, Dook. Who is he?"

"He is nobody now, Stevo. He was killed on the Somme. I painted a lot of soldiers during the war, and I've painted a lot of people since. One gets a bit muddled and mixed about them all. He was a young man named Cheffery . . . Chehling . . . something like that, I think. I forget . . ."

"Killed on the Somme, eh?" said Stephen. "Gosh! No wonder you forgot. There were plenty, weren't there?"

He had turned over, so as to roast his back, and he was kicking up his heels as he spoke. The Somme, thank God, didn't mean much to him. He was far more deeply interested in the doings of Captain Pentecost than in mine or Francis Chellew's. He leapt up and pulled on his shorts.

"I'll row you ashore, Dook. Time for morning coffee."

369

6

Everybody was there for coffee: my mother and Prue, Blanche and I, the two children, Ernie, Nobs and Miss Bunyan. Yes; that was indeed her name, and in the list she comes last because she was more self-conscious, more shy and retiring, even than Nobs. She was the latest of the governesses charged with the education of Frances, and from time to time, pulling Frances by the long fair plaits of her hair, Stephen would ask gravely:

"And how is our little pilgrim progressing, Miss Bunyan?" Miss Bunyan would giggle and blush, but never answer.

It often seemed to me that the education of Frances was a queer business. Each of these governesses came as a specialist. There was one who was supposed to teach deportment and dancing, and perhaps that was the queerest of all, for the idea of teaching "deportment" to a child having the swift and lovely grace of a hind! . . . then there had been a musician with whom Frances had tinkered at the piano; and Miss Bunyan's speciality was drawing in line and watercolour. Not till she had arrived at Tresco Vean did she discover that her pupil's great uncle was a Royal Academician and her uncle an A.R.A., and this threw her into a twittering dither whenever I looked at anything that she or Frances had drawn. The fact is that Frances could not draw, and neither could Miss Bunyan, but no doubt they had some amusing times together, and I saw no reason to intervene.

Reading and writing were such prosaic subjects that no one had been engaged to teach them. Frances had picked them up. She read voraciously anything she could lay hands on, and already wrote a more readable letter than her mother would ever write. Also, she had created a world of her own, as imaginative children often do. It was not a mere copy-world of ogres and fairies lifted out of nursery tales and mildly remodelled: it was a world of genuine imagination. There were odd creatures in it called Gnarls, who were twisted like old fantastic tree roots, and Firdunkins, whom I couldn't quite make out, and Slitherbellies who came from holes at night and whose slimy tails no Firdunkin could cross unless a Gnarl arched himself like a bridge to permit the passage. If he were in a bad temper he might refuse to do it, and then, should the poor Firdunkin be completely encircled by Slitherbelly slime, his days were as good as ended, for within these circles were bred the Mothymouths, creatures that were nothing but soft pulpy lips, with moth wings, that fed on Firdunkins. There was only one point at which any of this seemed to link up with reality: the Mothymouths had three chiefs who were called the Lutherans. I must confess that when I read that my heart missed a beat, and I wondered into what sort of abyss I was looking.

I came by accident upon the copybook in which all this was scribbled in pencil. Frances had been lying on the grass halfway down the slope between the house and the quay, writing away for dear life, and there had come a long "Coo-ee!" from the water: either Ernie or Stephen calling her. She had leapt up and ran, for she reacted to either of those voices as automatically as an electric light answering a switch. Soon afterwards a summer shower began to fall, and I went to rescue the book. The downpour worsened, and, pushing the book under my sweater, I ran into the shelter of the wood. There, sitting on a bench, I began to look at it. I was soon up to the ears in battle and intrigue: the Firdunkins, who lived in barrels in fir trees, pitted against the Slitherbellies and Mothymouths, with the Gnarls, old aboriginal creatures of earth, vaguely benevolent but apt to turn crusty, chipping in here and there with an unreliable bias towards the Firdunkins. There was a lot of this that I never saw, for the book was marked "Vol. 3". I was fascinated by this glimpse into Frances' mind, a glimpse of the unexpected, for she never appeared to be that thing called vaguely "a dreamy child". Slender as she was, she was as tough as wire; she seemed to like nothing better than to be on a horse's back or sharing with Stephen and Ernie the excitement of a bit of wild weather at sea.

I took a stub of pencil from my pocket, and in the margins I drew some pictures, consciously in the style of Arthur Rackham. I liked my Gnarls best. They were good rooty little bearded toughs who looked as though rheumatism were endemic in their tribe. But what Frances thought of them I never knew. I returned the book to her and she thanked me gravely for saving it from a drenching, but she never spoke of it or of what I had drawn in it.

I asked Blanche soon after this what she was getting at with Frances. What was the idea of this education by "specialists"?

"Well, the idea is that she has only one thing to worry about at a time, and so far as I'm concerned she needn't worry about that if she doesn't want to. So long as she has what's called a governess she's supposed to be getting educated and nobody interferes. That's all I care about: that no one should interfere. I suppose the truth is I don't believe in education — not what's called education — though honestly I haven't given the matter a thought. All I want is for her to grow up happy, and I think she's doing that. She spends hours in the kitchen, because she wants to, and she'll become a good cook, because she wants to. I think it's more important that she should *want* to make an apple pie than that she should *have* to know the names of Henry the Eighth's wives."

"What does Luther think of your methods?"

She looked at me sharply. "Luther? What's it got to do with him? If he wants to try his hand at educating a girl, let him get one on Christina Lake."

This was the only time I heard Blanche speak of Luther's women. I hadn't known that she was aware of Christina Lake.

That day as we sat at coffee on the terrace, I saw that Blanche was considering Frances with a more than usually acute regard, but Frances was unselfconscious, obviously not aware that her remark at breakfast time was charged with dynamite. I took Blanche aside later and told her what I had learned from Stephen. She had recovered from her shock and was able to smile. "You paint too well, Ted," she chaffed me. "That portrait gives everything away. I thought so myself as soon as I saw it. You've only got to exhibit the two pictures together and there'll be enough evidence to have me ducked in the village pond."

I told her then what I knew about the Gnarls and the rest of them, though I thought it best to omit the Lutherans. "She's living at the moment a highly imaginative life. She's created a whole little world of her own. You know very well that Luther doesn't mean much to her. *You've* seen to that. Very well, then. If she hasn't got in her life anything that fills her idea of what a father should be, she'll be on the lookout to create one. Seeing those two portraits together gave her the opportunity to do so. I don't for a moment think she *believes* the man she saw in the portrait is her father. I think she *imagines* it. It's part of an important game she's playing."

"Thank you, Ted," Blanche said. "That's a comforting way of looking at it. I hope you're right. Anyway, I'm glad to know what's at the back of it all."

"But don't forget," I warned her, "that imagination's a damned queer thing."

7

The next day came an odd encounter. I went to Falmouth to pay my respects to Uncle Kitto. The years had dealt kindly with him. He was a little thinner and finer-drawn, but he kept well, was still most active at his work, and was, as he put it, enjoying the reward of having all through his life avoided fuss and responsibility. "I am an example that humanity might well follow," he would say, polishing his eyeglass on a pale silk handkerchief. "I have never had a telephone or a gramophone, a wireless set or a motorcar. I have never seen what is so distressingly called a movie, and shudder to think of what is beginning to be spoken of as a talkie. I never read newspapers. I do not write letters and rarely answer those I receive. I am perhaps the only man in Europe who has never been to bed with a woman, and for half a century I have not felt even the desire to do so. I see no reason why I should assist in the creation of a being who would disturb my days and who could hardly hope to be as intelligent as I am myself. It would be an excellent thing if humanity decided to abandon the attempt to improve itself; and even to reproduce itself; and settled down to the conscious task of extinguishing itself with dignity rather than destroying itself catastrophically which, so far as I can see, is the purpose to which it is now dedicated."

He would run on like this for a long time, and the ironical gleam in his pale-blue eyes would invite you to take it all as seriously or as lightly as you chose.

Everything, when I called on him that morning, was as I remembered it to have been when I first set eyes on it – a boy expecting Uncle Kitto to be a tough-looking Viking – so many years ago. Sunshine filled the courtyard garden alongside the old chapel, falling on the stone figures and the flower-filled urns that were perhaps mossier, a little more – but imperceptibly – disintegrated. I walked to the steps that led down to the water, and the dinghy was there, as spruce as ever, and on the gentle swell rode the barge aboard which I had climbed with so much expectation. Outside the door leading to Henry Opie's quarter the verbena flourished, and instinctively I crushed a branch in my fingers as I passed and sniffed the lemon smell. Henry Opie was not at home, so I climbed the stairway leading to the studio, and I found the old man talking to a stranger. Kitto waved me to a chair, and he and his visitor continued their talk, looking through one of the windows that gave upon the harbour.

I was puzzled by something familiar about the face of this stranger, but for a long time I could not fix him. Then I went up to him and said: "Pardon me, but aren't you Tyson?"

He took my hand in a hearty northern grip and said: "Good lord! It's Ted Pentecost! When I came here this morning it had quite gone out of my head that you two were related."

There was in that word "related" just enough broadening of the "a" to tell anyone who had lived in the North that Tyson had lived there, too. But it was fined down now; in his speaking and in his dress and manners one read the story of "the young man who had got on."

I explained to Kitto that I hadn't seen Tyson since the day when I left Marquick and Marquand's. He was then the junior clerk who supervised the work of us office boys: a person of authority and dread to us, though not much older. He had not once come into my mind since those days, and I should not have expected him to achieve much, but clearly he had at least achieved a comfortable worldly position. I now found him to be the sort of man who likes to cling to any souvenir of the past, and I promised that I would take lunch with him that day. And so, when Kitto and I had spent an hour together, I telephoned to Tresco Vean to say I should not be back till late afternoon, and went on to the hotel where Tyson was staying. He gave me the whole works, as they say. There were cocktails to begin with, and brandy and cigars to finish with, and everything in between.

Tyson told me that he had a motor yacht in the harbour, but that he didn't live aboard when he could get into a decent hotel ashore. He looked anything but a yachtsman, and I guessed his yacht would be pretty posh. When he was aboard, he would probably dine in a dinner jacket. Now that he had this rather improbable association with the sea, he wanted some marine paintings for his house, and it was this that occasioned the call on Kitto.

I asked him how Manchester was getting on, and he said he hadn't seen the place for a year. "I cleared out as soon as I could. The Missus and I always used to holiday at Fowey, and that's where we set our hearts on living some day. Time after time we used to say 'That's the house. That's where we'll live some day' – you know, when there didn't seem a dog's chance. And that's where we're living now. Fell into the market just at the right moment."

Tyson snapped his fingers to a waiter and ordered more brandy. "A good place to be out of now, is Manchester," he said. "The cotton trade's gone daft. There's going to be one hell of a bust-up before long. Over-capitalisation, if you know what I mean. There've been too many clever boys playing about in Lancashire – chaps that are not interested in cotton, or in anything else but money. They're in one day, and out the next with the doings before you can say Jack Robinson. Chaps like Luther Brimlow. You've heard of him?"

I said that I had seen his name in the papers.

"Well," said Tyson, "that's the type. They buy the cow, milk it dry, and then sell it for more than they gave for it. It can't go on much longer. There've been plenty ruined already. Old Marquick for one. I seem to remember he was interested in you. We lads never got to the root of that, but we were always a bit nervous of you because of old Marquick's interest." He laughed reminiscently. "Did you know that?"

"No. That never occurred to me. You can't have been as nervous of me as I always was of you. I thought you were Jehovah."

Tyson laughed with pleasure, gripping his cigar in strong white teeth. "Well," he said, "I suppose I was always a good disciplinarian. You need to be to get anywhere. And I got there all right. There were fortunes to be picked up in Lancashire if you knew the way to go about it. But there won't be much longer."

The food and drink, and the heat there where we sat looking over the smooth wide sea, had reddened his face. He began to swell with self-satisfaction. I had a feeling that the "clever boys" he had so warmly condemned were nearer to his heart than he had cared to admit. I saw the old time junior clerk as a new time junior shark, lacking the courage of the bigger fish, clearing out after one clever tearing mouthful. Something like that, I imagined, was Tyson's story. I brought his mind back to Captain Marquick.

"Well," he said, "he's felt the draught. I wouldn't put it higher than that. I don't suppose he's among the utterly ruined, but I know he's taken a nasty knock or two."

Tyson said the Missus was on the yacht, and invited me to come aboard. I managed to excuse myself. He gave me his address in Fowey. "Don't forget," he said, "if ever you do a decent little bit of marine painting, I may be interested. I'll be keeping an eye on you from now on."

I never saw him again.

8

The two disturbing things that happened during that holiday – Luther's visit and Frances' remark about her father – had no immediate consequences. The holiday went on as though these faces had not momentarily looked in at the window of our bright room and then been withdrawn. *The Dook* did not again go out of the Helford River, but there was much sailing in the *Frances and Stephen*. She must have been close quarters for Ernie and the children when they sailed her to France or made a coastwise voyage lasting perhaps a week; for she had nothing that could be properly called a cabin. She was half-decked, and that provided only a rather poky forepeak with two frames hinged to the walls. These could be let down at night, and a couple of blankets turned them into what courtesy called cots. But the crew of three wouldn't have her changed. She was what they had always known, and proposals to put a cabin in her were rejected. Sometimes I was a little disturbed by this cabal of three. They were dreadfully conservative, incredibly exclusive. More than once I had asked Stephen whether he would care to invite a couple of his school friends to enlarge the party. "I don't see the point," he answered shortly the last time I had suggested this. "Still, if you like, I'll see what Fran thinks." A little later he told me: "Fran doesn't see the point, Dook."

Certainly, those two had I reached a stage where each seemed to find the other's company the only thing that mattered; and now that Stephen was capable of handling the cutter by himself; I sometimes wondered whether even Ernie Lingard could not at a pinch be dispensed with.

What was so lovely about this existence that we had contrived for ourselves at Tresco Vean was that the most entrancing things happened without premeditation. At teatime one day Ernie said casually: "There'll be a nice moon tonight. We could have supper aboard."

And so we did. It was the biggest party we had ever had on the *Frances and Stephen*. Even my mother came, though she had no taste for the water; and Amy Lingard and Miss Bunyan came, too. With the Cabal, myself, Prue and Blanche, that made nine of us; and it was on an occasion like this that we were glad the ship was only half-decked. It gave us an open cockpit that occupied two-thirds of the thirty feet, so that everybody was comfortable.

It is one of the evenings that remain in my mind more clearly than most that we spent there. It was seven o'clock when we set off. The western sky was already a smother of pink cloud and in the east the blue was turning to indigo. There was a great to-do conveying the passengers aboard, and the crockery and cutlery, and the baskets containing the supper, which was a secret, and which went into the ship like sealed orders.

The river was full of crepuscular quiet. The intangible breath of an autumn evening gave mystery to the light and turned the scrub oaks that lined the banks into a dark fleece. There was not a breath, but Ernie promised us a little wind once we were out of the river. We crept away slowly with the handy-billy purring hardly more loudly than a cat. There was no sense of "terrific engines". We stole past the darkening enigmatic creeks on either hand, past a few posh motor yachts moored in mid-stream with their riding-lights already on and their portholes glowing. Perhaps Mr Tyson was on one of them, changing into his dinner jacket.

Ernie and Stephen got hold of the main halliard, leaving Frances at the tiller, and the studs of the big Bermudian sail went rattling up through their channel. The open sea was before us. We found the wind we had been promised. The ship lay over a little to port and the engine was stilled. Strange how the cessation even of that small noise brought the silence among us like a presence. The jib and the foresail went up, and the breeze was so small and steady that there was nothing to be heard at all but the sigh of the hull pushing apart the sleeping water.

"Can you hold her, Fran?"

Frances did not deign to answer. Could she hold a kitten that wasn't trying to get away!

A line from an early Masefield poem came into my head. "Treading the quiet water like a fawn." I should have liked to be able to paint all that was said there.

Ernie looked up at the sails, adjusted the sheets a little on the cleats, and stood silent. There was nothing now for anyone, save Fran, to do, and little enough for her. Ernie handed me his tobacco pouch and we both lit up. It was a moment of great content.

The night was darkening, but St Anthony's lighthouse gleamed over the dividing sea like snow daubed on a black hill-face. Its intermittent light was reflected in the still water. We moved forward, leaning always a little to port, as though a gentle hand kept a steady pressure behind us.

The quietness, almost the solemnity, of our expedition did not break up till there came the small stir of dropping the anchor and running down the sails. We did this just off the lighthouse; and then there was the greater stir of unsealing the supper orders. Some of us sat on the bottom-boards with our cups and plates beside us; some luxuriously used the engine cover as a table. Everybody now was released, busy at the same time. Miss Bunyan was forking salad from a great brown casserole on to plates. Amy was slicing a tongue and my mother a ham. Blanche was pouring coffee from Thermos flasks and Ernie was handing the cups round. Prue was cutting up a loaf of bread, and someone produced pepper, salt and salad cream. Stephen and Frances, before the rest of us were served, were unashamedly at work with their knives and forks. Soon the bustle ceased; sitting, standing and crouching in the cockpit, we were all revolving our jaws and grunting with satisfaction. The ridge of the high land behind the lighthouse had for some time been luminous, outlined against a quiet pulsation of the sky, and now the full moon pushed her forehead over, climbed quickly, and flooded the sea with light. High tide and full moon, and "What's for afters?" Stephen demanded.

I looked up. He and Frances had to themselves the seat that curved round in front of the after-lockers. They had finished before anyone else, and there they sat side by side, the red of his hair, the pale gold of her plaits, shining under the moonlight. They were unselfconscious. Neither, I think, was aware of the other except within the bounds of the unspoken compact that grew out of their self-sufficient proximity. But this moment seemed to me so perfect, the possibility of anything better happening to any of us on earth seemed so unlikely, that Stephen's light question suddenly hit me like a question in a parable. "What's for afters?"

I suppose my mind had been mooning too much throughout the whole voyage. Anyway, for whatever reason, I found myself looking at the pair of them, almost shaken by dread at that childish question: "What's for afters?"

A renewal of stir lifted me out of this mood. There was cold apple pie and cream for afters, and Stephen had leapt down and was collecting used plates as Amy handed out clean ones. And when we had dealt with that matter, there was the question: "Anyone for the shore?" Only Ernie and the children and I went. The others all stayed to get on with the business of washing up and stowing things in baskets.

The cabal disappeared on the path towards the lighthouse, and I loitered about not far from where the dinghy had landed us. The bluish moonlight flooded land and sea. The scent of pines and bracken was sharp in my nostrils, and the tired unurgent fall of little waves without anger threaded a gentle sound through the quiet. I climbed, so that I could look down on the great panorama of land and sea. I was high up above the ship, lying so still with the mainsail bunched carelessly upon the boom, and the small dark figures moving upon her deck. She, and they, looked oddly isolated and defenceless. I lay down in the bracken, waiting for the children to come back.

9

The holiday ended soon afterwards. There were a few days in Hampstead; then I saw Stephen off to school; and, that being done, I decided to visit Captain Marquick in Manchester. This had been in my mind ever since my conversation with Tyson. I was not easy about my record so far as the captain was concerned. I had accepted so much from him, and I had given so little. It must be ten years, I reflected, since I had done so much as write him a line.

I remembered that Manchester could be lovely in autumn, and it was lovely during my visit. The weather, I mean. The heart of the town could hardly be lovely, except for enchantments of light when the evening was coming on, and the shop windows brightened, and harsh edges were everywhere rubbed off. But even at high noon the hazy autumn air, spiced with the first hints of frost, made the town a good place to move about in, and I spent a few days pleasantly enough, mooning round the art galleries, drinking coffee in the cafés, visiting the theatres at night, looking at the huge black façade of Marquick and Marquand's offices, and the window of Agnew's shop, and all the other places associated with a childhood that had been, in the main, so happy.

And when, at the end of this loafing, peeping and peering time, I did at last call on Captain Marquick, I was glad to find that he was not in such bad shape as I had expected. Didsbury, in that weather, had all that I remembered of beauty. Rowans were hung with coral clusters; Michaelmas daisies and dahlias and chrysanthemums were flaming and glowing in the gardens in such plenty that it was hard to believe one was so near the heart of the famous, the almost fabulous, city.

Yes; it was lovely under the tender blue of the autumn sky; lovely but unbearably fragile; and when I came to the captain's garden and pushed open the gate that was so familiar, the sense of dissolution seemed here to gather and thicken. The paths that had been so carefully raked were unkempt, grown with daisies and dandelions, carpeted with leaves that rustled and whispered beneath my feet. The big circular lawn had not for long known roller or mower. The grass was a foot high, and on top of that the leaves lay in brown and yellow drifts. But all the same, there came back to me my childhood feeling of an enclosed, enchanted spot. I felt it, if anything, with greater force, for the isolation was emphasised by the sense that no foot had walked upon the grass, where the tall rusty sorrel spires stood up, or disturbed this jetsam of red and gold that the season's tide, ebbing now so beautifully, had left around me. The serene, dispassionate light lay upon the front of the house, illuminating without warming it, and in the beds beneath the windows the Michaelmas daisies grew, save that they grew now companioned by weeds, as I had known them always to grow. There were bees at work among the flowers, and a few painted-lady butterflies drifted through the air. But upon the bees and the butterflies there was a sense of lethargy, of using up the last of a good thing, like bathers snatching the end of summer before the sea goes cold.

I stood for a moment, fascinated in this disturbing – this almost threatening – serenity, as though awaiting "some casual shout that broke the silent air," some breath that would dissolve the bubble hanging iridescent under the beautiful indifferent sky. Then I turned from it and rang the bell.

I was expected, for I had written to tell Captain Marquick that I would call, and a manservant took me to the big room – sitting room, study – which was all I had ever known of the inside of the house. The captain got up from his chair near the small fire and came towards me as certain of his surroundings as ever. He took my hand. "My dear boy!" he said. "My dear Ted! So long! So long!"

The change in him was great. His whole body had shrunk. He was an old man. His hair was rather long and quite white; his face had lost its florid health. He looked sedentary. And the oddest thing was this: one now saw at a glance that he was blind. He still looked straight at you as he spoke, but now you knew, as you had not known before, that he was not seeing you. I do not know why this was so, but so it was. Perhaps it was because the energy of the whole face had folded up.

A chair had been placed alongside his own, and I sat in this. As he spoke, from time to time he reached out a hand and laid it on my knee. Once or twice he squeezed my knee, as though assuring himself that I was there. Tea was brought in, and I looked after his needs.

"Well, you see how it is, Ted," he said cheerfully enough. "I've had to draw my horns in. Lucky to have 'em left. Plenty of poor devils have had them cut off and their shells trampled into the ground."

I gathered that he was living now with but the manservant who had admitted me, and with a woman coming in the mornings to "do" for them. "He was a mill manager," he said, speaking of his servant. "Fancy that, Ted! That tells you what the cotton trade's come to. But I think he's content here. He's a good fellow. We get on. He reads to me at nights, and he's a pretty good hand at the piano. We have a bit of music. I play the fiddle mostly now."

It was an odd picture: these two who had been hit by the wave that engulfed so many, solacing themselves thus.

"You must have noticed the garden," he said. "No gardener now, no chauffeur. But I'm not complaining, Ted. This place is mine, so there's no rent to pay, and I can hang it out here till the end. Fortunately, everything I had wasn't in cotton. But more than enough was."

It was a simple enough picture. He had been stripped of most things, but still had more than many – more than most – ever acquire. The pathos was wholly in contrast.

"I don't go out now," he said, "not to concerts or anything else. Every day when it's fine I ramble round the garden. I like to hear the leaves under my feet. And there's a robin that sings to me."

Yes; he was well off by any economic standard; but hearing him say this, I could have wept. I thought of his valiant air in the days when I had known him first, with the red-robin waistcoat flaming on his breast, and all his senses save one swift and apprehensive. It was unbearable to think of him shuffling through the year's perished glory, listening to the sere crackle, cocking his sightless face towards the cheerful twitter of the robin.

I refilled his teacup.

"Well, tell me your news," he said. "How is my dear little Blanche? How did she come to marry that damned scoundrel Brimlow? Mark me, Ted, we're not through with that fellow yet. There are more tears to flow. How does Blanche get on with him?"

I told him that Blanche did not get on with him, and gave him a picture of their strange divided life.

"Best news I've ever heard," he grunted. "Tell her from me not to let him get his fingers on her money. The man's pure poison. I don't give him much longer, anyway."

His hand sought my knee and squeezed it again. "Sorry, Ted. Forget all that. After all, I'm talking of your brother-in-law. But one gets bitter about some of the things that are happening in Lancashire nowadays."

I said that he would find it hard to offend me by anything he might say about Luther Brimlow. "I don't understand what he's up to," I said. "I suppose his affairs are sound?"

For the first time he smiled. "Sound as the Greenwood hat," he said.

The light was all but gone. The manservant who had been a mill manager came in and drew the curtains, switched on a table lamp, and made up the fire. When he was gone, I asked: "What was the Greenwood hat?"

"Give me some more tea. The Greenwood hat? That's a story J.M. Barrie tells. When he was a youngster in London, exalted persons like journalists were still expected to wear tall hats, especially when they called on even more exalted persons like editors. Well, Barrie and a man he shared a room with weren't very well off. They had one old tall hat between them, and whichever was going to see an editor wore the hat. Greenwood was the editor they called on mostly, and so they called it the Greenwood hat."

I said nothing, and he went on: "You wonder what that's got to do with Mr Brimlow, don't you? Well, look at it this way. A year ago, a lot of people who don't exactly like your brother-in-law were chuckling. One of his companies lost the best part of a million on one deal, and it was thought that when the general meeting came round that company would be found insolvent. It was also thought that if one of the companies was found to be insolvent an inquiry into its affairs would involve *all* the companies, and that might be very interesting indeed. However, when the annual general meeting came along, the company was not found to be insolvent. On the contrary, it was flourishing. I had a very old friend of mine staying with me at that time: a financier, but I think an honest one. Anyway, he was greatly interested in the Brimlow set-up; we discussed it for a whole evening; and it was he who evolved the theory of the Greenwood hat. Supposing most of Brimlow's companies are pretty wobbly, and that none of them could show an honest credit balance. Well, they are inter-related in a way that makes it possible for any one of them to lend money to any other. The swindle would be discovered if all the companies held their annual general meetings on the same day, but as the meetings are nicely spaced the switch-over from one to another is easy. Now the floating sum of money that does the trick is the Greenwood hat. Mr Brimlow can wear it with confidence so long, if I may put it so, as two editors don't want to see him at the same time."

"So that's it?"

"I don't know. It's only my friend's guess. But I think it's a pretty one. Hunt the slipper. There's only one slipper, and one of these days someone will be caught without it."

"It's like an office boy pinching a bob's worth of penny stamps and making good with a shilling from the petty cash when a junior clerk checks the stamps. Then, when the day comes to check the petty cash he makes good out of the stamps."

"Exactly. Most huge swindles are simply petty robbery magnified by the million. Not clever, but colossal. It doesn't need brains, only enormous nerve."

"And you must never panic."

"That's it."

"Because there's always a way out."

"Well, so they hope. But there's usually an extra juicy bit of cheese that springs the trap."

"Unfortunately, they're not alone in the trap."

"No. If one of them – well, say if Brimlow – came a cropper, tens of thousands of people would feel the draught."

"I wasn't thinking of them," I said. "I've got damned little sympathy with what's so romantically called 'the small investor'. They're always jiggering their money round from something that pays five per cent to something that pays seven and a half. And if something else offers ten, then they're after that. More and more for less and less: that's all they ask. Is it any wonder that crooks grow fat when there's so much credulous greed lying round for them to feed on? No; I wasn't thinking of them."

I was thinking of Blanche; I was thinking of Frances; but I didn't say that to Captain Marquick. Instead, I said: "Do you hear anything of old Anatole?"

"Anatole is dead," he said. "He's been dead these five years." It was a reproach to me.

"He was tortured to death," he added; and when I exclaimed at that, he said: "Well, what else would you call it – a man like Anatole trying to drive some idea of beauty into the heads of a lot of little stinkers? I don't see any other name for it."

I left him soon after this. "Well, goodbye, Ted," he said. "Give my love to your mother and Blanche. Tell 'em I often think of the old days."

He came with me to the front door and switched up the light in the porch. I rustled away through the fallen leaves, and at the turn of the drive I looked back, and he was still standing there under the light, his head turned in my direction as though to catch the last sound of my retreating footsteps. It struck me again how old he was looking, snow-white and shrunken.

"Au revoir," I shouted; and he shouted back firmly: "Goodbye, Ted. Goodbye."

And it was goodbye. The light snapped off. That was the last I saw of Captain Marquick.

10

I had been in Manchester for four days, and there was no reason now for staying any longer in the North. Unless I called on Iris Randle. I had picked up the *Liverpool Post* in my hotel and saw that she was in Liverpool, appearing in a week of Ibsen plays. It would be easy to slip over to Liverpool and make my return journey to London from there the next day. I had been thinking of this all the time I was in Manchester. I had been telling myself that I would and that I wouldn't; and on the morning after my call upon Captain Marquick I packed my bag and went. I had not seen her and I had not heard from her since the day when Luther Brimlow brought Stephen to her flat in St James' Square. She had not stayed in America long. Her adventures in Hollywood had found an echo in the English press. She did not appear in a film. *Wuthering Heights* was to be made into a film story, and I could well imagine that, though she was old for it, Iris would give a wonderful interpretation of the dark impassioned Cathy. She signed a contract to play the part, and she broke the contract, and it was the quarrel over this that reached the English newspapers. The trouble was that she had read the book and wanted to play what was in the book; and in both these matters she differed from what Hollywood expected. That was the simple essence of the thing, but it blew up into a terrific row. It made Iris' name known in the United States, and it gave a young American dramatist the idea of writing a play recognisably founded on what Emily Brontë had written. Iris was invited to play in this in New York. She did so; and as the row in Hollywood had made her notorious, this made her famous. She played the part of Cathy for a year, made a lot of money, parted with much of it to the film company, which won an action for breach of contract, and then returned to England.

This much I had learned from the newspapers, and from them I saw, too, that Iris' fancy had taken a turn to the most serious kinds of work. The process which had begun with her appearing in Alexander Durnford's plays had continued. Iris had now almost become an Institution, one of the few names one thought of when acting was mentioned.

I took a train which landed me in Liverpool in time to book a room at the Adelphi Hotel, wash myself, and go straight down to lunch in the restaurant. If I knew anything about Iris, she would be staying in the Adelphi, and with luck I might find her at lunch.

She was not in the room when I entered it, but she came in soon afterwards, and I must confess my heart gave a thump. There was no doubt about it: Iris had become a very distinguished-looking woman. It was pleasing to see men crane their necks to look at her. She was as thin as a hop-pole, and she was wearing a black suit. Small gold ornaments were clipped to her ears. Her pale face and black hair and those eyes which always seemed to be burning in her head gave her a rich gravity that was better than formal beauty. On a small scale, there was something almost rugged about the face. It sounds absurd, but it is the best I can do, if I say this: that if you can conceive Abraham Lincoln's face reduced to feminine proportions and served up with everything that could make it *soigneé*, you would begin to have some impression of how Iris looked. But I despair of putting it in words. Anyway, it was a face that had lived, and felt, and suffered.

A boy was with her. He looked about twelve years old. He was wearing long flannel trousers which gave him a lovable but rather absurd sense of grownupness, and a blazer with a gold design of star points on the pocket, and a school tie. Long, fine and rather curly dark hair fell in a wing over his forehead, which was exceptionally broad and white. Altogether a handsome child. I noticed how he nipped in before the waiter, drew out the chair for Iris, and gave her a smile before he climbed on to his own. Their heads came together as they consulted the menu card. They were gay and cheerful with one another.

Iris had not seen me, and she sat with her back to me. She and I had been rather late in beginning the meal, and by the time we had finished the restaurant had more than half emptied. When she got up to go, and the boy was putting a fur upon her shoulders, she saw me. For a moment she stood stock-still, one long white hand at her neck holding the fur. Then she came towards me, and the boy followed. I got up and pulled out a chair for her, and she said to the boy, who was standing by rather shyly: "Adam, darling, this is a very old friend of mine, Mr Pentecost. This is my son, Ted."

Adam . . . It seemed an oddly mature name for this beautiful child. He held out his hand and smiled at me. "I'm pleased to meet you, sir," he said gravely.

Iris said: "Will you excuse me and Mr Pentecost, darling, if we have a private talk for a moment?"

"Yes, Mummy. I'll go up to my room. I can do most of my packing now, ready for the morning."

When he was gone, Iris said: "Let us go to the lounge and drink some more coffee."

I followed her out, thinking of the last time we had met and of how that occasion seemed to be repeating itself. But then it was my son we had had to sidestep in order to talk. Now it was hers.

And mine? The question was in my head as I walked behind Iris and caught the faint perfume of her wafted back into my face. It caused no panic in my mind. Indeed, I was surprised to find with what pleasure I was thinking that this lovely child might be not only hers but mine. It taught me something about me and Iris that I had not realised till that moment.

We sat near a fire, and she gave my hand a brief warm squeeze before beginning to speak. "I'm so glad you know," she said. "I hate to think of Adam as a guilty secret."

There must have been a question in my eyes, because she gave a little laugh, and said: "No, Ted. You couldn't do anything so beautiful as that."

"I suppose not," I said humbly.

"It was someone who hardly mattered at all," she said, "except that he gave me Adam. Adam was a year old when I married Moreton Hampstead. I didn't conceal him, and I'm glad of that. Moreton Hampstead was sweet about it. He was a darling. He intended to adopt the child after the war."

"How many things," I said, "men have always intended to do after the war."

"Yes. Adam's father was killed, too."

"I wish you had told me. I should like to have known."

"There was no point in it," she said. "He was my affair. God bless us, I thought for a time that he was my misfortune, but now – well, you see how it is. One doesn't get younger."

They had not seen much of one another. Adam had spent his life in schools: nursery school, kindergarten, and now he was at a school in Derbyshire. They met only at snatched intervals when her work permitted. "I've stolen him for the last week," she explained. "He was due back at school a week ago. But I've got a good doctor friend here in Liverpool who has cooked up a certificate for me saying that Adam has some childish ailment or other. I sent that off and hung on to him. However, I've got to deliver him at school tomorrow."

She said that the holidays were a difficulty. When she was playing she couldn't be with the boy, and knowing what to do with him was a problem.

"You should send him down to us in Cornwall," I said. "We keep open house."

And as soon as I had said it, I thought: But do we? What of my efforts to make Stephen and Frances enlarge the cabal? "We don't see the point, Dook."

But Iris had leapt at the suggestion. "Oh, Ted! Could you do that? It would be too heavenly!"

So I couldn't withdraw, and we left it at that.

"I shall drive Adam into Derbyshire by car tomorrow," Iris said. "Does the trip appeal to you, Ted?"

It would be yet another day away from home, yet another day of solitude for Prue.

"It should be a glorious run in this autumn weather," Iris said; and I agreed to go.

11

It was, as Iris had promised, a glorious run. The cloudless autumn day broke after a night which had felt a little frost, and the red jovial sun had not much warmth to begin with. We were away by nine, with Iris driving, leaving behind us a city full of lilac mist through which tramcars clanged, and buses roared, and the restless crowds spewed in their thousands out of the railway stations. By the time we had left all this behind, the sun had climbed, the mist cleared, and we settled down to enjoy the day.

Adam had quaint, formal manners. As we stood outside the hotel and the luggage was being stowed in the boot, he said to me: "I hope you won't mind if I sit next to my mother, sir? I shall not be seeing her again for some time."

So I sat in the back, and left the morning to those two. I spoke hardly a word all through that drive. I listened to Adam chattering away happily about the coming term. He was hoping for plenty of snow and ice. In Derbyshire they would get it, if anywhere, and that would mean skating and tobogganing which he seemed to like more than football and cross-country runs. I was glad to receive the sense that school had no terrors for him, as it had never had for Stephen.

And that brought my mind back to the promise I had made last night: that Adam should receive an invitation to Cornwall. I saw no reason why he shouldn't fit in. He was twelve, so that in age he stood just midway between Stephen and Frances; and he had, I thought, the kind of manners which would make accommodation easy. I had found that he knew nothing of the sea, except as a watcher from the shore, but he was a swimmer, and no doubt Ernie Lingard could soon drill him into a good member of the crew.

So I sat there, watching the coloured pageant of the day unroll, and thinking pleasantly of this and that: of how I had enjoyed Iris' performance last night in *A Doll's House*, of the supper we had eaten afterwards in the hotel, of how she had got up and given me a light kiss, and said: "Good night, Ted. See you in the morning." I sat for some time after she was gone, full of content.

It was noon when we reached the school, which was an adapted and extended mansion in the deep heart of rolling agricultural country. We stood on the terrace in the quiet of that opulent day, and Adam pointed out this and that: the beautiful Dove, that Izaak Walton knew, flowing through the playing fields, the sweet rise of the Weaver hills, the field where a dangerous bull was to be avoided. Suddenly he said to me: "Do you glide, sir?"

I didn't understand the question for a moment, and imagined myself gliding over a ballroom floor, gliding over ice, or just simply gliding abstractly, as I had done in dreams.

"I should think," Adam said, looking at the distant hills, "that the Weavers would be a good place to take off from."

And then I knew what he was talking about, and in the few moments that were left to us I discovered his real enthusiasm. "One of our governors," he said, "is a marvel at making gliders," and he, too, it seemed, was engaged in the same game, though his gliders were only toys – "but absolutely scientific," he said warmly.

"And then – flying," he cried. "That's the real thing. Aeroplanes. Gliders are great fun, and I'd love to be up in one. It must be marvellous to move through the air with no sound at all except the wind. But I don't see where you're ever going to get with them, except for sport. But aeroplanes now . . ." And he went on to tell us that during the summer a couple of airmen had arrived at a field on the outskirts of the village near the school and had advertised "shilling hops". Adam had spent all his pocket money, and had then hung about so disconsolately that the airmen had given him a couple of free trips.

His formality and courteous reserve were broken down. This clearly was the spring to touch if you wanted to set Adam going. He would have run on for a long time if the matron had not appeared. Then, all in a moment, he was again a rather defenceless-looking little boy, being handed over to authority.

Iris did not kiss him. He shook hands with her and me, and ran happily enough up the steps and through the front door.

"Well," said Iris, "now you know what makes Adam tick."

"Yes. How long has this been going on?"

We got into the car, and now I sat beside her. "Oh, for a long time," she said. "An extraordinary thing happened last winter. I was playing in Manchester at the time when Adam's half-term holiday came round. I arranged for him to be put on the Manchester train so that he could spend the day with me. I met him at the station and said: 'Well, darling, what would you like to do with the day?' and to my amazement he said: 'I'd like to go to the Southern Cemetery.' I was flabbergasted."

"I should think so. What was the idea?"

"He wouldn't tell me till we got there. I ran him out by car. D'you know it? The flat miserable place on the Barlow Moor Road?"

Yes, I knew it. I had seen Jesse Cleghorn's coffin shoved out of sight there; and now, purring through the lovely day at Iris' side, I remembered that what had taken me to that funeral was the hope that I might see Prue.

"Well, when we got there, he said he wanted to see Sir John Alcock's grave."

"Who on earth was Sir John Alcock?"

"That's what I asked Adam, and he gave me a look – he *can* give you a look." I had noticed that.

"I had to inquire about the grave, and when we found it Adam said: 'That's who he was, but, of course, if you're not interested we'll go.'"

"I remember. He was the first man to fly the Atlantic. He flew with A. W. Brown."

"Yes; when I saw the grave I remembered too. But I don't think I've ever hurt Adam so much in my life. He tugged at my hand. He wouldn't stay. After I had seen him on the train I bought an enormous bunch of lilies and tied a card to it: 'In admiration. From Adam Randle.' Then I rushed back to the cemetery and put it on the grave. It was raining and the gates were just being closed. And I cried my eyes out."

We had begun to run downhill between the coloured autumnal hedges out of which the elms stood up, clouds of thin gold, transparent against the windless blue.

"Look what's coming," Iris said. "There's another way to my favourite farm, but I always come this way just for the fun of going through the water splash. One of these days some progressively-minded fool will take that water through a culvert, and then the fun will be gone."

She slowed the car and we sloshed through the water splash, a stream that here took the notion to wander from one side of the road to the other. The water hissed round the axles, and I thought of the hiss of shell-hole water round axles on the road to Amiens. Then we climbed again. "I've arranged about lunch," Iris said. "I'm expected to be alone, but experience teaches me that lunch for one in my favourite farm will easily stretch over three or four normal appetites. I always use the place when I can snatch a moment to see Adam."

At the top of the hill was a cluster of cottages and a little grey church in a tiny graveyard so different, with the crooked stones dreaming in the mild weather, from the Southern Cemetery, where the dead were packed as closely as the living about them. A short turn or two brought us to our destination: a red-brick farm, bloomed over with a sulphur-coloured lichen, shut off from the road by a low wall tufted with toadflax. At the roadside white ducks quacked on a pool, and the air was full of the pungent smell of a dunghill and a pile of grain, the offal of a brewery.

We got out of the car, and the wide peace folded about us, as Adam dreamed of knowing it in a glider, and as I had often known it when we had crept out of the river under the engine, and then had stilled it when the wind took over what was to be done. A few leaves spun through the air like golden feathers; a company of rooks went overhead, clamorous, discordant, yet somehow fitting into and emphasising the silence. We stood there without speaking, unwilling to break the perfect moment, and then our hostess, who had heard the car arrive, appeared at the front door.

She was a hale smiling woman, who overwhelmed us with hospitable welcome. A fire was burning in the stone-floored room in which we ate, and between those thick walls and behind the stone-mullioned window we felt we needed it, for it was a room that took the earliest hint when the year was done, a room which realised that all one saw without was but a pageant of ceremonious dying. We ate, and then we did not linger, for Iris must be back in Liverpool in time, she said, to have some rest before playing. It was a lovely and melancholy return. The air was turning chill, the mist was coming down again, and the street lamps were lit by the time we reached the suburbs of Liverpool. As soon as we arrived at the hotel Iris went to bed. I saw her play that night in *The Master Builder*, and we had supper together after the play. Then she kissed me good night. I was catching an early train in the morning. "I shan't be up, Ted," she said. "It's been a lovely meeting. One more jewel. And don't forget. Adam's holidays are always a bit of a problem. Well, now. God bless."

She kissed me again and went to the lift.

CHAPTER TEN

ONE THING and another happened to postpone Adam's visit to Tresco Vean. The chief thing was, I imagine, that Iris did not want to part with him if there were any possibility of his being with her. During some of the shorter holidays he stayed at school, and in the summer, if she were playing in London, she would keep him there, at the flat in St James' Square, letting him fend for himself in the evenings and taking him out into the country in the daytime. If she were on tour, he would go with her, staying at hotels in Manchester, Leeds, Birmingham, Newcastle, Liverpool, meeting actors and actresses, waiters, liftmen and chambermaids, knowing the insides of theatre dressing rooms and hotel bedrooms, how to dispense tips to some and charm to others. During the next few years I met Iris more often than I had done in the past, and sometimes Adam was with her. He had developed into a strange little creature, seeming both sophisticated and lonely.

On a summer day in 1930 I took Prue and Blanche to lunch at the Ivy. The school holidays had begun, and that morning Stephen and Frances had started off for Tresco Vean with my mother and Amy Lingard. There was no governess that time, and there never was again. Prue and Blanche did not go with the others because there was some shopping to be done in London: they would leave by road the next day: and as they were at a loose end in London I asked them to lunch.

We were hardly seated when Iris and Adam were conducted to the table next to ours. Neither Prue nor Blanche looked her best. It was a hot day and they had been tearing about the town. Iris looked as though she had come straight from the bath and wardrobe, as no doubt she had. Wherever she had come from, every man gave her a look of covetousness and every woman of envy.

I imagine it was many years since anyone had called Iris the Viscountess Moreton Hampstead. She liked to be called Miss Randle, and I now rose and bowed, and said: "Good morning, Miss Randle."

She had not met either Blanche or Prue, though years ago, I recalled, Blanche had seen a portrait I had painted of her. She had stood at my side, with Sapphira, outside Sir Harry Banfil's exhibition in Bond Street, when I had first come as a boy to London, and in the window was the abandoned portrait of Iris, nude to the waist, that I had painted for Sir Harry. Sapphira had commented on it tartly. I did not imagine that the distinguished woman, *soignée* to the fingertips, would recall that moment to Blanche's memory.

Iris had seen me, but had not appeared to do so. She had left me, with her perfect discretion, to do as I pleased with the situation. I had been half-turned away from Adam, who had not seen me, and I was aware of Iris' manoeuvre in arranging that he was seated with his back to me. Now the boy got up and made his formal bow to my women. Iris came to our table, and I introduced Prue and Blanche. None of us had begun to eat, and Iris said: "Adam, darling, see if you can arrange for a larger table where we can all lunch together."

When this small disturbance was over, I said: "I've known Miss Randle for a long time. She was one of my earliest sitters – oh, years before she was the famous woman she is now."

"And you were not the famous man, Mr Pentecost," Iris played up. "We had to take a chance with one another."

She managed perfectly to create the sense of two people who saw one another at odd times with pleasure and mutual respect, but between whom there was nothing more than that. So long, I thought, as Adam doesn't put his foot in it, saying something about Liverpool or the run into Derbyshire . . . But Adam's manners were as careful as Iris' make-up. He did not obtrude himself into the conversation. Happily, Blanche had seen the play in which Iris was then appearing. She began to talk theatre, and, given this opening, Iris took it. She talked shop, endlessly and gaily. "But we're boring Mr Pentecost to tears," she said at last. "I suppose nothing interests him less than what sitters do when they're not sitting."

"Oh, no," I protested. "It's what they do when they're not sitting that makes them worth looking at."

We had now got to the coffee, and it was now that an old dear who was all odds and ends of lace and ribbon and fichu, held together with a mad assortment of jewelled pins, came flapping up to Iris, and cried: "Oh, darling, I'm so glad I met you. I've got a terrible confession to make and a thousand apologies to offer. You'll be shocked and poor Adam will be desolated, but Charlie sent for me this morning and I've got a job after all and we go into rehearsal at once. So it's all off, and it would have been so lovely for Adam, with the Downs and all that, and Chanctonbury Ring in view from the bedroom window." She looked distraught, and added brokenly: "And the ducks on the pond."

"You make it so vivid, darling," Iris laughed. "I can almost hear the poor things quacking brokenheartedly."

"This is Miss Chirk," she explained to us. "She was going to be sweet enough to give Adam a holiday at her cottage in Sussex."

"And now the curse of Adam is upon her," said the boy. "She must work in the sweat of her brow."

"Oh, darling!" cried Miss Chirk, all her little bits and pieces trembling, "you're not desolated?"

"My life is in a thousand pieces," Adam said gravely. "I shall glue it together, but it will never be the same shape again."

"Darling, don't tease," Iris reproved him, and she dismissed the odd creature with assurances that somehow the blow would be recovered from.

2

It was not often that Blanche went to the theatre. She was going a lot at the moment, and she was seeking any other diversion that suggested itself. She was distraught and unhappy. She had the feeling, I know, that the storm which seemed to gather over our heads when Luther visited Tresco Vean three years ago, but then passed harmlessly, was now about to break. I had the same feeling myself.

In the winter before this Luther had asked me to dine with him in Bedford Square. "Just the two of us, Ted. Don't bother to dress." He was in an unusual, affectionate mood. He took my arm as we went together to the dining room, but I quietly disengaged myself and stepped forward, as I always did in that room, to look at the Boudins.

Luther came and stood at my side. "You've always had a fancy for those pictures, I notice, Ted. Would you care to have them?"

"But, good lord, man, they're worth – oh, I don't know, but quite a lot of money."

He laughed quietly. "I'm not *giving* them to you. I thought you might care to hang them at Hampstead or in your studio. There are some others you could have – all pictures that I'm sure would give you a lot of pleasure. And I thought of asking Blanche to take some to Tresco Vean. You could hang scores of pictures in that barn of a place. There's too much stuff here altogether."

A small cold finger stroked my heart. I had just been reading Anthony Trollope's *Autobiography*, and I recalled how the boy had been commanded one day to drive his father from Harrow to London. It was not till they were on the way that old Trollope told Anthony to drive to the Docks and put him aboard the Ostend boat. Having done this, Anthony drove home, and when he was near the house he was met by a man who warned him that the bailiffs were in possession. So Anthony turned about, drove off, and sold horse, gig and harness, saving that much out of the wreck.

Well, was I to help Luther to save something from the bailiffs? I did not, and I went home that night with a heavy heart. Luther had not pressed the matter. When I demurred, he went on to talk gaily of other things; but I had seen the first flash of the red light.

I began now to watch his affairs with anxious interest. His biggest concern, I knew, was the London Probity Finance Corporation, whose annual general meeting was to be held in a week's time. It was almost with a gasp of relief that I read the report of the meeting. The accounts showed a healthy credit balance. I had been worrying about nothing after all.

A fortnight later the London Probity suspended payment. It was capitalised at £1,750,000. Of this sum, £3,500 was, so to speak, in the kitty. The rest was air.

This bombshell burst just before Christmas; and by the end of January I gathered that the affairs not only of London Probity but of all Luther Brimlow's concerns were under official investigation.

Well, this was the state of affairs when we entered the year 1930. Blanche was living alone in Bedford Square. I gathered from her that a year before this Luther had tried to induce her to put all her capital at the disposal of his companies, and at his discretion. She had refused, and he had not pressed the matter. After the crash of the London

Probity he had tried again, and this time he had pressed the matter vehemently. She had again refused, and there was a flaming quarrel. For years they had lived together completely indifferent to one another, but keeping a front to the world and to themselves. Now the front crumbled; all their accumulated bile spilled forth. She gave him Christina Lake and a few others. He said he supposed she was holding on to her few ridiculous thousands of pounds for the sake of her bastard. "It'll buy her a husband."

"It was terrible," Blanche said, "terrible." I met her the next day, and she looked like death. "But terrible as it was, I was glad. I often wondered if he guessed, and of course he's only guessing now; but I was glad to think that the doubt has been torturing him all these years."

The façade never went up again. During the long investigation into his affairs Luther lived at Greenlands. Blanche, who had not been out of England since her honeymoon, took Frances to Paris. They had been back for a month on that August day when we met Iris and Adam. Blanche had filled the time madly with one distraction after another. And it was because she was still snatching at anything that promised the unusual that she now said to Iris: "Why not let your son come with us into Cornwall? We're all going tomorrow. There are other children already there, and it's a great rambling house where we could put up a dozen. Why not come yourself?"

Iris shook her head. "Why not? Work, alas! Our play shows no signs of dying. Would you like to go, Adam?"

"Yes, I think it would be rather fun. It's very kind of you to ask me."

Thus it was that Adam found himself for the first time at Tresco Vean.

3

In that winter when Brimlow's affairs were blowing up to a crisis a company of English actors and actresses had visited France. They were there for a month; they spent a fortnight in Paris and for the rest of the time toured the larger provincial towns. Iris was with them, and as Adam was freed by the Christmas holiday she took him along. Frances, as I have said, was in Paris with Blanche a little later in the same winter.

I was glad to be back here in the peace of Tresco Vean. Luther's affairs were, in a sense, none of my concern, but it was impossible not to be disturbed as the long secret investigations went forward which might at any moment end with a hand on Luther's shoulder and all the blazing publicity of the criminal courts. And so I had found it a wearing summer, and it was good to be lying on the grass with a handkerchief over my eyes listening to nothing more formidable than the chatter of the children. We were on the quay. Ernie was on the *Frances and Stephen* and we were all waiting for him to come ashore with the dinghy to take us aboard. Suddenly I thought: "But, good lord, they're *not* children. They're not children any more."

It was Stephen's voice which made me think this. Now and then it broke back into a boy's treble, but it was a man's voice. Stephen was seventeen; soon he would be leaving school. I took the handkerchief off my eyes and looked at them. Stephen, as usual down here, was wearing canvas shoes with a big toe sticking through a hole, a pair of khaki shorts, and nothing else. A man's muscles rippled in his arms and legs and down his back. Adam was fifteen. He was wearing a blue shirt open at the neck and long flannel trousers. He looked pale. Stephen was a regular tough alongside him. Frances was standing between them, as tall as Stephen, taller than Adam, though she was only thirteen. She was wearing a very short blue linen skirt and a red shirt. She was talking to Adam about Paris. They were discussing the crossing from Dover to Calais, which they had both made in bad winter weather. They admitted with a laugh that they had been very sick.

"Of course, it's all nonsense," Adam said, "crossing the Channel like that. A hop by air to Le Bourget – that's the way to do it, and I suppose that's how every intelligent person *will* do it before long."

"I beg to differ," said Stephen; and there was something in his voice that made me look at him sharply. He had stepped to the front of the other two and was talking with his back to them. He was prising a stone out of the ground with his toe, and at the same time looking out at the water. "I'm a fairly intelligent person," he said, "and I'd rather go in a boat – *any* boat – than fly in an aeroplane. Stinking things. Anyway, I thought Fran had done enough sailing to have learned how to keep her dinner down."

Frances laughed merrily. "You try it, Stevo, on a cross-channel steamer with half a gale blowing."

"Anyway," Stephen said, "why all the chatter about Paris? Isn't this good enough?"

And, of course, I thought, that's it. Why all the chatter about something in which I am not concerned? Why all the chatter about something that ranges Frances with somebody else and leaves me out? And I think, too, he was feeling and resenting the fact that he had grown away from Frances. Ten and fourteen is one thing. Thirteen and seventeen is another. I thought he would not have worried about that gap if Adam had not been there, so much nearer to Frances in age than he was, and, damn it, with things in common that he could not share.

It was two o'clock. We had come straight down from our midday meal, and it was understood that we would be back when we were back. Sailing is like that. Ernie, who had gone ahead to put things in order on board, now came ashore to take us off. "You got a sweater aboard, Fran?" he demanded. You'll want something more than that shirt. It's pipin' up outside." He looked at Adam's pale blue shirt and rather too well creased trousers. "You'll want something, too," he said.

"I've got a jersey aboard. He can have that," Stephen said. If we got a bit of spray aboard, that wouldn't worry Stephen. Nothing but cold would make him dress, and he was a warm-blooded animal.

Ernie wanted to go out under the engine, but Stephen was in a troublesome mood. "We don't need an engine," he said. "What are we? Sailors or mechanics?"

He stopped the handy-billy that Ernie had left turning over, and said: "Come on, Fran. Let's show Ernie how to hoist a mainsail."

Ernie had taken off the sail cover and the mainsail's ties and shackled the halliard to the peak of the sail. The sail was bunched loosely on the boom. Stephen and Frances swung on the halliard and up she went. Adam, with Stephen's old blue jersey over his shirt, tried to give a hand, but Stephen said gruffly: "Two's enough on this job."

We crawled down the river. In there, the sun was warm and the water was quiet. Ernie respected Stephen's mood and did nothing. Long gone were the times when he would stand at Stephen's elbow when the boy was at the tiller, gently advising and exhorting. "Bring her up a bit, Stevo." "Let your sheet out." "Watch that luff." Now he left it to Stephen. If he wanted to sail her out of the river, let him. "Wind's southerly outside," he said, "an' freshenin'."

"I can see that," Stephen said. "We're going to have a sail."

"What about a reef before we get outside?" It was the first suggestion Ernie had made.

"Why?" Stephen asked. "This isn't a toy. This is a ship. What do you say, Fran?"

Frances looked ahead. We could see now beyond the mouth of the river out to the open sea. It was a lovely lively sight, but rather an intimidating one to anybody not used to sailing. It was all a glister of sunshine on a green tumble flecked with white.

"I should say a reefed jib and a reefed mainsail and no foresail," said Frances. "But you're the captain."

"Out with the jib," Stephen commanded, and Frances hauled on the sheet. The sail was controlled by a roller-reefing gear. Frances pulled the sail half out and then began to fasten the sheet to the cleat.

"Right out!" Stephen shouted, and Frances obeyed him. We sailed out of the river with mainsail and jib fully extended. Frances stood ready to throw the foresail halliards off the belaying pins, and Stephen said: "No. We'll do without the foresail." It was his first concession.

Certainly, we had sail enough for that weather. The wind was on our starboard beam, and Stephen put the tiller down, bringing her up a little into the blow. She sailed swiftly, leaning steeply over to port, and there was a sudden clangour as some loose gear in the forepeak shot across the floor. The halliards were slapping on the masts and the blocks rattling.

"Tidy up that mess!" Stephen shouted.

There is a lot of rope in a mainsail halliard, and it was lying in tangles against the forepeak bulkhead. To coil this would have been an instinctive action on a normal day, but this was not a normal day. Ernie seemed to sense that, and there was a crusty obstinate look on his face. He glanced at Stephen, who was having to use both hands to the tiller, and left it to Frances to coil the rope. Adam had been standing on the starboard side, holding on against the tilt of the ship. He now let go, in order to give Frances a hand, although the job was such that only one person could do it. At that moment the *Frances and Stephen* heeled even farther over to port, the deck slope sharpened, and Adam shot down and crashed across the floorboards. The crest of a wave was flung inboard and drenched him as he lay there.

"Sorry!" Stephen shouted, and put the tiller down again, bringing the ship more upright.

It was an appalling moment, because Ernie, Frances and I were all aware that he had deliberately brought the ship round to put the wind abeam and tilt her as Adam let go his hold. It was the first time in the knowledge of any of us that something had been done aboard the *Frances and Stephen* for other than a sailor's reason. And so the fundamental rules that held us together at sea had been violated.

Frances was as agile as a cat, and the manoeuvre had not disturbed her. She said nothing. She did not even look at Stephen. She went on coiling the halliard, put a bight of cod-line round its coils, and hung it to a belaying pin. Only then did she turn to Adam, whom I had helped to his feet. He was white, his long dark hair was sodden, and there was a red bump in the middle of his forehead.

"Are you all right?" Frances asked.

"I loathe this," he said. "I'm frightened to death." And then he added politely: "Excuse me." He leaned over the side and was violently sick.

Ernie Lingard was looking like murder. He walked aft and said: "Are you satisfied about that jib, Stevo?"

"What's wrong with it?"

"There's a lot of wind in it, and you know as well as I do that t'canvas isn't too good. We agreed that it ought t'ave been renewed long ago."

"It'll see us through this trip, I expect."

"A sailor as is worth 'is salt," Ernie said slowly, "don't expect. 'E makes sure. An' what's more, 'e don't play bloody tricks wi' 'is ship. Us'll 'ave to 'ave an understandin', Stevo, before Ah sail wi' you again."

This was the first time I had ever heard Ernie swear. It was the first time there had been discord between him and Stephen. Stephen, his hair plastered to his head by spray, his bare torso glistening, did not answer. "Put her about," Ernie said sharply; and after a moment's hesitation Stephen sang out: "Stand by to go about."

He put the tiller hard down. There was only the jib to be handled. Frances uncleated the sheet on the port side and held it taut till the ship came round. Then Ernie hauled in on the starboard side as the sail filled out on the new tack. There was nothing for me to do. I sat with Adam at my side, watching the simple routine manoeuvre, but aware of a mingled anger and anxiety in Ernie's face. He was looking disapprovingly at the jib as the wind stretched its belly, and my eye followed the direction of his glance. Even as I looked it went. It was as though a knife, wielded by an unseen savage hand, suddenly slashed it through and through. What had been a taut sail was in a twinkling a tilted line of washing, thrashing and snapping in a wild wind. A smile of satisfaction appeared on Ernie's face. I could almost hear him thinking: That'll teach the damned young fool.

Neither Ernie nor Frances did a thing. The rags of canvas snapped like rifle shots, adding what must have seemed to Adam another menacing note to the hiss of water, the slap of halliards and the creak of blocks. He was not made happier when another wave top was blown aboard, soaking us all.

"How do you feel, Adam?" I asked him.

"Better, thank you," he said in his precise way. "I'm one of those fortunate people who are sick and have done with it. It doesn't hang about. But I feel cold, and I don't see where the fun comes in."

"It's not always like this," Frances assured him. "We don't often split a sail, and we usually take in a reef when necessary."

"Any road," said Ernie, "we're headed for home. We'll take you out on a better day than this, lad."

"Thank you. I'll consider it."

Meanwhile, the tattered sail continued to thrash noisily. A fragment broke away and rushed over the sea like a gull. Stephen could not but be aware that everybody was deliberately ignoring the situation that existed.

"Well?" he shouted at last.

"We're waitin' for t'captain's order," Ernie said.

"Take it in."

Frances loosed the sheet and began to climb on to the roof of the forepeak. Ernie's large paw fell on her shoulder, firmly holding her back. "Nay, Fran. Stay in t'cockpit. Never mind the roller-reefin'. Us'll run the whole thing down."

He threw the jib halliard off the belaying pins that were thrust through the edge of the foredeck, but it was a long time since the halliard had been used, as we relied on the roller-reefing gear. The halliard jammed in the block, and shake it as he would the sail wouldn't run down. Stephen shouted impatiently: "Leave it alone. It can stay as it is."

"Nay," said Ernie, "Ah'll not go into harbour lookin' like an amature as 'as been caught out."

He swung himself on to the foredeck, gripped the bowsprit with one hand and took the boat hook that was lying there with the other. He reached forward, hooked the luff of the sail, and gave it a hearty yank. The halliard freed itself and ran down; Ernie dropped the boat hook, pulled in the mess of tattered canvas, and smothered it under his body. He looked back over his shoulder and shouted: "Chuck us a rope's end, Fran."

She did so, and he lashed the sail into a bundle. "That'll do for t'time bein'," he said, and let himself down into the cockpit.

Stephen had watched this with annoyance. He now said quietly: "I told you to leave that sail alone."

"I heard you."

"I thought perhaps you hadn't."

"I heard you," Ernie repeated.

"When *you're* in command I obey your orders," Stephen said obstinately.

"Ay," Ernie answered reasonably. "But this isn't an ordinary occasion. T'captain's done some queer things today."

Stephen's face went a violent red. "Take the tiller," he said sharply, and Ernie obeyed him.

"I'd as soon sail in with the jib in rags as with that dirty mess on the foredeck," Stephen said. "If you had to play about with it, you should have done the job properly, and brought it down into the cockpit. I'd better do it myself."

I wished this voyage was over. Never before had I known an ill word aboard the *Frances and Stephen*, and that it should happen now, on the first day of Adam's being with us, filled me with shame. I glanced at the boy, holding to the bulwarks on the port side, with his hands behind him, facing down the slope of the deck. We were hissing along with the starboard gunwale almost under water. Adam looked dishevelled and unhappy. Worst of all, I had a sense that he felt a Jonah, that he was aware it was his presence that had brought dissension into the ship. I smiled at him, and he gave me a wintry grin.

What happened then was a matter of seconds. As soon as Ernie had taken the tiller, Stephen hoisted himself on to the foredeck. He didn't notice the hank of seaweed that the spray had brought aboard; he stepped on it, slipped, clutched at nothing, and shot down the slant of the deck. One second I saw him in the green racing sea; the next I saw his hand grip the gunwale; and there he was, towed along like someone gripping the mane of a furiously-racing horse.

Frances was the first to her feet. She sprang towards the foredeck, but before she could climb upon it Adam had slithered down the deck, caught hold of her from behind, and driven his knee into the back of hers. She fell to the bottom-boards, and Adam said sharply: "Stay where you are." He leapt as nimbly as a monkey on to the foredeck, and at the same time Ernie let the main sheet run out. The speed slackened, the slant of the deck lessened, and it was not too difficult for Adam, leaning over and seizing Stephen by the seat of his shorts, to haul him aboard.

But he didn't know, I was saying to myself; he didn't know that this could happen. He knows nothing about sailing, not the first thing. The slant of the deck, the speed of the ship: they must have seemed terrifying to him. He didn't know they could be so soon changed. He accepted them and pitted himself against them. I felt warm towards him, as proud as if he had been my son. He and Stephen clambered back into the cockpit. Adam was violently sick. "Sorry," he said. "I thought I'd got over it."

A few minutes later we were in the calmer water of the river, and Ernie handed the tiller to me, a person to be entrusted with it when nothing could go wrong. Ernie stood alongside Stephen. "OK?" he asked.

"OK," Stephen answered. They were grinning at one another rather nervously and tensely.

Presently Stephen said: "Just shows you." Nobody answered him, and he added: "What a bloody fool you can be." And from him, too, I had not heard that word before. A lot of things, I thought, were happening that had not happened before.

4

The three children were walking ahead of me and Ernie, tousled, dishevelled and damp. None of us had much to say. I heard Stephen say to Adam: "That was a good bit of work. Thanks."

All Adam said was: "I'll run on and get into a hot bath. I'm chilled."
He set off at a good lick, leaving the other two to plod on together.
Stephen shrugged his shoulders, aware that he had been rebuffed. He
and Frances had nothing to say to one another, which was unusual.
Normally, they would be chattering twenty to the dozen. It was odd
how what had happened had put a restraint on all of us. Ernie was
silent after one remark to Stephen. "We've got a new jib. We'd better
put it on her this evening, Stevo."

"Yes. I suppose so."

It was just teatime. We hadn't sailed far, and we had sailed quickly.
Stephen and Frances didn't take long to be ready for the meal. A rub
down with towels, a few dry rags: that was all they needed: and we
took the meal in the sunshine, which drove out all the chill of the last
couple of hours. We had almost finished before Adam joined us. He
was wearing white shoes, a new pair of flannel trousers, a cream shirt
with a crimson silk tie, and a navy blue blazer with brass buttons. His
long hair was dry and silkily brushed. He looked pale. "It's nice to feel
civilised again," he said. He consulted a beautiful little wristwatch. "I
apologise for being late."

Prue and my mother had gone in to Falmouth to see Kitto, who
was not well. Blanche poured out tea for Adam. "How did you like
sailing?" she asked.

He drank, said, "Ah, that's better!" and turned his dark eyes to her,
with a smile. "Sailing?" he said. "Give me the land or the air. The merry
Grecian coasters can have the sea."

"That's Matthew Arnold," said Frances; and she quoted:

"Freighted with amber grapes and Chian wine,
  Green bursting figs, and tunnies steeped in brine.

It's in the *Golden Treasury*," she said. "Old Kit-Kat gave it to me." It was
her name for Kitto.

"Good for him," said Adam. "My mother gave me a copy. I carry it
with me wherever I go. Look!" He took the book from his pocket.

"I can recite the whole of *The Blessed Damozel*," Frances cried. And
she said:

"There will I ask of Christ the Lord
  Thus much for him and me:

405

Only to live as once on earth
  With Love – only to be,
As then awhile, forever now
  Together, I and he."

She spoke it in her clear voice, with feeling. Strange matter, I thought, for your small fair head, dear child.

"Yes, that's good," Adam admitted critically. "My mother's mad on *The Ancient Mariner*. It's got some lovely stuff. But it's not in the *Golden Treasury*. Heaven knows why not. I like O'Shaughnessy:

"We are the music-makers,
  And we are the dreamers of dreams,
Wandering by lone sea-breakers,
  And sitting by desolate streams."

Isn't 'desolate' a lovely word?"

I wondered if anybody had ever talked to Frances about poetry before – ever, like this, swapped bits and pieces of immortal stuff. She was sitting with her elbows on the table, her face cupped in her hands, gazing into Adam's eyes. "Do you *write?*" she asked.

"Lord!" he said. "Not yet. I wouldn't have the nerve."

"Ernie, let's go and see to that jib." It was Stephen, breaking up a conversation that was incomprehensible to him. He didn't look at either of them; but Ernie asked: "Comin', Fran?" She shook her head and turned again to Adam. But he was finished with the matter. He got up and strolled into the house. Frances sat for a moment with me and Blanche; then leapt up suddenly and said: "I'd better feed the hens."

I took Blanche's hand. "How are you feeling?"

"Oh, bearing up bravely," she mocked. She was looking distraught this summer. "How much longer can it go on?"

She was referring to the investigation into Luther's affairs. "I've no idea. I suppose it depends on what they're finding out."

"I'm thinking of Frances. She's such a darling. And she's bound to be hurt." After a moment she added: "I'm more and more glad, day by day, that she's not his daughter. If the worst comes, should I try to tell her? Would it help?"

"I don't think so. Don't tell her just yet."

I still held her hand, and I was idly twisting the wedding ring on her finger. She withdrew her hand, took off the ring, and held it to me. "It's not the ring Luther gave me," she said. "It's like it; no one could tell the difference who didn't look inside. And as it's never off my finger, no one can."

I looked inside: "F.C. 1916. B.P."

"He gave it to me, and he had one like it for himself."

Perhaps it had remained intact. Perhaps some French peasant, ploughing a field, would see the minute glitter and pick up the ring, rub away the soil, and speculate on what was behind that inscription. Perhaps he would slip it on his own little finger and go on ploughing.

I wandered off to look for Frances. She was not feeding the chickens. She was in the small rough field where they were kept. They had gathered round her, as they gathered round anyone who went out at feeding time: a red and white and black commotion swirling about her bare legs, and she stood there in a mood of profound abstraction, looking at them as if they were the first chickens that anyone had seen on earth. And Adam was indoors. And Stephen was on the water. I walked away with a sigh.

5

All of us were at breakfast the next morning save Adam and Blanche. Blanche came down at last, when the rest of us had got to the marmalade and cigarette stage, and at once opened an envelope lying by her plate. She read the letter it contained, looked mystified, and passed it to me.

Dear Mrs Brimlow, – I must thank you for your kindness in asking me to Tresco Vean and apologise for leaving in a rather unceremonious way. I can't help feeling that my mother will be lonely in London and that I ought to rejoin her. There would be no point in putting you to inconvenience, so, during a walk last evening, I arranged with a taximan in Mawnna to pick me up at your gate early this morning and run me into Falmouth, where I shall catch the London train. Once again, my thanks to you, and my greetings to all.

Sincerely,

Adam Randle.

407

"Leave some toast for Adam. Don't eat the lot."

It was Frances, speaking to Stephen. He took the toast.

"They can make some more in the kitchen," he said. "Anyway, why isn't the lazy beggar up?"

"He is up," I said. "This letter explains that he is returning to London."

"Ah don't wonder," said Ernie Lingard.

Stephen's face reddened. "That's a remark that should be explained," he said.

Ernie was not perturbed. "You know what Ah'm talking about."

"I know," said Stephen hotly, "that you belly-ached enough when we were working on the boat last night."

"Ay, Ah did that. You don't catch me sailin' in a boat where tricks get played."

"I'm quite capable of sailing alone. Indeed, I intend to do so."

"OK," said Ernie. "Ah can find plenty to do round 'ere without sailin'."

He got up and went out. Frances ran upstairs to her room.

Stephen went through the open window on to the terrace. I handed the letter back to Blanche. "This letter seems to be dynamite," she said. "What's it all about, Ted?"

There was no point in telling them all that had happened on the boat. I said: "Adam isn't accustomed to sailing, and yesterday wasn't a good day to start. It was all right in here, but there was a bit of sea outside. For one thing, the jib was carried away. We all got rather wet and uncomfortable, and tempers didn't stand up to it. There were a few words."

"They must have been pretty sharp ones to make the boy walk out like that," Blanche said. "I shouldn't have thought he was difficult to get on with. He seems an intelligent person."

"He and Stephen might have got on if they'd had time to settle down to one another. They're so different. Don't think I'm criticising our offspring, Prue; oddly enough, I'm rather fond of Stephen. But he's a healthy young barbarian, you know, and he's got all a young barbarian's contempt for what he doesn't understand."

Prue leapt to the defence of her young. "I don't see much wrong with him, I must say. D'you want him to be hung round with airs and graces like a fairy?"

"No, no. I'm pleased with him as he is, and happy in the thought of what he may become. But he's collided with something very different from himself. I'm not saying young Adam Randle is better than Stephen. I'm only saying he's different. And they haven't mixed."

Blanche lit a cigarette. She was smoking continuously this summer. "I suppose it's Adam's mother," she said.

"I suppose it is," I agreed. "Till now, she's had him through all his holidays, and public school holidays make up a big part of the year. Any schoolmaster will tell you that one of his main headaches is what happens in the holidays. Well, Adam has spent his holidays in great cities, meeting rather unusual people, living in swagger hotels, and, what's more, with a head full of poetry. Stephen hardly ever meets a soul except schoolboys and us; and he meets us when we're down here in a schoolboy mood."

"You seem to think Adam an exceptional being," Prue said, sharply still; and I answered: "Well, he is, of course. His circumstances have made him so. An exceptional person is not necessarily an admirable one. We still have almost everything to learn about Adam; but for the moment the young beggar is denying us the opportunity. Anyway, Frances will miss him."

She missed him the more because Stephen decided to take himself off. He came in now while we were speaking, and, digging the carpet with his toe, not looking at any of us, he said to Blanche: "Auntie, would it be all right by you if I took the boat away for a few days?"

Blanche laughed. "My dear Stevo, I'm afraid my ownership of the boat is purely theoretical. Take her for as long as you like. The only thing is: what about Fran? Won't she want a bit of sailing?"

He looked up with a half-defiant smile. "Fran? Oh, she'll be all right. She's got – interior resources."

I thought there was a depth of young bitterness in the light words.

"I'll ask her, of course," said Stephen.

Frances, when asked, said lightly that she had no objection and that she was going to feed the hens. She was always going to feed the hens when she wanted to get away from something.

"There's a chap from school, holidaying at Portscatho," Stephen explained. "He's keen on sailing, but he hasn't got a boat of his own. I thought I'd sail over there and pick him up, and then we could go on

409

together. Somewhere new. I want to learn a bit more about charts and navigation. It's all getting rather toy-like, sailing round here."

About that time a lot of books were published by men who had crossed oceans in small boats. I knew that Stephen had been devouring them, that he was dreaming of landless horizons, not of our pleasant coastal pottering. He read hardly anything but such books as these, and Kitto had introduced him to *Moby Dick*. Kitto had written on the fly-leaf: "Salute to Young Adventure from Old Prudence, who is content to battle with Brainstorms."

But you couldn't divide things up so neatly as that. I remembered how, on the evening when Adam arrived, he and Frances and I strolled down to give him his first view of our little quay. The sun was set, and the western sky was a huge expanse of tender rose, down which drooped two clouds of feathery grey, themselves rosily luminous. Adam looked at them for a long time, smiling as though with delight in the presence of something he understood. "Wings!" he said. "Wings!"

And was that just a brainstorm, I wondered, a sensual recognition of a beautiful appearance; or was the young body itself transported in imagination to whatever was there speaking to it?

" Up there," said Adam, "you'd get the last of the light."

6

Stephen set off early the next morning. Everything necessary had been done the day before. There was nothing to do but go. I breakfasted with him and Frances. The others were not up.

"Well, so long, Dook," he said. "I'll be back inside a week."

'I'll walk down to the quay with you," I said. "Coming, Fran?"

"I haven't finished. Have a good sail, Stevo."

We walked together through the wet grass. He was quiet and thoughtful, more maturely companionable than was usual. Presently, he said: "I can't *always* be with Fran and no one else. She's only a kid."

I said nothing, and he insisted: "You do understand that, don't you?"

"Oh, yes," I said. "I don't think Fran is worrying about your going away without her. What's worrying her is what you did to Adam. You tried to humiliate him. And as it happened, he showed that he was a person not easily humiliated. He came out of it all rather better than you did."

I thought it as well to say these things and have done with them now that his mood had brought us together.

"So far as Fran goes," I added, "the point in her mind, as I see it, is not that you did it to Adam, but that *you* did it."

He didn't answer for a moment, and then said ruefully: "Fallen idol, eh?"

"In a sort of way – yes. Though I don't suppose she's thought it out and summed it up. She just feels hurt and perplexed."

"It was pretty low," he said. "I expect I should have got round to an apology if he'd stayed. He's not a bad kid, but rather touchy."

"Rather proud."

"Perhaps so. Anyway, there's nothing more to be done about it now."

"No –"

"Go on, Dook. Say it."

"Say what?"

"Nothing more to be done except learn your lesson and be a better boy in future. Isn't that it?"

"Well – perhaps –"

He looked at me and grinned in his old impudent way. We stopped, facing one another, and suddenly we both burst out laughing. He slapped me on the back, as though we were boys together. "That's better, Dook!" All the sulks and solemnity that had hung about us since Adam's departure evaporated in the morning air. My heart was uplifted and glad.

We had not expected to find Ernie at the quay, but he was there. "Ah've just been givin' things a look over," he said. "Ah've fixed that loose cleat an' put a new painter on t'dinghy. A dinghy can bang about a lot in an open sea."

"Thanks, Ernie. That's good of you."

"An' Ah've shoved a sea anchor into t'forepeak. You never know."

"No, you don't, do you? You might step on a bit of seaweed on the foredeck any day."

And then they two had a laugh, and it felt good there in the morning sunshine. A lot of shadows seemed to have blown suddenly away.

"Your petrol all right?" I asked.

"Petrol! I'm taking *no* petrol. It's time I learned to sail."

He got into the dinghy and Ernie pushed it out. We saw him climb aboard and begin swinging on the main halliard.

"Do 'im good, Dook," Ernie said. " 'E's all right, is Stevo."

We strolled up to the house, and I had another cup of coffee while the latecomers breakfasted. I felt good, as they say.

7

I thought I should have Frances on my hands that day. Good resolutions filled my heart. She mustn't be allowed to mope. Everything was for the best. There was no doubt about it, I told myself, that she and Stephen had become too dependent on one another. It was an excellent thing that they had been thrown apart, and it would be an excellent thing, too, if Blanche would take the child about, so that she could meet other children. There had been the short visit to France. I hoped there would be more of that. Meantime, the immediate thing was to see that Frances had a happy day. I looked about for her. She was not to be seen anywhere downstairs, and she was not with the hens. Her pony was in his stable. I went upstairs, knocked at the door of her room, and peeped in. She was sitting on the floor, leaning up against the wall, with one of her penny exercise books opened on her knees.

"Hallo, Fran! What's the drill for this morning?"

There was a frown of concentration on her forehead. "I'm working," she said.

"On a lovely day like this! Don't you think you ought to get out?"

"I'm writing a play."

"Well, this afternoon perhaps . . ."

"Perhaps."

She began to suck a pencil stump and to frown again at her book. I took it for a sign of dismissal. She had not plaited her hair. It was lying on her shoulders like ripe corn that the wind had dishevelled. The sun was shining through the window, caressing it. A most paintable picture, I thought: the short blue skirt, the long brown legs, the careless gold of the hair. She might value it in years to come. "Frances working." I kept a painting outfit at Tresco Vean, and now I wanted very much to paint her.

"What about painting you?" I asked. "I'd be as quiet as a mouse. You could get on with your work."

412

She put down book and pencil and looked up at me with a sigh, like an adult who must unwillingly rebuke an impercipient child. "It's so difficult here," she said, "to get a moment to oneself. And now that I've got it . . ."

I closed the door softly.

It turned out to be a day of bits and pieces. In the morning Ernie ran me to Falmouth in Lazarus. He, too, was loose-ended. I found him sitting on a log outside his quarters, ministering to Nobs who was cringing beneath a steel comb. When that was done with, he was rubbed up and down and almost inside out with a stiff brush, Ernie hissing as though he were grooming a horse. "You get a bit o' satisfaction out of attending to a dog like that," he said. "A good dog is like a good ship: it pays for what you put into it."

Nobs was getting old, and grey round the muzzle. He dribbled a lot and, more than ever, his eyes ran with tears. But Ernie looked at him with undiminished enthusiasm. "Ah sleep better at nights," he said, "when that dog's about t'place. Tha needs a good watchdog in a lonely spot like this."

He got out the old rattle-bone car, and off we went. I wanted to have a talk with Kitto, but I did not have it. He had taken to his bed, and Henry Opie said he was asleep. I went up alone, leaving Opie and Ernie talking together downstairs.

Uncle Kitto had been most successful in disembarrassing himself of all that was unnecessary. This one big room into which I softly stepped was all the shell the old hermit crab needed. Here he worked, and in the summer looked from these windows over the blue sea, and in the winter sat contentedly by this fireplace, and when the day was done got into this bed in which he now lay. One glance at him showed me that now indeed the day was done. He looked tranquil and composed. He lay on his back, with the sheet neatly under his chin. The trim pointed beard he had grown late in life lay upon the sheet. There was a glimpse of blue silk pyjama round his neck, and round his neck, too, was the broad black ribbon of his monocle. His right hand, resting on the sheet, was holding the monocle, as though he had removed it, lain quietly down, composed himself, and died without fuss. One would have said he was asleep, but I knew he was asleep beyond waking. What distinguishes sleep from death even in its kindest and least disfiguring shape I do not know. But it is a matter in which there is no making a mistake.

I felt no shock at my discovery, only an intense melancholy, an awareness of fugitive time. My antecedent generation was passing. My father had long been gone, and here his brother lay. The generation behind me was thrusting me forward, already asking for room. Stephen was aching for the sense of self-reliance. Even little Frances was finding her own affairs. For the first time, I was acutely aware that mine was now the generation that must next pass.

I sat for a moment by the bed, laid my hand on the small thin hand on the sheet. It was quite cold. The hand of Kitto Pentecost, whom I had imagined a Viking! I recalled the day in the barber's shop in Didsbury when, in an old Christmas magazine, I had first seen reproduced a picture signed Kitto Pentecost. What excitement — rapture almost! It didn't seem long ago. I felt I could reach out my hand and enclose the moment.

I went to the head of the stairs and softly called the others.

Henry Opie had not, as he said, "liked the look" of his master and, the day before, had taken upon himself to call in a doctor. I suppose, if it hadn't been for this, we should have had the fuss of an inquest. As it was, the doctor made his second call as we three stood round the bed, and he appeared not to be surprised at what he found. There was nothing that I could do except ask Ernie to remain for the night with Henry Opie, who was deeply distressed. Then, as I had never learned or wished to drive a car, I got on to a bus and returned with the news to Tresco Vean.

8

I spent the afternoon attending to melancholy formalities. I went back to Falmouth, saw an undertaker, a lawyer, and so forth. It was not being at all the sort of day I had expected, and I was not philosophic enough to rejoice that one of the good things about days is their ability to surprise us. When I got back to Tresco Vean I was worn out. I drank a cup of tea and went to bed. I stayed there till nine o'clock. Then I got up and dressed. I went downstairs and was in time to say good night to Frances, who was just going early to bed. Everybody was indoors, for the night had turned dark and wet. When we were at Tresco Vean, we were all much aware of tides and moons: things that we rarely thought of in London. I knew that the tide would be at its height in about an hour's time and that it would be a dark night. There would be no moon. It would be the darker because of the rain. Already, here in the lounge the lights were on, and Amy Lingard had been impressed as a fourth at cards. She sat at the table with my mother, Prue and Blanche. They were playing some childish game like Newmarket. None of them played cards seriously and they didn't play at all unless the weather shut them in at nights. I sat under a lamp in a corner with a book, listening to the soft moaning of the wind and to the spatter of water from a leaky gutter on to the stone of the terrace.

Prue looked up and said: "I hope Stephen's all right."

"I've no doubt," I said, "that he's in a snug harbour, lying in his cot, listening to the rain on the deck over his head, and feeling tremendously romantic."

The wind was nothing much, but if it were like this wherever he might be, the blocks would be knocking and the halliards slapping, and all the small straining, heaving, scurrying noises of a night at sea would be filling the little dusky space of the forepeak. I pictured Stephen there, with the lantern swinging from the beam overhead, a book in his hand, or perhaps his companion by now in the other cot. Anyway, I had no doubt he was very happy. Perhaps he had made the harbour at Fowey. The riding light would be burning steady on the tall mast of the *Frances and Stephen*.

I wonder, I said to myself, whether he is missing me as much as I am missing him?

What on earth will Iris think of us all now that Adam has so strongly turned us down?

I'm sorry Frances went to bed so early and that Ernie isn't here to be talked to.

My head was full of these random dispiriting thoughts, all reinforced by the wet weather and the background shock of Kitto's death. No one had told Frances of that. That would be a job for me in the morning.

Then I heard Ernie's dog whining outside the window.

"Has anyone fed Nobs tonight?" I asked; and it seemed that no one had.

"I'll see to him, and I'll take a look round the place."

I opened the front door and whistled to Nobs. He came in and followed me into the scullery. I fed him, and then pulled on wellington boots, an oilskin and a sou'wester. I went out through the scullery door and Nobs followed me. In his old age, he more than ever disliked being out of human company.

Trees grew close round the back of the house, and a light breath of wind shook the rain down from them to patter like hail on my oilskin. It was quite dark now: dark and wet, without a gleam. Always, last thing at night, either Stephen or Ernie, or both of them, would go down to the quay to cast a look at the *Frances and Stephen*, the despised *Dook*, and the dinghies. There were three dinghies now, but Stephen had towed one away. I decided to go down and see that everything was in order. It would be something to do. I cowered against a tree and lit a pipe; then set off. Nobs waddled after me.

I knew every pebble, almost every blade of grass, between the house and the water. Even on so dark a night, the vague shapes of familiar trees drew a workable geography upon the sky. But once I was under the ceiling of the wood I used a torch and went more quickly: more quickly still when, out on the water where *The Dook* lay at moorings, I saw a light.

I came out upon the quay and stood there in utter perplexity. Behind me the rain was falling among the trees, before me upon the black water. Mid-stream itself was impenetrable to my vision. I wondered whether Stephen had for some reason returned and decided to spend the night on the boat out there; and at once I saw that this was not so. On either side of the *Frances and Stephen's* forepeak there was but one port. On the water two portholes were gleaming side by side. That was *The Dook*. I flashed the torch along the steps up which the high tide had climbed and saw that now only one dinghy was there. I got aboard, untied her, and rowed out into the streaming darkness. Nobs shuddered on the thwart in the stern.

I put out fenders and went alongside very quietly. I heaved Nobs over the bulwarks, climbed aboard, and fastened the painter. Then I tried the cabin door. It was locked. I rattled the handle and shouted: "Who's in there?"

The door opened, and there was Frances, wearing pyjamas and a dressing-gown.

"You mad child!" I said. "What are you doing here?"

The rain was beating down, so I ducked into the cabin and shut the door. I dropped my hat and oilskins to the floor. There were a couple of disordered blankets on one of the berths. Frances had evidently been lying there.

"I wanted to see what it was like to spend a night alone at sea," she said calmly. She lay down and pulled the blankets round her.

"You might have scared your mother to death. What do you think would have happened when she went in to say good night and found you gone?"

"She doesn't always come to say good night. I stayed awake for hours and hours last night and she didn't come. But I left a note tonight in case she did."

"Well, I'm glad you had that much thoughtfulness." I spoke sharply, and to my consternation she burst into tears. I had never before seen Frances cry. Her body heaved with distress beneath the blankets. "I'm so *lonely*," she sobbed.

I tried to speak more comfortingly. "This is a queer place to come to if you're lonely, Fran. Wouldn't you have felt better in the house with people around you?"

She said a thing that surprised me. "Oh, you don't understand. It's not a matter of being *among* people. It's a matter of being *with* people."

At a stroke she had been deprived of the old easy companionship with Stephen and the new exciting contact with Adam, who had shown himself to be a sharer of what I guessed to be important things to Frances. She wouldn't be able to disentangle all this. It would he confused in her young mind; but how wretched it was making her! On the cabin table was the exercise book and stump of pencil that I had seen her using in the morning. "I'm writing a play." I supposed this was her way of creating people she could be *with*.

I didn't know what to do for the best. I stood there for a moment listening to the rain on the roof and to the child's diminishing sobs. I sat on the edge of the berth and took her hand, hot and restless. It clutched at mine as though I could save her; and I thought of how that morning I had sat by another bed and held a hand that had been lithe and full of skill and was now done with clutching at life. The thought made me very tender to the child.

> We must be tender with all budding things.
> Our Maker let no thought of Calvary
> Trouble the morning stars in their first song.

That was Yeats. I bent down and kissed her wet cheeks, and in her eyes I startlingly saw the eyes of my long-dead friend.

"Well, Fran, what are you going to do? D'you want to stay here? Or do you think you'd better come back and get into a warm bed?"

She had recovered her composure. "I think I'll stay here."

"Then I'd better stay with you. I must go back now and let them know what's happening. I don't know *what* they'd do if they found *two* people missing. Keep yourself warm. I'll be back as soon as I can."

I pulled on my oilskin and went out. The rain was falling more heavily than ever, but the water was flat. When I was in the dinghy Nobs stood on a seat with his forefeet on the gunwale, whining at me. I reached up, took him by the scruff of the neck, and lifted him in.

Although I knew that bit of water so well, I had to use my torch as I edged in to the steps, for the night was inky. The gleam happened to fall on Nobs, and to my surprise he was sitting up in the stern looking, for once, alert and businesslike. I thought of Ernie's remark about the good watchdog and I smiled. It was like Nobs to develop his senses on a night when not even an intelligent badger would crawl out of his hole.

"What is it, Nobs! Fetch 'em then!" I teased him in an urgent whisper. He replied with sudden agitated barking, and leapt out as soon as the dinghy lay against the steps.

I followed more slowly, made the boat fast, and stepped on to the sodden grassy quay, still holding the torch in my hand. An iron grip fell on my shoulder, the torch was struck to the ground; and a voice said: "Get in there!"

There was nothing to do but obey, for whoever this was had slipped behind me, pulled my arms together behind my back, and was shoving me violently towards the door of the boathouse that backed from the shoreward end of the quay into the bushes. The door was open; I was thrust inside; and the door was kicked to.

There were no windows in the boathouse, so a light could be shown without danger, and as I stood there, still held firmly from

418

behind, some other person flashed a torch in my face, himself unseen. Then a voice said: "Let him go. Well, Ted."

"That's Luther, isn't it?"

"Yes."

There was a moment of silence and darkness. Outside, I could hear Nobs whining and scrabbling at the door.

Standing there in the dark, I had an odd feeling of having known that this would happen. Something like this. Sometime. The shadow of this had been over me and Blanche all the summer.

Luther spoke again. "This is all most awkward."

I struck a match. A lamp hung from the ceiling. I lit it. I heard the man who had held me slip through the door and shut it behind him. As the light strengthened, I saw Luther and a woman standing side by side. I was beyond surprise. It would not have surprised me if the woman had been Christina Lake. But it wasn't. She was a young blonde woman, wearing a superb fur coat, sodden with rain. She looked no more than twenty. Also, she looked terrified. She clutched Luther's arm. "Vite, vite, chéri. Il faut partir," she said between chattering teeth.

Luther said: "Calmes-toi. Tais-toi. Nous avons beau jeu a échapper. Il n'y a rien à craindre. C'est mon beau-frère."

He was calm enough himself, though a tic in his jaw betrayed a hidden agitation. He was wearing a long rain-polished mackintosh. His towny shoes were saturated.

"There's little time to waste, Ted," he said quietly. "Sit down. Now that you've seen so much, you might as well know everything. Pauline doesn't know what we're talking about. Her English is small."

I shoved a plank across a couple of boxes, and the shivering woman sat down. Luther sat at her side. I remained standing.

"I'm going to talk quickly," Luther said, "and then I must be going. You doubtless remember that soon after I gave that motor launch to Frances I came down here rather unexpectedly. If I hadn't been able to make certain accommodations, I was done for. But not that time. It came out well. However, it *might* have been necessary, even then, for me to clear out of the country, and that motor launch was there for the purpose. It was my line of retreat. It's not the only launch of its sort in the country, you know. I took care to be acquainted with someone who understood the boat, and who knew enough navigation to get me to France."

"And now is the moment," I put in. "Don't let me keep you."

"Now is the moment, and you won't keep me longer than I want to stay. There's a warrant out for my arrest. That's the sort of fools people are. A little time, a little patience, and everything could be arranged. But no! Tens of thousands of simple people must be ruined because it pleases the jacks in office . . . Why, I could have."

"Don't go into it, Luther. You haven't much time."

He had lost a little control and glared at me. He stood up and shouted: "Surely you don't believe that! You don't think I'm just a bloody robber of poor men's purses!"

"Don't go into it."

"You don't understand. You never have understood me. You've always pitied me and despised me." He was shouting.

"No, no. I've always been sorry for you. Don't waste time, Luther."

He shot me a suspicious look. "What's to prevent you from tipping off the police as soon as I'm gone? Not that I shall be such a fool as to land in a port. There are beaches to creep into at night."

"There's no need," I said, "to tell me anything whatever of your plans. I'm not asking how you got here, or what provision you've made about petrol, or what you will do when you get to sea. You've always been a great planner, Luther, and all that, no doubt, has been child's play to you. Even I could have done it – and that's saying something. No; I'd rather be told nothing at all about it. And if you want to know why you're safe so far as I'm concerned, I'll tell you. It's because of Blanche. It would give me no satisfaction to have her reading of her husband's arrest and trial. The affair will be grievous enough for her as it is. I advise you to get away – the sooner the better. The tide's running out."

The door opened, and a man came in – presumably the one who had seized me. The whole business was unbearably melodramatic: Luther and his little French doxy, the shadows dancing as the opening of the door sent a draught to the lamp; and this fellow added the final touch, for he had bound a handkerchief about his face below the eyes.

"Come on, Mr Brimlow," he said. "If you hang round here chin-wagging much longer I shall leave you to it, and that's flat."

The woman added a silent entreaty, taking Luther's arm and urging him towards the door. Who on earth was she? Where had he found her? She seemed a pathetic piece of salvage from so colossal a wreck. She had pretty legs. She tottered forlornly on high heels.

"Well, come on," said the man. He picked up an iron belaying pin and weighed it in his hand.

"There's one thing more," I said to Luther. "Frances is on the launch. I shall have to go and bring her off."

The man groaned. "Oh, good Christ! We'll be here till dawn."

"You can go," I said to Luther, "as soon as you've heard us land and set off for the house."

The man said: "And be quick about it. This is getting beyond a bloody joke."

I held out my hand to Luther. "Goodbye, then," I said. "And good luck."

He took my hand in a sudden convulsive grasp, held it for a moment, saying nothing, looking into my face. His cheeks ticked in and out, and I saw now that his eyes were full of fear.

He dropped my hand and I turned to go, but the woman Pauline came up to me with a nervous shyness and held out her hand, too. I took it, and she smiled at me, forlorn and sad. I gave back what encouragement of a smile I could. She looked a lost and desolate little thing, not bad. "Merci, monsieur," she whispered. "Ayez pitié de lui. Il a beaucoup souffert . . ." I could have wept.

"For God's sake . . ." the man growled impatiently. He followed me out into the darkness, still weighing the belaying-pin in his hand.

I had forgotten Nobs, and now the poor beast rushed out from some dark embuscade, barking with pleasure.

The man shouted: "Oh, holy Jesus! That bloody dog! He'll bring all the world down on us."

It was so dark we couldn't see the dog, but the man lashed suddenly with the belaying pin in the direction of the frenzied noise of gladness. There was a bone-splitting thud, one sharp yelp of agony, and silence.

I stood still, the rain beating upon me, sick to the heart. It was so simple, so innocent and trusting a victim to have been offered up to this dark moment. It seemed to me that all that was vile and predatory in Luther Brimlow and in men like him rushed to consummation in

421

that blind killing blow in the darkness. My legs suddenly went weak. I said nothing to the man. He was a brutal clod, as unconscious of infamy as a falling rock that crushes a mouse. In the end, these were what Luther had come to: that woman and this man. I shuddered and walked towards the dinghy. My foot struck what I hoped was the torch that had been knocked from my hand. It was. I picked it up, walked back a step or two and turned the light to the ground. I hardly looked at Nobs as I picked up the body and laid it in some bracken. I didn't want Frances to stumble into that.

9

The electric lights which Ernie had put into *The Dook* were on in the cabin, and a smell of coffee greeted me as I pushed open the door. Also the foul smell of the Primus stove. Frances stood intently above its roaring, watching the coffee in a saucepan. Two cups were on the table, with a paper bag of biscuits beside them. "I brought everything with me, so that I could have breakfast aboard," Frances said. "Now we'll have supper instead, and then I'll read my play to you. And tomorrow, if you like, you shall paint me." She was in a repentant mood. "What did they say at the house?" she asked, pouring coffee from the saucepan into the cups. "Did they think I'm mad?"

What on earth could I say to the child? How could I get her to come away, and yet leave her mind untroubled? I decided to be as melodramatic as everything else was being that night.

"I'm afraid you're going to have a disappointment, Fran. We can't stay here. We must get back at once."

She looked up in sharp disappointment. "But, Dook—"

"I'm sorry, darling. When I was at the house there was a telephone call from the police. Had we seen any suspicious characters about the grounds? That sort of thing . . ."

Now her eyes were round with excitement.

"A couple of men, it seems, have escaped from custody. You know there've been a number of robberies from boats round here lately." Happily, there had. "Well, these men are believed to be the people concerned, and the police think they may board some boat tonight – perhaps get away to sea in it."

"But, look! Surely we ought to stay then, to see that they don't get away in ours!"

I laughed. "I'm too old to be as courageous as that, Fran. I'd rather give such gentry a wide berth. Anyway, your mother'd be worrying herself to death, thinking we were having our throats cut out here. Better dress."

"Well, let's drink the coffee, anyway."

"No, no. Please, Fran. I'll wait out in the cockpit while you dress."

She joined me in a few moments. She was depressed. The bubble of an unexpected excitement had been pricked, and she climbed without a word into the dinghy. She untied the one that she had come in, held the painter, and towed it behind us.

Now that we were ashore, I did everything in apprehensive haste. I was conscious of eyes in the darkness, of all the villainy that had shadowed Blanche's life and Fran's come to a head and lurking a few yards away, desperate with the urgency of fear. I prayed God that the child would not at this last moment take some fanciful notion to get something out of the boathouse or to do anything else that would hold us there. She did not. She stood kicking her heels while I secured the boats with fingers that trembled. Then we set off up the path.

"Now get straight to bed, Fran," I said when we were in the house. "I expect your mother will be up to say good night in a few moments." She went obediently. I felt a deep relief as I pushed home the bolts in the front door.

It was late. Only Blanche was up. She was in the lounge, smoking and playing patience.

"Blanche," I said, "I found Frances on *The Dook*, all settled down, ready to spend the night there. I've brought her ashore and she's just gone up to bed."

She swept the cards together and stood up. "The mad little fool! What is she up to?"

"I had to give her a reason for bringing her ashore. I said the police had been ringing up about some robbers at large. Go up and say good night to her. That's your cue for anything she says. But it isn't the reason. Something else happened tonight. Something we've been expecting."

She knew at once. "He's here?"

"He *was* here. I think he'll be gone by now. Go and say good night to Fran, and then join me and Prue in our bedroom."

When she was gone I put out the lights and went upstairs. Prue was sitting up in bed, reading. "Ted! Where on earth have you been? Do you know the time?"

There was a sunburst clock over the dressing table. It was midnight.

"And what's the matter with you? You look absolutely dithering."

She made her old gesture of lighting a cigarette, taking a puff, and handing it to me. "No, keep it, darling," I said. "It's against the rules in the bedroom, but I shall smoke a pipe.'

I lit the pipe, got into slippers and a dressing gown and sat down. Blanche came in, shut the door behind her with a queer conspiratorial quietness, and sat by Prue on the bed. "Well?" she said.

I felt myself to be in the same mood of conspiracy. I got up and drew the curtains across the window. There was only the soft glow of the bedhead light in the room. Blanche lit a cigarette, and almost before she had puffed it began tapping non-existent ash to the carpet with an agitated finger.

"Prue, I've already told Blanche. Now I must tell you. Luther was here tonight."

It relieved my tension to go through the whole story. I felt better when I had done. As carefully and fully as I could I told them everything, from the moment of my seeing the light on the water and finding Frances in *The Dook* right up to bringing her back to the house. Well, *almost* everything. I said nothing about the woman Pauline, nothing about Nobs.

"Well, that's it. That's what happened."

I got up and knocked the ashes of my pipe into the fireplace. No one spoke for a long time. We were all aware of being caught in a desperate coil. I, at least, was aware that I had committed a criminal act in conniving at the escape of a man wanted by the law.

At last Blanche said: "Can he get away? People like that always try to fly the country. They'll be on the lookout at every port in France."

"He dropped a hint," I said, "of what he intended to do. He said he wouldn't be such a fool as to land at a port – there were beaches. He knows France well. He speaks French like a Frenchman. I should say he's picked a skipper acquainted with the French coast. It would be possible to stay in mid-channel, out of sight from either shore, all through the daylight hours. At night they could sneak into some cove or beach, in Brittany, perhaps. Don't forget, there's a dinghy. Luther could be rowed ashore. He could make his way in the hours of darkness to a railway station. First thing in the morning he could be off and, with a few changes, he could be buried in the heart of France before the day was over."

We all considered this in silence. "And what would happen to the boat?" Prue asked.

"It's a boat like a good many others," I said. "Say this skipper he's picked up has its double in some yard on the Thames. Couldn't he have removed the plates with her name and port, and couldn't he put these on to *The Dook*? It would be no more than ten minutes' work with a screwdriver. What's to prevent him then from brazenly sailing home? The boat would be part of his pay for the job."

Blanche stubbed another cigarette into the pile in her ashtray. "Supposing he gets lost in the heart of France, as you say. What then?"

"I have reminded you that he talks French like a Frenchman. He could be Monsieur anything he liked. There are such things as forged passports."

I didn't imagine a forged passport would worry Luther. I remembered the forged letters of his boyhood.

"He could move into Switzerland, Italy, anywhere. He could grow a beard and take an Italian liner to South America."

"Well, my God!" said Blanche, "to think that we are sitting here, talking like this about my husband!"

But there it was. These shots from a melodramatic film were the sort of things we had now to consider as probabilities.

What, in fact, Luther Brimlow did, we never knew. He slipped through the fingers of the law, and he slipped from our lives, never to trouble them again. We decided that night that neither my mother nor Ernie, nor Stephen nor Frances, nor anyone but we three need know of what had happened down there on our peaceful little quay. With them all the fiction was maintained that *The Dook* had been taken away by thieves, and the children and Ernie did not mourn overmuch for her. She had never been loved. But Nobs had been loved and was mourned for many a day. Before anyone was up the next morning, I took a spade and buried him, wrapped in a piece of canvas, in a part of the wood where no one came.

CHAPTER ELEVEN

ADAM CAME into the studio chuckling, and, glancing up from my work, I thought, as usual, that he was a nice-looking boy. Unlike most undergraduates, he wore flannel bags that were carefully creased, and his brown shoes shone. A light blue shirt and a dark blue tie set off his wing of black hair, his eyes that a casual look might take to be black but were, in fact, of the darkest blue. He rarely wore a hat, but had the habit of taking a comb from hip pocket and pulling it through his hair. The only careless thing about him was his tweed jacket, which bulged with books stuffed into the pockets. Proust, T.S. Eliot, James Joyce — all sorts of people I didn't know.

He had a copy of the *Daily Express* in his hand. He passed it to me, with his finger pointing to a sentence, and I noticed that the nail of the finger was oval and polished. "Don't you think that's a jewel of a phrase?" he asked.

The paragraph was from a special correspondent in Melbourne. It described the end of an aeroplane flight from England to Australia. One of the airmen said: "It's been a lousy trip — and that's praising it."

"Very good," I said. "The traditional modest touch of the hero."

"By God!" he said. "What a trip it's been! They did 11,323 miles in seventy-one hours, and one engine phutted out over the Timor Sea. But they made it — on one engine!"

"The Timor Sea! That's the sea Bligh crossed, isn't it? Four thousand miles in an open boat!"

Adam laughed. "That's how old Stevo'd like to do it. Suit him down to the ground. *Belay there and avast! Don't throw those weevils overboard, bos'n. Let 'em breed. We shall need 'em yet.* Poor old Stevo! He's a delightful anachronism. How is he?"

"*How* he is at the moment," I said, "I can't tell you. But I can tell you *where* he is."

426

"Don't! Don't! I know it, Dook. He returned faithfully to work on the day term opened. Whereas others . . ."

"Yes, indeed, whereas others. I thought the Michaelmas term opened on October 13? It's now the 24th."

"I did go up and clocked on," he said. "But you know what the Black Widow is."

It was his outrageous name for his mother, who was rarely seen, off the stage, in anything but black. But not, believe me, the black of a funeral procession in Rochdale! I knew indeed what she was where Adam was concerned. Between them they concerted the most shameless wangles to explain his absences from Oxford, where he was reading English literature, contributing verses to the University magazines, and firmly refusing all invitations to run, jump, kick balls about, or row on the river. "A punt – yes. To read Proust in a punt, under the willows, on a summer afternoon: that's my idea of Nirvana. The river goes on and on like Proust, and Proust goes on and on like the river, till you don't know which is which, and don't care. They both smell beautifully of decaying matter."

"As a matter of fact," he said now, "I heard from Stevo this morning. He's busy with the set square and drawing board. But why Liverpool? I've been there. Indeed, I seem to remember it was there I first met you. A dreary hole, I think."

"Well, there are reasons. To begin with, the School of Architecture is very good, and then there's Bugsby."

"Bugsby! I could never understand how Stevo could be friendly with a man named Bugsby. There's a piece of the Thames, isn't there, called Bugsby's Reach? Bugsby would always make me think of a stretch of grey water."

"Perhaps it does with Stephen. Perhaps that's the attraction. Anyway, he and Bugsby were at school together for years, and then, as you know, they took to sailing together in the holidays, and now Bugsby's settled down in his father's office in Liverpool, and he's got a boat there. So you see, it all adds up."

"I suppose so. Nothing will ever cure Stevo of his wooden walls complex. Good Queen Bess would have thought him marvellous. He'd have got a knighthood for harrying the Armada."

"And modern life ties him to a drawing board."

"Yes. I expect he'll design yacht clubs. By the way, I really came up to tell you that Fran waits below."

"Well, I'm damned! It's taken you a long time to come round to it."

"Well, I'm damned! So it has! Let's go at once."

He was in a gay mood, but his moods could be black. He was as variable as an April day. But now, I say, he was in a gay mood, and so I might have guessed that Frances was about. "We've just been dashing round a bit," he explained, as I got ready to go. "We had lunch at Richmond and then had a look at the park. Beautiful on an autumn day like this. Blue mist. And the yellow bracken. And the deer. You know. 'And the running of the deer.' D'you remember that old carol? Lovely. Fran was incredibly happy." He picked up the *Daily Express*. "I shall want that. I must put that cutting into my aviation scrapbook. 'Lousy – and that's praising it.' Gorgeous phrase." He ran downstairs chuckling.

2

The small open car that Iris had given him, and that rushed to and from Oxford with a regularity which, I am sure, the university authorities neither knew about nor approved, was waiting in King's Mistress Yard. "It's odd," said Adam, looking at the sign over the pub door, "but that woman is remarkably like the Black Widow."

"Yes, I've often thought so," Frances agreed.

She was sitting next to the driving seat. I could see little of her but a canary-yellow sweater and a tanned face framed in sun-bleached hair. However, I thought, that would be enough for most men. She was seventeen. What was that idiotic phrase – sweet seventeen, and never been kissed. I wondered. I didn't think it likely. She slewed round, and asked: "Will you be all right in the back, Dook? Or is it too undignified for an R.A.? You can come here if you like."

"I shall manage."

The car was never intended to carry three. There was a lid that hinged up at the back, and you could crawl into a hole and lean back against this lid. The hole was not fit to receive anything but a suitcase. I managed to scramble in, and off we went. It was a time when London looked its best: late afternoon in October, with the lights coming on, the plane leaves not yet fallen, and a lilac dusk deepening.

We didn't talk any more. To be alive, and to be experiencing this, was enough.

It was not till we were almost at St James' Square that Adam shouted back to me: "I'm taking you to tea with the Black Widow. I'm afraid we're a bit late."

We were late enough for a few people to have already assembled. The flat looked charming. Iris had recovered from her arctic period of interior decoration; the room was warm and personal, full of bright colour. A fire was burning and a lamp or two, shaded in a creamy rose, mitigated without dispelling the gracious twilight. Three people were with Iris: that tattered old Miss Chirk whom I had once met at the Ivy, and who was now all the rage as a delightful grandmotherly poisoner in a play that couldn't die; a tall and taciturn dark man whom I knew to be a celebrated producer when he was introduced to me as Mr Cambridge; and a startlingly beautiful sophisticated young creature named Christine. I didn't catch her surname: no one called her anything but Christine. I took her to be an actress.

Iris kissed Frances and took her away "to put a comb through her hair." Adam, with easy familiarity, shook hands with Mr Cambridge and kissed Miss Chirk and Christine, calling both impartially "darling." All wished him many happy returns of the day. This was the first I knew of a birthday, and the first Frances knew, too; for now, coming in with Iris, she arrived behind a tea trolley pushed by a maid and containing a cake stuck all over with candles. "Why! It's a birthday!" she cried. "Yours, Adam?"

"Yes," he said; and I was glad he did not call her "darling," as he had called Christine and Miss Chirk. The word was becoming unbearably meaningless.

"Well, many happy returns of the day," Frances said. "Since you've kept it such a secret, it's your own fault that I've got no present for you."

"Well," he said lightly, "so long as you've got a future for me . . ."

Frances blushed. She was acutely embarrassed. She was not used to the superficial world in which Adam was so easily at home; and she didn't know whether his words were a moment's flippancy or something coming out of truth. She suddenly looked incredibly young alongside Iris and Christine: a child who could easily be hurt. It was old Miss Chirk who chipped in opportunely: "Well, Adam, darling, we expect some verses from you on an occasion like this." And Adam at once began to recite some nonsense beginning:

>"This is my birthday,
>   My nineteenth-year-on-earthday."

He had the situation well in hand, and settled down to be the good host, to light the nineteen candles on the cake and blow them all out in one breath, to receive presents and distribute words and kisses in return for each. Christine was all over him, as they say, greedy for him without more than a veneer of disguise, and he threw badinage to and fro with her, lightly and adroitly. I didn't enjoy the occasion, and I was glad when the party broke up. It was consoling to notice the books bulging in Adam's pockets, to be reminded thus of another Adam than this: of the boy who had stood with us on the quay at Tresco Vean looking at the beating wings of sunset and who thrilled at a phrase like "the running of the deer." I didn't imagine that Christine could have much to say to that Adam.

"The car's outside, Fran. I'll run you and the Dook up to Hampstead."

"Thank you, Adam," she said. "I really have had enough riding in a car for today. And we should make you shockingly late getting back to Oxford."

"As you wish," he said. "What do you think of my mascot?"

He was holding Christine's present: an atrocious plaster-of-Paris figure of a bulldog with a blue ribbon tied in a bow round the neck. "My reward for enduring nineteen years of human existence!" He laughed, and suddenly wrung the bulldog's neck. It came into two pieces, and he threw them into the hearth.

"Oh, Adam!" Iris cried.

"What the hell did she think I was going to do with it," he said savagely, "put it on the mantelpiece in my rooms in Oxford? Really, Mamma, the people you know!"

Frances and I went home by tube.

3

She and Blanche were now sharing the house at Hampstead with me and Prue. My mother was dead; for most of the time Stephen was in

Liverpool; and there was plenty of room in the house. Save that she no longer had the run of the house in Bedford Square, Luther's disappearance had made little change in Blanche's way of living. In the financial disasters of those years she had lost money, but she was still a well-to-do woman, rich enough to keep Tresco Vean going, though not as it had once been. The staff was cut down, inside the house and out. The gardens were wilder, but not, I thought, the less lovely for that. Ernie Lingard had married a Falmouth girl, and those two now lived alone in the house except at the time of our annual family trek. Then we took Amy, and we managed well enough. Occasionally, at other times than this yearly migration, Blanche would snatch Frances away to Tresco Vean for a week; for a month; one never knew. She was restless, an idle purposeless woman, but not so edgy as before Luther had gone.

It had become the thing for Adam to join us in the annual visit. He had even become reconciled to sailing, though he treated it as rather a joke, a primitive picnic, and when young Bugsby turned up, as he always did – an odd, diffident fellow, who seemed glad when the moment came for him and Stephen to set off on a longish voyage, leaving us all behind – Adam saw the boat sail with no pretence of regret. But he and Stephen had come to an understanding. A wary respect, each for the other's overmastering passion, was the basis of a friendship that seemed secure.

Frances had, so to speak, a foot in each camp. She was happy at sea with Stephen and the blushing Bugsby; but when they were gone she could turn with equal candour to Adam, reading her plays to him – which she never did to me – and absorbing the books in which he was careful to keep her up to date. But the plays were the thing. In the course of his strange upbringing, Adam had picked up a lot of technical knowledge – about acting and producing; and especially of late, when he was developing this through working with the O.U.D.S., Frances found him a preordained victim of her passion for the theatre. He didn't mind. He submitted with good humour, and they would argue for hours about whether a line that sounded lovely on paper would really "get across" when uttered on the stage.

For me, I had become a Cornish property owner. Kitto had bequeathed to me the old chapel-studio looking over Falmouth harbour, with the proviso that Henry Opie, in return for giving me his services as he had given them to Kitto, should continue to occupy his quarters. Henry was left three pounds a week. The old fellow was beginning to feel his years. I rarely disturbed him. A studio over Falmouth harbour was not of much use to a fashionable portrait painter. But it made an amusing *pied à terre*.

This, then, was our position in that autumn of 1934. Except that Iris had said to me: "If I'm free next summer, Ted, I'd like to see this Cornish paradise that has seduced Adam from me. D'you think it could be arranged?"

We had talked it over at Hampstead, and it was now understood that Iris was to be of the party next summer if she could manage it.

4

But there was spring before summer, and there was the delicious month of May that is neither spring nor summer but a time still full of the one's innocent virginity, yet with a hand resting on the other's richness and fulfilment. It was in May that Adam invited me and Prue, Blanche and Frances, to visit him in Oxford. It so chanced that at the same time Stephen wrote from Liverpool suggesting a visit, and Prue decided to go. Blanche said she would go with her. It was many years since either of them had been in the north of England. They worked up between them the scheme of quite a sentimental journey: Withington and Didsbury, and chocolate éclairs at Meng and Ecker's in St Ann's Passage, and then on to Liverpool.

So it came about that on an opalescent morning Frances and I were leaning over Magdalen bridge, watching the slide of the water and rejoicing in the feel of the fresh early hour that promised later heat. We saw Adam go down to the landing stage, and walked round to greet him. He was putting promising-looking baskets into a punt, and glanced up to say: "Ha! The first arrivals!"

"Are there to be others?"

"One other. Mamma should be here at any moment. It's going to be a heavenly day." He strewed multicoloured cushions about the punt.

The day seemed to me already heavenly. The sky was a haze of milky blue that soon would be azure. Magdalen tower stood up in the languid air, with a few rooks circling lazily round it, lazily calling. The light smouldered but not yet sparkled on the river. Beneath the arches of the bridge the water was darkling, and to lift the eyes from that to the triumphant green shout of the trees was like opening the ears to the burst of a glorious overture.

Frances had not been in Oxford before. "Oh, Adam!" she cried. "Is it always like this?"

He straightened himself and stepped out of the punt. "Except that it often rains, and sometimes snows, and that here as elsewhere the leaves fall from the trees and the mist creeps up from the river and crawls with ague into undergraduate marrow: apart from a few considerations of that sort, it's always like this. For centuries the little victims have played, unconscious of their coming doom. This is the last enchanted chamber before youth steps out into reality. Oxford is full of bells. They have been sounding for centuries, and they always sound the knell of passing youth. This, my dear Fran, is a very sad city. It is the city of perpetual farewell."

She looked at him with round serious eyes. He was laughing. How handsome he was! He was all in cream: cream flannel trousers, cream shirt, and cream blazer touched with some bright colours of heraldry. He ran up the slope to meet his mother who had stepped out of a taxi.

Iris kissed Frances, with an arm around her: a kiss, not the conventional rub of cheek to cheek. I felt that she liked the girl.

"Well, Ted. This is charming. I didn't know you were to be here."

"Nor I you. Fran and I stayed at the Golden Cross last night."

"And I at the Mitre. Adam, darling, you do arrange the most enchanting surprises."

"Yes, Mamma. I am a wizard. Shall we get aboard? That is, if Fran agrees that to step into this oblong box is to get aboard. I must say it's my idea of the perfect ship, and the perfect voyage:

> Where falls not hail, or rain, or any snow,
> Nor ever wind blows loudly."

Iris had settled herself, and Frances, getting in after her, said:

> "But it lies
> Deep-meadowed, happy, fair with orchard lawns
> And bowery hollows crown'd with summer sea."

433

I got in, and Adam pushed out the punt, crying:

> "So said he, and the barge with oar and sail
> Moved from the brink, like some full-breasted swan
> That, fluting a wild carol ere her death,
> Ruffles her pure cold plume, and takes the flood
> With swarthy webs."

We glided past the banks where the anemones lie like blue stars on the grass, and the sun came out, turning into chains of silver the water falling from the punt pole.

"But there's one thing," Frances said. "I don't know what he means when he talks about 'bowery hollows crown'd with summer sea.' A bowery hollow surely is on the land. How can the sea crown it – that is, be over it?"

"You horrible little literalist," Adam said. "Give the bard his head. Old Alfred liked words as words. He liked to see them sparkling off his pen like this water sparkling off the pole. So long as there's a silver gleam in 'em . . ."

"Yes, that's all very well, but–"

They were happily away. The banks moved by, and the sun strengthened. The river smell was in our nostrils, and a gentle slap-slap sounded under the bows. Iris caught my eye and smiled. I was very happy.

5

How do you keep so young? I wondered, watching her. She was, as usual, in filmy black, and a sunshade of chiffon in black and white kept the sun off her face. She was full breasted like the swan Tennyson had written about, and her clothes made no attempt to conceal that, or to deny the slender length of her limbs. Here, I thought, in this varnished gliding box, are four people in love. But I am also in love with Prue, and Frances is also in love with Stephen. Frances is in love with whichever of them is with her: Adam or Stephen. And I am in love with whichever of them is with me: Prue or Iris.

6

I remember kingcups – such kingcups as Blanche and I used to find edging with their green and gold embroidery our enchanted pool at Northenden. We would take them home clutched in our hot hands, the stems hanging like queens' limp necks, unable to sustain the burden of their crowns. My mother would put them into "the Truro pot" and by morning they would have drunk deep and strengthened themselves: the hollow green tubes would be rigid, holding up bravely the golden clusters. I remember cresses trailing in the flood, and the smell of mint, and places where the broken banks sloped in ramps of brown clay to the water and the cattle came out of the fields and stood there knee-deep, looking at us with their velvet eyes as the punt slipped by. Adam standing up against the sky's blue, his shirt-sleeves rolled above his elbows; Frances singing quietly to herself; Iris half-asleep; the blue air untroubled by a single cloud, warm as the air of June, vibrant with sun and the multitudinous murmur of creatures that lived brief lives upon the wing.

"For a poet, darling," Iris said, "you have sound ideas about food."

Adam laughed. "There's a lot of it," he admitted; "but it's all manna and ambrosia."

The punt was tied to a willow, and upon the grass of the bank he had spread rugs and disposed the bright cushions. Then he unpacked the baskets and laid out the cutlery and crockery. He unwrapped the damp napkins that held the sandwiches. "You see! Pâté de foie gras. Cucumber. Caviare. And these tarts that melt in the mouth – 'with jellies soother than the creamy curd, and lucent syrops tinct with cinnamon.' Well, sit you all down. Let us recreate Manet's *Déjeuner sur l'herbe*."

"It will be only an approximation, hardly a recreation," I advised him.

"Yes," he said. "Convention forbids. This is not Parsons Pleasure."

7

The warmth lasted into the evening. There was a dance, and Adam was to take Frances to it. We were to dine first at the Golden Cross, and now Adam and Iris were there with me, sitting in the courtyard, sipping sherry as we waited for Frances. It was quiet. A few vines climbed upon the walls; a few shrubs stood about in tubs on the flagged pavement. We seemed to be centuries removed from the traffic that hardly made itself heard in Cornmarket, beyond the ancient archway. Adam, in full fig, made me feel old and shabby: I had not changed from my flannel bags and tweed jacket. He was silent: not morose, but collected within his own thoughts. Presently he said "Mamma, you've never played in Shakespeare."

"No, darling, somehow that's never come my way."

"Every actress," he assured her, "should play in Shakespeare before she dies."

"I expect I shall. I'm not dead yet, you know."

He took her hand with the spontaneous affection that was so beautiful in him and that she prized. "No, no. I'm not thinking of sitting upon the ground and telling sad tales about the death of kings – or queens. But this courtyard makes me think of Shakespeare. You know, it's ten to one he saw it, more or less as we see it now. He was here a lot. Just think, Dook, when you go to bed tonight you may be in a room where he lay awake, tossing on his bed and thinking out his lines. The death of Ophelia. He could have been on the river, just as we've been today. It would give him the mood, wouldn't it? – and the imagery. 'There is a willow grows aslant a brook, that shows his hoar leaves in the glassy stream.' It could be."

"Yes, it could. I wonder what he would have written about today?"

"Everything on God's earth, and in heaven and hell, as he would have done whenever he had existed," said Adam. "And of course nowadays that includes flying."

"Are you flying now?"

"Oh, yes, whenever I get a chance."

Frances stood for a moment framed in the old doorway of the inn, and upon the ancient background, dark with dead centuries, she was like a daffodil blooming against a winter that has lasted too long. This was the first time I had seen her in evening clothes. I was so accustomed to another Frances, to a long-legged, brown ragamuffin climbing in and out of boats, careless and dishevelled, a creature of woods and winds, that I caught my breath as she paused, smiling in the dusk that was thickening into one more night of the many nights that had added up into so many years, so many lives here come and gone. She was wearing a dress of gold lamé. It clasped her body like a skin and belled into wide skirts from beneath which her gilded shoes peeped forth. Her hair, that I had been accustomed to see bound anyhow to her head so that it should not fly as wildly as the spray that wetted it, was gathered over either ear into a gold-lacquered whorl. There was a gravity about her as well as a beauty, as though this were a conscious moment of stepping upon a new scene for the opening of a new act. She was nineteen. She came forward, and in the evening quiet the dress made a metallic rustle, like the scraping of beetles' wings.

Adam and Iris, who were sitting with their backs to her, turned at the sound, and Adam got up to place a chair. She did not at once sit down, for Iris, without rising, took her hand and looked her carefully up and down. "My dear," she said, "just before you came I was saying to Adam that I'm not dead yet. But I don't know – really, I don't know."

She got up and kissed the girl, and Frances said she would not have sherry, and we all went in to dinner.

There is one other thing I remember of the evening. We strolled about the streets, Iris and I, when those two were gone, aimlessly beneath old towers and past dark crumbling gateways, and along lanes and alleys shut in by walls on whose crenellated summits tufty weeds were etched against a starry windless sky. We had little enough to say, for the thoughts of both of us were with those others rather than with ourselves, but we went sedately at random, arm in arm, and presently we found ourselves on Folly Bridge. There we came to a stand, leaning upon the bridge and listening to the water whispering by in the darkness.

Iris said: "Did you notice how *proud* of Frances Adam looked?"

"Yes, and that's something – to have Adam proud of you."

"She's a beautiful child, and a great darling. What a bitch I was when I was her age! I feel that I soil her with my eyes."

"You are still a beautiful woman, my dear, and you were always a generous one. You know that I love you, don't you?"

"Yes, Ted, and I love you, too. My life has narrowed down to you and Adam."

After a moment she said: "How badly I put things, darling. My life has deepened to you and Adam."

I took her hand and kissed it, and said: "That is sweet of you. I hope it's true."

"Yes; it is true. Quite simply true."

"I am very happy to think that those two can have the sort of lovely day they have had. How different my childhood was! And yours, too."

"I regret nothing in it," she said. "After all, we had what it takes to give this to those we love. I'm rather tired. I shall go in now."

We walked back to the Mitre, and there I said good night to her, and, rather tired myself, went to my inn and to bed.

8

"Of course," said Stephen, "this sort of thing will soon be coming to an end."

"But for me it's only beginning," Iris reminded him.

We were eating our first evening meal together at Tresco Vean in the late summer of that year, 1935. Prue and Stephen and I, Blanche and Frances, Iris and Adam. We lingered at the table because the evening had settled in with rain, and there was no call to go out of doors. A fire had been lit.

Stephen was right: this sort of thing would end soon, for what he meant was the endless-seeming holiday that summer was at Tresco Vean.

"Before long now," he added, "I shall be through my course, and you'll be done with Oxford, Adam. We'll have to join the respectable ranks – the toiling masses with a fortnight's holiday a year."

And that, I thought, will be the end of my own second youth. Visiting Stephen's school at half term, sneaking over to Oxford to see Adam, dallying here with the young growing things through long summer weeks: it had all given me a spurious but happy sense of being young myself, and I now looked almost inimically at these three. Any one of them might at any moment be so unpardonable as to make me a grandfather, a great-uncle, something abominable like that!

Amy Lingard came in with the coffee. Suddenly I remembered the roly-poly girl who had returned to Hampstead in 1919 after serving with the WAACs. Amy was stout and rather breathless. Her hair was grey. She was still what one called a well-preserved woman. But, good God! I thought, what does one mean by preservation if not artificially arresting the processes of decay?

"Yes," Stephen went remorselessly on, charging his briar pipe. "We're well on the way to becoming the new generation of wage-slaves. What are you going to do, Adam?"

"Join the RAF."

"What on earth for? There's no sense in an air force unless there's a war, and there's no sense in it then, either. Good lord, man, a decent naval gun would shoot a squadron of you out of the sky."

Adam smiled. "My dear antediluvian child! We should come and sit on your funnels and lay eggs in your boiler rooms."

Stephen flushed. "Eggs would be about the weight of it," he said. "What do you think an aeroplane could do against a first-class battleship – or even a destroyer? You'd be like a lot of damned wasps trying to sting a rhinoceros."

"That remains to be seen," Adam said equably. "Anyway, Stevo, I'm surprised to hear you speak up for anything that doesn't sail. I should have thought you'd want to fit out the *Cutty Sark*, or dig the old *Victory* off her moorings, and sail forth pouring broadsides through your wooden walls, with the breeze gaily filling your bedsheets and pocket handkerchiefs."

"They did a job, those ships," Stephen answered, "and that's more than any aeroplane has done in wartime yet. And let me tell you that a man trained in sail would be a better man for that if he found himself in a warship." He said after a moment: "As I should be found if it came to the pinch." His pipe had gone out. He lit it, looking red and agitated.

The conversation died for a time, swallowed in a profound silence. I think we all in that silence heard the future, grisly with sounds that were vague and ill-defined, but menacing.

Presently Adam said: "Well, Stevo, let's enjoy this silken dalliance while we may. When the time comes to lay it in the wardrobe, it's not going to be much fun on sea or in the air."

Stephen got up and brusquely said: "Where's Ernie? I want to go down and have a look at the boat."

Frances said: "I'll come with you. We can manage without Ernie."

A moment later we saw them, crusted in oilskins and seaboots, going arm in arm through the rain. Adam had risen and was standing at the window smoking a cigarette. "I think I'll find an oily and go with them," he said.

Iris said: "Oh, darling! Should you desert me on my first evening here?"

He crushed the cigarette into a tray and said patiently: "Very well, Mamma." He stood at the window watching them till the wet wood took them from sight.

9

There was not a puff of wind. The *Frances and Stephen* had crept out of the river under the engine, the day so unpropitious for sailing that we had not even bothered to take the cover off the mainsail.

"Anyway, it's a nice ride in a taxi," Stephen grumbled, looking up into the unpromising heaven and over the sea that wasn't dappled by a catspaw. We turned down the coast but didn't go far. There was a golden beach, embraced in an arc of rock. We dropped the anchor in three fathoms of water so clear and undisturbed that we could see the crabs crawling sideways over the yellow floor, and shoals of mackerel bait swimming in orderly platoons that wheeled and turned, silver-flashing, as though at a command, and jellyfish wambling near the surface like opened parachutes. Landward, the green water was mottled with lilac, and on the yellow sand a languid tide drew a design of undulant lace. Kittiwakes and herring gulls were shapes of white loveliness upon the sky's breathless blue. For Stephen, it may not have been much of a day, but for the rest of us it was paradisal.

We piled the luncheon baskets into the dinghy. "You row the women ashore, Dook," Stephen said. "Adam and I will undress here and swim it."

Frances, who was barefooted, in a couple of wriggles shrugged herself out of a sweater and skirt. She was wearing a light blue bathing-suit that fitted her like a skin. She threw the skirt and sweater and a towel into the dinghy, and as we moved off she climbed on to the gunwale, stood for a moment surveying the wide prospect of sea and sky, then shot into the water like a blue arrow. The impetus took her under the dinghy. I turned my head and saw her rise to the surface. She trod water, laughing, and when we reached the shore, she was there to give me a hand in pulling the boat through the foam.

We left it there on the edge of the water, for the tide was beginning to ebb, and carried the stuff up the beach to the shadow of the cliff. Adam and Stephen were ashore by now, and we all set to work collecting driftwood. There was plenty of it lying about, bone dry. We built a fireplace of stone, and the fire was started. Adam, Frances and Stephen ran back into the sea. "I'll bathe while the kettle's boiling," I said. "The finest cup of tea you drink in the year is the first one after the first bathe in the summer."

Prue and Blanche were poking sticks under the kettle. "Well, don't be too long," Prue said. "This fire's going like mad. The kettle will soon be boiling."

Iris asked: "Can I help?"

Prue looked up from kneeling on the sand and answered, rather shortly I thought: "Oh, no, thank you. This is a job that looks after itself. And I've become so used to providing Ted's creature comforts. It's a thing I like doing."

"Then I, too, shall bathe," said Iris.

She was standing up very straight, looking down at the other two crouched over the fire. For this holiday occasion she was not wearing black. She was wearing a short-sleeved white linen blouse and a linen skirt in broad vertical stripes of green and white. She wore no stockings, and through open green sandals her painted toenails peeped out. Prue looked at them with distaste, and repeated to me: "Don't be long."

Iris disappeared among the rocks in one direction, and I in another. Presently we stood side by side, with the foam whispering over our feet. She was wearing a white bathing suit as uncompromising as that which emphasised Frances' youthful figure. A white rubber cap confined her hair. Far out, the three young people were shouting and thrashing the water into a sparkling agitation. Frances' clear voice and the deeper voices of the boys came through the crystal morning like the final note that gave meaning to the harmony of air and sky and sun-slashed water. Paddling lazily out, with Iris doing a comfortable breaststroke beside me, I watched Frances' long brown arm come up in a lovely arc, throwing a big rubber ball, and the boys, with powerful trudgen movements, tearing after it, as though life itself depended on being the first to reach it. Iris, too, was watching this play, and now, turning on to her back and floating with her hands finning on either side, she said: "It's more than play out there, you know, Ted. I'm afraid it's a rather desperate situation."

"The oldest one in the world," I said, looking down at her face which seemed beautiful and fulfilled, pillowed on the blue water.

"Yes," she agreed. "Old – but new every morning. Did you notice how Adam wanted to rush after them last night? I had to stop him as best I could. Rather clumsily, I'm afraid."

"You look like Ophelia on her watery bier," I said. "I should like to kiss you as you lie there."

Her eyes had been closed, but now she opened them and gave me a look of utter fright and distraction. "No! No!" she said. And again, "No."

She rolled over and began to swim towards the shore. "I love you, Ted," she said breathlessly. "I love you, love you. But we're old, darling. We're too old to pull things down in ruins. We haven't the strength left to climb over them. We should simply sit among them and weep to see what we had done."

We walked through the fringe of foam, and then she ran as lightly as a girl towards the rocks where she had left her clothes.

10

I came back towards the fire, dressed. Iris was already there. With a smile, Prue lit a cigarette, took a pull, and handed it to me. "I know you like one as soon as you've bathed," she said.

"Yes. Thank you, darling."

The bottom-boards of the dinghy were laid on the sand, and the cups and plates were spread upon them. Prue filled four cups. "We won't wait for the children," she said. "Really, once Stephen gets into the water, you might as well try to lure a porpoise ashore as him."

However, they were already on the way; and with the happy carelessness of youth they did not keep us waiting by bothering to dress. They came as they were to the improvised table, Adam and Stephen wearing nothing but slips, Frances in her bathing suit. The sun was hot. They dried out in a few moments. They were all panting a little. Nothing much was said as we sat there, crisping our toes in the hot sand, munching our pasties, drinking the hot tea tinctured with woodsmoke. It was a rough-and-ready meal compared with the one that four of us had eaten not long before on the river bank near Oxford. Somehow, it seemed to me, this was Stephen, as that had been Adam. I squinted under half-closed lids at the glistered water, at the boat lying out there with her tall naked mast as steady as a flagpole, at the reach of sea and beyond it the white of St Anthony's lighthouse, pastel-blurred by the haze, and I listened to the wild sad crying of the seagulls as they soared and dived. I looked at Frances, and she was wrapped up in this moment, at home in it, loving its dear familiar attributes, as she had loved the new shock of grey towers and crumbling stone and river water and trees white and pink and yellow under the bomb-burst of May. So we all ate, giving our bodies to the sun and our minds to the silence.

Suddenly, Stephen cried: "Gannets! Gannets! We don't see many of them round here!"

We all looked up into the blue, and there they were, two of them, as ethereally white as mountain snow, with a smudge of black: so white and pure that the white of the gulls looked tarnished, so swift upon the wing that now we saw them clearly and, in a matter of seconds it seemed, they were distant crumbs of snow. Then they were back again, and one of them hovered, quivering for a second against the sky, then fell like a white meteor hurled from the blue. The smitten water leapt up in a brief glittering fountain, and Adam shouted: "By God! Well bombed, sir!"

Frances was staring like the rest of us at the beautiful display of speed and precision. She held a teacup in her hand, and at Adam's words she looked at him with a world of sad reproach in her eyes. She put down the cup, and I heard it rattle unsteadily on the board. "Don't, Adam," she said in a low voice. "Don't say things like that."

"But, my dear Frances," he began, "there are such things as bombs in the world." And then, seeing her stricken face, he said: "Oh, darling! I'm sorry. Please – please don't be hurt. It was silly of me."

Before us all, he put an arm round her waist, drew her to him, and kissed her gently on the forehead. There was something beautiful and instinctive about the gesture. It moved me deeply.

Frances coloured violently, and pushed him away. "No. Please," she said. She snatched up her skirt and sweater and ran away to the rocks.

She had been sitting between Adam and Stephen, and as soon as she was out of sight Stephen leaned over towards Adam and said: "Your remark was unnecessary, and your attempt to recover it was offensive."

443

Adam looked astonished. "Well, really," he said, "I seem to be in the wrong with everybody. I apologise, Stephen. I apologise most sincerely if what I did was offensive to you."

"It was offensive to me and it was offensive to Frances."

Adam looked at Stephen's hot flushed face thrust towards his own. He said quietly: "Are you so certain that it was offensive to Frances?"

Stephen slapped him in the face.

For a moment no one spoke. Adam and Stephen looked at one another, and on the face of each was a look of utter surprise. Blanche and Prue seemed shocked, and, as for me, I felt as though a horrid experience that had been boiling up in dream had suddenly become true on waking.

At last Adam said: "If I deserved that, I suppose you had to do it. But I still don't think that I did."

He was calm. Stephen's bare body was heaving with agitation. "Well," Stephen said, "what are you going to do about it?"

"Do? What is there to do? I don't carry my rapier when I bathe. Besides, I am not interested in horseplay."

His attitude, tinged with a faint disgust, left Stephen defenceless.

Blanche said fatuously: "You'd better shake hands and make it up."

Adam looked up at her, his deep blue-black eyes seeming filled with a wonder that naiveté could be so complete. Those eyes considered her for a long moment from under the raven wing of his hair. He said nothing. She endured that pregnant look for a while, then her glance faltered and she cried fussily: "Well, we'd better gather up these things."

Prue said: "Yes; it's time we were making a move. Give us a hand, Stephen." He began obediently to help them.

Iris had said nothing. She sat there, a hand on either side of her pressed down into the hot sand, watching the drama with a look almost of exultation on her face. She was enjoying the moment: there was no doubt about that. It was something she understood far more deeply than either Prue or Blanche. It was a fight for a woman that had openly declared itself. The sight of those two young almost naked bodies confronting one another by the sea, under the sun, was pagan and immemorial. It stirred and excited her. I felt that she was pleased with Adam. There had been no need for her to intervene. He had chosen not to declare his hand, to keep all his guns masked.

444

Adam said: "I'll go aboard and dress." He pulled the dinghy into the water, and Iris said: "You might as well put me aboard while you're about it." He lifted her up easily, carried her through the shallows, and put her down in the boat. I knew that she wanted to talk to him alone.

I filled my pipe and went along the beach to the rocky spur behind which Frances had disappeared, leaving so much agitation in her wake. I saw her, dressed, wandering on the sand a long way off. She was walking slowly, her eyes on the sand, and she paused now and then to pick something up. I quickened my pace and overtook her, and said: "Hallo, Fran. What are you up to?"

"Oh, hallo, Dook. I'm looking for cowries. They're usually to be found on this beach." She opened her hand and showed me half a dozen of the lovely little shells lying in her palm.

I joined her in the search. Without looking up, she asked presently: "Where are Stephen and Adam?"

"Everybody's packing up. Time to be getting home."

She straightened and said: "Oh, but it's so early! I thought we were making a day of it? I know that Mother packed the tea-things. Amy made a lot of little cakes, and . . ."

Her voice petered out. She looked at the rosy shells lying in her hand, but she was not seeing them. Suddenly she threw them away. "I suppose there was a row," she said.

"Yes."

We stood silent, looking out at the sparkling water. We could see the *Frances and Stephen*. We could see Adam and Iris leaning on the rail, their dark heads together.

"Everything's ruined," Frances said forlornly. "Everything's finished. And it was so lovely. All this . . . the sea and the sand . . . the birds and the cowrie shells . . ."

She was fighting hard not to cry. I began to chaff her. "You ought to know better, Fran – you, a playwright! If this is the end of anything, it's not the end of the play – only of an act. Act One, at that."

She looked at her hands that had lately held the pretty toys, and dusted off a little sand. "Do you remember," she asked, "the first time Adam came here, and how he went away the next morning?"

"Yes, I remember it well."

"And here he is, as though that had never happened."

The thought seemed to give her comfort.

445

"Of course," she said, "if he and Stephen have quarrelled, he'll go away again."

"I'm afraid there's no doubt about that."

We began to walk back towards the others. "Fran," I said, "be as sharp as you please with me if you think I'm an interfering old fool. You can tell me to go to the devil if you like. But I feel I've got some sort of right to know where we all stand. Stephen was infuriated because he saw Adam put an arm round you and kiss you. When you were gone, he slapped him in the face."

She winced.

"There. Now you know exactly what happened. Had you given Stephen any right to feel so resentful?"

"He wants to marry me."

"Are you sure of that? Has he said so?"

"Oh, yes."

"And Adam?"

She stopped. She was barefooted. I saw her toes curling violently into the sand and her fingers clenching. "Oh, for God's sake," she cried, "leave me alone!"

"I see. I'm sorry, darling. Cry, if you want to."

She did. We had come to the spur of rock that hid the stretch of beach where the others were waiting. In the shadow of the rock she came into my arms and laid her head upon my shoulder. She shook with sobs for a long time. Then we heard Prue's voice calling: "Ted! Ted! Everybody's waiting!"

Frances pulled herself together. A freshwater rill tinkled down the rocks, and I dipped my handkerchief in it and handed it to her silently. She pressed it to her eyes and nose and forehead. "Now," she said, "if you've got a cigarette . . ."

I lit one and gave it to her, and bravely enough she stepped out with me to meet the party on the beach.

11

Bugsby, who had seemed an almost inevitable diffident intruder into our holiday at one point or another, did not arrive that year. He had become engaged to be married, and proposed to do some sailing from the Mersey with his girl. Stephen mentioned this in the course of a difficult lugubrious dinnertime. We were all being appallingly polite and formal about passing the salt and suggesting a second helping, but beyond this, conversation did not get far till Stephen produced Bugsby.

"Then your annual voyage is off?" I asked.

"I don't see why," he said. "I can handle the boat alone. It would be rather fun to do it. Unless you'd like to come, Fran?"

"I don't know," she answered. "I should have to think about that."

"There's one thing," he said, "before I go there'll have to be some ballast shifting. I don't like the way she's lying. Seems to me to be a bit down by the nose. I'm going along now with Ernie to have a look at her. Coming?"

He pushed back his chair. After a moment's hesitation, Frances got up and followed him.

"You know, Mamma," said Adam, "even in vacation the Anglo-Saxons pursue me. Will you all forgive me? I must go to my room. I don't suppose I shall see you again tonight, darling." He kissed his mother and went.

Twilight filled the room. The lights had not been put on. "Well, now," said Iris in a voice of reasonable accommodation, "I could do the thing in accordance with custom. That is, I could send a telegram from the post office in the nearest village, recalling me and Adam to London. Or, in the morning, we could just pack up and go. Which do you think would be the better?"

With one voice Prue and Blanche began to protest.

"Oh, but you're not going away? You've hardly arrived. You haven't begun to see what there is here."

And: "Just a boys' quarrel. You can't break up a holiday for that! Why, in a day's time they'll be playing together like puppies."

Iris looked at them both, and her look was the deeply understanding look that Adam had turned on Blanche when she advised him to "shake hands and make it up." She didn't bother to answer them. She understood too much.

"I imagine," I said, "that Adam is packing at this moment. We can dispense with the telegram. I'll get Ernie Lingard to run you into Truro in the morning. That'll save you the bother of changing out of the Falmouth train. If you're ready to leave at about half-past nine you'll have plenty of time. You'll be in London by five, and you can get lunch and tea on the train."

447

Iris laughed. "What an assemblage of comfortable hard facts! You sound like the man from Cook's, Ted. It's obviously untrue that artists are woolly-minded. But you're quite right. We must go. Will you all forgive me? I'll join Adam in his Anglo-Saxon studies."

That night, when we were in bed, Prue said: "Does it strike you, Ted, that tonight you did something you've never done before?"

I thought it over. I didn't like the sound of Prue's voice. "No," I said. "I can't think of anything."

"You've never before had one of our visitors taken through to Truro. If it was a bother to change out of the Falmouth train, at least it never bothered *you*."

"Well," I said placatingly, "Iris and Adam carry rather a lot of luggage. It would have been an awful bore hauling it round the platforms."

"There are porters."

"Of course. So there are. Well, good night, darling."

"I'm glad that woman's going. I don't like her."

"Why? What's wrong with her?"

"Everything. The way she looks at you. The way you look at her."

"Darling, you're imagining things."

"And that white bathing dress. When she came out of the water it was positively transparent. I thought it disgusting for a woman of her age. She must be as old as you are yourself."

"She's older than I am."

"You know *everything* about her."

I tried to laugh it off. "Prue, darling, please remember you're speaking of a viscountess."

We had been lying in the dark. She sat up and switched on the bed-light. "That's another thing," she said; and it was clear to me that much that had been below the surface was suddenly coming up. "That's another thing. What about that boy? Randle is her stage name. It's not the name that belongs with her title. Why is *he* called Randle? Perhaps he doesn't belong with the title, either. Where does he come from?"

For the first time in my life I felt ashamed of Prue. "Really, my darling," I said, "is that any of our business? Adam is an exceptionally charming young man. I'm pleased to know him, and I'm sorry that for the second time Stephen has caused him to leave this house."

"I'm not sorry," she said with conviction. "Anyone could see with half an eye that Stephen's head over ears in love with Frances and she with him. I want Stephen to be happy, and I don't want to see Frances married to a — a—"

She couldn't get it out. "A bastard," I helped her. And as I spoke the word I could see Blanche turning the ring upon her finger, slipping it off, and showing me the inscription: "F.C. 1916. B.P." And Chellew had worn a ring like it when he dissolved into the bright air. There was so much that Prue didn't know: so much, I thought, about so many things. A huge cloud of sadness weighed me down. "Let us try to sleep," I said. "He won't be here to disturb Frances and Stephen after tomorrow."

12

It was three days later that we went down to the quay to see Stephen and Frances set off on their voyage. He was in the highest spirits. Frances, in corduroy slacks and a blue jersey, looked businesslike but reserved. Stephen took a bundle of charts into the dinghy, shouting: "Something new this time. We shall make for Cork. Perhaps we'll call in at the Isle of Man on the way back. Then the Mersey. We'll look up old Bugsby. Surprise of his life."

It was the first we had heard of the route. They would be away a long time. We watched them climb aboard, tie the dinghy astern, and haul up the mainsail. The buoy splashed overboard and the boat began to move. Blanche and Prue stood there to watch them out of sight, but I gave them a wave and turned away.

The post had come when I got to the house. There was a letter from Iris:

Dear Ted, — I am at a place called Redcar, which they tell me is in Yorkshire, though it feels like Timbuctoo. I am here because Adam, too, has a Bugsby, but with the more agreeable name of Freemantle, who is with Adam at Magdalen. Freemantle's people live in a palatial house in the country outside the town, and Adam and I are in a rather sad hotel. But we put up with it, I because Adam is here, Adam because Freemantle is there, with a private aeroplane. The thing terrifies me every time I look at it. They spend hours together playing with the engine and fastening bits together in what looks to me a dreadfully chancy fashion. Occasionally I see them sailing over my head, and then I shut my eyes tight and pray to God, especially when they go over the sea, though I suppose that would be softer to hit than the land. Then they come down with faces shining like seraphs and fasten up another bit which they think wasn't too good. It would be quite all right now, they say, for me to come and have a flip, but I tell them I have my public to think of.

Rather a wearing life, my dear, but there's going to be a change. I'm being persuaded, very hard, to go out of the country: a long tour, South Africa and Australia. I think soon I shall succumb. If I do, Adam says he will throw his hand in at Oxford and come with me. I'm afraid he's deplorably inconsequent about his Oxford career. By the way, it's a Shakespearean tour at last. I should do Lady Macbeth, and Portia, and the Queen in *Hamlet*, and so forth. So I shall need all your prayers. Adam says: "Send my greetings to the Dook," and here they are,

with all my love.

Iris.

CHAPTER TWELVE

W HEN MY birthday came in 1938, Blanche handed me a pipe across the breakfast table, wished me "Many happy returns of the day," and said: "Next time, you will be fifty." "Never mind next time," I answered shortly. "I am in my forties."

It seemed important to emphasise that. When you are in your fifties, the next thing you will be in is your sixties, and that's really getting near to closing time.

Time, gentlemen!

"I'm pretty young for a grandfather," I said. "I should say a grandfather in his forties is rare enough."

Blanche soothed me. "Yes. And, of course, artists are notoriously long-lived."

"I wish I had been born a few months later," I said. "February is a poor month for a birthday. Mother once told me that I was born in a snowstorm. She lay there groaning, and watching the snow driving past the window. I suppose that's why I hate English bedrooms that never have any warmth or cheer."

"It was pleasant enough," Blanche recalled, "that birthday of yours when we met Captain Marquick. Do you remember? We came down the road from Northenden, and his victoria nearly ran us over. We went in and had tea with him and talked about you wanting to paint and me wanting to dance. What a funny pair of kids we were! Ah, well! My dancing days were few, and soon ended."

She got up and walked to the sideboard to refill her teacup. Yes, I thought, poor Blanche! You don't look a dancer now. She had thickened. Arms and legs were heavy. Her face had a placidity that was almost stupid. It was a placidity that had nothing to do with serenity, life's last and hard-won guerdon. It was almost, indeed, vacuity. I brought before my eyes a picture that I could put there at any time, complete and shining: the picture of Blanche, thin, long in the leg, with her skirt tucked up, swooping and dancing in a springtime field.

"If I could choose," I said, dutifully filling the presentation pipe, "I would be born in May. Then, when I was in my fifties — which please to remember I am not yet — I could look back on the wonderful birthdays of my youth. In a punt on a river, with the trees exploding into bloom, and a girl and a lunch basket. Perhaps in the evening she would come to a dance with me. That would be something like a birthday."

"We'd better give Amy a chance to clear up. What shall you do today? I suppose you won't be going to the studio?"

"No. This morning I shall potter about. This afternoon I shall go and see Frances and John. Are you coming?"

She lit a cigarette. "No. I'm going to a bridge tea at Mrs Elland's. Where is my *Vogue*? Have you taken away that box of chocolates?"

She began to fuss around, and I went upstairs to my den to fill a seasoned pipe.

2

In this house had been my mother and my wife, Frances and my son. Now there was only Blanche. I lived with her in a state of nervous irritation. She was increasingly untidy, loose-ended and aimless. A fool would have called her lucky, would have thought that life had given her everything. I bore with her as tenderly as I could, because I knew it had given her nothing. Nothing of value except one shining hour, which, like her dancing days, was soon ended. I did not know how far, now, even that had significance for her. Once Frances had married Stephen, and they had both resisted and overcome her efforts to make them live with us, she had disintegrated with pitiful speed.

Amy Lingard had lit a fire in my room. It was a day without heart or spirit: not cold enough to invigorate, but damp, dun and unprepossessing. The clouds beyond the window were like tangled grey knitting.

Not a cheerful birthday, but at least it had not the horror of my birthday last year. That was the day of Prue's funeral.

Jesse Cleghorn's portrait that I had painted so long ago — dear God! I thought, the first, the very first of all the portraits I had painted, except the youthful self-portrait that set me on the way – was on the wall facing me; and my mind went in a dizzy backward march among the princes and potentates, the generals and admirals, the Lord Mayors and Vice-Chancellors, the playboys and society girls, reaching back and back through time to the morning when two young men in knickerbockers had ridden their bicycles to our little house in Didsbury, and one of them had said: "Ah, Prue!"

I felt a bit cheered as I looked at the picture. Certainly, that boy in Manchester had had something. Here in this face was the serenity that more and more seemed to me the golden gift that could not be striven for, but that a fortunate few who lived wisely might find at the end to be the climate of their lives. Old Kitto had had it, and a few others I had known. It seemed to be what was left in the sieve when all that was superfluous had been riddled through.

There was much between me and serenity that birthday morning, and especially there was all that had darkened the end of my time with Prue. I recalled the morning when Stephen and Frances sailed away. Presently Blanche and Prue came up from the quay, and the three of us sat down to drink coffee on the terrace. Nothing was said for a time, and I think that we all felt unspeakably dreary. I am sure that I did. There had been seven of us, and now there were three, and of the four who were gone three were youth and hope and the future. I felt as though a dark door had been banged in my face, and there was, on this side of it, nothing but the memory of how Stephen and Adam had collided, how Frances had wept, and how Prue had chided me.

On the morning when Ernie Lingard took Iris and Adam to Truro I reacted as Frances used to do to her misfortunes when she was younger. I went to feed the chickens. They had a run wired off under some fine old beeches, well away from the house. It was a quiet, reassuring spot to browse and linger in if one felt below the weather. I filled the water bowls, threw the handfuls of golden maize, watched the scrambling birds for a time, and then, determined to keep away as long as possible, began to clear the mess from the dropping-boards in the henhouse. The door darkened, and I looked up to see Prue standing there. I came out of the house, filled my pipe, and said: "Well, they got away. I really think it was a good idea to send them in to Truro."

Prue, who was usually a calm and equable person, was clearly in a state of distress. For a time she did not speak, then she said, the words coming in an urgent rush: "Ted, I want you to promise me not to see that woman again."

I did not answer this, and after waiting for a moment she asked: "How long have you known her?"

"Oh, I've seen her off and on during a fair time. Some years now."

"How many years?" she persisted.

"What does it matter? Some years."

"Do you recall the first time Stephen met her?"

It had slipped my mind, and I said: "What's the matter, Prue? What are you getting at?"

"Let me remind you. It was more than what you call some years. It was a good many years. You were to meet him in London when he came down from school, and you weren't there. He tried to find you, and at last he went to Luther Brimlow's house. Luther took him to a flat in St James' Square, and there you were, and there was a lady. Oh, yes, he told us all about it when he came on to Cornwall. You see, it had been quite an adventure for him – having to seek you out like that, and the afternoon on the river at Richmond, and all the rest of it. It's a long time ago, isn't it? And how long before that? Do you still call it a few years?"

She looked old and tired – more old and tired than I had ever seen her. "Do we need to go into all this, my darling?" I asked.

"Now that we've begun it, let's finish it. That was a miserable holiday for me, Ted. I kept saying to myself: 'If he tells me about her, it's all right.' Because you did – didn't you? You told me about every sitter you ever had. We've had many a laugh over them – haven't we? And all through that holiday I waited, and you told me nothing. You didn't even speak of forgetting to meet Stevo. It was as though you shut the whole thing away in a place that I couldn't get at and I was afraid. I've been afraid ever since."

All around our feet the hens were pecking over the last of the grain. There wasn't much left.

"I didn't like Iris from the moment I met her, but I tried to, for your sake. Of course, I didn't guess who she was at first. But when I found that her flat was in St James' Square I began to wonder, and when Adam said one day: 'Mamma, how long are you going to stay in that old flat? You've been there for years and years,' I knew that you had known that flat for years and years, too."

She began to cry. "Oh, Ted, can you imagine what it's like, can you understand how beastly and horrible one feels, when one listens for stray words that add up against someone you love?"

I took her in my arms, and said fatuously: "Darling, don't worry about Iris. She's a good woman."

"I don't care," Prue burst out, "if she's the best woman God ever made. It's horrible and degrading to feel used, and ordinary and unexciting. And that's how she makes me feel to you."

"No, no," I protested.

"Oh, don't talk nonsense to me," she said. "She's famous, and she's striking to look at, and I'm neither the one nor the other, and never was. I've never been anything but a woman who liked looking after men – first my uncle, and then you. I suppose it's not enough."

"Let's go in, darling. Let's leave this alone. You've nothing to worry about."

She stood away from me, and said: "It hasn't been easy to begin, but now that I *have* begun I shall say all that's in my heart. There was a day when I was in town, just before this holiday started. I called at your studio, thinking we might have lunch together, and you weren't in. Then I walked out into the yard, and I noticed the signboard of the public house there. You could hardly fail to know who it was, could you? And I knew you had painted it. Oh, I've never been of the slightest use to you in your work, but at least I know it when I see it. So I went into that public house to pry on you. All my decency urged me not to, but I went, and ordered some filthy drink that I didn't want, and chatted with the landlord. I said that his sign was remarkably like a portrait of Iris Randle, and he answered: 'Oh, yes, it's Miss Randle all right. Mr Pentecost painted that, he did. I've known the times when they were in and out here a lot, them two.' Them two! You can imagine how I loved to hear that! And then she came down here, and I hated her like poison. I hated the way you looked at her, and the way you got up when she came into a room. It's a long time since you've done that for me. And I was glad – ay, glad with all my heart – when Stephen struck that boy, because I knew then that they'd have to go."

At last she had finished, and at that moment Stephen and Frances went by, outside the hen run; and Stephen shouted: "Fran and I are running in to Falmouth. We've decided on a voyage together, and there are a few things we must buy – we need some new rigging screws for one thing."

So that they should not see the agitation of our faces, we stayed where we were till the car was gone. Then Prue gathered the eggs from the nests and left me.

3

The few days that followed before the children sailed away were horrible – horrible with the necessity to play one's part with a normal face while walking on the edge of chaos; and the nights were worse: the nights when we did not say "Sleep well," but got wordlessly into the great double bed and took care to lie apart from one another.

And so the morning came when Stephen and Frances went, and I walked up alone from the quay and read Iris' letter with a ghastly sense of guilt. I put a match to it in the lounge fireplace and watched it shrivel to ashes. I stirred them with my foot, and then, seeing Prue and Blanche come up, went out and joined them at coffee on the terrace.

It was as lovely a day as we had ever known at Tresco Vean. All the world was full of the light of a temperate sun, and the great trees, through whose walls on either hand the lawn ran down to the quay, were tranced in the majestical pause that lies between knowledge of what has been and acceptance of what is to come.

But all this had no power over our hearts.

"I have been thinking about this place," Blanche said. "I have decided to sell it."

Neither Prue nor I answered her. Even a few days ago I would have reacted with a shocked protest. Now the words sounded inevitable, almost expected.

"What's the use of it any longer?" Blanche asked. "Stephen was right. The long holidays are over."

The trees, which had been utterly still, all trembled to a breath so gentle that we did not feel it. It was as though they had shuddered, and then were still again.

"It costs me a lot of money," Blanche said, "and from now on there'll be very little value in return."

"What will you do with Ernie?" I asked.

"Oh, I expect that whoever takes the place will be glad to keep him on."

"He may not want to stay with strangers. He's known us a long time."

"That's his lookout."

What on earth was the matter with us all? Why should Blanche answer with so sharp a bark? I got up and walked away, offended with her; and my heart said to me: "Oh, God, man! Do try to *understand* something. Isn't *her* heart broken, too? Is it easy to know that so much is finished, and that so little remains to be done?"

4

There was no boat to sail, and rowing a dinghy in the river wasn't much fun. Prue and Blanche were melancholy companions, and the holiday which I had hoped would be one of the best we ever had was the worst. It was filled not only with present distress but also with an apprehension of finality: of being in a dark place that would not lighten. I walked a great deal alone: I walked for miles and miles, puffing a pipe and swinging a stick. The perfect weather was an ironical benediction: a hand uplifted in blessing in the condemned cell. I could not see a sail upon the blue without a prayer that it was bearing Frances and Stephen unexpectedly homeward. I yearned for young life: in the crying of the curlews there was an ancient and terrible beauty. Every part of life's atmosphere and envelope was beautiful: the majestic flying of the wild swans; the green and white, the lilac and amethyst of the sea lying beyond the yellow sand of little coves; the fresh air of the morning and the burning splendour of the sun's down-going. But all this was beyond me and outside me: the vital duct through which it might have flowed was choked and atrophied.

Ernie Lingard was my only human comfort. We spent hours together with a two-handed saw, preparing wood for winter fires, not saying much, but close together. Even in this soothing occupation there was a sting, for the question rose up: "Who will sit by these fires? Will Tresco Vean be gone from us before winter comes?"

457

"It's a bit dull like, without t'children," Ernie said, pausing to mop his forehead. "There don't seem much for me to do 'ere nowadays. Stevo likes to do it all himself."

"They grow up, Ernie. They leave us in the lurch."

"Too true, Dook. This place is beginnin' to give me t'creeps. It's like an empty nest when t'birds 'ave flown."

Well, we all flew a few days later. The holiday was being so manifestly a failure that Blanche announced brusquely that she was packing up. I think that, having decided to sell the place, she wanted to leave it at once. Prue and I returned to London with her. A note was written to await Frances and Stephen, asking them to follow. There is nothing more to be said about Tresco Vean. It was sold before the year was out. It was resold a year later; and then it became a country hotel, with fancy trimmings added to the old building. Everything went: even the dinghies, even the *Frances and Stephen*. I understood why the trees had shuddered.

I was glad to be able to lift Ernie clear of the wreckage. Old Henry Opie was dead. For some time my chapel-studio had been without a caretaker. Ernie and his wife moved in there. I bought him a motor launch, and during the months of Falmouth's "season" he used her as a pleasure boat and made enough to live on during the winter. I hung on to the old chapel because it reminded me of my youth and of Kitto, and because now it was all the stake I had in Cornwall, the memorial stamping ground of the Kittos and the Pentecosts.

5

I had known Sir Ernest Wittering for a long time. He was one of the few architects to become Royal Academicians, and that, among other things, had brought us together. During Stephen's first vacation from the School of Architecture in Liverpool I had taken him out to lunch and we had run into Wittering in the restaurant. The three of us lunched together, and I discovered for the first time that Wittering was a keen sailing man. He had a converted Brixham trawler lying at Burnham-on-Crouch. It had long been Stephen's ambition to sail something bigger than a Falmouth quay punt, and a Brixham trawler was just his idea of the sort of boat he wanted to have. It was not surprising that he and Wittering got on well together. They were blue water enthusiasts: I was left out of the conversation. Wittering invited

Stephen to go down at the weekend and have a look at the trawler, and the boy went gladly.

From this propitious beginning, Wittering's interest in Stephen developed, and it became understood that when Stephen was finished with Liverpool he should enter Wittering's office. He did this; and then he and Frances married.

When they came back from their voyage together they were very close to one another. Those days of placid weather that we had spent at Tresco Vean had not been universally placid. The *Frances and Stephen* had run into a good deal of bad weather. A Falmouth quay punt is a stout and serviceable little boat, but it is a little boat, and it was not the weather for fools to be at sea in little boats. Each learned how far the other was removed from being a fool. They had to rely on one another, and they found with what completeness they *could* rely on one another. They made the voyage they had intended to make, despite Bugsby's advice to leave the boat at Liverpool and go home overland. They returned radiant with achievement and with confidence in one another.

The autumn was almost upon us then, and at my studio I received a letter from Iris, telling me that she had decided to make the Dominions tour. Adam would go with her. I saw and heard nothing more of her or Adam till the spring, and then it was only from the newspapers that I learned they had sailed. Nor did I hear anything further until the autumn, when a letter came from Adam, giving me a full and humorous account of the "Black Widow's" tour and triumphs. It ended like this:

"She has decided to retire from the stage, and I think this is the moment for her to do it. *Finis coronat opus.* She has had a hard life, she is wealthy, and she is tired. This will reach you when autumn is lapsing into winter, which is to say when, over here, spring is growing into summer. Why should we come back to endure your fogs and the black wintral miseries of London? (I think Frances will like the word wintral.) The bathing beaches near Sydney are beyond compare, so we shall make no comparisons, but see the summer through here. Then we shall ship home and lay hold at once of *your* summer, learning from the wisdom of the swallows. Perhaps then it will be possible to tie together the threads so harshly snapped at Tresco Vean? Or perhaps not. How can I know? I can only say how happy I should be if it were possible, although my time is not likely to be my own. I shall join the Air Force as soon as I return. I have had some good flying here, but the Widow still insists on keeping her pretty feet firmly anchored to earth. Bless you, my dearest Dook. All our love. Adam."

I didn't know whether or not "wintral" would appeal to Frances; but I was sure it was the sort of question that would never enter Stephen's head. I decided that this was hardly the moment to test her in such a matter. She and Stephen were to be married next week. For some weeks after her return from the voyage she had gone anxiously to the letter tray in the hall each morning, but for a long time now she had not done this.

6

I shall interpolate here two small incidents of that year 1936. The clash between me and Prue in the hen run at Tresco Vean made a deep mark on my mind for many reasons. Not least because what boiled up then had been simmering in Prue's mind for years. Few things, I think, are more terrible, more destructive of harmony and integrity, than furtive sipping at a hidden poison. I was almost glad when it was out. Now at least we could face one another with clean if painful wounds. It was a situation which made me ponder upon many things, and I thought of the day, years before, when I had picked up the book full of Frances' infant scribblings and had come upon the Lutherans. I thought, too, of the strange, solitary remark the child had made at that time – that Brimlow was not her father. Whether time had lightened what was evidently a real, if unrecognised, obsession I did not know, but I did not want Frances to enter upon marriage with bogies clotting her imagination. I spoke of this to Blanche, who was ready enough to leave the task to me.

I arranged the matter as obviously as I could. I asked Frances to take tea with me in my studio, on the pretence that I wanted her to choose a picture as a wedding present. During my holidays it was agreeable to take a rest from portrait work by doing an occasional landscape, and there were a dozen or more of these, all painted near Tresco Vean, in the studio. While waiting for Frances to come, I took the portrait of Francis Chellew and my childhood portrait of Frances and hung them side by side over the mantelpiece. It was a dusky afternoon; when Frances arrived the fire was lit, and the only other light in the studio came from the concealed strips over the two pictures.

We sat near the fire and I gave her tea. Her glance again and again sought out the portraits. Presently she knocked me off my perch by asking frankly: "Why the rearrangement of pictures, Dook? What do you want to tell me about those hit-me-in-the-eye portraits?"

There was nothing for it but to be equally frank. "I believe there was a time when you were impressed by a similarity between them?"

"I didn't know you'd been studying psychoanalysis," she said. "Or is it the police method of confrontation? Let me give you some tea."

"I thought I was the host here."

"Look at your hand. I wouldn't trust you with the teapot."

Indeed, my hand was trembling; but so was hers. The tea slopped into the saucer and onto the cloth. She left the cup half-empty and put the pot down.

"I suppose I don't need to tell you," she said in a hard voice, "that I loathed my father like poison? That's the beginning, isn't it? I didn't see much of him, as you know, but even as a child I found that little was too much. I used to tremble when he spoke to me and shudder when he kissed me. I hated him."

She examined her clenched hands, and I said: "By accident, I happen to know that. I chanced to pick up something you had written about the Lutherans."

"Do you know, Dook," she said, "I was such a little fool that for years I thought I'd made the Lutherans up. I didn't realise that they had anything to do with him. I only knew it one night after he had struck me. Did you ever strike Stevo?"

"I'm afraid so."

"Well, I imagine that was different. He came into my bedroom in Bedford Square one night when I was asleep. He was all dolled up. I suppose he'd been to some dinner. I woke up, and there he was. He was even wearing an opera hat. I think he was a bit tight. There was a red carnation in his buttonhole. The dreadful thing was, I had been dreaming about that stuff I used to write – I often did then. And there he was. I wanted to let out a scream, and couldn't, just as if it was a nightmare. I put my hand in front of my mouth, and I imagine I looked absolutely terror-stricken."

I managed now to pour her out some more tea, and she drank it eagerly.

"He had been smiling in a silly affectionate way, but suddenly his face went livid. He walked to the bed, pulled my hand down from in front of my mouth, and said: 'You silly little bitch! I only came in to kiss you good night.' I continued to look at him, with his reality all mixed up with my dreams, and my terror must have infuriated him. Anyway, he suddenly gave me a slap in the face that jarred the teeth in my head, and went out of the room. When I got to sleep again, I dreamed some more."

"I wish you'd told someone," I said.

"Ah, well, I was one of those little fools who tell it all to themselves. Perhaps I still am. Anyway, I began from then on to take refuge in telling myself that he wasn't my father. It was just about that time that I found these two portraits in your studio, and on the strength of the likeness I began to build up the fantasy that *this* was my father."

Her eyes lifted again to the portrait of Chellew.

"Would you be surprised," I asked, "to know that it was?"

She was calmer now. She was even smiling. "Not a bit," she said. "You know, Dook, growing up as I did, it was impossible not to know that things weren't right between my father and mother. I often wondered about it. I continued to keep it to myself but it wasn't fantasy now. It was something I could reason about. I couldn't help seeing that they were nothing to one another – nothing, except as a matter of form. If there had been anybody else, then it was likely to be someone you, too, were acquainted with, and as you have an incurable habit of painting your acquaintances – well, that, combined with a more than striking likeness, made me at least *think*. However, I've gone on, as you see, telling it all to myself. Even in these emancipated days, one doesn't like to think certain things about one's mother, or relish the idea of being a bastard."

"This tea's nothing but cold slops. Let me make some more."

I hurried into my small scullery to give her a chance to compose herself. When I had come back and refilled the cups, she lit a cigarette and said: "Your turn, Dook."

I told her the story of Blanche and Francis Chellew. She was silent for a time, turning upon her finger the ring that Stephen had given her. When at last she spoke, my heart was filled with happiness. "I'm so glad you told me," she said. "I feel cleaner."

Presently she added: "I'd better tell Stephen."

"No, no," I said. "Don't do that. This is something that concerns only you and your mother. I felt you'd be happier if your mind had no tangles. That's all that matters."

"My mind *is* happier," she said. "I feel that I've sloughed a dirty skin. But all the same . . ."

However, I persuaded her to leave the matter where it was.

7

The other thing that happened was this, and it happened when the winter had come, after the young people were married. A series of lectures upon art was arranged by the Manchester Art Galleries Committee, and I was invited to visit the city and deliver the first of them. I had no wish to linger in Manchester. All the ties that had bound me to the place were snapped. My father and mother were dead. Anatole Lop and Captain Marquick were dead. Jesse Cleghorn was dead. The place was like a graveyard, and out of it a ghost arose.

I didn't reach the city till late afternoon, and I stayed at the Queen's Hotel so as to be near the London Road station for an early departure in the morning. I had had a few hospitable invitations, but I declined them all. I would arrive, have dinner, deliver my lecture, get straight back to my hotel, read for an hour or two in bed, and be away as soon as I had had breakfast in the morning. What was there in Manchester that could concern me now?

It was filthy weather. I walked from the station to the hotel through flurries of snow, and underfoot the pavements would have been white but for the people churning the snow to slush. The weather remained bad, and the consequence was that my lecture was delivered to a patient and optimistic handful of people. I was glad when it was over and I was making a zigzag journey through the back streets between the Art Gallery and the hotel. There was hardly a soul about. There never is at night in Manchester, except on a couple of main streets. The snow was falling and beginning to settle now that traffic was ended for the day.

I found myself in George Street and paused in front of the building that housed the Literary and Philosophical Society. There was nothing about it to attract a glance, except that John Dalton had lived there. It had been a home, and that was something, a warm point of human reminiscence amid the vast and silent impersonality of trade and commerce.

It was weirdly quiet as I stood there for a moment looking at the house from the other side of the street, with the snow dithering down between: not a vehicle of any sort, not a passer-by. I could almost hear the snow settling upon the road. Looking up, I saw it lost in a roof of blackness.

Then there was someone shuffling towards me: an old bent man, as I saw from the rays of a lamp. There was an icing of snow on his hat and on his bowed shoulders. He came to a stand at my side and said: "Forgive me for following you, Ted. If you could find time for a word . . ."

How they were gone, how utterly they had been sponged out of my mind – the Brimlows! And here he was, Luther's father, the man who had brought my own father Over the Line. His nose still dripped, his eyes still watered, but he was not the man he had been, and that had never been much. He looked shrunken and hollow, a half-inflated thing of parchment, a fleck of the residuary scum left on the surface when Luther had sunk. In the silence the snow wuthered round me and this pitiful piece of wreckage.

I said foolishly: "You shouldn't be out on a night like this, Mr Brimlow." And indeed he looked as if he would at any moment disintegrate into the disintegrating night.

He began to cough, and I half-suspected that it was a stage cough, that he was a good deal of a wily old fox. "I saw your lecture advertised," he said. "I thought it would be a good chance to have a word with you. So I waited outside and followed you."

A cold wind suddenly charged along that snowy canyon, driving the flakes in a mad horizontal rush. "We can't stand about in this," I said, catching my breath. "What is it you want?"

"Money," he answered briefly.

I had guessed as much. He had the look of the furtive bloke who sidles up at an unfrequented corner with a few boxes of matches on a tray. I was about to answer harshly, but I remembered my childhood, my happiness, Blanche and the chestnut tree, the days when a blue sky was everlasting heaven. Incongruously this snow-powdered scarecrow was part of that.

"Well," I said, "we can't talk about it here. You'd better come with me."

He shuffled along at my side, and we were soon at the hotel. "This will be a lark," I thought. "They're not used to customers like this at the Queen's."

It gave me a grim pleasure to hand old Brimlow's sodden dirty overcoat and disgraceful hat with my own to the porter. "Come up to my room," I said.

I switched on the electric fire and rang for a waiter. "You'd better get something warm into you," I said. I had often heard him declare, "Wine is a mocker, strong drink is raging," so I added: "What about coffee and a sandwich?"

"I'll have a double brandy," he said.

I ordered sandwiches and two double brandies, changed into my slippers, and sat down to have a look at him. Stripped of hat and overcoat and seen in a good light, he was more deplorable than I had thought. He was as bald as an egg and all his features had shrunk and withered. A woollen muffler of black and red check concealed, I imagined, the absence of collar and tie. His creased and dirty suit hung on him loosely; his boots were cracked and obviously leaking. I didn't like him. I didn't like the something sly and sneaking that had replaced the bogus sniffling humility of his heyday. But pity for him smote me, and when the waiter was gone I said: "Take off your boots and warm your feet. You must be frozen."

"Ay, Ted, I am," he said. "Whom the Lord loveth He chasteneth."

The words came with the automatism of a phrase shrieked by a parrot, and they infuriated me. He sat with his wet socks stretched towards the fire, steaming. They were filthy things, holed all over. "Listen, Mr Brimlow," I said. "It may surprise you to know that I have some religious feelings. To hear you babbling words from the Bible that mean nothing to you offends me. I've got a spare pair of good thick socks in my bag. I was thinking of offering them to you, but if you'd rather cast yourself upon the Lord, have it your own way."

He grinned, and answered with brazen incorrigibility: "The Lord will provide. I could do with them, Ted."

He pulled off the wet socks, and I knelt down and chafed his cold feet with a towel from a warm rail. The turn-ups of his trousers were tattered and soaking. As he sat there wriggling his bare toes luxuriously before the fire I pulled a little table between us and gave him his drink. He tasted it with smacking relish.

"Since when have you learned to drink that?" I asked.

"Oh, I started with Luther. Just an odd one now and then. It didn't seem wrong, drinking with Luther. And I got a taste for it."

A tinge of colour came to his cheeks as he ate and drank.

"Where is Luther?" I asked suddenly.

He looked sly and crafty. "How should I know? D'you think Luther bothers with the likes of me?"

I didn't press the matter, but I felt certain that he knew.

"He did you no good in the long run," I said without pity.

Old Brimlow looked into his empty glass. "Oh, I dunno," he said. "We had a grand time while it lasted. Mother and I used to go to the races to see Luther's horses run. He paid all our expenses and gave us some good tips."

It flashed an amazing picture before my eyes: Mr and Mrs Brimlow at the races! Mrs Brimlow approaching a bookie, cashing in on her good tips! I remembered a day when I had gone to Epsom and among the tatterdemalion maniacs was one carrying a board inscribed: "Jesus Christ is the only sure tip for the Everlasting Stakes." I wondered how Mr and Mrs Brimlow would react in the days of their glory to an apparition of that sort. But it was idle to speculate.

"After the bust," said old Brimlow, as casually as if discussing the bankruptcy of a corner shop, "there was nothing. My little business was sold up when things began to get sticky. You'd think they'd have left a little thing like that, wouldn't you? Of course, I'd had nothing to do with it for years, except live on it; and when it went I was out of touch, and too old anyway."

He had eaten my sandwiches as well as his own, and the drink made him garrulous. He rambled on, and I gathered a picture of the misery of the Brimlows' latter years. They were living in two rooms in Salford. He did odd jobs of addressing envelopes and such like when he could get them; his wife cleaned offices. There was no word to suggest that he thought his son had treated him, or anyone else, badly. The luck had run out: that was all. If Luther had turned up again that night, as crooked as a corkscrew, he would have been well pleased. I recalled the shed that had served him as an office long ago, the shed in which he had terrified me, with the card hanging on the wall: "Thou God seest me." I remembered even the words that the occasion had scorched into my young mind: "God is not only looking into this room. He is looking into my heart. And yours." Well, well, I thought. You dodged the look, old man, and the trouble is you don't know it. Because you never, really, knew that the look was there. My pity for him was ebbing out in disgust.

He pulled on the new warm socks and put his feet into the steaming boots. "Well, Ted, it's been nice having a talk with someone who belongs to the old times. I've been gassing along and forgetting what Mother said: 'You nobble him,' she said. 'Them Pentecosts owe us something!'"

So it was "Mother" who had put him on my track. I might have guessed it! My heart hardened.

"And what do the Pentecosts owe to the Brimlows?"

He looked up from lacing his boots. "Didn't Luther marry Blanche? Didn't he raise her up?"

I didn't know whether to laugh or to strike that foolish bag of bones.

He was happy with unaccustomed drink, and went on: "There's one thing Mother thought I might say. Mind you, Ted, you must forgive me for mentioning this. It's just an idea Mother's got, arising out of some hint Luther let fall. He wasn't certain that Frances was his."

Again the sly look shot at me sideways out of his face. For a moment I was knocked backwards; then I said: "And that's one of the things Mrs Brimlow thought you might mention?"

"Ay, Ted. It was just one of her notions."

He stood up and I took out my wallet. I counted five pound notes into his ready hand. He put them in his pocket, and then, in a blaze of anger, I took him suddenly by the dirty muffler and shook him to and fro till the teeth rattled in his head. A riot of emotions and recollections left me hardly knowing what I was doing. I saw his office and the small boy cowering there. I saw Mrs Brimlow's glittering *pince-nez* on the day when she first invaded our house; I saw Luther, wearing an opera hat and a carnation, striking Frances across the face;

and I heard the sharp cry of agony as Nobs fell under the blow of the belaying-pin on the quay in the wet dark at Tresco Vean.

I let him go, and he stood looking at me, dazed and shaken. "Tell Mrs Brimlow," I said, "that I am delighted to have her message. Tell her that I am pleased she knows the truth. Tell her the Pentecosts are glad that that lousy snake Luther never got a child on Blanche. There's no Brimlow in Frances. Tell her we all thank God for that."

He eased the muffler round his neck, rolled his old socks into a ball and put them into his pocket.

"It was my job," I said to him, "to tell Frances that Luther wasn't her father. You can tell Mrs Brimlow what she said. She said: 'I feel cleaner.'"

I might as well have shaken and harangued a jellyfish. "Give our love to Blanche," he said.

"Blanche will be enchanted," I railed. "She's got a hell of a lot to thank the Brimlows for."

I went downstairs with him, and helped him into his overcoat. His brown watery eyes looked into mine like the eyes of an old dog that has learned a few tricks in its time. "Thank you, Ted, for helping the poor and afflicted. It will be remembered in the latter day."

I watched him cross the road, dodging a tram that came clanging round a corner. A moment later he was hidden by the snow that was now driving about the city in a blizzard.

8

I did not often go away to deliver a lecture, or for any other reason. These occasions were simply the breakings of a rule by which I kept myself to myself and to my work. I travelled back the next day asking myself as usual why ever I had done it. Why now, of all times, leave home?

The fact was that I was worried about Prue. We were no longer living together in any sense of the word that had meaning. We were not living *together*. We were living side by side. So long as Frances had been about the house all the time, and Stephen occasionally, it had been possible not to be too oppressed by Prue's grey lethargy, the sad weariness of her spirit. She herself had found some escape in the preparations for the wedding, but now that the young people were married she had collapsed into utter apathy. "She said I am a-weary, a-weary. Would God that I were dead!" Prue never said it, but the unspoken words filled our house at Hampstead like a fog that nothing could disperse.

Since that day at Tresco Vean she had never mentioned Iris Randle's name. She had never again so much as hinted at the things in her heart that she had then painfully revealed. And the pain, for her, lay as much in the sense that she had failed me as in the knowledge that I had betrayed her. I knew that in my bones. She hadn't been able to blaze so inextinguishably that no other fires could warm in her presence. Her pride was touched, and she winced. She recoiled upon herself. "Nay, I have done. You get no more of me."

What could I do? There were all the traditional rules for meeting a situation of the sort. I could have assured her passionately that no woman but herself *really* meant anything to me; and I should have been lying. I could have showered her with gifts and attentions: brooches and flowers and dinners in town, and she would have shuddered to see me acting like a whipped dog coming to heel. It wasn't "a situation of that sort." It was our own situation, distinct from every other. It wasn't a game of chess in which there were regulation moves: it was a dreadful fog that had blanketed Prue's heart for a long time and now had swirled forth to envelop us both. And the truth was that I couldn't see a footstep ahead.

These melancholy reflections occupied me as we moved through the dirty environs of Manchester, smoking under a winter sun that lit with pale blue-shadowed rose the snowy roofs and chimney pots, giving them a brief ironic beauty. I was in a mood to see all life as dust and ashes patched here and there with a skin of loveliness that was essentially without meaning.

I lunched on the train, and as soon as I reached London went straight out to Hampstead. Neither Prue nor Blanche was at home. Amy Lingard said they had been out since eleven o'clock and had not told her where they were going. They came in as I was sitting down to tea. I had had the table laid for three, in case they should return, and I poured out tea for them. Blanche took up her cup, put it down again before it reached her lips, and began to cry. She got up from the table, said brokenly: "I couldn't eat or drink a mouthful," and hurried out of the room. Prue was drinking her tea. I looked at her questioningly, and she said: "Well, Ted, I've got my death warrant."

It was cancer; and the knowledge of this, too, was something that she had hidden in her heart for a long time. She died soon: in the following February. She had kept her pains to herself too long.

9

I did not know, nor did she, how short the time left to us now was. I am glad that we had that time. It would be nonsense to say that it was a happy time; but it was a better time than we had had for months. All uncertainties were now resolved. Prue had reached the point when she knew that there was nothing more that she could do about anything, and this had a calming effect upon her spirit. The greyness lifted from her; the simple and straightforward goodness of her heart came out like the sun when fog has blown away. She had never been boisterous or demonstrative; a kindly and understanding gravity that could say much with no more than a smile was what I had loved in her; and it was this which now once more uncovered itself. It was as though she now knew this to be, as it was, the essential thing, and allowed everything that clouded it to be dispersed.

I don't know whether it would give me any satisfaction if I were able to write that at the end we frankly talked over our differences and she said: "It's all forgiven, Ted." Anyway, I can't write that. She would not allow the matter to be discussed. There was one evening when I wanted very much to discuss it. December had given way to January, and I had spent the afternoon, restless and self-distrustful, wandering about the West End streets. The florists' shops were gay, and should have been heartening, glowing with the haphazard colour of daffodils and hyacinths, snowdrops, anemones, tulips and crocuses. Bowls and baskets, vases and urns, were bursting with this loveliness, snug and warm behind the plate glass, while out in the street a searching wind made me shiver as I loitered with my coat collar up and my hands in my pockets. I could not but think of spring: of daffodils in the wood at Tresco Vean and primroses showing shyly at the mossy roots of the trees there; of the kingcups Blanche and I had gathered when we were children, and all the things that wakened earliest: the winter heliotrope, the yellow aconites wearing their green ruffs, the catkins dangling on the hazels and decorating with silken buds the rosy shoots of the willows.

And the thought of spring was unbearable: these shops and all that they stirred in my mind seemed as ironic as the tender winter sun on the snowy roofs of Manchester: that sun which, by the very warmth of its smile, must unmask the filth that for a moment it transfigured.

Prue would not see the spring again. She might live through the season to which we gave that name; but the rising sap, the stir, the resurrection miracle: she could never feel these again.

I was filled with an intense desire to justify myself to her, or, if there could be no justification, at least to let her know that many years had passed since Iris and I, to put it plainly, had been to bed together. Not, indeed, since that time when Stephen's boyish prattle of his visit with Luther to St James' Square had first brought Iris' existence to Prue's mind. It seemed to me important that she should know this.

I was glad when Blanche went out that night. There was a lecture by some swami, some Indian mystery man. She was agog for such sensations. With bridge parties, they dropped some crumbs of occupation on to her empty plate.

When she was gone, Prue put on her spectacles and sat with a book by the fire. It was one of Jesse Cleghorn's books, and Jesse Cleghorn did not write for the million. But Prue undoubtedly was getting something out of it. "You know, Ted," she had said to me a few evenings before, "you should read my uncle's books. He's better than I thought. He gives you something. But then, of course, he always did. He was one of the few men I have known who gave me something simply by existing alongside me. You are another."

I was too surprised, too moved, to reply, and she had gone on reading, as though forbidding me to comment on what she had said.

And now I looked at her sitting there with the spectacles on her nose and her hair grey, communing with the spirit that had been housed in the flesh docketed as Jesse Cleghorn. "Prue," I said, "could you bear it if I said what I think you ought to know about Iris Randle?"

She put her book down on a table by her chair and laid the spectacles upon it. "Yes," she said, "I could bear it. I only wonder whether it's necessary."

It was an agitating moment. I got up to fill my pipe from a tobacco jar on the mantelpiece, and my fingers were trembling. Prue said: "Sit down, and let me tell you something. It's about a man called Richard Franklin."

"Never heard of him," I said.

"No. I knew him in Manchester, but not very well. He was at the University there. Jesse Cleghorn was excellent with young people, you know. He was 'at home' to them, as they call it, one night every week. I used to make the coffee for them and bake the buns. They were simple cheerful evenings, with a lot of talking and laughing and smoking, and no doubt all those young men got something out of my uncle, as I did. Richard Franklin was one of them. He was the only one of whom my uncle would talk to me occasionally when the others were gone. Old Jesse thought of him as a promising young man, and he liked him, too, in a personal way. So did I. He was a dark, ugly youth, at the University on scholarships. His father kept a barber's shop. I remember him telling us that one night in a rather sour defiant way, and Jesse said: 'Like J.M.W. Turner's father,' and so Richard couldn't be sour about it or make one of his inverted boasts about it any more. He disappeared, as they all did sooner or later. I understood that he had gone to some school as a teacher. Anyway, we never heard another thing about him while we lived in Manchester.

"I met him again in 1916. You were in France. I was walking along Piccadilly one day when an infantry lieutenant saluted me and said: 'Hallo, Prue!' It was Richard. He looked well in uniform. He was not so dark and savage as I had known him; I was pleased to see him. It was teatime, and it seemed the most natural thing in the world to be taking tea with him. It was a dance-tea, and we danced together, though I was never much of a dancer. Between dances we sat and talked. He had just got home on leave. He had been through a lot of fighting, and he wanted his leave to be a good one. He frankly asked me to help him to make it so. I was young, you know, Ted, and not bad-looking."

I was amazed. There was nothing I could say. I got up and put some coal on the fire, knocked the ashes out of my pipe, and waited for her to go on.

"I told him that I was married, that I had a child, that I was a respectable woman; but I said it all laughingly. I was surprised to find that I was not shocked. I liked him more than ever. He wanted me to go back with him to his hotel, then and there, but I excused myself and went home. However, I promised that I would have lunch with him the next day. Your mother, you remember, was living with me then. I invented a story for her which would permit me to be out as long as I liked, and the lunch engagement stretched to include tea and dinner and dancing after dinner. They were excitable days, you remember, Ted, and you had been away a long time. Dancing with Richard Franklin, whom I liked very much, was not exactly soothing to a passionate woman. He was persistent, and adroit, and charming."

She paused for a moment, looking into the fire, as though living again for a moment in those hectic days that the years had smothered with their dust. I had lived through them, too: the days that any barrel-organ could call up. "If you were the only girl in the world." The days of the doomed young men and the pitying women. Still, it was strange to think that they had touched Prue.

"Two days before his leave was over, he took me all the way home to Hampstead in a taxi – to this house. It seems strange to think it was to this house. But, of course, the taxi stopped a few hundred yards away and I walked home. He had won. I had promised to make it a really good leave, as he kept on calling it, at his hotel the next afternoon. But it never happened. When I got there and asked for Lieutenant Franklin I was told that he had left an hour ago – recalled from leave. There was a note for me – the most bitter little note I have ever read: 'You were a long time coming to a decision. Too long. I shall die a virgin.' I don't know whether he died or not. There was never another word from him or about him. And that's the story of Mrs Pentecost and Richard Franklin."

And so Prue never assured me: "It's all forgiven, Ted." She merely said after a moment's silence: "I don't see why we should ever mention Richard Franklin again."

10

I saw her doctor privately. I wanted to know how much of hell Prue might have to endure before she was released. He was a man I had known pretty well for years, and he talked to me frankly. We lunched together. "I can give you very good news, Pentecost," he said. "Her heart's in a shocking state. I've said nothing to her about that; she thinks it's only the other thing. If it were, I should say the news was bad – God knows how long, and getting worse all the time. But it may end soon – very soon – and suddenly."

He chattered on: "I was talking to a Danish doctor not long ago – a man who's worked among the Eskimos – the ones farthest north. They're riddled with tuberculosis, you know, glandular and pulmonary. But there's never been a case of cancer among them. It's odd –"

Odd enough. Life was full of odd things. It was odd to be sitting here feeling a lightening of the heart because Prue would probably die sooner than I or she had expected. Most odd. The wagons trundled about loaded with hors d'oeuvres and luscious sweets. Waiters hurried by, balancing trays of drinks at shoulder height. There was a coming and going of pretty girls and cheerful eupeptic men. And Prue might die any day. And I was glad. Yes, it was odd enough.

That was how it went; that was the manner of my last days with Prue. I set off for my studio every morning, as regularly as my father, years before, had gone to work with his basket over his shoulder. I did not spend an evening away from home. Usually we were alone together, for Blanche's trivial affairs seemed more and more demanding on her time. Perhaps once a week Stephen and Frances would look in from their flat on Parliament Hill. They knew nothing of the state of things, and they were too wrapped up in one another to be observant. More often than not, there were just the two of us, sitting by the fire, reading, having little to say to one another because words could say so little and there was so much that could be said without them. Even in such moments, I sometimes thought of Iris, far away in the summer sunshine of Australia, and I could think of her without agitation or shame. I loved her; I loved Prue. Someone had said that monogamy was the greatest triumph of the female over the male. Well, monogamy was one thing, a matter of legality. Love was another. The world was cold enough, and both for me and for the world in general it looked like being colder. In such a moment, love was not a thing to deny.

The last evening we spent thus together, Prue looked up from her book and said: "Did you know that old Jesse's books, for some reason or other, are having quite a little boom?"

I hadn't known it; and she said: "The last half-yearly returns from the publishers were the best ever. Jesse's been a drug on the market for a decade, but the last half-year brought me in a couple of hundred pounds."

Cleghorn had bequeathed to her the income from royalties on his books.

"It's too bad," she said, "that I should not have discovered him till now when I'm dying." And she said it as casually as if she had said, "now that I've finished arranging the flowers." She said: "I suppose no orthodox parson would like Jesse's idea of God. What I find moving in him is his loathing for any sort of coercion of the individual, and his equal loathing of the individual who throws his weight about. How he would smile to hear me trying to condense his philosophy into a couple of rags of sentences like that! The individual, subdued yet fortified by an apprehension of God: that's what he's getting at. I hope this little boom doesn't mean that the world, like me, is coming to Jesse on its death-bed."

Apart from the casual small-change talk of good night and good morning, those were the last words Prue spoke to me. I was called hastily from my studio the next day, but did not get home in time to speak to her again.

11

Well, then, this was the background of my recent life as I sat in my den on my birthday in February of 1938, a dun and dingy day that didn't cheer up from one end to the other. In the afternoon I waited till Blanche had set off for her bridge tea and then went to see Frances. Blanche looked what they call nowadays "tatty" – a good descriptive word that I like. She was increasingly without substance in every sense but the physical. An untidy smear of lipstick, which of late she had taken to using artlessly, was gashed upon her face. That and her generous powder made her look like an old clown. At the door she paused to say: "Ted, I'm afraid I may be giving you a terrible shock before long."

"I shall try and bear it," I laughed. "Tell me. Get it over."

"I may be leaving you."

I took the news as gravely as I could.

"Mind you, it's not absolutely certain," she rattled on, "but you know Kitty Delabole's husband has gone off with that dreadful little secretary of his? After being married for twenty-five years! Actually, it was on their silver wedding day that he went."

475

I knew Kitty Delabole, Blanche's favourite companion at bridge, lectures, cinemas, and in the eating of cream buns at all sorts of odd hours. It seemed to me that any man who had endured Kitty Delabole for twenty-five years had earned a free pardon. But I said it was incredible what men would do in these days.

"Well, there it is," Blanche said. "Actually, one of those charming little houses on Well Walk can be rented, and Kitty and I are talking about setting up house together. You mustn't be offended, Ted. But I do feel lonely. You're at your studio all day and in your den all night . . ."

That was true enough, but it hadn't affected Blanche's way of life. She had found all the company she wanted, and of the sort she wanted. The truth was, she was letting me out of a dilemma. There seemed to me no sense in keeping on this house in Hampstead, but I had hesitated to suggest to her that I could live my widowed life comfortably, and more conveniently, at my studio in Chelsea.

"I shall be all right, Blanche," I said, trying not to sound too eager. "Really, I shall get along. Do what you find most convenient."

"Well, actually," she said, "it's as good as settled. You're sure you won't mind?"

"Bless you, I shall manage."

I watched her go, went back to my den to fill my tobacco pouch, and set off to see Frances and John. John was the newest Pentecost — six months old.

12

It was a Saturday afternoon, so possibly Stephen would be there as well as Frances and John. It had to be John, of course. There was only one Pentecost who meant much to Stephen, and that was Captain John Pentecost of the packet *Termagant*. It was after him that our little John was named, but actually, to use the word Blanche infuriated me by using again and again, he was all Chellew. (*Actually* was one of the things Blanche had got from Kitty Delabole. I wondered whether Delabole had run away with his secretary because she did not say actually. That would be amusing, but not at all improbable.)

I bought a large mixed bunch of flowers: tulips and daffodils and mimosa, and toiled up Parliament Hill. Frances would welcome the flowers. Stephen's pay didn't run to extravagances, but the young people were in the stern and independent stage. Blanche had wanted to settle a small weekly sum on Frances, but they wouldn't have it. They would manage all right, thank you very much, and it wouldn't be long before Stephen was able to move out from the poky little flat into a house of their own.

Sometimes I wondered about this. The fact is, Stephen not only was not much of an architect now, but he didn't show promise of ever becoming a good one. He was a hard and earnest worker, but there wasn't the original endowment to work on. I know that nowadays Jack's as good as his master and it's a self-evident proposition that all men are created equal, but it chanced that Stephen was an exception to this otherwise happily universal rule. I never understood why he took up architecture. He had not shown a bent that way; but then he had never shown a bent in any direction except that of physical occupation. Years ago, I had gone so far as to suggest that he should be trained on the *Conway* or the *Worcester*, or even enter the Navy, but in a puzzling way this idea that he would make an architect had hold of him then, and now here we were.

The house they lived in was almost at the top of the hill, and they lived in rooms at the top of the house. John's pram was in the passage. I climbed the stairs. The place had never been properly transformed into flats. It was simply an old-fashioned, not very convenient, house let out in rooms. There was no lift. They had two rooms, a cupboard called a kitchen, and, under the tiles, a bathroom with a bath that belonged to the dawn of sanitation. The bathroom was lighted only by a skylight. Standing on the edge of the bath, you could put your head through the skylight and thus obtain the only view of the Heath that the flat afforded. The first time I did this I was reminded of Didsbury and of hurling conkers at Luther Brimlow, hopping on one leg below and singing hymns.

I knocked at the sitting room door and went in, my bouquet preceding me like a sunburst. "Hallo, Fran? All alone?"

She was sitting by an electric fire, a vast piece of black machinery that enshrined in its heart a small tentative glow. Like the bath, it was an instrument of pioneering days. She got up and kissed me and thanked me for the flowers. When they were arranged in a few vases the place looked more cheerful.

"Well, where's Stevo?"

"Burnham-on-Crouch."

"Oh! What's to do there at this time of year?"

"My dear Dook," she laughed, "I don't know whether you've ever had a mistress, but you should at least know that a mistress is more demanding than a wife."

"A mistress!"

She laughed again and tugged my hair, which was long and grey. "You old literalist! No, no. I mean *Rosalie*."

Rosalie was Wittering's Brixham trawler. "I should have thought she'd be on the hard or in a shed. They're not fitting out surely in February?"

"You ought to know enough about ships, Dook, to know that those who want to play with them can do so from one year's end to another. There's always something. Stevo and Sir Ernest are like a couple of kids down there. They live in dungarees, playing with planes, chisels, gluepots, grease and varnish. If there's nothing else to do, they scrape off one coat of varnish and put on another."

"What time do you expect him back?"

"I don't expect him back – at least not till Monday night. They'll be spending the weekend in Sir Ernest's cottage there."

"Well, I suppose it's all right for Wittering. He's a widower."

"And I'm a widow, with one child."

She was still laughing, but I looked round the dull little room and wondered. Over the mantelpiece was the picture of John Pentecost lifting the cannon. Damn John Pentecost, I thought.

"By the way," I said, "it's my birthday, and, being of an eccentric turn of mind, it's my habit on my birthday to give presents to my loved ones. Have you received the electric fire? It should have been here by now?"

She looked at me, puzzled. "No, Dook. Nothing's come. And do forgive me. Really, I didn't know it was your birthday. Let me give you another kiss, darling. There! Stevo ought to have told me."

"Stephen's a very forgetful young man," I said sternly. "He forgets to praise the Lord for all his benefits. Well, now. I must leave you for a moment. But I'll be back. Indeed, I am staying to tea. But I must go at once and see why that fire was not delivered."

I had seen a pretty electric fire down in the village, and I hurried to the shop and bought it. There was an attractive lightshade, too, of rosy pink, and I bought that. A shilling to the messenger boy standing there doing nothing induced him to return to the flat with me, carrying the gifts. At a confectioner's I bought a dozen muffins. Toiling up the stairs behind the boy, I damned Captain Pentecost again.

We shifted that villainous piece of ironmongery on to the landing and put the new fire in its place. We fixed the new lampshade and drew the curtains. "Now," I said, "give me a toasting fork, or, if you haven't got so necessary an implement, give me a knife."

There was no toasting fork. I wrapped a handkerchief round my hand to protect it from the heat, impaled a muffin on a knife, and began to toast it at the new fire.

"Mind you don't scorch your hand," Frances said. She was always solicitous about my hand.

"My hand's all right," I told her crustily. "You make some tea, young woman. There are other things in question as well as my hand. I intend to talk about them. Put a plate down here where I can keep these muffins warm."

Well, this was cosier. The place was more human. We sat close to the fire with a little table between us. On my right was a bookcase. I looked at the titles. All the English poets, a lot of plays, *Knots and Splices*, *The Yachtsman's Year Book*, *Falmouth for Orders*, the *ABC of Boat-building*, *Laying Up and Fitting Out*. A lot of stuff of that sort.

"What's happened to the potter's thumb?" I asked her, biting into a muffin.

"What do you mean, Dook?"

"That inky ridge you used to have on the index finger of your right hand."

"Oh, Dook," she said, dodging me. "Only very young amateurs get ink on their fingers. You can tell a pro by the fact that he has none."

"At least they have inkpots, and presumably a desk."

"Oh, no. A fountain pen at any old table."

"Look here, Fran. Honestly, are you doing anything at all?"

"There's no time, Dook. Really there isn't."

"Is that all there is to it?"

"Well –" She hesitated and looked perplexed and pained. "When Stevo's here there's so much else to talk about, and when he isn't – well, it's more than solitude somehow. It's a desperate terrible loneliness that so upsets me I can do nothing."

"I see." She was trembling a little, and I didn't know whether I ought to go on. But I asked: "Is he away much?"

"Most weekends. Of course, I used to go with him till John came. It was jolly down there. I used to cook for the pair of them. And now, of course, there's the R.N.V.R., too. That keeps him out some evenings."

Even with the new fire and lampshade and buttered muffins the afternoon didn't seem too good.

"Is Stevo the least bit interested in what you used to try and do?"

She was a long time answering, and then she said: "I don't know how you managed to do it, Dook, but you begot a Puritan. Stephen's a darling. I'm very happy with him, but aesthetically he's by Baden-Powell out of Mrs Grundy. Don't think I'm not happy with him," she added hastily.

I waited for her to continue. "Reading poetry, and trying to write it, and to write plays, is no *use* to Stephen. He doesn't see the *point* of it. I did a bit before John came. Stephen never disapproved, but he used to laugh. 'Come on, Fran. You'll be growing whiskers like Bernard Shaw's. Let's get out and draw a bit of God's fresh air into our lungs. Time you limbered up.' That sort of thing. And, of course, when you *were* out, it was marvellous: rushing over the Heath with Stephen and coming back as fit as a fiddle to a good heart-to-heart talk about anti-fouling and copal varnish."

"I see."

"There was one evening when I really *did* want to work. I felt I'd *got* something, if only I could have peace to worry it. You know what I mean?"

"All too well, my dear."

"In the middle of it Stephen put on the wireless. There was to be a talk by the master of a Finnish barque. Well, that was a night! I didn't get on with the work, and he didn't hear the Finn. We argued. It wasn't a row, mind you, just a reasonable argument, each side stating its point of view. I was convinced, utterly and absolutely, by sheer force of logic."

"And that was the end of it?"

"That was the end of it. And let me tell you, Dook, that you've turned me into a woman unfit for motherhood this afternoon. Rain, hail or snow, John Pentecost should be put into his pram and trundled over the Heath. You've made me neglect my duty. D'you want to see him?"

He was sound asleep in his cot in the bedroom, looking as though he didn't care whether he slept on the Heath or under the tiles, so long as he slept. "You see," said Fran. "I've got something. I'm not without resources."

She helped me on with my overcoat. "Thank you for coming, Dook," she said, "and thanks for the presents. I'm so sorry we forgot the birthday."

"I must look in more often."

"Yes, do," she said, "do."

But, going down the stairs, I remembered that soon I should be shifting to Chelsea and that the chances were I should not see her even as often as I did now.

CHAPTER THIRTEEN

T HE KING'S Mistress was a free house. That is not to say that you could get a drink there without paying, which is what I thought it meant when I was a boy. A lot of things had changed since I was a boy. There was pub after pub in those days bearing the notice: "Accommodation for Man and Beast." A useful and necessary class distinction, but one that was now wearing a little thin. Men really went about then dependent on horses. Now the very Guards were "mechanised". I remembered the files of horses and mules, patient head-down, mud-bellied beasts, that I had seen slogging along the wartime roads of France and Belgium, and someone had told me that when tanks were first used at Flers in 1917 the idea in some generals' minds was to clear a way for the cavalry to get through. I don't know.

Well, I thought, sitting there in the pub, if we're going to have it all over again, I'm glad the horse at least will escape. I suppose there'll still be some of them, but not many. The knight and his gallant steed had had a long sentimental run. It was about time the knight did his own dirty knightly work.

"Remember last time, Mr Pentecost, when they killed that bloody Archduke? I can see you an' Mr Chellew sittin' there arguin' the fat about it as clear as if it was yesterday."

So could I.

I was glad that this was a free house. That meant that it was Joe's own property. No brewery could push him out. Here he was. He was getting old and garrulous; but here he was. He gave me a comfortable sense of continuity. There was not much that Joe and I didn't know about one another now. He and I, the old plane tree, his pub, my studio: these seemed the unchanging things in King's Mistress Yard. We were closer than ever now that I lived altogether at the studio. I took all my meals at the pub. Joe's wife was an excellent cook, and Joe's daughter, who was behind the bar at opening time, kept my rooms in order. My life was more comfortable and convenient than it had been at any time since Prue's death. Amy Lingard was with Blanche and Kitty Delabole at Well Walk in Hampstead.

"They're dishin' out the pigs' snouts tonight," Joe said. "You goin' along?"

"I don't know. Perhaps it'll blow over." The word of the moment was Munich.

"P'r'aps it will," Joe assented. "P'r'aps 'Itler's bluffin'. There was a bloke in 'ere the other night. Just back from Germany. Saw one of them big parades 'Itler's always stagin' to impress people. Tanks by the score rattlin' through Berlin. An' a bloody tradesman's cart got out of 'and and run into one of 'em. Went right through it. Cardboard it was. This bloke saw it with 'is own eyes. Laugh! 'E says 'e nearly wet 'imself."

"Yes. One hears such things. Remember the Russians in the last war, Joe? Snow on their boots! I met a dozen men who saw them."

"Aw, that's different. I *know* this bloke. Been comin' 'ere for years."

Joe swiped a cloth over the mahogany and left me to enjoy my evening pint.

The door was pushed open and a head came through, eyes scanning the room. "Ah, there you are! I always know where to find the old tippler."

It was Adam Randle in Air Force blue, one ring round his sleeve. He came in and sat at my table. He looked very brown and handsome, but very grave. When his drink came, he raised the pewter to his lips, saying: "Well – here's to you, Dook. Good health; and – just in case – good luck."

It was almost unbearable. "You sound very – valedictory," I said gruffly.

"Well, I'm just dashing round – in case, you know. I took the Widow to lunch, and then I dashed out to Hampstead to shake hands with Fran."

"Oh, you did, did you?"

"Yes. It was a lovely domestic occasion. I caught up with her just as she was pushing the pram on to the Heath. We walked sedately for an hour. Every passer-by must have thought: 'What a charming couple. And with a baby, too. Dear, dear! I hope he comes through all right!'"

"Shut up!" I said savagely. "How was Frances? She must be worrying about Stephen. He'd have to go, of course."

"Thank you," he said, "she's as well as can be expected in the circumstances." In a moment he added with an intense bitterness: "And bloody fine circumstances, too."

He put down the tankard and stood up. "Well, I must be off. It took a hell of a lot of wangling to get away as it was. If I'm not back at Tangmere before long I'll be for the firing squad. State of emergency."

I walked out into the yard with him. A small open sporting car was standing there. He climbed in and clanged the door, leaned over it, and took my hand. He held it hard for a long time – the boy who had looked at the sunset, breathing with ecstasy: "Wings, wings!"

He dropped my hand. "Well, once more, Dook – just in case. All the best."

I stood there in the quiet evening after he was gone, feeling utterly lonely, bereft and sick at heart. The old plane tree seemed to be holding its breath. The caretaker who lived in one of the houses came along with her small child. In their hands the pigs' snouts, as Joe called the gas-masks, were dangling. "But what are they *for*, Ma? What are they *for*?" the child was whining.

The woman looked distraught. "Oh, shut up!" she said. "Shut up, for Christ's sake."

They disappeared into their house; and the words lingered on in the dusk: For Christ's sake. For Christ's sake . . .

2

I took a turn by the river, then climbed the stairs to my studio and put a match to the fire. I thought about Adam and Frances. It was in June of 1937 that Iris and Adam returned from Australia. Iris sent me a casual postcard to say that they were back and I went along to see them in St James' Square. I told them my news: of the marriage and of Prue's death; and Adam told me that he had already put things in train for joining the Royal Air Force. Iris confirmed what Adam had said in his letter: that she would do no more acting. Nor, she said, did she intend to spend much more time in England. She wanted the sun. Perhaps she would be in London for a month or so in spring or autumn, the two seasons when the place was tolerable; but she intended to find a small house on the French Riviera and live there.

Adam had a dinner engagement with his friend Freddy Freemantle, who was already in the Air Force. Iris and I spent the evening together in the flat.

"What do you think of this idea, Ted – this Riviera business?"

"I think it will be lovely – for you."

"You could come and visit me."

"Oh, yes. I certainly should do that."

"You don't sound happy about it."

"I'm not happy about it. Why should I be happy about it?"

She came and sat on my lap. She was as light as a bird, and I was rather substantial. She put an arm round my neck and kissed me and laid her cheek to mine. Incredible woman! It seemed as though she were indestructible, as though the years could do nothing to her. As I embraced her supple body I could feel that she still had no need to hold herself together with a casing.

"Did Prue ever guess?" she asked, keeping her cheek close to mine.

"Yes."

"Did you have a very bad time, darling Ted?"

"No. A better time than I deserved."

"I love you still. All the excitement of that tour! And then the long time alone with Adam. If anything could have made me forget you that would have done. And here I am, and that's all I can say: I love you still. Odd, isn't it?"

"I don't see anything odd about it."

"You don't think we're a pair of silly old self-deluding fools?"

"No, I don't. Will you marry me?"

She stood up and looked down at me and shook her head. "No."

We were silent for a moment in the dusky room, then she repeated: "No, Ted. Some day I shall. I *know* that. I've known it for years. But I'm superstitious about it. I'm sure it must *happen*. It mustn't be arranged. All these years we've never arranged anything, have we? And yet it looks as though nothing can part us. I haven't even written to you – not much, only when it was necessary. I've done nothing – have I? – to keep you. And yet I can't get away from you."

"You've done plenty to keep me, believe me."

"I've given Fate a fair chance to take you from me," she said. "One of these days I'll give it no more chances."

"We're getting old, my darling. Perhaps Fate won't give *us* any more chances."

"We should be getting old whatever happened."

"What do you mean by Fate, Iris, my darling?"

"I mean what gets you in the end because of what *you've* wanted to get from the beginning."

It was a strange comment. It set my mind racing back across the years. "I should like to tell you something, my sweet. Something that happened a long time ago – twenty years ago. Do you remember that concert for the troops near Amiens? I met you there, and we went back into the town."

"Yes. I remember it very well, darling. I shall never forget it. *The many men, so beautiful, and they all dead did lie . . .*"

"I stayed in Amiens for a day or two after you were gone. I ran into a young Catholic priest and we went to his lodgings and talked about this and that. He talked about Fate. To him, it was the love of God. That was man's destined end. Man might dodge it, but so long as he did he would know no peace. It's the idea Francis Thompson works out in *The Hound of Heaven*. Do you know that poem?"

"Yes. It's one of Adam's favourites. He reads a lot of poetry to me."

"Well, there it is. This priest quoted *There is no armour against Fate* and drew a picture of silly men piling up armour upon armour when all they need to do is not resist but submit. Lay themselves open to the love of God."

There was again a moment of silence, filled by all the years between that time and this; and then Iris said: "Ted, my dear one, do you think I'm a fit person to be discussing such things as this?"

"My darling, why ever not?"

"Oh," she cried with sudden passion, "I've been so cheap! You and Adam and Frances are so good to me. You treat me as though I were one of yourselves. And I'm so – oh, I've always been worse than nothing."

I comforted her and kissed her. She was crying; and she said: "Go away now, there's a darling. I'm not fit to be seen."

3

This was in June of 1937, and when I called on Frances on my birthday in the following February she had not, I knew, seen Adam since his return from Australia. I was preoccupied then with my move to Chelsea, and I was very lonely. Adam was in the Air Force. Iris had closed the flat she had had for so long in St James' Square and had moved to a cottage near Cap Ferrat. There was at least the consolation of letters. She now became, for her, quite communicative and wrote about once a fortnight. I learned much of Berthe Montjolis, a forthright peasant woman who looked after her, and of Berthe's husband Albert who pottered about the house and garden and could drive a car.

It was rather a miserable time for me. On a Saturday in June I set off after my pub lunch to see Frances at Hampstead. When I reached the top of her abominable stairway I paused for a moment to catch my breath and was surprised to hear laughter from the other side of the door. I knew that Stephen was away, crewing on the *Rosalie*, so I knocked ostentatiously. Usually, I just barged in. The door was opened by Adam Randle. He looked very happy.

"Well, Dook!" he cried, and seized me by both hands and drew me in as though it were his own home.

It was a hot day. The window was wide open and the muslin curtains fluttered in a little breeze. Young John, as naked as a newt, lay kicking on the hearth rug. He was being brought up as, I remembered, Stephen had been. Prue had positively winced to see clothes on him. Frances, looking very beautiful, was sitting at the table where a few sheets of paper were laid out. There was a smudge of ink on the index finger of her right hand. She got up and kissed me. Her face was cool and smooth.

"Good lord!" I cried. "You don't mean to say you're working, Fran?"

"I found the girl bursting with ideas," said Adam.

"Oh, it's just a notion for a play," Frances said diffidently. "I've been thinking it over for some time, and naturally, when Adam called, I mentioned it to him."

"Naturally."

"And he insisted on trying to get something roughed out. However, let's pack it up and take John into the air."

She swept the pages together and put them in a drawer. John was rendered fit for the public gaze by being thrown unceremoniously into one slight garment. Adam hoisted the child on to his shoulder, and we all trooped downstairs. "What's he going to do, Fran," he asked, "work his way up from powder-monkey to admiral?"

We walked on the Heath, Adam and I disputing for the honour of pushing the pram, and when teatime came I took them into a small tea shop called the Haven, and we ate poached eggs on toast and drank tea. Then Adam had to go. We all shook hands outside the tea shop, and I wondered whether, if I had not been there, he would have tried to kiss her, and whether she would have let him.

"Well," he said in parting, "keep it up, Fran. It's a good idea. And now that you're in touch again with your old collaborator, it wouldn't be a bad idea to report progress now and again. Promise?"

"I'll see," she said.

It was of this and suchlike things that I was thinking as I sat by the fire that day when the word Munich was tolling like a bell of fate.

4

"My dear Iris," I wrote, "I expect you have been through the same sort of emotional, almost hysterical, experiences in France that we have known here. I have never seen anything quite like it. The funeral bell that was tolling in our ears turned suddenly to a wedding peal. The whole funeral procession broke up and began dancing like mad on the village green. Ribbons in hats, hats in the air, and everyone whirling round the undertaker, shaking his hand and patting him on the back. It seems to have escaped the general notice that the corpse is still there, the grave still open, and the funeral only postponed. I mustn't pose as a superior and far-seeing person. No, indeed. I was as lunatic as the rest. After all, plenty of us remember the last war and know that the next one, when it comes, will make that one seem like a march of the Boys' Brigade. It is not to be wondered at if we expressed with some enthusiasm our sense of joy that the world and all that dwell therein are not immediately to be battered to pulp or scattered into dust. It is hardly surprising to find that men prefer life to death. We shall be in a bad way when they don't. All the same, everything has its price. You can't have 'peace at any price,' as they say. You can have peace only at the price of peace, and the price is pretty high. It certainly hasn't been paid in the last few years, and I doubt if it will be paid now. I have a feeling that it's too late, even if the debtor now wanted to pay. The creditor is determined to foreclose.

"Forgive these woolly metaphors, my dear. All I am trying to say is that I am afraid. Stark, staring fear of the future is with me day and night. I am afraid for myself; I am afraid for you; I am afraid for our children. Won't you consider coming back to England? Shouldn't we, now, all be together while we may . . . ?"

And so on. It's extraordinary, I thought, that you are willing to use anything, even the threatened collapse of the world, to get this woman back to you. But she didn't come. In the spring of 1939 I reminded her that she had said she would come for some time to England each spring. But she didn't come. Adam spent his leave in France with her. The year moved on, and in July Stephen and Frances went with John to Burnham-on-Crouch for a fortnight. I didn't go with them: and as for Blanche, I was almost out of touch with her. By chance, I met her with Kitty Delabole in Regent Street and sounded her about her intentions. It was Mrs Delabole who answered for her: "Well, actually, only this morning we booked very nice rooms at Frinton."

I wrote to Ernie Lingard, telling him to have the studio ready, and I set off alone for Cornwall. I had often made that journey alone, but never before to a lonely end. To go to Cornwall had been a gregarious experience: the children would be at Falmouth station with Lazarus. Ernie would seize the luggage. We would rattle away to Tresco Vean, and Prue would be there, and my mother and Blanche. A nondescript governess would be in the background, and in some years there was Adam. The enigmatic Bugsby would drift across the scene. Even Nobs, even the hens, would always haunt the place for me with silly ghosts. And, once, Iris was there.

Well, this year there was nothing. Ernie was not at the station to meet me. He was out on the bay, giving a pleasure run to trippers. I felt rather hurt, but Ernie had to live. His wife had tea waiting for me on a little table by a window overlooking the harbour, one of those excessive Cornish teas that the children had delighted in, and that revolted me: stewed fruit and cream, cakes, splits, jam, and God knows what. I fiddled with the food, looking at the harbour's customary beauty, precisely the scene that I had looked on from this same window when, a boy, I made my first call on Kitto: yachts with gaily painted top sides and sails of red or white, dinghies breaking with their oars the placid blue, the noble headland of Pendennis crowned with its castle, and the corn ripening on the hills over Flushing. But then it had been morning, and now the sun of late summer was already sloping towards the west.

I went downstairs and into the little courtyard garden, crushing the lemon-scented verbena in my fingers as I passed through the doorway that once had led to Henry Opie's gleaming brass and glowing copper. Nothing was changed, because I had given orders that nothing must be changed. The same plants climbed upon the crumbling walls; the mossy statuettes of lead and stone stood upon their plinths over the flags of the pavement, sprouting with herbs. As I have always known them to come, carefree voices came clearly over the water, and through the soft western air the sun's declining rays bent like light through gauze. It was a timeless moment, and I could have screamed with the agony of it, because I felt poised on the edge of chaos, ready to tremble and dissolve. If Ernie had painted the statues green, if he had torn up the ancient pavements and planted pink geraniums edged with lobelia, it would have given me a salutary shock; but this timelessness, this sticking it out even to the edge of doom, undermined me, so that I should not have been surprised if the solid scene had wavered before my eyes and stirred uneasily beneath my feet.

I did not stay long. Once or twice I joined the crowd on Ernie's launch. I took the boat to St Mawes and Percuil and sat in the tea garden where I had first seen Ernie and Nobs. I followed the road to Portscatho. I bathed. I drank a pint in one or two pubs. But there was no savour in any of it. There were still beaches to be found where a man could be as lonely as Crusoe, untroubled even by a footprint. There were cowries in the sand and there was ripe corn on the hills. There was wind on the sea and a breathless hush of heat in the brakes, humming with the vibration of insect wings, where the blackberries were ripening and the bracken sheeted the ground with gold and umber. You could find spots, out of sight of roof and road, where nothing seemed to have happened since the beginning of time, and one would behold without wonder a Phoenician keel kissing the yellow sand. Never had Cornwall seemed more beautiful. Never did

I flee from its enchantments with less regret than I did three days after my arrival in that late summer of 1939.

5

I do not intend to write a history of the war, beginning with Chamberlain's Sunday morning broadcast and the sirens' swift ironic comment upon it. I shall not even write of blazing cities and smashing bombs and the poor wretches living like cattle in infernal subterranean corrals. All this, disturbing enough, was but the physical integument of a spiritual tragedy. It was a matter for reporters, and they have done their duty amply.

I shall write here only of one or two matters that concern the story of my own life.

It is a very moving thing to see one's son for the first time in the panoply of a warrior. Bugsby was with Stephen, and let us now drop the childish nickname, for Bugsby has put away childish things. This is Lieutenant Timothy Begbie, R.N.V.R., a shortish tubby young man, fresh-faced and reliable-looking, wearing a dark blue uniform with two wavy rings round the coat cuffs. Stephen overtops him by inches. He is similarly dressed: Lieutenant Stephen Pentecost, R.N.V.R. On the couch are two peaked caps with golden devices. I pick up one of them and turn it over, examining the workmanship of gold wire, but I am aware not of the cap but of the two young men who have done so much together on the sea they have loved. Now they will need all their love and all their skill.

Stephen has been in the R.N.V.R. for some time, but it chances that I have never before seen him in uniform. The wavy rings, the white collar and black tie, the slip of white cuff showing beneath the sleeve, the neat gold cuff link. It is all very becoming. The double-breasted jacket with the brass buttons embossed with anchors. My heart swells with pride, and shrinks with agony.

Tim Begbie had stayed overnight at the flat, sleeping on a couch. I had come out early from Chelsea to take breakfast with them. I was up fussily at six o'clock, and the taxi I had ordered was there at half-past. It was a morning of what Adam might have called Septembral enchantment: webbed with mist waving its scarves through the branches of the plane tree, breaking overhead now and then into a tender blue that came and was obscured again. I had boiled a kettle, and I took the taxi-driver up to the studio, where we drank a cup of tea and talked in quiet voices. We talked, as men of our age will, of the "last time", and I found that he and I had been wounded the same day in 1916, not far from one another. And we talked of our sons. He had two; already both were gone. He was a grizzled old fellow; I wondered whether to strange eyes I looked as old and life-beaten as he.

Certainly I felt old now, with breakfast finished, and nothing remaining but for Stephen and Timothy to take up their suitcases and go. I was out of the picture. Whatever had to be done now would be done by these, and such as these. I felt trivial and humble as I shook hands with them.

Frances came out of the bedroom, carrying young John. Stephen kissed the child, and so did Begbie, blushing madly. Then Stephen took Frances by the elbow and steered her back into the bedroom and shut the door. Begbie and I stood uncomfortably together near the table littered with the breakfast things.

"Those were good times down in Cornwall, sir," Begbie said.

"Yes, something to remember."

"One thing I remember is this. We anchored for the night in that little harbour at Portscatho. I was fool enough to leave the W.C. gadgets improperly adjusted. We didn't keep watch, of course, being anchored in harbour, and Stevo woke about two in the morning and shouted: 'Good God! We're full of water!' It was nearly up to the top of the engine cover. We got cracking with buckets, hurling the water over the gunwale. It was quicker than pumping. A bit of wind had come up and was swaying her from side to side. You'd never believe what a nasty feeling it is when a whole boatful of water wallows from side to side. It was pitch dark. We did all we could with the buckets, and then Stevo said: 'Finish off with the pump.' I said: 'Have a heart! I'm fagged out.' Stevo gave me a clip across the ear, and said: 'Finish off with the pump. You pee'd after I did, so it's you who did the damage. Now get cracking.' It was a lesson. I never forgot it. I hope I manage to stay with Stevo through this lot."

Begbie seemed glad to have this anecdote to fill the moment. Frances and Stephen came out of the bedroom, and there was a sound of heavy steps on the stair. Knuckles rapped on the door. It was the taxi-man. He picked up the suitcases and went away. The two young men put on their caps, pulled on their kid gloves. It gave them a look of completion.

"Well, now," said Stephen. "Ready, Bugs? Don't come down, you folks. I hate being seen off. So long, Fran. All the best, Dook."

Frances and I listened to the sound of the footsteps going down the stairs. We heard them clearly on the oilcloth which led to this top landing, faintly on the carpet below, and then we heard them no more. Even when we heard them no more, we both stood there for a moment, intently listening to nothing. This nothingness was unbearable to listen to, and presently we relaxed with a simultaneous sigh.

6

I took train to Chichester and put up at a pub. There was at least a chance, I thought, of seeing Adam before events swallowed him up. I hadn't written to him. It was no time to impose upon a young man the demanding affection of an old one.

He walked into the pub with three other pilots as I sat there drinking a pint. They all looked very young, very excited, the wings above their breast pockets very new.

"Well, Dook! Of all the damned apparitions!"

He introduced his companions. One was Freddie Freemantle. I ordered drinks, and, with a nice consideration, the other boys moved off with theirs, leaving me and Adam alone.

"Well," he said, "a year ago doesn't seem far off. A year hence – I wonder. Do you remember a year ago, Dook?"

I did. He had come to the studio to say goodbye – "just in case". He had been to see Frances, and they had pushed John round Hampstead Heath in a pram.

"Did you say goodbye to Frances this time?" I asked him.

"No. It couldn't be managed." He took a pull at his beer. "I shouldn't have gone, anyway," he said. "Fran was getting a damned sight too fond of me."

"She was always fond of you."

"I didn't say fond, Dook. I said too fond."

I couldn't think of the answer to that. Adam had our tankards refilled, and we sat for a time in silence, swigging and smoking. At last he said: "I used to go round to Hampstead a lot. There was nothing much else to do during weekend leave – at any rate, nothing else that I particularly wanted to do. The Widow had deserted me, and I was at a loose end. So I wandered up to Hampstead one weekend and found Stevo away. What's more, I found he was away almost every weekend. And, for a time, going up there became a habit. I thought it was worthwhile for one thing because it set Fran off again."

"Writing?"

"Yes. She'd got a bit under the weather, you know, so far as that went. She'd not only stopped writing, but she'd got into a bad way of laughing about it, as though it were all nonsense anyway. Well, I didn't like that. I had to cure her of it."

"I never see what she does," I said. "By accident, I came on some of the stuff she was writing as a child. But I know nothing about her work now. Is it any good?"

Adam shrugged his shoulders. "So, so. Immature. But what does that matter? Whether it's good or bad isn't the point. The point is that she believed in the importance of something outside herself. She believed that something immaterial was valuable, and she was losing that belief. She was selling the pass to the Philistines, and, by God, we mustn't do that."

His handsome boyish face blushed at his own enthusiasm and he added apologetically: "I hope you don't think I'm talking poppycock, Dook."

"On the contrary," I hastened to assure him. "I believe what you say is right. I must believe it or die."

"Where do we get to without it?" he demanded. "Look at this bloody business. Don't think I'm going into it like a playboy. I'm not. I know what it's going to mean. I'm a fighter pilot. I've got a Hurricane. I shall meet Messerschmitts and what not, and if it isn't me it'll be him. It'll be some poor damned Boche smashed to blood and bones in a pile of wreckage. That doesn't sit nicely on my stomach, Dook. And that's not all. Maybe I shall transfer into bombers, and then what? Well, if you shoot down some poor sod, at least it's a battle. There is you, and there is your enemy. You're face to face. It's your guts and skill against his, and you know all that there is in it. Some elements of decency are left. But bombing – by Christ! You see nothing. You know nothing. You're an inhuman force blowing children out of the womb and old men out of their armchairs by the fireside. Let's stop boozing and go out."

He waved to his friends who were getting noisy in their corner, and we went out and walked in the cool dusky streets.

"So you see how it is, Dook," Adam said. "If I can't believe in something outside myself, where the hell am I? Can I, as me, do that sort of thing? I can do it only if I'm not me any longer – only if I'm a mere instrument of something that is not me: call it what you like – justice, truth, liberty – but it's got to be something damned important, something that survives."

He was deeply troubled. At any time since I had known Adam I could have guessed the sort of things that both disturbed and fortified him, but he had never before uncovered them to me.

"England, my England, is no good to me," he said, "except insofar as she means this damned important thing I'm talking about. If she doesn't mean that, then she's nothing but *me* a bit bigger; and if she does mean it, then she's not England: she's just the box that happens to hold a bit of the spikenard. And it's the spikenard that matters, not the box. The spikenard, wherever it is."

We walked in silence for a while, and then he said: "Excuse the woolly metaphors. Just like a bloody poet."

I put my arm through his. I felt very near to him. "I'm glad you've said all this," I assured him. "You know, I don't myself think poets bloody."

"No, Dook. I know you don't. You've always been a comfort to me. Forgive the outburst of exhibitionism. We've wandered a long way from Fran. What I was getting at was this: I just hated to see her going dead, because, oddly enough, I *believe* what I've been talking about. Religion and the arts are the things outside ourselves which we just can't afford to betray unless we are ready to sell everything to the Philistines. I'm not. That's all I'm trying to say."

I said: "I don't think, my dear boy, you need worry over-much about Frances. When I was younger, I was in touch with people holding what I took to be odd religious views. For example, once saved, saved forever. There might be backsliding, but the lamb could not finally fall to the wolf. It would at last return to the fold. Perhaps they were right. Perhaps Fran is like that."

"I don't believe it," he said decisively. "I believe you can be born with the light in your eyes and still turn from it. And that is the grand refusal. That is the thing that is worse than having never seen the light at all. I don't think Fran is in that danger, but I sometimes wonder whether the whole world isn't."

I had not expected this sort of conversation with Adam, but I was glad we were having it. "Tell me anything you like," I said, "about you and Fran. I know that you love one another."

"We do. Well, as I say, I used to go out to Hampstead a lot at weekends. I never felt happy about it. I had stumbled quite by accident on the fact that Stevo was not at home at those times, and I always went away feeling that I'd taken a mean advantage. I knew that Fran was not telling him of my visits. Well, one Saturday night I was there very late, and she said: 'Why bother to go back to your hotel? I can give you a shakedown on the couch.' So I rested on the couch that night, and I might as well tell you I didn't get much sleep. I'm human. The next weekend Fran said: 'I expected you'd bring your things with you. Why stay at a hotel? Why don't we have all the time together that there is?' It was a pretty big question, Dook, and I had to find the answer. I never went again unless there was good reason to think Stevo would be there. Once, he wasn't. Fran had guessed pretty well why I hadn't been coming at weekends, and we were very nervous with one another. You know, excessively polite for a time, and then the whole façade broke down. There were mutual confessions, and old Stevo was there in the room all the time like a self-confident unsuspecting ghost – a complacent ghost, rather pathetic. Nothing passed between us but words – pretty broken words, believe me – and a kiss or two. That was towards the end of last July. I haven't seen her since."

Freddie Freemantle and the others came along the street. Their voices were loud and gay. They were singing *Come, landlord, fill the flowing bowl*, simple souls, choosing even in their cups the first simple words that came to mind. Adam steered me into a dark turning till they had gone by, and then, at a distance, we followed them towards the camp.

"Tell me," I said, "have you any news of your mother?"

"Yes. She's still at Cap Ferrat, and she says she's going to stay there. I've asked her to come back to England, but not she. She's going to see the war through where she is. I wonder."

We reached the camp gates and shook hands. "Well, Dook, thank you for coming. You know, this is one of those dawns in which it's blessed to be alive, but for the young the chances of finding very heaven are abnormally high."

"Any message for Fran?"

"No. I think not."

"When are you off? If you're allowed to say."

"Honestly, Dook, I don't know. I'd tell you if I could, and to hell with security. Good night now."

As soon as I had had breakfast the next morning I hurried down towards the aerodrome. I leaned upon a fence, and a long way off, vague in the misty autumn air, I could see a group of aeroplanes squatting on the ground. It was a peaceful September day – a day for picking blackberries – a silvery-blue day that would be warm later. I filled my pipe and paced about there for an hour as the strengthening sun sucked away the mist and drew outlines more sharply. Then I saw a handful of men running across the aerodrome. They were too far off for me to see their faces. They ran clumsily in great flying-boots; they were padded out like huge badly-tied parcels. They disappeared into the cockpits of the machines. Soon the machines were taxiing across the ground, and then one by one they rose into the now-clear air. They beat up the aerodrome for a while; then the whole squadron formed into line astern, so gallant, so vulnerable, upon the blue. When the sound of their going was dead, still with my eyes I followed the diminishing specks; and when they could be seen no more, still I stood there, biting on a cold pipe, and followed them with my heart.

7

One would imagine that this war had been organised as a piece of spite personally addressed against Blanche. "Just as we were settled down so comfortably," she kept on saying.

It was an unpleasant day, dark and lowering. I had called on Frances, and Blanche came in just as we were sitting down to tea. She complained about the stairs. She complained about the dimness of the little sitting room. She complained in retrospect saying that what she had had to put up with in the last war nobody would ever understand; and she advanced her complaints into the future. Soon enough, she supposed, we shouldn't be able to meet like this because there simply wouldn't be anything to eat. "And when it's all over there'll be years and years of misery."

"Actually, Frances," she said, putting more butter onto the buttered toast that Fran had provided, "actually, I called to see whether you wouldn't come away with me and Kitty. And bring John with you, of course."

"But, Mother, I didn't know you were going away. This is the first I've heard of it."

"Well, it's all settled. We got the final letter this morning. It stands to reason that the fewer people there are in London the easier it will be for the government if serious bombing starts. Anyone who can go ought to go, I say. Kitty and I thought for a time of going to America, but that had to be ruled out. I should feel most uncomfortable with people who haven't joined us in the struggle. If they had come in, it would have been another matter. Then I'd have gone like a shot. As it is, we've found a very nice couple to take over the lease in Well Walk, and we shall go to Torquay."

"I hope you'll be most comfortable," Frances said dutifully.

"As I've been trying to make clear," Blanche insisted, "it's not a matter of comfort. It's a matter of our patriotic duty to relieve the government of anxiety. I hope you will see it like that and come with us. John will be a bit of a trial for Kitty, but she's willing to see how it works out."

"Give her my thanks," said Frances, "and tell her I fear he'll be too much of a handful. He'd better stay here where I can wrestle with him. And Torquay wouldn't be very handy for Stevo, would it?"

"Well, the decision's yours," Blanche said, satisfied at having done her duty, but not without a look of relief. "I don't know Torquay, but Kitty does. She says the hotel she's chosen is most comfortable, but not so big that some greedy government department will want to snatch it. Good gracious! What a mess this richly-buttered toast makes of one's fingers! I must wash my hands, child."

Frances took her into the bedroom while I carried the tea things to the kitchen and washed up. When I returned to the sitting room Blanche was ready to leave. I said I would go with her as far as Well

Walk. My overcoat and scarf were thrown on the bed, and when I went to get them I took a look at my face in the mirror over the washbasin and drew a comb through my hair. My eyes were caught by a gleam in the filter over the waste pipe, and, fishing with a hairpin from the dressing table, I pulled out a plain gold ring. No doubt it was Blanche's. It had been buttered off her finger. I remembered how she had shown me this ring once at Tresco Vean, and I looked for the inscription within the band. It was there no longer, but there was evidence of recent work by which it had been erased.

I find it hard to explain why I felt as if I had received an all but mortal blow. It was as though I had known for a long time that Blanche's life was flickering out, and had at last been told that she was dead. I had, too, an extraordinary sense of Francis Chellew's presence, as though we were looking at the ring together, as though we shared this disillusioning moment of insight into the treachery life could impose.

It was a December evening. Darkness was come and a bitter wind was blowing as Blanche and I walked down Parliament Hill. She was swathed to the eyes in expensive furs.

"What are you going to do with Amy Lingard, Blanche?"

"Well, actually, Amy was a bit of a problem. We couldn't have taken her to Torquay, could we? I mean, what could she have done there?"

"She's done plenty in her time. I don't suppose she'd have objected to taking it easy for a while."

"No, Ted. I couldn't see her doing it. She's not the type to take things easy. Not that that's the word. The contemplative type is not necessarily taking things easy. However, Amy didn't give us a chance. She took the decision right out of our hands."

"And what did she decide?"

"She's going into munitions. Don't you think that's splendid?"

"Yes. She's been with the Pentecosts for a quarter of a century, you know."

"Indeed I know! And then to come to a decision like that, without a moment's hesitation! It shows you that all this stuff one hears about British decadence is pure poppycock."

"Blanche, you dropped your ring – your wedding ring – in Fran's wash-basin. I fished it out. Here it is."

She drew off a long silver-grey fur glove and slipped the ring on to her finger. In the blackout there was not even an efficient street lamp to show me her face. We walked on in silence for a moment, then I said: "Do you ever think of Fran's father nowadays?"

"Of course I do," she said with a kind of defensive asperity. "I think of him day and night."

I wished she had been honourable enough to say: "No. That's all done with, Ted. Francis has been a ghost for too long, and now he's vanished utterly." But her voice sounded as hollow as a tin can that has lost its contents.

"How could I leave that inscription in the ring?" she asked petulantly. "As a matter of fact, it slipped off my finger once before. Mercifully, I found it in the washbasin. Supposing Kitty had found it and looked inside? What on earth would she have made of it? She loathes impropriety. She wouldn't take back that husband of hers if he came crawling to her tomorrow."

There seemed nothing more to be said. When we reached Well Walk, Blanche asked: "Will you come in? We can give you a decent glass of sherry. We took care to lay some in before it becomes unobtainable."

I pleaded an appointment, and when her front door was shut I hurried back to Frances' flat. John had been put to bed, and Frances was sitting by the electric fire reading Donne's poems. I didn't know Donne's poems myself, but looking at Fran's almost lint-white hair shining under the light I remembered that Adam had once commended them to me. My heart was filled with grief for Fran's loneliness and sorrow. We read to one another and talked and cooked a sketchy supper. As I was about to leave I said: "Fran, why not come and live with me at the studio? What's the sense in your being here all alone? I'm lonely, and so are you. John will be no trouble at all, and there's a homely full-bosomed barmaid who looks after the place."

"Dook, you are a darling. And you make that last consideration sound irresistible."

"You'll come, then?"

"I should love to."

She kissed me, and I went home feeling happier than I had expected to be.

8

Blanche was gone and Frances was installed at Chelsea, and I began to live with more content than I had known since Prue died. Fran and I were able to spend a good deal of time together, for Joe's daughter took a liking for little John and was not only willing but anxious to push the pram in the afternoons. Then Frances and I would ourselves go for a walk, arriving back as dusk was falling. Our best times were after tea, with the long curtained evenings before us. I gave up going to the King's Mistress for an evening meal. We had a good meal there at midday, and at night Fran would cook a snack, so that we had not to bother to go out. We liked to feel that once the curtains had been drawn and the fire made up, what was left of the day was ours. We read to one another, or I read to myself while Fran did a bit of writing. We even played childish games with counters, and I am sure a good deal of stress and tension was eased out of Frances' mind. Now and then we went to a theatre. I sounded Joe about what could be done with John if Frances and I were out in the evening, and he answered without hesitation: "You bring 'im in 'ere, Mr Pentecost."

I must admit it was a hesitant Frances who wrapped John in a shawl, when we were ready to go out that night, and carried him across the yard. She had not attained my fullness of faith in the humanity of British pubs and pub keepers.

"In 'ere, Mrs Pentecost," Joe invited heartily, and we passed through to his private parlour where, from time to time, I had had the privilege of being his guest. I shall not linger over a description of that room which my mind still treasures as the most perfect survival I have known of the Victorian lower-class domestic interior. Now, added to its congestion of monumental furniture and aery bric-à-brac, there was an oak cradle near the hospitable fire, and by the cradle stood Mrs Joe and "our Bess". A blanket, lying in the cradle, overflowed onto the floor on either side. Bess took John in her arms, laid him down, and folded the blanket about him. We all five stood looking down at him, undisturbed, unawakened, ready, it seemed, to make an excellent night of it whether in a parlour behind a pub or in a ship's crow's nest. Joe stirred the cradle lightly on its rockers with his toe. "Ay," he said reminiscently, "our Bess' that was. Fancy, Mother, you used to put 'er in it just like that. An' look at 'er now."

501

Well, Bess certainly would have needed an ampler bed now to do justice to her charms. "Cheese it, Pa," she said. "Where's that net?"

A villainous red tomcat, with torn ears and other honourable scars won in the lists of love, rose on a chair, yawned, and regarded us with contemptuous yellow eyes. Bess tied the net taut over the cradle. "There you are, Percy," she said. "That keeps you out." Percy rearranged himself with a paw tight over his nose as though sleeping on a baby's face was the last thought that would enter his mind. "You never know," Mrs Joe said. "Nearly lost our Bess once that way, we did. It's not that they mean any 'arm. They don't think. After all, they're not 'uman."

"No," said Joe. "The way 'uman beings are thinkin' about one another's peace and comfort today is a hell of a consolation to all concerned. Wot about a quick 'un, Mr Pentecost, before you go?"

9

"My dear Dook," Adam wrote,

when you have sufficiently enriched the National Portrait Gallery and retire to a 'nice little place' in Cornwall, you may need to lay some land drains in one of your fields. Just ring up the Air Ministry and ask to have Flight Lieutenant Adam Randle – or perhaps by then Air Vice-Marshal A.R. – detached for this temporary duty. However hoary I may have become, I shall not have forgotten how to dig. My God! I thought I should be Icarus, singeing my wings in the sun's corona, and I am Adam after the fall, Adam laboriously turning up flints and earthworms and rasping his spade occasionally on fundamental gneiss. We have moved Hither and Thither, and you must remain in profound darkness as to where those two villages are. All I can tell you about them is that they exist in many places on the map of France, and that, when you arrive at either, you begin to dig. Someone is most sensitive about the value of our young lives. We must have trenches to leap into. The other day Freddie and I, beginning ten yards apart, were confronted in no time. 'How now, old mole? Canst work i' the earth so fast?' I cried, and Freddie answered: 'Shut up, you silly sod. Get on digging.' Thus is life resolved to its elements.

However, we have bathed and boozed, we have played football, and we have even flown, but life has its dull and earthbound patches. So our autumn has passed and our winter is passing. We are minus some of those who began this adventure with us, and the Boche is minus some of his. I have been amongst those responsible for this, and you'd never believe with what little satisfaction I contemplate that fact.

I have made my first visit to Germany, and from 26,000 feet it looks remarkably like France, or England for that matter. All that happens to me at that height is that I don't want to go home. I get a beautiful muzzy feeling, Dook, with the blue above and snowy rafts of cloud below, and vague supra-physical dreams wambling about in my skull. I have to take hold of myself, remind myself that Icarus' wings are only gummed on, and that he is not in fact lighter than air, and that he'd better watch his step.

I wangled some leave about a week ago and spent it in Paris. The Widow came up from Cap Ferrat, and we had a couple of wonderful days together. She is looking very well and sends her love to you. I would rather she were in England than in France, and I told her so. But no, no. Mamma knows best. She is content where she is, and she will see the war through in her chosen paradise. I am not happy about it.

It fills me with salutary remorse as I realise that this is the first time I have written to you since coming out. I'm glad I was able to spend that last evening as I did instead of boozing with the boys. I don't know how the bomber boys feel – a nice little crew of them all together; but, believe me, a solitary fighter, ranging the sky like a condor looking for prey over the Andes, gets some funny thoughts. At such times I occasionally push the buttons of my guns, just to reassure myself with the sense of a power that I can call up at my own will; and then I think 'Stop it, you B.F.! You may need every last bullet.' When you see another condor, and finally decide that he's not one of yours, the funny thoughts vanish and you realise the meaning of 'the sticking-point' – everything clicking together to make you a machine of skill and craftiness. And then, when it's over, and you are wandering slowly homeward, alone in the sky once more, the funny thoughts come back again and you are glad that there's a bottle or two in the mess and you can get plastered. And this is an especial comfort if someone you have been expecting to join you fails for some odd reason to do so. I miss Freddie Freemantle very much. My love to you, Dook, and to anyone else who cares to accept it.

Adam.

10

I began from Stephen's letters to piece together some picture of his way of life. There was "the old man", a "regular R.N. type", whom I discovered later to be what I should have called a nice-looking boy in his late thirties. There was Number One, and there was the Doc, and there was, of course, old Bugs, who was in the same destroyer. There was the grey midwinter Atlantic, and there was oiling; occasionally there was a foot briefly ashore, and, looming like a beacon of hope, there was a boiler-clean. "I shall almost certainly get home for a day or two if we are ordered a boiler-clean."

He came in March. The evenings were lengthening. In the parks daffodils and almond trees were in flower. It was possible, in the early days of that spring, to hope again. Nothing had happened. Freddie Freemantle was dead. A boy from Bootle had been washed overboard from Stephen's destroyer and drowned. Millions were uprooted from their homes and occupations all over Europe. Amy Lingard was working in a Yorkshire factory. But everything was at a pause, hesitant: nothing much had happened in the swift cataclysmic sense that we had all dreaded when the war began. A letter from Iris had got through to me. She wrote of the mimosa in her garden and of a whitlow that she was treating on Albert Montjolis' thumb. Yes: I think of that early spring of 1940 as the last time when it was possible to hope. It was possible to be such a fool as to listen to some who said that, as nothing much had happened, so nothing much would happen.

Stephen was at home for four days. I lived in the pub with Joe, leaving the studio to Stephen and Frances. Every day they went off on some jaunt together. Bess and I between us looked after little John. In the evenings I would spend a few hours with the young people in the studio. Stephen had nothing much to say about his life at sea, except that destroyers were too big for him.

"But, Stevo, I've always thought of them as the whippets of the fleet."

He was confident and sure of himself. His uniform was no longer an advertisement for Gieves. He stuffed his hoary-looking pipe with tobacco which he could buy at an enviably cheap price. "They're too big for *me*," he said. "What would be absolute death would be to be transferred to a battle-wagon. I couldn't stand the pie frills. I want a command of my own."

"What sort of ship are you thinking of?"

"Oh, something with a crew of about a dozen that goes out and does a buccaneering job. Something like the German E-boats."

"I've never heard of them."

"Neither had the Admiralty, apparently, when the war began, although the Germans have had them for years. I expect their Lordships'll get round to it in time. Then we shall see. It'll be too small beer for the R.N. types, of course. It'll be a hundred per cent R.N.V.R. force, and we'll have some fun. All pie and no frills."

This was the last evening of his leave, and I remember it for one thing because it was the last time that he and Adam met. Adam came in at about nine o'clock. He did not know that Frances was living at the studio or that Stephen was on leave. He unceremoniously pushed open the door after a perfunctory rap on a panel and walked in amongst us. It was a raw night. The collar of his greatcoat was turned up and he was carrying a suitcase. His sudden coming in like that out of the night – I had almost written his materialising – had an air of the dramatic to us sitting there in ease at the fireside. We looked at one another in surprised silence for a while; then Adam lowered his suitcase to the ground and said: "Well! I seem to have broken up something."

He had. There was no doubt about that. An air of tension came into the room with him. To relieve it, I got up and shook hands with him. "Take off your coat and come to the fire," I said.

He dropped his coat onto a couch and threw his cap upon it.

He was wearing the ribbon of the D.F.C. We all saw that at once, though no one said anything about it. But it was there, a small eloquent résumé of hazard beyond our earthbound experience. He shook hands with Fran and Stephen and sat at the fireside. I gave him a drink. He raised his glass to Stephen, and said: "To the exceptionally Silent Service."

Stephen seemed to give himself a mental shake. "Sorry, Adam," he said. "You must admit you've been a bit sudden. You've taken the wind out of our sails."

Adam sipped his drink and smiled. "Observe, Dook," he said, "that even now this boy can't pull himself out of antiquity. He means I've taken the oil out of his boilers."

"He means," I said, "that you've still to explain a somewhat abrupt apparition."

"It's very simple. Every hotel in London appears to be full. I'm going North tomorrow, and I thought you might give me a shakedown tonight. I expected you to be alone. That's all."

I explained the situation. I told him that I should be sleeping at Joe's, and that I had no doubt he could sleep there, too.

"Well, then," he said, "let's be going."

He got up and pulled on his overcoat, and at that Stephen woke to life and began to urge him to stay longer. Frances said nothing. She had said nothing since Adam came into the room. Adam would not stay. "No, really, Stevo. I'm tired to death, and I shall have to be up first thing in the morning. I've got a long journey before me."

Nothing would persuade him. "Well," I said, "I'd better come with you and fix things with Joe. See you in the morning, Stevo."

"What about you, Adam?" Stephen asked. "Shall I see you?"

"Oh, dear, no. I shall have to be a very early bird. *Au revoir* and happy landings."

He shook hands with him and Frances, and we went out together into the bleak night. As soon as we were under the sky he dropped his suitcase and leaned against a wall. "Well, of all the damned things!" he said. "I'm sorry, Dook. I wouldn't have had it happen for the world. D'you know, I've been boozing round town all night, fighting with a bloody little devil who's been urging me to go to Fran's flat at Hampstead. I win. I feel gallant and virtuous, and I walk into that! His last night of leave, too. My God! Of all the damned things!"

He was deeply upset. "It couldn't be helped," I said. "You couldn't know. I ought to have told you she'd shifted."

"Is there any possibility of getting a taxi at this time of night?" he asked.

"I think I could raise one. I know a private-hire man. Why?"

"Because I'm going straight to the L.N.E.R. station. I shall not spend a night here. I shall sleep in a waiting room."

I did my best to dissuade him, but he held out. I went with him, and in the taxi he was silent for a long time. At last he said: "This is the most heart-breaking business. It begins with this awful balls-up, and do you know how it goes on?"

How could I guess?

"I'm going to spend my leave with Freddie's people. Can you imagine what that's going to be like? The old boy keeping a stiff upper lip, the old girl getting me into corners to show me photographs of him at his kindergarten and things like that. And then the moment when one of them says at dinner with a brave smile: 'Well, now, we don't want to talk about it, but just for once, and to get it over, how did Freddie die?' There's all that in front of me, Dook. I did my best to get out of it, but, seeing that my mother is in France, they thought it would be a kindness to give me a nice homely leave."

"I see you've got the D.F.C."

"Oh, bugger the D.F.C. There are plenty who deserve it more than I do, and they're in such little bits that you couldn't find a place to pin it on them."

There was nothing to be done with him in this mood. I said goodbye to him in the draughty echoing station, hell-lit with vague blue lights, and the next morning I said goodbye to Stephen. And after March there was April, and then there was May.

11

It was in May that the dams burst and the iron flood of the barbarians swirled across Europe. Norway, Denmark, Holland, Belgium, France. But again let me say that it doesn't come within my intention to write of all that. At the end of May I received the last letter that ever reached me from Iris.

My dearest Ted – I am very well. The weather is lovely and I have begun sunbathing. Last week I woke up in the night with an ache in my left knee. I haven't felt it since, and no doubt it was nothing more than a rheumatic twinge. But this was quite literally the first ache or pain I have ever had in my life, barring the pangs of Adam's birth; and therefore it infuriated me! I am a bag of bones, but such healthy bones that a creak in one of them seems indecent and not to be endured. And so I have been going back to gymnastics. I find with pleasure that I can still lie on the ground and touch the floor over my head with my toes. I can do a handspring and walk on my hands. And I am fifty-four years old! How I must love and trust you to make that confession!

I am as brown as a coffee-bean, and this morning I had my first swim of the season – all part of my defiant campaign against that traitorous pain in the night! I *will* not grow old, my darling. Every right-thinking woman should remember that old French dear who was captivating lovers in her seventies. I hasten to add, dear Ted, that I am captivating no lovers here.

Do you know: when I was swimming this morning I thought that if I could swim to England I would. It would – would it not? – be a surprise for a grumpy old Academician, suffering from increasing *embonpoint*, to see this brown reed haul itself out of the water under that old chapel of yours at Falmouth. But I decided against it, because I'm not much of a swimmer. However, lying on that beautiful blue water, and looking up at the beautiful blue sky, I thought of many reasons why I would have done it if I could. For one thing, it was all so lovely that I began thinking of you, darling Ted. I wanted so much to be with you – whether here or there. I have told you before that I shall marry you, and this morning I felt such a longing for you that I am sure I have been wrong to wait. I have been happy here – most happy. My life has been such a harum-scarum affair that the idea of this pause in it at first terrified me. But really, Ted, it has been a great success. I see hardly a soul except my two old French people; I read what Adam sends me; and I find that my own company, after all, is nothing to be afraid of. It has done me a lot of good, but now at last I am beginning again to feel restless, and this happens when I think of you.

Well, that's one reason why this poor fish wanted to swim to England; and another is that the atmosphere here has become disturbed. Briefly, my Montjolis couple have developed the jitters. So long as the extraordinary static war continued they were valiant and talked of the Maginot Line as a cliff on which the Germans would batter themselves to pieces. But now that there is movement, they sway between melancholy and bitter anger. I am not very good at French, but I understand enough of their chatter to know that they are afraid, and that they endlessly discuss what they shall take with them if they fly. Where they will fly to I don't know, and I don't think they do, either.

I am still optimistic enough to feel that we are as well off here as anywhere; but all the same the joy is going out of things. Their fears are beginning to infect me. If a reasonable chance of returning to England were to present itself now, I'm not sure I wouldn't take it. At the same time, I feel some responsibility to these old people. Though I fear that I am becoming in a way an embarrassment to them, still, if I went it would be the perfidious English saving their skins again. I can understand how they feel, because in the last war, when they were children, they knew it all. They both lived, then, in the track of the invasion.

Well, my dearest one, this letter, which began with a certain gaiety, is turning melancholy. But don't let that be the last impression. Think of me as one who is thinking of you and who finds much consolation therein. I have Adam to think of, too. God bless and preserve him. Was ever woman more fortunate than the one who can think of Ted and Adam and say 'They are mine. They love me.' So splendid –

That sentence was never finished. Perhaps the postman was coming. Perhaps some domestic crisis arose. I shall never know. "All my love, Iris," was added, as if in haste.

12

It is all behind me as I write. What was then beginning is now ended. If there is any ending in the ceaseless concatenation of cause become event, and old event giving birth to new cause. It is difficult to see "ending" written over the huge graveyard of Europe and Asia. The ghosts will squeak and gibber yet to some effect.

I am writing in Falmouth, in this old studio that was Kitto's and now is mine. I went this morning to see Iris' grave. My ghosts are widely scattered. I have graves in Manchester and Falmouth, in

Highgate and in a drear village on the East coast. This is June, and this morning the sun was shining and singing birds were shaking dew from the trees in the graveyard. I was there early and my shoes were wet in the long grass. There was no one else about: nothing but the trees and the singing birds, the dew, the sunshine and the dead. The graveyard is on sloping ground. Looking down, you see a long mere glistening at its foot, with reeds thick at the edges. In the winter, when they are dry, the wind rustles them in a dirge. This morning they were green and silent. I walked down from Iris' grave to the flat ground at the bottom. There, a long oblong of earth with a flagstaff in the middle is sown with the crosses of those who died off our bit of coast. R.N., R.N.V.R., R.N.R., the inscriptions run; and there are "unknown sailors," Frenchmen, Dutchmen, Chinese cooks, a V.C., all come in out of the stormy deep, out of the last bitter moment of flood or flame, to lay their bones in this quiet corner by the mere, where I have seen otters playing, and where the reeds are silent in summer and full of whispering sadness when the winter dusk comes down early. I walked along the orderly rows of those who are Iris' mute companions forever and ever. The many men, so beautiful . . .

It was on a day like this, a June day of blazing sunshine, in the month following the month when Iris' last letter reached me, that I left Frances in Chelsea and travelled down to Falmouth alone. No one who lived through those few days will ever forget them. How often the great moments of human destiny are summed up in the name of a town, a village, a mere hamlet. You have but to utter the name and it becomes a window through which you look out upon watersheds, upon the traffic policemen of history, waving the milling human hordes along this road or that of splendour or disaster. Nazareth, Waterloo, Cambrai, Munich; and now it was Dunkirk.

With so much in the balance, it was a triviality that was taking me to Cornwall. The motor launch that Ernie Lingard used, though his in all that mattered, remained technically mine. Some commission or committee or what not of the Admiralty had been combing the waters about Falmouth in search of small craft, and the launch was among those that they had decided to acquire. There were some formalities to be gone through, some papers to be signed, and it was this that took me to Falmouth.

Ernie met me at the station. On his left sleeve he was wearing an armband with the letters L.D.V. We did not speak of that or of the anxiety eating at our hearts of which these laconic letters were one of the symbols. "How did you leave Fran?" he asked.

"Very well, considering," I said.

"About time Ah saw Stevo's boy. 'Fore we know where we are Ah s'p'ose Ah'll be teaching 'im to sail. What's the news of Stevo?"

I had none to give him. I could have given him a picture that was in my heart of that fateful lane between Dover and Dunkirk, that artery through which now the lifeblood was being pumped back from France to England, pumped back through a congestion of ships wrecked, ships ablaze, ships limping, loaded with weary undefeated men, while the sky darkened with fatal wings and the sea leapt and quivered. Perhaps Stephen was in that. Perhaps not. I had no means of knowing. My heart was with him all the time, remembering the pain and puzzlement in his face the morning after I had seen Adam away on his journey to visit the Freemantles. We took a turn or two together in King's Mistress Yard, talking trivialities for a moment, and then suddenly he blurted out: "I wonder what brought Adam here last night?"

"Simply the need of a bed," I assured him.

"Did he know that Fran was here?"

"Oh, no. I'm sure he didn't. I hadn't told him, and how else could he have known?"

He lit his pipe and said between puffs, as he held his hands cupped round the bowl: "That's all right, then. I just wondered. Does Fran write to him?"

"No."

"That's all right then," he repeated, and added earnestly: "I'm very fond of Fran. You understand that, don't you? Look after her for me."

"I'm doing my best."

"I know. I wish I'd done so. I don't think I did, you know. All those weekends away. It wasn't good enough. Fun for me, but rather dull for her. When this lot's over I'll organise a new regime. Well, here's the taxi. Thanks for listening to my bind."

Ernie and I walked down the station approach and turned onto the sea front, silent, each closed in his own thoughts. In a few minutes we were at the old chapel. I stood at the window, looking out onto the harbour. The merchant ships no longer sported gay bands and devices on their funnels or any colour on their topsides. From truck to waterline they were a grim repellent grey. But the sea was its old burning summertime blue, the sky was cloudless, and a few yachts were on the water. Ernie, who had gone down to the kitchen, appeared at my side with a tray. "Better have a cup o' tea, Dook."

He put the tray down on a table, and we stood there side by side while the tea got cold and nothing was eaten, and we felt old and useless men. The very tranquillity of the scene bit into our hearts. It was a way of life, a way of peace, and we could feel its foundations trembling.

As we stood there, a dirty-looking coaster, belching villainous smoke into the clear air, crawled slowly into sight, stopped, and ran out an anchor. I took up the glasses that always stood on the window ledge and brought her into view. She was flying a tattered French flag, and she was crowded with men, women and children. I gazed at her in astonishment. Never in my life had I seen the like. They were standing in her from bows to stern. They were stuck in thick clusters upon the housing. There was not an inch where they did not seem to grow like bunches of grapes on an unthinned vine.

I handed the glasses to Ernie. "What on earth do you make of that?"

He gave her a long look. "Some of 'em are soldiers," he said. "Never saw such a mix up. Soldiers an' civvies. Women and children."

She was the first, and in the days that followed there were such scenes upon the harbour as it can never have known before and I hope to God it will never see again. Ernie and I went down to the pier head that evening and joined the group looking speculatively upon this apparition which brought a chill reality into the tranquillity of the summer night. It was not difficult to guess what lay behind the dirty ship and her teeming freight, what disruption of homes, what tearing asunder, what closing in of an enemy, sweeping them to the shore, sweeping them on to the sea.

"Where's she from?"

"Bordeaux."

Bordeaux . . . the edge of the waters . . . Ernie and I walked back through the warm quiet night, and my mind was full of the picture of the edge of the waters and the barbarian flood swirling towards it, piling upon it thousands of hapless wretches praying for an inch of iron deck, life reduced to the contents of a handbag and the sea's uncertain hazard.

They continued to come in during the next few days: sailing boats and steam boats, boats big enough to be called liners and things no bigger than the *Frances and Stephen* that a couple of men could sail and that were now congested with thirty or forty. A vast armada, anchored or tied to buoys, almost touching one another, they lay upon the harbour, with dinghies plying between them and official launches hurrying from one to another upon whatever affairs so unprecedented an invasion required to be done. The heavenly weather continued. The June sun burned down. The water was unrippled. Standing well out to seaward in the launch which was still ours, Ernie and I saw all those ships silhouetted between us and the shore over which the midsummer sunset smouldered with a drift of pink feathery clouds slowly turning to grey. Funnels, spars, rigging, a sail or two, the quiet darkening water and the dying day; voices calling through the dusk from ship to ship, the jigging music of a mouth organ, soldiers singing and a child crying: we moved, with the engine throttled down, through all this; and Ernie said: "I hope to God, Dook, no bombers find this lot," and miraculously none did.

They came ashore. Soldiers camped on the beaches; performances were suspended in the cinemas and the homeless sat there for hour after hour. They were given food there; they slept there. The streets were full of foreign tongues, and the banks were besieged with people fluttering sheaves of foreign notes that they wished to change. It was a phenomenon as old as the hills: war's brutal kicking over of the anthill, the scurrying of the ants; but it was new to us, and we walked through the familiar streets in wonder to find them so changed, to see the hopeless desperate eyes, to hear the shrill alarmed voices and the occasional heartbroken sob.

13

I was almost unknown in Falmouth. A few Royal Academicians had lived in the town: Tuke and Hemy and Kitto Pentecost, but they had *lived* there and become known there. I never had. Falmouth had not been for me more than an occasional holiday place. I was a short, stout, grey-haired person with no eccentricities of dress, and I could walk through the streets, thank God, without causing a head to turn.

Among the few people in Falmouth who knew me was a Nonconformist parson named Mathews. He had called upon me to ask me to speak to some guild or society in which he was interested. I had declined, but I had liked the man, and when we met we would stop and exchange a word or two.

During that week when the Bordeaux refugees arrived, I was sitting in the cool of an evening in the garden alongside the studio. It was a place of quiet and retirement. Few people, even of those who lived in Falmouth, knew of its existence. You turned into a lane off the narrow noisy main street, walked fifty yards or so to a gate, went in, and there you were. In a minor way, it was like leaving the racket of Fleet Street and finding oneself in the cool and quiet of the Temple.

I was sitting there smoking, thinking with pleasure that I should be returning in the morning to Frances and John, when Mathews came into the garden. He was accompanied by a man whom I took to be one of the refugees: a small gnarled mahogany creature with a long grey drooping moustache. He was wearing a greeny-black suit, a dirty, dented peaked cap that might once have belonged either to a sailor or a chauffeur, and brown leggings. Mathews looked tired and grave. I was not surprised. He was the sort of man who would expend himself ruthlessly on the situation that existed. I got up and shook hands with him and urged him to rest himself in my chair.

"I'm afraid there's no time, Mr Pentecost," he said. "This is Mr Montjolis."

The little man nodded his head vigorously and said, "Oui. C'est ça. Montjolis." He laid his fingers on his breast.

It was a beautiful evening, serene and cloudless. Suddenly it was dark. As never before, in one swift killing thrust I knew the meaning of the words "Brightness falls from the air."

I knew what Mathews was going to say next. "There is a lady named Randle in the hospital. She came in one of the ships. She is dying."

I put my pipe into my pocket with trembling fingers. I could not find a word to say. Mathews looked surprised to see me so stricken.

"She is someone – dear to you?" he asked.

I nodded, and he put a hand on my shoulder. "Let us go at once," he said. "We may be in time."

Montjolis was looking with small bright puzzled eyes from one to the other of us. Suddenly he said: "Madame est très malade. Faut se dépêcher. Elle va mourir."

He turned and began to walk away, looking back over his shoulder, like an eager little dog anxious to lead his owner to the scene of some discovery.

We walked along the main street, then turned up the hill towards the hospital. Montjolis was trotting ahead.

"This man Montjolis –" Mathews began, and Montjolis turned and said: "C'est moi. Montjolis. Je vous conduis à Madame." He placed his cap on his breast, bowed, and went trotting on.

"He has told me the story," said Mathews, carefully leaving out the man's name. "I won't bother you with it now, Mr Pentecost. He had heard Mrs Randle speak of you."

"Miss Randle," I corrected him. As if it mattered. As if anything mattered. "To be correct," I said, surprised to hear myself speaking such nonsense, "you would have to call her the Viscountess Moreton Hampstead. The title dies with her."

Everything dies with her.

"Oh," he said. "This man doesn't seem to know that."

"No."

"She was very ill indeed when the ship was coming into Falmouth. When they left Bordeaux they didn't know where they would land. But when it became apparent that it would be Falmouth, she was still well enough to understand that. Then she told this man that you might be in the town and that he must get in touch with you. She was delirious when they brought her ashore."

"What is the matter with her?"

"Pneumonia."

I learned it all later, the story of the long journey by road north-west through France, Montjolis driving the open car, his wife and Iris sitting in the back. They spent one night in the open, drawn up to the side of the road in a little wood, and they 'woke in the morning wet with dew. During the next day Iris began to shiver, but no one bothered. It was, Montjolis assured me, "un rien – un peu de fièvre." At Bordeaux they had not to wait as long as some, but it was long enough. They spent hours hanging about in warehouses and on draughty quays. Iris forbade Montjolis and his wife to fuss about her condition, which grew worse. She feared that a sick woman might be a complication that no ship's captain would add to a situation already desperate. So at last they all three got aboard a small cheerless ship, and Iris spent the first night at sea sitting on a coil of rope, leaning against the bulwarks. By the morning she was so obviously very ill that Montjolis informed an officer of the ship. For the rest of the voyage she was in a crowded cabin, receiving such attention as could be given her. It was not much. It was not enough. That is the simple story as I detached it later from the excited elaborations of Montjolis.

Mathews was known in the hospital, and it was known that he had gone in search of a friend of the unknown woman who was dying. Unknown except for a name. He and I were taken at once to a ward of which I remember nothing except the dim lights and the screen round a bed in a corner. I saw that she was living and that she was dying. She never knew me. She was now beyond knowing anything. Her hands lay upon the counterpane. Her eyes were closed. We had arrived at the utterly last moment.

Mathews was a simple instinctive man. He knelt at one side of the bed with his hands folded and his eyes shut, as no doubt he had done when a child, before climbing in. I knelt on the other side of the bed and watched his lips moving. As I have said, he was a Nonconformist parson, and it therefore surprised me, when he opened his eyes, to see him outline a cross in the air over Iris' breast. Somehow the antique gesture comforted me. At the same time it brought tears to my eyes, and, seeing the tears flow, Mathews smiled at me. It was odd to be here at the last with a man I scarcely knew; yet I was glad he was there, because through him all human forgiveness and compassion seemed to flow into my heart. Our faces were almost touching over the narrow bed, and I was surprised to hear myself whisper to him: "We should have been married if she had lived."

He reached out and took my right hand and laid it upon hers. Then he held both those hands in his, and whispered: "In the name of the Father, and of the Son, and of the Holy Ghost. Amen."

He got up, and I got up too. A nurse looked round the screen. "There is nothing more," Mathews said.

I kissed Iris upon the forehead and we went away on tiptoe as if fearing to wake her. Mathews remained behind in the hospital. I went out into the last light of the day. There would be no moon and there were not yet any stars. It was the anonymous moment between day and night, when the turmoil of living and the majesty of dying stand at truce, and one can believe in forgiveness or at least in forgetfulness. But what, I wondered, was there to forgive? And I was certain there was nothing I would forget.

CHAPTER FOURTEEN

I T WAS lonely in Chelsea when Frances and John had gone away. I was not doing much work, and at times I thought of closing the studio and going to live in Falmouth. Life was very noisy and dirty, disagreeable and dangerous in that year 1943. It was pointed out, of course, that it was also full of endurance, courage, the splendour of disaster borne by rich and poor alike with equal fortitude. One was asked to admire the orderly lives of the troglodytes in the tubes. They had established a model democracy which was conducted with humour and forbearance. And if London was in ruins, how magnificently it would rise again! It was almost possible to believe that a panel of theologians and architects had arranged the war as a means of promoting the immediate spiritual salvation of the people and the eventual architectural redemption of the city.

However, I was unable to enjoy the consolation of these fortunate illusions. I had lived long enough to see many things twice. I did not believe that fraternal emotions engendered in wartime persisted in peacetime. No whiff of nobility reached me from the fetid stinks of the tubes. I saw there nothing but poor wretches making their sorrowful best of the disastrous mismanagement of their governors. Nor was I enchanted by the loveliest things in London knocked down before the Germans began to take a hand in the game, and, contemplating what had gone up in place of them, I was not amused.

No. There was not much that tempted me to stay in London. I stayed merely because, if I had been in Falmouth, the East coast would have been a long way off. Fran was there with John, and I could get there pretty quickly. Fran had been fortunate enough to find a bungalow. She had wanted me to share it with her, but I preferred that she and Stephen should have every opportunity to be together, with no one between them.

I had thought it strange and moving to see my son in his naval uniform. It was even stranger, more deeply moving, to find him known and talked of. "By God, Pentecost, you must be proud of Stephen!" This was Sir Ernest Wittering, slapping me on the back in the vestibule of the Café Royal. A great man, Sir Ernest, on all sorts of boards, panels and consultative committees that were already blueprinting the New Jerusalem, never bothering their happy heads about who would pay for it. Their tens of millions glittered in the air like celluloid balls dancing over a fountain in a fair. They never seemed to think that someone would come along with a pop-gun and blow them down. We had a drink together, and he raised his glass, and said: "To Stephen! May he long continue the good work."

Frances had persuaded me, rather against my will, to have a wireless set in the studio, and it was about a week before this that she turned it on just as I was bringing the coffee to the table at breakfast time. We ran right into the middle of a breathless excited sentence: "– so accounting for three German E-boats without the loss of a single man from our gunboats. And now here is Lieutenant-Commander Stephen Pentecost, D.S.C., who will tell you in person just what these dogfights are like."

It was a grey morning of late autumn. I can see that moment now: the dun light; the few big ginger-headed chrysanthemums that Fran had bought standing among the cups and plates; she, wearing a green linen overall, arrested in the act of pulling out a chair, myself, struck suddenly to immobility with the coffee pot in my hand. We looked at one another and waited. There was a sound of a throat clearing itself with unnecessary violence, and then:

"Well, it's all in the day's work. All in the night's work, I should say. We're night birds, you know. Well, the great thing is to get to windward of 'em. You pick up the sound of 'em, you know, and your own sound has a chance of being borne away in the wind. Still, you make as little sound as you can. You wait for 'em to come down the lane that you know leads to home. Well, you don't bother about keeping quiet then. You burst on to 'em out of the darkness and give 'em everything. Personally, I like to have my boats in line ahead and go round 'em – one after the other of us – giving 'em all we've got. Don't let 'em have time to think. If they're in line ahead, too, so much the better. You go – well, sort of like darning – you go darning through 'em, blasting away, one after another. Well, that's how we do it. Last night we were lucky. Of course, you're not always lucky. You can't sink three every night. Wish we could. Well, I think that's all. Thank you."

"Thank *you*, Commander. That was Lieutenant-Commander Stephen Pentecost, D.S.C., giving an account of last night's engagement with German E-boats, three of which were sunk. We are now taking you over—"

Fran snapped the thing off. I was still standing there with the coffee pot in my hand. When suddenly she began to cry, I laid it down and put an arm round her shoulder.

2

One of the stupider papers had a headline: "Darner Pentecost tells us how he sews 'em up," and that is how Stephen became known as the Darner. At Ambling on the south-east coast, where his flotilla had its base, "Where's the Darner?" "Where's Darner Pentecost?" were questions you could hear at any time. "The Darner, D.S.C.," was the next allusion I saw to him in a headline. It was clear that the papers, which like to personify all the anonymous heroism of wartime, had picked Stephen out to be the symbol of the men who went forth in the little ships, the ships whose very littleness gave them a glamour, a touch of the romance that lights up any David with a sling. Stephen was not the only one; but round his name there began to assemble a special legend of impudence and hazard. The flotilla he commanded, operating mainly towards the Dutch coast, was no place for the timorous or circumspect. No officer or man posted to that flotilla could be certain, when the gunboats roared out into the growing North Sea dusk, that before the night was out he would not be engaged in circumstances that another commander would regard as overweighted against him. Only once more did I hear Stephen broadcast, and that was after another spectacular engagement which earned him a bar to his D.S.C. He said then: "An ancestor of mine was Captain John Pentecost who commanded one of the Falmouth packets in days when, as now, England was at war. The orders to those old packet captains were not to seek out the enemy and not to fight except as a last desperate resource. I think my ancestor on more than one occasion found himself so illiterate that he couldn't read his orders, and certainly when our gunboats go out now the intention is to seek the enemy in every hole and corner, and to fight him as long as there's a shot in the locker and a man able to crawl to a gun."

Lieutenant Begbie, D.S.C., commanded one of the ships of the flotilla. I met him briefly in London, and I recall a phrase or two of a hurried conversation. "Well, it depends how you look at it. Some of us hate him, but then on the other hand some of us love him."

I had a vision of the little ships huddled in the dark waiting for their prey. I could hear Stephen's voice speaking over the loud-hailer, and I had no doubt what would be the emotions of Begbie's heart as he listened to it. I shook his hand warmly; he saluted and went off in his shabby suit and battered cap.

3

Adam Randle was grounded. That is to say, returning in his bomber from an operation over Germany, he had just managed to bring the damaged machine over English soil and there had made a landing that left him with a broken leg and a few ribs stove in. He had been put together, but was not yet fit for flying again.

In December of 1942 I had pulled on my overcoat, Frances had fussed about the cold night and twisted a muffler round my neck, and I was leaving the studio. I didn't like going out at night, abandoning Fran and John, but this was an engagement that had to be kept. Adam came up the stairs as I was going down them.

"Oh, Dook!" he said. "You're not going out?"

"Sorry, my boy. This is one of those nights when I *have* to. They happen about once a year. You've drawn the unlucky number."

He took me by the sleeve. "Wash it out. Stay in."

"The impertinence of the young!" I laughed. "They think their simple affairs override everything. No, no. I must be off."

"I'm sorry. Still, if you must – I'll walk a step with you."

We went down into the dark yard. We might as well have been walking in a pit. Not even the King's Mistress showed a friendly gleam.

"I always feel the last thing has gone wrong with humanity," I said lightly, "when a pub can't send out a cheerful blaze. This is the second time I've known the poor old King's Mistress compelled to hide her charms. I knew it before 1914, you know. Fran's father and I used to have a pint there together occasionally. Joe tells me it was the last place he visited before going back to be killed on the Somme."

Adam laughed. "Dook," he said, "this war has gone on far too long. It's making even your mind slip. Fran's father wasn't killed on the Somme. You're mixing your references."

I could have kicked myself. It had slipped out. I had sometimes wondered whether Frances had told him. Now I knew she had not. Well, it was her affair. She, or no one, must do it.

"You're right, my boy," I said. "It's true that Luther Brimlow and I used to drink there a bit in those days, and this other man – Chellew his name was – occasionally joined us. Yes; memory's an odd jumble when you get to my age."

"Ah, well," Adam said, "I fear the truth is, Dook, that too much of your life has been associated with this hostelry. You and the King's Mistress are one and indivisible. Old Joe is staggering on his last legs. It wouldn't surprise me to learn that you had bought the pub and settled down to end your days there with buxom Bess."

"It's an idea. Might do a lot worse."

"Well, this is where I turn back to have a word with Fran. Coming?"

"No, no. I must go on."

"Well, I asked you, Dook."

I went on and he returned towards the studio. Squadron Leader Adam Randle. His poems were appearing now and then in the reviews. His short book *Icarus*, dealing with the deeds of his squadron up to Dunkirk, had recently been published. Battle of Britain fighter pilot. One of the few in it at the beginning and still in it at the end. Bomber. Bar to D.F.C. The sort of potted biography that might go under a photograph in a newspaper. I shuddered in the raw December air. A photograph in a newspaper was an ominous idea nowadays.

I walked on. I was going to dine with an A.R.A. who lived not far off. A week ago his son's photograph had appeared in *The Times*, and the old man, with a pathetic gesture of defiance, had called a few friends together for tonight. Life must go on. We must pretend there is no spectre at the feast. After all, it's the sort of thing the boy would approve of.

I didn't like it. I felt assured of a wretched evening, but I couldn't disappoint old Briggs.

Feeling rather than seeing my way through the few streets between my studio and Briggs', I thought of Adam and the moment, two and a half years ago now, when I had met him for the first time after Iris' death. I had stayed in Falmouth for the funeral, which Mathews conducted. Ernie Lingard and I were the only mourners. It was an afternoon of midsummer heat, cloudless and radiant. As I turned away from the grave a Falmouth newspaper man approached me and asked whether this was *the* Iris Randle, and wasn't she in fact the Viscountess Moreton Hampstead? I said that it was so; and the news was telegraphed to the Press Association in London; and thus, when I met Adam, he already knew that his mother was dead. Nor was she all that death had taken from him. That little flight of planes which (it seemed now a long time ago) I had seen rise from the ground on an autumn day at Tangmere, had contained much that was dear to him, much that was now dead. It was but a remnant that watched the streaming roads of France, the black smoke billowing, and that flew back to England when June was halfway through.

I met him in town. He did not look tired and he had taken care to be spruce. We went to a quiet tea-place, and it was not till the tea was before us that he pulled out of his pocket a newspaper, folded over at a picture of Iris and an article about her career. He slapped it on the table, and said: "A generous allowance of space, don't you think, considering the size of the newspapers nowadays? Of course, if she'd died in a flat in London she'd have got ten lines. But the journey from Bordeaux and all the rest of it gives the thing glamour. Nothing like a bit of glamour to give death a popular appeal, don't you think?"

I laid a hand on his arm, and he looked round the tea room apprehensively. "Sorry. Was I shouting?"

I nodded.

"All right, Dook. I'll try not to. They tell me it's becoming a habit. But I'm like the little birds in the advertisement: I've got something to sing about."

He put the newspaper back into his pocket. "It'll make a nice *finale* to her scrap-book," he said. "She never bothered about it. But I always kept it up. She used to laugh at me. She used to laugh. Odd to think that, isn't it?"

"I don't think so. It would be odd indeed, if I could ever think of her without remembering how she laughed."

"You were fond of her, Dook, weren't you?"

"More than I can say."

"Well, then, let's shut up, shall we? We'll just shut up and remember."

We left it at that. But I felt that, for him as for me, they were becoming too many: those concerning whom there was nothing left to do but shut up and remember.

4

I didn't get away from Briggs' till eleven o'clock. I expected that Frances would be in bed, but she was still up. "Poor darling," she said. "Was it terrible?"

"Painful enough. But never mind. It's over."

She took my hat and overcoat and brought my slippers to the fireside. "Old Briggs is a teetotaller, isn't he?" she asked.

"Yes. And he imposes his views on his guests."

"Then you shall have a drink." She had the tray ready and poured out the whisky. "You see, I can look after you as well as Joe's Bess. She's too fat."

"What are you talking about?"

"Adam says that you're at a dangerous age and that artists often fall into the hands of comfortable unintelligent women. There was J.M.W. Turner. He says there's so much to be said in favour of such marriages that we must at all costs prevent you from contracting one."

I sipped my whisky and she sat on the other side of the fire smoking a cigarette. There was an inner excitement about her, almost a radiance.

"Oh, he told you that, did he? What else did he have to tell you?"

"That Luther Brimlow wasn't my father. He says you let the cat out of the bag and made a snatch at its tail but couldn't catch it."

"He seems very bright tonight. So for that matter do you. You look beautiful." You look in love, I thought.

"I'm sorry about the cat," I said. "I thought I had recovered it."

"Please don't bother," she laughed. "Adam was enchanted. He said the last blot had now been wiped away and I could leave the court without a stain upon my character. We thereupon spent some time in admiring the portrait of Francis Chellew, and agreed that he was Hyperion to a satyr. Having said that, Adam recited the passage in which it occurs, and, of course, that led to other passages. We began swopping our favourite bits."

"You did that the first time you ever met."

"Yes. He remembered that, and reminded me. He even remembered the bits."

"So it was a wholesome literary evening."

"Oh, culinary, too. I knocked up an omelette, and we found a bottle of your Château Piada. Adam said it was too sweet, but I like sweet wine."

"I seem to have missed a thoroughly festive occasion. How long did he stay?"

"Not terribly long. After supper we talked for a while and he read me a few things he's been writing."

She yawned suddenly: red mouth, white perfect teeth, little twitching tongue; and as she yawned her body stretched itself in luxurious content and then relaxed. I knew that Adam had been her lover that night. I had let the cat out of the bag, and that had led to confession. And there had been nostalgic reminiscence. Confession and reminiscence, dangerous things, had led to tenderness, and tenderness had ended in consummation.

"You'd better get to bed, Fran. You must be tired."

"Tired? Why, Dook, I feel like a house on fire!"

However, she came across the hearth rug and kissed me as I sat there, and her mouth was warm and tender.

"Good night, darling," she said. "I shall sleep like a top. What on earth do people mean when they say 'sleep like a top'? How does a top sleep?"

"Fran," I said, "when the house is on fire it's odd to be discussing whether one should say geranium or pelargonium."

She looked at me, a little startled, and I said: "Well, I may be wrong, but I've always imagined it to derive from 'comme un taupe.' However, good night."

I didn't feel like going to bed. I poured myself another whisky and got up to reach down my tobacco jar from the mantelpiece. I stepped on something hard and bent down to see what it was. I picked up a jewelled pin that had been hidden in the folds of the fleece rug, and I knew then that I had not been mistaken in my imaginations about that night.

It would be about a year ago that I had accepted an invitation from Adam to visit him at his aerodrome. After a meal we had sat talking in the anteroom. There were a number of young officers about, boys in their early twenties most of them, with tired wary eyes, but apt to revert to the horseplay of the childhood that lay not far behind them. One had had too much to drink, and Adam told me quietly that this was because of old Rockers. At this time yesterday, it seemed, this boy and old Rockers were all in all to one another, but since then, so brutally swift and decisive are the things that happen to these children, Rockers had been seen going down like a blazing comet over the target for the night. This boy, his friend, was sitting by himself, occasionally laughing quietly; then he got up and began going the rounds, slipping a finger under the tie of each man he came to and twitching it out. They took no notice of him. They smiled and put their ties back.

Presently the boy came up to Adam, and Adam said: "No good, Tony. My tie's anchored."

Tony looked at him with a glazed eye, put a finger behind the tie, and twitched. The tie stayed where it was. Then Tony took a real grip of it and hauled. Adam got up and put the boy gently aside. "Let me show you, Tony," he said. He unbuttoned his tunic and showed how the end of his tie was fastened to his shirt by a pin. He undid the pin, buttoned his tunic again, and said, with a smile: "Now have a go."

Tony pulled the tie out, seemed satisfied, and wandered away, a forlorn, lost figure. Adam handed me the pin – a beautiful little piece of jewellery set with rubies. "A queer thing, don't you think, Dook, for a tough airman to wear? Still, I'm never without it. It belonged to my mother."

This was the pin I picked up from the hearth rug, and I thought there was no need to wonder what agitation had caused Adam to drop it when he had taken off his tie. I found a piece of tissue paper, wrapped it up, and put it in a safe place.

In the morning Frances was preoccupied and subdued. "In the cold reasonable light of morning." A nice *cliché*, true like many of them. The time for second thoughts. She was short-tempered with John, a sure sign that she was dissatisfied with herself, and at breakfast she was unusually silent with me. "Dook," she said at last, "I'm thinking of leaving you."

This did surprise me. I looked at her tenderly. The dilemmas of these young people were heartbreaking. "Why, Fran?" I asked as lightly as I could. "Am I so unbearable?"

"It's not that," she said shortly. "I feel I ought to be with Stephen."

I was glad. "I shall be sorry to see you go," I said. "I shall have to comfort myself with Bess after all. Still, I think it would be a good thing."

"If I could get a small house at Ambling, there's no reason why you shouldn't come, too. I fear to leave you with Bess," she said, venturing on the first light word she had spoken that morning. "I'm afraid you'll find her buxoms irresistible."

"You must let me dree my own weird. I've dreed a good many weirds in my time. I'm quite expert at it."

"Well, I'm afraid it's a weird-dreeing situation all round. I wish you'd come, if I can find a place. You're doing very little work."

"No. Write to Stephen, and if he can find room for you there, you go and take John with you. I shall be all right."

Nothing would have induced me to go after what had happened last night. That she and Stephen should be together, should have a chance, seemed to me the most desirable thing in the world.

"There's one thing I ought to tell you about last night," she said, and the words made me tremble. I did not feel capable of handling a confession.

"Adam is back in bombers."

I thought it was dreadful news, but I sighed with relief.

"I say I ought to tell you," she went on; "but of course I ought *not* to tell you. He ought not to have told me. He and his crew and two other crews are practising an operation."

"I don't want to hear about it. He certainly ought not to have told you. Did he tell you when it's to be?"

"No. That's one thing he wouldn't say. But it'll be tremendously important – if it comes off."

"He's a lunatic to have mentioned it at all."

She looked as if I had struck her. Her face went white. She got up and began clearing the things away into the scullery. Then she came back, after a lot of noisy clattering, and leaned towards me over the table with both hands clutching it desperately. "Lunatic!" she said in a hard controlled voice that evidently wanted to shriek. "That's the best word you can find, is it? A man who could have stayed out of it if he'd wanted to, who begged to be let in on it! He'll have to go through hell to do what he's trying to do, and ten to one he won't come out of it alive. And that's all you can say about him — a lunatic! Of course they're lunatics, all of them, or they'd never risk their lives for the sake of a lot of rotten, worthless—"

I went round the table and took her in my arms. She was trembling violently. I didn't speak. There was nothing I could say. She had clutched on to me as if I were a lifebelt in a maddening sea. Her shuddering eased away, and I sat her in a chair. "Take it easy, Fran," I said. "Shall I write to Stevo about this shift, or will you?"

She blew her nose and wiped her eyes. "You write," she said.

5

She didn't go at once because Stephen couldn't find a place for her to live in at Ambling. Moreover, he didn't seem anxious to have her there. He came up to town early in 1943 for a weekend leave and did his best to make her stay where she was. The three of us talked it over one night at supper. "I don't like it," Stephen said. "I'm seeing too much of it down there. Several officers in my flotilla have their wives in the village. It's just like these RAF types having their wives living near the aerodromes. They hear the planes go out and lie awake waiting to hear them come back. That's no good to them, and it's no good to the men in the planes. Not even to the ones who get back. They have to tell some Jill or Jessie about George or Jack who's gone for a Burton. No, I don't like it. And it's the same with us. You see those girls on the quay watching the gunboats go out, and the minds of the men in the gunboats are apt to be on them instead of on their work."

Frances said quietly: "I'm told that Lord Kitchener wouldn't have married men on his staff."

"And I wouldn't have them in my boats if I could help it," Stephen said flatly. "Or at least I'd keep the women well away from the base. There was far more common sense about a war fought overseas in the old days."

"I'm afraid, Stevo," I said, "wars overseas are things of the past. They will come closer and closer home, and a good thing, too, in my opinion. Not that the old time wars were at all what you imagine. If you had taken the trouble some day when you were down in Cornwall to have a look into Mylor churchyard, where your great-grandfather is buried, you would have seen an interesting if atrocious memorial. It is to soldiers and their wives and children who were returning from the Peninsular War and were wrecked on the coast near Falmouth. The women and children tagged around with the troops in those days. You may remember that the officers rushed to Waterloo from the arms of their women in Brussels. So this situation is not as new as you suppose."

"I don't like it, anyway," Stephen persisted. "I've got the morale of my flotilla to think of. It's pretty high, and anything that tended to weaken it would have to be thought about carefully."

Frances got up, leaving her food unfinished, and went and sat by the fire. "I'm sorry," she said desperately. "Not for the world would I do anything to undermine your fighting efficiency."

That was the end of the meal. Stephen and I could not pretend to go on with it. He began to pace the room, looking at her with affectionate exasperation. "Oh, you don't understand!" he burst out. "What has it got to do, Fran, with the love between you and me? That's there, isn't it? Nothing can touch that. You know it, and I know it, and if we were a thousand miles apart instead of an hour's journey it would be all the same. But every boat in the flotilla, and every man, is on my mind as something I've got to expend and save at the same time. It's not easy, Fran, and it takes all I've got. It's a job outside what there is between you and me, and it's better to keep the two things separate. If you imagine I don't think of you, you're mistaken. I have to force myself *not* to think of you. I *dare* not think of you too much."

He paused and rammed tobacco into his pipe. "D'you know what I *do* think of sometimes?" he asked. "Sailing! There are plenty of nights, you know, when nothing happens. Moonlight nights and a calm sea. Perhaps you're lying there with engines stopped, and in the moonlight you can see the other boats and sometimes hear voices from them. Perhaps I hear old Bugs chewing the fat about something. You have an extraordinary feeling of happiness and companionship. You can't believe in what you were doing last night and will perhaps be doing tomorrow night. Those are the times when I'm in danger of wool gathering. All the sails we had. That marvellous sail to Ireland. And all the sails we shall have. I want to try and buy back the *Frances and*

Stephen. We'll put a cabin in her, when this lot's over, and we'll give little John his baptism. We'll lounge around the seas till my gratuity's spent! How about that, Fran?"

She got up and put her arms round him and laid her head on his shoulder. "Oh, Stevo," she said, "you're such a dear child. Let me come to Ambling. I want to be with you."

His fierce red hair over hers was like a sun over ripe oats. That is the picture of them I think I shall always see: his strong arm coming round her waist, with the three wavy gold rings upon the cuff, two broad and one narrow, the little bits of colour upon his breast, that stood for so much valour, snared in a vagrant tress. He looked at me over her bowed head, and an impudent grin lit his blue eyes. "Fran," he said, "I think it's time we sent Father back to his pub. Well, you'd better come to Ambling and be my Emma."

She looked up, smiling. "Emma? Why? Have you got a wife somewhere?"

He looked at her, infatuated. "Have I not! That's just what I want to prove to you."

I thought it was high time I was away.

"Let's hear the nine o'clock news before you go," Stephen said, and clicked on the machine.

We listened, and we heard an account of an operation over Germany. It was entirely successful. A cool voice paid tribute to the courage and daring of those engaged. "From this operation three of our escorting fighters and one of our bombers failed to return."

I looked at Fran, who was standing behind Stephen. Her face was pale and rigid. "Is that John?" she asked, and disappeared quickly into the bedroom.

Stephen switched off the wireless. "Well," he said, "that's how it goes. That's what I mean, Dook. There were men in that bomber and there were girls waiting for news. You see what I mean?"

"Yes," I said; "but do your best to have Fran near you. Be very kind to her."

"As if you needed to tell me to do that!" he said.

6

It was soon after this, in one of Stephen's most desperate battles, that a gunboat of his flotilla was sunk, and a wife who had been living with two small children in a furnished bungalow at Ambling had no need to live there any more; and Frances moved in with little John.

When they had been there for a few days I travelled down, taking some things to give the place a personal sense: a couple of pictures and such-like; and, as the early spring flowers were once more in the shops, I took bunches of these, too, to brighten the house. Our minds were lifted up a little, because the news of Adam was better than we had feared. He had dropped by parachute, and was a prisoner of war, unharmed. "Give him plenty of time to write poetry," Stephen said grimly; and Frances assented with a laugh. She was gay now.

I have never liked the flat East coast, and Ambling would have been a dull place wherever it had been planted. The war had given it a bit of kick and bustle by making it the lair of these modern freebooters who went slipping out at dusk and sneaking in at dawn. I watched them off several times during the few days I spent there, and it was touching to see the pigmy ceremonial with which they went, the handful of crew dressed on the vibrating decks, the flags valiantly whickering in the winter nightfall. The powerful engines filled the dusk with their roaring as the boats moved off in line ahead, their knife-bows slicing back the white parings of wave, their sterns so low that you imagined them, when they were full out, racing along on their tails. Orders on the loud-hailer came across the water, but soon voices and engines alike were swallowed up in the night striding hugely over the sea. Then there was nothing to do but go back to the bungalow and think. I began to see Stephen's point of view.

The springtime came, and in May I was at the bungalow spending a week. Frances had begged me to come. I knew that, like the other women there, she found the nights unbearable and longed for company. The weather was good, and I pottered in the ten yards or so of garden, frustrated, worried, wondering whether in a few months' time other eyes than ours would be looking on the results of what I was doing. Already the question was in my heart that has been in it ever since, and never more than in these days ironically called days of peace; whether anything one did was worth the doing, whether men were not such incurable fools that one might as well retire from the struggle and leave them to accomplish as soon as they could the self-annihilation on which their hearts seemed set. Stephen had taken me aboard his gunboat and enthusiastically expounded its beauty, the

531

fearfulness and wonder with which it was made. I had tried to echo
his praises of this and that, but it had seemed to me nothing but a
highly-charged and literally infernal machine, lit by bright inhuman
gleams. Frances was with us, and we left him there when we went
ashore.

"You hated it," she said.

"Yes."

"So did I. Loathsome."

There were these things on the water – and they were but the small
fry of monsters infinitely more complex and deadly – and through the
air the aeroplanes droned over, lovely and luminous in the soft spring
light, and they were deadly too. Man seemed to me to be like a child,
and not a very bright child at that, half-awake and playing with toys
that some fatal nurse who loathed him had left for his destruction.

Frances went back to the bungalow, and I wandered on the dunes
amid the sea holly and the spiky grass. The misty May morning sun
dropped a leaden sheen upon the eastward-stretching water. I thought
of a May morning not many years ago – oh, but thousands of years
ago! – when this same sun lighted the water by Magdalen bridge, and
Adam put the baskets into the punt, and four of us slid past the blue
anemones over green water undulant with greener weeds. "This," said
Adam, "is the last enchanted chamber before we step out into reality."
I thought of Adam and I thought of Iris. I wondered what reality for
her had lain beyond the narrow bed in the Falmouth hospital.

I slept badly that night and rose at dawn. I dressed myself and
peeped into Fran's room. She was sleeping uneasily, lying on her back,
with one arm thrown up out of the foaming bed clothes, like an arm
glimpsed as it rose in despairing appeal above a wave. John was
sleeping in his cot alongside her bed. The picture of Captain Pentecost
of the *Termagant* was on the wall over the fireplace. Stephen had hung
it there.

I stole quietly to the kitchen, shivering in the dawn cold, and made
myself a cup of tea. I lit my pipe and wandered down to the quay to
which the gunboats returned. I had never done so before. I knew that
Stephen disliked it. Mrs Begbie was already there, a fragile little
woman with violet-blue eyes. She was wrapped up in an immense
cape, sparkling with the misty hoar of the morning. She looked like
nothing but a great dewy sack with this charming, blue-eyed wistful

face rising out of it. Her exceptionally long eyelashes, too, had taken these tears from the morning.

We talked in low tones for a while, as though the day were asleep and we did not wish to wake it for fear of its news. Soon to our straining ears there came the well-known throb-throb-throb that meant the boats were coming home, and at the same time the base doctor, hardy and without an overcoat, came along. The vivid red of his calling, interwoven with the wavy gold on his cuff, looked startling in the dun miasmic air. Then an ambulance came, and he said brusquely: "Come along. Make it snappy. Back her in here."

The ambulance was backed in to the quay's edge; the men got down from it and began flapping their arms across their breasts.

The surgeon lieutenant-commander came up and saluted. "Good morning, Mr Pentecost. Good morning, Mrs Begbie." He was a fresh-faced sanguine young man who did not seem afraid of the morning. "We got a message from Darner to stand by," he said. "They ran into a spot of bother last night."

Neither Mrs Begbie nor I could ask what we wanted to ask. The throbbing sound of the distant boats was getting louder. He took pity on us. "Nothing to worry about," he said.

A few sailors began to appear, standing by the bollards to which they would fasten the lines, and presently the gunboats could be seen taking shape out of the grey east. Now the throbbing had become a roaring; then the roaring subsided as they throttled down, became hardly more than a purring as they slipped slowly towards the quay. There was nothing but this, and a great sense of expectancy, till Stephen's voice came over the loud-hailer. "Hallo, Doc! Are you there?"

The doctor cupped his hands round his mouth and shouted: "All ready, Darner! Everything on the top line!"

Now the boats could be clearly seen, and in the side of Stephen's there was a hole as though a mighty iron fist had been smashed splinteringly through it. All the boats had an appearance of being tired and overdone, of having come through great tribulation.

Stephen's boat sidled into the quay; orders rang out; ropes were flung and made fast. The morning came alive in stir and bustle. Stephen leapt ashore, a heavy-looking mass of duffle coat, muffler and sea boots, his eyes hard, his face drawn and tired, his cap on the back of his head. "Come on now. Snap into it!" he shouted.

Two stretchers were carried ashore. On one was a man with a bandage, red-stained, tied roughly round his head; on the other one whose hurt was not apparent. His shattered leg was hidden by a blanket. Stephen walked alongside the stretchers to the ambulance and saw them put in. Then he lit two cigarettes and stuck one in each man's mouth. "Well, thank you, boys," he said. "Don't fall in love with the nurses. That'll delay your convalescence, and I can't have that. I want you back. As soon as you can make it. Can't do without you."

One of them said: "Ay, ay, sir," and the other said: "OK, Darner. Be seeing you soon."

The doctor climbed in, and the ambulance drove away.

Stephen stood still for a moment in the middle of the road, looking after the ambulance. With one hand he raised his cap and thoughtfully scratched his head. The sun came out. He turned, saw me standing there, and, as if refocusing his mind, recognised me. "Don't bother about me at breakfast time," he said. "I may not be there. There's a lot to do."

He turned abruptly, shouting: "Where's Mr Begbie? Is Mr Begbie ashore yet?

He was; and I saw Mrs Begbie walking away smiling.

7

Well, that was the sort of thing, and it made you think. A hole above the water line could as easily be below it. A shot that glanced a head could as easily take a head off; and a sailor in an ambulance could as easily be one man as another. Stephen's was not the only damaged boat that morning. They all had the disreputable air of drunks that had been slamming round in a rough house.

I walked thoughtfully to the bungalow. Frances was preparing breakfast. "I heard them come in," she said. "Everything all right?"

"They're all back, but they seem to have had a tough night. Two men wounded. The ships rather battered."

"Oh, well. That's not so bad."

I knew it was not her heart speaking. I thought of the girl I had peeped at two hours ago, with all defences torn off by sleep, muttering a few indecipherable words. How apart they were, these young people, how far, in their waking pride, beyond the reach of compassion! What contemporary equivalents of the Lutherans, I wondered, terrified Fran's dreams?

"Stevo says we'd better get on. He may not be up for breakfast. There's one thing: I should imagine it'll be some days before the flotilla's fit to go to sea again."

We were early breakfasters in those days. The clock pointed to seven. "Well," said Fran, "even if he comes, you may be sure we shall hear little from him. We'd better have it from the velvet mouth of the BBC." She switched on the wireless.

We learned that a flotilla of gunboats, operating from an east-coast base under the command of Lieutenant-Commander Stephen Pentecost, had encountered soon after midnight a flotilla of German E-boats, of superior strength, which had left their base on the Dutch coast to intercept a convoy sailing to a British port. A long-sustained fight "ensued". "The Germans pressed the attack with great determination, but not one of them was given an opportunity to land so much as a single shell upon any ship of the convoy. Not only were they diverted from their purpose, but three of them were sunk, at least two others were badly mauled, and the flotilla was pursued back to the base from which it had emerged. Our chase of them was pressed almost to within range of the enemy's shore guns. This was one of the most brilliant and successful of our small-ship operations, for not only was the attack on the convoy frustrated and severe damage inflicted on the enemy, but we did not lose a single gunboat, though three were damaged, and our casualties amounted to no more than two seamen wounded, one of them lightly. Truly this was the Nelson touch."

"Balls," said Stephen, who had come in and heard the end of this. He switched off the wireless. He was still swathed in duffle and muffler and looked too tired to take them off. He sank down at the table. Frances kissed him and placed hot coffee before him in a large thick china mug that he liked to use. He sat with both hands wrapped round it as though he were still cold, staring moodily in front of him.

Presently he said: "Once you get talked about by the BBC and the newspapers, the oddest people write to you about the oddest things. I've shown you some of the letters, Fran. We've had a laugh over some of them, and there were others that made you want to cry. I received one yesterday, and wondered if I ought to show it to you. I think I had better."

I felt that something desperate was about to come up. What came was incredible. Frances, who, too, was puzzled by his manner, looked at him expectantly and, I felt, with apprehension.

"Did you ever meet your father's mother – Mrs Brimlow?"

"I may have done," Fran said. "But if I did I remember nothing about it. She didn't play much part in my childhood, you know."

"It is she who has written to me. She sent the letter under cover to a newspaper, asking them to send it on. Their naval correspondent knew where to find me. He's been down here looking at the flotilla; and so the letter came to me."

He took a letter from his pocket, and handed it to Frances, and while she was reading it, he began, with an assumption of indifference, to eat and drink. I watched Fran, and saw the page of cheap paper trembling in her fingers, saw her face go white. When she had finished reading, she passed the letter to me without a word. It began with appalling brutality:

Dear Sir, – You ought to know that your wife is a bastard. My son, Mr Luther Brimlow, was never her father. I am as certain of this as that God is my maker. Her mother was a bitch, and who her father was perhaps she knows. I don't. It is a shame that a fine brave man like you should be deceived, and I'll bet you are being deceived. I don't suppose you know these facts. And like mother, like daughter, I shouldn't be surprised. Blanche Pentecost deceived my son Luther when he was on active service for his country, and if I were you, I'd look out. My only object in writing this letter is to assure you that I am a sincere admirer of your gallantry, and your well-wisher

Mrs Brimlow.

I crumpled the poisonous thing into a ball, with fingers quaking in rage, and threw it into the fire. Stephen did nothing to hinder me. "Well, Fran?" he said.

She answered quietly: "All through my childhood I knew nothing of this, but I have known for some years that Luther Brimlow was not my father."

"Did you know it before you married me?"

"Yes."

"But you thought this rather important fact was not one I should know?"

She was moistening her lips and looked terrified. "Well, Stephen, I didn't—"

I intervened savagely. "Stephen, for God's sake what is this all about? Are you going to allow a venomous letter from that old bitch to come between you and Frances?"

"A letter, Father, which Frances tells me contains the truth."

"What does it matter, true or not?"

"Simply that I should have been *told* the truth. I assure you the truth would have made no difference to my feeling. It's this withholding of the truth. Surely to God the matter was important enough for me to be told?"

"It was not of the slightest importance to anybody. So unimportant that when Adam Randle learned of it he laughed and turned it into a joke."

I saw at once that my anger had betrayed me into saying the wrong thing. Stephen got up, looking outraged. "So Adam Randle knows about it, does he? Adam Randle seems to be more intimately privileged than Frances' husband. Has the good news been bruited round to any others that I should know about?"

He reached for his cap, and I laid my hand on his shoulder. "Stephen – please – for heaven's sake—"

He shook himself free, and said: "It was a nice letter to be thinking about all last night, don't you think? If I'd *known*, I could have put it in the fire and laughed. That's what – what *hurts* – me. I seem to have been thought such a stupid-minded fool that I wasn't to be trusted with the news."

Fran said pleadingly: "Oh, darling, it wasn't that. Really, it wasn't that."

"Well," he said, "I'll be back when I'm back. I must get down to the boats. I know Brimlow was a bloody swine, and I'm glad there's no Brimlow in John. All the same, one of these days you may think that I'm among those privileged to know who is in him." He took a letter from his pocket and threw it on to the table. "Incidentally," he said, "that's my answer to Mrs Brimlow. You may both care to read it, and then you can post it."

When he was gone we read the letter.

Dear Madam, — I receive many letters from admirers, but none has given me more heartfelt pleasure than yours. It has lifted a great weight from my mind. The thought that my wife was the daughter of one of the dirtiest crooks of our time has never been easy to bear, and now I need bear it no longer. Your advice to me to 'look out' for my wife would have been important if, indeed, Mr Luther Brimlow had been her father. Now I am strengthened in what I have always believed of her — that never in word, thought or deed would her conduct give a moment's anxiety to the man who loves her with all his heart. I could not love and admire her more, else what you tell me in your letter would make me do so.

Yours faithfully,

Stephen Pentecost.

I went out and posted this letter, leaving Fran with her head lying upon her arms which were stretched across the table. She was crying as if her heart would break.

8

I had not seen Blanche since she went to live at Torquay, and I knew no more of her doings than could be gathered from the occasional six-line letters which served her turn. Now she sent me a brief cry from the heart. Kitty Delabole was a traitor and everything was upside down. Would I go to Torquay and see her? I went, although it wasn't a place I cared for.

The journey west was becoming more and more environed with war. Rusting dumps of barbed wire as high as gasometers, sentries on bridges, vast parks of armoured vehicles, barriers of complicated steelwork standing in the tidal shallows, and barbed wire, in and out of which children played, looped and festooned about the beaches.

What had happened to Kitty Delabole had a fine ironic simplicity. Her husband had found a job in a ministry and the ministry had offices in Torquay. And so it happened that George Delabole, walking on the front one day, met his wife whom he had not known to be in the town. She had not known him to be there. It was a lovely day of late spring, and no doubt that had something to do with it. No doubt, too, the surprise helped. Anyway, George Delabole seems to have thought that his wife looked charming, and I imagine that his black dispatch case, with G.R. monogrammed over the lock, so that any thief might see at once that it contained official documents, his wing collar and civil service trousers, looked excellent in her eyes. Well, there were the palm trees rustling, and the sun was shining on the sea, and "actually," as Kitty explained to Blanche, "we decided that we'd been a pair of silly fools, and we made it up." Actually, they went at once to a tea shop that Kitty knew still supplied cream cakes; then to a jeweller's where George bought her a sapphire brooch; and then, as ministerial calls were not pressing and others were, to bed. In short, the matter could hardly have been more conclusive.

This was all very simple, and it surprised me to find, during the three days I spent in Torquay, how it could be served up at breakfast, lunch and dinner, with infinite variation. Blanche handled it with the mastery of an army cook handling bully beef: plain and spiced, as rissoles, shepherd's pie, faggots and haggis. The upshot of it all was that she would stay in the hotel, where there were some quite good bridge players, and that she would never speak to Kitty Delabole again. I wondered why she had brought me to Torquay to tell me this.

It was not till my last evening there that Blanche asked: "How is Frances? Do you see her at all now?"

"Don't you hear from her? Or write to her?"

"Not much. There's so little to write about."

I told her what I could. I gave her some account of John.

"It's strange," she said, "how little desire I have to see him. I hate being a grandmother. I positively hate it. I still can't believe that I am one."

We were the grandparents of the same child: Blanche and I, who had once been inseparable, presenting a united front against the Brimlows. Well, we had kept them out of this, anyway. I did not often reflect on this joint heritage of ours; her daughter, my son, continuing in our grandchild. It made me feel tender towards her, but, really, she had become a very silly woman.

"There's one thing," she said. "Though I shall stay on here, I shan't stay for long. I've been hearing from Amy Lingard. She'll be out of munitions soon."

"She should never have been in them."

"Oh, I wouldn't say that. She thought it her duty, and that being so I considered it only right that my comfort shouldn't stand in her way. But now she finds that she's really not up to it. She's willing to come back to me. So what I shall do is look round for a little labour-saving bungalow, here in the west country, and when I'm ready to move in Amy will join me. That she should be free now seems too good to be true. It's providential."

"Yes," I said, "we should never give up our faith in God. From time to time these little things come along to remind us of His existence."

9

I had an idea that what had happened before I left Ambling would be to the good in the long run, and perhaps not so long as all that. Stephen's letter to Mrs Brimlow, I knew, had touched Frances to the quick. Her heart was torn between two men, two men so different, and I truly think that in the presence of either of them she suffered from a sense of infidelity. Stephen's plain declaration of belief in her faithfulness to him must have both hurt her and exalted her, and I thought it likely that their happiest moments were now there to be enjoyed.

I took care to remain away from Ambling. When I returned from Torquay I busied myself with painting a portrait of Stephen. I had, during my visits to the east coast, made innumerable sketches of which he knew nothing, and now I began to paint. It filled the days of a hot weary summer week, and they were made the more endurable by Fran's letters, infused with a serenity that told me all was well.

Towards the end of June I thought I might venture on another visit. I arrived late one afternoon, and Frances, with John in a small pushcart, met me at the station. It had been fine sunny weather, and the pair of them looked as the children had always looked after a week in Cornwall. "We go out every day," Fran explained, "and hide ourselves in a crinkle of the dunes and offer up all we decently can to the sun god." She was happy; radiant even.

I had brought the portrait with me, and they were both kind enough to speak well of it. I must say I liked it myself. I had overcome a temptation to do a nice ancestral picture with a clean jacket, shining gold rings and proud blobs of medal ribbon. Instead, I had painted a young man with an anxious face, carelessly wearing a grey woollen muffler and a toggled duffle coat, with a battered cap whose badge had dimmed and faded in the wind and weather. For background, I used the mere ghostly outline of a gunboat, away on the river that was blanketed with morning fog. It was, so far as I could get it, the moment of return, of extreme exhaustion, the moment when the legendary warrior becomes the familiar son, the boy to whom the heart goes out, young, tired, and ready for bed. I felt that we were in danger of forgetting this aspect of the matter. Men, more and more, were becoming indistinguishable from material, mere expendable stuff. Not that there was anything new about this. We had been that on the Somme all right.

However, Stephen didn't have anything to say about the ideas behind the picture. He merely assured me that it was "jolly good" and hung it alongside that of Captain Pentecost. He, like Frances, was in a good mood. I felt sure that they had found one another again. I puzzled a lot about what it was that made their relationship different from the relationship between Frances and Adam Randle. That there was a difference I was certain, and it seemed to me probable that it was this: Stephen and Frances were a boy and girl happy together, happy in many shared memories, many shared likings for things on a physical plane. It was an association that could bring great content. But with Adam, it was not an association: it was a fusion. Only the things of the mind and spirit can generate the heat that fuses, and it was on that plane that Frances and Adam met. They met not as boy and girl but as man and woman. I had no doubt whatever that physically, too, they were extremely attractive to one another.

If these speculations were uncovering any part of the truth, I could not pretend that the outlook for the future was bright, but there was not then, any more than there is now, much reason for concerning oneself with the future. The day's good and evil must be sufficient unto themselves. It was good that Adam was alive and well. It was good that Stephen and Frances were as happy with one another as they had contrived to be, in the main, when they were children together at

Tresco Vean. It was lovely weather. Stephen was due for leave, and took it there on the spot. We found an old dinghy. We rowed about in it and fished. We bathed and sunbathed. We carried lunch over the dunes and lit fires and boiled water and made tea. For a day or two we could look eastward at the glinting sea and forget that it was a battlefield. We lay stretched on the ground and saw blood-red poppies trembling between us and the blue. John staggered about naked and brown, while we three lay doped by sunlight. From time to time I would see Fran's hand reach out and take Stephen's, or his reach out and take hers, and they would lie there with fingers interlocked on the baking sand. They would talk of "after the war," as Francis Chellew had so often talked of it to me in days when it was possible to believe that from the trough the wave must rise and we had not learned to stare with fascination into depths undreamed of and unsunned. Stephen's mind turned again to the *Frances and Stephen*, which remained for him the symbolic embodiment of childhood and youth with Frances. He urged me to go, next time I was in Cornwall, to the hotel which Tresco Vean had now become, to find if she were still there, and to buy her. I promised to do this. He would make neat little architectural drawings of the cabin he proposed to fit into her, with handy lockers, a galley in place of the old Primus, two hunks instead of the swinging cots.

"And you know, Dook," stretching his toes in the warm sand, "I'm not at all sure about Bermudian rig. There's a lot to be said on the other side. I'll probably change that and have a gaff."

So through the sunny daylight hours Stephen had to do no more than lift his hand to touch his boyhood and draw about him again its warm enveloping folds. But when night came his mood deepened to gravity, and I wondered whether we shouldn't have gone right away from that place for our holiday. Begbie was commanding the flotilla, and as a matter both of discipline and of respect for his old friend Stephen would not go down to the water, but when the time of departure came he was as restless as a wild animal in a cage, and even when the sounds which told us that the flotilla had left had faded into the east he was not happy. Only when the boats were in Ambling did he know any sort of quietude.

It was at this ticklish moment of one evening, when Fran and I were sitting in deckchairs in the little garden and Stephen was prowling restlessly to and fro, that a boy in a very new suit, with a gleaming cap badge and one glistening wavy ring on his cuff, came up, opened the gate, and entered the garden. His breast was innocent of any decoration and his face of guile. He looked like some mother's son fresh from school, but with a pride – oh, such a pride! – in his face.

He saluted Stephen smartly and said: "I've been sent to this flotilla, sir. I thought I'd better report at once to the commanding officer."

"Did you report to the office?"

"Yes, sir."

"Did they tell you there that Lieutenant Begbie is in command of the flotilla?"

"Yes, sir. Temporary command. I thought – er – I'd like to meet *you*, sir." This with infinite hero-worshipping shyness.

"You'll meet me soon enough, I can assure you. Meantime, understand that an officer in temporary command is entitled to all the respect of his command. Lieutenant Begbie is entitled to be reported to by you. He and no one else is so entitled. Report to him in the morning. What is your name?"

"Phipps, sir. Sorry if I made a mistake, sir."

"Very well, Phipps. Good night."

The boy was walking away, looking half the size he had been, when Stephen called: "Phipps!"

He came back, and Stephen held out his large red capable hand. The boy took it.

"This is a tough flotilla, Phipps."

"Yes, sir. That's what I hoped."

"Welcome to it. And good luck to you. Report to Mr Begbie in the morning. Done any sailing?"

"Only national dinghies, sir."

"Good enough. You'll do. Good night to you."

The boy went away, looking once more as big as a sixth-form prefect. "Poor little devils," Stephen said.

10

Phipps was crying at the graveside. And no wonder. It wrings the heart, all that ceremonial with which the Army and Navy dispose of their dead when the opportunity occurs: as if to make up for the many who go unhouseled, unannealed, sinking beneath the wave, disintegrating into the clay, or dispersed unrecognisably upon the bright air. The slow music, the muffled drums, the reversed arms, the flag upon the coffin, the heartrending bugles. And so Sub-Lieutenant Phipps was crying. He was very young to be thus sharply reminded of the price of glory. When a boy, I read Erckmann-Chatrian's *Le Conscrit*. One phrase only remained in my mind. *Voilà à quoi sert la gloire*. All through the proceedings, standing there amid the men of Stephen's flotilla, with the July sun burning down, and the white gulls flashing upon the blue, and the padre's voice uttering the immemorial words, the phrase recurred again and again: *Voilà à quoi sert la gloire*.

I could not share young Phipps' tears. I envied him the power to shed them. My own eyes and heart were too dry. Moving as it all was, it was following a formula. I knew every step of the way, and I wished it would end. Overhead, half a dozen aeroplanes were sweeping in majestic circles, and I saw now that they were descending in a vast spiral which converged upon what must seem to them this small handful, this unconspicuous and anonymous slit in the earth. And then the formula broke. They were bombers, and when the first was over us at no great height the bomb doors opened and a rain of flowers drifted down. They were not wreaths or crosses; they were just piles of flowers, and all were red: roses and poppies. The first aeroplane flattened and climbed, and then the second was over us, and before the first flowers had reached the earth this lovely tribute rain was refreshed. So it went, and for a long time, it seemed, the air was full of roses whose heavy beauty hit the earth and of poppies that whispered down. Then, in line ahead, the bombers dipped their wings and the noise of them died away.

And then I cried, my heart fuddled and maudlin with a confusion of words and images: "O Knights, O Squires, O Gentle Bloods," and I thought of the war I had known and of roses blooming in Picardy and poppies in Flanders fields. And, oddly enough — but perhaps not so oddly — I thought of Adam Randle, for this was such a thing as he would have done. Some of the flowers had fallen into the grave: a rose and a poppy: the joy of life's day, the opiate of death's night. I felt as though, from far away, Adam's hand had reached out and placed them there; and as I walked from the graveside I thought of some verses that Adam had written.

From air and land and sea
Our young hands reach to thee,
O Death!
But ask thee not to break
Our holy bread or take
Our breath.

Let us with Life today
Enjoy our holiday,
So bright.
We'll meet in your dark room
From air and land and spume
Tonight.

11

I was glad that Frances was not there. As soon as the news had come, I telephoned to Blanche and asked her to go at once to London. Frances and John had joined her there, at the Chelsea studio. I had myself gone up with Frances and then returned when Blanche had come. And so, being lonely, and feeling the sadness of those likelier to be lonelier yet as the years peel off one by one down to the last core of life, I was glad to have Sub-Lieutenant Phipps to share my walk back to the bungalow. I made some tea, and we drank it sitting on the bit of lawn where, little more than a week earlier, Stephen had been so abrupt with Phipps. The boy was shy and still shaken by what he had gone through: not only the harrowing beauty of the ceremonial but also the event that had preceded it. He was a young romantic who, as I had guessed, had gone straight from school into the Navy. He had thought it too good to be true when chance sent him to this flotilla, for he had read with enthusiasm of Stephen's buccaneering work. "I always hoped," he said, "it would be with the Darner or Peter Scott or Dickens. Preferably the Darner."

Stephen had drafted him into his own gunboat, and it was with his head in this boy's lap that he had died. It had been a lovely summer night and they had cruised through the few dark hours and seen nothing. There was nothing at all to worry about: the sea was friendly and there was no enemy. They were off the Dutch coast in the dawn when Stephen gave the order to make for home. Making home in the other direction was a flight of German bombers with an escort of fighters.

"We were all in rather a gay mood," little Phipps said. "The night before had been grim. This had been such a contrast. It was like a summer cruise for fun. And with the sun coming up and warming us, we all felt good. We didn't bother much about the planes, though naturally everybody stood by to do what would have to be done if the need arose. But they were so high up, and it didn't look as if they were interested in us. It was a pretty safe bet that at that time of morning the bombers had laid everything they had. They passed over us, and we watched them disappearing towards the Dutch coast when one of the fighters suddenly peeled off from the bunch and swerved round towards us. He flew right ahead of us and then turned in. We were sailing in line ahead, and there he was, losing height, and coming to meet us. It all seemed to happen in no time. He shot along the line, emptying his machine guns into us, and we blazed at him with everything. But we didn't get him. He rose and tore after the others. Darner ordered his gunboat to slacken speed, and as the other boats went past us one by one he shouted over the loud-hailer: 'Every one all right?' Everyone was. Not a man had been hit, and we were ready to laugh at the whole thing when Darner said: 'That's good then,' and turning to Number One he added: 'Bugs, I'm hit. Shut up about it, but take command of the flotilla.' He stood steady for a moment, and then he slid to the deck."

That was how it happened. A bullet had shattered his collarbone and passed slantwise down into a lung. He spoke only once again, and that was to say: "Well, Phipps, I warned you that this was a tough flotilla." He was dead when the boats came into Ambling.

And now, as we drank our tea, and I looked at the bright annual flowers Fran and I had planted in the garden, the swallows were hurtling through the air with shrill cries, the day was in its decline, the flotilla would be going out with Begbie in command, and I should be left to another night of the intolerable quiet of the bungalow.

"I think, sir," Phipps said with the absurd deference that I felt we ancient life bunglers so little deserved, "the Darner would have appreciated that gesture by the RAF types."

"I'm sure he would."

"I hope I'm not imagining it, but I believe he got rather fond of me in the few days we had together. Anyway, I shall always like to think that. He used to call me Phippo. When things were quiet, he and Mr Begbie used to talk to me about sailing and the times they had in Cornwall. I hope you won't mind my mentioning it, sir, but they were both terribly fond of you."

Rub in the salt, rub in the salt.

"They both wished you were a better sailor," he added, with a boy's smile that I found enchanting. "But I was talking about the RAF Darner would have liked that because of his friend Adam Randle. I expect you know about him, sir. He often mentioned him. 'Now there's a man,' he used to say. Just like that. 'Now there's a man.'"

We carried the tea things into the bungalow, and I gave him one of the sketches I had made of Stephen. He seemed to be deeply touched. In the morning I packed my few belongings and took a last look round to see that there was nothing I had missed. In a shed I found John's folding pushcart, overlooked in the hurry of Fran's departure. I folded it and laid it alongside my suitcase. Then I went down and said goodbye to Begbie and his wife. Begbie was as enigmatic as ever. He did not then mention Stephen's name – he had not done so since his death – and I knew this was because he dared not: the small lost schoolboy whom Stephen had fortified with chocolates before tying a label to his coat. I felt that Begbie had so much to remember that at the moment his burden was heavy. I hoped he would live to remember Stephen some day with a lighter heart.

I hoped he would live; I hoped little Phipps would live; and all these men of the flotilla who knew me, but to whom I had not been made known, and who looked at me with a shy respect and solicitude. Oh, my heart was full of a longing for life for all of them! Gentle Bloods, my longing would have made you immortal.

Well, this was the end of it. I should not be here again to hear the boats go out or see them come in. Sub-Lieutenant Phipps walked with me to the station. I carried the suitcase and he the folded pushcart. I leaned out of the window of the compartment to exchange a last word with him, and suddenly he said, blushing: "I hope you won't think it heartless of me to mention such a thing, sir, but is there any hope that I might get hold of the bungalow? It would be nice to have my wife down here."

"Good God!" I could not restrain myself from saying. "You're not *married?*"

"Yes, sir," he said, smiling proudly. "Last January. I thought the flowers in the bungalow garden looked nice. Eunice is very fond of flowers. She could sit there. She's expecting a baby."

"I think you have a good chance," I said, marvelling at the beautiful courage of youth.

We shook hands, and the train began to move. The boy stood there at the salute, and that was the last I saw of him or of any of them: the shining ring upon the cuff, the gleaming badge in his cap: emblems of honour that bitter life had not yet had a chance to tarnish.

CHAPTER FIFTEEN

WHEN THE war ended in 1918 I was in London and I was twenty-nine years old. I have confused memories of the night: of battling my way into the Café Royal with a few friends, of passing quickly from excitement to delirium; of a music hall, of shouting and singing, and of arriving in Hampstead lashed like a piece of luggage to the top of a taxicab. A distinguished novelist was lashed by my side, and how many people were inside I can't remember.

When this recent war ended I was fifty-six and I was in Falmouth. Frances and I were reading in the studio when Ernie Lingard climbed the stairs and said: "There seems to be summat up outside." He was wearing the uniform of a second lieutenant of the Home Guard. We parted the curtains cautiously and saw that on the other side of the harbour, in Flushing, the street lights were on. One by one lights unmasked themselves on the ships that crowded the water. Sirens began to be sounded and house windows to send forth light. In a remarkably short time the night was full of commotion. The howling, warbling and bleating of sirens, all morsing the V-sound, filled the ear. The sky was hung with necklaces of tracer bullets. The ships of the fire service pumped lacy geysers into the air and upon these the searchlights of other ships threw their beams. Coloured fires floated high up and slowly fell. It went on for a long time.

"Better rouse John and let 'im see this," Ernie said. "It's summat 'e'll remember."

Frances dropped the curtains, pulled them sharply together. "No," she said. "Let him sleep."

Ernie went downstairs, and a few moments later we heard him and his wife going out to join the people in the streets.

549

The lamplight fell on Frances' fair head. She took up her book again. "Rejoicing!" she said. "Well, let them rejoice. With half the world in ruins, they'll find out soon enough what there is to rejoice about."

2

We came down to Falmouth immediately after Stephen's death, and we stayed there. I was fortunate enough to let my studio in Chelsea to an American war correspondent who had just arrived in London with his wife. Americans played more and more a part in our lives. Falmouth became an American town. Hotels, shops, houses were commandeered for them, and the harbour was full of their ships. They went about with their names stencilled on their buff wind breakers: "Jim, Elkhorn, Ohio," and "Fritzy, Athens, Pa." With their vast range of physiognomy, it was as though all Europe had paradoxically swept into our town from the West instead of the East, and all Africa, too.

I had expected to take a holiday till the war was over. Falmouth was not a portrait painter's paradise; but the coming of the Americans changed that. The English are reticent about intruding on strangers. Never once till now had anyone called upon me to pay his compliments because I was Edward Pentecost, R.A. But the news that I was living in Falmouth spread among the Americans, and I never knew at what time of day there might not be a knock at the door and a deferential young man asking to be allowed to shake me by the hand and take a look round the studio. If it were afternoon, they were asked to stay to tea; and Fran and I were deeply embarrassed, because this small courtesy was usually so heavily repaid. Our visitor would come back in a day or two, and leave behind him sugar and tea, tins of fruit and cigarettes, with a charming disregard for the burdens of the American taxpayer. But there was nothing we could do about it without being boorish and uncivil.

There was a young naval lieutenant – Lieutenant Galer – who came often. His face interested me because it showed so clearly the Red Indian bone structure that many American faces have. It was very obvious in Woodrow Wilson's face. I asked to be allowed to paint him, and he agreed. There were processions, after that, to see Galer's portrait; and, without having intended any such result, I got as many commissions as I cared to handle.

I don't know whether all these attractive young men would have called on me if Fran had not been there. I suppose not. They got to know about Stephen, and they treated her with that deference and courtesy that is a bit alien to Englishmen, as though she were precious porcelain. John was a godsend to them. They brought him "candies," but Frances forbade chewing gum. He was a "cute little guy," and to see him thrown up onto a manly naval shoulder, holding on to hair above a smiling face decorated with formidably perfect teeth, and with Fran standing by: this made (as I think the young men hoped) a fine picture of domesticity such as would have been a certain Academy winner a couple of generations before my own.

Young Galer invited us to lunch aboard his ship, a tank-landing craft, an iron box with a drop front. There were odd things indeed on the harbour in those days. I think John enjoyed that outing more than Fran and I. He was round-eyed with wonder when negro mess servants brought on the tough chicken, the ice cream and the rest of it. He loved the cute little cabins and the gramophone records that you could throw to the iron deck without breaking them, and the vast warehouse below decks in which the tanks would be housed. Galer contrived to leave him behind while he showed me and Fran his cabin. I felt that he would have liked to leave me behind, too, but Frances wouldn't have that. "Come on, Dook. You mustn't miss this."

There were a few photographs scattered about the little iron room. "That's my mother," Galer said, "and this is Sis. I'd like to have you know them some day, Mrs Pentecost. I guess you'd find the States pretty swell. This is the college, taken from the campus." He was a lecturer in literature in a Southern state. We hovered, looking at the photographs.

"You haven't seen the bathrooms, Mr Pentecost. Just along the corridor there. It's a cute little outfit."

"Oh, let us see them," Frances cried, taking my arm.

"Mrs Pentecost," said Galer desperately, but with a smile, "since we can't shake off this man, I must ask you in his presence. What about coming to a dance with me? Would you have any objection to that, Mr Pentecost?"

I shook my head and walked out into the corridor. Frances followed, and we looked at the bathrooms. Galer turned the taps, to show that water really ran. "Look," he said. "It's a dance at a swell place. I've been there. The Tresco Vean Hotel. We'd run out by car."

We heard John's voice, and Frances ran out to find him. "Looks like this is not my lucky day," Galer said.

The voices of Frances and John were fading in the distance. Galer and I sat on the edge of a bath. "You might have been luckier," I said, "if it hadn't been Tresco Vean."

"I don't get that, Mr Pentecost."

"The house belonged to Frances' mother. She was brought up there. Her husband, you know, was also her cousin, so that she knew him from childhood. Tresco Vean was where they ran round, and rode horses, and learned to sail boats." I didn't add: "And where she first met a boy named Adam Randle." I said: "So you see the place is mixed up with a lot of things she's lost. She wouldn't want to dance there."

Galer looked dismayed. "We could go some place else," he said, "except that I guess I've scared the bird."

He broke open a packet of Chesterfields and offered me one. "Yes," I said. "I suppose you could put it like that. She'll have to come to life again some day, and she will. But for a long time it'll be easy to scare her back."

He was a nice boy. You could feel a goodness in him, a soundness. I didn't want him to be hurt – or Fran, or Adam. So, as we sat there absurdly on the edge of the bath, I said: "There's another thing. She's waiting for someone else. That's what's the matter with her. She's waiting. And it's being a long wait."

He got up and we went to look for Frances and John. Well, Mr Pentecost," he said, "whoever she's waiting for is a lucky guy. I confess I was – I am – mighty attracted. But I guess this is where I sidestep."

There wouldn't be much point in recording this if it were not to show how Fran was in those days. For a girl as attractive as she, life was there then to be taken with both hands. There were young men in plenty, American and British alike; and the Americans had in abundance what we had in meaner measure: food and drink, money and petrol, with all that that word means to the modern young. She was not attracted. She was beautiful, and she took great care of her looks. She was as fanatical a sunbather as ever, and the light blue eyes in the golden face had never looked lovelier. She was attentive to the young men when they called, but only as a good hostess should be.

She was like a rose without perfume, a rose in ice. She who had loved two men found her life deepened down to an intolerable longing for the one who was left.

He came at last, without warning. There was no letter, no telegram, no telephone call. It was a summer evening. John had been put to bed. Ernie Lingard and his wife had gone to a cinema. Fran and I walked down into the little paved garden, haunted now by more memories than those of Kitto. There was not much shipping on the harbour. That amazing armada of odd eccentric shapes that no old sailor would have recognised as ships had gathered here and long since dispersed; but in the garden the memory lingered of the young men from those ships who had come ashore, and sat here with us for an hour, and now were gone to fulfil what destinies we knew not. The night had come when the lights danced and dazzled, and Fran had drawn the curtain, not wishing to look on them too long. And now we could tell ourselves that it was peace: the time when, some say, you reap the benefits of war, and others that you pay the price of it.

So there we sat in deckchairs, with the scent of the herbs in the pavement and of tobacco plants under the walls rising into our nostrils, when a voice said: "Well, Fran, home is the hunter."

I looked up, and he was standing at the back of her chair, with his hands laid lightly over her eyes. It was as though I did not exist for him. Nor, when she got up, for her. She said: "Oh, my darling, my darling!" gave a great sigh like a spring breeze that steals up suddenly on winter, and fell upon his shoulder with her eyes closed and her arms about him.

I went in and left them there.

The next day they travelled to London. I was dazed with sleeplessness as I went with them to the station. There had been talk and talk till four in the morning: talk of the prison camp and how it had broken up as the Russians advanced from the east, of the tattered tail pushing westward day after day with their belongings on homemade sledges or perambulators, and finally on their backs. "Even then," said Adam, "I managed to make a few notes each day."

He had managed to hide his notes all through his imprisonment, and now they were to be made into a book. "So we'd better be off first thing in the morning, Fran. We can be married in a registry office. And then we'll settle down and begin work."

That's the mood he was in, and Frances was in the mood to deny him nothing. With the heartless egotism of the young and happy, they put me out of their lives. And why shouldn't they? I thought. I was glad to see the light in her eyes, to be aware of the perfume of her reawakened being. It was fortunate that the American correspondent who had leased my studio had moved on into Europe. They could have that. It would be a good place for Adam to work in. They accepted the offer. They even thanked me, and Frances kissed me; but it was the sort of thing they expected. The gods were smiling on them, and it was right and proper that paths should straighten.

And so, within a few hours of Adam's appearing, he had disappeared again, and Frances had disappeared with him. I watched the train vanish, and then I turned homeward feeling suddenly as though a tornado had passed, flattening out everything. Why, I thought, she has not even told her mother! Poor Blanche! How she had become meaningless! How she had drifted to the farthest circumference of life! I rested for twenty-four hours, and then, taking John with me, I went to visit Blanche in the cottage she had found behind Torquay.

3

There is not much left to say. All I have sought to do here is to present myself and some of the men and women I knew in the act of life. Inevitably, such an intention arrives at a lonely point. One moves along the street, and here and there a door opens and a companion disappears, not to be seen again, and towards the dark end of the street one walks alone. Living is the only fatal malady: it gets us all down in the end.

I must confess that when I had returned from my visit to Blanche and, a few days later, had put John on to the London-bound Riviera Express in charge of an acquaintance, I entered upon a period of profound melancholy. I had not been in London for some years, save for flying visits, and was beginning to feel the need of it. And I wanted to be near the young people who were now all I had. Thus, I was not sorry when a letter reached me from Adam.

My dear Dook, – Now that Frances and I have been married for a month, we have sufficiently returned to sanity to remember some of our obligations. They seem all to be to you. It is vilely selfish of us to perch ourselves here in a home to which you may well be wanting to return, and so we have been looking for a place of our own. You know, or can guess, what London is like in these days, and it hasn't been easy; but at last, at great cost, we have found a burrow and crept into it. If, therefore, you want to be back here in your old studio there's nothing in the way, and it will be a great delight to us to have you about. Our burrow is only ten minutes' walk from yours. The book is making headway. It is nothing but autobiography, but I'm casting it in the form of fiction. There'll be plenty of books like that, I imagine, during the next couple of years – till the publishers find us out and say, 'No more.' So I am trying to get in early. I work every morning from nine to one, find it quite easy, and reckon to finish in six months. For lack of other space, I write in the bedroom, and it is amusing to hear Fran hushing the faintest signs of life out of the exuberant young John. One would imagine I was a Major Prophet making his contribution to the Bible, with the Oxford University Press complaining that copy was overdue, or Shakespeare stuck for inspiration halfway through Hamlet. Really, I don't mind if the boy yawps a bit or the muffin man rings his bell under my window – not that such a lovely phenomenon is ever likely to trouble us again; for I find myself to belong to the happy breed that writes undisturbed by noise. But, of course, for dear Fran, all writing is the Sacred Word. I have no intention of saying it again, Dook, but that, too, is what Fran is to me, if you can disentangle the meaning from so cryptic a remark. That is what she is and always has been; and I thank you – also something I shall not do again – for looking after her for me. She loves you. My women folk make a habit of that, and may I say that I don't wonder. However, let us end on a phlegmatic British note – just a hearty assurance that we'll be glad to see you haunting these parts again. Your friend Joe has been called to fill the drinking horns of Valhalla. His daughter Bess, married – don't break your heart! – to a Mr Smith, continues to dispense the lesser *post bellum* beverages that are permitted to mortals.

As ever,

Adam.

And so I went back to London, and throughout the following year I fear I shamelessly twined my life about these young lives that were all I now had left. There seemed no reason to me why a long time of content should not lie ahead of me. But it was not to be. Adam's book was finished and found a ready publisher, but, when he had read the proofs, there was a long delay before publication. He learned of paper shortage, of difficulties with binding, of this and that. He had no immediate task, and this filled him with restlessness. He had time on his hands to become aware of hindrances and frustrations in whichever direction he turned. The hold-up of his book became for him a symbol of spanners in many works. He had dreamed behind bars of England and now, in England, he found himself hedged with impalpable bars. He came across old comrades who had started in small trades and businesses, and were filling in six forms to get a yard of planking or a dozen bolts and nuts, and then not getting them. There was no personal reason why he should worry. His mother had left him well-to-do. But he was not a man who could sit down and treat life as if it were a bell hop, leaping at his orders.

I had been aware for a long time of his inward fume and fret, but this did not prevent me from taking a heavy shock when he said one day in my studio: "Dook, I'm wondering whether this is the country for me after all."

There it was in the open at last – what I had been fearing for months. "What's wrong with the country?" I said sharply.

"If I could tell you that," he answered, "I suppose I should devote my life to politics, which is the last thing I want to do. What I want to do is to *enjoy life*. Does that seem selfish? Anyway, I believe it's the only thing worth doing. We've all *got* life. *Something's* got to be done with it, and what ninety-nine people in a hundred want to do with it is to enjoy it – make it a thing of joy – just that. The trouble is that so few of them know how it's to be done."

"Do you?"

"Yes. It's to be done by working – but only by working at the one thing on God's earth that you feel worthwhile. So that, paradoxically, I'm a hedonist who can only realise himself through slave-labour – utter slavery to doing something for a worthwhile purpose."

"You're suffering from an old trouble, Adam. You're an artist appalled by the useless activities of an industrial civilisation."

"There are two things to be said about that," he answered. "One is that they're not only useless – they're dangerous. They ruin everything that's truly important, and more and more they tend to shake the world to pieces. And the second thing is this. You say I'm suffering from an old trouble. I know that for a hundred years industrialism and its attendant commerce have been getting between men and the enjoyment of life. But now there's something new in it. There's the horrible word *total*. That means that the slaves who had a chance to revolt against individual oppressors are gaily handing over this last rag of their birthright. They – the very slaves themselves – love the word and rejoice to consider themselves not men but masses. That is the meaning of this hailstorm of rules, forms and regulations. The slaves are now addressed as one single body and told what to do. It all makes an atmosphere I can't breathe in."

"Do you think you'll find a better atmosphere anywhere else? Isn't all this a world phenomenon?"

"Whether it is or not, it isn't a happy phenomenon. The world's predominant feeling is of despair."

"I believe you're right," I said; "but it doesn't follow that there's any ground for the world's feeling. Victorian Liberalism took a crazily optimistic view of man's possibility of advancement. We have been shown how idiotic that view was. Perhaps we shall be shown how idiotic is the view that from this point onward the road goes down to hell."

"I hope you're right, Dook, but I feel like Gulliver when he woke up and found horrible little spider-men running all over him. Lousy little men, with permits, visas, rubber stamps and Homburg hats. I didn't fight to help lice of that sort to breed."

"Well, what do you want to do?"

"I don't know. My instinct is simply to get away."

"There used to be a convention in fiction that when a lover was rejected he went to Labrador to think it out."

"Yes. It's something like that. I'm not a planner. I'm not going to pretend that I know what I want to do. I only know what I don't want to do. I don't want to spend my life writing in capital letters on dotted lines."

"I'm afraid, my boy, you're a difficult son for a paternal State to handle. It wants to offer you everything, and you haven't a spark of gratitude."

"Have you noticed, Dook, two amusing manifestations of the modern spirit? I mean among that pestilent breed called the intellectuals. They are all out to destroy the influence of the father in the home. The poor creature who has sweated his guts out for centuries to hold things together is now discovered to be the epitome of evil. He saps the vitality of his young. Every one of his litter would be a glorious independent lion cub if Daddy's baneful influence didn't turn it into a mewling kitten lapping milk at the parental saucer. The psychologists have been roped in to invent words for it like parent-fixation. Well, then, out with father! But at the same time, in with the parental State. The lion cub who was corrupted at the domestic milk saucer will roar in mighty independence when fed at the municipal milkbar. Father loosened the thews and sinews by sending Jack off to school on his own two legs, but the State binds them up by taking Jack to school in a motorbus. Frankly, it all looks damned fishy to me. I know as well as the next man that the parental idea can be corrupted. I know that in the industrial north big families were welcomed because children were economic assets — wage-earners from early days. When I ask myself why the super-parent, the State of these total times, takes such an interest in its sons, the answer isn't reassuring. For myself I don't expect it to be any more humane than Daddy. I expect it to insist that Jack shall turn in all it wants out of the pay packet, and that when things blow up into a dirty row with the family next door Jack shall do what he's told, and do it pretty quick at that."

I looked at Adam with disturbed speculation. I could see that he was desperately unhappy and disappointed. I asked him again: "What do you want to do?"

"I don't know, Dook. Honestly, I don't know. But I'm young, and I feel inclined to try and find out."

4

It was soon after this that he met Sam Nicol. There was an episode in Adam's life that I have not yet recorded. Several times during the Battle of Britain he was, as the young men used to put it, "in the drink." Once he was shot down and was picked up by a trawler; and once he baled out and was picked up by a rescue boat commanded by Sam Nicol. They liked one another, but the chances for liking to develop into friendship were slender enough in those days and they drifted apart. On a summer evening Adam and I were walking on Chelsea Embankment when we saw a bulky – almost a square – man leaning in contemplation over the river. We walked on a little way, and then Adam looked back, and said: "I believe I know that man. There can't be two backs as broad as that in Great Britain."

It was a blue back, and the man was wearing a sailor's cap. Adam went up to him and said: "Aren't you Sam Nicol?"

A happy but truculent face turned towards us. "Yes. Who are you?"

The explanations were soon made and contact re-established. "Well, I'm damned," Sam kept saying. "Fancy! You! I lugged so many of you birds out of the drink you can hardly expect me to remember you all. But you were the first, and I remember you all right. Like women. You know. Isn't it Kipling who says the only women we remember are the first and the last?"

He was a voluble creature with a short rough beard and this uniform that I couldn't make head or tail of. His cap badge was decorative but conveyed nothing to me, and on his cuffs was a lot of unorthodox-looking gold lace. But he wore a few medal ribbons that spoke eloquently. He was not unaware of the staring way in which I tried to size him up, and he burst into a gust of laughter. "Interested, Mr Pentecost?" he said. "I think it's pretty fruity. Made it all up myself. There's no law against wearing fancy dress. Not yet, anyway. I expect it'll come."

We went to what Adam called his burrow, where Frances was just preparing supper, and I didn't leave till hours later. Sam Nicol was more than ready to talk. The question, so common then: "Well, what have you been doing with yourself since you got out?" set him spouting like a geyser. Before getting out, it seemed, he had commanded a corvette, and then:

"There I was. I'd never learned to do a damned thing, you know. Straight into the Navy from Harrow. Well, I'd made up my mind I wouldn't come on the old folks at home, but what to do? I mooched around a bit, and then I had a brainwave. Paint! That's what the country seemed to me to need – a bit of make-up, so to speak. Well, slapping paint on wood didn't look difficult. After all, when I joined the Navy I didn't know one end of a ship from another, but I soon learned, and this seemed easier. So I scouted round and found a village that was more down at heel than most and I took lodgings there, and damn me if I didn't set up as a house decorator. I blued my gratuity on ladders and paint, and varnish, putty, turpentine, sandpaper and God knows what all. It was a fair hoot, I can tell you. I used to go round roaring with laughter. I painted 'Sam Nicol, Decorator,' on the ladders, and bought a truck to push the stuff round on. I started in on the pub. They left the colours to me, and I can tell you it was a pretty nifty hostelry when I'd done with it.

"Then I got cracking on the rectory. It looked as if it had suffered a bitter blow at the Dissolution and had gone on dissolving ever since. But I made a job of that, too, a tasty shade of bright blue on the door that looked like a bit of heaven peeping through the trees. There was a flagstaff on the lawn and I had a slap at that. I made a bosun's chair and a little carrier for my pots and brushes and hauled myself to the top, praying to God the thing wasn't as rotten as it felt. Well, there I was on a fine spring day whistling like a thrush on the top of that pole, when a damn great car comes whizzing up the rectory drive and I expect nothing less than the Archbishop of Canterbury to leap out and congratulate me and ask me to have a slap at Lambeth Palace.

"But, no. Blow me down if it isn't some lousy little coot in a black coat and a bowler hat with a portfolio under his arm. 'Hey, you,' he says, standing at the bottom of the flagstaff. 'Wot you doing?' 'Working,' says I. 'You got a licence to work?' he says. 'No,' says I, 'just an urge to earn my living.' 'You come down off that there flagstaff,' he says; so down I comes.

"Well, it was a hell of a do, I can tell you. Some louse in the village had written to some louse in a ministry, saying that there was a man working; and the word ran through the ministry like news of treason. So this bloke was sent two or three hundred miles on public petrol to see what S. Nicol, house decorator, was up to in the way of destroying his country.

"The poor old rector was routed out just as he had written 'see 2 Corinthians, 3, 6,' and he was asked where was his licence to have his door a tasty blue and his flagstaff a virgin white? He was trembling as if the Court of Arches was hemming him in for having married a couple within the prohibited degrees.

"Well, this piece of ration cheese in the bowler hat kept on telling us just how near we all were to Dartmoor, me and the parson and the pub-keeper, because we hadn't in the first place asked anyone for permission to apply for permits; consequently we hadn't applied for any permits, and it was doubtful if we would have had permission to have permits, even if we had been permitted to apply. 'As for you,' he says, addressing this ex-corvette commander, 'if you want to work, apply for employment by a licensed decorator.' So off I go the next day to two or three of the nearest specimens of that ilk, and they, Methodists to a man, with large drooping moustaches, laugh heartily. 'employ you?' they say. 'How the devil do you think we can go on employing the people we've got, what with Rule 2XA, sub-section Y, and one thing and another?' 'Oh, well then,' says I, 'to hell with this for a skylark,' and I finish painting the flagstaff, sell my ladder to the parson, who had just received his Easter offerings, and my paints to the pub-keeper, who had probably just watered the gin, and off I go where lousy little men in bowler hats can't find me."

It was a fine sustained effort, and S. Nicol had certainly earned the drink that Adam did not need to press upon him. "And what are you doing now, Sam?" he asked.

"I am trembling on the verge of a great adventure," Sam answered. He produced from his pocket a folded newspaper, which I saw with surprise was the *Falmouth Packet*, a journal I had never before had the pleasure of seeing in London. "Get in touch with world opinion," Sam said with a grin, pointing a large flattened finger-end at a paragraph.

As Adam read the paragraph I saw a look of speculation in his eyes. He handed it to me, and I learned that a small steamship, the *Henry B. Thompson*, now at Belfast, had been bought by Captain S. Nicol and Captain Egbert Muir, and would sail shortly for Falmouth. There she would take aboard a hundred passengers who were anxious to make their way to South Africa. "To wait for a passage in the normal way," said the paragraph, "would be to wait for months at least, and possibly for years; but so eager are these people, some to return to their homes, some to find new adventure, that they have agreed to lend a hand with the running of the ship. The men will keep watch, the women will cook, and so forth . . ."

"So you're a captain, Sam?" Adam asked.

"Well, yes, in the same sense that Egg Muir is. It's a Pickwickian sense, but it'll work out. Egg and I thought it would be good for discipline."

"This ship must have cost you a pretty penny."

Sam gave a laugh that would have shaken the rafters of an Elizabethan alehouse. "We've got her more or less on tick," he said. "I think it's a hoot to have a steamship on tick. It was Eggie's idea in the first place. I was with him at Harrow. He raised five hundred off his old man and I raised the same off mine. That's what I'm doing in London now. I've been fixing things with the owners, entering into bonds and recognisances and things. The way we figure it is this. We're charging a pretty steep fare, and the passengers do most of the work. What with the takings that way, and running a cargo back to England from Africa, we reckon we'll clear up what we owe on the ship out of the first voyage. After that, it's money for jam."

"Are you all right on navigation, Captain Nicol?" I asked.

"Oh, fair to moderate. I don't think we ought to worry too much about refinements like that. Africa's pretty big. We'll hit it somewhere and wangle our way on from one port to the next. It's a chance, like Columbus took."

"How are you making out for passengers?" Adam asked; and that was the question I was dreading to hear.

"They're the plague of my life. We put an ad in a couple of London papers, and there were enough applications to found a colony. We've worked it on the basis of first come first served, and the lists are closed."

I was glad to hear it, but I was determined to blow up this fantastic adventure. "I suppose you've got a couple of good doctors?"

"Oh, do you really think that necessary? I'm putting a bit of first-aid stuff aboard, and one of the passengers has been a district nurse."

"What about wireless? You'll employ an operator for that?"

"Well, that's a snag, Mr Pentecost. The old barque, you understand, has knocked round a bit during the war and she never was what you'd call a liner. There are one or two defects in her, and the wireless set isn't on the top line. Still, I shall fiddle round with that when we get to sea. I'm not bad on mechanical things, and perhaps I shall make something of it. But I'm not worrying. Columbus had no wireless."

"When d'you reckon to sail?" Adam asked.

"Well, that's rather a matter of God's will. Egg should be berthing in Falmouth tonight, but he's rather chancy. Then we've got to get a few stores into her and what not. The passengers have all been ordered to assemble in Falmouth by Friday, to be ready for anything."

"I'd like to come down and have a look at her," Adam said. "What d'you say, Fran?"

"It'll do John good to get out of London."

"It'll do us all good to get out of the country."

I left them talking, and went home with this ominous remark in my mind.

5

They went the next morning, and a week later I knew that I was to be alone. Adam came tearing back to London with the news that a few of the voyagers, having at last set eyes on the legendary *Henry B. Thompson*, had recoiled from the adventure. He and Frances and John were to go with the ship. He burst into my studio with this news, then rushed off to pack trunks and see to formalities that had to be dealt with. He was in London for three days, and on the fourth he and I travelled to Falmouth. In the train we talked of his plans. Or rather in the course of talk I discovered that he had no plans. "I rather fancy that when we get to South Africa we'll make our way to Kenya. It's a long way round, but everything's a long way in these days. Anyhow, we'll see. I don't want to tie myself down. I'm young, Dook, and the world is wide."

I didn't doubt him. There were no fears in my heart about Fran's future or John's. Adam was in a phase of disillusionment, and so was the world. He was a man who would always feel the world's pulse throbbing through his own. Some day, I imagined, he would be recalled as urgently as he was now repelled. What was squeezing my heart was the Saharan desolation, for me, of the time between. I was dismayed, too, by the suddenness with which things had happened. It had been almost literally a last-minute decision. The ship was due to sail at dawn tomorrow.

I was appalled when I went aboard, late that evening. Ernie Lingard, who now had a new motor launch, ran us to the ship at about nine o'clock. There was no one to throw us a rope or take ours, and we bobbed there for a long time under the rust-stained hull in the placid dusk till Adam grabbed a Jacob's ladder, climbed aboard, and saw to things himself. He made us fast, dropped a rope, and hauled up the suitcases tied to this one by one. Then John ran like a monkey up the Jacob's ladder, Fran followed, and I went after. We landed on decks that were foul and slippery with oil, littered with uncoiled ropes and cables, and crowded with confused and bewildered people, all trying, without anyone to control them, to do things that they were unaccustomed to doing. Some were chopping up packing-cases for firewood to start the galley fires, and both on deck and in the corridors and cabins below self-constituted cooks and bottle washers were falling over one another in a chaos of unrelated endeavour. For a moment I caught the flash of Sam Nicol's impressive gold, and then he was gone, shouting a stentorian order I didn't understand to someone I couldn't see. That was my last glimpse of him.

Ernie Lingard, who had so carefully instilled into Stephen and Frances the notion of keeping a ship tiddly, looked round him with utter bewilderment on his aged, rugged face. He scratched his head and gave it up. "Well," he said, "Ah don't know . . ."

Adam seized my arm. "Come and see our quarters," he said.

I followed him, ducking my head in the low corridors, to the bows of the ship, where a bit of rough carpentry had enclosed a triangular space that they could just fit into. There were three wooden shelves for them to sleep on, and there was precious little room for anything else. "We're lucky to get this to ourselves," Adam explained. "It's a favour from Sam. Most people seem to be shoved in with utter strangers."

An odd-looking girl in purple slacks and wearing violent lipstick pushed past us, peeped into the tiny cabin and withdrew. "Oh, sorry," she said. "I'm looking for the W.C.s."

There was a hellish bumping and banging on the iron deck over our heads. "It'll sort itself out in time," Adam said confidently; and John, who had not forgotten the Falmouth Americans, said, "Sure." He, at least, was undismayed. His eyes shone with excitement. He was going to Africa. Quite suddenly and unexpectedly, he was going to Africa. The thought exalted him. He hauled Ernie Lingard by the arm. "Come and see the engines. They smell beautiful."

Ernie said: "Well, I'll see the engines, then I'll go down and wait for you in the launch, Dook. So long, Fran."

She was wearing the clothes she had worn on the *Frances and Stephen*: the patched corduroy slacks, the comfortable blue pullover. How many thousands of times had Ernie seen her like that, and Stephen with her? He looked at her for a long time before turning to follow John and Adam, and I knew that he was seeing Stephen standing at her side. He looked old and grave and sad. He tried hard to carry off a casual air. Then suddenly there were tears in his eyes and he took hold of her roughly, pulled her to him and gave her a long kiss on the mouth.

"Dear Ernie," she said. "Goodbye. I shall remember it all."

"Me, too, Fran," he said, pulling out his handkerchief, and then we heard him blowing his nose loudly in the corridor.

I, too, I thought, shall remember it all. So casual in their passing, the things which in the long run are the things we remember: a mackerel splashing aboard, full of the sea's beauty and vitality; a dinghy being rowed through a rough sea to a golden shore; the smell of woodsmoke; the taste of smoky tea; the wind drawing in the sails; the anchor chain rattling through the fairlead. These things and a few names – Prue, Iris, Adam, Stephen, Frances – made up so much. There wasn't much else that I wanted to remember.

We couldn't stand upright in that shabby hole. We sat side by side on one of the wooden shelves, my arm around her and her head on my shoulder: the daughter of a man I had known so little time and of a sister from whom life had estranged me. Yet I wondered whether I did not love her more than any other.

There were tears in her eyes. The encounter with Ernie had brought them there, and she kept them for me. "You mustn't think badly of me, darling," she said. "I should love to stay, but Adam is unhappy here, and I must go with him. I love him so."

"Yes, Fran, of course."

She raised her face and looked at me with those eyes of light scabious blue that she had dabbled with my handkerchief on the day when Stephen struck Adam on a beach not far from here.

"You've been so good to me," she said. "You gave me everything: my father, Stephen, Adam. I should have had none of them but for you. Don't be too unhappy, darling."

"I shall do my best."

"We shall come back, never fear."

"I hope so, Fran; but whether you do or not, you leave a lot with me. You and all the others. I've got that, anyway."

"Ah," she said, "I don't want to leave you only memories. I want to leave you hope. We shall come back."

I knew that she was trying to comfort herself as well as me. "Yes, yes," I said, hoping it would be true. "There is that, too."

They were leaning over the rail when the launch chugged away with slow reluctance: Francis Chellew's daughter, Iris' son, and Stephen's son. Other people's children. But they were all I had. It was dark by now, and I did not continue to see them for long. Everything to do with Sam Nicol and his ship had seemed to me so casual, ramshackle and impromptu that I should not have been surprised to find them there in the morning. But for once, something happened at the time arranged. In the morning they were gone.

6

I had not visited Tresco Vean since Blanche sold it, but that day I got on to a bus and went down there. I left the bus half a mile before we reached the gates and walked along the country road enclosed by high hedges full of blackberries. It was an afternoon full of autumnal mildness, and I strolled along with my mind almost numbed by recollection. At every step I made I seemed to be walking on my own heart. I had driven along this road, when a small shabby boy, with Sapphira Kitto in her mouldy-smelling carriage. I had seen Blanche, young, proud and beautiful, riding along it on her horse, and after my marriage in Falmouth I had driven this way with Prue's hand in mine. Here, with the small Fran beside me and Stephen earnestly concentrated at the wheel, the bone-shaking car called Lazarus had many a time smelled home and the beginning of holiday. Iris and Adam had walked here; my mother, too; and, in days before I was thought of, my father and Uncle Kitto had here known days like this: days of blackberries and of swallows gathering for flight.

I did not want to see any of it again. If Frances and Adam ever returned, perhaps we would all make a sentimental pilgrimage. If not, this was goodbye.

Here were the gates and the long drive to the house. It had always been, when I knew it, a tunnel of overarching green. Now it was opened up and bushes of hydrangea bordered the sides. I walked along like a ghost revisiting the places it had known, wondering what the years would have piled up for it to find. Well, where I had left a house I found a hotel, and there seemed little more to be said. It was all right as far as hotels go, but with me they have never gone far. I hadn't the heart to look deeply, to try to see again some of the rooms I had known and to discover what had been their fate. I walked straight through the place to where the old terrace had been, and found it caged in with glass, making a room in which a party of swarthy gentlemen were unhealthily stewing and discussing stock exchange prices. If the place had been allowed to moulder and decay, I should have felt happier in it, more at home with it, than I did that day. The very fact that here and there were things familiar to me made the whole more alien and inimical.

Most familiar was the land, running down beyond this glass cage to the glimpse of water. Nothing there had changed, and when I had taken tea I passed through the glass doors and of their own volition my feet went the way they had gone a thousand times before. The great beeches were wearing their rich autumnal copes and, the evening now coming on, the spaces between them were remote and mysterious. I did not linger, because I should see too many figures, young and old, flitting there, and hear too many voices that it would not be good to hear with my mortal ears again.

Down on the landing stage I had the world to myself. Indeed, everywhere now I should have the world to myself. It was a moment of melancholy beauty, full of the year's dying fires, and the crying of the curlews seemed the very voice of loss and dissolution.

The *Frances and Stephen* was lying there, listing on the edge of the water. Her mast and bowsprit were gone. She was old, shabby and derelict. No one had loved her since we had left her, and a boat, like the rest of us, needs to be loved. I walked down the steps and crunched over the shingle and laid my hand affectionately on her timbers. They felt rotten, and I saw that she was holed. She would fill at every tide. We had been so proud of her, and she had been so proud.

I returned to the quay and looked at her, and at the water beyond her, and at the farther bank where the russet foliage still hid the branches of the scrub oaks that would be naked and writhing in winter. Winter was not far off. The mist was thickening. It had condensed here and there into scarves that were caught in those distant trees and that streamed out on the air like long white arms, waving in farewell.

Mylor: January 4th, 1947.
Falmouth: April 2nd, 1948.

HOWARD SPRING

ALL THE DAY LONG

Maria Legassick was born in 1876, the youngest daughter of a Cornishman. She lives with her two sisters Louisa and Bella and her brother Roger in a large house close to the sea in Cornwall. *All the Day Long* is a powerful saga, set against the backdrop of the dramatic and often hostile Cornish scenery. Howard Spring sympathetically chronicles the lives and loves of his engaging characters, telling their compelling stories with freshness and a gripping honesty.

FAME IS THE SPUR

Born into poverty, Hamer Shawcross is arrogant and ambitious. Entering politics he becomes a cabinet minister, then Viscount Shawcross. Ann, his wife, loves her husband but will allow nothing to diminish her commitment to the Suffragette Movement. This passionate novel is set against social and political changes of the early 20th Century — the rise of the Labour Party, Suffragettes, the challenge to the power of the landed gentry and the aftermath of the 1914-18 war.

Howard Spring

The Houses In Between

Born in 1848, Sarah Undridge was three when she witnessed Queen Victoria opening Crystal Palace. Throughout her life Crystal Palace remained for Sarah a shining symbol of hope. However its glory was always obscured by 'the houses in between'. This powerful tale chronicles an eventful life that lasted almost one hundred years. Set mainly in London and Cornwall, it is crowded with Cornish fisherman, politicians, saints and sinners – the many people who knew and influenced the indomitable Sarah Undridge:

Hard Facts

In 1885 the young curate, Theodore Chrystal is struggling to come to terms with life a working-class district of Manchester – a shock after having lived amongst the dons and landed gentry of Cambridge. Dan Dunkerley is the ambitious young printer who establishes the penny journal, *Hard Facts*, to help create a new future for himself, his family and those around him. Here, amongst poverty, violence and prostitution Theodore must learn some 'hard facts' of his own.

Howard Spring

I Met a Lady

In 1916 the impressionable fifteen-year-old George Ledra is sent from Manchester to Cornwall because of his ill-health. Here he meets Hector Chown, a professor of Greek. Hector is living in a derelict house with his actress niece, Sylvia Bascombe and her young daughter, Janet. The story of how their lives become entwined spans the years of uncertainty between the two world wars and ever present in the tale, the house becomes a symbol of the fragility of their world.

Time and the Hour
(Third in the *Hard Facts* trilogy)

Time and the Hour opens in Bradford in 1912 with a group of young people who later move to London. In the mid 1930s they are confronted by the influx of persecuted Jews and the looming tragedy of the Second World War. This is a compelling saga of personal challenges, a tale where a child discovers the true identity of his mother and where romance is tempered by the terrifying reality of the growth of fascism in Europe.

OTHER TITLES BY HOWARD SPRING AVAILABLE DIRECT
FROM HOUSE OF STRATUS

Quantity	£	$(US)	$(CAN)	€
All the Day Long	7.99	12.99	19.95	13.00
Dunkerley's	6.99	11.50	15.99	11.50
Fame Is the Spur	8.99	14.99	22.50	15.00
Hard Facts	6.99	11.50	15.99	11.50
The Houses In Between	7.99	12.99	19.95	13.00
I Met a Lady	7.99	12.99	19.95	13.00
A Sunset Touch	6.99	11.50	15.99	11.50
Time and the Hour	7.99	12.99	19.95	13.00
Winds of the Day	6.99	11.50	15.99	11.50

ALL HOUSE OF STRATUS BOOKS ARE AVAILABLE FROM GOOD BOOKSHOPS
OR DIRECT FROM THE PUBLISHER:

Internet: www.houseofstratus.com including author interviews, reviews, features.

Email: sales@houseofstratus.com please quote author, title, and credit card details.

Hotline: UK ONLY: 0800 169 1780, please quote author, title and credit card details.
INTERNATIONAL: +44 (0) 20 7494 6400, please quote author, title, and credit card details.

Send to: House of Stratus Sales Department
24c Old Burlington Street
London
W1X 1RL
UK

Please allow following carriage costs per ORDER
(For goods up to free carriage limits shown)

	£(Sterling)	$(US)	$(CAN)	€(Euros)
UK	1.95	3.20	4.29	3.00
Europe	2.95	4.99	6.49	5.00
North America	2.95	4.99	6.49	5.00
Rest of World	2.95	5.99	7.75	6.00
Free carriage for goods value over:	50	75	100	75

PLEASE SEND CHEQUE, POSTAL ORDER (STERLING ONLY), EUROCHEQUE, OR
INTERNATIONAL MONEY ORDER (PLEASE CIRCLE METHOD OF PAYMENT YOU WISH TO USE)
MAKE PAYABLE TO: STRATUS HOLDINGS plc

Order total including postage:_____Please tick currency you wish to use and add total amount of order:

☐ £ (Sterling)   ☐ $ (US)   ☐ $ (CAN)   ☐ € (EUROS)

VISA, MASTERCARD, SWITCH, AMEX, SOLO, JCB:

☐☐☐☐☐☐☐☐☐☐☐☐☐☐☐☐☐☐☐☐☐☐☐☐

Issue number (Switch only):

☐☐☐

Start Date: Expiry Date:

☐☐/☐☐   ☐☐/☐☐

Signature: _____

NAME: _____

ADDRESS: _____

_____

POSTCODE: _____

Please allow 28 days for delivery.

Prices subject to change without notice.
Please tick box if you do not wish to receive any additional information. ☐

House of Stratus publishes many other titles in this genre; please check our website (**www.houseofstratus.com**) for more details